Another Woman

Another
Woman
Penny Vincenzi

THE OVERLOOK PRESS
New York, NY

This edition first published in hardcovder in the United States in 2012 by
The Overlook Press, Peter Mayer Publishers, Inc.

141 Wooster Street
New York, NY 10012
www.overlookpress.com

For bulk and special sales, please contact sales@overlookny.com

First published in the United Kingdom in 1994 by
the Orion Publishing Group

Cataloging-in-Publication Data is available from the Library of Congress

Manufactured in the United States of America

FIRST EDITION

2 4 6 8 10 9 7 5 3 1

ISBN 978-1-59020-357-6

For my family, all of it,
with much love

Acknowledgements

As always there are people without whose help this book could not have been written.

In no particular order, but with equal gratitude, for their knowledge, expertise and patience in the face of my interminable questioning I would like to thank Felicity Green, Caroline Baker, Karen McCartney, Sian Banks, Sandra Lane, Robert Carrier, Stephen Jones, Mary Anne Champy, Ursula Lloyd, Tony Rossi, and Dr David Storer.

Nobody could enjoy more inspired publishing; could I thank in particular Susan Lamb for constant emotional as well as practical support; Katie Pope and Caroleen Conquest for exemplary patience and attention to the nuts and bolts which would otherwise surely all have fallen out; and Rosie Cheetham, who is everything an editor should be: patient as well as hard-headed, inspiring as much as truthful, and above all optimistic in the face of such considerable odds from her author such as ever later delivery, much noisy anguish and a complete inability to predict even in the vaguest terms how the book might finish.

And as always, a special thanks to my agent Desmond Elliot, who is also the wisest, funniest and most wonderfully encouraging friend.

Prologue

It was going to be the perfect wedding.

Of course everybody always said that about weddings, but nobody sitting round the great pine kitchen table of the bride's home that perfect July evening doubted it for a single moment. How could they? When the couple themselves were so patently and blissfully happy, sitting together, holding hands, smiling round at their families, at indulgent fathers, proud mothers and assorted friends smiling back at them. When the sun was finally setting on a perfect day, night drifting over the deep Oxfordshire valley, with just a touch of mist promising another still more perfect one tomorrow, the thick, rich scent of the roses drifting in through the open door? When Maggie Forrest, mother of the bride, could finally relax, knowing that everything was in order, the pink and white marquee up and decked with flowers, the tables half set, the champagne (vintage) delivered and in crates in the utility room off the kitchen, the food in the process of being transformed from dozens of pounds of salmon, chicken, beef, mountains of strawberries, raspberries, eggs and cream into the most splendid wedding feast by the caterers, and the cake, four exquisitely iced tiers, standing on the dining-room table?

What could possibly go wrong now? they might have asked one another. For such a perfect match, between Cressida, younger daughter of the immensely successful and distinguished gynaecologist James Forrest, and Dr Oliver Bergin, also a gynaecologist, only son of Mr and Mrs Josh Bergin of New York City. Cressida, so pretty, with her fair English-rose beauty, so enchantingly mannered, so extremely well suited to the life and husband she had chosen; and Oliver, so dashingly handsome, and almost too charming for his own good, as Maggie Forrest had remarked, laughing, to Julia Bergin on the first occasion they had met. The guest list was long, but not too long, just 300, for Cressida had insisted on being married in the little stone church in Wedbourne where she had been christened. All over England the women on the list had been buying dresses, choosing hats, mulling over the wedding lists (the General Trading company and Peter Jones), and checking on their husband's morning suits; and the chosen eight whose small children were to be attendants had been trekking up and down to the London studio from where Harriet Forrest, Cressida's older sister, ran her fashion empire, and where the dresses had been made – not Harriet's usual sort of thing, but charming nonetheless, sprigged muslin Kate Greenaway style for the girls, white linen sailor suits for the boys. Cressida's dress had been made at the Chelsea Design Company, a wonderful creation in heavy cream silk, studded with pearls and with the palest, tiniest pink silk roses drifting down the train. It hung upstairs now in the attic room that Maggie used for sewing, swathed in its muslin cover, the veil beside it in a box, waiting for its tiara of fresh flowers to arrive in the morning, along with her bouquet (cream and pink roses) and the baskets of daisies and scabius that the attendants were to carry into the church. In the dining room of the Court House the presents were stacked, ready to be shipped over to New York, when young Dr and Mrs Oliver Bergin settled into their new home in East 80th. Marvellous presents: glasses, china, linen, silver, all listed, the thank you letters long since written.

A few miles away in Oxford the string quartet that was to play at the wedding was practising a rather difficult Mozart piece which the bride had specially requested; the vicar of St Stephen's, Wedbourne was running through the few wise if predictable words he always spoke at weddings and the organist was rehearsing the choir, and in particular the dazzling-voiced small boy he had just discovered in the neighbouring council estate, in 'Love Divine'. A few miles away in the garage of the Royal Hotel, Woodstock, the silver vintage Bentley belonging to the bride's godfather, the famously powerful and rich Theodore Buchan, was being given a final and quite unnecessary polish.

Everything ready; everything perfect. For a perfect wedding for a perfect bride.

And who could possibly have thought, on that golden scented evening, entertained a suspicion even for a moment, that the perfect wedding was never to take place at all?

The Evening Before

Chapter 1

Harriet

Late, she was going to be late, for the bloody pre-wedding supper. God, her mother would never forgive her. She could see her now, carefully serene smile growing tense as she looked ever more frequently at the clock, could hear the barbed comments, about how she, Harriet, was always late, always had so much, so many terribly important things to do; and her father would be trying to calm her, to make light of her lateness, and Cressida would be saying of course it didn't matter, it didn't matter at all, everyone else was there, telling her mother not to fuss, but making in fact the lateness more noticeable, more important. Well, it was all very well for her mother and for Cressida. They didn't really have immense claims on their time. They didn't have to worry about leaving London mid-week for a Thursday wedding. Thursday! Why not a Saturday like everyone else? Of course her mother had worked very hard on the wedding, but it had been the only thing she had had to think about, and Cressida's job with her Harley Street doctor was hardly stressful, she could take time off whenever she needed to, at the bat of her long eyelashes. They didn't have a business to run, collections to design, stock to deliver, books to balance. Or not balance. Harriet suddenly felt so sick, so frightened that she braked violently and pulled over onto the hard shoulder. She sat there, breathing deeply and slowly, hauling herself together. Don't panic, Harriet, don't; don't look down even. It'll be all right. Well, it probably won't, but you'll be all right. It's not a hanging offence, going bust, going bankrupt. It may be the end of a dream, but she could survive that. She'd survived the end of others after all.

Her head ached, and her throat felt dry, scratchy; it was a bit like a hangover. Only she hadn't had a drink. She'd wanted to have a drink all day, several drinks, but she hadn't. She'd had to keep her head clear for the endless phone calls, the faxes, the decisions. All to no avail, it seemed. She was almost certainly done for: stymied; defeated. She needed more money than she could possibly even imagine getting hold of, within twenty-four hours, and the one person who might be able to supply it was the one person she couldn't possibly ask. So that was that really. She just had to face it, and rethink the rest of her life. Harriet looked at herself briefly in the rear-view mirror; the events of the day showed with awful clarity on her face. It wasn't just that she was pale, most of her make-up gone, her hair uncombed, not even that she looked tired; her dark eyes were heavy, her skin somehow dull, her mouth drawn and taut (rather like her mother's, she thought with horror, consciously relaxing it, forcing a fake smile into the mirror). Her mascara had smudged, adding to the shadows under her eyes, and the collar of her white linen shirt was crumpled. Her earrings were hurting her; she pulled them off and felt her ears throb painfully, and for some reason that was the last straw and she felt hot tears stinging behind her eyes.

'Oh, for God's sake, Harriet Forrest,' she said aloud, wiping them irritably away, 'don't start crying now, just because your ears hurt.' And she turned on the engine again, pulled back onto the road and put her foot down, forcing her mind away from the day behind her and on to the one ahead. Her sister was getting married, and she had serious responsibilities, not the least of which was to get to the Court House as soon as ever she could. Sitting on the M40 feeling sorry for herself wasn't going to solve anything. Against all logic she felt suddenly better, more in order, better in control; she was even able to appreciate the beauty of the evening, the darkness settling onto the shadowy Chiltern hills. It would be nice to see everyone, especially Rufus and Mungo, and Merlin would be there, bless him, she hadn't seen him since he got back from Peru, although she'd heard him talking on *Start the Week* or something, his wonderfully strong voice sounding more as if it belonged to a twenty- than an eighty-year-old. And then she switched on the radio, and Pavarotti was singing 'Che gelida manina' from *La Bohème* and that really was too awful, too cruel, and although she did not stop again, she saw the last twenty miles of her journey through a dreadful haze of pain.

'That was mean of You, God,' she said aloud again, as she finally turned the Peugeot into the gravel drive of the Court House. 'You really had it in for me today, didn't You?'

James

James felt a rush of intense relief as the lights of Harriet's Peugeot beamed into the darkness. It wasn't just that he had been, as always, worried about her, for she drove much too fast (and in that way, as in many others, she was very much his daughter, the carrier of his genes), it was that her arrival would create a stir in the room, a regrouping, would make it possible for him to leave it, to escape briefly from its claustrophobic perfection. He was finding it almost physically stifling, having enormous difficulty in sitting still; indeed had got up so often to refill the glasses, to offer more coffee, to pass fruit, cheese, biscuits, that Maggie had finally said sweetly, but with a just discernible touch of irritation, that he was making everyone feel exhausted, and that he should relax and let people help themselves. As if she of all people knew about relaxing, with her overcontrolled calm, her near-manic, all-encompassing smiles. Susie, for all her energy, her eager vitality, had a well of calm within her that was truly restful. He looked at her now, as she sat chatting easily, happily to Josh Bergin, to Cressida, to Oliver, and wondered resentfully as he had a hundred, a thousand times if Alistair recognized his intense good fortune in having her as his wife. She had taken that marriage in all its distinct lack of promise and turned it into something happy, constructive, strong. He had never in all the years heard her complain about, even belittle it; it was her job, her career and she had been hugely successful at it. And now, by some extra-ordinary, almost evil quirk of fate, it was threatened. She had come over to him in the garden where they'd been having drinks in the scented early evening, before supper, her dark eyes just a little wary, and said, 'Jamie, we have to talk.' And a little later, while Maggie was putting the final touches to her supper, and Alistair was, in his beautifully mannered way, helping to carry glasses in from the garden, he walked with Susie through the rose garden and she said, her voice half amused, half anxious, 'Jamie, you're not going to believe this, but Rufus tells me he wants to get married.' And he said, 'Well, is there any great problem in that?' And she said, 'Just possibly, yes, there is. He wants to marry Tilly Mills. I'm not sure quite why, but I think it might very well open a rather large can of worms, don't you?'

And ever since he had been so afraid, so deeply uneasy, that he had had trouble swallowing Maggie's perfect supper, and had been more consumed with longing for a drink than he could remember in the whole of the – what? – twenty years that had passed since Tilly Mills had been born.

It was the forced inactivity that was so frightful, his absolute powerlessness to do anything about it. Any other night, he would perhaps have talked to Rufus, questioned him casually, gently about his life, about his plans, would have been able to form at least some impression of how serious things really were. But not tonight, with all the family gathered for his daughter's wedding, when he had so many other worries and concerns, slight in absolute terms, but of immense importance in the immediate future, and so he had simply had to sit and watch Rufus, as he sat at the table, displaying the slightly old-fashioned charm that was his trademark, talking with huge and courteous interest to his mother, (he was famously devoted to Susie), to Julia Bergin, to Maggie, to Janine Bleche, Cressida's French godmother (amazingly glamorous still, even if she was over seventy), and know that before he could explore the matter any further, at the very least twenty-four hours would have to elapse. It was almost unendurable.

He looked with intense envy at his godfather, slumbering sweetly in the corner by the Aga: Sir Merlin Reid, famously eccentric explorer (and making discoveries still, even in his ninth decade, with the world so much smaller, so much more familiar than when he had begun his travels, sixty-five years earlier). Merlin had cut short his last expedition (travelling the Central Cordillera by mule) in order to be at the wedding. He had never married himself, had said no woman would stand for him, nor he for any woman, but James was a son to him, and Cressida and Harriet granddaughters: he would not have missed being in the family, he said, at this time for the world. He was still, in his eighties, wonderfully erect and youthful, his white hair thick, his blue eyes brilliant; he was much given to bargaining for everything, not only in the souks and casbahs and bazaars of the world, but in Harrods and Sainsbury's and even on British Rail.

'Give you five guineas for that tie and that's my last word,' he would say to some flustered young salesman, or, 'If you think I'm paying twenty quid to travel twenty miles you can think again, fifteen's my last offer,' and just occasionally someone would give in to him, either to humour him, or to amuse themselves, would sell him a shirt for half price or give him two pounds of apples for the price of one. He had never managed to persuade British Rail or London Transport to drop their rates for him, but London cabbies occasionally would, especially if he had regaled them with some story of his travels, a journey into the unknown or a brush with a hostile tribe which they could pass on to other customers.

The passionate envy James felt as he looked at Merlin now was not only for the sweet sleep he was so patently enjoying, but for the long peaceful life, devoid of any complexity or wrongdoing, that lay behind him. Merlin might have risked acute danger at the hands of hostile tribes, deadly wildlife and savage environments, but he knew nothing of guilt, of remorse, of wrecked relationships, of ruined lives.

And then James thought that there was at least one thing he could do, that would make him feel a little better. He could tell Theo. As he had done in every other crisis of his life. He would call Theo at his hotel – the bugger should have been here anyway, what was he doing for Christ's sake, spending this important evening alone with his new little bimbo of a wife? Despite everything James grinned to himself at the thought of what Theo was almost certainly doing with the new little bimbo – and talk to him. Not now, of course not now. But first thing in the morning while everyone was busying about, occupied with things like hair and flowers and dresses and hats, he would go and talk to Theo, lay his troubles before him, and ask him what he thought he should do. Theo would have an idea. Theo always did.

Tilly

Far away in Paris, Tilly Mills, despite every resolution to the contrary, heard herself saying that yes, she would like to go to Les Bains Douches with the new big screen hotshot, Jack Menzies, who might have a face like an angel with a past as *Arena* had put it last week, but also had a serious personal hygiene problem. She knew it was crazy, that she had an early call, that it had been a tough day, that if Mick McGrath should be there he would kill her, that she had been late the night before, that it might hit the papers and upset Rufus, but she had to do something to distract herself from the thought of what was going on in England. The frenetic atmosphere of what was still considered one of the chicest discos in Paris would surely take her mind off the twin spectres of a self-congratulatory James Forrest leading his younger daughter down the aisle, watched by roughly 300 adulatory friends and family (Rufus Headleigh Drayton amongst them), and the colour and added interest she might have brought to the occasion had she yielded to temptation and Rufus's fairly intense pressure and attended the wedding. She could have been there right now, in England, a few miles (or not even a few miles) from the heart of the Forrest home, casting a six-foot-one-and-a-half-inch shadow over James Forrest's happiness.

'Shit,' she said aloud, 'shit, shit, shit,' then she stood up, tugged her Lycra dress down so that so long as she stood absolutely straight it just covered her buttocks, and sashayed across the room towards the exit, feeling rather than seeing every pair of male eyes (and a good few female ones as well) fixed upon her, and sensing rather than hearing her name being passed from mouth to mouth, table to table, and then as she hit the street, walked through the door of the restaurant followed by Menzies and his minder (Christ, what was she doing with this Holly-wood riffraff when she could be with Rufus?), met the inevitable wall of flashbulbs, went into further automatic pilot, and in one swift movement smiled at them, made some crack about giving them a flash and slid into the Menzies limo. And wondered as it shot off into the night, not for the first time, how she imagined she could possibly move with any degree of permanence from this world into the sweetly ordered, old-fashioned one inhabited by Rufus Headleigh Drayton.

Theo

Theodore Buchan, sitting alone in the bar of the Royal Hotel, Woodstock, embarking on his fourth Armagnac, and waiting with a fair degree of impatience for his fifth and fairly new wife Sasha to return from what she still insisted on calling the girls' room – he must have a little chat with Sasha about the things which were beginning quite seriously to irritate him – was also concentrating his formidable energies on not thinking about the wedding at which he was to play a considerable part the next day.

'Of course you must come,' James had said, when Theo had first tried to make excuses, offering perfectly genuine-sounding alibis in the form of conferences, company launches, merger announcements, a long-postponed and promised honeymoon with the new Mrs Buchan. 'Of course you must come. Cressida is your goddaughter for Christ's sake, and you're my oldest friend, and how could you even think we could do any of it without you? How could I get through the day even? Besides, you love weddings – even when they're not your own. And since when, Theo, could a conference, let alone a honeymoon, not be put off?'

He had been genuinely and deeply hurt; Theo had recognized the fact, promised to come and spent the following months preparing himself for the ordeal.

The wedding itself of course would be wonderful: the daughter of one of his oldest friends marrying the son of another. Dear old Josh, who'd been at the International School with him, with whom he'd gone on sexual rampages in Geneva, whose best man he had been at his wedding to Julia. That marriage had lasted. Only Josh's second, and the first had been very swiftly over. And Julia was a good wife to him, of course. That helped. Intelligent, (whatever the Forrests thought), gracious, a little intense – but then she was an American – and very sexy. Very very sexy. There'd been that rather strange incident one night when Josh was away – Theo wrenched his mind away from the incident: one of the few times he felt he had behaved really well – and she had been a terrific mother to Oliver. Although she did rather over-love him, Theo felt. But the boy had survived her spoiling, was really very nice indeed. A perfect husband for Cressida. The whole thing was nearly perfect. The only thing that could have improved on it would have been Cressida marrying his own son, his beloved Mungo, named by his doting parents after an obscure Scottish spirit in honour of the country of his conception, but that would have seemed almost incestuous, so closely had they grown up together. Worse still, if she'd fallen in love with – Theo switched his mind away from the one unthinkable, the one he and James never even spoke about, and concentrated instead on Oliver. Charming, brilliant, good-looking Oliver. A little lacking in humour perhaps, but still a golden, blue-eyed boy. Literally as well as metaphorically. Not only graduated summa cum laude out of Harvard medical school, not only winner of a research scholarship to the Mount Sinai, but a superb sportsman too, played tennis for Harvard; wasted, in a way, on the medical profession, but he would no doubt make a fortune out of his specialty, as they called it out there. He was already doing brilliantly.

Funny how history repeated itself. The gynaecologist's daughter marrying the gynaecologist – and this was third generation. Well, at least Cressida was Oliver's first choice, the love of his life. Not entirely predictable, perhaps, gentle, sweet little Cressida – several people had remarked that Harriet seemed more his style: hopelessly wrong there of course, but then people were usually wrong about such things and few people knew and understood Harriet. But certainly he needed a Cressida, a loving supportive wife, someone who could run his home, entertain for him, back him up, raise his children perfectly. And Cressida was extremely socially accomplished: despite her gentleness, she wasn't shy, and she was very efficient – although undeniably impractical: it was a family joke, Cressida's physical incompetence, it wasn't just that she couldn't change a plug or thread up a sewing machine, she could never even get the right station on the radio, or fill up the windscreen wash on her car. But she was superb at persuading people to do things for her, at delegating; she would be a perfect wife. For a rich man. Not so good for a poor one, maybe. Well, that was all right. She wasn't marrying a poor man.

Funny, how marriage as an institution went on and on. People said it had had its day, that everyone simply lived together these days and so on and so forth, but the fact remained that in the end they usually wanted to formalize things. He'd read somewhere that statistically there were

more marriages than ever. Well, thought Theo, waving at the barman –
Christ what was Sasha doing in the lavatory, giving herself a blowjob? –
he certainly kept up the batting average. Five was quite a good total. It
was his compulsion to own things, of course, that had led him to it:
companies, houses, paintings, cars, horses, all neatly packaged up and
labelled 'property of Theodore Buchan'. And women. He'd tried not
owning them, tried just having mistresses, but it never worked. Most
recently and most terribly it hadn't worked. He was too possessive, too
distrustful to love and let go, in that awful modern psychobabble phrase.
It was fine, having a mistress as well as a wife, you could love her and let
go, although even then he found that painful, when he was very involved
with them, with the mistresses, and they started having other relationships. That was how he'd arrived at marriages three and four: both wives
had originally been mistresses that he hadn't been able to face losing.
Then somehow there'd still been something missing in the relationship,
risk, intensity, and he'd had to find a mistress as well . . . and so it had
gone on. Until – well, until. And then there'd been Sasha and she'd gone
straight to ranking as wife. He'd met her at a race meeting in Longchamps, she'd been with someone he'd been trying to do a deal with,
and he'd taken one look at her, so edibly delicious, so perfect, with her
peaches-and-cream skin, her tumbling hair, and a body that he could see
would soothe and ease him out of the considerable pain he was in, and
he'd had to have her. She was lonely, she told Theo, her blue eyes wide
with innocent distress (and so was he, rawly, desperately lonely), and she
didn't like being on her own, she was no good at it, she really needed
someone to care for. And Theo had offered himself up to be cared for,
and that had been that. And without looking too far forward and by
sheer force of will refusing to so much as glance backwards, he had
married her. And it had worked to a surprising degree. Theo was still
slightly shocked at how well it had worked. And he'd managed to avoid
thinking too much about what had happened before until tonight. And
tomorrow. When he had to confront it, face it, face – well, face the
whole damn thing. He didn't know how he was going to handle it. He
felt, if the truth was to be told, shit-scared. Which was a situation Theo
wasn't used to at all.

He waved at the waiter again, asked for a cigar; he was just drawing
it into life when Sasha came hurrying across the room, slightly flushed,

freshly made-up, hair reshaped, a cloud of that heavy sexy smell she wore – what was it called? Obsession, great name – hanging about her. She sat down beside him, kissed him, took his hand, smiled into his eyes. Theo looked at her, at her swelling breasts in her black dress, at her perfect thighs, disappearing into her short skirt, at the delicately rounded stomach, and felt his erection beginning to form, to stir with its profoundly powerful precision. He didn't say a word, just stared at her for a moment, stood up quickly, pulled her up almost brutally, and then dropped her hand and stalked out of the bar and into the lift. She followed him, half anxious, half excited; he stood aside to let her pass, then shut the door and pushed her against the back of the lift. His face must have been easy to read, for she smiled at him, very slowly and confidently, and pushed up her dress; she was wearing no pants, no tights.

Slowly, gracefully, like a dancer, she raised one of her golden legs and wrapped it round his waist; Theo felt her hand unzipping his fly, reaching for his penis. His blood sang, his entire energy focused on her, on reaching into her; and as he felt her, sank into her wetness, stood there braced against her, feeling the glorious pulling pleasure so intense it was near to pain, holding her small buttocks, kneading them, reaching for release, he was able for a brief but timeless time to forget, even to care about, what he had to face the next day.

Susie

Susie felt terribly tired. Like James, she looked enviously at Merlin sleeping so very soundly in his corner. The day seemed to have gone on forever. Normally she never felt tired, certainly not in social situations; she tried to ignore the fact now, afraid of its implications, concentrated even harder on Josh and the stories of his youth. She liked Josh; he was so uncomplicated, so charming – and so very good-looking. Susie could never understand why women said they didn't like good-looking men. In her experience, they were no less interesting and no more conceited (which was the charge women tended to set against them) than plain men, and at least you could enjoy the looks if they were being boring.

Alistair was good-looking; it had been a factor certainly in her decision to marry him. She really couldn't see why that was so terrible. If you were going to live for the rest of your life with someone, you wanted them to be the kind of person you'd be happy with; Susie would not have been happy with a physically unattractive man.

She looked at him now, being charmingly attentive to Maggie, and thought how good he was. He found Maggie something of a trial, she knew, although he greatly enjoyed her cooking, and had had two helpings of her salmon en croûte that evening, and one and a half (mindful of Susie's watchful eyes) of the chocolate mousse. He was always telling her how wonderful it was to be given things like cream and pastry and roast potatoes, after the food he got at home: it was one of his jokes that even the water in Susie's kitchen was low-fat. Just the same, he looked wonderful on the low-fat water, ten years younger than his fifty-nine years, his dark brown hair still thick and hardly grey, his lean body muscley and strong, his blue eyes brilliant and amusedly alive. In fact she had to admit he actually looked a lot better than James these days. James had put on a lot of weight lately, and he often looked terribly worn. He did now; well, that was partly her fault. Perhaps she shouldn't have told him. But if she hadn't, Rufus might have said something; not the kind of thing James would be able to handle in the middle of his daughter's wedding day. And he had other things on his mind as well, poor Jamie: Maggie increasingly – what? – difficult, his practice increasingly demanding, and shorter term, there was tomorrow to worry about. Not that anything major would, could possibly, go wrong, but he had a speech to make, hundreds of guests to receive, a strung-up wife to steady, a daughter to lead down the aisle. Not easy, any of it.

She saw Janine looking at her, smiling, and smiled back. Dear Janine; how lovely she was still, and how very Parisienne, with her jet-black bob, her pale face and dark eyes, and her tiny, trim figure. She was dressed in a plain linen shift, made Maggie look very gross; Susie wondered, as she so often had, if Maggie had any idea that Janine had been Jamie's first love, had schooled him in sexual matters when he'd been a raw boy of eighteen and she a sophisticated woman of thirty-three. And then decided she couldn't possibly. Maggie was a darling, but she wasn't overburdened with intuition. Thank God . . . Susie looked at her watch: almost half past ten. It was getting late. The bride should be getting her beauty sleep. She looked as if she needed it; beneath her happiness was a heavy shadow of tiredness.

Although Harriet looked a lot worse. God, she was thin. Even to Susie, who saw thinness, not cleanliness, as next to godliness, Harriet looked thin. And pale and exhausted. Poor little thing. She had a lot to carry in that business of hers, and no help from anyone really. Of course she wanted it that way, had turned down a lot of offers of partnership (including a very generous one from Theo), had a seeming obsession about making it on her own, (and you didn't need to be a psychoanalyst to work out that one, Susie thought), but when things got tough she must surely yearn for an arm to lean on.

Thinking of arms made Susie suddenly sharply aware of her own, aching dully (probably it wasn't, probably entirely psychological) and the phone call she had to make in the morning. She'd almost decided to leave it until the day was over, but she liked to face things, did Susie, liked to know what she was up against. If the news was there, she needed to hear it: for better or for worse.

The phrase, singing through her head, made her think again of the morning, of Cressida's wedding day, of the need for them all to go, to leave the family in peace. She stood up, held her hand out to Alistair.

'Darling, come along. We should get over to the Beaumonts. And Cressida should go to bed. Maggie darling, wonderful meal as always. You really are marvellous, feeding us all, tonight of all nights, when you've so much else to do. Thank you. Cressida, sweetheart, sleep well. And you too, Harriet, you look exhausted. Maggie, send her up to bed. Goodnight, everyone, see you in the morning. Merlin, darling, don't get up, you've been having such a lovely sleep. I'm so glad you got back in time, from – where was it? Ecuador?'

'Peru,' said Merlin. 'Think I'd have missed this? Told the pilot chappie I'd give him a bit of a bonus if he got us down ahead of time.'

'And did he?' asked Harriet, taking the glass of wine her father had handed her, sitting down between Susie and Alistair in an attitude of profound weariness.

'No. Useless these commercial chaps. No fire in their bellies. No incentive I suppose. Still, at least we got here. Susie, you're not going, are you? Night's still young. Hoping to get that husband of yours to play chess with me. What do you say, Alistair?'

'I'm sorry, Merlin, I'd have loved to, but Susie has other plans for me,' said Alistair. 'Rufus, are you coming with us or what?'

'I'm not sure – Mungo, what do you think?'

'I think we should get Oliver safely back to his hotel,' said Mungo. God, he was delicious, thought Susie, looking at him, smiling at him (few people could look at Mungo without smiling), trying to analyse for the hundredth time what made him so extraordinarily attractive: the nearest she had ever got was to express it as a kind of messed-up perfection, as if something had got hold of the genes that had given him his straight, heavy dark hair, his deep brown eyes, his square jaw, his aquiline nose, his classic mouth and shaken them vigorously so that they fell back not exactly true, the hair determinedly untidy, the eyes just slightly too deep-set under the winging brows, the nose a trifle flaring, the mouth a millimetre fuller (and therefore infinitely sexier). He was, she had to admit, in a different league of looks altogether from her own beloved Rufus; Rufus, who might have been sent from Central Casting to play the archetypal Englishman, blond, tall, slightly languid, not overtly sexy at all. Mungo was all about sex; Janine had once remarked laughing that he made the simple act of handing you a cup of tea into an invitation to bed. And yet it was apparently so unstudied, so unselfconscious, as undeliberate as breathing or blinking (while at the same time of course you knew he was aware of it, knew what he could do to you, should he so choose); that was its greatest charm. Lucky boy, she thought: dangerous boy. As dangerous as his father. He saw her smiling at him now, smiled back, just at her, for a brief, intensely attentive moment, then at all of them again, around the room. 'I'm taking my best-manly duties very seriously, you see,' he said.

'Mungo dear, we can take Oliver back to our hotel,' said Julia Bergin, smiling her neat, well-ironed smile.

'No, Mother, let them. I'd like that.' Oliver stood up, kissing Cressida briefly. 'Now you do realize, don't you, this is the last time I'll see you, Miss Forrest.'

'What on earth do you mean?' said Maggie. She sounded genuinely alarmed.

'Mummy, don't look like that,' said Cressida laughing. 'He means tomorrow I'll be Mrs Bergin. Goodnight, Oliver darling. Sweet dreams.

Harriet, come up with me, will you? And Mummy, come and kiss me goodnight. Promise. And you, Daddy.'

'May I come up too?' said Julia. 'Or would I be intruding on this very special occasion? I'm just so excited to think I very nearly have a daughter.'

'Of course,' said Cressida. 'Just give me ten minutes to get into bed and then you can all file in one by one and pay your respects.'

What a perfect daughter, thought Susie fondly, watching her leave the kitchen, arm in arm with Harriet. And what an absolutely perfect bride she was going to be.

Mungo

All Mungo had wanted to do all evening was get to a phone. A private, quiet phone, not one of the Forrest extensions, with people picking them up and putting them down all over the house. He could hear one ringing even now, adding to his anguish. He'd tried twice to make an excuse to go out and use the phone in Rufus's car, but he'd been stymied. For some reason he hadn't actually wanted to tell Rufus: which was seriously stupid, actually, Rufus was such a gent, would never have asked him who he wanted to call or why. It was just that somehow, against all possible odds, nobody had the faintest idea that he was so desperately in love, not even that he was having a serious relationship, and he wanted to keep it that way as long as he possibly could, a quiet, gentle secret. Like his quiet, gentle Alice. Of course he could have pretended he was calling his banker, or his lawyer (faintly unbelievable on such an occasion, and at such a time, although he could always have said the call was to New York). Anyway, in the end he'd decided to leave it, until he got back to the hotel. It wouldn't be too late. Alice never went to bed until well after midnight, and then they could talk for hours, undisturbed. God, he was missing her. All this family togetherness and lovey-doveyness was making his balls ache, he missed her so much. Well, maybe in a few months it would be his wedding everyone would be turning up for. Only of course he didn't want a big affair like this one. Weddings were a bit devalued in Mungo's currency. When your father had just got married for the fifth time, in a huge haze of publicity, you wanted something a bit alternative for yourself. Maybe a beach wedding, or perhaps they could dash up to Gretna Green. That would be very romantic. And then spend a few days in the Scottish Highlands. Mungo had never seen the Scottish Highlands. Like most immensely wealthy, over-indulged people, he was more familiar with places the other side of the world than those near to his own doorstep. Anyway, he was sure they were very beautiful and, even if they weren't, seeing them with Alice would surely make them so.

God, he loved her. He felt sick, he loved her so much. He'd spent the whole evening thinking how wonderful it would have been for her to be there, how well she would have fitted in, how much everyone would have liked her, and wondered how he could stand not having her there. Well, it wasn't for much longer. He would tell his father tomorrow, he had decided, after the wedding, and then once he'd done that, he would tell everyone else. And then they could be together for the rest of their lives.

Surely, surely his father would be pleased, surely he wouldn't put up any resistance. He would just be delighted that Alice was going to – what was his phrase on these occasions? – take Mungo on. That was what he'd said when he married Sasha. Thanked her for taking him on. And it would be such a perfect day to tell him: Cressida's wedding day. When everything else was going to be absolutely right.

The Wedding Day

Chapter 2

Harriet 6am

Cressida must have gone for a walk. Of course, thought Harriet, looking into the empty room early, very early, only just after six, on this perfect morning, misty, golden, gathering its beauty about it for the day ahead. Obviously. It would have been exactly like her. She would have gone down to the stream to sit on the little bridge (*her* little bridge as she liked to call it, so irritatingly, it was no more hers than anyone else's), to be still and calm, to savour what lay ahead. She'd always done that, ever since she was tiny, before some important event (her first day at a new school, the presentation of some great new love to the family, the announcement of her own engagement); taken herself off, wanting to be alone. There was nothing, nothing at all odd about it, that she wasn't there; nor in the fact that her room was so tidy, that her bed was made up, apparently unslept in. Cressida was the neatest of people, had been so right through adolescence even. While Harriet's room was permanently shell-shocked, Cressida's, whether she was using it or not, was pretty, charming, sweetly ordered, and there was no change that morning. There were rather more flowers in the room than usual, grand flowers, roses and freesias and lilies, as well as the blue and white jugful of more homely varieties that stood on the pine chest of drawers; and her going-away hat, jauntily red and befeathered, stood on the 1940s hatstand she had been given for an engagement present (she had a passion for hats). And of course there was a rather larger pile of letters than usual on her little desk, already neatly stamped, waiting to be posted, late thank yous for late presents, but otherwise it was exactly, completely as usual. A perfect room for a

perfect daughter. No wonder, thought Harriet, Cressida was their
mother's favourite: the apparent embodiment of all Maggie's ideal
virtues. Cressida even looked like Maggie, with her English-rose skin,
her fair, just curly hair, her wide blue eyes, her sweetly curving mouth.
Harriet, with her die-straight mink-brown hair, her faintly olive skin,
her grey eyes, her sculptured cheekbones, looked, as her mother often
told her slightly edgily, exactly like her grandmother – James's adored,
wonderfully vibrant mother Rose. Rose who until her death had given
Maggie such an inferiority complex. No wonder Harriet's resemblance
to Rose distressed her.

Harriet hardly minded any more about Cressida's first place in her
mother's heart, it was a fact of her life, like always being late, the one in
trouble, the one everyone thought of as plain. The nagging lifelong
anxiety that their father also favoured Cressida was harder to endure.
Harriet adored her father; he had always seemed to her, even since she
had been grown-up, exactly what a father, a husband, a doctor for that
matter, should be: loving, caring, conscientious.

She hoped he would enjoy today: it was a special thing for a father, to
lead his daughter down the aisle, and the way she was going, it would be
a long time before it happened again. Well, the weather was doing its bit
for them: it was perfect. It might be nice, Harriet thought, looking at the
dew-spangled meadow beyond the house, to go for a walk herself. She
certainly wasn't going to go back to sleep now; the anxieties which had
invaded her sleep, made her dreams fitful and wearying – all night long
she seemed to have heard voices, phones ringing, faxes bleeping – were
crowding back in upon her, making her feel panicky. She might even go
and find Cressida; the kind of conversation they would have would
guarantee at least a degree of distraction. Just as long as her mother
hadn't got there first. The thought of having to listen to the two of them
discussing the guest list made her feel suddenly worse. She looked at
Maggie's bedroom door: firmly shut. She was obviously still fast asleep.
Good. The longer she slept the better. For all of them, thought Harriet,
and then hastily crushed the thought. Her mother wasn't that bad. Just
a panic machine.

She was just closing the door again on Cressida's room when she
realized suddenly that yes, there was something not just, not quite as
usual; the window, which Cressida kept always open at night, a crack in

the winter, wide in the summer, was closed, and the room was slightly hotter, just a little less fresh-smelling than usual, and the curtains hung unusually lifeless and still. Now why . . .

'Harriet, *mon ange*, is Cressida all right?' It was Janine's voice, very quiet; she had come out of her own room looking concerned, pulling her silk wrap round her.

'Yes, of course. Well I think so, she's not there. Why shouldn't she be all right?' said Harriet.

'Oh – I heard her earlier. She was – vomiting. I got up to see if she needed help, but the bathroom door was locked. Nerves, of course, *la pauvre petite*, but still –'

'Are you sure it was Cressida?' said Harriet, anxiously. Cressida's delicate stomach was a nightmare. 'Daddy said he was going to give her something in case.'

'Oh, but of course. Her door was open, the cover thrown back. And then I heard her go back to her room.'

'Poor old Cress. Well, I suppose it is pretty traumatic. Anyway, she's obviously all right now, room shipshape as usual, and she's gone for a walk. To the bridge I expect.'

'Ah, the bridge. What would you all do without that bridge?' said Janine, smiling. 'Harriet, I would so like a cup of tea. Would you make me one?'

'Yes, of course. I was going down anyway. You go back to bed, Janine, and I'll bring it up.'

'No, I would rather come down with you.' She followed Harriet quietly down the stairs into the kitchen, then shut the door, smiled at her again. 'Now we can speak more easily. We do not wish to awaken your mother, do we?'

'We certainly don't,' said Harriet. 'Hallo, Purdey, I'll take you out in a minute, you'll need a walk.' She bent to stroke the old labrador, who was fast asleep in her basket. 'She'll have to be shut in the utility room later, poor darling. That's funny –'

'What is that?'

'She's wet. And her paws are muddy. She must have gone out with Cress. But then she'd have stayed with her surely. Purdey, what have you been up to so early? Rabbiting I suppose.'

Purdey raised one weary eyebrow, lowered it again and sank back into her slumbers. She seemed exhausted. Harriet looked at her and smiled tenderly.

'She's getting so old, poor darling. There, Janine, one cup of lemon tea. I'll just drink mine and then I think I'll go and find Cress, make sure she's all right –'

'You are worried, my darling, are you not?' said Janine. 'About other things than your sister. I could see it last night.'

'No, really Janine, I'm fine,' said Harriet, forcing a smile, fighting down the awful realization that Janine would suffer from her incompetence along with, more than, the rest. 'Just the usual traumas, you know? But nothing serious, I promise. Nothing that's going to spoil today anyway –' Her voice trailed away and Janine said of course, she quite understood, and smiled at Harriet, and as she met her brilliant dark eyes Harriet could see that, as always, Janine was not remotely fooled by any of it, and she was suddenly a small girl again, crying behind her bedroom door, and she could hear Janine's voice, quietly reasoning with her father at the foot of the stairs . . .

'Jamie, don't be angry with her. Don't. It is not right.'

'Janine, I'm sorry, but this is none of your business. Harriet is my daughter and I have to be firm with her. She has to learn she can't behave like this.'

'Like what? James, Harriet is only nine years of age. And she is terribly upset at the moment. She needs discipline, yes, I agree, but she also needs kindness and sympathy.'

'Oh Janine, really.' Her father's voice sounded almost amused. 'I thought the French were supposed to be tough on their kids. You sound like one of those American softies. It was only a puppy, for God's sake. She hasn't suffered a major bereavement.'

'Only a puppy! Jamie, how can you say such things! That is being very, very tough, as you put it. To her *of course* it is a major bereavement. And since we are discussing the French attitude, I think there is much to be said for it. I would say we are not so much tough as demanding. We expect much of them. We treat them in a mature way. But we do try to understand them. And at this moment, I think Harriet needs much understanding.'

'Well, I suppose so. I'm not very good at being understanding, I'm afraid. These days. All right. We'll try a bit harder. But she's so – awkward. It's difficult, when –'

'When the other little one is so easy and so good. Yes, yes I can see that. But –' There was a fraction of a pause.

'Yes?' said James, his voice wary.

'Well, it is no business of mine, of course. But I don't think sending her away to this school is a good idea. That is certainly one thing we would never do in France. She is so young, Jamie, so tiny. She should be at home.'

'Janine, forgive me, but it is none of your business. Maggie is finding her impossible, she's disruptive, both here and at school, and this place we've found specializes in difficult children.'

'Well I suppose you know what you are doing.' Janine's voice was cool, then she said, 'I am going up to my room now. I am a little tired. Goodnight, Jamie.'

'Goodnight, Janine. Sorry to have involved you in all this.'

'Oh, don't be foolish. I am family – nearly. I like being involved. In the rough and the smooth as well. I only wish I could help.'

' 'Fraid you can't,' said Jamie and his voice was heavy. 'It's – oh Christ, there's my phone. Not the hospital, not tonight, please God.'

'I will ask Him for you too. Goodnight, my dear.'

Harriet heard steps on the stairs, coming down the corridor, hid under her duvet, screwing her eyes up tight. There was a gentle tap on the door, then she heard the handle turn.

'Harriet? Are you all right, *mon ange.*' The voice, the voice she loved so much, so pretty, so much more interesting than her mother's, was concerned, gentle. She lay silent: determinedly, deadly still.

'Darling, I'm sure you must be awake. Do you want to talk to me?'

'No,' said Harriet, sniffily and reluctantly.

'All right. But if you change your mind, I am going to bed, but I do not expect to sleep. I plan to read for quite a long while.' Janine bent to kiss Harriet, her perfume, expensive, rich, seeming to surround her. Harriet put her arms out suddenly and gripped her neck.

'You're my favourite grown-up,' she said. 'My favourite grown-up of all.'

'Darling! What a nice compliment. But –'

'It's true. Daddy's so cross all the time, and Mummy – well, Mummy hates me.'

'Harriet, of course she doesn't hate you. You must not say such a thing.'

'I do say it, because she does.' She pulled a tissue from the box by her bed and blew her nose. 'You'd hate me too, if you had to live with me. Anyway, they're not going to have to live with me any more, are they, they're sending me to this boarding-school place, getting rid of me –'

She was crying again now, harder than ever. Janine reached forward, drew her into her arms. It was funny, Harriet thought, that she was so small and thin, not cuddly and cosy-looking like her mother, and yet her arms were gentler, more comforting. She snuggled into the arms now, rested her head on Janine's breast. 'You should have been a mummy,' she said.

'Well, I would have liked that. But it didn't work out so well. And I have you and your sister and –'

'I wish you were my godmother. Not hers.'

'I will tell you a little secret,' said Janine, brushing her lips across Harriet's head. 'I wish I was your godmother too. I love Cressida very much of course, but I feel you are more like me. Not so perfect, not so good.'

'She's not perfect,' said Harriet, her voice muffled again in Janine's soft jumper. 'She's not perfect at all.'

'Of course not,' said Janine. 'Nobody is perfect. But she is nearer to it than I, I think.'

'No she isn't. I hate her. I've always hated her.'

'But why?'

'Because she's so pretty and goody-goody and she's always being sickly sweet to everyone, and she's mean to me so often, and nobody ever realizes.'

'Harriet, you exaggerate I think.'

'I don't, I don't. Once she threw my lovely baby doll, the one that cries you know, out of the window, and she got stuck on the flat roof and she was there for days in the rain, and another time she took my new pen that Grandpa Merlin had given me and lost it, and she told my best friend at school that I didn't really like her and was always saying mean things about her and – oh I know you won't believe me either, grown-ups never do.'

'I believe you,' said Janine unexpectedly, 'of course I do. But all sisters squabble, Harriet, I certainly used to with mine. And I am sure you are not perfect either. And,' she added with a spark of amusement in her dark eyes, 'it certainly was not a good idea to throw your soup at her this evening.'

'I know. I know it wasn't. But she was giving me her look, you know? Her horrible goody-goody look, while Mummy was telling me not to be rude. And I thought – well I knew – it would make me feel better. And it did for a bit,' she added with a sheepish, tearstained grin.

'But now you are in terrible trouble, and not allowed to go to the party tomorrow, and your mother is very upset, and your father is angry. Do you still feel better?'

'Yes,' said Harriet, surprising herself with her own certainty. 'Yes, I do. It was still worth it. Seeing her face change.'

'You might have changed it forever. If the soup had been hotter.'

'I know. And I know it was wrong. But she's oh – oh I don't know. And they both love her so much. And –'

'And her puppy hasn't just been run over, and she's not being sent away to school. Is that it?'

'Yes,' said Harriet. 'Yes, that's it.' And she started to cry again.

'Harriet, listen. It was dreadfully sad about Biggles. Even I cried, and I do not greatly like dogs. Although I'm sure Biggles was a very special one. I still have the photograph of him you sent me. But you can have another puppy. Your parents have said so and –'

'And what's the point of that,' said Harriet, 'when I'm not going to be here with it? Oh Janine, it was so awful. The worst bad dream you ever had, only much much worse than that. I can't stop thinking about it, it just goes on and on over and over again, in my head, like something on TV. I see it happening, I look out of the window and the gate's open and I know I've shut it and I'm running and running down the drive and calling and calling him, and I can see him there, looking at me from the opposite side of the lane, sitting in the long grass, and then the lorry coming and him suddenly starting to pad over the lane towards me, rather slowly, wagging his tail, and then – and then the lorry on him, on him, Janine, tons of lorry, what do you think he felt like, can you imagine, and all my fault, all of it – oh Janine, how could I have done such an awful thing? I didn't deserve him, did I, I didn't deserve to have him. I wish I'd been under the lorry with him –'

'Oh Harriet, my darling, *chut*, *chut*, please, don't say such dreadful things. That would be no better, it would be a million times worse.'

'Well I do. And then Mummy appeared, and she just led me back into the house, wouldn't let me see him, wouldn't let me near him, and Cressida was on the stairs, and do you know what she said?'

'No, I don't.'

'She said, "Well it was your fault, you know, Harriet, you should have shut the gate." Even Mummy was cross with her. And her horrible kitten was fine, sitting there on her bed washing itself. I'll never forgive her for that, never. Of course she said she was sorry, Mummy made her, but she didn't mean it, and she was holding her kitten at the time, stroking it. It's all right for her, she's still got something to love. Anyway, I don't want another puppy, I want Biggles.'

'Well,' said Janine, 'well, my darling, it is all very sad of course. But the pain will get better, I promise you. That is the first important lesson you are going to learn in life, Harriet. That pain gets better. All pain. And when it gets better, you will find you do want another puppy, and you won't forget Biggles, but you will love the new one, a little bit differently of course, and –'

'But I've told you,' said Harriet, 'I'm not going to be here. I'm going to this stupid school. So I can't love anything, differently or not.'

'Well,' said Janine with a sigh, 'perhaps you will like the school and perhaps it will not be stupid. Now then, would you like me to stay here and read you a story until you are feeling a little bit more like sleeping?'

'I'm frightened to sleep,' said Harriet, 'I dream about it all. What happened. Every night. I try to stay awake, but I can't. In the end I go to sleep and the dream comes.'

'*Allons, allons, mignonne,*' said Janine, taking her in her arms again, stroking her hair. 'You shall come to my room, if you would like that, and sleep in my bed with me tonight. And if I think you are dreaming badly, I will waken you. All right? And very possibly, I think, once you have slept one night without the dream, it will not trouble you again.'

'I think it will,' said Harriet, 'but that would be lovely, yes. I'd like that. Thank you.'

Janine held out her hand. It was such a beautiful hand, very white, with long slender fingers and brilliant red nails. Not the sort of hand you'd think would be comforting, but it was, warm and soft; Harriet closed her own round it and followed Janine along the corridor and into her room. And in the morning, she was still in Janine's bed, and she realized she had slept all night without having the dream at all.

All the same she didn't get another puppy; she said she didn't want one. If they thought they could make her less upset about sending her away, just by doing something easy like buying her another puppy, they could think again. She still couldn't believe it was all happening. She watched the trunk that had been her mother's filling up slowly with her new uniform, she was bought new shoes, a lacrosse stick, a rather formal-looking watch, she had a medical check at the doctor's, she was taken to the dentist, she had her hair cut, all in readiness for this dreadful event and she was taken to tea with another little girl who was already there, at St Madeleine's, who told her it was lovely, great fun, much better than being at home, and she counted the time that was left until she had to go, first in weeks, then in days, finally in hours, and right up to the last minute when she was dressed in her new uniform, all brown and blue, she really expected her father to come into the room and say, 'OK, darling, it's all right, you don't have to go if you really don't want to,' but he didn't; it was all coming true, the nightmare.

She behaved, in her rage and terror, even worse than usual; she shouted at everyone, she refused to eat at mealtimes, (raiding the larder when no one was around for cakes and biscuits so she wasn't hungry), she was rude to any of her mother's friends who asked her kindly if she was looking forward to going to her new school; and she fought endlessly with Cressida, on one dreadful occasion pushing her from the top to the bottom of the stairs and knocking two of her front teeth out. They'd been loose anyway, so she couldn't really see what all the fuss was about, and she said as much to her parents when they sat her down and asked her if she wasn't ashamed of herself.

'Harriet, darling,' said her father (for he was more tolerant, tried to be more understanding of her behaviour than her mother was), 'why did you do it? I don't understand,' and she said nothing, nothing at all, knowing that he wouldn't believe her if she told him the reason, that Cressida had told her she couldn't wait for her to go away.

The night before she went she lay in bed so frightened she thought she would die, her heart beating in great painful thudding bursts, her hands clammy with fear, determined not to cry, struggling not to cry; and there was a gentle knock at the door and Cressida came in, looking so sweet, so concerned. 'I shall miss you,' she said, 'I don't really want you to go,' and she climbed into bed with her. To her great astonishment Harriet discovered that that made her feel better, all her hostility suddenly vanished, and they fell asleep in one another's arms. She woke later, much later, to hear her parents whispering in the doorway.

'Look,' her mother was saying, 'isn't that sweet? Would you have believed it possible?'

And 'No,' her father said, 'but it's very encouraging. Maybe the separation really is going to be the best thing for them.'

'I hope so. I'm so glad they've made it up, that they're parting friends. Cressida's had to take such a lot from Harriet these past few weeks. If she wasn't such a sweet, forgiving little thing . . .'

Go on, Daddy, go on, say something nice about me, say something that shows you don't think it's all me, thought Harriet, feeling quite weak with the huge effort of keeping still, breathing quietly and steadily when she wanted to leap out of bed into their arms, beg them, for the last time, not to send her, promise to be good.

But 'Yes I know,' he said, 'let's hope this school can really do something for Harriet, make her a little bit sweeter too. Come on, we don't want to wake them, all hell will be let loose.'

And they went out, closing the door with infinite care behind them, and Harriet lay awake for hours, seething, aching with misery, and when she finally went to sleep she dreamed for the first time in ages about Biggles and his tiny golden velvet body settled into the long grass by the side of the road, the last look of adoration he gave her as he set off towards her on his fat paws, and the hideous sound of the lorry's brakes screeching and then the dead silence that settled on everything, and nothing to be seen of Biggles but a small trickle of blood leaking out from under one of the lorry's front wheels.

❋ ❋ ❋

The school was horrible. She could never remember feeling so lonely, so permanently, utterly unhappy, so literally sick with longing for home. They all wrote, even Cressida, but she wasn't allowed to phone because the staff said it would be unsettling for her, and new girls weren't allowed even a Sunday exeat for the first half of the term because that was supposed to be unsettling too. Harriet couldn't imagine being any more unsettled than she was already; she felt permanently sick, she had terrible diarrhoea almost all the time, she couldn't sleep, and she seemed to hear and see everything from the end of a long tunnel. She watched herself getting up in the morning, getting dressed, picking up the awful breakfast, trudging from the house over to the school; going to lessons, playing games, doing prep, and then going to bed again, and lying awake hour after hour, unable to sleep. The other girls began by trying to be kind, but they gave up in the face of her awful, blank-faced hostility and started teasing her instead, calling her Po Features and Farty Pants, imitating her as she ran endlessly, doubled up, to the loo.

She did badly at everything, made dense by misery, her considerable facility for games wrecked by increasingly poor health. When they came for her at half term, she fell into her father's arms, sobbing helplessly; she was even pleased to see Cressida, and held her hand in the back of the car all the way home.

When it was time to go back, she locked herself in the lavatory and refused to come out; it was only when they promised that if she wasn't feeling better by the end of term she could leave that she agreed to return. Then Cressida wrote to her, warning her not to believe them, that she had heard them saying the school was doing her good, that she was bound to settle down in time, and she realized that if she was ever to escape she would have to take some action herself.

The best thing, indeed the only thing, she decided, was to get expelled; once she had thought of it, she was excited at the sheer simplicity of the notion. She embarked upon her plan with the nearest to enjoyment she had felt for a long time, and started stealing the other girls' things, over a period of a few weeks: a watch, a bracelet, a transistor radio, and some money from the lost property fines box, left unattended one day on the secretary's desk. She left everything in her locker, which was duly searched when the alarm went up. Harriet stood in the headmistress's study, looking at all the things on the large desk, and waited to hear the wonderful words, 'We've asked your parents to come and take you home again.' She had even begun to pack a few things in her attaché case before she was sent for, so confident was she.

Only the wonderful words didn't come; instead the headmistress went droning on for hours about letting herself and her parents down and instead of being expelled, she was taken to the school psychiatrist, a droopy woman with greasy hair who said things like 'Nobody is angry with you, Harriet, just very upset' and 'You must learn to understand yourself better, Harriet, and then you will know why you do these things.'

She had to spend an hour three days a week, learning to understand herself; the psychiatrist, who dressed in sagging beige garments and whose name was Dr Ormerod, asked her endless questions about her family, whether she felt they loved her, how she felt about her sister and whether she was angry about being sent away to school. Harriet certainly wasn't going to make Dr Omerod's job easy for her and give her the satisfaction of telling her she hated her sister, that she knew her family didn't love her and she was extremely angry at being sent away to school; and besides she knew that if she did that, she would be labelled disturbed and unhappy, rather than bad, and crush any hopes of getting expelled. She said she loved her family and especially her sister, and she loved school, but she had lost her watch, she didn't like the girl the bracelet belonged to and she'd needed money to buy the new David Cassidy LP.

She'd confidently expected this to do the trick and that her parents would be finally phoned and told to come and collect her immediately, but Dr Omerod who had sat listening to her very carefully, clutching her beige cardigan tightly around herself, her crumpled beige face very solemn, had suddenly smiled and said, 'Well done, Harriet. You've made some very big progress. You've learnt to confront yourself, be honest about yourself. A lot of grown-ups can't do that, you know. I'm proud of you. I'm going to talk to Miss Edmundson again, and see what she thinks, but I would like to see this whole thing set behind you. We need some more sessions of course, but I think we're very well on our way.'

Harriet gave up, resigned herself to a life sentence.

And then Sir Merlin turned up.

✿ ✿ ✿

She had always adored Sir Merlin. Even when she was tiny, only two or three, his visits were wonderful occasions, exciting, unpredictable; he brought her extraordinary presents, a stuffed monkey, a real shrunken head, a baby python. She loved the python and slept with it for a few weeks, but it began to grow rather large and feeding it was a problem. Sir Merlin came to an arrangement with the local abattoir where it was let loose on the large rat population, but Maggie, finally driven beyond endurance when it rose up at her one morning from the depths of the airing cupboard where it liked to sleep, insisted slightly hysterically on it going to the zoo. When Harriet was only six, he took her on a four-day camping expedition in a remote part of the Pyrenees; she returned exhausted, sunburnt, covered in mosquito bites and blissfully happy. Since then he had taken her on a trip every two or three years to all manner of marvellous places, as once he had taken her father. Together they had travelled to India, Morocco, Egypt, and had driven the length of America in a boneshaking truck; Harriet, while loving every trip more than the last, had come to associate travel with acute physical discomfort. And the best thing of all about her journeyings was that Cressida had shared none of this enchantment, had never shown the slightest desire to go. Even as a child she had liked her comforts.

'Bit of a softic, your sister,' Sir Merlin had remarked one night as they lay together in the confines of the truck, gazing at the glories of the Arizona night sky. It was the nearest he had ever come to criticizing Cressida, but Harriet knew he didn't like her, and it made her happier still.

Cressida did not miss out altogether, because Theo, who thought she was wonderful, took her on long, exotic, sanitized holidays, staying in five-star hotels, flying in private planes, sailing on luxury yachts: all very far removed from the wondrous, vast, magical experiences that Harriet shared with Sir Merlin. The unique bond between them, forged by their first shared adventures, was strong and powerful; and Merlin had fought hard alongside Janine, Harriet knew, to spare her the miseries of St Madeleine's. But he had not won.

She was sitting on a bench in the playground playing cat's cradle with herself when she heard the familiar poop-poop of his beloved dark green Lagonda; hardly able to believe she wasn't dreaming, she looked up and flew across the tarmac to him, flinging herself into his arms.

'You're looking very thin,' he said, picking her up and setting her down again on the running board, and his brilliant blue eyes were concerned. 'Don't they feed you here?'

'They try to,' said Harriet with a shrug, 'but I can't eat it.'

'Damnfool idea, the whole thing,' he said. 'I've come to take you out for lunch. Just got back from Java. Wonderful place. Tell you all about it. Come along. I suppose we should warn someone.'

'Grandpa Merlin, they won't let me out for lunch,' said Harriet, her eyes round with horror. 'We're not even allowed out on Sundays and this is Tuesday.'

'Oh rubbish. I'll just tell 'em. Come on, Harriet, where's your spirit gone?'

'Dr Omerod's busy killing it off,' said Harriet with a sigh.

'Who's she? Never mind, tell me later. Hey, you!' He waved his stick at one of the staff who was walking towards him.

'Grandpa Merlin, you can't do that,' said Harriet, 'you have to be polite to staff.'

'What for? If they can't look after you properly they don't deserve politeness.'

'I'm so sorry.' Miss Foxted, the Latin teacher, as beige and droopy as Dr Omerod, her bosom hanging almost to her waist, with plaits coiled over her rather large ears, was hurrying over to them, out of breath with anxiety, 'You really can't park that car there.'

'Why not?' said Sir Merlin, looking at her in genuine puzzlement. 'What harm's it doing? I don't see any precious plants beneath it, anything like that.'

'Well, it's . . . it's the playground. It's dangerous.'

'Stuff and nonsense. Girls aren't blind, are they? Can see a car when it's moving, I imagine. Now look here, I'm taking Harriet out for the day. Have her back by bedtime if you like.'

'You can't do that, I'm afraid,' said Miss Foxted, her beige face strained with anxiety and disapproval. 'It's a working school day, you know. And we insist on formal appointments, even for day exeats. Besides, I'm afraid I don't even know who you are. It would be irresponsible of me to allow Harriet off the premises.'

'Well, I can see that,' said Sir Merlin, suddenly reasonable, holding out his hand, 'I'm her father's godfather. Sir Merlin Reid. How do you do. Want to phone I expect. We'll wait here for you.'

'Sir Merlin, I really can't–'

'Look,' said Sir Merlin, 'look, go and talk to your boss, whoever she is, will you? We haven't got all day.'

'But – I really don't see – that is –' Miss Foxted's voice trailed into helplessness.

'Tell you what,' said Sir Merlin. 'We'll come with you.'

They followed Miss Foxted across the playground towards the headmistress's study, stood outside while she went in; they could hear her voice, and Miss Edmundson's voice, slowly rising. Finally Miss Edmundson came out. She smiled her gracious, understanding smile at Sir Merlin, held out her hand.

'Sir Merlin! How nice to meet you. Now then, I understand you want to take Harriet out for the day. I'm afraid that will be quite impossible, against all our rules. Later in the term, one Sunday perhaps–'

'Have you phoned her father?'

'Certainly not. There is no question of her going out, therefore no question of phoning him.'

'Look, woman –' said Sir Merlin, and his white bushy eyebrows began to bristle; it was a sign to those who knew him that he was losing his temper. Miss Edmundson did not know that; she stood her ground, flushed.

'Sir Merlin, I really don't like–'

'I don't care what you like. I don't like what I see of this child. She's shockingly thin, she looks as if she hasn't had any fresh air for months. What have you been doing to her?'

'Sir Merlin, I assure you–'

'I'm not interested in your assurances, I'm interested in Harriet. And I'm taking her out.'

'But–'

Sir Merlin took Harriet's hand, went to move away, then turned back.

'Incidentally,' he said, 'what are the fees in this establishment?'

'I'm afraid I don't–'

'They must be at least a thousand a term. That's about – let's see –' He pulled a calculator from his pocket, and beamed at her over it. 'Wonderful things these. You should get one if you haven't already. Pay for themselves time and time again. Now then, thousand a term, let's say twelve weeks, that's eighty-four days, eleven pounds point 9047 pence a day. That's a lot of money, wouldn't you say? That you're saving on Harriet today. I'll tell my godson to dock it off the fees next term. Good day to you. Can't wait any longer for you to make some damnfool phone call. I'll have her back for bedtime, don't fret.'

'Sir Merlin–'

The Lagonda was halfway down the school drive before Harriet dared even to breathe.

Sir Merlin accomplished what the stealing, the illness, the misery, the tears, the begging letters to her parents, had not. Harriet was removed from St Madeleine's; she first heard of this decision not from her parents, or even Miss Edmundson, but from Cressida. 'I'm so excited, they've said you can come home,' she had written in her neat, careful handwriting, 'but I heard them say if you're at all naughty you've got to go again.'

'I think I'll go down to the bridge and find Cressida,' said Harriet, putting down her mug of tea. 'She's obviously feeling more nervous than we all thought. Funny, she was so amazingly calm last night. I'll be back in a minute, Janine. Purdey, walk?'

But Purdey raised one weary eyebrow and sank back into her dreams.

Harriet went into the utility room, pulled on her mother's old Barbour over the long T-shirt that was the nearest thing she possessed to a nightdress, stuck her feet into a pair of the long line of wellies that stood there and went out into the golden morning. The air was fresh, almost tangibly sweet; it was like breathing champagne, she thought, surprised at herself for thinking it. She was not greatly given to poetic observations. She walked across the small brick-paved court-yard outside the back door, through the walled rose garden that was her father's pride and joy, and across the lawn. In the far corner was a small gate and beyond that a field leading to the stream and the little double-arched bridge. It was an absurdly pretty spot: the setting for countless family photographs, both formal and informal. A weeping willow trailed into the water, and on the other side of the bridge was a stone seat, set into a small grassy mound, with ferns growing round it.

Harriet had half expected to see Cressida standing on the bridge playing Pooh-sticks with herself, as she had done all her life at times of emotional turmoil – good or bad. She would stand there, leaning over, staring intently into the water, waiting for her stick to come through, a bundle more of them in her hands (Cressida never did anything without being carefully prepared), and usually Purdey would be sitting beside her, watching the water with the same concentrated gaze. Only this morning Purdey wasn't there, and Cressida wasn't there either; nor was she in the little spinney beyond the bridge, or at the top of the meadow opposite. She was nowhere to be seen.

Frowning slightly, Harriet turned and walked – quickly, anxiously, while telling herself that of course there was no need for anxiety – back across the grass, towards the house. And noticed, as she should have done earlier, she told herself, that there was only one set of footprints in the thick dew and they were her own; and no doggy prints either. So where had Cressida gone, with Purdey, and where was she now? Back in the house of course, Harriet told herself, she must have missed her, she would have gone down the lane, maybe towards the bridlepath, she liked that walk (but so early in the morning? so far on such a day?).

She walked across the courtyard and into the kitchen, her heart pounding just a little too hard, smiled, carefully casual, at Janine, said (her voice just slightly strained), 'Cress back?'

And 'No,' said Janine, sounding surprised, 'no, she is not back, was she not at the bridge?'

'No,' said Harriet, 'no, hadn't been there actually. Well, I expect she wanted to go a bit further, calm her nerves. I'll – I'll get dressed and go down to the shop in the car and get a paper, I think, probably pass her in the lane. If she's not back already.'

'Yes of course,' said Janine, 'and *chérie*, I will go and take a bath and we can all meet again here in a little while. I expect your mother will be down soon.'

' 'Fraid so,' said Harriet, with a grin.

❀   ❀   ❀

It was still very quiet upstairs; her mother must have taken a sleeping pill. Otherwise she would have been pacing the house by now. Harriet looked at her watch: quarter to seven. That meant Cressida had been gone for at least an hour. A long time for a wedding morning. Or maybe she'd come back, through the front door, and Harriet had missed her. She knocked gently on Cressida's bedroom door: no answer. She opened it, looked in: the room was exactly the same – still, lifeless, neat. It was almost as if – Harriet shut the door again, stood very still for a moment and then, feeling slightly sick, her heart thudding uncomfortably in her throat went to her own room, pulled on some leggings and a clean T-shirt and ran downstairs again. Bloody Cressida, she thought, feeling suddenly angry: this was playing the drama queen just a bit too thoroughly. She must have realized they'd all be getting up by now and would start worrying: shit, where had she put her car keys? Probably on one of the hooks on the dresser, where they all hung their keys. Yes, she remembered now, she'd put them next to Cressida's – hung on that irritating key ring of hers, with the naff 'First Class Toilet' sign – the night before. Harriet reached for them, and then saw that Cressida's weren't there: not on the hook, not on any hook, she thought, her eyes racing over the dresser. She ran out to the drive: no red mini there as it had been last night. Well, of course not, she said to herself, hanging onto calm with great effort. James had told her to put it away, said they must clear the drive, either he or Cressida must have put it in the garage. Harriet went over to the garage, stood looking at the big white double doors, taking deep breaths, confronting what she was afraid of; then put out her hand to turn the knob and noticed that her hand was shaking, her palm slippery with sweat. She pulled the door back and looked cautiously, almost fearfully in.

And what she saw was precisely what she had been afraid of seeing: the only car in the garage was Maggie's little Renault; Cressida's car was gone.

Chapter 3

Theo 6am

Theo woke up feeling, as he so often did, in serious need of sex. He could never understand why people didn't want sex in the morning; after a night of close proximity to someone, curled, wrapped round them, the smell of them, the shape of them, the feel of them, what else could a normal person desire? It was the logical, natural sequence of events: first the foreplay, then the act. One of the main reasons he had made Sasha (apart from her blonde hair, wide blue eyes, impressive breasts and extremely good legs) the fifth Mrs Buchan was that she was wonderfully responsive in the mornings. 'Oh, Theo,' she would say, laughing, turning to him, kissing him, feeling for his penis, stroking it, fondling it, 'Oh Theo, you are so wonderful.' It was the best possible way to start the day; he would rise, after it, refreshed, as sleep alone could never make him feel, and stand in the shower, singing in his curiously tuneless voice, before heading for the gym and his religious-like progress round it. After that, and another shower, he would make his way through glass after glass of orange juice, bowl after bowl of coffee (wherever he was Theodore liked coffee in the French way) and a proper breakfast too, two very lightly boiled eggs followed by a great pile of croissants and pains au chocolat and tartine, and then he would take his great six-foot-five, 100-kilo frame into his dressing room and clothe it, and finally, still feeling wonderful, would pronounce himself ready for the day.

Only today, little of this progress through pleasure was to be granted to him. The Royal Hotel at Woodstock was extremely good, but there was no gym, no indoor pool even, nowhere for him to exercise. God, he should have told Jamie to check on that. So it would have to be jogging which he didn't enjoy these days, now that he'd got so heavy, and what they called a Continental breakfast was no doubt a piddling little glass of orange juice and a couple of chewy croissants. He could have the English, which was clearly excellent, he'd studied the menu the night before, bacon, eggs, sausages, mushrooms and black pudding – God, it was years since he'd had black pudding – maybe that would see him through to the wedding luncheon which would not be until nearly teatime.

James had asked him if he and Sasha would have supper at the house that night, after everyone had gone; he was still trying to get out of that one, an emotional evening in the bosom of the Forrest family, with its own particular attendant torture, think of an excuse, but so far he'd failed. James had been quite hurt enough that he'd stayed at the hotel the night before, and . . . Theo wrenched his mind from the problem and decided to have a shower; but the thought was not tempting, an English shower, feeble, trickling, he'd spent half an hour the night before trying to get the soap out of his hair. God, where was Sasha?

It was only just on six, she couldn't possibly have got up yet. Sasha liked to sleep late, usually slumbering peacefully (after satisfying his demands so deliciously) while he exercised, occasionally sitting up sleepily to be fed morsels of breakfast and sips of orange juice and then often dozing again until he got dressed and made the half-dozen or so phone calls that heralded the beginning of his working day.

'Sasha?' he called fretfully in the direction of the bathroom. 'Sasha, where are you?'

No answer; Theo felt a rush of something close to real rage. She didn't have to do much, for Christ's sake, just be there for him. That was what women were for, in his opinion: to be there for men. When he had first met Sasha, she was actually working in a public relations company, and she'd told him she wanted to carry on with her work: her insistence that she was in some way important, contributing to the running of the company, amused and almost touched him, indeed he had enjoyed teasing her about it at the time, especially in front of his friends. 'How was the board meeting today, Sasha?' he would say, or 'Tell us about that big deal you've got going through, Sasha, the one with that bank,' and she would blush prettily and say, 'Oh Theo, I can't, you know it isn't like that,' and he would say, 'No, no, if it's important to you, then we're all interested, I'd like you to tell us all about it.' And he'd listen, smiling indulgently as she stammered through some story of a decision to take on two extra account executives, or a new contract with a client in the City, and then he would ask everyone their views on whatever it was, and she would sit only slightly discomfited, looking at him adoringly. But once they were married, he'd insisted on her severing every connection with the company; he was her partner now, he said, with just the merest shadow of menace in his voice, and the only deal she need concern herself with was the one with him. Yes of course she'd said, she completely agreed and understood, and she could quite see that looking after him was going to be not only much more important than anything else she might be involved in, but a great deal more interesting and fun. And she had tried, she had tried very hard, and in the nine months they had been married had made him very nearly happy. Not quite, but that wasn't her fault. She was only thirty-one years old (to his fifty-nine), loving, thoughtful, charming to his friends and associates, a surprisingly talented housekeeper, a good cook (a talent she didn't often get a chance to display) – and if she wasn't exactly clever (a fact which he gently reminded her of from time to time, when she showed any real interest in his business affairs) she was bright enough to chatter away amusingly in any company. She was also extremely good at spending money. Theo had told her he wanted her to look the part of the wife of an inter-national businessman and she'd taken her duties seriously, becoming a personal customer at such disparate places as Chanel, Valentino, Ralph Lauren, Jasper Conran and Jean-Paul Gaultier. Theo raided the jewellers of the world for her, and was said to be seeking a knighthood, simply so that Sasha could have a tiara; meanwhile her collection of gems was dazzling, although mostly stored in the vaults of various banks, her preferred jewellery chosen from Cobra and Bellamy and Butler and Wilson.

Theo's five children, with the exception of Mungo, detested her, seeing her as a totally unscrupulous gold-digger, and his two elder daughters by wife three no longer spoke to him, since he refused to have them in the house unless they could be genuinely friendly to Sasha. His eldest son, Michael, by wife one, was distantly courteous to her, since his life and personal fortune were too caught up in the business to be otherwise, but Mungo, by wife two (always said to have been Theo's one great true love, and who had died tragically of cancer after five very good years), made his father very happy by being patently fond of Sasha, said she was gorgeous, that it was nice to have someone his own age around, and that from where he was sitting, anyone who would take his father on deserved any little rewards that happened along her way.

What he meant also, Theo knew, was that anyone who could distract his attention from Mungo's misdemeanours, or make excuses for them, was extremely welcome; wife number four in particular had been less than fond of Mungo, feeling, perhaps with some justification, that never having done what anyone would actually consider a day's work in his life, and having lost at least a million at the poker table, a little discipline was called for, albeit somewhat late in the day, and had urged Theo to cut Mungo's allowance, stop giving him the run of the Buchan homes, and make him at least consider the possibility of casting his mind in the direction of doing something in the way of gainful employment.

Well, she had been right, had number four, Jayne by name: Mungo's behaviour was a great deal less than exemplary; but Theodore was hard-pressed to upbraid him on it, having led an almost identical life up to the age of thirty himself, when he managed to find the rush of adrenalin, hitherto only experienced at the poker game, in the business world and had trebled the fortune his father had left him by the age of thirty-five.

'Business is just like poker,' he was fond of saying, 'it has nothing to do with chance or luck, or the cards you are dealt, and everything to do with how you read the situation. You can turn a terrible hand to a good one, simply by patience, and watchfulness.'

This maxim was much quoted in the business press. There was, as the financial journalists argued, a little more than patience and watchfulness to making a couple of billion pounds, which was what Theo was currently said to be worth, via his various companies (mostly food, oil and timber), but he would smile charmingly and say no, no, not at all, and if they ever cared to play poker with him, he would prove it to them.

He lived in one of three homes: a fine London house in The Boltons, a large apartment of breathtaking beauty in Paris, on the Ile St Louis, on the Quai Bethune, a chateau in the hills above Nice. He also owned a small island near Mustique, and another even smaller off the west coast of Scotland, a castle in County Cork, and an apartment in Trump Tower,

New York – but they were for occasional visits, he explained, they were not homes. His favourite was undoubtedly Paris; Paris was where he had grown up, he said, where he had spent his happiest times, where he had his closest friends.

'Paris is a sexy city,' he liked to say, 'people know how to enjoy themselves, how to please themselves.'

Sasha, on the other hand, preferred London.

Theo got out of bed, pulled on his bathrobe and went over to the window. It overlooked a quiet courtyard at the back of the hotel; in the distance he could see the glorious lyrical parkland of Blenheim. It was a perfect day; well, that was good. Probably be too hot, but the sun would shine on the bride, and they would all be able to wander about in the garden, drinking the champagne that he knew would be excellent because it had been his wedding present to James (not Cressida, to whom he had given a bed of considerable splendour, a late eighteenth-century French four-poster, with exquisitely painted and fluted posts and wonderful cream brocade curtains). 'I don't want any bloody nonsense,' he'd said firmly, when he called to say twenty cases of Veuve Clicquot were being delivered to the Court House, 'expensive business getting married, Christ, I should know, and you're not a rich man.'

'I'm quite rich enough, thank you,' James had said with a touch of irritation, and Theo had said it was impossible to be rich enough and that James wasn't rich at all by his standards, which was true, and couldn't he give an old friend a little something to launch his daughter into married life?

As he looked down into the courtyard, frowning, increasingly displeased at Sasha's absence, he suddenly realized that his car was missing. It was his favourite car: the silver Bentley Continental, immensely valuable. He kept it garaged in London through the winter and drove it with great pleasure down to the South of France every spring; he had driven it back up this summer, so that Cressida Forrest could have it for her wedding, and Theo's chauffeur, who had sat wretchedly in the back of the Bentley for most of the journey up from Nice, was due to drive it over to the Court House at 1:30 to take first Maggie and the bridesmaids and then Cressida and James to the village church. And the last thing

Theo had done last night before getting into bed was look fondly out of the window at it; now it had gone.

He turned to the phone and called reception: where was his chauffeur?

'In his room, Mr Buchan. Shall I call him for you?'

'Yes please. Tell him to get up here fast and send up some tea, would you?'

'Certainly, Mr Buchan.'

'And have you seen my wife?'

'Yes, Mr Buchan. She went out about half an hour ago. She said she was going for a walk.'

A walk? Sasha's idea of a walk was from one department of a shop to another. What the hell was going on?

There was a knock at the door; it was Brian, the driver. He looked nervous; he was wearing his dressing gown.

'Yes, Mr Buchan?'

'Brian, where the hell is my car?'

'Your car, Mr Buchan?'

'Yes, Brian. You know what a car is? Motorized vehicle, four wheels, engine, that sort of thing. I have a few. Special favourite parked in the courtyard here last night. Any suggestions, Brian?'

'Well, Mr Buchan, I do have one.'

'Well, one is better than none, Brian. Come along, let's have it.'

'I think Mr Mungo might have it, Mr Buchan.'

'Mungo? Took the Bentley? Brian, I do hope not. For both your sakes.'

'I'm afraid that is what has happened, Mr Buchan. I'm sorry.'

'But why did you let him, for Christ's sake? And when did he take it and where?'

'Well – he took it last night, Mr Buchan. Very late.'

'Brian, for Christ's sake why did you let him? You know that car is priceless. And that Mungo drives everything as if it was his Maserati. What was he doing taking it, late at night? He'd had at least a bottle of champagne and God knows how much wine at dinner. Sweet Jesus, if anything's happened to that car I shall personally drive what is left of it over first him and then you.'

'Yes, Mr Buchan.' Brian looked as if such a course of action would be welcome.

'OK. Let's get some sense here. Why did you give him the key?'

'I – didn't. Well, not at first. He'd had rather a lot to drink as you say, and he said he felt like a drive. I told him he couldn't have it, no matter what, and he said he'd win it off me. At poker.'

'Oh really? You embarked on a game of poker, with my car as stake. Brian, you are fired. As of this moment.'

'Mr Buchan, of course I didn't. I said he couldn't have the car whatever he did. And then he said quite right, Brian, spoken like a man. Let's have a game anyway. He said he couldn't sleep. So I said all right, and he went off and came back with some cards and a bottle of Scotch and young Mr Headleigh Drayton.'

'Rufus? So he's in on this as well.'

'Yes, Mr Buchan. Well, we started and we played for – oh a couple of hours. Then the phone rang. It was reception. They said was Mr Mungo here, and I said yes. He took the call, and he seemed very upset. Genuinely upset. He was very white. He asked me to excuse him and Mr Headleigh Drayton for a moment, and they went outside the door. When they came back, he said "Look, Brian, I absolutely have to go somewhere. It's a real crisis, I swear. Let me have the car." He'd left his in London, as you know, and came down with Mr Headleigh Drayton. I said he couldn't and that I didn't trust him, told him to get a taxi. He said how was he going to get a taxi at two thirty in the morning in the middle of the country. He did seem terribly upset, Mr Buchan, they both did.'

'Dear me. I suppose they were in tears.'

'Mr Headleigh Drayton was very near tears, sir.'

'Good God,' said Theo, concerned for the first time at something other than his car. 'And they wouldn't tell you what it was about?'

'Well – not really. They said they couldn't, but they had to get over to see someone, that it was literally life or death. I said they should call an ambulance, but they said they would do less damage by dealing with it themselves. "I swear to you, Brian," Mr Mungo said, "I swear on my mother's grave I'm telling you the truth." Well you know as well as I do, Mr Buchan, he just wouldn't lie in such a way.'

'No, no, I daresay he wouldn't,' said Theo impatiently. 'All right. So did they say where they were going? Give you any clue? Or say when they'd be back?'

'They said whatever happened, they'd have the car back by this morning, Mr Buchan. But that was all. And I believed them. So I – I let them have it. I'm very sorry, sir. But I felt it was worth the risk.'

'Well I hope for your sake, Brian, that it was. I very much hope so. Oh, incidentally, have you seen Mrs Buchan this morning?'

'Yes, sir. About an hour ago. I saw her going out of the front of the hotel. She had low-heeled shoes on, sir, she looked as if she was going for a walk.'

'The world's going mad,' said Theo, 'that's what they told me in reception. I'm going back to my room. Let me know the moment they return, Brian.'

'Yes, Mr Buchan.'

Theo went back to his room, and was about to get in the shower when the phone rang. 'Brian? What –'

'No, Theo, not Brian. It's me. James. How are you?'

'I'm about as all right as could be expected under the circumstances. My car, my son and my wife have gone missing, but otherwise everything is normal. They're not there, are they? Any of them?'

'No,' said James, 'no, not as far as I know.'

He sounded very odd; strained, his voice under tight control. Nerves, Theo supposed; he'd seemed all right last night at dinner.

'Jamie, are you OK?'

'No, not really,' said James. There was a silence, then he said, 'Theo, I've got to talk to you. Could I come over?'

Theo had heard those words, in that desperate over-controlled tone, twice before. 'Sure,' he said, trying to sound reassuring.

'I'll be there in ten minutes.'

'Fine. I'll put the kettle on. Suite 2. First floor. Come straight up.'

That was an old joke of theirs about the kettle. He ordered some more tea and coffee and sat back to wait, remembering, remembering the first time, thirty years, a whole lifetime ago.

James had walked in the door, looking terrible. His face was white, drawn, as if he was bleeding internally. He looked a lot older than his twenty-nine years.

'I've got to do something terrible,' he said.

'What do you mean, you've got to? If it's upsetting you that much, don't do it.'

'I do have to. I don't have any choice.'

'What sort of something?'

'Finish with Susie.'

'I'll have her,' said Theo cheerfully.

'Theo, don't. Don't joke about it. It's not funny.'

'No, I can see that. I'm sorry. Tell me about it.'

'Well – it's quite simple really. I have to finish with her.'

'But why? I thought you and she were finally getting it together. After all these years.'

'Christ Almighty, Theo, don't make it worse.'

'Well, why are you going to finish with her when it's clearly making you so extremely unhappy?'

'Because I'm getting married.'

'Good God, Jamie, who to?'

'Maggie Nicolson.'

'Oh Jamie, Jamie, no.' Theo was surprised at the depth of emotion in his own voice. 'Don't do it. Please. I'm deadly serious, you can't do that. You can't.'

'Of course I can, Theo,' said James. His voice was calmer: it was as if Theo's reaction had steadied him. 'I'm going to.'

'But why?'

'Because – because I want to. Because I love her.'

'Bollocks.'

'Theo, don't be offensive. Maggie is a great girl. I'm very lucky.'

'Uh-huh. So great you've hardly been near her for weeks. Hardly out of Susie's bed.'

'Don't be filthy,' said James wearily.

'I feel filthy. It's filthy news. What are you up to, for God's sake?'

'I'm not up to anything. I'm getting married. Christ, Theo, give me a drink. A very big, very strong one. Then I'll go and see Susie.'

'Not if I can help it you won't. This is suicide, Jamie. Suicide of the soul.'

'Yes,' said James, suddenly. 'I know. Christ I'm a shit, Theo.'

And he sat, drinking Scotch after Scotch, turning the glass in his hand, his voice increasingly blurred; and Theo sat listening to him, also drinking hard, trying to grasp what James was saying, what he was going to do, and to work out what he could do to help him.

❊ ❊ ❊

In the end, all he could do was support him. James's mind was made up, irrevocably; he had asked Maggie Nicolson to marry him and she had accepted. Plump, sweet-natured, dull little Maggie, whom he had known for a couple of years now, whose father was the senior consultant gynaecologist at St Edmund's Hospital (where James was a registrar), who had an undoubted crush on him, whom he had taken out from time to time, flirted with, danced with, and even (James now confessed to Theo) had taken to bed a few months earlier – 'Don't look at me like that, Theo, she's a lovely girl, and actually quite – how can I put it –'

'James, don't tell me she's sexy. I can't bear it.'

'She is. She's potentially very sexy. I'm – very lucky.'

'So you proposed, did you?' said Theo. 'Just like that? Swept off your feet?'

And 'Yes,' said James, 'yes I did.' And went on to say that the Nicolsons were delighted, were cracking champagne all over the place, the announcement was going in *The Times* and the *Telegraph* in a matter of days, and that Maggie was a lovely girl, she would make a marvellous wife, he was a lucky sod, and Theo had to be happy for him.

'And what's in this for you?' asked Theo, in a pause in this soliloquy. 'Apart from gaining a wonderful wife, I mean?'

'I don't know what you mean,' said James.

'Of course you bloody well do. Old man Nicolson's bought you, hasn't he? Look at me, Forrest, and tell me he hasn't. You can't. Come on. What's he offered you?'

Jamie was silent. He stared at the floor for a long time. Then he suddenly got up and rushed to the bathroom. Theo heard him vomiting. He went in after him, and sat with him, proffering him tissues, towels, glasses of water.

'You silly bastard,' he said equably, 'here, come on, come back into the other room. Look, I don't give a shit what you do, Jamie, as long as you're happy. But you're not going to be.'

'I might be,' said Jamie.

'No, Jamie, you won't.'

'Well I have to try to be. That's all.'

'What exactly is it? That he's giving you?'

Jamie walked into the sitting room again and sat down heavily on the sofa. He didn't look at Theo. Finally he said 'His full support, as he puts

it, for Senior Registrar at St Christopher's Cambridge. That means a hell
of a lot. Almost a guarantee, you could actually say. The medical
profession is just as open to politics as any other. And the same thing for
junior consultancy at Teddy's when he retires from the NHS in three
years' time. Honestly, Theo, I listened to him, and it was like Christ in
the wilderness. Temptation beyond endurance. My whole life set up for
me. Success, money, status – guaranteed. I'm getting bloody nowhere,
Theo. And all I have to do is marry a sweet girl I'm terribly, terribly fond
of. Who will make in any case the perfect consultant's wife. Which Susie
wouldn't.'

'Of course she would. She'd be very good at it, chatting up all the
patients.'

'No she wouldn't. Too frivolous. And she is so appallingly extravagant,
she needs a seriously rich husband. Which I'm never going to be. It just
can't work, Theo. Not ever. And she's putting a lot of pressure on me.
We had a terrific row about it only two days ago.'

'How convenient for you. Or rather for Maggie.'

'Oh, go screw yourself, Theo. I really can't even think about marrying
Susie. Ever. Anyway, sitting there, at the table at Simpsons, with a lot of
claret poured down my throat, I was suddenly looking at a golden
future. And I just couldn't turn it down. Of course it was all very subtly
done. I mean not like I've made it sound at all. But it was made very
clear that none of it would happen if I didn't marry Maggie.'

'And you want it that much?'

'Yes,' said James, sounding slightly surprised. 'Yes, I suppose I must
do. Bloody hell, Theo, you've no idea what a jungle the medical
profession is. Everyone thinks it's all so gentlemanly, but it's just as
corrupt as everything else. Jobs for the boys, all fixed long before you go
for interviews, the boards going through the farce of talking to you,
pretending to consider you. Six senior registrarships I've applied for in
the past nine months, and sixty-six ahead I'd say. I want to be a
consultant; to earn some money, to have some status before I'm an old
man, Theo. And without a helping hand I'm not going to get any of it.'

'I still can't believe it,' said Theo, looking at him morosely. 'It's
disgusting. And I can't believe any man would sell his daughter like that.
They must both be desperate. She's not in the pudding club is she?'

'No, of course she's not,' said James wearily. 'And neither of them are desperate, as you put it. But Maggie and I are very fond of each other and I think he can see I'll be the sort of son-in-law he wants. Shit, Theo, half the world runs on arranged marriages. Look at the French even. They work very well. You ask Janine.'

'Oh for Christ's sake,' said Theo. 'Jamie, you're crazy. I just hope you know what you're really doing, that's all. And I hope Maggie doesn't. Poor cow.'

'Maggie is very happy,' said James slightly pompously. 'Very.'

'At the moment, I daresay she is,' said Theo. 'It's all the other moments I'm worrying about. All the rest of her life. I hope she never gets to find out about Susie.'

'She won't because there'll be nothing to find out,' said James. 'I'm going to finish with Susie. Completely. Obviously.'

'Oh yeah?' said Theo.

About three weeks before the wedding, he had dinner with Maggie. James had been going to join them, but got caught up at the hospital. Theo sat and became extremely drunk as he listened for what seemed an extremely long time to Maggie telling him how wonderful James was, how happy she was, how perfect their life was going to be. She really didn't deserve what was coming to her, he thought; she was such a sweet, pretty girl, so extremely naive, so desperately in love. Well James was right about one thing: she would make the perfect consultant's wife. She was a well-bred English rose, twenty-four years old, she did all the right things, knew all the right people. She had been a deb, done a history of art course, (and a cookery course) and worked at a gallery in Bond Street. She shared a flat in Kensington with four other girls, and was busy decorating and furnishing the charming little Fulham cottage she and James were going to move into after the wedding. Her father had put down a very large deposit on it as a wedding present. 'I still can't believe it all, Theo,' she said, helping herself to a second dollop of whipped cream to go on her trifle. 'It's all too good to be true. Of course I always knew Jamie liked me, and we'd had some lovely times together, but I thought he'd gone off me actually, until a few weeks before he proposed. I mean I did think there was someone else. But it was just that he was so busy.

They work the most horrendous hours and days at that hospital, you know.'

'Oh I know,' said Theo. He kept his eyes firmly on his plate.

'Theo,' said Maggie suddenly, 'I want to ask you something.'

Christ Almighty, she's going to come out with it, thought Theo; what on earth am I going to say?

'Yes, Maggie,' he said.

'Theo, look at me.'

He raised his eyes reluctantly, met her candid blue ones, anxious in the candlelight. 'I hope it's not serious,' he said lightly.

'It is. Well, it is to me.'

'Ask away.' He poured himself another glass of wine. Maggie was on water.

'It's just that you know Jamie better than anyone in the world, I should think. And so I thought you'd know.'

'Know what, Maggie?'

'Well – if he minds about my father.'

Jesus Christ, this is getting worse every minute. 'What about your father, Maggie?'

'Well, the thing is, Theo – oh dear, this is so difficult, so embarrassing –'

'Maggie, I'm not easily embarrassed.'

'It's just that – well, there are some things we never talk about. And –'

'Maggie, maybe I'm not the person to talk to about this.'

'Oh Theo, I think you are.'

She leant forward suddenly, her hands clasped. Her face was flushed, her eyes brilliant. Her fair hair with its loose curls was tumbled on her shoulders; her dress was quite low-cut and a very pretty full white bosom swelled up from it. He could smell her, feel her warmth; for the first time he understood how James could be marrying her. She was, in her own way, very attractive, quite sexy even. He smiled at her.

'Go on then.'

'Well, you see my father is quite – dominating. He likes to control things. And people.'

She had guessed. She knew. Not so stupid after all. And very brave. Theo put his spoon down, took both her hands in his. 'Maggie, I can't tell you how –'

'Let me finish, Theo. Please. Then you can have your say. It's hard enough anyway. Now the thing is, Jamie's parents are quite hard-up. They're lovely people, but they really haven't got any money. Well, you know that. And my father has a lot. And he's just throwing it about all over the place, buying the house, paying for the honeymoon. He's so tactless. And I just wondered if Jamie minded. He's never said anything about it – in fact if I try and ask him he changes the subject.'

I bet he does, thought Theo, I bet he bloody does.

'And I don't want him to feel – well, humiliated. Or his parents, come to that. It's all so delicate, Theo, don't you think?'

Theo felt as if he had suddenly surfaced after a rather long spell under-water. He smiled at her, released her hands, sat back with his glass of wine. 'I really don't think you should worry too much about Jamie,' he said finally. 'He's not really the sensitive little plant you seem to imagine. He can look after himself, old Jamie can. I don't think he'd mind any of that in the very least.'

And 'Oh Theo, thank you,' said Maggie, 'that is such a relief. What a good friend you are.'

Afterwards, after dropping her off at her flat, he wondered if he should actually have told her the truth, and knew that in fact he had not been a friend to her at all.

It was a measure of Theo's anxiety about James that he had forgotten about his beloved car as he sat and waited for him. It was also a measure of his faith in his son – which was both considerable and oddly justified. Mungo might have been expelled from two schools (once for smoking cannabis, once for what the headmaster had described as fornication), he might not yet have shown a great interest in anything remotely resembling a career, (although he was currently masquerading as an estate agent and had an office in Carlos Place, whose earnings were, Theo was forced to recognize, just beginning to balance out with its costs); he consistently lost large sums of money at the poker table, consumed awe-inspiring quantities of alcohol, and his idea of being faithful was not being in bed with one woman while another was actually under the same roof; but he was fundamentally honest, loyal and, when the occasion demanded, sensible. And Theo knew that this occasion demanded sense. Mungo would be back, and he would bring the car back; things just might be a little tense in the meantime. He wished he could feel as certain about Sasha. He wasn't going to stand for this sort of thing from her. He was lighting the first cigar of the day, as a comment on his uncertainty, when the phone rang.

'Theo, good morning.'

'Yes, Mark?' Mark Protheroe was his personal assistant; he ran the London office with a towering efficiency that at times awed Theo himself. He also had considerable power. He had a watching brief on the companies worldwide, handled all Theo's charitable ventures, and dealt, together with Theo's personal secretary, with his diary, a work of some complexity. Mark was on paper an unlikely candidate for the job, a Wykehamist, with a double first in mathematics; he was tall, stooping, and extremely thin, with a hawklike nose, huge bony hands and very faded blue eyes which could absorb the contents of a company report, a balance sheet or a computer screen faster than most people could note the date at the top of it. He reported directly to Theo rather than to George Harding, managing director of Buchan International, a fact which caused Harding to complain vociferously that the swift path he liked to tread was often obstructed by the need to involve Mark Protheroe in considerable and absurd detail. Theo shrugged off the complaints, saying that it was his company, his system and if George didn't like it he knew what he could do, and that Mark's brief was simply to receive and transmit information which should in no way affect any decision-making Harding was involved in. This was not strictly true and Theo knew it and Harding knew it, but generally speaking the arrangement worked, mainly by virtue of Mark's ability to sift through information at a rate which at times seemed almost instantaneous and decide which of it needed Theo's urgent involvement and which did not. It was a dangerous brief that he held; 95 per cent of the time he got it right. Theo had met him at a business convention Mark was attending in his capacity as lecturer in economics at the Manchester Business School, had made him an offer that quadrupled his salary as well as putting the use of his private plane and the company apartments in New York and Tokyo at his disposal, and was still surprised when Protheroe accepted.

Mark's voice, level, calm as always, came over the phone now. 'Morning, Theo. Just an update. London market's steady, Japan looks slightly unsettled, New York closed well up.'

'Fascinating,' said Theo.

'Yes indeed,' Protheroe earned his salary as much for unruffled good-natured fielding of Theo's quixotic responses as for any of his more technical skills. 'Only two other things to watch at this stage. Tokyo Electron have dropped for some reason, only three points but they dropped four yesterday; and I'm afraid we've missed out on Tealing Mill.'

'How for Christ's sake?' said Theo scowling into the phone through his cigar smoke. Tealing Mills was a timber company, family owned and in trouble; he had been watching it obsessively, convinced he could buy into it and turn it round, had instructed Mark and George Harding to pounce. It was such obsessions, such convictions that had made Theodore Buchan into a billionaire.

'They've – well they've sold a 20% share apparently,' said Mark, his nervousness just detectable. 'Twenty-four hours ago.'

'How the hell did we miss it?'

'We blinked,' said Mark. 'It happened that quickly.'

'I pay you not to blink,' said Theo furiously. He groped for the lighter; his cigar had gone out. Christ, this was turning into a bad day. 'Can't I leave anything to you guys to see to? You know how much I wanted that company. Timber's going through the roof. What the hell are you doing Mark? And who's bought the bloody thing anyway?'

'Private individual. New York based. I've got the New York people on it. They're getting back to me.'

'Private individual! Shit a brick. Can we get hold of any more?'

'Difficult at the moment I'd say. They've got enough money to see them through a bit.'

'Bloody brilliant. So we've totally goofed.'

'Well – yes. If you regard this company as really important. George and I don't. It's doing OK, but that's all. You have interests in far more profitable timber companies.'

'Yes, but not ones I can get a hold of. I can turn Tealing white-hot. Correction. Could have done. Stay on it, Mark. Ring me when New York opens at the very least. Tell them to find out who this person is. And keep trying to get hold of some more of the shares. Someone must be offering them.'

'Sure. Er–'

'Yes?'

'Won't you be in the church?'

'Ring me on the mobile. It'll be with Brian.'

'Yes, all right. Oh, and Exmoor phoned, want to check you'll still be going on Saturday.'

'Of course I will. What a bloody silly question.'

'Yes indeed.'

The Exmoor Foundation was a small community for the mentally handicapped Theo had financed and built from nothing on the edge of Exmoor; it was one of his favourite projects, and he took a personal and oddly tender interest in it.

'All right, Mark. Speak to you later.'

He put the phone down scowling and poured himself another coffee. God, it was filthy. He dialled room service, complained about it, ordered some more, and was trying once again to relight his cigar when Sasha walked in. She looked gorgeous; she was flushed, her hair was in a tangled blonde cloud, and she was barefoot. Her blue eyes as she looked at him were innocently wide, but just slightly wary. Theo looked back at her without smiling.

'Where the hell have you been? And where are your shoes, for Christ's sake?'

'They're outside the door, Theo. They're muddy. I've been for a walk.'

'Sasha, since when did you like going for walks?'

'Since this morning,' said Sasha. 'It was lovely. I really enjoyed it. I think I might take it up as a regular thing.' She spoke as if walking was a rather unusual occupation like scuba diving or rock climbing.

'Well, next time, you might tell me where and when you're going. I've been worried out of my head about you. Come over here.'

He held out his arms; Sasha went over to him and put her arms round his neck, kissed first his cheek, then his lips, very gently. He slid his hand into her raincoat and met a bare breast.

'Mrs Buchan! What is this?'

'A breast. I think.'

'Sasha, most people wear clothes before going for country walks. If you're going to make it a regular activity, you'd better get the equipment for it. Stand up.'

She stood up. He undid the belt of her raincoat; it swung open.

Underneath she was stark naked. Theo caught his breath, sat staring at her, feeling his skin prickle, his balls stir, his breathing deepen. Shit, she was gorgeous.

'You're gorgeous,' he said simply. 'Take that raincoat off.'

Sasha took it off. She was smiling gently now, clearly assured of his benevolence, his trust. She leant towards him gently; Theo put out his hand and pushed her upright again.

'A moment, my darling. I'm not yet absolutely into my dotage. Would you mind telling me exactly why you developed this sudden urge for early country walking after – what? thirty-one years of sleeping late? Well, maybe only thirty. I daresay you woke early as an infant.'

Sasha looked at him slightly less confidently. She shivered slightly and reached for her raincoat. Theo put out his arm and held hers.

'No, don't put it back on. I like the slight sense of disadvantage you're at, and besides it's very nice for me. Just tell me, Sasha, I'm not going to beat you up.'

'Oh, Theo –'

'Don't Oh Theo me. I don't like being lied to. Or prevaricated with.'

'Theo, I would like to get dressed.'

'And I would prefer you didn't. Why did you go out?'

'Theo, for God's sake, I told you –'

There was a knock on the door. 'Yes,' shouted Theo.

'It's me,' said James's voice and he walked in.

*

'Christ I'm sorry,' said James. 'You did tell me to come straight up.'

'Don't worry about it,' said Theo expansively. 'We're pleased to see you, aren't we, Sasha?'

'Yes of course,' said Sasha, smiling automatically. She had put her raincoat back on. 'How are you, James? Er – would you both excuse me? I have to have a bath.'

'Sure,' said Theo. 'Close the door, darling, won't you? This is a private conversation about to be held. Very private.'

Sasha looked at him, her blue eyes suddenly dark with hostility. Theo was surprised; she was normally totally acquiescent. She turned and walked through to the bathroom and slammed the door. Taps started running very hard.

'You're a bastard,' said James. He managed to smile rather weakly.

'You really can't talk to your wife like that.'

'On the contrary, I can, and frequently do,' said Theo calmly. 'Coffee, Jamie?'

'Yes, please,' said James. He sat down and took a cup. His hand was shaking visibly. He drained the cup, held it out for more.

'You look as if you need a brandy,' said Theo. 'Want one?'

James shook his head. 'Of course not.'

'Sorry. One of these days I'll crack that resolve of yours.'

'Of course you won't,' said James irritably. 'Never.'

'OK,' said Theo, refilling the cup. 'What is it? What's wrong?'

'It's Rufus.'

'Rufus! What on earth has Rufus been doing? Nothing in my car I hope. You haven't heard from them I suppose?'

'No. Sorry.' James looked at him, tried to smile and then suddenly put his head in his hands. Theo looked at him in alarm.

'Jamie, come on. It can't be that bad.'

'It's quite bad,' said James. 'Rufus is in love. Says he's going to get married. Susie told me last night.'

'So?'

'So it's with – with someone he has no business to be in love with.'

'Oh, for God's sake, Jamie, do stop talking in riddles,' said Theo wearily. 'Who's the boy in love with? And what's it to you? Apart from the little matter of – well we won't go into that now.'

'We might have to,' said James. 'He's in love with Ottoline Mills.'

'Shit,' said Theo, 'shit a brick.'

Chapter 4

Tilly 6am

'Fuck off,' said Tilly politely, slamming down the phone on the well-spoken robot who had just informed her that it was *six heures*. She tried to open her eyes, but they felt raw and scratchy, and her head throbbed horribly. 'Shit, shit,' she said aloud, she shouldn't have had all that red wine last night, she should never have gone to that bloody place with that little nerd, it always always had this effect on her, she really should have learnt by now. It would show too, on her face, on her skin, she would look terrible, and she only had – what? Three-quarters of an hour, not long enough to go for a run, maybe the hotel sauna – yes, that would help. God, it had better be open; of course it would be, this might be Paris, but she was in a small piece of America, that's why she had chosen to be here rather than somewhere more romantically French – who needed that on a trip? Tilly unwound her long legs from the foetal position they liked to spend the night in, sat on the edge of the bed, her head in her hands, her long red nails pushed into her short cropped black hair, trying to force the pain out.

'Come along, Ottoline,' she said, 'pull yourself together,' and she stood up, fighting the nausea, the pain, wrapped herself into the thick white bathrobe that the Intercontinental Hotel had loaned to her, and padded along the corridor to the elevator.

The Fitness Centre was not only open, it was busy. Complacently lean, tanned Americans and earnest Japanese walked, jogged, stepped, rowed: every machine was in action. Tilly looked round the room, swept it the half-inviting, half-contemptuous smile that accompanied her down the catwalks on the most prestigious fashion shows in the world, and walked into the sauna, ignoring the pile of towels on her way in. It was empty, thank Christ; she took off her robe and sat down naked, as wearily as if it had been night-time (if only, if only it was), on the wooden slatted seat, drew her knees up, sat hugging them, her head thrown back, waiting for, feeling already, the hard dry heat take possession of her, reaching inwards for her aching bones, her sore stomach. Trickles of sweat were forming between her breasts, her thighs, on her forehead, it was good, so good this, healing, soothing, and she felt suddenly she could cope with it, the long awful day ahead, the heat of the city, the bad temper she was going to encounter, from French fashion editors, hairdressers, make-up artists, and that bastard of a photographer McGrath. God, she hated him, with his bald head and his ponytail, and those dreadful glittering, evil eyes. The real Evil Eye, maybe he had that even, and maybe he could – Tilly realized suddenly that her thoughts were drifting dangerously free, she would be asleep again in a minute, and she stood up, feeling the room swim nastily, nauseously. Outside the sauna she breathed the suddenly fresh air, and without daring even to pause, jumped into the ice-cold plunge pool, feeling its shock on her skin, her veins, her lungs. Christ Almighty, she was going to faint, she was going to die. She hung onto the rail, her eyes closed, counting; get up to sixty, Tilly, and you can get out. But could she stay there deathly, mortally cold for so long? Yes, she could, she must . . . forty-nine, fifty . . . fifty-five, nearly there, now, fifty-nine, sixty. Thank Christ. She opened her eyes, started to climb out, realized she had left her robe in the sauna, realized there was a smiling, cocky bastard – French, he had to be, in those grey jersey shorts – standing at the top of the steps to the plunge pool watching her climb out, realized her breasts – the nipples hard and stiff with the cold – were already out of the water, and that the rest of her must surely follow. Well, OK, fine, if that was how he wanted to start his day, getting his rocks off on a bit of voyeurism, let him. She continued to climb, enjoying the moment as she finally stepped right out when he saw that she was taller than him, by two, maybe three inches, looked down at him, first at his face and then, pointedly, consideringly, down at his crotch, and walked slowly, gracefully past him, retrieved her robe and made for the elevator.

✳ ✳ ✳

Back in her room she did feel much better: tired, but at least likely to stay alive. She stood in front of the bathroom mirror, drenching herself in Opium body lotion, looking at herself dispassionately as she was able easily to do (indeed it was one of the essential qualities, one that separated a good model from a great one, Felicity her agent had told her once), at the small head set on the long proud stalklike neck, the great slanting brown eyes, the chiselled lips above the tiny pointed chin, and the great slender height of her, six foot one and a half inches, the breasts that managed to be full on her wraithlike torso, the awesomely narrow hips, the flat stomach, the high, taut buttocks – slightly darker than the rest of her body, which was what the arty-farty girl from *Vogue* had labelled cocoa-butter brown in her copy – and then the legs, forty-five inches from hip to floor, legs that fashion editors at once loved and loathed, necessitating trousers specially made for sessions, false hems on skirts, legs that propelled her along without seeming (as another arty-farty journalist had said) to make any true contact with the ground. She brushed what there was of her hair: it was good, the short cut, very good. After ten days she still liked it. It had been the right thing to do. Tough, like the plunge pool, but right. Nicky Clarke had been telling her to cut it for months and she had resisted him, saying there were too many black girls around with short crops. 'Not the way I'll crop it,' he'd said, and had spent a whole afternoon working round and round her head, caressing it tenderly, sensuously with his scissors, getting it exactly the right shortness, a perfect carved cap with a lick of length over the nape of her neck. Clever boy, Nicky: very clever.

She hauled on a pair of leggings and a big T-shirt, heard her stomach rumble ominously; she should eat. Otherwise that row would be going on all day. She'd pick up a baguette on the way down to the studio, eat it in the taxi. She might throw up, but it was worth the risk.

In the taxi, blind to the golden beauties of early-morning Paris, going towards the Marais, to Mick McGrath's studio, munching the baguette, feeling steadily better, she looked at the real people – as opposed to the fantasy folk, like herself, like Susie Verge the fashion editor from *Sept Jours* she would be working with today, like Laurent the make-up artist, like McGrath – and felt sharply ashamed of regarding her day with foreboding. What she did, what they all did, was, as Nöel Coward had so memorably said, better than working; and as her mother had also said, slightly less memorably, 'Ottoline, you don't know what the word work means.'

Her mother certainly knew what work meant: it meant sewing, eight, nine, ten hours a day, in a sweatshop in Brixton, putting sequins, pearls, diamanté, frills, onto the bodices of the sort of evening dresses that still sold on great bushy rails in street markets. Sewing with an aching head and sore eyes, and for years and years a gnawing anxiety about her child, first with the childminder (all right, but not good – too many children, too few facilities), then at school (poor, not even all right – far too many children, hardly any facilities), and finally not at school at all, but bunking off, hanging around with her friends at McDonald's and Burger King, making a milk shake and a cigarette last all day. She had tried so hard, her mother had, to persuade her to get her GCSEs, to get something behind her: 'You'll never get anywhere, Tilly, not without qualifications. I got my school cert and it made all the difference.' And she had looked at her mother's poor, weary, pale face, and been too kind, loved her too much to say what nonsense, it had got her nowhere. And of course she, Tilly, had got everywhere without them, both literally and figuratively, had travelled all over the world, in the company of the world's most famous photographers and fashion editors, and appeared on the cover of every glossy magazine, had been, at only eighteen, signed by the Deep Blue jeans label company, for a rumoured half million to promote their new perfume, d'Accord, had been the star of fashion shows in London, in Paris, in Milan, in New York, with an annual income that ran easily into six figures. She owned a Ferrari (which she couldn't drive), a large flat in Kensington, (which she seldom saw), a small roomful of designer clothes (which she rarely wore); was admired, pampered, quoted, sought after: all on the strength of (as she often said, laughing, in interviews, to the despair of parents of teenage girls everywhere) straight Es in third year; after which she had been spotted by Felicity Livesey of Models Plus in Ken Market one day, as she sat on the floor, endless legs stuck out in front of her, sharing a strawberry shake with her friend Mo, watching the world go by.

* * *

'Excuse me, but I wonder if I could have a word with you?'

'Pardon?' said Tilly. 'What've I done now?'

She was, at fourteen, constantly expecting trouble; she often found it. The woman looking down at her thoughtfully was young – well, youngish, probably a good twenty-five actually, and dressed a bit too trendy. People that age should stop trying so hard, thought Tilly, licking the straw with relish.

'Nothing,' said the woman. 'Except look rather interesting.'

'Oh puh-leeze,' said Tilly. 'What is this, a pick-up or something? Look, lady, I'm not interested.'

'It's not a pick-up,' said the woman, looking at her calmly. 'Well, not in the sense you mean. I'm from Models Plus. I thought maybe you'd like to come and see us.'

'Oh sure,' said Tilly, 'and my name's Cindy Crawford. Listen, I don't want to be rude, but I really have got places to go, things to see.'

'OK,' said the woman, shrugging. 'That's fine by me. But take my card. Discuss it with your mother. And if you're interested come and see me, preferably with her. I won't tell her you were quite clearly bunking off school,' she added, with the glimmer of a smile, and turned away and walked off in the direction of Kensington High Street.

'Cheek!' said Mo.

'Gross,' said Tilly.

'Let's see the card.'

They looked at it. Felicity Livesey, it said. 'Director. Models Plus. 748 Old Brompton Road. 071–467–0873.'

'Wow!' said Mo. 'Hey, Tilly, do you think –'

'Nah,' said Tilly, her voice very firm. 'It's a fake. I know she's some dyke.'

'Yeah, probably. Still, you could ring.'

'Mo, do me a favour. This is the oldest trick in the book. I wouldn't even think about it. Got any money left? I could do with a ciggy.'

'Hi,' she said, noticing with some anguish that she had only two units left on her phone card. 'Is Felicity Livesey there, please?'

'I'll see. Who is it calling please?'

'Oh she won't know me. She spoke to me in Ken Market yesterday.

Tell her the black girl. Outside the jewellery store.'

'Just hold on please . . .'

Shit, thought Tilly, snooty cow. She watched her two units dissolve into one, and listened to the chatter on the other end. It didn't sound like a put-up job, she had to admit. Come on, you bitch, get a move on . . .

'Hallo? Can you ring back in half an hour please? Miss Livesey is interviewing at the moment.'

'Oh – yeah, OK,' said Tilly and put the phone down. Bugger. Phone card dead, no more money, now what did she do? Reverse the charges? No, they'd never take a call from her. Shit. It'd have to be Ron. She hadn't asked him for a while. Well, not for two days. But it'd have to be lunchtime, so he'd think she was actually at school – better go home and put her uniform on – so she couldn't ring back in half an hour. Well, if this Felicity person was on the level she could wait for her. She had better things to do than run around after her.

'Hi, Ron. How're you doing?'

'Fine thanks, love. How about you? I hope you've been at school this morning.'

'Ron, course I have. What do you take me for? I'll tell you what I did if you like, biology, we did the digestive system of the rat, it was gross, first we –'

'OK, OK, girl, that'll do. Why aren't you there now?'

'Because it's lunchtime. I came out for a sarnie.'

'Ciggy more like it,' said Ron tartly.

'Ron! Would I? Well-brought-up girl like me.'

'Well brought-up, yes, but something went wrong along the way.' He grinned at her over his stall, over the military-straight rows of vegetables, crisp white cauliflowers, gleaming peppers, shining glossy tomatoes, set out to tempt the customers, who were then given slightly less white, gleaming, glossy produce from behind the counter. 'How's Mum? Got over that cold yet? Here, have an apple.' He handed her a big, golden russet; Tilly hated russets, but she bit into it obediently, to please him.

'Yeah, she's better. Tired though.'

'Course she's tired. She works too hard. Here, darling, mind the shop for me one minute, would you? Call of nature.'

Tilly ducked under the stall, took up position behind it, gazing out at the market; it looked so different from this standpoint. She loved doing this: she'd begged Ron for a regular Saturday job, but he said he couldn't afford her, and he wouldn't exploit her, make her work for nothing. So she did the odd hour when he was really busy in the middle of the day, earned a couple of quid – 'Now that's not for fags, Tilly, understand?' 'Course not, Ron, what do you think I am?'

He was back very quickly, grinning up at her with his little monkey face. He was at least nine inches shorter than she was.

'OK, my love. Thanks. I needed that. You all right then?'

'I'm fine. I must get back to school though. Ron, you couldn't – well –'

'Lend you a quid? Tilly, I've lent you five this month already. I'll have to start keeping a slate. What do you do with them all?'

'Buy chips. The school dinners are gross. And I get so hungry. Please, Ron, I'll pay you back.'

'Yeah, and pigs'll fly. Oh – all right. But it's the last one. For a long time. OK?'

'Sure. Thanks, Ron.'

She pushed the pound coin into her blazer pocket. It was about three sizes too small for her, the sleeves way up her wrists, the bottom hardly skimming her waist.

'And bring your mum round Sunday, OK? I'll do you a Chinese.'

'Great,' said Tilly. She dreaded Ron's Chineses, greasy, slimy stir fries, usually ducked out of them, but she might have to eat this one. She'd pushed her luck with him lately.

'Hi, this is Tilly Mills again. Is Felicity Livesey there?' Now come on, you stupid cow, put me through.

'No, I'm sorry, but Felicity asked me to tell you to come in and see us. With your mother.'

'Well – I don't know. When?'

She could hear the girl shrug. 'Doesn't matter.'

'Tomorrow morning?'

'Yeah, sure.'

'OK. Thanks.'

Tilly walked up and down the Old Brompton Road several times before she finally plucked up the courage to go through the door marked Models Plus. She had spent hours getting ready, washing and blow-drying her hair – God, it needed straightening again, already – ironing her only skirt and the blouse her mum had brought her home from the workshop, making up her face with great care, sticking on her false eye-lashes. She had expected number 748 to be rather glamorous, some huge building like a film studio; it was actually a small entrance by a sweet shop. A sign told her to go to the second floor; she went up, feeling slightly sick, still half expecting the whole thing to be some awful hoax.

It wasn't. She found herself in a large room filled with an extra-ordinary number of people. A girl sat by the door, manning a switch-board; beyond her there was a big round table, seating about four more girls and two men, each with a telephone and a Rolladex; beyond them was a pair of sofas, each containing at least three girls with a couple of boys perched on the arms, all talking; and beyond that a desk, on its own, with its back to the window. It was empty.

Tilly looked uncertainly at the girl by the door; she looked back, her eyes blank and slightly hostile.

'Hi,' said Tilly. 'I've come to see –'

'Sorry,' said the girl. 'We're not seeing anyone at the moment. Books full. Got any pictures? You can leave them with me.'

'No, I haven't got any pictures,' said Tilly, trying not to sound rude, 'and I'm here because you told me to come.'

'What's your name?' asked the girl, sounding more bored still.

'Tilly. Tilly Mills.'

The girl looked at her diary, shook her head. 'Sorry. Must be a mistake.'

'Look,' said Tilly, 'there isn't a mistake, and I rang yesterday. Felicity Livesey told me to come and see her.'

'Oh,' said the girl, looking slightly less bored. 'Well – I'll ask. She's not here anyway. You can sit down over there.'

'I'll stand, thanks,' said Tilly. She wasn't going to be told what to do by this stroppy cow. She saw the girl raising her eyebrows imperceptibly towards the round table; another girl got up and walked over to her.

'Hi,' she said, 'you want to be a model? We're not taking anyone on at the moment, but you can leave your pictures, if you like, and we'll get in touch if –'

'Look,' said Tilly, 'I don't really want to be a model, but Felicity Livesey told me to come in and see her. If she's not here and you're not taking anyone on, that's fine by me, but I'm going.'

'Sure,' said the girl, smiling at her, rather patronizingly, 'fine. But it would be better to leave some pictures. You never know . . .'

'I know, thanks,' said Tilly and walked very swiftly, propelled by disappointment and hurt pride, towards the door. As she reached it, it opened and Felicity walked in.

'Hi,' she said, 'nice to see you. How are you? Where's your mum?'

'At work,' said Tilly firmly. Well, it was true.

'No school today?'

'No. It's a half-day. For – for study leave.'

'Oh I see,' said Felicity, smiling at her slightly conspiratorially. 'Well look, I've just got a couple of calls to make, and I'll be with you. Mary Anne, would you make two coffees please? One for this lady; could you wait there?' she added, indicating one of the sofas. Mary Anne had the grace to look just slightly shamefaced.

Tilly sat down, looked around, tried to pretend she felt all right. She felt terrible, dressed in her neat little skirt and blouse, as if she was naked and they were all dressed, as if they spoke a language she didn't understand. The girl next to her on the sofa, a fragile whey-faced blonde in army trousers and DM boots, was saying to one of the boys, 'I've been down at Petty France all morning, bastards won't give me a passport till tomorrow and I have to leave tonight, or I'll lose the booking.'

'They suck,' said the boy agreeably, retying his ponytail. 'I lost mine last year, you should have heard the fuss. You got any gum?'

'Yeah, sure.' She offered him a stick and then one to Tilly; Tilly took it gratefully.

'Thanks.'

'You new?'

'Yeah. Well, maybe.'

'You have a great look,' said the boy, smiling at her. His eyes were very blue, his eyelashes very long. Tilly blushed.

'Thanks.'

The girl from the round table who had told her to go away came over; she looked just slightly awkward.

'I'm Jackie. Could I just take a couple of Polaroids?'

'A couple of what?' said Tilly.

'Polaroids. Photographs.'

'Look, I told you, I don't have any,' said Tilly irritably. 'I'm waiting to see Felicity.'

'I know that,' said Jackie, with immense, bad-tempered patience. 'I'm going to take the pictures. With this camera. See?' She waved it at Tilly.

'You're a bully, Jack,' said the boy with the blue eyes. 'Can't you see she's scared? Go on,' he said to Tilly, 'it really doesn't hurt much.'

'Oh, – OK,' said Tilly, trying to look cool.

Jackie took her onto the landing, told her to look into the camera, took one full-length photograph and one close-up, then walked back into the room without a word. Tilly followed her, slightly uncertainly. She longed to see the pictures, but didn't like to ask.

Felicity was waving to her from her desk. 'Come over here. Sit down, and drink that coffee. Or don't you like it? Sorry, I should have asked.'

'What? Oh, yeah, thanks,' said Tilly. She looked at the Polaroids which were in Felicity's hand.

'Right,' said Felicity. She had a form, which she started to fill in.

'What's your name?'

'Tilly. Tilly Mills.'

'Just Tilly? What were you christened?'

'Ottoline,' said Tilly, embarrassed.

'Ottoline. That's a great name. I love it.'

'You can't. It's a crazy name.'

'It's great. How old are you – Ottoline?'

'Sixteen,' said Tilly.

'Uh-huh. Address?'

'Fourteen, Gareth Road, Brixton.'

'Right. And how tall are you?'

'Five eleven,' said Tilly.

'Still growing?'

'Yeah, I think so.'

'Stand up,' said Felicity, 'and turn round slowly. Mm. Yes. Yes, that's fine. Let me look at your hands. Oh, nice hands. It's unusual, you know, in a girl your age. You obviously take care of them. I'd be a bit worried about that scar on your cheek. How did you get that?'

'Fell off the swing,' said Tilly.

'Well – maybe it wouldn't matter.' She leant back in her chair again. 'Sit down again, Tilly. Have you ever thought about modelling?'

'No. Not really,' said Tilly.

'I think possibly you should. But I do need to see your parents. When could they come in?'

'I haven't got a dad,' said Tilly, 'and my mum works. Like all the time. She couldn't come in here.'

'Not even on a Saturday?'

'Well – maybe. I'd have to ask.'

'Of course. Because, you see, I can't go ahead without her permission. I presume you do go to school sometimes? Or at least you're supposed to?' She grinned at Tilly.

'Yeah, course I do. I'm coming up to my GCSEs.'

'Good. Because we don't like taking girls away from their studies. Until you were sixteen you'd only work after school or in the holidays.'

'And you really think I could make it?' said Tilly. She felt slightly dizzy suddenly as if the room was whirling, very slowly; she put her hand out onto Felicity's desk to steady it.

'Well, Tilly, I really don't know. I never, ever make any promises. This is a funny fickle business, fashions change all the time. All I can tell you is you look pretty OK for now. And I can tell from these Polaroids you're photogenic. But you may be awkward in front of the camera, you may hate the whole thing – and that shows – you may just not catch on. And it's a long hard haul, Tilly, be warned. It's not glamorous and it's not easy. But I'll say all this to your mum. Try and persuade her to come in next Saturday for a chat. I'd so much like to meet her.'

'Yeah, OK,' said Tilly, trying to stay sounding cool. 'Yeah, I'll try. Can't promise anything though. Thanks,' she added, standing up. Outside she had to resist a strong temptation to do cartwheels right down the street.

* * *

Her mother was very unhappy about even going to see Felicity Livesey.

'It'll never come to anything, Tilly, and it's an awful world. I wouldn't want that sort of thing for you.'

'Oh Mum,' said Tilly, 'don't start on that sex and drugs and rock'n'roll thing. Listen, you should meet this woman. She's cool. I liked her. You'd like her.'

'I wouldn't like her,' said Rosemary Mills firmly. 'Filling your head with all that nonsense. It's immoral.'

'Mum, she was not immoral. She won't even let me have my test shots done without talking to you.' This was true; Tilly had tried to get away with telling Felicity her mother was going away.

'What are test shots?'

'The pictures they take to see if you're going to be any good. Then they go towards making up your portfolio and your model card,' said Tilly. She felt rather pleased with her mastery of all this technical jargon.

'But Tilly, I can't afford to have expensive photographs taken.'

'You don't have to afford it. The agency pay. They reckon to get it back later.'

'You seem to have had a very long conversation with them,' said Rosemary wearily.

'Mum, that's the whole point. She's nice. She's careful. I swear you'd like her. And think. If I make it I'll make lots of money, and we can get a smart house up West somewhere, and you can leave that foul job.'

'Oh Tilly,' said Rosemary with another heavy sigh. 'Don't start day-dreaming too soon. You're just going to be more and more disappointed. When – when could we see this woman?'

'Saturday,' said Tilly, sensing victory. 'She said she'd come in any time. We could go just before teatime and then we could go round Uncle Ron's for a Chinese. He asked us the other day, I forgot to tell you.'

'Oh – well, I suppose there's no harm talking to her,' said Rosemary.

'Oh Mum, thanks!' Tilly flung her arms round her mother's neck. 'You're ace, Mum. Listen, do you want a cup of tea or something?'

'Yes please. Something. Camomile. There are some leaves in the jar.'

Tilly sighed. Her mother loved all that herbal rubbish. It was a hangover from her seventies youth. Tilly hated the smell of it even, it turned her up. But she'd have gone out and grown the leaves herself, she was so happy. She went over to the kitchenette, made the tea, singing.

'You won't regret this, Mum. Honest. I'm gonna change our lives.'

Rosemary took the cup, smiling slightly anxiously at her. 'Tilly, please don't get too hopeful. It's a fairy story really.'

Tilly looked at her mother sitting on the saggy old sofa, at her pale worn face, her long, rippling, faded blonde hair, her still beautiful hands, oddly graceful in her long flowing skirt, and thought how much she loved her. It wasn't cool to love your mum, most of her friends hated theirs, never spoke to them from one week's end to the next except to row with them or ask for money. But then she and her mum were different, battling away alone against the world, just the two of them, fighting for their corner and their place in it, no dad to come between them, no brothers or sisters to claim attention – and then, as she so often did on such an occasion, at some important point in her life, Tilly thought about her, about the other one, the other one who should have been there, sitting with them. Would she have been part of this adventure, would Felicity have approached her too, seen the two of them? Maybe she would – if she had been an identical, as much like her as, say, Gary Redburn was like Garth, with the teachers not able to tell which of them was in the lesson and which wasn't and who was fighting and who had bunked off and not knowing who to punish.

Well, no use even wondering. She wasn't here, she wasn't anything, never had been, not for a minute, not even for a moment probably, and that was that, thanks to that bastard. Bastard. One day, thought Tilly, settling into the familiar, outraged contemplation that was almost meditative, one day she'd get him. She'd get him as her mother, too gentle, too sick at heart, too overawed by him had finally failed to do, she'd get him and tell everyone and make sure he suffered for it.

Her thoughts clearly showed, for Rosemary suddenly said, very softly, 'Tilly, I know what you're thinking, and don't. Sometimes, I wish I'd never told you.'

'I'm just so glad you did,' said Tilly, hauling herself back to reality. 'I'd still feel there was something of me missing and I wouldn't know why. More tea, Mum?'

It was history now: a short sweet history of almost instant recognition, of a too tall, awkward, rebellious schoolgirl become a superstar, a top

model, sought after, at only fifteen years old, by the haut monde of the
fashion business; of photographers, fashion editors, art directors fighting
to book her from the moment Felicity had released her first upon
London, then Paris and New York; of dozens, hundreds of fawning
articles about her, interviews with her, of her face on television, on
hoardings, on buses. Famous she became, known simply as Ottoline,
swiftly, suddenly famous, gazing with her raw, rich, gawky sensuality out
of the pages of every magazine in the world, stalking down the catwalks
with her light, arrogant tread, photographed at airports as she arrived
for collections, at charity shows, and soon, surprisingly soon, in the
gossip columns, for like all creatures famous for their beauty she was
required to bring that beauty to grace all number of occasions: parties,
premieres, charity openings. Right through the latter part of the eighties
she queened it, an icon for her time, smoothly rough, sharp, flashy,
newly rich, outrageously sexy; there were famous affairs, with the glitzy
superstars of the eighties, with photographers, rock stars, designers, and
she took to it with delighted ease, loving it, laughing with patent,
infectious pleasure at it all.

By the time the decade had drawn to its painful Armageddon-like
end, lurched into the frugality of the nineties, she was safe – rich,
famous, still hugely in demand. She had bought her mother not the
smart house up West, which Rosemary had in any case not wanted, but
a pretty little cottage in Peckham Rye, from which Rosemary ran her
own business as an aromatherapist. It had been Tilly's idea that; she had
done a beauty photograph for *Vogue*, and the make-up artist was
studying aromatherapy.

'You'd love it, Mum, right up your street, all herbs and God knows
what. I've brought you a pamphlet, you should do a course and get going
on it.'

'Don't be silly, Tilly, how can I do a course at my age and who'd pay
for it?'

'I'd pay for it,' said Tilly, carelessly happy at her new power to give.
'It's nothing, only a few hundred quid, and you could do it from home,
it'd be great.'

And Rosemary had first remonstrated with her daughter for speaking
of 'only' hundreds of pounds, had warned her of seven-day wonders and
houses built on sand, and then had sat down to read about aromatherapy

and at the end of the evening had said to Tilly, smiling, that she did think
it sounded very nice, very interesting and she'd certainly like to consider
it as an option.

'Bloody hell, Mother, you'll be pushing the daisies up before you've
done anything at this rate,' said Tilly impatiently and made inquiries
herself, and before she knew what was happening Rosemary was
studying aromatherapy and loving it as Tilly had predicted.

Tilly had started out living in Peckham with her, but on her
eighteenth birthday had moved out to Kensington: 'We're going to start
fighting otherwise, and you're going to get upset and I'm going to get
awkward and I don't want that, and nor do you. I'll be round to you lots
and lots, but not all the time. OK?'

'OK, Tilly,' said Rosemary.

She got to the studio at seven. Mick McGrath, looking even more seedy
than usual, was sitting drinking coffee, reeking of garlic, reading the
London *Times*.

'Hi, babe.'

'Hallo, Mick,' said Tilly coolly.

'Good day. The light's really nice. I've told that group of freeloaders
in there to pull their fingers out and get you ready fast. I want to be out
by eight o'clock latest. In the Place des Vosges, in your wedding frock.'

'OK, OK,' said Tilly, rummaging in her bag for her Gauloises. 'But don't
blame me if they don't deliver. You know what Laurent's like, he starts out
slow and gets slower as he warms up.'

'Hey, that's good,' said McGrath, smiling at her. 'I like that. You're
getting witty in your old age, Til. Yeah, well I'll keep on his tail. Oh, and
you have to call your agency. Soonest. Felicity's at her desk waiting for
you now. Keep it brief, for Christ's sake, though. Coffee?'

'What do you think? Black.'

She called the agency. Felicity's calm voice came down the line: 'Tilly,
hi.'

'Hi, Felicity.'

'I know I've got to be quick. Mick told me so in his inimitably
charming way. But it's important. Tilly, I've had a call from Meg
Rosenthal.'

'Yeah?' said Tilly. She was struggling to find her cigarettes, and couldn't; she dropped her bag, everything spilled out on the floor. 'Shit.'

'Not quite the reaction I was expecting.'

'Sorry. Spilt all my make-up. Including that gorgeous powder she gave me.'

'Who, Meg? Have you tried the foundation yet? It's all gorgeous, I must say. And the colours –'

Rosenthal was the new word in cosmetics: more haute couture than Lauder, more brilliantly fashionable than Saint-Laurent, more expensive than Chanel. Launched simultaneously in Britain, America, France and Italy, sales were soaring after only nine months, and rich women everywhere were filling their dressing tables and make-up purses with it.

'Yeah, they're great. Love it all.'

'They want you, Tilly.'

'You mean – really want me?'

'I mean really want you. A two million-dollar contract and that's just for starters.'

'Shit,' said Tilly again. Mick's tiny office spun slightly. It wasn't just the money, nor was it the thought of the fame; it was that a top-of-the-range cosmetics company should decide to stake everything on her. A black girl. Not Christy, not Cindy, not Linda, not your archetypal WASP glamour babe, but her. She knew what it meant, and it was quite literally breathtaking. It meant they saw her as twice as beautiful, twice as inspirational, twice as desirable, as all of them: simply because she was black. It was that simple. For a black girl to sell beauty to rich white women, she had to be twice everything. Probably three times. She had to be perceived not as black, not as white, not as anything – except absolutely, one hundred percent beautifully, glossily, stylishly perfect. No messing. That was the only way it wasn't a gamble, wasn't a political gesture, wasn't a statement. These guys were only interested in one thing and it wasn't statements. Well, except financial ones. 'Shit,' she said, for a third time, and then, 'What's it mean?'

'Most relevantly, money apart, it means you have to move to New York almost at once . . .'

'Why?' asked Tilly.

'They're in a hurry. They want to announce it, promote you, start touting you around absolutely straight away. They really do need you, Tilly. It's just huge.'

'Yeah,' said Tilly. She was trying to take it in, to work out what it might mean to her, today, tomorrow, next week, next year. Belonging to someone else, that's what it meant, becoming a piece of property, her every move mapped and studied and ordered. The one thing she most hated, most dreaded. On the other hand – well, on the other hand, it was a lot of what Tilly called the fuck-off factor. It would turn her into a very powerful force. Very powerful indeed. Which meant – 'Oh God, Felicity,' she said, 'Felicity, I don't know. What do you –'

'For fuck's sake, Tilly, I told you to be quick. Get off that phone.' Mick McGrath's black eyes were snapping dangerously.

'Felicity, I have to go. I'm sorry. And I have to think. I'll – I'll call you tonight. Promise. With an answer.'

'OK, I think that's fair. I'll tell them. Bye, Tilly.'

'Bye, Felicity.'

Tilly put down the phone, stood there briefly concentrating on what she had just heard, what she was feeling, and then almost visibly shook herself back into the present. She would think about it later, maybe tonight: not now. One of the reasons she was so successful, so sought after, was the way she gave herself entirely to the job in hand, whether it was a million-dollar deal or a one-off editorial shoot. She went into the dressing room; a small pale creature, with a wild mop of black hair, dressed in black T-shirt, black trousers and black plimsolls sat playing cat's cradle with a very long hair ribbon.

'Hi, Laurent.'

'Hi, Tilly.' He looked at her, dropped the ribbon. 'Who cut your hair? It look like sheet.'

'Thanks, Laurent. I'll tell Nicky.'

' 'Oo is Nicky?'

'Laurent, you know perfectly well who is Nicky. Nicky Clarke. Très famous.'

'Très terrible as well. Oh well, I must try. Let us start with the make-up. You are to be a bride, *n'est-ce pas?*'

'Yeah, that's right,' said Tilly absently. Suddenly, sharply she properly realized what day it was. Cressida's wedding day. Of far more importance than any job, any deal, any contract. And what was she doing? Leaving them to enjoy it in peace, leaving Cressida to mince down the aisle on her father's arm, and him to smile complacently upon her and the congregation as she did so.

'You're crazy,' said Tilly aloud, 'fucking crazy.'

'*Comment?*' said Laurent, distracted from a deep study of whether navy or purple mascara would suit Tilly's surprisingly long eyelashes better. '*Qu'est ce que tu as dit?*'

'Nothing,' said Tilly, 'just thinking aloud. Christ, Laurent, you're not putting that filth on my mouth? And if you are I want another coffee first.'

'Tilly, you cannot have another coffee,' said Laurent, his rather small mouth setting petulantly. 'Mick wants you all done by eight and is already ten off eight now.'

'Oh – all right,' said Tilly. 'Where's the frock?'

'Here,' said Mick's assistant and stylist, a rather fierce Sloaney girl called Emma. She had got the job against fierce competition purely by virtue of her background; Mick, who had been raised in a council block in Tower Hamlets, was famous for his ferocious snobbery and while being foul-mouthed and deeply unpleasant to almost everybody he ever came in contact with, could be unctuously charming in pursuit of an invitation to a charity ball, a weekend at a country house, a society wedding. He liked to hear Emma's clipped bossy tones on the phone, arranging bookings, demanding things, telling people he was too busy to speak to them; it made him constantly, gloriously aware of how far he had come.

'It's going to be a bit too short, even if you don't wear any shoes,' said Emma, 'so we'll have to shoot a bit carefully. They just refused to let it down.'

'I expect they did,' said Tilly. 'What's it cost, a million francs?'

'More I should think,' said Emma. 'Pretty, though.'

Tilly looked at the clouds of cream slubbed silk, studded with pearls, and sighed. It did seem doubly ironic that she should be modelling wedding dresses today of all days.

'Best get going then,' said Emma. 'Mick's having a baby out there. You'll have to put it on there, Tilly, no way you can walk along in it, and we certainly can't get you into a car. It's only a five-minute walk and you can change in a shop doorway. OK?'

'OK,' said Tilly equably. She was famous for her unfailing good humour. She had once posed naked in a rainstorm on the top of Beachy Head and, while everybody else shivered and complained, had got the giggles and stood there shrieking with laughter for a full five minutes. The pictures had made headlines round the world.

They walked along the narrow, still quiet streets; the Place des Vosges, the sun shafting through its vaulted arcades, had a cathedral-like quality. It had been worth the effort, the early start. Tilly looked at her watch: still not eight, not quite seven in England. She was standing in the doorway of a shop that sold outrageously expensive bric-à-brac, dressed only in her pants, the dress supported by Emma and Laurent poised over her head, when Mick's portable phone rang.

'Yeah,' she heard him say, as the dress settled around her, 'yeah, she's here and, no, of course she can't come to the phone. She's working for fuck's sake. You heard of work, mate? It's what she gets paid ten thousand a day for. Yeah, well, it is a lot of money. Tell me about it. What? Is it really urgent? Oh, all right. But make it quick, OK?' He handed the phone to Tilly. 'It's for you,' he said. 'I wish you'd tell your boyfriends not to call you on the job.'

'Oh go fuck yourself,' said Tilly equably, fiddling with the silk roses on the neckline of her dress. 'Who is it?'

'It's Rufus somebody something. Very upmarket, darling.'

'Yeah?' said Tilly sharply, freezing in her task. 'Give me the phone, Mick. Rufus? Yeah, it's me. What's the matter?'

Rufus's light, public-school voice, high with anxiety, cut into the peaceful, golden morning.

'Tilly, I'm sorry to ring you there, but I simply had to speak to you. Something awful's happened, it's an absolute nightmare. Mungo and I've been up with Oliver most of the night. He says – well, he says he can't go through with it. It was Mungo's idea to call you. Tilly, what the hell do we do?'

Chapter 5

Susie 8am

Susie liked waking up. Being an intrinsically happy person, she enjoyed surfacing slowly into the day: reflecting upon it and its content, the shape she had planned for it, the people she would see. She would lie there, smiling, going through the gentle stretching and relaxing programme that her body trainer had taught her (for Susie did not like to waste so much as a moment), and then reach out for the thermos jug that contained her hot water, pour it into the cup on her bedside table, add two pieces of lemon from the covered container at its side, and leaning on one elbow would sip it slowly, consideringly, before getting up and pulling on a swimsuit, tracksuit and trainers and running down the stairs and out into the street where her silver Mercedes convertible was parked. She lived with her husband and her two younger children (Annabel, aged seventeen and Tom fifteen) in a house of extraordinary beauty on Chiswick Mall; it was a short drive therefore to the Riverside Health Club, where she swam thirty brisk lengths. She was back in the house, bathed and dressed by 7:30, listening to Annabel's complaints that her alarm hadn't gone off, that her head/stomach/back hurt, that someone had taken her tights, that there was no orange juice, that the spot on her chin was worse, and to Tom's desperate groans as he sat at the kitchen table trying to do two hours' prep in fifteen minutes. And then, when they were finally gone (Annabel to St Paul's, Tom to Westminster), she would take a large cup of strong tea, with two sugars, up to her husband, wake him with a tender kiss and tell him his bath was running. Susie was exceptionally nice to her husband; she felt it was the least she could do after marrying him when she did not love him in the least. She had made him very happy, and he had provided her with a very pleasant life; it seemed to her a perfectly fair exchange. The fact that she had conducted an adulterous liaison with another man for most of the twenty-nine years of her marriage seemed to her neither here nor there. Susie was not given to introspection; what mattered was what lay on the surface of life, and the surface of hers was calm and charming.

But today was a little different. In more ways than one. Today was threatening, the waking less gentle than usual, the thoughts and memories that came into her head troubling. There was no question of her shaping the day ahead, that was all done for her, and for the other 299 guests at the wedding of Cressida Forrest and Oliver Bergin. There was the phone call to make; and there was no pool within reach, no comforting, happy routine in which to hide herself, to slough off the disturbing thoughts. She wished fervently she had insisted after all that they should drive down from London that morning, instead of staying with the Beaumonts, near neighbours of the Forrests, it would in every way be easier, more comfortable for her; but Alistair had said he'd rather they started the day down there, he didn't want to be worried about traffic, and Annabel had said if they did drive down from London her outfit would get creased and Tom had said at least if he had to go to the horrible wedding he would be able to play tennis before and after it. (She thanked God that Lucy, her eldest, was in New York and needed no consideration in the matter). And so she had given in, as she always tried to, for the sake of ease, of greater pleasantness. Only Rufus had expressed no preference, had given her his sweet smile and said it didn't matter where he began the day, he didn't care, as long as he could end it with Mungo in London.

'Darling,' Susie had said, 'darling, as long as you both get Oliver to the church on time, I don't care either.'

And Rufus had kissed her and said he would, of course he would, but it was hardly a danger, Oliver being so exemplary a citizen; their responsibilities were likely to begin and end with making sure he didn't get to the church too early. 'His stag night was the shortest I can ever remember, Mum, all over by midnight, and we had to send the stripper home. He's a great guy and I'm very fond of him, but a lot of the time I do feel he's another generation.' Susie had laughed and said in that case she could relax and stop worrying about it all. In any case there seemed no excuse for them to stay in London, and so it came to pass that they travelled down and she was waking this morning in the Beaumonts' large, indisputably charming but extremely uncomfortable house, with its even more uncomfortable guest room. One of the worst things about staying with friends, of course, was that she and Alistair had to share a room and in this case a bed; they had had separate bedrooms for years, not as a reflection upon their sex life, which was modest, though pleasant, but on the erratic hours Alistair kept as an international lawyer, and his insomnia. Well, the insomnia hadn't been too much of a problem the night before, Susie reflected, since she hadn't been able to sleep either, and had been quite grateful to be able to pretend to be reading, but the night had been a torture nonetheless. She had finally fallen asleep at four and dreamed of Jamie's anguished face, exactly as she had last seen it in the garden of the Court House the evening before; and now it was – what? – after eight. God, she hated waking up late – and she felt wretched, thick-headed, slightly sick, and with this general sense of unease. And no swimming pool to work it off in.

She got up, looked out of the window. What she saw lifted her spirits. The sky was clear; there was just a very slight trace of mist drifting still in the small valley below the house. The Beaumonts' two hunters were grazing in the paddock; Janet Beaumont, smiling peacefully beneath the brim of her large straw hat, was in the rose garden clipping the huge white roses, some of which Susie knew would adorn the breakfast table. On the tennis court, just beyond the rose garden, Tom was playing tennis with Mike Beaumont, his normally cheerful face contorted into ferocious concentration, his heavy dark hair flopping into his eyes. Susie looked at him, and her heart tumbled over with love. Mothers weren't supposed to have favourites and of course she didn't; it was just that Tom was her baby, her last-born, and she felt more protective, closer towards him than the others. When Rufus had been fifteen, he had seemed almost grown-up, but then the way she felt about Rufus had never seemed to have much to do with the way she felt about her other children. It was a love that was differently shaped, differently experienced – scarcely recognizable as mother-love at all. But Tom – Tom was still to her a small boy. All mothers said that of course, that the baby stayed the baby; but there was something different, special about Tom. He still needed her, needed her a lot; and oh Christ, she thought, the ugly fear rising in her throat, hitting her hard, how would he be if –

'Oh shut up,' she said aloud, 'don't be negative, Susie, it'll be all right, and you'll know for sure in an hour or so.' She forced her mind back (Susie's mind was in general very biddable) to the day and to admiring Tom's service, which was impressive; indeed she spontanously clapped an ace, winging down the line past Mike Beaumont.

Tom looked up at the house, saw her and waved; she waved back, and decided to go and join them on the court. Susie was never troubled by self-doubt, by the thought that she might not be welcome anywhere: she knew with a sweet certainty that she was. And sure enough, as she left the court, three-quarters of an hour later, hot, happy, her ill-ease worked away, she heard Mike Beaumont say, 'Your mum's top of the range, Tom.'

Susie rewarded him with one of her most dazzling smiles.

She was lying in the stained roll-top bath in what had once been the nursery bathroom, idly soaping herself, anxiety creeping back into her head, when she heard the phone ringing in the hall downstairs. Janet answered it.

'Maggie!' Susie heard her say, in her low, headgirl voice. 'Hallo, dear. Lovely day for you. All set I – what, dear? No, no of course not. Well, how extraordinary. I can't imagine – oh, look, Maggie, of course she can't be far away. I expect she's gone for a walk, calming her nerves a bit. Or a little drive. I – oh I see. Well, dear, I wish I could – yes, Maggie, of course I will. At once. Yes, of course. Can I phone anyone for you? Yes, all right, my dear. Don't worry, I'm sure it's perfectly all right.'

Susie sat up, dropped the soap in the bath. The sense of foreboding had suddenly increased, and it had nothing to do with Jamie. She climbed out of the bath, put on her robe and padded down the stairs. Janet was standing at the kitchen window, staring out.

'Janet, what did Maggie want? What's wrong? I heard you on the phone.'

'Oh – nothing's really wrong I'm sure,' said Janet, turning with a quick, rather stiff smile. 'It's just that Cressida's gone walkabouts. I'm sure that's all it is. But I can see why Maggie would be worried. That she's not there, I mean.'

'Well I can't,' said Susie. 'And we all know how Maggie worries. Poor darling,' she added hastily, anxious as always that not a breath of criticism might drift from her in Maggie's direction. 'I mean, it's not even nine yet. I expect she's gone to find some peace and quiet.'

'Susie, dear, I think there must be a little more to it than that,' said Janet, a touch of reproof in her voice. 'Apparently she's been missing for well over an hour, Maggie said. It does seem very strange. I would be beside myself, if it was my daughter. She'd have to be feeling very upset, surely, to disappear for so long. Without saying a word. And you said she seemed so calm last night, not nervous at all. What on earth could have happened to her?'

'I can't imagine,' said Susie. 'And yes, she did seem very calm. But maybe it was all an act. She's a very good actress, Cressida, always was. I honestly think the most likely thing is she's just gone off to be by herself for a bit. Such an ordeal, one's wedding day. However lovely.'

And she was back vividly, clearly, at her own, twenty-nine years earlier, alone in the house with her father, waiting to leave for the church. He had handed her a glass of champagne, and she'd caught sight of her face in the drawing-room mirror, so pale it was almost corpselike, her dark eyes huge, and she'd seen her hand tremble as she took the glass.

Neil Carrington came over to her, gave her a bear hug.

'Darling, there's no need to be quite so frightened. It's not like you. Where's the girl who was calmly playing tennis an hour before her coming-out ball?'

'A bit older and a bit more thoughtful,' said Susie with a rather shaky smile.

'You're not – doubtful are you? Because if you are, it's still not –'

'Oh Daddy,' said Susie, hugging him back, a great rush of love filling her for a man who could genuinely contemplate cancelling a wedding for which a church was already filled, a lunch prepared, champagne iced, ten bridesmaids dressed, and a huge amount of money spent. 'Daddy, you're an angel and of course I'm not doubtful, Alistair is an absolute darling and the perfect husband, and I'm a lucky girl.'

'All right. As long as you mean it. I've never actually heard you say you love him –'

'Haven't you?' said Susie, draining the glass quickly. 'Well, you must have missed all the occasions when I did. Of course I do, who couldn't? He's sweet and kind and good and –'

The phone rang suddenly, shrilly, through the house. She knew who it was; she froze, hesitated just for a moment, then said, 'I'll get it. It'll be Bunty calling from LA, she promised she would.'

'Bad timing,' said her father. 'The car's just arrived. Be quick, poppet.'

'They can't start without me,' said Susie, going out into the hall.

'Susie?'

'Bunty! Hallo.'

'Who the hell is Bunty? It's Jamie.'

'You're sweet to ring, Bunt. Really lovely. Perfect timing! Daddy says I have to be quick.'

'Susie, don't, please don't. I can't bear it. I love you. You know I do.'

'I don't know, actually,' she said, hearing her voice, cold and controlled. 'And as you couldn't be with me, I've had to do it without you. Very sadly. I know you'll be thinking of me though. Look, the car's here, I have to go. Sweet of you to call. Bye, Bunty.'

She put the phone down, very carefully, as if it might shatter, and stood there quite still for a moment, staring at it; then she lifted her hand and pulled down the short veil over her face. A tiny tendril of dark hair had escaped from the crown of lily of the valley on her head; she left it, falling onto her forehead, symbolizing, she felt, a last-minute, last-moment bid for freedom, a last look at love. Then she walked back into the drawing room, took her father's hand. 'Come on, Daddy,' she said, 'time to go.'

She smiled and she smiled and she smiled until she felt that her face would never ease into any other expression. She smiled at the guests and she smiled at Alistair and she smiled at the best man and the bridesmaids, and she smiled at her mother; she smiled at the cameras, she smiled at the manager of the Dorchester, she smiled at the maître d', and she smiled most determinedly and blindly at Serena Hammond, her best friend and chief bridesmaid, as she helped her to change out of her dress, her exquisite wild silk, rose-strewn Belinda Belville dress, so suited to her dark beauty, and into the cream silk Ossie Clark suit in which she was to embark on her first journey as Mrs Alistair Headleigh Drayton.

'It was wonderful, wasn't it?' she said, setting down her bouquet, looking at it, pulling one single pink rose out of it, handing it to Serena. 'Would you be terribly sweet and press that for me, give it to me when I get back?'

'Of course,' said Serena, 'of course I will. Are you – OK, Susie? I mean really OK.'

'Serena, I feel wonderful,' said Susie. 'Absolutely wonderful,' and then quite suddenly her heart, her aching, tender heart, which had through the long day grown physically heavier, until she felt she must hold with her hand the area beneath which it lay, to support it, to keep it from falling, crushed, somewhere deep and desolate within her body, it stirred, that heart; and the pain was sharp, uncontrollable suddenly, and she winced, heard a faint strange whimpering sound escape her, so faint she wondered if it had indeed been real, and then she saw Serena staring at her alarmed, and she sat down on the bed, and buried her head in her hands and wished she could stay there forever in the quiet darkness and never move again.

'Susie,' said Serena, 'Susie, what is it, are you ill?' And she could not answer, dared not move even, in case the tears came, broke free, alongside the grief. She sat for what seemed a long time, was indeed a long time, on such a day, such an occasion. She heard first the phone ringing, then a knock at the door, heard Serena say, in an anxious whisper, that she was all right, but had a sudden headache, needed five minutes to recover, that they must all wait, Alistair, the guests, everyone, was that so much to ask?

She sat there, thinking of Jamie with such longing, such love that he seemed to be physically beside her; she saw him, saw his slightly untidy face, with its wide, laughing blue eyes, his wild fair hair, heard his voice, his slightly husky voice, saying 'Christ, Susie, I love you, I love you,' and then, harsher, colder, filled with brutality, saying, 'I'm going to marry Maggie Nicolson, I'm sorry, Susie, but that's what I'm going to do.' And she saw him again, no longer laughing, his face no longer untidy but neat, controlled, forbidding; and she felt him now, felt his hands on her, felt her body rising, throbbing with desire for him, heard her own voice, her own laughing exulting voice saying, 'Jamie, Jamie, this is heaven, this is so good' and then that same voice, dead, leaden, saying, 'Fine, absolutely fine, I understand, I hope it works for you, Jamie.'

And then because she was well disciplined, well behaved, because she had chosen this day and what it was to do to her and her life, she finally lifted her head and said, still dry-eyed, still somehow smiling, 'Sorry, Serena, I'm so sorry. Just a bit faint, that's all. Give me my hat, there's a love, and I must go down quickly, they'll think I've done a runner.' And she stood up, seized her flowers, and almost ran to the door and out to the landing where Alistair waited, anxious, and she smiled at him too, and said, 'Darling, I'm so sorry, bit of a hiccup with the buttons,' and together they went down the stairs where she paused and threw her bouquet and was careful that Serena, whom she loved, would not be able to catch it, for she felt that anything associated with pain could not possibly bring anything near to happiness.

'Mummy!' It was Annabel, appearing in the doorway, the great fall of dark hair so like her mother's, half covering her face. 'Mummy, I've forgotten to bring any tights. Can I borrow some of yours?'

'Yes,' said Susie, endeavouring to hide the irritation in her voice, smiling determinedly at Annabel, 'well, yes, you can, but I've only brought a couple of pairs myself. So –'

'Well, I can't see why you need more than one,' said Annabel. 'So that means there's a pair for me.'

'I like to have a spare pair,' said Susie mildly, 'in case of accidents.'

'Yes, well, this is an accident. In a way. Honestly, Mummy, I'm only asking for a pair of tights. Not to borrow your entire outfit. Oh, and can I use your make-up, it's so much nicer than mine?'

'It's nicer than yours because I don't leave everything open all over the dressing table,' said Susie.

'I don't actually and anyway, yours is obviously nicer because it's better. I can't afford Estée Lauder and Chanel.'

'All right,' said Susie with a sigh, 'but please put everything back when you've finished with it. How are you feeling, darling, anyway? Sleep well?'

'No, not terribly, I had awful dreams and I've got a really bad headache.'

'Too much wine at supper, dare I suggest?'

'I hardly had any wine, that's not fair, about a quarter of what you were drinking. Honestly, Mum, you're turning into a real alkie.'

'Thanks,' said Susie.

'Well it's true. Oh and by the way, Rufus has gone missing.'

'Dear God,' said Susie cheerfully. 'I hope he hasn't run off with Cressida.'

It was a flip, thoughtless remark; she regretted it instantly, seeing Janet's face set into reproach, Annabel's into intense curiosity. 'Sorry!' she said. 'Sorry, Janet. Bad form. Sorry, Annabel. Bad joke. Do you mean Rufus is not in his room as of now, or he hasn't slept in it?'

'Hasn't slept in it,' said Annabel, clearly enjoying the potential drama.

'Well that's all right, darling. He went off with Mungo Buchan after dinner last night, he's probably at the hotel with him still.'

'If he was with Mungo, I should think they're pissed as newts in some gambling den somewhere,' said Annabel prissily. Susie sighed: if Tom was the nearest thing she had to a favourite, Annabel was the furthest from it.

'Darling, that's not fair. Rufus is quite sensible really, and he certainly wouldn't let Mungo do anything awful on quite such an important occasion.'

'Rufus isn't sensible at all,' said Annabel irritably. 'And anyway, you know he just follows where Mungo leads. They're a lethal combination, and we really should have kept them under lock and key last night.'

'Oh rubbish,' said Susie, realizing that Janet Beaumont was looking increasingly uncomfortable, 'you're being over-dramatic, darling. Go and have a bath or something and I bet you anything you like Rufus and quite possibly Mungo too will be here to join you for breakfast.'

'Anything?' said Annabel.

'Anything.'

'Peugeot 205 then. When I pass my test.'

'Well, darling, I didn't mean quite –'

'Mummy! That is so exactly like you. Backing down when the going gets tough and –'

'I'm not backing down,' said Susie, almost crossly, 'and all right, Annabel, if they –'

There was a scrunch of tyres in the drive and Theo Buchan's silver

Bentley appeared; Rufus jumped out of it and it reversed sharply again, vanished down the lane.

'Thank God,' said Susie, as he walked into the kitchen. 'Rufus, I am particularly pleased to see you. You've just saved me about eight thousand pounds and your father's wrath.'

'Oh,' said Rufus, 'how come?'

His voice was oddly expressionless, his voice heavy. Susie looked at him sharply. 'What's the matter?'

'Oh – nothing. Nothing really. I think I'll go and have a shower. If that's OK. Sorry if you were worried.'

'Is – is everything all right?' said Janet, 'With – Oliver, I mean?'

'Oh – yes. Yes, he's fine. Nothing to worry about.' He walked out of the room in silence.

'Well really,' said Annabel, 'talk about the spectre at the feast.'

'What feast?' said Janet darkly.

'Oh, there'll be a feast,' said Susie. 'Of course there will.' She glanced at her watch, felt her heart thud, fiercely, uncomfortably. 'Janet, could I make myself a cup of coffee and then a phone call? To London? I promise to be quick'

'Yes of course,' said Janet Beaumont, 'use the phone in my room, dear, it'll be quieter. I'll make you a coffee, we could all do with one I should think.'

'Thank you,' said Susie, and stood there watching while Janet with agonizing, awful slowness plugged in the kettle, searched for the coffee pot, cut open a fresh bag of coffee, discovered all the cups were in the dishwasher, washed out four by hand, poured the coffee, fetched some milk from the doorstep, asked everyone if they wanted sugar, and all the time she thought of Mr Hobson arriving at his consulting rooms, drinking his own coffee, putting in the phone call to the lab, making a note of it, setting it aside, and then waiting for her to phone as she had said she would. He'd wanted her to go in for the result, said he didn't like giving these things over the phone, but she'd said she had to know, she couldn't wait another day, that there were reasons besides her own impatience, her own anxiety, that he knew how sensible, how steady she was, she would be fine, and he had given in, saying very well, as long as she promised to come in the next day, with her husband if possible, so that they could discuss the next steps – if indeed next steps had to be taken. And finally she had the coffee and sat on Janet's bed, looking at the phone and feeling very sick; she took a large swig of it, as if it was something much stronger, and quickly, almost feverishly, dialled the number.

'Mrs Briggs? Mrs Headleigh Drayton. Is Mr Hobson in? I've arranged to ring at this time.'

'Ah, Mrs Headleigh Drayton – good morning. Yes, he's here, I'll put you through.' And was she imagining it, or was Mrs Briggs's voice slightly lower, gentler, more carefully concerned?

Mr Hobson's voice, smoothly easy, came on the line. 'Mrs Headleigh Drayton. Good morning. What a lovely one for the wedding. All well down there?'

'Yes, yes, fine,' said Suzie (for what was a vanished bride, set against what she might be about to hear?). 'Thank you. Mr Hobson, do you have the results of the mammogram?'

'Yes, I do,' he said, and his voice had changed, she knew it had now, this was not imagined. 'Mrs Headleigh Drayton, I – well, there's no point beating about the bush. I know you've no time for that sort of thing anyway. Now I've had a look at your ultrasound as well as the mammogram, and I'm not entirely happy, I'm afraid. It isn't just the lump, there's a bit of microcalcification as well – close by it.'

'Oh.' She felt odd: not upset, hardly touched by it even, but just very distant, as if she was sitting, very small and still, in the middle of a large empty space. She knew Mr Hobson was still talking, but she couldn't really hear the words; she sat there, trying to make sense of it all, trying to get herself back to reality.

'. . . so I'd like you in as soon as possible,' she heard finally. 'Later today if that's feasible.'

'It isn't,' said Susie. 'It really isn't. But – well, I suppose – I suppose tomorrow, if –' To her horror she heard her voice, or rather the voice of the small still creature, shaky, trembling strangely, felt something on her hand, looked down, saw a splash of wetness – how absurd, was she crying? She never cried, certainly not easily, like this. She hauled herself together, smiled into the phone.

'Yes, tomorrow, that would be fine. Of course I have to talk to my husband –'

'Of course. I'm so sorry, Mrs Headleigh Drayton, and especially to be breaking the news to you on the phone on such a day, but that was –'

'I know, that was my idea.' She smiled again, brightly, as if he could see her.

'What you have to bear very much in mind is that even the worst possible scenario is nothing like it was. There are many treatments, the prognosis is good –'

'Yes. Yes of course,' said Susie, thinking of a friend who had had that treatment, who had undergone chemotherapy and its attendant tortures, the nausea, the weakness, the weariness, the baldness – and still died. 'Yes, I understand.'

'So – tomorrow then. You can arrive any time, but the earlier the better. I'll tell Mrs Briggs to make the arrangements. Nothing by mouth after midnight. Now would you like me to speak to your husband? Explain things to him?'

'Oh no, no that's fine,' said Susie. 'I'll talk to him. He'll be fine. He's very – supportive.'

'Good. Exactly what you need. I'm so sorry to have cast a shadow over your day.'

'It's all right,' she said, smiling again determinedly. 'It really isn't your fault.'

'No, but I do always feel somehow responsible. Goodbye.'

'Goodbye,' said Susie.

She put the phone down and sat there, staring out of the window; she realized she was cradling the breast in her hand, the left breast, that had been invaded so swiftly and silently by this obscene, all-consuming monster.

Cancer. There was no doubt in her mind as to Mr Hobson's conclusions. She had known anyway, for a while. Apart from the lump, discovered as she tenderly, lovingly massaged her Chanel body lotion into her breast, it had been one of her days for meeting James. She had been excited, happy, and there it was, small, sinister, predatory. She hadn't said anything to James, of course; had waited indeed for two weeks, telling herself it was probably just a purely temporary thing, that it would disappear after her next period. It hadn't. She'd lost weight, too, had been aware of it for a little while; not a lot, but enough to notice. She had stopped having to be careful; she'd tested herself in fact, had eaten all the things she always refused, for over a week, chocolates, puddings, potatoes, cheese, and at the end of it, stubbornly, defiantly the scales had shown a drop of almost two pounds.

'So,' she said aloud, 'so, Susie, what to do?'

And as she sat there, trying to digest the news, to face the fact of her possible, probable death in – what? – six months? a year? a painful, ugly, hideous death, when she was still young, still beautiful, still happy, she knew exactly what she was going to do. She was going to have James, all to herself, for as much of that time as she possibly could. He owed her that much; they all did. She had earned it.

Chapter 6

James 10:30am

He knew there must be something wrong as he pulled into the drive: Maggie was standing by the back door, her plump face tense, white, and Janine beside her, holding her arm. His first thought was of course that Cressida must be ill, and he wondered briefly, almost idly, what he could give her, what shot might settle a stomach, ease panic, cure the migraine that occasionally plagued her. And then Harriet, her face as white as theirs, eyes wide and frightened, came running out to the car, and he stared at her through the open window. 'What is it?' he asked. 'What on earth's going on?'

'It's Cressida,' said Harriet, quite quietly but with an undertow of panic in her voice. 'She's gone.'

'Gone?' said James, getting out of the car, looking towards Maggie and Janine and then back at Harriet, aware even as he spoke the words how stupid, how dense, how unhelpful he must sound. 'What do you mean gone? Of course she's not gone.'

'Daddy, she's gone,' said Harriet. 'And her car's gone, she's been missing for ages – probably hours –'

James had once been in a car that had skidded and turned over twice; he had felt then a chilled, blind terror, a sickness that had consumed all his senses. He leaned against the car to steady himself; Harriet's face and voice seemed to be very far away, her voice echoing and odd, rather slow. 'Three hours?' he said, and was aware how foolish he must sound. 'Cressida's been missing for hours, but that's absurd, she was here when I left about – what was it, seven o'clock?'

'How do you know she was here then?' asked Harriet quickly. 'How do you know, did you see her?'

'Well, no – but her door was closed, everything seemed calm –'

'Where on earth have you been anyway?' said Maggie. She had walked over to the car; her voice was high, shaky with tension. 'What have you been doing all this time?'

'I went for a run, as usual,' said James easily, blessing his infinite capacity for deceit, 'and then I realized I hadn't got enough cash for the waiters today, so I drove into Woodstock to the cash machine. I'm sorry. Anyway, Harriet, where were you at seven? Why on earth weren't you raising the alarm then rather than waiting three hours?'

'Daddy, I was looking for her,' said Harriet, quietly, patiently, her dark eyes nevertheless angry, 'and trying not to raise a panic. I felt sure she'd turn up. Anyway, we've been looking for her for ages now, making phone calls –'

'Who have you phoned?'

'Well, Mummy phoned the Beaumonts, I tried to get hold of Mungo, only he's not at the hotel, and Theo's line is constantly engaged –'

'What about the Bergins? Does Oliver know anything?'

'We haven't phoned them,' said Harriet.

'Why on earth not, for Christ's sake?' Careful, James, you're sounding hysterical now; don't add to this panic. He made a huge effort to level his voice. It was surprisingly difficult; there was a fierce, hot sensation behind his eyes, a constriction in his throat. 'If she really is – well, missing, then surely he is above all the person who has to know. He also might very well know where she is. She might be there, with him.'

'Oh, of course she's not with him,' said Maggie. 'That's absurd.'

'I don't see why. It seems at least a possible explanation to me.'

'James, of course she's not with Oliver,' said Maggie. 'She was so insistent she didn't see him after midnight even, don't you remember last night, it's absurd to talk about –'

'Oh, for God's sake,' said Harriet, 'don't start arguing about it. You phone them if you think it's a good idea, Daddy. We weren't prepared to, that's all, not yet . . .'

'I'll phone them,' said Janine quietly. 'It would be more discreet, I think. Can I use the phone in your study, Jamie?'

'Yes, of course. Thank you, Janine.' She disappeared into the house; they all stood looking after her, staring at her small back as if in some way she was carrying with her the answer to the mystery.

'Well, we may as well go in,' said James finally. He was beginning to feel slightly steadier, able to think. 'No point standing here. What about her flat in town? Have you phoned there?'

'Yes, of course. We keep ringing it. No answer.'

'And – I suppose you haven't – that is, should we phone the – the police?'

Maggie had reached the doorway; she turned to look at him, her face puzzled.

'No,' she said, 'no of course not, why should we phone the police?'

'Well, because there might have been – Cressida might have had – well, you know – an accident.'

'Oh, don't be absurd,' she said, 'of course she hasn't. Of course we shouldn't bother the police with it. Harriet, make some tea, would you? I feel – I feel –'

She looked terrible suddenly; no longer just pale, but grey with fright, her eyes huge, the pupils dilated. She walked forward and staggered slightly; James caught her arm and helped her to a chair in the kitchen. She was very hot, he noticed, almost with distaste, sweating heavily; but her hands were cold, her lips white. She was about to go into shock, he thought. He turned to Harriet, said, 'Darling, make that tea quickly, would you, lots of sugar for Mummy,' and pushed Maggie's head down between her knees. Her neck was wet with sweat, her hair clinging to it, and there was a damp patch on the back of her velour tracksuit top. What on earth was she doing dressed in something so warm on such a day? he wondered, and then knew: she was covering herself up as much as possible, as always hiding the heavy body she was so ashamed of, hated so much and yet seemed incapable of doing anything about.

Harriet came over with the tea; Maggie sat back, took the mug with a hand that shook.

'Better?' asked James. He watched her as she sipped at it, saw a slight colour seep back into her face.

'A bit.'

'Good. Don't worry, darling, she'll be –'

'Look Jamie,' said Maggie, and there was an edge to her voice that he found almost comforting in its normality, 'I'll try to keep calm, I'll do whatever is necessary. But don't tell me not to worry and don't say any more you're sure she'll be back. I can't stand it.'

Janine came into the kitchen; she smiled quickly, carefully at them.

'What did Oliver say?' asked James. 'Did he –'

'I didn't speak to him,' said Janine. 'I was put through to Josh and then to Julia, unfortunately. I said I wanted to talk to him about a little present I had for Cressida which I was going to ask him to give her on the plane.'

'That was clever,' said Harriet.

'Well, she seemed to accept it. Anyway, Oliver was asleep.'

'So late? How odd.'

'He was up playing poker with the boys until three, Julia said. She sounded a little disapproving. She is absurd, that woman, she behaves as if the boy was two, not thirty-two. She was very reluctant to wake him up. I couldn't really – well, I didn't want to force her. At this stage.'

'No – no, I suppose not. I must say that doesn't sound like Oliver. He's not a poker player at the best of times. Bridge is more his style. But maybe he couldn't sleep, and those two can be very persuasive. But anyway, did Julia sound – well – quite normal?'

'Oh yes. Very normal. She said what a wonderful day it was, and she hoped we were all feeling as great as she and Josh were.'

'Dear God. Well, it certainly doesn't sound as if there are any clues there. You were right, Mummy,' said Harriet. 'Daddy, should we phone the police do you think? And – and the hospitals?'

James stood by the window, constantly expecting, hoping, praying, that Cressida's little car would pull into the drive, that she would jump out, run in, full of apologies; he was afraid himself of ringing the police, of what it meant, that they were making it official, the disappearance, that they needed help. He felt very sick himself suddenly; he forced himself to smile at Harriet.

'I think maybe we –' he said, and then the phone rang. Maggie jumped up, moving with extraordinary speed across the kitchen, snatched it up.

'Cress – oh – oh Mary.' There was a sharp intake of breath, and she handed it to James, shaking her head.

'Hallo, Mary? Yes, this is James. Yes, she's fine. A bit panicky. Busy morning here as you can imagine. What can I do for you? Oh really? Well, yes of course you can. We'll see you then. Bye, Mary.'

He put down the phone. 'That was Mary Fortescue. She wants to drop Belinda off a quarter of an hour early, and then get down to the church and check the flowers in the porch. Apparently that's her bag.'

'James,' said Maggie, and her voice was only just under control, 'James, I don't want Belinda Fortescue here early, rushing around in her bridesmaid's dress. The child is a nightmare at the best of times, I never wanted her as a bridesmaid anyway and –'

Tyres scrunched onto the drive; they all stiffened. It was the florist's van. He knocked at the open back door, loudly, stood there whistling. Harriet went to the door.

'Oh! Mr Spragg,' she said, 'good morning.'

'Morning, Miss Forrest. Got some lovely things for you here. One bouquet and eight posies. And the coronets. Now do you want them or shall I take them away, try and find someone else who can use them?'

They all stood there, staring at him, frozen. His words seemed horribly prophetic, his bonhomie hideously misplaced. He looked at them, and his smile slowly faded.

'Nothing wrong is there?'

'No,' said Harriet, smiling quickly, 'no of course not. How lovely, Mr Spragg, do bring them in. Maybe if you put them in the utility room, it's cooler in there.'

Mr Spragg's face eased out of anxiousness; he turned and went to his van, carried first one and then a second box of bouquets. He was whistling again, loudly and tunelessly – 'Here Comes the Bride'. James felt as if barbed wire was slowly tightening round his heart.

'Right, and there's the buttonholes. Sign here, Miss Forrest. Beautiful they are. Now you all have a lovely day and give your sister a kiss from me. I can remember making up her first bridesmaid's posy, pink sweetheart roses, I can see them as if they were here now. Well, I expect you're all very busy so I'll be getting along. Mrs Spragg's going to pop down to the church at two, if that's all right, just to see the bride. I would but I've got a very busy day. I hope all goes well.'

'Oh – yes, thank you, Mr Spragg.' James forced his voice into action; it was extremely difficult. 'I'm sure we will.'

The van disappeared down the drive. Maggie looked at James as if for comfort and then suddenly started to cry, tears rolling down her face. She started drumming her hands on her knees; Harriet stepped forward. 'Mummy, don't –'

'Stop it!' Maggie's voice was loud, raw. 'Don't touch me. Just find her, go and find her.'

'Maggie, pull yourself together,' said James, aware of the desperate edge to his voice. 'This won't help anyone.'

'I can't, I can't,' cried Maggie, her voice a wail. 'She's gone, she's gone, and we shall never find her, never, she's run away, and the whole day will –'

Yet again the phone rang. Christ, James thought, it was like some ghastly persistent torture, he felt the ringing physically, like a probe entering his brain, somewhere behind his ears. He picked it up.

'Yes? Oh, Julia, good morning.' He looked at them, over the phone, his eyes asking for guidance. They all stared at him, helpless. 'How are you?' he said. 'Sleep well, I hope? In spite of everything. Good. Yes, indeed, a lovely day. I'm sorry? No, she's not here just at the moment. She's – in the bath. Can I get her to – yes, of course I will, Julia. How kind. How very kind. Goodbye. Yes, just before one we said, didn't we? For a glass of champagne. Excellent. See you then, Julia.'

He put the phone down again. 'She rang to speak to you,' he said to Maggie, his face carefully expressionless, 'to say she was sorry she missed you earlier when Janine rang, but she had just got out of the tub, as she calls it, and to – I quote – to tell you good morning, wish you the happiest of days. That's all.'

'She is very American that one,' said Janine lightly.

'Well she would be,' said Maggie. 'She *is* American. Nothing else? Nothing about Oliver?'

'No. Nothing. He's obviously still asleep.'

'James, what do you think we should do?' Her eyes were on him, strained, frightened.

'I think,' he said rather heavily, 'I think, quite honestly, we should phone the police.'

'So do I,' said Harriet.

A small pained cry escaped Maggie.

James braced himself to confront the truth. He phoned first the vicar, then the police, and he phoned all the hospitals in the area; there had been no accidents, not even minor ones. The Chief Constable, whose daughter had been delivered of a fine strapping son in her own front room by James Forrest one December a few years earlier when all the roads for miles around had been closed by freak weather – James had trudged on foot through the snow to get to the house – made half a dozen calls to all the major units in the country. There were no serious accidents on record. 'And I've had the hospitals checked out too. Nothing. I wouldn't worry too much, Mr Forrest. She's probably just – well, there is one thing you could do –' He hesitated.

'What's that?' asked James.

'You could phone the Missing Persons' Bureau. Very good people they are, very experienced in this sort of thing.'

'Well I might. A little later,' said James, shrinking from further phone calls, explanations, forms, details, red tape, further confirmation that Cressida was precisely that: a missing person. 'Thank you.'

He looked at his watch: moving towards eleven. Christ, this was getting out of hand. They'd have to start notifying people soon, couldn't go on like this. It was madness. But it seemed crazy, irresponsible, not to tell Oliver first: they should have done it hours before.

He phoned the Bergins' hotel. While the number rang interminably, he stood staring out of the window, thinking inconsequentially that the white roses would actually be at their best next week and what a pity that was, what a waste, and it was several seconds later, when the hotel switchboard answered, before he forced himself to the realization that of all the possible, indeed almost certain, waste of today, the roses constituted the very least.

'Lambourne Park Hotel,' said the girl's breathy voice, 'how may I help you?' And again James found himself distracted by minutiae, by how much he hated that phrase, so awkward in its syntax, so redolent of learnt-late rather than instilled good manners; then he pulled himself together, back to reality, and said, 'Dr Bergin, please, Dr Oliver Bergin.'

'One moment please,' said the voice and there was the abstract clicking of computer keys and a long pause; then 'Dr Bergin doesn't appear to be answering at the moment, sir, can anyone else help you?'

'No,' said James irritably, 'no they can't, I'm afraid,' and then suddenly Julia's voice came on the line, just slightly less well modulated, marginally quicker than usual: 'Julia Bergin speaking.'

'Oh,' said James, thrown into total confusion, 'oh – Julia, this is James Forrest. I – I was actually hoping to speak to Oliver.'

'Why?' said Julia, and again this was not the rather fey, carefully flirtatious woman he normally spoke to, it was someone businesslike, quick, almost sharp. 'First Janine, now you. Why do you all want to speak to Oliver, James?'

'Well – I wanted to check something with him.'

'And what was that, James? Maybe I can help?'

'I don't think so Julia. It was about the – the best man's speech. I wondered how – how long it might be.'

'I would have thought you should have spoken to Mungo. He would surely have more idea.' She sounded more herself, the voice softer again.

'Yes, but he's on the tennis court.'

'I see. Well, Oliver isn't here right now.'

'He isn't?' Dear God, had the entire world gone mad, disappeared?

'No, he's in the tub. No doubt reflecting on his future as a married man. A very fortunate married man, of course. Will I have him call you?'

'Oh – yes, Julia, yes please. As soon as he's out of the – er – tub. Thank you. I'll be by the phone.'

'All right, James. Goodbye for now. My, it's getting late, isn't it?'

'Yes,' said James, looking helplessly at his watch and the clock on his desk: another ten minutes had passed, it was indeed getting late, after eleven now, after five past. 'Yes it is. Well – thank you, Julia.'

'And there's nothing else?'

'No, no, nothing. Thank you again.'

Silly woman. Fussing over her little thirty-two-year-old boy, hanging around in his bedroom on the morning of his wedding. What on earth was she doing in there, and would she be soaping his neck for him in a minute, checking he'd rinsed his hair properly? God, Cressida had a tough row to hoe with Julia for a mother-in-law.

'Only maybe you won't,' he said aloud, and sat down at the desk, buried his head in his hands, his eyes tightly closed, his thumbs pushed into his ears as if to shut out as much as possible of the world, willing it away. As he always did, always had, in moments of appalling crisis. As he had, almost exactly twenty-five years ago, as he finally left the delivery room at St Edmund's Hospital at five in the morning and stumbled exhaustedly into his room, wondering how, how in the name of God, he was ever to recover from the sheer awfulness of what he had done.

'Mr Forrest? Staff Nurse Jackson here. We've got an admission into the labour ward, and I'd really like you to come over and have a look at her.'

'Ah,' said James, playing for time, 'ah, yes, Staff. Yes, yes, I see.'

'She's very small, the baby seems to be quite big, and she doesn't seem to be getting anywhere. And she hasn't been coming to antenatal clinics.'

'Isn't Dr Meadows there?'

'No, it's young Tim Davies on duty, and I really don't think he's got the experience, and we've got three others in labour anyway –'

'Ah', said James again. He looked at his watch: one thirty, dear God, and he was in no condition to look at anything, except possibly another stiff whisky; he'd already had a great deal of wine, he'd known it was foolish, that he was on call, but he still found entertaining the Headleigh Draytons a strain. He wished Maggie would stop insisting on being quite such close friends with them, asking them for dinner and so on. He'd promised himself just one drink before dinner, but somehow the one had led to another and then he'd had to listen to bloody Alistair banging on about his bloody career and his bloody family and how he'd put his bloody son down for Eton already. If only, James had thought, if only he knew; he had sat there, glass after glass of claret going down, (surreptitiously because they all knew he was on call, well diluted with a great many glasses of water), looking at Alistair's handsomely good-natured face, and then at Susie's beautiful one, listening to her lovely husky voice as she regaled them with some amusing story, not hearing a word of it, wondering with the old, sick, illogical jealousy how she could possibly have married Alistair.

'Yes, all right, Staff,' he heard himself saying, quite clearly, quite coherently. At least it would get him away from this filthy evening. 'I'll come over. Be about fifteen minutes. All right?'

'Thank you, Mr Forrest.'

He had drunk almost a whole bottle of water and two mugs of strong coffee and gone; they had all looked at him anxiously and asked was he really all right, but he said yes, fine, he'd only had a couple of glasses, and that was hours ago (hoping no one had been counting). And went out to his car, and drove the few miles to St Edmund's where Rosemary Mills was lying in the labour ward.

She seemed incredibly young, but then most of the mothers did these days. She was nineteen, she told him, her eyes resting trustingly on his, large blue eyes in a small pale face. She was very small; James looked at her narrow hips, small, childlike legs, either side of the huge stomach as he examined her, and sighed silently. Then he smiled his careful consultant's smile, patted her hand gently.

'Right,' he said, 'everything looks all right. Your cervix *is* dilating although it's slow. But there's nothing to worry about.'

'It doesn't feel all right,' she said, her face contorting as a contraction hit her. She panted heavily, fiercely, her eyes fixed on him, clinging to the hand of the student nurse who was with her; he could see what she was doing, desperately trying to relax her body. One hand was clenched, the other flexed open.

'Been to classes?' he asked carefully, when she was finished, had swallowed, drawn breath, the midwife had wiped her dry mouth.

'Well – not here.' Her voice was pretty: slightly husky, with – what was it? – a West Country accent. 'But to yoga classes. I – know what to do.'

'Hmm. I'd advise some pethidine. Help a lot, you know.'

'Oh no,' she said quickly. 'No, I don't want drugs.'

Oh God. This was going to be tough.

'Well – it could be a long night. Think about it at least.'

'I have thought about it,' she said, 'and I know I don't want any. I want to have my baby naturally.'

She sounded fierce; very fierce for such a gentle creature. She had been brainwashed by some bloody natural-childbirth freak. James would have them all bound and gagged and made to watch a long, tough breech birth, without benefit of pain relief.

'Well, we'll see how you get on. Of course,' he added carefully, anxious not to alienate her, 'that's best if you can manage it, and if everything is straightforward. Now according to Staff Nurse, you haven't been coming very often for your prenatal care. In fact, the last time we saw you was three months ago. That was silly, you know.'

'I know,' she said humbly. 'I'm sorry. I hate hospitals.'

'Well you're here now. With your husband?'

'No,' she said quickly, 'with my yoga teacher and my mum. Can they come in – later?'

'I don't know. We allow husbands, but not –'

'Oh God, it's starting again,' she said and started panting.

Staff Nurse Jackson patted her hand briskly. 'Good girl. That's right. You sure you wouldn't like some pethidine?'

Rosemary Mills shook her head. Her teeth were gritted. The student nurse looked as white and exhausted as she did.

'She's very large,' said Nurse Jackson. She had asked him to come into the corridor. 'Don't you think? Especially for a primagravida?'

'Not really,' said James curtly. He turned away from her, afraid his breath must smell of drink. It was too late: she knew, and she could see he knew she knew.

'Dr Forrest, are you all right? You look very – tired. Would you like me to try and find someone else? Even now.'

'No,' said James. He found a packet of peppermints in his pocket, started chewing them. 'I absolutely would not. This is a perfectly routine case. She's already 5 cm dilated. She may have a tough time, but that's all. Still, I'll stay and see her through.'

'How was the heartbeat?'

'The heartbeat was fine.'

Staff Nurse Jackson met his eyes. 'I'm sorry, Mr Forrest, but I just don't like the look of it. Her waters broke over an hour ago, she's been going hard for almost six hours as far as I can make out. And in mild labour for much longer than that. And she's only thirty-six weeks. And as I say very big.'

'Thirty-six weeks. Yes of course,' said James quickly. He hadn't noticed that. Shit. Did she know he hadn't noticed?

'Mr Forrest.' The eyes were more contemptuous still. 'I do think this one might be a Caesarian. Should we tell theatre, have them on standby?'

'Staff, I'll make my own decisions, thank you. Now you can get me a coffee, I've had a very long day, I'd only been home a couple of hours,

and then you can try and persuade that stupid girl to have some
pethidine. All right?'

'Yes, Mr Forrest.'

He drank the coffee, sent for some more. He still felt odd, slightly
distanced from reality, but not drunk any more. Of course not drunk.
God, what was – well, maybe three glasses of wine? And a gin and
tonic of course, but that had been many hours ago. He had frequently
drunk much more than that in the past and gone on to beat Theo at
poker. He was just tired. Terribly tired. And upset. That was all. Maybe
he could get a few minutes' sleep before he had to deliver the baby.
He closed his eyes; the room swirled briefly. He drank some water,
tried again, hung on through the swirling, and dozed for a while. His
phone woke him. It was Staff Nurse Jackson. 'Mr Forrest, she's been
pushing for almost half an hour, not getting anywhere. Could you
come down please?'

'Yes, of course.'

He stood up; he felt sick, still slightly odd, but much more sober.
Good, the coffee had worked. He sook another slug of water, hurried
along to the delivery room. Rosemary Mills was wide-eyed with terror
and pain; her face was white and contorted.

'Ah,' he said. 'How are you? Pushing I hear. That's good. How about
some gas and air?'

'No. No, I really don't want any. Please don't make me.'

James struggled to sound patient. The slight sense of unreality he was
feeling, the sense of physical distancing from the room, from the girl,
from her pain, helped. He managed to smile at her, to pat her hand. 'No,
not as long as you're coping. And you're pushing now, Staff Nurse tells
me. That's the good part. It will soon be over, and the baby will be here.
Now I'm just going to have another look at you. Tell you how you're
getting on.'

He examined her; the tummy was very big. Staff was right. He did an
internal. The head needed turning. That was it, that was what was
holding things up. The heartbeat was absolutely fine, nothing serious
there. Just a bad hour ahead for the poor girl; well, she should have
some pain control. Silly bloody nonsense, all of it.

'Right,' he said, 'now everything's fine and you're doing well, but the baby's head is in slightly the wrong position.'

'What does that mean?' Her white face was panicked. 'Is it dangerous?'

'Not at all, no. It's facing the wrong way – just slightly. That slows things down. But it may turn as it comes into the birth canal. All right?'

She nodded dully. Then a contraction came; she pushed. Another; she pushed again. And again. After twenty minutes, nothing had happened; the baby hadn't budged. She was yelling now, her courage finally deserted her, her face contorted with fear as much as pain. 'Get it out,' she kept crying, 'get it out, get it out. Please, for God's sake, just get it out.'

'All right,' said James gently, 'all right. I'm going to use forceps and give you a local anaesthetic, something called a pudendal block. And you'll have to have an episiotomy. It will help us turn the baby's head and get it out. Do you understand?'

Rosemary Mills moaned helplessly as her legs were placed in the stirrups. She looked like a small animal in a large trap. James looked at her. He had not known many births as bad before. He still felt sick and his head ached horribly. Christ, this was a nightmare. 'Get me another glass of water,' he said curtly to Janet Adams, the student nurse, 'and call the paediatrician.'

He put the blades on the baby's head – turned it and began to tug, gently. The baby proceeded, smoothly, easily now down the birth canal. He manipulated the head between contractions. Released from some of her pain Rosemary Mills was quieter, biddable. He felt better: in control, excited almost, as he often did before a birth. The baby was face downwards now; he did the episiotomy, gave a final pull and the head delivered. It was a very dark head, the hair very black. A pair of small brown shoulders followed, he gave an injection of syntometrine and the rest of the body emerged. A little coffee brown female body. He lifted the baby, slapped her gently, heard her cry, handed her into her mother's pale, shaking arms.

'She's lovely,' he said.

'Yes,' said Rosemary Mills, her voice little more than a croak. 'Yes, she is. Really lovely. I can't believe it.' She looked up at him, gave him her trusting, childlike smile. James smiled back just slightly awkwardly. He felt he could have served her better. But: 'All well then,' he said to Staff Nurse Jackson.

'Just as well,' she said, 'there's a crisis in the theatre, baby with a heart problem.'

'Ah,' he said. 'Well, we were lucky.'

'Thank you,' said Rosemary, 'thank you for everything.' She was high now, with pleasure and relief, smiling, laughing almost, stroking the baby's black head, her small pudgy nose, looking at her dark blue eyes.

'What are you going to call her?' he asked as he delivered the placenta and prepared to stitch her up.

'Ottoline,' she said.

'That's a fine name.'

'I know. After Lady Ottoline Morell. She's a great heroine of mine. And her daddy's.'

'And where is her daddy?' asked Staff Nurse.

'Oh – he's off working,' she said quickly, bravely. 'He's in a band.'

It all made sense suddenly. She wasn't going to see a great deal of the daddy. Probably after a while she wouldn't see him at all. She had a tough time ahead. But meanwhile, the miracle had been worked again, a baby had been born, given life, love, tenderness; and it was all worth it.

James smiled at her. She smiled back at him. Staff Nurse Jackson smiled at them both. And then Rosemary Mills was sick. That was quite normal. It was the syntometrine. As she vomited, as Staff Nurse rushed for a bowl, James patted her hand, took the baby from her. And saw a bulge in her vagina, a nightmare sight, a second bag of membranes making their way out of the birth canal.

'Staff,' he said, his voice light, shaky with urgency, 'Staff, take this baby. There's another one in there.'

'Ah,' said Staff Nurse quietly. She laid the baby in a cradle, told the junior midwife to take her away.

'Right,' she said, her calmness icy, reproachful. 'I'll try the paediatrician again. You –'

'It was a singleton,' he said, 'I know it was a singleton. There was no other heartbeat, no sign –'

Nurse Jackson looked at him, and her eyes were very contemptuous. 'I did say –'

There was a great gush of water over the bed, and a small foot appeared. Rosemary Mills groaned; James with difficulty stopped himself from doing the same. Twins, and this one a breech. God Almighty.

'I'm sorry,' he said to Rosemary. 'I didn't – didn't realize. It was very high up, you see, it's very often difficult to tell in those circumstances. Nothing to worry about though, soon get this one out.' God, if only he felt clearer-headed, less exhausted. 'Now you're going to start pushing again, and I'm going to deliver your baby.'

She tried; she tried desperately. But she was very tired. Progress was terribly slow. 'What's the heartbeat, Staff?'

'Still a hundred.'

'Good. Thank God. Now come on, there's a good girl. Push, Rosemary, push.'

He was fumbling now; his hands, normally so skilful, seemed awkward, undeft. He hurt her; she cried out. 'Sorry, Rosemary. Sorry. Won't be long.' Right. He eased the buttocks out; progress. And then there was a trickle of fresh blood. Shit. That was the second placenta separating. Keep calm, James, you still have time. 'Heartbeat, Staff?'

'Seventy.' She sounded stern, almost angry.

'Right. Good. Another push. Good girl. Well done. Ah, you have another daughter. That's something to keep you going. And now the shoulders. Soon be over.'

'Mr Forrest, this is too slow. Much too slow.'

Stupid bitch. How was that going to make the girl feel? Anyway, it wasn't. The baby was coming. Although the head seemed to be very large. Never mind. It would be all right. Perfectly all right. Only – Christ, now the cervix was begining to close down. That was the syntometrine at work.

'Mr Forrest, it's been almost half an hour. We have to get her to theatre.'

'No, no, it's too late for that.'

'Mr Forrest, the heartbeat's down to fifty.'

'Shut up,' he said. 'Shut up and help me.' He was sweating, everything was very hot and strange. He had the forceps on the head now, and was tugging, tugging really hard, with all his weight. Get it out. Get it out.

'Ah. Here she is. All's well, Rosemary. Well done.'

Only it wasn't. The baby was a strange colour: paler than the other one, almost chalky, and blotchy. And it wasn't all right. There was no heartbeat.

He intubated the baby, ventilated it on the Resuscitaine. Still no heartbeat.

'I'm so, so sorry,' he said to Rosemary Mills, as the second baby was handed over to Staff Nurse, to be taken away to the mortuary, 'so terribly sorry. There was nothing, nothing more we could do. The baby was so big, you see, and you were so tired, and it was a breech. We did all we could.'

'Yes,' she said dully, 'yes. I see.'

Her eyes were almost closed, her body seemed to have collapsed. Her face was grey, drawn with pain and grief; she was not properly conscious of anything. Ottoline had been taken away to the nursery, to be checked, monitored, just in case there were any complications, but Rosemary Mills seemed scarcely aware of it.

'Well,' he said, 'I think we should get you stitched up now. Then you can have a nice sleep. And have your Ottoline with you, if you like, if there's no need for her to stay in the nursery.'

'I don't see,' she said suddenly, 'I don't understand why you didn't know. Surely you could have felt it. The other one.'

'Oh no,' he said, and felt a rush of fear in his bowels, 'Oh, no, not possibly. I assure you, Rosemary. The other baby was very high up, you see, and the heart was under your own ribs, so it was quite undetectable. All I could feel, hear, was a normal singleton – that's what we call a single foetus.'

She sighed. 'It sounds so much less important when you say foetus, doesn't it? Not a baby, not a twin baby, not a dead baby.'

'Perhaps to you. Not to us.'

Clever little line that. It sounded caring, properly concerned.

'But I still don't see why you couldn't –'

'Look, Rosemary,' said James, gently firm. 'I hate to say this. I really do, but if you'd come in regularly to antenatal for check-ups we would have –'

'Oh no! No, no.' The cry was a wail of agony, fiercer, keener than anything she had uttered in childbirth. 'Is that really true? Do you mean it was my fault, that I could have saved the baby myself . . .?'

James took a deep breath. He hated himself for doing this, but he had to start covering himself now. If there was trouble over this, if it ever emerged he'd been negligent, drinking for Christ's sake, he'd be done for. He had to force the fact home, that she was actually responsible; and anyway, she was, dammit, she was.

'I'm sorry,' he said, quietly, steadily, 'but that's exactly what I do mean, Rosemary. If only we had been able to look after you –'

She suddenly started to cry, with a new frantic energy; her sobs rose, became hysteria. Staff Nurse Jackson came hurrying in from the corridor where she had been trying to get hold of Jason Benjamin, Rosemary Mills's boyfriend.

'Don't,' she said, 'don't upset yourself. Please, Mrs Mills. It's all right. And Ottoline is doing beautifully. You can have her with you very soon now.'

Rosemary stared at her. 'Sorry,' she said, between rasping gulps for breath, 'I'm sorry. I know I'm lucky, I have one lovely baby. But Dr Forrest was just explaining how it was my fault, how I should have come to prenatal. I just didn't think, didn't know –'

'Of course not,' said Nurse Jackson soothingly, and the look she shot at James across the bed was white-hot fury, total disgust. 'Of course not. You mustn't allow yourself to think that way. Really you mustn't.'

'But I have to. It's true, isn't it? It's my fault. All my fault. Oh God, I wish I was dead too.'

'Now what good would that do?' said Nurse Jackson, sternly kind. 'Then who would care for little Ottoline? And as you say, you do have one very lovely baby. Mr Forrest, could I have a word with you?'

'Not just now,' said James, settling down at the foot of Rosemary Mills's bed, preparing to complete his sutures. 'I'm busy, looking after my patient. As you see. Perhaps later.'

He forced himself to look at her and saw what he had feared. She knew exactly why the twin had been undetected, and why it had consequently died; and exactly why, moreover, he had told Rosemary Mills that the blame lay actually with her.

He visited Rosemary each day, on his ward round, and was always kindly, courteous and sympathetic towards her (although careful not to seem excessively so, least that might be in some way interpreted as displaying guilt); she was a sweet girl, anxious not to be a trouble and even apologizing for her frequent weeping.

'I know I shouldn't,' she said to him on the fourth morning after the birth, dabbing her eyes rather helplessly with a very soggy tissue, 'and I know how lucky I am that Ottoline is alive and doing so well but I just can't stop thinking about the other one. And feeling bad about her.'

'I know, I know,' he said, handing a clean tissue, 'and that's natural, indeed you *should* grieve for her. It would be wrong not to. But you're right, and you do have a lovely baby, and she is doing beautifully, and you should be very proud of her. What does her daddy think about her?'

'Oh –' She flushed, looked down at her hands. 'Oh, well, he's very proud of course. He hasn't actually seen her yet, because he's away on this tour you know, but he sent me those flowers, look, and he's rung twice. He'll be back for when I get home, he's promised me that.'

'I should hope so,' said James lightly, smiling at her, going along with the soothing fiction that Mr Benjamin was indeed such a very busy man he couldn't possibly be expected to take time off to visit his baby daughter and traumatized girlfriend, and torn between a sense of outrage on Rosemary Mills's behalf and an unbidden sense of relief at the realization that she was going to be very poor, very under-resourced and highly unlikely even to consider taking any action against him and the hospital.

'Oh,' she added, looking up at him rather nervously, 'Tamsin, that's my yoga teacher, I hope you don't mind, she'd like to have a word with you. About – about everything. Would that be all right?'

'Yes of course,' said James easily, 'perfectly all right.'

He thought that Tamsin was one of the most frightful women he had ever met. She had long plaits, steaked with grey, falling from a centre parting, a high, lined forehead, and an earnest pale face with unpleasantly small eyes. She wore long flapping Indian skirts, and although it was October, open sandals showing very unsavoury feet. She had a large number of beads around her neck and bangles virtually up to her elbows. She smiled at James, but her small eyes were cold.

'Dr Forrest. I'm Tamsin Smith.'

'How do you do – Miss? – Smith.'

'Ms please, Dr Forrest. How is Rosemary coming along?'

'She's fine, Ms Smith. Recovering well.'

'She seems very emotionally labile to me.'

'Most women are emotionally labile after childbirth, Ms Smith.'

'The women I work with are not. They tend to be on a very high emotional plane.'

'I don't understand,' said James, looking at her coldly. 'In what way do you work with these women?'

'I bring them through their childbirth, Dr Forrest. Lead them into motherhood.'

'And how do you do that exactly? By the way, it's Mr Forrest. I am a consultant, an obstetric surgeon.' He knew that was silly, that it would antagonize her further, but he couldn't resist it. 'You were saying, you brought these women through childbirth? I don't quite –'

'By being with them. By using the yoga method, relaxation, visualization, acceptance of pain, the opening to the birth experience. Sharing women's emotions, helping them to overcome their fears, to reach the final exaltation of birth. I feel Rosemary was robbed of much of that, Dr Forrest.'

'I see. I have to tell you, Miss Smith, that left to accept her pain Miss Mills would have experienced a great deal more and there would have been no exaltation of birth whatsoever.'

'Just the same, one of her babies died.'

It came swiftly, that lash, catching him unawares. He managed to meet her eyes; he hoped his own were steady.

'There was nothing that could have saved that baby.'

'Indeed? I have reason to doubt that. I believe there was negligence.'

'That is a very serious statement, Miss Smith. I would not advise you to repeat it. And whatever reasons you have, no doctor here would accept them.'

'No doctor, no. Of course not. But I happen to know there has been – gossip. To the effect that you could have saved the baby, had you been more – competent.'

'Oh, really?' He took a deep breath. Steady, James, don't let her rattle you. Keep cool. 'Miss Smith, I would like you to leave. I find your remarks offensive and I am really not prepared to discuss this with you. There will be an inquest on the baby, an inquiry into my handling of the birth. There is nothing more to say for now.' He stood up, hoping she would do the same; she didn't, just sat there, staring up at him, oddly in command.

'I will leave, Dr Forrest. But I wouldn't like you to think you have heard the last of this. I intend to take legal advice on Rosemary's behalf and to see justice done.'

'I shall wait with interest. Good afternoon, Miss Smith.'

He went over to the door, held it for her; finally she stood up, walked slowly out. She didn't say goodbye, didn't say anything. It was very unnerving. James watched her walk down the corridor, her bracelets jangling, and then went back to his desk and sat down again. God, what he'd give for a drink.

He reached for his phone, rang the labour ward, asked for Staff Nurse Jackson. She was just coming off duty; he asked if she would come and see him.

'Yes, of course,' she said. 'I'll be along in a minute. Any problem?' She sounded slightly disdainful. Christ, was this a further mistake? Too late now if it was.

'No. Not at all. Thank you, Staff.'

She came in, looking tired. 'Tough birth. Prem. Saved it though.'

'Good. It's a tough business. Nobody really understands that.'

Why did everything sound like a justification suddenly?

'Oh, I think they do. What's the problem?'

'Oh – nothing really. Just had a visit from that dreadful friend of Rosemary Mills. The yoga woman.'

'Oh – her. And?'

'She threatened me with legal action. Silly bitch.' He smiled cheerfully.

'Well, the committee will find you whiter than white,' said Staff Nurse Jackson. Her face was politely blank. 'So I'm sure you shouldn't worry.'

'Oh, I'm not worried. There was just one thing though. She said she'd heard gossip. I wondered if you –'

'Said anything? Mr Forrest, what about? Of course not. But you know, there always is talk on these occasions. And the little student – what's her name, Adams, was very upset.'

'But she hasn't said anything to you?'

'No. Although she did ask me something.'

'Which was?'

'How I thought you could have missed the twin. She said she just couldn't understand it.'

'And? Why didn't you tell me?'

She shrugged. 'Nothing to tell. I said it wasn't always easy. That the heartbeat was muffled by the ribs.'

'I see. Well – thank you for that. Was there anything else?'

She hesitated. Then she said 'Well – she did say you'd seemed very tired.'

'I was, dammit,' said James. He could feel the sweat breaking out on his forehead. 'Terribly tired. It was four in the morning for Christ's sake.'

'Yes, of course,' said Jackson.

'So did you –'

'I told her you were fine. And that it was nothing to do with her. But she's a silly little thing. She may have – chatted a bit. To her friends. These things always escalate.'

'Do they?' said James. 'Oh God. Should I say anything to her?'

'Of course not. That would look very –' She paused. 'Well, anyway – don't. If I pick up any gossip, I'll stop it. To the best of my ability. And, as I said, I very much doubt if the medical inquiry will find against you. I wouldn't worry too much, Mr Forrest, if I were you. These things happen. Unfortunately. Just the same –'

'Yes?'

'You were very tired.' The real meaning was plain. James looked down at his hands. He remembered how useless they'd been that night, awkward, unsure, feeble. Christ, what a mess. What a bloody awful mess.

Later, much later, the matter was dealt with in the usual way: with bland reassurances, with carefully worded justifications on behalf of the hospital and a carefully coded conversation between James and Mr Nicolson, who asked exactly what had happened, and when told nodded and said that if a patient refused prenatal care, then in his book that amounted to criminal negligence, and assured James that the medical union would back him to the hilt, especially as he intended to write a personal expression of confidence in his medical judgment and skills. There was, naturally, an official investigation: the post-mortem had shown that the baby's death had been due to separation of the placenta and lack of oxygen supply to the brain, and the verdict of the official inquiry was that every effort had been made by the hospital staff to save it in an untenable situation.

Staff Nurse Jackson had still been a considerable source of anxiety to James, but, as he pointed out in another carefully coded conversation, she too had failed to establish the presence of a second foetus; she was also about to be promoted to Sister, and she told the inquiry committee that both she and Mr Forrest had done everything possible, given the very difficult circumstances – an uncooperative patient, a large baby in the breech position, and a separating placenta. Rosemary Mills, discharged from hospital, still experiencing considerable emotional trauma as she struggled to come to terms with the death of one baby while rejoicing over the birth of another, was told in a coldly formal letter that while the hospital naturally regretted very deeply what had happened, there was nothing more they could possibly have done, and had she only come for regular prenatal checks then there might have been a better chance for twin two.

At no time was the slightest breath of criticism directed towards Mr James Forrest.

There was just one thing he could do, one act of contrition he could make, that just might help at another time, another crisis, another birth, and he did it. He gave up alcohol forever.

'May I come in?'

He was so lost in the past, in the nightmare of it, that he half expected Staff Nurse Jackson, Rosemary, even little SRN Adams to walk in the door; he turned and the relief as he saw Janine was so intense he forgot the terrors of the present.

'Janine! Come in.'

'You look better, *chérie*. Is there good news from the Bergin household?'

'I'm afraid not. No news. Unless you could regard Oliver being in the bath as news.'

'I fear not. Does he –'

'Couldn't speak to him. Only mama.'

'*Tiens!* How I dislike that woman. Terrible clothes, terrible hair, terrible perfume.'

In spite of himself James laughed. 'Really, Janine! You can't dislike a woman because of her perfume and her hair.'

'I can. Very easily. And besides, I don't trust her. There is something about her that is – two-headed.'

'Two-faced,' said James, smiling tenderly at her. Janine's occasional lapses into less than perfect English never failed to enchant him. 'Janine, we are all two-headed at times. I don't think we can condemn poor Julia on that basis.'

Janine shrugged. 'Perhaps. But she is not to be trusted. Believe me. She likes to appear so sweet and charming, but when the mask drops, just for a moment, she is very very different. There was a little incident last night, and I did not like it.'

'What was that?' said James, intrigued.

'Oh, Cressida came in from the garden with a bunch of sweet peas, and she gave them to Julia, in the kitchen. It was a pretty gesture. Julia took them and smiled and kissed her, and said how very lovely of her, all those little things she does, and then Cressida went to change and I said I must go too, and we left Julia. But I had left my spectacles, and when I came back, Julia did not hear me, she had her back to me and she was pulling the flowers to pieces, taking their heads off and putting them one by one into the dustbin. Then she saw me and tried to pretend she was simply sorting them out – she said some of them were half dead.'

'Well, that doesn't sound too dreadful to me,' said James lightly. 'Maybe she just doesn't like sweet peas. I don't think you'd get very far in a court of law with that one, Janine.'

Janine shrugged. 'Maybe not. But I have observed other things. Anyway, the fact remains, I do not trust the belle Julia. Now then, what I really wanted to say was that I think you should try to give poor Maggie a little something. She is becoming hysterical, she will make herself ill, and that will not help anyone. What do you think?'

'Oh God,' said James, 'inevitable I suppose. She's increasingly hysterical these days anyway. I'm worried about her. Yes, all right, Janine. I'll get her something.'

'Will she take it?'

'Oh, yes,' said James with a sigh. 'She'll take it. She'll take anything, any pill, any potion. Grabbing at straws.'

'What for? Why should she be grabbing at straws? In what is she drowning?'

'Her own sense of inadequacy,' said James. 'Poor woman. I should never –' The phone rang. 'James Forrest.'

'James, it's Oliver. Mother said you called. About Mungo's speech. What –'

'Oh – Oliver. Yes. Look, it wasn't about Mungo's speech. I'm afraid I told your mama a small fib.'

'She tells plenty of those herself,' said Oliver cheerfully, 'so don't worry about it. What did you want to talk to me about?'

'Well, it was – you see – oh God, Oliver, there's no way of dressing this up. It's Cressida. She –'

There was a very long silence; the room seemed stifling, claustrophobic. James could hear the blood pounding in his head, was suddenly aware of the clock ticking on his desk, of Janine's light breathing close beside him. Then: 'She hasn't gone, has she?' said Oliver, and his voice was very quiet and totally without emotion. 'She hasn't actually gone?'

Chapter 7

Harriet 11:30am

'Harriet, you got a minute?'

It was Merlin, in the corridor outside her room (where she had retreated briefly, with a bottle of iced lemonade, to take a break from the telephoning), his weather-beaten old face with its brilliant blue eyes, its shock of white hair, looking surprisingly cheerful, a touch of normality in this nightmarish day.

'Yes. Yes, I suppose so,' said Harriet.

'Could I use that computer of yours? Got an article to write, promised I'd send it off this morning if I could. Might as well put all this time to good use. Jannie suggested I ask you. Damned attractive woman that. Sort of woman who makes me think of settling down.'

'Merlin, darling,' said Harriet, laughing, 'What are you saying? Have you finally sown all your wild oats?'

'Well, I don't want to end my days a lonely old bachelor,' said Merlin. 'Been thinking about it for some time as a matter of fact. Never met the right girl, you know, that's been the trouble.'

'Well, maybe she's been here all along,' said Harriet. 'And yes, of course you can use my machine. Only you won't find much peace anywhere, I'm afraid, Merlin. Mummy keeps coming in here, and –'

'Good Lord,' said Merlin. 'Can't face that. Maybe I won't –'

'No,' said Harriet, 'you certainly should. I tell you what, we'll take it up to the big attic. No one ever goes up there, except Mummy, to sew, and she won't be doing that today. You'll be perfectly quiet up there. Hang on a minute, I'll unplug it. It's very portable.'

They went down the corridor silently, tiptoeing like two guilty children, and up the back stairs to the attic. It was very hot; Harriet pushed open the big skylight window, and the sweet fresh air rushed in, full of birdsong, cooling the room.

'It's such a lovely day,' she said, staring upwards at the perfectly blue sky, 'It seems so terrible . . .'

'Oh, I don't know,' said Merlin briskly. 'Be even worse if it was raining. Can I move this sewing machine of your mother's, use the table?'

'Yes, of course you can. And I've got the extension lead, look, we can set you up in no time.'

Merlin sat down at the table, started tapping his way into the computer. 'Lovely things these,' he said happily, 'transformed my life, I can tell you. Should have brought my own, but I didn't think I'd get a chance to use it. Bloody silly really, you never know what's going to happen, do you? Right, then, here we are, bless you, Harriet, that's marvellous. I'll just sit here quietly, won't be a bother to anyone. Not like that sister of yours,' he added darkly. 'Causing all this anxiety. Very selfish if you ask me –'

'Oh Merlin, don't,' said Harriet quickly. 'Something must have been terribly wrong for her. Poor Cress. Oh God, Merlin, there's her dress, I'd forgotten just for a moment this is where they'd put it. Such a lovely, lovely dress too.' She shook herself. 'Listen to me. As if a dress mattered.'

She went over to the dressmaker's rail, where Cressida's dress had been hanging for over two weeks now, swathed in its muslin wrap and gently, tenderly, without knowing why, stroked it, as if it was Cressida herself, Cressida in distress, in need of comforting. And the room suddenly felt stifling again, and her head felt as if it was being crushed, crushed in some kind of vice, and she stood there staring at it, trying to make sense of what she saw. For as she touched the dress, the wrap, which was not fastened in any way but was simply draped loosely over it, started to slither off and what Harriet was looking at was not Cressida's wedding dress at all, but an old ballgown of their mother's.

And the wedding dress, like the bride it had been made for, had gone.

Chapter 8

James Midday

He was walking along the first-floor landing when he heard the sobs coming from Cressida's room: soft, muffled, desperate. Christ, she was back, back for help, for comfort: afraid to face them all, hiding, rather as Harriet used to do when she was little. What had happened to Cressida, what could possibly have gone wrong in those few hours, to change her from radiant bride to desperate runaway? He was almost afraid to go in, to face all her pain; stood outside the room for an absurdly long moment before knocking gently and opening the door.

'Cress?' he said. 'Cress darling?'

And the figure lying on the bed, weeping into the lace cushion, turned to him slowly, turned a ravaged face: only of course it wasn't Cressida at all, it was Harriet, and she had clearly been crying for some time.

'Daddy,' she said, reaching out for his hand, 'Daddy, I'm so sorry, it's only me.'

He took her in his arms, rocking her gently, kissing her, smoothing her hair, hushing her, trying to ease her pain away. After a while she stopped crying and said, 'There's something new. I was – going to come and tell you. I haven't told anyone else.'

'What?' he said. 'Have the police –?'

'No, no,' she said, 'not the police, or the hospitals, no news. But Daddy, I just went up to the attic, and – it's so weird, so spooky, I just can't think –' Her voice trailed away, silent tears began again, rolling down her face. James set her away from him, stared at her.

'What, Harriet, what is it? For Christ's sake, Harriet, you've got to tell me.'

'Yes, of course. I'm sorry.' She swallowed, took a deep breath. 'Daddy, her wedding dress is gone.'

'Her wedding dress? What on earth do you mean? How can it be gone, why, what could she –' His own voice trailed away, he sat staring at her, equally shocked.

'I don't know. I don't understand it. I just can't think why she should have taken it. But it's gone. And not just ripped off the stand, there's another dress where it was, under the wrap you know? She obviously wanted to take it, didn't want us to know.'

'Oh, for God's sake,' said James. He felt very tired suddenly; he couldn't take much more of this. 'Harriet, has she run off with someone else? To get married to – oh, it's preposterous. It makes no sense at all.'

'I know. I know it doesn't. But she obviously did plan it. The disappearance I mean. She must have done. Well at least we know now she hasn't been abducted, which was one of Mummy's wilder fears.'

'No. I suppose we should tell her. Or shouldn't we?' They started at each other, visualizing the fresh trauma this news would inflict upon Maggie, wondering if it was worth it.

'Yes, I think we should. I think it's better.'

'I'll go down then. In a minute.' He sighed, sat very still, staring out at the day. 'Harriet, has she ever said anything to you, anything at all that might indicate she wasn't happy about marrying Oliver?'

'No,' said Harriet, 'no. Nothing. But then I haven't seen much of her lately. What with – well, work and everything. I kept thinking we ought to spend some time together, but somehow – oh God.'

'Well,' he said, 'if she'd told anyone she'd have told you.'

'No, she wouldn't,' said Harriet flatly.

'What do you mean? Of course she would. You're so close.'

'Daddy, we're not close. Everyone thinks we are, but we're not at all. I really don't know what goes on in Cressida's head, never have. She's always been very – self-contained – with me. Since we were tiny. And I – well, anyway, she hasn't.'

James stared at her; if she had announced she was working for MI5 or had signed up for the next space project he could hardly have been more astonished.

'Well,' he said finally, 'who do you think she might have talked to?'

'I have no idea,' said Harriet and her voice was oddly blank, cool. 'No idea at all. I really don't know who her friends were, who she might have confided in. She was a mystery to me. More than I realized,' she added with the shadow of a smile.

'But darling – you were fond of each other, weren't you?' He could hear the pleading note in his own voice; it seemed very important somehow.

'Yes, we were,' said Harriet quickly, 'very fond. Of course we were.' James chose to believe her. For the time being. It was simpler that way.

'Do you think,' he said, looking rather helplessly round the room, 'we should look through her things? For addresses, contacts? Would it be –'

'I have,' said Harriet, with a slightly apologetic grin. 'I've been right through her desk. Very neat, very tidy, nothing in the least helpful or – incriminating. No address book though –'

'What about bank statements? They might give us a clue –'

'No bank statements. Nothing like that at all. I did think that was interesting. It all points to her covering her tracks.'

'Well, I don't know. She'd probably keep that sort of thing in her flat, wouldn't she?'

Harriet sighed. 'I suppose so. Yes of course. I hardly ever went to that flat, you know.'

'None of us did,' said James. 'She always told me, when I suggested I come to see her there during the week, that it was horrid and she hated it, and she'd rather come to me. I don't think I've been there since – oh, before last Christmas. We don't have a key for it, I suppose?'

'No. All her keys are gone.'

'I wonder if we ought to go up there anyway, have a look round?'

'Daddy, you can't go. Not today. I will if you like –'

'No,' he said with a sigh, 'no, let's leave it for now. Maybe this evening if – oh God, Harriet, this is a mess. A bloody awful mess. I feel so guilty, as if it's all my fault somehow.'

'Well it isn't,' said Harriet. 'Of course it isn't. You've been a wonderful father to Cressida.'

'Not wonderful enough it seems.' He sat looking round Cressida's painfully neat, perfectly pretty room, and his heart ached physically with the pain of her loss. The cancelled wedding, the trauma of the day seemed nothing; he just wanted her back, safe, so that he could comfort her, find what the trouble was. His lovely, gentle, sweet daughter; where was she, where had she gone, what had distressed her so dreadfully, that she would do such a thing?

'Do you think we should actually ring the bank? Her account is still here in Woodstock, isn't it? It might give us a clue. What do you think?'

'Well – I suppose I could. Oh God, I hate sitting here in her room prying into her life.'

'Come into my room, you silly old thing. I've got my mobile in there anyway.' She smiled at him; James felt tears sting his eyes.

'All right. Thank God for you, Harriet.'

'Oh,' she said, 'you won't get rid of me so easily.'

He shuddered. 'Don't joke about it.'

He phoned the bank. The manager, Tony Bacon, with whom he played golf occasionally, was out until late afternoon, his assistant was pompously unhelpful. 'This is extremely confidential information, Mr Forrest. We would never disclose any details of a customer's affairs.'

'Not even under exceptional circumstances? We are extremely worried about her.'

'I'm afraid not.'

'But my daughter does still have an account with you? She hasn't closed it in the last few days or made any large withdrawals?'

'I'm sorry, Mr Forrest, I really can't help you.'

'Oh all right, all right. Would you get Mr Bacon to get in touch with me please? As soon as he gets in.'

'I will certainly ask him to ring you, Mr Forrest.'

'Self-satisfied jumped-up little creep,' said James, switching off the phone with unnecessary violence. 'Any other good ideas, Harriet?'

'Doctor?'

'She saw someone in London. Haven't the faintest idea who. Oh, this is hopeless.'

'What about having another word with the vicar? See if Cressida might have talked to him? She was so good about doing the flowers in church and everything, they chatted a lot – you never know –'

'Well, we could try,' said James, 'but I'm sure his code of practice or whatever would forbid him telling us anything. Aren't priests supposed to take secrets to their grave?'

'Yes, but it might not be a secret,' said Harriet. 'She might have said something quite openly to him. Like she was worrying about going to live in New York or something –'

'Yes, I suppose so. Yes, all right.'

'Daddy, try not to worry. The police were so reassuring.'

'Yes, well, she's not their daughter,' said James. His voice sounded very unsteady even to himself. He dialled the Vicarage.

'Mrs Hodges? James Forrest again.'

Sylvia Hodges' careworn voice came down the telephone: it suited her perfectly that voice, he thought: if a voice could be lined, pale, scrubbed, then Sylvia's was.

'Oh, Mr Forrest. We've been so anxious. Has she –'

'No, I'm afraid not,' said James, cutting her off. He couldn't stand anyone thinking, even for a moment, that Cressida had returned. 'No news yet.'

'You mustn't despair,' said Sylvia Hodges, 'you must have faith. Not a sparrow falls, you know, –'

'Mrs Hodges,' said James, perversely irritated by her concern, 'I am nowhere near despair. I assure you of that.'

'We're praying for you here,' she said, 'and thinking of you so much. Such a wonderful, sweet girl. We're both so fond of her. I was saying to Alan only last night, oh for a daughter like that – oh dear –' Her voice trailed away, as she realized her tactlessness.

'Well, thank you. Is your husband there? I just wanted another word with him.'

'He's out in the garden. Hoeing. And working on the compost. He always does that when he's upset. He finds it healing.'

'Well, I might try it,' said James with an attempt at cheerfulness. He winked at Harriet. She smiled back.

'Alan Hodges here, Mr Forrest. No news, I gather?'

'No news,' said James. 'But – well, we're turning over every stone here, Mr Hodges. As I'm sure you can imagine. Talking to everyone who just might have some ideas to toss into the equation. Now of course I'm not asking you to breach any confidences, but did Cressida ever say anything to you about – well, express any doubts at all about her marriage?'

'I quite understand what you're saying. And I'd like to help. Now let me see. Well, let me begin by saying I can honestly tell you she certainly never told me anything that would be classified as confidential. That any help to you?'

'Yes, I suppose it's comforting in a way. You mean she never told you she was planning to take the veil or anything like that?' He winked at Harriet again; she had looked at him sharply. God, maybe that had crossed her mind; maybe it should have crossed all their minds.

'Oh no, Mr Forrest. Most definitely not. Not the veil.' The voice, as earnest as his wife's, sounded shocked. James smiled into the phone in spite of his misery. Alan Hodges had not so much been in the back row when senses of humour were handed out, he hadn't even been in the room.

'Well, I didn't really think that. But – well, she never talked about her plans –'

There was a silence. James's flesh began to creep. There was something; he could feel it.

Then, 'No. No, absolutely not. She seemed very calm and settled. Except – well –'

'Yes? Except what?'

'The other afternoon. Good gracious, it must have been only the day before yesterday. The panic about her passport, you know?'

'No,' said James sharply. 'What passport?'

'Her new one. Didn't she tell you about it? Oh, maybe she didn't want to worry you. She certainly didn't want Mr Bergin to know. She'd left renewing it until terribly late. She was afraid she wouldn't be able to get away on her honeymoon.'

'I didn't know, no,' said James, carefully.

'Well, obviously, she was keeping her worries to herself. It was only by chance I met her, in the post office in Oxford, she was getting one of those short-term passports you know, that do for a year. It was all she had time for, I suppose. Nasty little cardboard things.'

'Yes, but that wouldn't have been any use anyway,' said James. 'She – they were going to New York. It wouldn't have got her there.'

'Indeed not. I hadn't thought of that. Well, she seemed very upset, distraught almost, I would say. Quite out of character. Although of course brides often do get into a bit of a state. Anyway, if I think of anything else, Mr Forrest, I'll certainly ring you. And I'll ask my wife if she has any thoughts as well. And try to keep your spirits up. I'm sure she's all right. We're praying for you all. Please know that. And if there's anything more I can do . . .'

'Thank you,' said James. 'Thank you very much, Mr Hodges.'

He put the phone down and stared at Harriet. 'Did you know anything about Cressida's forgetting to renew her passport?' he asked. 'I mean just in the past few days?'

'No, of course not. In fact I know it was all right, because she had to get her visa, don't you remember? About a month ago. So there can't have been a problem surely. And Oliver's got it anyway, because of the honeymoon being a surprise and everything. Why?'

'Well, for whatever reason, she was applying for a new one the day before yesterday. Alan Hodges met her in the post office in Oxford. Oh God, Harriet, this is getting worse and worse.'

Chapter 9

Mungo Lunchtime

He had the worst job of all, it seemed to him; standing at the church, missing out on all the drama, in order to head off any arrivals. It would be a while yet of course: surely nobody was going to get there before one, not even the most neurotically punctual guests, but all the same, maybe some of the bridesmaids' parents – anyway, James Forrest had said that someone should be there, just in case, and Rufus had volunteered, saying that he, Mungo, should stay with Oliver. Mungo had studied the two options and hastily opted for lychgate duty; Rufus would be far better doing his support number, it was just his sort of thing. Bit of a goody-goody, old Rufus. Mungo was very fond of him, but he longed just once to hear he had done something truly horrendous, like getting two girls pregnant at the same time, or embezzling some of the bank's funds, or just running up a humungous debt somewhere and being unable to pay it. It was highly unlikely, of course. Rufus was upright, charming, and self-disciplined; Mungo had only seen him properly drunk once, and that had been to celebrate getting a first at Cambridge. What on God's earth Tilly could see in him, he couldn't even begin to imagine: Tilly, with her wonderfully outrageous approach to life, her overt sexuality, her staggering beauty, her interestingly individual morality; but she certainly saw something.

It was the most extraordinary relationship: sweet, tender, defying any kind of logic. Mungo watched them sometimes, caught together in a charged, almost tangible stillness, not even touching, excluding everything and everyone around them, and knew he was looking at love. It charmed him, even while it baffled him, made him happy, gave him pleasure. It had probably, he thought, been the inspiration for his own

passionate, all-consuming love affair. The one he had to speak to his
father about, that he could hardly believe in himself (so unpredictable,
so unexpected it had been), the one he hadn't shared with anyone, not
even Oliver, not even Harriet, the two people he probably felt closer to
than anyone in the world. Now there was compatibility. Stange, so
strange, he thought even now, that Oliver had chosen Cressida, sweet,
gentle, softly spoken Cressida, when he could have had Harriet. Harriet
who was so original and clever and go-for-it and successful, who had
always seemed to know what Oliver was thinking before he knew it
himself, who loved doing all the things that he did, sailing and riding and
rock music and travelling. They had once gone on a trip together with
Merlin, when they were both about fifteen, had gone down the Amazon
in a small boat, just the three of them and a guide, and had disappeared
for days, come back charged with excitement, with wonderful tales of
crocodiles (stunned at night by shining a light in their eyes) and sweetly
smiling friendly dolphins and great shoals of fish, and monkeys and the
brilliantly coloured parrots they had seen on a trek through the steaming
jungle, so thick that their guide had often had to chop a way through it
for them; the chattering, screaming noise by day and the deathly silence
at night, the feeling that they had travelled back thousands, maybe tens
of thousands of years. Cressida had listened to their stories, her eyes
wide with horror, and said she couldn't imagine anything more horrible
and Oliver, reacting to her with barely disguised scorn, had said that he
and Harriet were going to set off on their own as soon as they were
allowed. They planned the trip for years, right up to the age when they
both left school and no longer spent family holidays together. The adults
teased them about it, asking them when they were off, how much money
they had saved, whether it was to be China or India or the Arctic Circle
this year, and Merlin would defend them, saying they were a fine pair of
travellers, he was proud of them. But they had never gone, and Oliver
went backpacking on his own in his college vacations and Harriet threw
all her energies into building up her fashion business and wanted only
to lie on a beach and recover in the short weeks available to her, and now
of course it was quite forgotten and their wonderful joyous closeness
had gradually disintegrated. Oliver had changed, naturally, had become
grown-up, seriously grown-up and fiercely ambitious – and maybe that
was a factor in choosing Cressida, so much more suitable these days,

more – well, more wifely than Harriet, more the person he needed to be married to.

Only it was beginning to look like she wasn't. Mungo wrenched his thoughts back to the present, and his task, refusing to allow himself to contemplate for more than the briefest wildest moment the glorious prospect of climbing into the car and just driving away, and wondered if there was anything he could do for Oliver, apart from getting him so hammered he wouldn't even know his own name. He decided there wasn't.

The Forrest women, as he thought of them, and especially today, Maggie, Janine, Susie, Harriet, were all at work on different telephones, Maggie in her bedroom, Janine in the study on James's line, Harriet on her portable phone, and Susie at the Beaumonts', all working through sections of the guest list, telling people that Cressida was ill, that the wedding was postponed, that they were desperately sorry, that they would be in touch just as soon as it was possible to rearrange, refusing offers of help with the notifications (lest wires should be crossed, messages overlaid, lists muddled).

Christ, thought Mungo, what an incredible, filthy mess. The whole thing. Not just Cressida's disappearance either, it had started hours before that, the nightmare; and he relived sharply, suddenly, the terrible scene at two that morning, when he and Rufus had driven over to the Bergins' hotel, gone up to Oliver's suite and found Oliver head in hands, horribly drunk, tears pouring down his unshaven face, saying he couldn't go through with it, couldn't marry Cressida, that even now, even at this late stage, they had somehow to get him away, get him out of it, that if they didn't he would kill himself.

'But why, Oliver, why?' Rufus said over and over again, and Oliver just looked at them, his blue eyes almost black with pain, his fair hair wild where he had been pushing his hands through it endlessly, hopelessly, and said he couldn't tell them, it was all too horrible, they just had to do something, help him, save him. He was extremely drunk, but there was a kind of quiet sanity about him as well. Mungo found the combination strangely terrifying.

'If you don't, I'll do something desperate, I swear I will,' he said, and as they tried to calm him, tried to find out what the trouble was, what had happened, he suddenly got up, walked almost calmly into the bathroom and locked the door. They looked at each other, Rufus and Mungo, thinking, hoping even, that it was over, that it had been simply a rather extreme case of last-minute nerves; then he'd walked out again, and smiled at them, with a sweet serenity, and said, 'That should settle it, then.'

'What should?' Mungo said rather stupidly, and Oliver smiled again, more serenely still, and said, his voice slurring, 'Taken something for it.'

Rufus looked at him thoughtfully and then got up and went into the bathroom himself; he came out with an empty half bottle of aspirin in his hand. 'Ollie, did you take these?' he said gently, and Oliver nodded and said, 'Yes. Had to do something.' And sat down, picked up a copy of *Sporting Life* and started reading the Goodwood report. To the end of his life Mungo was to associate horse racing with personal tragedy.

Rufus was wonderful. He went very quietly down to the hotel dining room and found several salt cellars, which he emptied into a jug of water and made Oliver drink. Then he took him into the bathroom. Mungo who was squeamish sat outside, trying not to listen and wondering if he should go and get Julia or Josh Bergin. After ten minutes Rufus came out with Oliver and laid him down tenderly on his bed.

'Ring room service for some coffee, and some bottles of still mineral water,' he said, 'and ask them to leave it outside the door.'

'Should I tell the Bergins?'

'Christ no. He'll be fine now. We caught it in plenty of time. Poor old boy.'

They both looked at Oliver who lay glassy pale, his eyes closed, half asleep.

'How did you know what to do?' said Mungo.

'Girl I knew at Cambridge did exactly the same thing. She lived with a medic. He got me to help. As long as you're really quick, there's no lasting damage done. But we have to keep pumping fluids into him.'

'What on earth do you think it's about?'

'Can't imagine. Just nerves I expect,' said Rufus, his voice rather determinedly easy. 'They seemed perfectly OK at supper.'

'Yeah. I wonder if Cressida's been over, if something's happened since.'

'It hasn't,' said Oliver's voice, very quiet, rather hoarse, from the bed. 'Haven't seen her since I left the house. Don't worry. I'll be fine now.' His eyes closed; Rufus took his pulse.

'He really is fine,' he said quietly. 'Don't look so scared, Mungo.'

'Sorry,' said Mungo. He was feeling rather sick himself. 'It's just so terribly unlike him. He's usually so calm, so steady. He never even gets drunk.'

'I know. I know.'

The coffee and water arrived; they fed it to him alternately, tenderly, as if he was a sick child. It was a long night; he had to be helped into the bathroom quite frequently. He slept a lot, fitfully at first, then more soundly. At around five, he woke and seemed almost himself.

'Must have a pee,' he said, standing up, smiling at them. 'Don't worry, Rufus, I won't do it again. Can't think what came over me. I'm so sorry.'

He came out again, walking rather slowly and painfully. 'I guess this is what old age feels like,' he said, 'bloody awful. Every joint aches.'

'It's dehydration,' said Rufus. 'Drink some more water.'

'I'm full of bloody water. I'll start leaking in a minute.'

He drank another tumblerful, lay down again with a groan. 'You are such good friends,' he said simply. 'I owe you my life, don't I?'

'Doubt it,' said Rufus with a grin. 'You'd have called someone else, if we hadn't been here. You weren't doing it for real.'

'No,' said Oliver, pulling himself together with a clear effort. 'No, of course not. Panic, that's all. Awful thing to do though.' There was another silence; then he said, 'I'm so sorry' again, and closed his eyes.

'Oliver,' said Rufus gently, 'Oliver, is it really all right? The wedding? Because it's not –'

'What? Oh God, I expect so. Maybe. I don't know.' And then was asleep, deeply and sweetly, in minutes. They sat looking down at him.

'I think we should stay with him,' said Mungo quietly. 'I don't like the thought of leaving him alone.'

'Yes, of course we should. Poor old sod. What a nightmare. What do you think we ought to do? About it, I mean.'

'Christ knows. Should we talk to someone, do you think? Try and find out if there really is a problem?'

'Well yes, probably, but I can't think who,' said Rufus. 'Cressida? Harriet? His mother? I mean think of them all last night. They all looked like a commercial for soupy happiness.'

'I think we should talk to Tilly,' said Mungo suddenly. 'She's very close to Oliver. And uninvolved enough to maybe have picked something up from him. Didn't they have dinner two nights ago?'

'Yes, they did,' said Rufus. 'I was furious because she wouldn't let me join them. She wanted to give him a present, apologize for not coming to the wedding.'

'Why wasn't she coming, actually?' said Mungo. 'She was going to come. She told me she was looking forward to it.'

'She suddenly had to work,' said Rufus. He sounded defensive. 'You know how in demand she is.'

'Yes, but –'

'Well it doesn't matter why. She just couldn't come. But she did see Oliver. You're right. It's a good idea. She might have picked up something. I'll call her. Very soon.' He looked at his watch. 'Six thirty in France. I'll get hold of her in an hour or so. Christ, what a night. Let's try and get a bit of sleep. Shall we toss for the other bed?'

'Not me,' said Mungo with a weak grin, heading for the door. 'I'd honestly rather take the floor in his sitting room.'

They were woken by Julia Bergin; she came in, without knocking – well, she was his mother, thought Mungo, but it still seemed odd – and practically tripped over him. She stood there, looking down at him, her face white with shock – and that was strange too, he thought, for she was fully made-up already, at – what? seven in the morning, and neatly dressed in trousers and a sweater.

'What the hell are you doing here?' she said, and her voice was harsh and angry.

'We thought we should stay with Oliver, he wasn't well last night,' Mungo said, sitting up, feeling slightly sick again.

'What do you mean not well?' she said, and Rufus came out of Oliver's bedroom, pushing his hair back, closing the door gently behind him.

'He was – very drunk,' he said carefully, 'and – well, we were worried about him. Taking care of him. That's all.'

'And why was he so drunk?' asked Julia Bergin, and Mungo thought how strange it was that the graciously charming woman – over-gracious indeed, absurdly charming – he had always known had become this hostile, harsh creature. 'Were you drinking with him? I thought you were going to go back to your hotel last night, when we left the Forrests, not coming over here causing trouble –'

'Yes, we were,' said Rufus gently. 'But Oliver phonedand asked us over. He said he was – nervous. He wanted company.'

'I was here,' said Julia, and the expression in her eyes was heavily antagonistic. 'He could have talked to me.'

'Yes, of course,' said Rufus, 'but I – well, I expect you were asleep. It was quite late.'

'Well you can leave him to me now,' said Julia. 'And I'd like you to go, get out. Immediately. I still don't quite understand what you're trying to tell me. Was there some problem that I should know about?'

'I – don't think so,' said Rufus. He still sounded calm and quiet. Mungo was impressed. 'But he was quite – sick. Perhaps you could keep an eye on him.'

'Rufus,' said Julia Bergin, and her voice shook a little, 'Rufus, I am Oliver's mother. I have looked after him for thirty-two years now. I don't need to be told what to do with him in any situation.' She went through to the bedroom, looked down at her sleeping son. They couldn't see her face. 'He looks perfectly all right to me. I have to tell you I find your story a little hard to believe. I would suggest that what really happened was that you both wanted a drinking partner and came over here of your own volition.'

'Well, you can suggest whatever you like, Mrs Bergin,' said Rufus, more determinedly equable than ever. 'My only concern is for Oliver.'

'Mine also,' said Julia Bergin. 'Now please leave.'

They left, too exhausted to argue.

'Weird,' said Mungo, as he started up the Bentley. 'Seriously weird.'

Well, even this boredom, waiting for guests who clearly weren't going to come, was better than being back in that nightmare room. Mungo wondered how, in fact, Oliver would be taking the news of Cressida's disappearance; it was not something he would like to have to predict with any accuracy. But however it was, things were going to be difficult. Mungo was not too familiar with difficulty; if he saw it coming he moved swiftly and determinedly in the other direction. Certain things he had had to face, had had to deal with: his mother's death, his father's marriage to his next wife – and the next one, bitches both of them (but he approved of Sasha, she was a peach, pretty, fun, not too bright, kept his father permanently in a good mood; and he'd been so terribly down, so wretched in the time just before he'd met her, really not himself at all, Mungo often wondered if something had happened he hadn't heard about).

A couple of the schools he'd been sent to had been a bit grim, especially that awful English prep school stepmother one had insisted on, but when she went, so did the school. Since then life had been pretty much all right, he'd loved the school in Geneva, enjoyed the Sorbonne, and hadn't even minded too much his father's efforts to initiate him into the business. It had been boring and, he could see, frustrating for his father, but distressing it hadn't been. He had tried most of its facets, the supermarkets, the foodbroking, the hotels, the chemical division, before sitting the old buzzard down and making him face the fact that none of it was for him. His father had been angry and bawled him out, but he was used to that; the rages, the threats of disinheritance (also uttered when he had some particularly large gambling debt to settle) meant no more than the ones he'd had to listen to when he had been naughty as a small boy: threats to beat him with a leather strap, to cancel his birthday or Christmas, to send his pony back, to confine him to his room for a week. None of them ever carried out: just a few hours of mild anxiety and then his father would come up to his room or out to the stables when he was sitting with his pony, and look slightly shamefaced and say 'I hope you're sorry, Mungo' and Mungo would say, his eyes filled with the great tears he could summon at will, 'Yes, I'm really sorry, Dad' and he would get first a playful cuff round the head, then a hug, and his father would say, 'Well, we'll let it go this time. But never again, all right, never again?' And he would hug him back, and say 'Course not, Dad, never again,' and there would be no more talk of punishment until the next time – and never any actual punishment at all.

Looking back now, he could see he had got away with murder; he could also see why wives three and four had hated him so much.

His father loved him best, and they knew it, better than them, better than the poisonous little sisters they foisted upon Mungo, Careena and Dido by wife number three, Christina by wife number four (still very young, Christina was, an overripe, overweight thirteen-year-old, sanctimonious and spotty, thank God her mother would hardly let her near any of them). He wondered if Sasha would have a baby: that would be good – Mungo liked babies. He had always imagined having lots of children. It was one of the things that just slightly troubled him about Alice . . .

'I love your kids,' he said to her, lying beside her on the pillow, looking at her beautiful face, her streaky blonde hair, her clear blue eyes with just a very few lines round them. 'I think they're great. Honestly. How do they feel about me?'

'Oh Mungo,' she said, putting out her hand, stroking his cheek, 'they love you. Of course they do. You're such fun for them. Like – well, like a big brother.'

'Yes, well, that's fine,' he said, 'but it isn't quite the same as being a dad, is it?'

'No, it's not, but you're not their dad.'

'If we get married, I will be.'

'Mungo, darling, can we not talk about getting married? It's so –'

'So what?' he said, sitting up suddenly, 'Alice, so what? I keep telling you I want to marry you.'

'I know, I know you do.'

'And you say you love me.'

'I do love you, Mungo. Very much. But –'

'But what? But you don't love me enough? But you don't want to marry me? But I'm not good enough for you?'

'Mungo, maybe I love you too much. To marry you.'

'But why, why? I don't understand.'

'Mungo,' she said with a gentle smile, 'Mungo, I'm thirty-nine. You're twenty-seven. That is a great many years' difference.'

'No it's not. It's twelve years. It's nothing, nothing at all.'

'It isn't nothing. I'm a middle-aged woman. You're a very young man. If you were thirty-seven, and I forty-nine, that might be different.'

'I don't see why,' he said, and panic rose in him, panic and fear of losing her, of not being able to keep her forever.

'Then I'll tell you,' she said, her voice enragingly patient, reasonable. 'You're young and you have a right to a young wife.'

'I don't want a young wife. I don't like young women.'

'Mungo, that's ridiculous. Of course you do. You want a young wife, who can give you children – '

'You can give me children.'

'Well – maybe, maybe not.'

'I thought you were getting all that checked out.'

'I have.'

'And?'

'Well, in theory I can still have babies. Or at least one baby.'

'Well then.'

'But in practice, it may not be quite so easy.'

'Then,' he said, leaning over and kissing her, 'then we shall have to put in lots of practice. To make it easier.'

'Oh Mungo. Darling Mungo. What can I say?'

'Nothing. Just that you love me.'

'I love you, Mungo.'

'Now don't say anything else.'

And he slithered down in the bed again and began to make love to her. Making love to Alice was quite unlike making love to anyone else he had ever known. She was at once so gentle and so strong; she would lie, apparently passive, as he aroused her (and she was so deliciously, swiftly easy to arouse, fluid, soft, sweet), and so gloriously yielding as he entered her, unfolding to him in all her warm tender depth; and then suddenly she would change, would grow fierce, almost violent, would turn him on his back and mount him, plunging down on him again and again, using him, working at him. 'Don't,' she would say, 'don't come, not yet, don't, don't,' and he would lie beneath her, trying to wait, to distance himself from the leaping, desperate climax that grew, thrust, forced itself within him, up to her. 'Wait' she would say, command him, 'wait,' and would climb from him, kneel above him, tantalizing him with her wetness, her heat; and then finally she would fall onto him again, yelling, crying out with hunger, and come, over and over again, great unfoldings of tension, he would feel them, pulling, clutching at him, and then she would slowly fall again into stillness, and was the old Alice again, no longer predatory, no longer fierce, but the still, calm woman he loved. He loved them both, both his Alices, loved them with a binding love. She was beautiful and desirable and desiring; she was also fun and clever and wise. She was perfect; he loved her. And he wanted to marry her.

He had met her over the New Year skiing in Val d'Isère; she was there with her children, staying with friends in their apartment. She was waiting in the queue for the ski lift, and the first thing he noticed about her was her perfume, which was one he knew and loved: strong, sexy, and very potent.

They got talking: he liked her. He bought her a hot chocolate at the café at the top of the mountain; she was coolly, amusedly friendly. They did the long tough run down to the town together, and he was impressed by her courage and her skill, bought her a hot wine as the dusk fell, arranged to meet her for lunch the next day. She had a superb figure, and an extremely sexy voice, husky and low. They went over to Tignes for lunch, skied back into Val d'Isère together, met for dinner that night. By the end of the week, he was quite sure he was in love with her.

She was divorced and lived in London with her three children; she worked as a secretary to a children's charity, not for the money, but to amuse and interest herself. 'My husband is very generous, but I'm easily bored.'

She had been divorced for three years; her husband was an investment banker, now married to a girl younger than Mungo. The children (two girls and a boy, aged fifteen, twelve and nine) were remarkably nice and well adjusted: testimony, Mungo felt, to Alice's skills as a mother. The eldest, Jemima, was at boarding school, Katy and William still at home. They lived in a pretty little mews house in Chelsea, just off the Kings Road; Alice had decorated it charmingly, and it had an enchanting tiny walled garden which was her pride and joy. Mungo went there very often for Sunday lunch, which was invariably delicious, always bearing expensive presents for everybody, and they would all go for a walk in Richmond Park or Kew Gardens in the afternoon with Lottie, the King Charles spaniel. It all seemed wonderful to him; he had never known ordinary family life. It became a tradition that he took them all out to tea somewhere afterwards; occasionally somewhere very special like the Savoy or the Ritz, but often somewhere quite ordinary, even occasionally McDonald's. Jemima, who had her mother's blonde beauty and was rather sophisticated for her age, liked the posh Sundays, and so did Alice, but the others preferred the more modest ones. Mungo liked going to McDonald's best of all. The children had no idea how extraordinarily rich his father was, or indeed how serious he was about their mother; they just all enjoyed him, although Jemima had a rather half-hearted crush on him, which he encouraged, and when they got back on the Sundays she was home, he would give her what he called flirting lessons. She didn't actually need them. And then, much much later, they would sit alone in the tiny garden, he and Alice, surrounded with the lush scents of her roses and lavender and stock, and drink the bottle of extremely good champagne he also always brought with him, and sometimes talk and sometimes be quite easily and peacefully quiet. To Mungo who had spent his entire life in a rather frenetic pursuit of pleasure those Sundays seemed almost magically sweet.

He saw Alice in the week as well of course; he would take her to dinner or the theatre, and then they would go back to his flat in Sloane Street and experience some extremely joyful sex. She had refused to go to bed with him for quite a long time, telling him that it was foolish, dangerous even, that she did not want him reading more into their relationship than he should; but one night, after a particularly happy evening, when she was sitting on his small balcony, smiling at him, her lovely face soft in the dusk, he suddenly said, 'I love you, Alice. I really do.'

And she had said, 'Oh Mungo, don't.'

'Don't what, Alice? Don't love you? Or don't say it?'

'Don't even think it.'

'But why?' he said, hurt, shocked almost. 'Why can't I think it, when I know it?'

'Because you don't. You are a young, young man, free to do whatever you choose; you have no business to be thinking you're in love with someone almost old enough to be your mother.'

'Oh for Christ's sake,' he said, 'you're not, and anyway, what I choose to do is be in love with you. I don't want anything else. Please believe me.'

He heard almost to his own surprise a catch in his voice as he spoke; looking at her, he saw her face soften into tenderness, concern, saw her almost speak, then hesitate. Mungo was a past master at manipulation; the years he had spent working on his father's emotions had been a superb training. He found that the easy tears were still at his command; he looked at her, knowing his eyes, his dark brown eyes, were huge and dark with them, felt one even roll over and splash down his cheek.

'Oh Mungo,' she said, putting out her hand, wiping the tear away with her finger, 'darling Mungo, don't cry.'

'I can't help it,' he said, 'it hurts me so when you talk like that. Don't you feel anything for me at all? Am I just someone to fill your lonely evenings?' He wondered briefly if he had gone a little far there, moved into Act Two of the melodrama when Act One was not even complete; but 'Of course you're not,' she said and her voice was at once also hurt, but full of tenderness. 'I love being with you, spending time with you. But –'

'But you don't love me? Not in the least?' Another tear, another splash.

'Well – oh Mungo, don't. I can't bear it. Yes, yes all right, I do love you. Quite a lot. There now, I've said it, I'm afraid.'

'Why afraid? Alice, why afraid?'

'Because I have no right to be telling you. Involving you.'

'Alice,' said Mungo, kneeling in front of her, taking both her hands in his. 'I am involved. We're both involved. We can't help it. We're in love with each other. And it's wonderful. Nothing to be afraid of. Now, can we please do the sensible thing, and go inside and go to bed?'

And 'Yes, Mungo,' she said finally, after an endless silence. 'Yes, Mungo, of course we can.'

She had been from the beginning appalled by his idleness, his willingness to live off his father; it was entirely due to her influence that he took the office in Carlos Place, started his estate agency only a month after their meeting. He knew very little about the business, but he had at least an instinct, a sympathy for it, and he hired a small but excellent team and bluffed his way along. There was after all no great hurry to get into profit; his father was so delighted by the whole thing, Mungo knew he would back him for five years if necessary. It was also due to Alice that he gave up gambling, apart from the occasional poker game, started drinking less and completely gave up even soft drugs. Alice felt very strongly on that subject; she said that apart from her own distaste for anything to do with drugs, she had the children to worry about, and any bad example they might be exposed to.

'You've reformed me,' he said to her one night, early in May, soon after they had first gone to bed together. 'My father won't recognize me when he next gets back.'

'Where is he at the moment?'

'Mexico. With Sasha.'

'On holiday?'

'Good God, no. My father doesn't believe in holidays. Sasha's honeymoon was twenty-four hours at the Bel Air, en route to San Francisco and a conference he was chairing on AIDS research.'

'It doesn't sound very romantic. Poor Sasha.'

'Oh, she's all right,' said Mungo easily. 'She has a great time. She just shops. She's very good at that.'

'And what else?'

'I don't think anything else. Well, you know, the usual things my father wants, looking great, being nice to him, sex, I suppose.'

'I see,' said Alice.

She had known about his father of course; her husband had even, she thought, met him once or twice.

'He must be quite a hard act to follow,' she said sympathetically.

'Oh, not really,' said Mungo, vaguely, 'I've never really seen myself as following him. Up to now.'

He had started asking her to marry him in late May; initially she had assumed he was joking, then as she realized he wasn't, had refused, resolutely at first, then slightly more half-heartedly.

'It's ridiculous,' she kept saying, 'I can't even let you think about it.'

Mungo told her she was in no position to tell him what or what not to think and continued to ask her. He asked her by phone, letter, motorbike messenger (cards accompanied by bottles of champagne, jewellery and the perfume he loved so much) and even by singing telegram. And in person on every possible occasion, and in every conceivable situation, in bed, over dinner, in the car, while they were out riding with the children (the children well out of earshot), at concerts and theatres, and once, most romantically, in his father's box at Covent Garden. They were watching *La Bohème* at the time; Mungo did not greatly like opera, but Alice loved it and it seemed to him a most appropriate situation. He ordered a bottle of champagne for the interval and it was brought in by one of the uniformed lackeys, together with a dozen red roses and a note which he handed to Alice.

'Oh my God,' she said laughing, kissing him, 'oh God, Mungo, what am I to say to you? I can't cope with this very much longer.'

'Say yes,' he said, 'it isn't very difficult,' but she managed not to, managed to keep saying it wasn't a good idea, that she really couldn't, until finally one night he lost his temper at yet another refusal, stormed out of her house and walked very fast back to Sloane Street.

When he got in, there was a message from her on his answering machine.

'I love you,' it said, 'and yes, perhaps I will.'

Now all he had to do was tell his father.

Mungo moved into the shade of the lychgate. He was terribly hot, and thirsty as well. This was ridiculous. Nobody was going to come yet, nobody at all. He wondered if he could sneak into the pub for a quick beer. It would only take ten minutes. He was severely tempted. He looked up and down the lane: no sign of anybody, let alone wedding guests. It was as if the nightmare had stopped the whole world, held time still; there was a tiny drifting breeze ruffling the long grass just inside the churchyard, a bird sang half-heartedly in the hedge, the noise of a thousand bees at work in the perfect flower garden of the little cottage opposite the church: those were the only sounds, the only movements. It was almost spooky, the silence; the whole thing had somehow shades of a ghost story. It seemed as reasonable an explanation as any suddenly, something supernatural, Cressida spirited away perhaps, into some strange half-world. For want of anything better to do, Mungo moved into the churchyard, started reading the gravestones. He had never done such a thing before, was startled, instantly saddened by them, by the brutally brief lives ended there: a young couple dying in 1601 within days of one another, a young mother (twenty-four years old) 'taken at Christmas-time 1797, mourned by her five beloved children', of countless babies dead in the first year of their lives. A shadow covered the sun for Mungo; he sat down abruptly in the grass, thinking of Alice. Life suddenly seemed very fragile, happiness brief. They must be together quickly, he thought, must waste no more time. And then he heard a car coming down the lane and looked over the wall and it was Harriet's with Sasha driving it; she pulled up by the lychgate, got out, leant on the wall.

'Hallo, Mungo. I thought you should know what's happened. And I've brought you some beer. You must be terribly hot.'

'Glad someone thinks of me,' said Mungo, standing up, taking the cans gratefully. 'You're a doll, Sasha. What has happened? They haven't found her, have they?'

'No. Not her. But they've found her car.'

'Oh shit.' Mungo sat down abruptly again, feeling sick. 'Crashed? Is she –'

'No, not crashed at all. The car was fine. Parked neatly in a country lane. Somewhere in Essex.'

'Essex? What on earth was she doing in Essex?'

'Picking up her plane.'

'Her plane? Sasha, this is purest fantasy. Cressida can hardly handle the lawnmower.'

'Well, maybe not, but she can handle a plane. She has a pilot's licence. What's more, Theo has been paying for her lessons. He didn't know about the licence, though. She swore him to secrecy. Mungo, what the hell do you think is going on?'

Chapter 10

Theo 2pm

Theo felt terrible; guilt suffused him. He shrank from what James might have to say to him about Cressida's flying lessons; he would see it as an appalling betrayal of friendship, of trust. Theo set aside as determinedly as he could the remembrance of another, greater betrayal – or what James would certainly see as one – and concentrated on this one, the part he had played, however unwittingly, in Cressida's disappearance. It was ridiculous, he told himself, to feel so bad, he had only paid for the bloody flying lessons (and promised Cressida not to tell anyone about it), but the fact remained that if he hadn't done it, she couldn't have taken off quite literally into the blue. OK, if she'd been desperate enough to vanish, she would no doubt have gone anyway; but he had certainly made it easier for her. And he'd kept his promise not to mention it to anyone: 'Please, please don't tell them, Theo,' she'd said, her blue eyes wide with anxiety. 'You know how hopeless I am, I'll have such trouble with it, probably never master it at all, and then they'll all laugh at me. I'll tell them when I've finally cracked it and it'll be wonderful.'

And he had agreed, unable to refuse her as always, had kissed her and told her to tell the flying school to send their bills to him. 'On one condition. You take me up on your first solo flight.'

'Of course I will. Of course. I promise.'

That had been over eighteen months ago, and she never had taken him up: had confessed to him, ruefully, whenever they were alone together that it was exactly as she had feared, that she was indeed completely hopeless, still hadn't got the hang even of keeping the nose steady, although she did love it, loved her lessons, and hoped he wouldn't mind if she went on, and no, he had said, of course he didn't mind, it was fine by him, she should go on for just as long as it took. He did wonder (as she'd been having so much trouble) if she was actually at the best flying school, but she assured him they were wonderful, terribly kind and patient. She'd told him it was somewhere in Wiltshire; quite what she was doing flying out of Essex he couldn't imagine. Maybe she'd just had a few lessons there. It had never occurred to him to check on the school; he had rung his secretary and she had confirmed that yes, all the bills had come from some place in Essex, a very intensive course, several hours a week, but that they had ceased in April that year. 'Apparently she got her licence last September. Just went on flying with them once a fortnight. They said she was very good. Very good indeed.'

'And she took one of their planes?'

'Yes. They're very upset. They want to speak to you.'

He had called them, spoken to the owner of the school, Richard Crooke, who had personally instructed Cressida. She had turned up that morning apparently, at eight thirty, asked if she could take one of the planes up and not returned. No said Crooke, she hadn't seemed at all upset, she was her usual steady, highly competent self. She'd said she'd be back in an hour. There was enough fuel on board for about five hundred miles. Had Mr Buchan any idea where she might have gone and when she might be back?

Theo said he had no idea, no idea at all, but of course he would contact the school immediately they heard from her, and trusted that they would do the same. Crooke asked if, in the event of the plane not being returned, Mr Buchan would be underwriting the cost. Theo said there was no question of the plane not being returned, and asked if Cressida was really a good pilot.

She was excellent, Crooke said; from the very first lesson she'd been a natural, shown a complete grasp of the whole thing. No nerves, no mechanical problems. 'And she loved it. She was laughing with pleasure from the moment the plane started taxiing down the runway. All the things that people usually don't like at first, banking, landing, she just took in her stride. Her first solo flight, she was off, straight over the sea.' He hesitated. 'She didn't mention to you that she had asked me to look out for a plane for her?'

'No,' said Theo. 'No, of course not.'

'Well, she did. In fact I'd found one. Just a tiny one, a Cessna, two-seater. That was what she liked best. Said the four-seaters were too cumbersome. She said she was going to come over and see it last weekend. But she never did.'

'But that's not the plane she's gone off in now?'

'No. That's one of ours. The one she flew most. Got her licence in. She said it felt like a pair of running shoes to her, that plane, she was so comfortable, at ease in it. She was a lovely girl, Mr Buchan. I hope to God nothing's happened to her.'

'Yes, well, I hope so too,' said Theo. He'd put the phone down feeling rather sick.

He wished Sasha was with him, but she had gone to see Mungo with some beer, and to tell him the news. He needed her, he needed her very badly. To distract him. What he should have done, he thought, staring morosely into his glass of whisky, was gone to meet Tilly at Heathrow, instead of letting Merlin go. She was coming over, had managed to catch a lunchtime flight. That would have cheered him up, distracted him from his guilt. His marriage to Sasha had not dulled a response to a sexuality as raw, as uncompromising as Tilly's. But he could see that he couldn't have left his post; and besides, her imminent arrival was probably causing James as much anguish as the disappearance of his daughter. Bloody silly idea getting Tilly over really; he had tried very hard to dissuade Mungo and Rufus from doing it. But Mungo had said her presence would help, she was so full of common sense and Oliver was so fond of her, and anyway things could hardly be worse. Theo had said shortly that they could be worse, much much worse actually, and Mungo had asked why; and short of giving him a full explanation (which was really not his to give) Theo had been forced to let things run their course. In any case, maybe it was better that she came, that the confrontation between her and James was finally forced; the drama of the aborted wedding might take the edge off it. And there was no doubt that Tilly would cheer things up.

Extraordinary set of coincidences that had brought things thus far, almost unbelievable. That this girl should not only have met Harriet, but become a friend, quite a close friend indeed, and then to all of them, their tight little circle, and finally that Rufus should have fallen in love with her – it was bizarre, nightmarish. The only thing that saved the situation was

Tilly herself. She was superb. In every way. He'd known she would be beautiful, sexily, raunchily beautiful: he'd seen dozens, hundreds probably, of pictures of her. But he had expected her to be tough, self-seeking, and quite possibly extremely stupid. He'd waited to meet her the first time, expecting to dislike her intensely. And she had walked into the room like some graceful, rangy black lioness, smiling her impossibly wide, glorious smile, and had taken his hand and shaken it, and it had been like a man's handshake, so firm and strong, and said, 'Hi, Mr Buchan. I'm Ottoline Mills.' And he'd looked at her, at the slanting eyes, the wild mass of hair, at the long narrow body (dressed in a long slither of a black dress under a black leather jacket), and had not just responded to her, been charmed by her; he'd liked her. It was nothing to do with her beauty or her sexuality or the fact that, yes, she was tough, but humorously so, and that, no, she was not stupid, quite the reverse indeed, coolly, sharply clever; it was the fact that she was plainly extremely nice. He could see it was a little early to reach such a conclusion, that he could be accused of being overwhelmed by her, but he was sure of it nonetheless. And everything that had happened since had reinforced that view.

He could scarcely blame Rufus for falling in love with her, in spite of the appalling complications of the thing. What was less clear was why she should reciprocate that love: Rufus, however sweet, was patently not the sort of man with whom Ottoline Mills had spent much time or indeed would have been expected to enjoy spending time. Himself certainly (Christ, if only), Mungo perhaps (God forbid, especially now the boy seemed to be settling down finally – something was having a good effect on him). But Rufus, with his gentle manner, his tender heart, his old-fashioned charm – very unlikely. But love him she plainly did; further proof, Theo felt, of her niceness, that she should value such old-world, intangible virtues. Rufus was not rich, he was not particularly witty, he was not stylish, he was not even chic, he cultivated an almost deliberate shabbiness. If you looked at him and Mungo together, Theo had once remarked to Janine, Rufus looked like some slightly well-worn classical building and Mungo like some stark, perfectly conceived piece of modern architecture. But Rufus was clever, articulate, cultured, original. Of all those qualities, Theo supposed, it was the last that had won Tilly's heart. She was certainly something of an original herself . . .

* * *

Josh Bergin had rung suggesting a walk, had come into his room looking grey with strain, and Theo had been unable to refuse. He hated walking, it seemed to him the most dreary of physical activities, if indeed it could be dignified with such a name; but he couldn't think of an alternative. Josh was hardly in a state (nor did it seem suited to the situation) to swim, or to play golf; walking was at least sober, respectable.

Well, at least there was good news about Tealing Mills. The New York individual, whoever they were, had put their shares – at a huge profit incidentally, they were obviously extremely canny – back on the market. Theo had instructed Mark to buy. 'And while you're about it, tell George I think it might be time to get on with buying some more of those CalVin shares. I know I said softly softly, but that was my policy with Tealing. That is one baby I don't want to lose. Or rather have you guys lose it for me.'

'Sure,' said Mark. 'I'll get back to you.'

Theo put the phone down; he wished to hell all he had to worry about today were his companies and their conduct. His pleasure over the Tealing business was intense, almost sexual in nature. Theo could never quite decide which gave him the greater buzz, women or deals. He thought probably deals; certainly the pleasure was longer-lasting. And now if he could just wrap up CalVin, the day would at least have had something in its favour.

Theo poured himself another large whisky (God, why wasn't it working, why couldn't he get drunk?) and sat reflecting upon CalVin: not a Scottish company this time, but an extremely profitable little wine-producing company in the Napa Valley, California (hence the name). Not only was it profitable, it was an exquisite place; he rather fancied making a home there, building a house. Not as a major home, more of a refuge; he might not even tell Sasha about it, he thought, smiling into his glass. It could be extremely useful, in the just-possible event of his wanting to be on his own, or almost on his own, for a few days: secluded, peaceful, utterly private.

Well, that was for the future: meanwhile there was Josh to be taken care of. He couldn't put that off any longer. He picked up the phone again. 'When my wife gets back, tell her I've gone for a walk with Mr Bergin, would you?'

'Certainly, Mr Buchan.'

God, she'd been a long time. Disappearing seemed to be the order of the day altogether.

Josh didn't say anything for a long time; he led the way rather determinedly through the hotel grounds, over a stile and into some woods in total silence. Theo, who disliked any silence that lasted for more than twenty seconds, stuck it out for as long as he could and then said, 'I suppose in twenty years or so we'll all be laughing about this.'

'Maybe,' said Josh. 'I certainly hope so.' He looked at Theo. 'It really is one's worst nightmare, isn't it?'

'Oh, I can think of much worse,' said Theo carefully, thinking how Josh really did look more English than the English, tall, blond, quietly dressed; he even talked like an upper-class Englishman. Well, that old-money New York crowd prided itself on its cosmopolitan character; he had been to banking dinners there with Josh and wondered at times whether he was actually back in London. Especially now that the London financial scene was so overrun with barrow boys. Wall Street seemed better.

'I can't,' said Josh. 'I really can't think of anything much worse. Poor Oliver. Poor old boy.'

'Yes,' said Theo, 'poor old boy.'

'He's so upset. He's much more easily hurt than anyone realizes, you know. He comes on very controlled and upbeat, but he's actually extremely sensitive. And he adored Cressida. Really adored her.'

'Yes, well, we all did,' said Theo. 'Mustn't speak of her in the past tense, Josh. She'll be back.'

'Yes. Yes of course she will,' said Josh. He didn't sound terribly certain.

'Definitely,' said Theo. There was another long silence.

'We didn't all actually,' said Josh suddenly. He sounded rather strained.

'I'm sorry?'

'We didn't all adore Cressida.'

'Really? Who didn't? You?'

'Oh – yes. Yes of course I did.' He sounded even more tense. Theo looked at him curiously.

'So – who? Who didn't?'

'Julia didn't.' The words came out almost defiantly.

'Oh, really?'

'No. In fact I would go so far as to say she didn't like her. Christ, Theo, I've been keeping this to myself for months now.'

'Well, old chap, mothers of sons don't often like their daughters-in-law. Jealousy you know. Freud at work. Thought you Yanks were heavily into all this psychiatric stuff.'

'Oh, yes, of course, I know all that. And I'm the first to admit that Julia is – what should I say – highly strung. She virtually lives with her analyst. She seems very cool and in control, but she's a hotbed of emotions underneath. Rather like that crazy old father of hers.'

'How is dear Vernon?' asked Theo, laughing at Josh's contorted face.

'Well, I fear,' said Josh, relaxing suddenly and laughing back. Vernon Coleridge, Julia's father, lived as a virtual recluse in Palm Beach; Julia, the focus of his life, was now almost his only visitor.

'Anyway, this was rather more than just jealousy, I think. She often said she – didn't trust her.'

'Really? Why? Whatever made her feel that way?'

'She said Cressida had – lied to her.'

'What on earth about?'

'Oh – this and that. Small things mostly, that didn't really matter, I suppose.'

'Go on, like what?'

'Well, for instance, she told her that she'd had a bad riding accident as a child and had completely lost her nerve. When Julia asked Maggie about it, Maggie told her she certainly couldn't remember it. And she said she'd always wanted to go to boarding school, and that because Harriet hadn't liked it, she wasn't even allowed to try. Again it turned out that she'd always said she didn't want to go, had become hysterical at the very suggestion. Oh yes, and she said she'd always desperately wanted a puppy, and because Harriet had had one and it had been run over, that was that.'

'None of it sounds very serious to me,' said Theo lightly. 'Typical rewriting of childhood history. Sympathy bids. I expect she was just trying to get Julia on her side. She probably sensed she didn't like her.'

'Well – maybe. And I expect you're right. There was a lot of jealousy. Oliver being not just the only son, but the only child. Julia does – what shall I say? – like to mother him still. But there was something rather more serious. That I never discussed with her as a matter of fact.' He looked at Theo. 'Are you sure you want to hear all this? Maybe this isn't the time.'

'I think it's exactly the time,' said Theo. 'And I do want to hear it.'

'Well – she'd been staying with us in New York for a week or so. Earlier this year. Julia was away, gone to see her father, he had a chill or something. Cressida had been out shopping all day and arrived home at around six thirty, terribly upset, said some man had been following her. She hadn't been able to get a cab and she'd been walking the few blocks home up Madison. As she turned into our street, there's a small florist on the corner, he'd pushed her into the doorway, started trying to kiss her, and got his hand into her blouse. She only got away by kneeing him in the crotch. She certainly looked a bit roughed up, she had a bruise on her face and another on her arm, and she was very shaky and tearful. I wanted to call the police, but she begged me not to, said everyone would fuss and she just wanted to forget about it. She especially didn't want Oliver knowing about it, he'd freak out, as she put it, and she couldn't face going over and over it.'

'Where was Oliver?' said Theo.

'He was with a patient. Delivering a baby. Anyway, rather reluctantly I agreed. I sent her to bed, told Oliver when he came in that she wasn't well, and not to disturb her. She didn't appear again until the morning, and then she seemed better. We talked after Oliver had gone. She insisted no real harm had been done to her, and she wasn't hurt at all, although she was still upset and a bit subdued. She said she just wanted to try and forget the whole thing – she really didn't want any more fuss. She said, quite rightly, that both Julia and Oliver would berate her for walking up the street, not getting a cab, and I had to agree that they would. I said they'd be right moreover and she said she was very sorry, she knew it was stupid of her. But she was going the next day and she didn't want her last evening with Oliver spoiled. So I said I wouldn't say anything. She told him she'd hit her face on a door, when he noticed the bruise, and I tried to tell myself no great harm had been done.

'A couple of days later, the hall porter rang up. He had a limo driver with him, and he'd brought in a pair of Cressida's gloves. Said she'd left them in the limo, the night before last, that they looked expensive and he thought he should bring them back. Well that was the night of the alleged attack. I asked him if he was sure it had been then and he said sure he was sure, the next two nights he'd had off, his wife was in hospital or something. I asked him where he'd brought Cressida from and he said up from Brooklyn. That she'd hired him for the day, and he'd taken her down there at lunchtime, dropped her by some subway station and been told to pick her up three hours later. He'd brought her right to the door. I – well I don't know what you make of it, but it sounded pretty odd to me.'

'Very odd,' said Theo. 'Bizarre. And you never – taxed Cressida with it?'

'No. Well, I told you, she'd gone back to England.'

'And you didn't mention it to Oliver?'

'No. No I didn't. It was an almost impossible conversation to have. I'm sure you can see that. And then we didn't hear from her for weeks, by which time the wedding plans were in full swing. It didn't seem – appropriate to start implying she was a liar.'

'I'm sure she wasn't,' said Theo. 'I mean isn't. What about Julia, what did she say?'

Josh looked awkward. 'I – well, I didn't tell Julia either. Now of course I think perhaps I should have done. But it was all so inconclusive, so insubstantial, and Julia would have made such a terrible performance of it. Used it to prove her feelings against Cressida. And I thought – well, it seemed better, more positive, to believe Cressida. So I kept quiet. Until now.'

'I see,' said Theo. He felt outraged, defensive on Cressida's behalf. The sensation he had been struggling with all day, that he was in a nightmare and was about to wake up suddenly, revived with great force. 'Josh, I've known that child all her life. Really really well. She's been like a daughter to me. A sweet, adorable daughter. She just doesn't tell lies. Well, maybe white ones, to spare people's feelings or whatever, but nothing major –' His voice faded slowly. Was persuading him to pay for her flying lessons and making him swear not to tell anyone about it really a small white lie? Harmless, perhaps, but quite substantial actually: involving someone else in a deception as well as herself. He suddenly didn't feel quite so sure about Cressida Forrest.

Chapter 11

Tilly 2pm

She made it. Sweet-talking the cab driver, jumping the queue at the check-in, haring up those fucking awful travelators at Charles de Gaulle, waving her passport and ticket wildly at the departure gate, she had fallen into the cabin of the plane with one minute to spare, had stood there, gasping for breath, laughing, dressed just in a vest T and her cut-offs, still with all the make-up on; had walked through, more slowly now, into the first-class cabin, enjoying the stares – some hostile, mostly appreciative – of the businessmen self-importantly stacking up their laptops, files, organizers for the journey, and slumped into her seat, next to a particularly oyster-eyed old geezer, smiled at him, fumbled in her bag for her cigarettes, started to light up, been reprimanded by the steward and offered a peppermint in return (a peppermint, for God's sake, what use was that in a crisis?) and sat watching Paris slowly shrinking beneath her.

'Champagne, madam?' It was the peppermint-bearing steward.

'What do you think?' said Tilly, grinning at him, taking the glass from the tray. She could never understand the mealy-mouthed crowd who survived transatlantic flights on distilled water and a couple of mouthfuls of celery; she took everything she was offered and enjoyed it.

'Lovely day,' she said cheerfully to her companion.

'Indeed,' he said slightly coolly, and opened the *Herald Tribune*.

Tilly shrugged and drained her glass, waved it at the steward. 'Could I have another? Maybe with a little orange juice?'

She had scarcely finished that and the plate of smoked salmon they brought her when the pilot announced they were beginning their descent. She looked out of the window, and saw the orderly green patchwork of England below her. God, it was always so nice to get back; she'd only been away ten days, but it still felt like forever. She enjoyed travelling – for around forty-eight hours. After that homesickness set in. Tilly was famous for her homesickness; she had even declared herself hungry for England in the middle of winter from a beach in Barbados. If she did this thing with Rosenthal, she'd never be home. Oh God . . .

She wondered who might meet her. Rufus had said it probably wouldn't be him. She'd promised to get a cab if there was no one there for her. It really was time she passed her test. Bloody thing. She didn't know anyone, anyone at all who'd failed three times. And there was her car, her beautiful Ferrari – 'Bit like you,' Mungo had said when she showed it to him, 'long and sleek and fast and black.' He was a great guy, Mungo. Much more her style with those amazing, dramatic dark looks, the sexy chat, the instant easiness with her world. Mungo had spent most of his life kicking around with the sort of people she worked and lived with, international, glamorous people, moving with ease from country to country, continent to continent, intensely fashionable, individual and, OK superficial, but amusing, interesting, fun. Rufus's world, measured by such things as schools, accents, career structures, and the still stately pattern of upper-middle-class English life, was far stranger and more difficult for her to enter. If she didn't love Rufus she'd be off with Mungo before you could say fuck. Or alternatively his gorgeous great bear of a father. But she did love Rufus, she loved him to pieces and it was having a strange effect on her.

Tilly had not known love before. She had known sex and desire and pleasure and bed-based friendship but not, most assuredly not, love. Love had come creeping up on her, sly, unexpected, with a sweet smile and a pair of soft brown eyes under a heavy blond fringe and the sort of voice that had always sent her into fits of mirth. Love had spoken to her politely, held doors open for her, pulled back chairs for her, asked her how she was, waited patiently outside photographers' studios for hours while jobs overran. Love had sat in fashion shows, watching her, smiling in appreciative wonder at her, and had cheerfully cancelled tables for dinner afterwards because she had to be up at five, four even, the next day. Love had read her poetry, and taken her to romantic films, to concerts and to High Mass at Notre-Dame and Sacré-Coeur, to Versailles, studying enraptured her myriad reflections in the Hall of Mirrors, to Giverny to take her wandering through the tumbling, dreamlike colours of Monet's gardens. Love had taken her to bed and pleasured her to an astonishing degree, and finally, only a week ago, had lain on the pillow beside her and asked her to marry him.

'Marry!' she'd said. 'Marry you!' and 'Yes,' he'd said, his brown eyes hurt at the reaction, 'marry me, Tilly, please. I love you. I love you so much.'

'Yeah, and I love you too, but people like me don't marry people like you. Why do we have to get married anyway? Risk spoiling everything. This is great.'

'I want to make you mine,' he said simply. 'I want to live with you, and grow old with you, and have babies with you –'

'Oh no,' she said swiftly, sitting up, reaching for her cigarettes, lighting one, 'no babies. Absolutely no babies. Sorry Rufus. No way.'

'Oh, not now,' he said, misunderstanding, 'of course not now while you're working, but when you've finished, when your figure doesn't matter so much –'

'Fuck my figure,' she said, 'my figure has nothing to do with it. I just will never ever have a baby, OK? I couldn't face it, couldn't go through with it.'

'But why?'

'Because it scares the shit out of me, that's why. All that pain, all that danger –'

'Darling Tilly, there isn't any danger, not now –'

'Oh, really?' she said, and noticed that the hand holding her cigarette was shaking, feeling rare tears behind her eyes. 'You tell that to my mum, Rufus Headleigh Drayton, you tell her there was no danger. I'll – oh shit, can we stop this please? No babies, that's all, Rufus, no babies.'

And he had held her and comforted her and said of course no babies if she minded that much, if she was that afraid, but she had to tell him why. She ducked the issue (of course, because she had to, she had still not decided what to do), said maybe she had seen too many horrific childbirth scenes in films or something, but anyway, she was phobic about it and that was that.

'In any case,' she said finally, 'I don't see how I can marry you. I mean, think what sort of wife I'd be to you. How many lawyers have wives like me?'

'Not many, poor things,' said Rufus, kissing her gently. 'I'll be the envy of every court in the world.'

'Don't be stupid,' said Tilly irritably. 'I know the sort of wife you need and she isn't black and she doesn't come from Brixton. And she's very happy to spend her time doing the flowers and having the house done out and being on charity committees and inviting important people to dinner.'

'You do know, don't you?' said Rufus, surprised.

'Rufus, I know lots of things. I've been around. I've been to a few of those power dinners, I've seen those women at work. I'd be a total disaster. I have a much better idea. You get a suitable wife and we'll meet once a week for a fantastic fuck.'

'No,' he said, and his brown eyes were very tender, very honest, 'no, I'm sorry, I couldn't do that. I'm like my dad. A one-woman man.'

'And is your mother a one-man woman?'

'Yes of course she is,' said Rufus, half indignant. 'You'd love my mum, Tilly. And she'd love you. She's the best. She's so pretty and she's such fun and when she's there everyone always has a good time.'

'And a good lawyer's wife?'

'A great lawyer's wife, yes.'

'And I suppose she went to the best schools and all that garbage?'

'Well yes, she did, but that doesn't mean –'

'Rufus, I know what it means. I love you, but I'm not going to marry you. I'm not going to marry anyone. I never want to belong to anyone that much.'

'But Tilly, love is about belonging,' said Rufus, looking hurt. 'I feel I belong to you anyway.'

'Yeah, I know, and I kind of feel the same thing, but that's a different sort of belonging from being married.'

'I don't understand,' said Rufus.

'Rufus, all my life –'

'Such a long life –'

'I thought you wanted me to explain.'

'Sorry.'

'All my life, and I mean all, since I was really really tiny, I've wanted things to be down to me. Independent, you know? Not having to ask for things, not having to be grateful. To be in charge. My mum spent most of her life being grateful for lousy jobs she should have thrown back at people, for the odd bit of money she could persuade my dad to give her, for droppings from those self-important turds that call themselves the social services. Christ! And she's worth so much more than any of them. I hated it so much, Rufus, watching it, watching her. And I decided I was going to do it all my way, stay free, stay clear. Not have to take, from anyone, not put myself at risk.'

'That seems to cut out me altogether,' said Rufus. He sounded very sad. 'You won't be at risk from me, Tilly, I'll never ever leave you, let you down. And isn't it worth it, taking, if you really love someone? I would.'

'You say that,' said Tilly, 'but you don't know. You've always had so much you don't know you're taking. Anyway, of course it doesn't cut you out. It doesn't cut out anything we have. It doesn't cut out love or fun or sex or being together.'

'It cuts out giving,' said Rufus. 'Tilly, won't you even think about it, marrying me? Not even one day? I want it so much, I want to know you're mine, I want everyone to know you're mine.'

He looked so wretched Tilly was shocked. She leant over and kissed him tenderly.

'Rufus, I *am* yours. And everyone does know. I'm not going to leave you. I love you much too much. I just don't want to marry you. I don't want to marry anyone. And like I keep saying, I'd be the most terrible wife for you anyway. You need someone like – well, like Cressida. An English rose in frilly blouses.'

'I don't want an English rose in frilly blouses,' said Rufus irritably. 'I want you.'

'You've got me.'

'I mean married to me.'

'Rufus, I can't. You haven't been listening. But I tell you what. You're lovely to ask me. Thank you. Maybe we should get to sleep now.'

'I shan't be able to sleep,' said Rufus.

But he did, curled around her, his head buried in the nape of her neck. It was Tilly who couldn't sleep, lying awake for hours, thinking not about Rufus and marriage, but about her mother's anxious, troubled life, and her inability to do anything about it, and childbirth and its attendant terrors, and the tiny plaque in the Crematorium Garden of Remembrance that read 'Beatrice Mills. Sister to Ottoline. Born and died, 20 October 1974'.

'Miss Mills?' The voice was charming, courteous. Tilly looked at its owner, tall, taller than she was, and very erect, despite what was clearly considerable age. He was dressed in a manner that seemed slightly eccentric even to her, a white shirt, very baggy khaki shorts and a morning coat; but the legs beneath the shorts were not spindly old men's legs, they were strong and very tanned, as was the rest of him, and the hand he held out to her was large and firm.

'Yes,' she said, grinning at him, shaking his hand, 'yes, I'm Tilly Mills. Hi.'

'How do you do. I'm Merlin Reid.' Tilly had heard about Sir Merlin, and had longed to meet him; he'd sounded like her kind of person.

'Young Rufus asked me to meet you. Said he thought we'd get on. I can see we will,' he added. 'Got any luggage?'

'No,' said Tilly, 'only this' – indicating the leather rucksack on her back.

'Good girl. I only ever take a rucksack myself. Most people take far too much luggage. Follow me, then.'

He led the way out of the airport; a stout, ferret-faced female traffic warden stood by what was clearly his car (1930-ish, Tilly thought, dark green, with a running board, brown hood folded down), writing out a ticket.

'Oh wow,' said Tilly, walking round the car, stroking it, totally ignoring the warden. 'This is some car. What is it?'

'I'm glad you like it. I'm very fond of it. It's a Lagonda. We've been together for about thirty years. Driven her all over Europe.'

'Really. It really is f – very beautiful.'

'You can't park here,' said the warden, clearly as enraged by being ignored as by the flagrant disregard for parking restrictions. 'I have to give you a ticket.'

'I think you should brush up on your grammar,' said Merlin. 'Quite incorrect, that sentence. Clearly I can park here, or I wouldn't have been able to do so. What you mean, I imagine, is that it is against your horrible rules for me to park here. You should make yourself plainer, madam. Now please remove that piece of paper from my windscreen.'

'I can't do that I'm afraid.'

'Wrong grammar again. Of course you can. By raising your arm and lifting the ticket with your hands. I can do it too. Look. Now take it back and get out of my way. I'm very busy.'

'I have to warn you you are still in breach of the law,' said the warden, groping on the ground for the ticket which she had dropped. 'I have your car number and I shall issue a duplicate ticket which you will receive through the mail. There could be an additional penalty, moreover, for trying to obstruct the course of justice.'

'Oh get out of my way, you ridiculous woman,' said Merlin. 'It's you who are causing the obstruction. Pity you weren't born fifty years earlier. You'd have been of great value to the Third Reich. Good afternoon to you.'

He opened the passenger door for Tilly, cranked up the car and drove off in a cloud of smoke; the warden stood staring after them, her mouth a wide O.

'Dreadful people,' said Merlin cheerfully. 'Should be put away. Are you comfortable, my dear? Good. We have a little drive ahead of us, so we can get to know one another. Like an apple?' He produced one from the pocket of his morning coat. 'They were selling them in the village shop. Awful little things, I told the woman I'd take them off her hands. She tried to make me pay, we had a bit of a barney, but in the end I beat her down to half price. Anyway, they're better than nothing.'

'They certainly are,' said Tilly, biting into the classic country-shop apple, small, soft, slightly withered. 'Do you want a beer? In exchange. I have a couple here, in my bag. It's travelled from Paris, but it's probably all right.'

'Oh yes, rather,' said Sir Merlin. 'That would be fine. As long as it's not that German stuff you all drink now. Buddy something or other.'

'Do you mean Budweiser?' said Tilly. 'That's American. But this is Dutch. Would that be all right?'

'Yes, fine. Some of our finest allies, the Dutch. Thank you very much. Take the top off for me, would you?'

'It's really kind of you to come and meet me,' said Tilly, handing him the beer.

'Oh, not at all. Relief to get away as a matter of fact. God, there's a to-do going on at the house. Poor old Jamie.'

'Well, I suppose it is worth a bit of a to-do,' said Tilly, grinning at him. 'I mean it is Cressida's wedding day and –'

'Lot of fuss about nothing if you ask me,' said Sir Merlin.

'Oh, Sir Merlin, you can't say that, surely.'

'Indeed I can. I can and I do. Your grammar is a little at fault as well. Look, my dear, when you've lived as long as I have, you'll know nothing is really very important. Twenty years after some event that you thought catastrophic, you're wondering what it was all about. Or you can see it wasn't catastrophic at all.' He took another swig of beer, looked at Tilly thoughtfully. 'Give you an example. All my young life I dreamed of going in the army. My grandfather was a field-marshal, Father was a general; place all ready for me at Sandhurst. Got turned down at the medical. Dicky ticker, they said. Although I can't say it's ever bothered me since. Well, I was very upset at the time. I'd have fallen on my sword if I had one. But now I can't think of anything worse. I'd never have really travelled, never have learnt what I've learnt, carried on seeing the native as fuzzy-wuzzies instead of fine, civilized chaps. More civilized than we are, most of them. Well, I don't know why I'm telling you that. Where are you from? Somalia by the look of you.'

'Brixton really,' said Tilly, 'but yes, my dad was from Somalia.'

'Thought so. Fine people. Anyway, you mark my words, Miss Mills, in a few years you'll be wondering why on earth there was such a fuss over this. Oliver's a tough young nut. He'll get over it.'

'Well – I suppose so,' said Tilly slightly doubtfully. 'And please call me Tilly.'

'Right you are. You haven't got another of those beers, have you? It was jolly good. Excellent people, the Dutch. Excellent. Lived in an attic in Amsterdam for a year or so with six of them. Never a cross word.'

'Why did you do that?'

'Well, it was in the war. Had a little sailing boat, made a few trips over to Dunkirk, you'll know about that I trust. Picked up some chappie who had a Dutch wife. Jewish. She was with her parents just outside Amsterdam, he was desperate to get her home to England. Well, I pulled a few strings you know, managed to get over there and went to see her. Nice girl. Wonderful people, put me up. Just leaving with the girl when the Gestapo started on the village. Local baker let us hide in a little attic, above his grain store. Had a hidden door. Just for a few days, we thought. Well the few days turned into a few months. Pretty exciting. I have to tell you I enjoyed it. Got a bit restless, but we made out. Wonderful fellow the baker. They – well, they shot him in the end. And his wife. And found the attic, dragged the family out, put them on a train to Bergen-Belsen. All dead, I'm afraid. Well, when you've seen things like that some damn silly girl running off in her wedding frock doesn't seem very important.'

'No,' said Tilly. 'No, I can see that.' She was completely engrossed in the story. 'Why didn't they take you as well?'

'I was out on the roof. We'd made a sort of trapdoor, took it in turns to climb out each day, get some fresh air. It was my turn. Felt terrible about it, but giving myself up wasn't going to help anybody. After that I made my way to the border, got out. I had a very good German passport some johnny at the Foreign Office had done for me. And I speak their filthy language of course. Anyway, where was I? Oh yes, the Dutch. Lovely people. Survived that terrible winter, never broke. How did you meet young Rufus then?'

'Through Harriet,' said Tilly. 'And Mungo and Oliver. In Paris. Um – did you say Cressida had run off in her wedding dress?'

'Well, she took it with her. Don't suppose she was actually wearing it.'

'Why on earth should she have done that, I wonder?'

'God knows. Dreadful behaviour altogether. Always thought she was spoilt. Harriet's worth ten of her. Work for Harriet, do you? Bit of sewing I suppose?'

'Um – not exactly,' said Tilly carefully. 'I'm a model.'

'Oh are you? What, walk up and down on the – what's it called – catwalk, that sort of thing?'

'Yes, that's right.'

'Had a girlfriend who was a model once. In London, just before the war. Worked for the chappie who makes clothes for the Queen. Norman Hartnell. Never let me near her, in case I creased her frock. You don't strike me too much like that. What do you think of Harriet?'

'I think she's great,' said Tilly. 'Really great. And clever too. She's going to be really big.'

'You mean successful? I think so too. Gave her a bit of money, you know, helped get her going.'

'That was kind.'

'Yes, well, haven't got any nippers of my own. Always had time for Harriet. Took her travelling with me a bit. Wouldn't have taken Cressida. Not in a million years. Not surprised she's done this between you and me. Not surprised at all.'

Tilly looked at him thoughtfully. 'Really? I don't know her very well. I only met her once or twice.'

'Not worth meeting much more often. Not for a girl like you anyway. Only thing that ever impressed me was that she played a fine game of poker.'

'Poker!' said Tilly. She thought about Cressida, with her soft sweet manner, her slightly helpless charm, and tried to imagine her at a poker game. It was almost impossible. 'That's amazing. When did you discover that?'

'Oh – a couple of years ago. We were stuck in Charles de Gaulle Airport. I was on my way back from somewhere or other, stopped over to see Harriet and Cressida was there staying with her, said she'd travel back with me. Well, you know what the French are like, go on strike as soon as look at you. We were there all night, made friends with a couple of young chaps and one of them suggested a game. I expected Cressida to say she couldn't play, but she was very good. Didn't win of course, I always do that, but –'

'You do?' said Tilly, grinning at him. 'You played with Mungo Buchan?'

'Of course I have. Many times. He did beat me once, I think. Anyway, she asked me not to mention to the family she could play. She said she'd been learning and was planning to surprise them at Christmas or some such nonsense. What do you think of Mungo then?'

'He's cool,' said Tilly.

'I take it that's a compliment. I agree with you. A most interesting young man.'

'Yeah, I suppose,' said Tilly slowly. She was still trying to imagine Cressida playing poker. 'Yeah, he is.'

'So how do you fit into all this?'

'I told you. I know Harry.'

Careful, Ottoline, don't even think about the other connection; not now.

'Rufus seems very fond of you.'

'Yeah, he is. And I'm very fond of him,' she added with just a touch of defensiveness.

'Good,' said Sir Merlin. 'Wouldn't want him hurt. Very fond of his mother,' he added slightly unexpectedly.

It was an exhausting drive. The novelty of being in an open 1930s convertible rather than an air-conditioned limo very soon wore off. The fumes and the noise on the M4 were appalling, and as the car never went above 45mph, the journey took a long time. Tilly drifted into a confused agitated sleep, and woke to hear Sir Merlin singing 'It's a Long Way to Tipperary' very loudly. 'Have to sing,' he explained. 'Only way I can keep awake. Sing with me, won't you?'

Tilly didn't know many of the songs in his repertoire, so they settled for 'London's Burning' and 'Ten Green Bottles'. She was inordinately relieved when they turned off the motorway and he announced they were almost there. She was to be taken, Sir Merlin told her, to where Rufus was staying, at the Beaumonts', old friends of both the Forrests and the Headleigh Draytons. 'And after that I think I'll head over to the hotel where young Theo's staying. Get a bit of peace and quiet.'

'I'd much rather go there,' said Tilly. 'Can't get along with these country types.'

'Nor me, my dear. Can't stand them. But Rufus has told me to take you there, so I have to, I'm afraid. You'll like Susie, though. Lovely girl. Lots of guts. Ah, here we are, our turning. Hasn't she done well, the old darling?'

It took Tilly a few moments to realize he was referring to the Lagonda rather than Rufus's mother.

Rufus was standing in the Beaumonts' drive. He looked rather pale, but cheerful.

'Tilly! It's so wonderful to see you. You seem to have got here very quickly.'

'Sir Merlin and I made good time,' said Tilly tactfully, getting out of the car and kissing him briefly, feeling her heart lurch as always at the sight and sense of him and marvelling as always that she could feel such tenderness and such passion for someone who was so patently a product of everything she disliked and disapproved of. And thinking, too, that if she went to New York they would be forcibly separated for a great deal of the time, and that would be at one and the same time almost unbearable and a very neat way out of her dilemma. 'It was very kind of you to bring me,' she said, hauling herself back to the present, holding out her hand to Sir Merlin. 'Thank you. I enjoyed it. I hope we meet again.'

'Oh, I shall make sure we do. I enjoyed it too. Good afternoon, my dear. Everything all right, Rufus?'

'Oh – well, you know, sir. As well as can be expected. Everyone's a bit hysterical.'

'Lot of silly fuss,' said Sir Merlin, turning back to his car. 'I'm off to have a stiff drink and a nap. See you later, boy. Give my love to your mother.'

'Yes, I will, sir. And thank you again.'

'Pleasure. You've got a good one there,' he said, indicating Tilly.

'I know,' said Rufus, giving Merlin his oddly sweet smile. He took Tilly's hand and led her towards the house.

'Do we have to go in?'

'Well – just for a bit. Mum's here. I'd really like you to meet her. And I can tell you what's been happening. After that, we can go and see Oliver. He was so pleased you were coming.'

'OK.'

They went into the house. Tilly having admired the exterior, which was large and modestly grand, was amazed by what she found inside, an extraordinary blend of ripped sofa covers, kicked-about paintwork and what were clearly extremely expensive bits of furniture dotted about. A great many silver-framed photographs of children in various stages of development stood on a large table in the hall and what was obviously a valuable oil painting of a woman in a red crinoline hung above the stairs. The stairs themselves were covered in extremely theadbare carpeting, the floor of the hall was stone, and of the drawing room very unpolished wood. A woman with wild grey hair held back from a pleasantly plain face by a velvet Alice band came down the stairs. She was wearing wellingtons, a floral, full-skirted Laura Ashley dress and a sleeveless quilted jacket. She held out a very rough hand with rather dirty nails to Tilly.

'How do you do. You must be Tilly. Jolly nice to meet you. So good of you to come all this way.'

Tilly looked at her in horror. If this was Rufus's idea of a pretty, fun person, then they really did have no future together. She smiled slightly nervously and said, 'No problem.' The heat, the long journey and her anxiety made her suddenly feel rather dizzy.

'Now what about a cup of tea? My goodness, I've made a lot today. Rufus dear, bring Tilly into the kitchen – you don't mind a kitchen tea do you, Tilly? Careful, dear, of that dog, she's blind and deaf and gets a bit snappy if she's startled. Now then, I expect you're hungry, that drive with Merlin must have been jolly tough, I've got some cake or would you prefer a sandwich or something? – William, darling, I've told you not to bring bridles into the house, take it out to the tackroom.'

'But Mum –'

That was funny, thought Tilly, she could have sworn Rufus's small brother was called Tom.

'Take it out at once. Now, Tilly, would you like China or Indian?'

'Indian please,' said Tilly, 'with lots of sugar.' She sat down thankfully at the huge wooden table, which was covered in newspapers, mugs, letters, a pile of snapshots, a dog's lead and a lot of crumbs, removing something excruciatingly unfriendly from beneath her buttocks which proved to be what looked like a cross between a metal brush and a comb.

'Great,' said William, swooping on it. 'My curry comb. It's all right, Mum, I'm going.'

'I'm glad to hear it. Dreadful child,' she added, smiling at his disappearing back. 'Seems to have been home forever already and we're only three weeks into the holidays. Rufus dear, tea for you? Now – ah, Susie, there you are.'

And into the room, smiling, came a woman who Tilly could indeed recognize as extremely pretty and who could quite clearly be tremendous fun: a woman with dark brown hair, tied back loosely from a perfect oval face, large dark eyes, perfect, almost unlined skin. She was wearing beige shorts (revealing very tanned, very good legs) and a white T-shirt and she looked about thirty.

'I'm Susie Headleigh Drayton,' she said, holding out her hand to Tilly. 'How do you do? It's lovely to meet you and it's so nice of you to rush over from Paris. All the boys seemed to think you would make them feel better. I can quite see why.'

Tilly smiled back at her, took her hand, knew she was going to like her immensely, knew also at once why Rufus was as he was. 'I can't really,' she said, 'but I'll do my best.'

'What were you doing over there? The shows?'

'No, they're over. It was a photographic session for *Sept Jours*. Wedding dresses,' she added, after a pause.

'How ironic,' said Susie lightly. 'On such a day. One of my favourite magazines that. Do you enjoy modelling?'

'Yeah, I love it,' said Tilly briefly.

'I did a bit when I was young. I was with an agency that's gone now, called Peter Hope Lumley. I never really got going because I wasn't tall enough, but I did a few shows and lots of head shots. Mostly with Barry Lategan, does that mean anything to you?'

'Yes, but he doesn't work much now,' said Tilly, both impressed and irritated that Rufus hadn't mentioned this crucial piece of information about his mother. 'He was great, though. The guy I was working with today, Mick McGrath, he has a kind of shrine to Lategan in his studio in Paris.'

'Really? He was such a sweet man. I loved him. Anyway, I never got very far. But it taught me all kinds of useful things, like how to do my hair and put on false eyelashes, and I developed huge muscles in my arms, carrying my bags around, all those shoes, my goodness –'

'You don't have to do any of that these days,' said Tilly. 'They have hairdressers and make-up artists and the fashion editors bring everything, down to the last pair of tights.'

'So I understand. Aren't you lucky! Well, I'm sure they make a much better job of it than we did.'

God, she was nice, thought Tilly. Really really nice. She wanted to get to know her: properly know her. She sat there trying not to stare at Susie, at her lovely, fine features, her curvy mouth, her slender, young girl's body, and as she looked, Susie looked back at her, and Tilly saw within the depths of the velvety dark eyes an odd expression, something close to wariness, to anxiety. And she noticed something else too: a heavy shadowing beneath the eyes, a tautness to the jaw when the smile relaxed. There was something going on here, Tilly thought, some unhappiness beyond the disappearance of a close friend's daughter. She was intrigued, and more than intrigued – concerned. She smiled at Susie, and Susie smiled back, warmly, sweetly, and Tilly thought, in recognition of her concern.

'Mum, unless there's anything you want me to do, I thought we'd go over and see Mungo and Oliver,' said Rufus. 'Mungo's running out of positive thinking and wants to talk to Tilly and Oliver's in a very weird state apparently. His mother's totally freaked out and his dad's gone for a long walk.'

'How extremely sensible,' said Susie. 'About the best thing he could have done, I would think. If I was Josh I'd spend my whole life going for long walks. That woman is exceedingly irritating.'

'Fearfully glam though,' said Janet Beaumont, coming over to the table with four cracked mugs, a milk bottle and an exquisite silver teapot. 'Wish I had a figure like that. You have of course, Susie. Lucky you. How about some cake? Tilly, what about you?'

'Mustn't,' said Tilly, 'it looks delicious, though,' she added politely, eyeing the wonderfully solid, large iced chocolate cake on the dresser. 'Is Harry around? I'd love to see her.'

'Who?' said Susie. 'Oh, you mean Harriet. Yes, she's on her way over. So please wait for her, Rufus. Poor girl, she's worn out, trying to console her mother and keep calm herself. She's so fond of Cressida, of course.'

There was something about the 'of course' that struck Tilly rather forcibly; she looked at Susie sharply. But Susie was relaxed as she looked back at her, smiled her lovely, radiant smile.

'How well do you know Cressida?' she asked.

'Oh, not very well,' said Tilly. 'Harry's my friend. She was how I met Rufus.'

'Well, bully for Harry,' said Susie lightly. 'I have to say she is my favourite of those two girls, although of course one shouldn't be saying any such thing. Not that Cress isn't adorable, but Harriet has so much gumption. The way she's built up that business of hers, almost single-handed, I really do admire her. And she had a tough childhood –'

'Really?' said Tilly. She thought of her own childhood and wondered what tough meant to Susie Headleigh Drayton.

'Yes. Very tough. Sent off to that awful school when she was only nine – Janet dear, this is wonderful cake –'

'Glad you like it. I thought everyone would be hungry when we got back after the wedding. Oh dear –'

'Yes, well, we're all hungry before it,' said Rufus cheerfully. 'So it hasn't been wasted. Yes, I'd forgotten Harriet was sent away. Didn't last long though, did it? Merlin rescued her, like a real wizard.'

'Yes, but if he hadn't . . . And I always thought it was so unfair that Cressida was allowed to stay at home. Still, Harriet always says now it was the making of her –'

'It probably was,' said Rufus. 'Look at all of us. Stuff the British Empire was made of –' He winked at Tilly.

'Rufus darling, you know perfectly well none of you went away until you were thirteen. And Tom hasn't gone at all.'

'Yes, well, you spoil him. Your baby.'

'I do not,' said Susie serenely. 'I don't spoil any of you. Never have.'

'Maggie says you always spoiled me,' said Rufus. 'She said it at lunch yesterday, didn't you hear her?'

'Oh really?' For the first time she seemed less relaxed. 'I don't see that Maggie is in any position to know such a thing. Or to make such a judgment.'

'You know Maggie,' said Janet Beaumont, taking a second slice of cake. 'So tactless. Always speaks her mind. I do feel rather sorry for her though,' she added. 'She doesn't have an easy time.'

'She seems to have quite an easy time to me,' said Susie briskly. 'Neither of the girls at home, Jamie in London half the week, plenty of help – oh I know she's had the wedding to do, but –'

'Well I wouldn't like to be married to James Forrest,' said Janet.

'Really? Why not specially?' Susie's dark eyes were very brilliant suddenly. Now why should that be, thought Tilly, what is he to her? (feeling her own flesh crawl, her pulse quicken at the name).

'He's such a demanding creature. Everything in the house has to be perfect. Maggie was telling me he threw a terrific wobbly a couple of weeks ago because she still hadn't got the drawing-room carpet and curtains cleaned.'

'Doesn't sound too unreasonable to me,' said Susie lightly.

'I know, but there's always something. She has to run around after him, seeing to his clothes like some sort of valet. And you know how vain he is –'

'Is he?' said Rufus. 'I didn't know that.'

'Oh terribly. Mike teases him about it sometimes. That's my husband,' she added to Tilly.

'Yes, well no one could call Mike vain,' said Susie laughing. 'I doubt if he even knows where a single mirror is in this house. Alistair's quite vain as a matter of fact. If you call fussing about clothes vain. Still, I don't think Jamie's all that bad to live with. He's very good and supportive to Maggie, and frightfully good-tempered really –'

'Yes, well, you always see the best in people, and anyway he's got a bit of a soft spot for you,' said Janet winking at her.

'Rubbish!' said Susie cheerfully. 'No more than for any other pretty lady. Oh, there's Harriet's car now. Rufus, go and bring her in, give her a cup of tea.'

Tilly was sorry Harriet had arrived so soon; she could have sat listening to stories about James Forrest for a very long time.

Harriet came into the kitchen looking tired; she smiled round the table at them, and then went over and hugged Tilly.

'It's lovely to see you,' she said, 'thank you so much for coming.'

'Lovely to see you too,' said Tilly. She hadn't seen Harriet for three or four weeks; she looked terrible.

'How's your mother, Harriet dear?' asked Janet Beaumont, passing Harriet another cracked mug.

'Pretty bad,' said Harriet carefully. 'But Janine is doing wonders with her. I've told you about Janine, haven't I?' she said to Tilly. 'My wonderful French fairy godmother.'

'I thought she was Cressida's godmother,' said Janet.

'She is, her real one. But she and I have this secret code. She's always been so good to me. Don't tell Mummy for heaven's sake,' she added.

'No of course not.'

Maggie Forrest seemed to need a great deal of protection from life, Tilly thought; she wondered why.

'Anyway, there's some news about Cressida. Extraordinary news. No, she hasn't been found, but her car has. Somewhere in Essex, of all places. And, even more peculiar, she's got a pilot's licence. Nobody had the faintest idea. And she took a little plane from her flying school this morning, really early, and hasn't come back –'

'Good God,' said Susie, staring at her. 'Cressida! I can't believe she's capable of it. Not just learning to fly, but doing something like this. It's so calculated and – and tough, somehow. She's always seemed so sweet and – well, helpless. And what on earth is she doing taking flying lessons in Essex? It's such a long way away.'

'I know, I know,' said Harriet wearily. 'Anyway, Daddy's phoning round every little airport, and big one for that matter, in the country . . .'

'And abroad, presumably?' said Rufus.

'Yes. We thought at first she couldn't have gone abroad.'

'Why not?'

'Because Oliver's got her passport. Ready for going to Mexico today. But apparently she's got one of those post office jobs – the vicar saw her getting it.'

'Good God,' said Rufus. 'How absolutely extraordinary. You've spoken to Oliver presumably about this?'

'Yes. Yes of course. He had no idea she could fly. No idea at all. He's – well, he's very shocked.'

'Let's get over there,' said Rufus, standing up, taking Tilly's hand. 'Are you coming, Harriet?'

'Oh – are you going already? I was hoping to talk to Tilly.'

'You can talk to Tilly later,' said Rufus. 'I honestly think we should go and support poor old Mungo. And we both thought Tilly would be able to help.'

'I would have thought it was Oliver who needed the support,' said Susie. 'But anyway, yes, I'm sure they'll welcome you.'

'I – I think I'll stay here for a bit – if that would be all right, Janet,' said Harriet. Her voice was almost deathly quiet. 'I don't think I can face any more scenes.'

'Oh Harriet, please come,' said Rufus. 'I know it would help, and I'm sure Tilly would – '

'Rufus, leave poor Harriet alone, for heaven's sake,' said Susie. 'She's absolutely worn out. Harriet darling, you're very pale. I bet you haven't eaten anything all day. Why don't you have a sandwich or something?'

'No – really, I'm not hungry,' said Harriet. 'But thank you anyway. Lovely tea, Janet. I'll see you later, Tilly. Maybe back here or something. I'd ask you over to the Court House, but –' Her voice trailed away.

'Oh I don't think that's a very good idea,' said Tilly quickly. 'Rufus can sort something out. You stay here, Harry, you look rotten. We can talk later. Come on, Rufus, let's go.'

They drove over to Woodstock in Rufus's rather uncharacteristically flashy Porsche. Tilly suddenly felt desperately tired and slightly surreal; she had planned to talk to Rufus about the offer from Rosenthal amongst other things, but she drifted off instead into a strange half-waking, half-sleeping state. She woke in the courtyard of the Royal Hotel to see Sir Merlin's car parked next to an extremely large and beautiful Bentley. 'My God,' she said, unwinding herself with difficulty from the confines of the Porsche. 'You lot do have a corner in good cars.'

'Yours isn't so bad,' said Rufus. 'Oh Tilly, it's nice to see you. I hope I've said that.'

'You haven't,' said Tilly, grinning at him, 'but I kind of took it for granted.'

'Good. I love you.'

'I love you too,' said Tilly, kissing him on the mouth, putting her arm through his.

'Have you thought any more about marrying me?'

'I've thought about it, yes.'

'And? What are you thinking?'

'Nothing very different,' said Tilly, kissing him gently again, 'just that I love you. But I have something else to talk to you about.' She smiled at him. 'Is Mr Buchan here? I hope so. He's really wild.'

'Theo? I'd forgotten you knew him. Now I feel jealous. Yes, I think so. He certainly was. Anyway, Mungo will know. What's the something else like?'

'Oh – business,' said Tilly. 'It can wait.'

✵ ✵ ✵

Mungo and Oliver were in Mungo's room. Oliver was extremely drunk.

He was still in his striped trousers and his white shirt; his fair hair was wild and his blue eyes were bleary, dark shadows etched heavily underneath them. A half-empty bottle of bourbon stood on the table by him.

'Hi,' he said, 'so good of you to come. Welcome to my bridal feast. Hallo, Tilly. Specially good of you. Long way from Paris.' He got up and went over to her, gave her a hug. She hugged him back. He smelt very strongly of bourbon and the extremely expensive aftershave he always wore. The mix wasn't exactly good, but it was very sexy. Oliver wasn't conventionally, overtly sexy, but there was a tension, a tautness about him that was very attractive, almost challenging, Tilly had thought the first time she met him. She had danced with him once, and felt that tension, felt it right through him, a physical thing, and she imagined then that once released it would have a power of its own, strong, possibly dangerous. She had considered (not having then met Rufus, fallen in love with him) working on it, on him, exploring him, the challenge had been as arousing as Oliver himself, and she'd stood still on the dance floor briefly, just looking at him, contemplating him and what his rather awkwardly moving body might do for her, and he had recognized it and stood still himself, looking back at her, and then pulled her to him, quite abruptly, and she felt his erection rising against her, felt his face against her neck, his lips on her ear, and a flood of quite extraordinary warmth had filled her, and she'd slithered one hand slowly down his back, towards his buttocks, and as it moved she felt the tension beneath it leaving him, easing, and his hand joined hers, echoing the charge in him, and he'd said, 'Tilly, you are just – just –' and then the music had changed, grown faster, and she'd said laughing, 'What am I, Oliver, what am I?' And he'd stood back, and she'd watched him gather himself together again, look over at where Harriet was dancing with Mungo, and he said 'Gorgeous,' lightly, but carefully, and then 'Come on, let's get a drink.' And the others saw them going to the bar and joined them, and she had never been in a situation to explore him again. Now sharply she remembered and standing there, close to him, felt confused, almost embarrassed. She smiled at him, kissed him on the cheek.

'It was a long way,' she said, 'but it was worth it.'

'You haven't got Harriet with you?'

'No. She's at the Beaumonts'.'

'Ah. Well, do have a drink, all of you. Help yourselves. Mungo old chap, you do the honours. Tilly, what'll you have?'

'Diet Pepsi, please,' said Tilly. .

'Rufus, old man?'

'Oh – the same.'

'So she's up in the sky somewhere, then,' said Oliver. 'My bride. My beautiful bride. Oh God.'

'Yes,' said Rufus. 'Yes, so it seems. You had no idea she could fly?'

'None.'

'How odd. So unlike Cressida to have a secret like that.'

'Oh yes. Very unlike her.' He sounded bitter suddenly, angry. It was hardly surprising, Tilly supposed. Poor Oliver. Grief apart, the humiliation of this was fairly heavy. And he had one hell of an ego, Oliver. He was nice, he was clever, but he did have an attitude.

'Mind you,' said Rufus, 'she did surprise one now and again. Didn't she?'

They all looked at him.

'Did she?' said Mungo. 'I always thought you could read Cressida like a book.'

'Yes. A mystery book,' said Oliver and laughed shortly.

'What do you mean, Rufus?' said Mungo.

'Oh – nothing much. She just wasn't quite as straight-forward as she seemed.'

'In what way? Give us a for-instance. You never know, it might help.'

'I'm sure it won't, but – well, for instance I never knew she could speak such perfect French.'

Mungo stared at him. 'She can't.'

'Yes she can.'

'Rufus, she can't. When she came to stay with my dad and me in Paris quite recently, it was embarrassing. She insisted on trying out some very schoolgirly stuff one night in a restaurant.'

'Well I'm sorry but she can. I've heard her.'

'When?'

'Well,' said Rufus, clearly enjoying the mild furore he was causing, 'she was in Paris visiting Harriet once, and I arrived in Harriet's flat and she was on the phone, I don't know who to, but it was about some money she was having transferred into a French bank or something. And she was absolutely fluent. A lot better than me.'

'Did you ask her about it?'

'Yes. She didn't know I was there at first – she was a bit embarrassed. Not about speaking French but about the conversation. I told her I hadn't taken any of it in, which was true really. I said I was impressed by her French and she said she'd just done a crash course, she'd always regretted not going on with it at school.'

'I see.' Mungo looked at him thoughtfully. 'How odd. Did you – did you mention it to Harriet?'

'No, Cress asked me not to. She said it was a bit of a sore subject, Harriet had always had trouble with the language and she'd cracked it so easily.'

'Oliver, did you know she could speak perfect French?'

'Not really. It wasn't the sort of thing we discussed,' said Oliver blearily.

'Oh well. You must have got things muddled, Mungo. Must have had dinner with her before she did the course.'

'Rufus, we had dinner with her about a month ago.'

'Well, she was obviously fooling around. I can't think it's very important.'

'No. No, of course not. Tilly, do you know anything surprising about Cressida?'

'I don't know her well enough to be surprised by her. If you see what I mean,' said Tilly. 'I've only met her about three times. Twice in London and once in New York.'

'Oh yes, last Christmas? When she was staying with Oliver and we all had dinner?'

'Yeah. The only thing that ever surprised me was how different she was from Harriet. Not to look at so much, there was some kind of family look, but their personalities. It was hard to believe they were sisters. Harry's so positive and independent and ambitious, and Cressida's so – gentle and feminine and all that stuff.'

'Everyone said that. Says that,' Rufus corrected himself. 'We mustn't start talking in the past. I'm sure she'll be back. Soon.'

'Yeah,' said Mungo. 'Of course she will.'

'Oh yes, and there was something else,' said Tilly, 'something really surprising. I only learnt today. Sir Merlin told me. Did you know, I suppose you did, that she was really good at poker?'

'Poker! Cressida! Oh that's ridiculous,' said Mungo. 'I tried to teach her once. She gives everything away all the time, can't remember anything, doesn't concentrate –'

'Merlin said she was great. That she's planning to surprise you.'

'Well she certainly will,' said Mungo. 'I'll believe it when I –'

Oliver suddenly stood up. 'Oh God,' he said, 'going to throw up,' and he rushed into the bathroom. They waited for a long time; in the end Tilly stood up and went in after him. He was sitting on the lavatory, his head in his hands. She sat on the edge of the bath, and stroked his hair gently.

'Oh Til,' he said, 'oh Tilly, what a frightful bloody mess.'

He looked up at her and his eyes were red; a tear rolled down one cheek. She reached out and stroked it away.

'Oliver, I'm not going to say anything stupid, like you mustn't worry. But you have to hang on in there. She'll be all right. I know she will.'

He shook his head, took both her hands, clung onto them. His eyes as he looked at her were tortured, agonized.

'No. No, I don't think she will be. And even if – oh God, Tilly, this is so terrible. So much more terrible than you can imagine even. I –'

He stopped, bit his lip. Tilly looked at him, waited.

'Yes? You what, Oliver?'

'Oh – nothing. Shit, I'm going to be sick again.'

Tilly stayed with him, held his head, fetched him some water. He sat down on the bath beside her, put his arm round her. 'You're a great girl, Tilly,' he said, 'the best. Should be marrying you really. Only Rufus wouldn't like it.'

'Not too much,' said Tilly lightly. 'And anyway, it would be a terrible idea.'

'Well, thanks. You really know how to make a man feel better.'

'You know what I mean.'

'Yes, I suppose I do. I bet we'd have a good time in bed though.' He smiled at her, distracted just momentarily from his misery.

'Maybe. Oliver –' Perhaps this wasn't the time to mention this morning, but Tilly believed in directness, in getting things said. 'Oliver, Rufus phoned me in Paris this morning. He said you were terribly upset, that – that you felt you couldn't go through with the wedding. You can tell me to take a running jump if you like, but – well, what was that about? I mean is there some kind of connection, do you think? I'm sorry, Oliver, if I shouldn't have mentioned it, but – well, what did you –'

Oliver stared at her; he looked first startled, then wary. 'Oh,' he said quickly, 'I didn't mean anything. Not really. Just nerves, wedding-day nerves. I'm sure lots of bridegrooms say things like that.'

'Yeah,' said Tilly. 'Yeah, I'm sure they do.' But most bridegrooms don't take an overdose, she thought, don't cry for help that loudly. Well, he clearly wasn't going to tell her. There was a silence. 'It's terribly hot in here,' she said. 'Why don't we go for a walk or something? Just you and me, Oliver?'

'No,' said Oliver, 'I don't think so. Nice idea, Til, but I think I ought to stay by the phone.'

There was a knock on the door. It was Mungo. 'OK, Oliver?'

'He's fine. I was just trying to persuade him to come for a walk with me, but he says he ought to stay by the phone.'

'You can take my mobile,' said Mungo. 'I think it's a really good idea. You have a chat with Tilly, and we'll ring you if there's any news at all. Anyway, you don't have to go far.'

He was clearly desperate for a break, Tilly thought. She stood up, held out her hand to Oliver.

'Come on. I'm not used to being turned down. I might get difficult.'

'God forbid,' said Oliver, and for the first time he smiled. 'OK. We'll go. Thanks, Tilly. Thanks, Mungo. For everything. You've been one hell of a best man, you know that? You too, Rufus.' He smiled at them all weakly, and followed Tilly out of the room.

As they walked out of the front door of the hotel, a Jaguar pulled into the drive.

'Christ,' said Oliver, 'it's James Forrest. I wonder if there's any news.'

'Oh God,' said Tilly. She stood quite still, staring at the car, at the shadowy figure inside it. Her heart was thudding so hard she felt it might break right through her ribs; she felt sick and very hot, and at the same time oddly clammy, as if she might faint. It had happened, finally: she was going to come face to face with this man who had wrecked her mother's life, as good as murdered her baby, greatly damaged her physical and mental health, and deprived Tilly herself of a twin sister – and had refused to make any recompense for any of it. God, how was she going to deal with it, what was she going to say?

And then he got out of the car, James Forrest, and walked towards them slowly, and she could see he recognized her, knew who she was, and was as totally thrown, as horrified as she. But any anxieties about what she might say or do were swept away as Tilly stared into his face. At a set of features so familiar to her she could scarcely believe she was looking at them on a different person, at a head of thick wavy hair that despite being more grey than fair was instantly recognizable, at a way of moving – slowly, almost carefully – that was one she knew, had studied tenderly, lovingly, at a body that was tall, narrow-hipped (despite a burgeoning paunch), but with surprisingly broad shoulders. Only the eyes were different, blue not brown, but otherwise, God, God Almighty, how could anyone not see it, the almost astonishing resemblance? Presumably it had always been there, developing so slowly no one had taken it in – and as she stood there, staring, drinking him in, her enemy, learning who he really was, she knew with a rush of sadness and something close to rage that even setting aside all her other reasons she could never ever marry Rufus now.

Chapter 12

Susie 2:30pm

Susie decided not to say anything to Alistair that day, about her breast, her conversation with Mr Hobson: there was enough drama, enough crisis going on. There would be plenty of time tomorrow. In any case she didn't know quite what she was going to say, not until she had spoken to James. But she longed to talk to James, more than she ever had in her life, to lay her fear and her misery on him, to ask his advice, to draw on his strength. Until she had done that, she would wait, head in sand.

Anyway, Alistair had always hated scenes, emotion, conflict. It was one of the reasons Susie had married him. Partly because she hated them too, partly because she knew he would never become overanalytical about their marriage. A marriage to someone she didn't love Susie could handle (especially when the someone was charming, rich, civilized and clever). Having that marriage and its foundations examined, queried, fretted over, she could not.

Alistair had left that afternoon, just after two. 'Darling, of course you must go,' Susie said. 'No earthly point in you being here in the middle of this nightmare, there's absolutely nothing you can do, and you'll be much much happier back at your desk.'

'Well, that's certainly true. I must say this has revised my view that nothing could be worse than a wedding. There not being a wedding. Where do you think the silly girl's gone?'

'God knows,' said Susie with a sigh. 'I just hope she's all right. One hears such awful things and Cressida is so trusting and sweet. I fear for her, I really do.'

'I think she's well able to take care of herself actually,' said Alistair.

'That sounds interesting. Why do you think that?'

'Oh – nothing really.'

'Alistair! You can't do this to me. What is it?'

'Well – I've never told you this. Didn't seem very important. But I was once dancing with her, you remember, that terrible New Year thing we were all at, at Hurlingham, and she came on very strong at me. Tried to dance me out of the ballroom.'

'Alistair! You must have been drunk.'

'Susie, you know I never get drunk.' That was true; he didn't. 'She was, though. Extremely.'

'And?'

'And I just gently disentangled myself. Took her back to the table.'

'Was she upset?'

'No,' said Alistair briefly. 'She was furious.'

Susie saw him out to his car. 'I expect I'll be up later, but it may not be till tomorrow. Would that be all right?'

'Yes of course. As long as you keep the children down here. I really don't want to have to worry about Annabel.'

'You don't have to worry about Annabel, I promise,' said Susie, kissing him. 'Anyway, she's still hoping to make an impression on Mungo Buchan. So she'll be more than happy to stay.'

'I hope she's not successful,' said Alistair, plainly alarmed at the prospect. 'That boy is serious trouble.'

'He isn't actually, but you don't have to worry. There's no danger of him taking any notice of Annabel. I happen to know he has a perfectly lovely girlfriend somewhere who is fortunate enough not to have been asked to this nightmare, and he can't wait to get back to her. So Rufus tells me anyway. Annabel may seem very lovely to you and me, but to Mungo she's a very immature, slightly overweight schoolgirl. Incidentally you didn't really tell her you'd buy her a car as soon as she passed her test, did you?'

'No, of course not. I wouldn't unleash that child out on the roads with a shopping trolley.'

'I thought not. Only she implied it was on the delivery truck now, just round the corner from the house, unless I was evil enough to send it away. Anyway, you get back up to London, and don't worry about anything here. And I do assure you, your family is safe from the Buchans, my darling.'

'Even my wife?'

'Alistair! Have you not studied the lovely Sasha? Sex on legs, and Theo is mad about her. And they've been married less than a year.'

'She seems very stupid,' said Alistair cheerfully, throwing his leather Gladstone into the boot of the Jaguar. 'I don't give it more than another year. At the most.'

'I fear you may be right. It would be so nice to see Theo properly settled. These bimbos are all very well, but he needs something a bit more – substantial.'

'Sasha seems quite substantial to me. Especially in the pectoral area.'

'You know I don't mean physically. I just wish he could find another Deirdre. The one real love of his life.'

'Only because she died.'

'Alistair!'

'I'm sorry, darling, but it's true. I can't help my incisive legal mind. If Deirdre had lived, Theo would have been fooling around within the year. You know he would.'

'Well – I *don't* know actually. I think I take a slightly more benign view of Theo than you do. Anyway, there's nothing we can do to help him, I'm afraid.'

'No, he's beyond help,' said Alistair. 'Well, my darling, I'm off. How will you get back to London?'

'In Rufus's car.'

'Oh yes of course. What's the superstar girlfriend like? Wish I hadn't missed her.'

'Glorious.'

'Well I know that. I've seen her pictures.'

'No, but she's intelligent and funny too. I really liked her.'

'Do you think they'll get married?'

'Oh no,' said Susie coolly, opening the car door for him. 'Definitely not. They couldn't.'

'Why not?'

'Oh – it just wouldn't work.'

'Pity. Bit of exotica in the family might have been nice. Bye, darling.'

'Bye, Alistair.'

He kissed her fondly, patted her neat, well-exercised backside and climbed into the car. Susie waved him off, smiling, and then went back rather wearily into the house. She was stunned by the swift, almost cataclysmic change the news from Mr Hobson had wrought in her feelings about everything. Including Alistair, including her marriage. Until today, she had been very clear about it all. Alistair was a dear, sweet man, whom she was extremely fond of and with whom she got along extremely well. As a marriage it had seemed very near perfect. She had always wondered why people got so worked up about being in love with the person they married. Alistair had the occasional affair – he was probably off to see his latest girlfriend now, a little bonus of time Cressida had provided him with, so some good had come of this fiasco – and she had Jamie and no harm had been done to anyone. (Not, she was fairly sure, that Alistair knew about Jamie, and certainly, most certainly, not about Rufus.) It had all worked perfectly, and she had known as surely as she had known her own name that it was an infinitely more practical arrangement than the other way, endless misery and tears and divorce. She and Alistair would no more have thought of getting divorced than – Susie struggled for something sufficiently unlikely – than moving to the country. They would agree – had they ever discussed it, which they had not – that divorce would be disagreeable, disruptive and extremely expensive. Marriage was a business arrange-ment, and as long as both parties adhered to the original principles, the business thrived. The French knew that; French marriages had always been based on the principle of convenience.

But now, today, she felt completely differently. She needed Jamie, because she loved him, she needed to be with him, she needed them to be a couple, a strong united force, she needed his support, his overt support, not the rather vague intangible awareness of it buried deep within herself and her life. She needed to wake up with him and to go to sleep with him, she needed to have a home with him, to be recognized as his wife, as the woman he loved. It was the only way she could survive, survive the pain and the fear and the prospect of the awful, final separation. The children might be upset, Maggie might be deeply wounded, but they would survive. They were strong, they were whole, healthy people who were not going to die. If they didn't like it, she thought, then that was absolutely their problem. She did not, could not care. The time had come for selfishness. She wanted to be with the person she loved.

She wondered suddenly if that might have been why Cressida had run away: thinking that she didn't love Oliver enough, or that he didn't love her. I should have made an effort to spend some time with her, she thought to herself, over the past few weeks, maybe she needed a confidante, some reassurance, she was such a romantic, naive little thing. She and Cressida had always been able to talk, and enjoyed one another's company, and Maggie was so neurotic and hopeless, no use at all in such a situation.

Then she remembered what Alistair had said about Cressida making a pass at him at the dance, and she reflected that perhaps Cressida was not quite so romantic and naive after all . . .

'Susie dear,' said Janet, as she went into the kitchen. 'That was Janine on the phone. She said could you perhaps go over there, take over for a bit, she's absolutely exhausted, and Jamie's disappeared somewhere. I must say that's a bit bad of him, but –'

'He's probably gone to see the police or something,' said Susie. 'Anyway, if I was Jamie today I think I'd have disappeared by now. Yes, of course I'll go over.' God, that was all she needed, feeling as she did, having to comfort and cheer Maggie. 'Is Janine still on the phone?'

'Yes.'

'Janine, hi. How are things?'

'Not fun,' said Janine. 'Jamie has been trying to persuade Maggie to take something, just to calm her down, but she won't. She veers between hysteria and terrible deadly silence. I'm running out of smoke, I'm afraid.'

'Steam, darling, steam,' said Susie. 'All right, I'll come over. You've earned a break. I'll have to borrow a car.'

'I'll come with you.' Harriet's voice was behind her. 'I've got my car here.'

'Oh – all right, darling. Thank you. The cavalry's on its way, Janine.'

* * *

Harriet looked rotten, Susie thought. Well, it was hardly surprising. She'd taken a great deal today. Poor little thing. She was so fond of Cressida. Always been the big sister, looked after her, protected her.

'You all right to drive, poppet?' she asked as Harriet swung her Peugeot 205 away from the Beaumonts' house.

'Yes, I think so,' said Harriet. 'What a bitch of a day.'

She braked suddenly, switched off the engine and burst into tears. It was extraordinarily out of character; she never cried.

'Oh, sweetie,' said Susie, putting her arm round her. 'Darling Harriet, you cry. You need that. You must feel so terrible.'

'I do,' said Harriet. 'Absolutely terrible.'

'It's so – harsh somehow. So sudden. And Cressida of all people. So well behaved, so – perfect. Everyone loving her, wanting her to be happy.'

'That's Cressida,' said Harriet. 'Well behaved. Perfect. Everyone loving her.' Her voice sounded dead, almost bitter. Susie looked at her sharply.

'Sorry,' said Harriet, lightening her voice with a clear effort. 'I'm so sorry. I'm upset, Susie, I didn't mean anything.'

'You sounded as if you did.'

'No, honestly. It's – well – I just don't know what to do.'

'Of course you don't, darling. None of us do.'

'No, but – ' She slumped back in her seat and looked at Susie. Her eyes were very dark, very shadowed.

'Harriet, has something happened? Something new? That you haven't told us.'

'Oh – well, yes and no,' said Harriet with a sigh.

'Want to tell me about it? I promise not to pass it on,' she added, 'I'm very good at keeping secrets.'

'Are you?' Harriet looked at her, seemed to be trying to decide something. 'Yes, I expect you are.'

If only you knew, thought Susie, and thank God you don't.

'Tell me,' she said, 'I might be able to help.'

'I don't think so,' said Harriet, bleakly. 'Not unless you could give me a couple of million pounds.'

'Ah,' said Susie. 'Possibly not. It's the business, is it?'

'Yup,' said Harriet briefly. She sighed. 'I've got myself into the most filthy mess, Susie. Mostly through my own arrogance. Wouldn't listen, wouldn't take advice. And now – oh Susie, you can't begin to imagine.'

And Susie sat there, listening sadly, sorrowfully, to the quintessential nineties story, of overexpansion, high interest rates, lower profits. Harriet had overexpanded, mostly in France: her little shop in Passy making a fortune, she had bought the right to a lease on another – 'the most beautiful shop, in the rue du Bac, right by the Conran shop it was, and I looked at it and it was perfect. Loads of people pouring past every day, the very chic-est area, and terribly expensive. But I could just see it, my clothes in it, my name over the door, the interior all done out in my lovely silver and white, and I wanted it. I had to have it.'

'Well, it doesn't sound too silly, so far,' said Susie gently. 'Good sites are what good business is all about.'

'Yes and no,' said Harriet, blowing her nose. 'I mean you're right, but that wasn't actually what it was about. Not a shop, not a site at all, Susie, it was about my bloody fucking ego – sorry –'

'That's all right, darling.'

'I have to be so important, you know, have to have everyone looking at me. I mean what was wrong with the dear little shop in Passy? Nothing, nothing at all, except it wasn't big-time stuff. And I wanted to be big-time. To get my name on the fashion pages, be one of the in-crowd. I mean what a pathetic, pitiful ambition. God, I'm ashamed of myself. And it was so much money, that lease. You know how it works in Paris, you buy the right to rent a place. Two million francs it cost me, only it wasn't me, it was – oh shit, Susie, I'm so ashamed of myself.'

'Who was it?' asked Susie quietly.

'It was Janine. Darling Janine, who's been there for me all my life. She insisted I took it, said she wanted to help. It's a lot of money, you know, it's –'

'Yes, I know, it's two hundred thousand pounds, give or take a bit. Well I'm sure she could afford it if she offered it.'

'No she couldn't. Not easily, anyway, not so it didn't matter if she lost it. I mean of course it was a loan, and I'm paying her interest, well I was, but lower than the bank would take. But it's gone, Susie, all of it. The shop never even broke even, and then I remortgaged the shop in Covent Garden, just to keep it open, and you know how big the turnover on that one is, and even that didn't support the loan.

I really, really should have listened to Rufus, he said right from the beginning –'

'Rufus?' said Sue sharply. 'What does Rufus have to do with it?'

'He told me I should get a proper business adviser, rather than just Johno –'

'Who's Johno?'

'He's my accountant. Has been right from the beginning. And he's sweet and lovely and clever, but he just isn't up to all this stuff. Rufus even had someone in mind for me, someone he knows. But no, I had to know best, had to be able to manage. I wasn't satisfied with being a good designer, I had to be a brilliant businesswoman as well, Jean Muir and Anita Roddick rolled into one. Someone actually wrote that about me in an article a few months ago, well, not quite that, but said I had the makings of one. No doubt there'll be plenty now saying that I haven't.'

'Harriet darling,' said Susie, 'you really mustn't be quite so hard on yourself. You've done so well, and everyone makes mistakes. And I can't believe that just a little bit of over-extending could really bring your whole business down. I mean you have lots of shops, surely –'

'Susie, don't. Yes, there are other shops, other Harry's. But none of them are actually making real money any more. Oh, the turnover's fine, but they mostly just about break even. And this is pack-of-cards stuff. It's all going to come tumbling down very very fast. I certainly can't sustain this debt. And I'm going to look such a fool, and I have to get rid of all those lovely girls. You know Ellie, in Covent Garden, she's worked for three weeks now without money, because she believed in me, and now what do I say to her? Sorry Ellie, sweet of you. Here's your reward, one P45 and the directions to the DHSS. But it's Janine, that is absolutely the worst thing, I mean she's quite an old lady now, she's going to need that money, and – oh Susie, what am I going to do?'

'Well,' said Susie briskly. 'I don't know exactly, but sitting and sobbing and berating yourself certainly isn't going to help anyone, least of all Janine. Listen, Harriet, Janine is a very wise, very worldly woman. I can't believe she would have lent you that sort of money if she hadn't been ready to risk losing it. I'm amazed she's got it, but that's beside the point. And I'm also sure she didn't just give it to you without a second thought, I mean presumably she saw some kind of business plan –'

'Well – yes she did. But it was a bit amateurish and optimistic. I –

well, I was so sure, so confident. I just made certain it was all presented in a very positive way. Rounded figures up, that sort of thing. Not much, don't look at me like that, only a few thousand here and there. But enough to be just that bit more persuasive. And then I threw my flat into the ring. As surety.'

'Well then,' said Susie, surprised to find how relieved she was, 'that's all right. You can still sell it. I don't see what you're so upset about. Of course it will be sad, it's a lovely flat, but –'

'Susie, it's worthless. In cash terms. You see before you an outstanding example of negative equity. I bought my flat at the height of the boom, knew it was desperately overpriced, but there I was, flying along, got a ninety-five per cent mortgage. It's worth about – oh, I don't know, sixty per cent of what it was.'

'Ah,' said Susie quietly. 'Ah, I see.'

'So – Harry's goes into liquidation. Tomorrow, actually. I was blocking it out of my brain, not thinking about it until after the wedding. And now there's no wedding.'

'Can't you find someone to buy the business?'

'It isn't easy. Have you noticed how many shops are empty in so many high streets at the moment? Half South Molton Street even is for sale. But yes, I have tried. I've done so many presentations, I go into my spiel in my sleep. Twice I thought I'd done it, been saved, and then at the last moment they pulled the plug on me. Trotting out the usual platitudes about return on equity, too much long-term investment needed.'

'How – how much are you prepared to give away?' said Susie, trying to sound as tactful as possible.

'A lot,' said Harriet. 'I know what you're saying, but honestly, Susie, I'd lost most of my pride. At first of course I wanted to keep control, have it all my way, but I'd long since stopped that. My only condition in the end was the final word on design, when my name was literally on the line. Which is fair enough. I mean I wasn't going to have some purple lurex number with "Harry's" stitched into it. And I'd almost got to the point where I'd have given way on that. But it still wasn't working. There was just one last hope, a guy called Cotton. You may have heard of Cotton Fields? Nice clothes. Cheap and cheerful, but nice.'

'Yes of course,' said Susie. 'Annabel buys quite a lot of them.'

'Well, there you are. I'd have gone in with him quite happily. He's

American. His head office is in New York. Anyway, I really thought he was going to make me an offer – not huge, but enough. I'd been really, really honest with him, told him all the problems, but he still wanted to buy. I thought. We were down to the small print. And then he backed off. Much as the others did. Yesterday, actually. He sent me a fax saying he wasn't interested after all, and when I tried to ring him, to talk about it, right up to about midnight, his secretary just kept telling me he was in meetings.'

'Well,' said Susie, 'that does sound strange. But maybe if he was reading the small print, rather than just writing it –'

'Yes,' said Harriet. 'I know. Anyway, I can't do anything about it. That's it. Finito.' She smiled a slightly wobbly smile at Susie. 'I'm so sorry, Susie. To burden you with this. But you did ask –'

'I know, darling. And I'm glad you did. I wish to God I could help. But the only person I know with that sort of money is Theo. I suppose you couldn't –'

'No,' said Harriet quickly. 'No I couldn't. Not possibly.'

'He's very fond of you. I'm sure he'd like to help.'

'Well – I just can't. It's too – close to home. I might ask him for Janine's money, if I absolutely had to, but nothing else.'

'Oh well. That's your decision. It's nothing to do with me. Now look, I'll have a think about all this, and if you'll let me, maybe ask Alistair if he knows anyone who might be able to help. He really does know every investor in town.'

'Susie, it's sweet of you, but I honestly do think I've turned over every possible stone –'

'I bet you haven't,' said Susie, 'and it's surely worth giving it just another couple of days. Now look, we really have to get over to your mother and relieve poor Janine. She's at the end of her tether. Would you like me to drive?'

'No, I'm fine,' said Harriet. 'And thank you for listening.'

There were an awful lot of tethers being stretched that day, thought Susie, as she lay back slightly wearily in her seat. Her own felt pretty taut. Now that she knew there was a reason for her constant tiredness, she felt suddenly, sharply worse. While she had first assumed and then hoped she was simply feeling her age, and fighting it with her usual blithe determination, it had seemed merely a nuisance, a slight brake on her activities. Since it had become something different, a painful, heavy reality, she was finding it already harder to handle; her head, she acknowledged, actually ached, and so did the small of her back, and what she wanted more than anything was to close her eyes, to shut out the dazzling flashing light of the afternoon, to give in, just for a moment, to rest.

'Go on, Susie,' came Harriet's voice, half amused, half gentle. 'Take a nap. You've earned it.'

'I can't stand people who take naps,' said Susie.

'Nor can I. But you do look absolutely rotten.'

'Thanks a lot.'

'Sorry.'

'That's OK,' said Susie, smiling at her. 'I know you meant it kindly. But I'd rather chat.' She was intrigued still by Harriet's tone when she'd said 'Everyone loves Cressida'; she was hoping to lead her back to that.

'How did you like Tilly?' said Harriet.

'I loved Tilly.'

'So does Rufus.'

'So I understand.'

'You know he wants to marry her?'

'Yes, I do.'

'And?'

'And I think that's – fine. If it happens.'

'But you don't think it will?' Harriet's voice was gently insistent.

'Harriet, I don't know. Let's say their lives are very different. I don't want Rufus hurt.'

'Well,' said Harriet. 'I know. I know what you're saying. And I don't want him hurt either. He's just one of the loveliest people I know.'

'I think so too,' said Susie, smiling at her again. 'But then I would.'

And then she did close her eyes, remembering briefly, fiercely, how nearly Rufus had not been born at all.

They had agreed she should have an abortion. It was the only thing they could possibly do. There was no way Susie could bear James's child –

and she knew it was his child, Alistair had been away most of the month and certainly at the time of conception, and her hormones ran with clocklike regularity – Alistair would quite possibly work it out, Maggie would come to hear of it, there would be at best dreadful recriminations, anger, ugliness, at worst divorce. They both had children already: Harriet was two, Lucy one. It was unthinkable they should put all that at risk.

James had arranged the whole thing, had booked her into a nursing home somewhere near Luton.

'Luton, Jamie, why Luton? It's the most terrible place,' Susie said, when he told her. She was hanging on, with great difficulty, to her sense of humour.

'I thought you were unlikely to know anyone there,' he said rather helplessly. 'You can't go very far out of London, and central London would be dangerous. I'm sorry. Anyway, what does it matter?'

'It doesn't,' she said, trying to smile. 'Of course it doesn't. I'll go even to Luton for you, Jamie, don't worry.'

'How do you feel?'

'I feel fine,' she said. 'Pregnancy suits me. I felt wonderful with Lucy.'

'You would,' he said morosely, 'you bloody well would feel wonderful. Maggie was sick every single day.'

'Yes, well, I think we'd best not talk about Maggie. Under the circumstances.'

'Sorry.'

'I'd better go now,' she said, looking at her watch. 'Bathtime beckons. Nanny's night off.'

'Good luck, darling. I love you.'

'I love you too, Jamie.'

She couldn't think how she could possibly still love him. After all he had done to her. But she did. When they had met for the first time after their respective weddings, innocently, at a drinks party, she had felt quite faint with longing for him. And hatred. He had smiled at her across the room, come over to her, and she had stood there, just staring at him, refusing even to speak.

'You look lovely,' he said, 'quite lovely.'

She was silent. 'I miss you,' he said, 'I really miss you.'

Susie raised her eyebrows, took another sip of champagne.

'How is Alistair?'

'He's very well. As you see.'

'Doing well?'

'Of course.'

'Good. Aren't you going to ask if I'm doing well?'

'No,' she said, and there was such suppressed fury in her voice that he looked round nervously, fearing Maggie, Alistair – anyone could have heard. 'No I'm not. Of course you're doing well. You would be, wouldn't you? You married to do well.'

'Susie, don't –'

'Oh fuck off,' she said quietly and turned away, went to join Alistair. She slipped her arm through his, smiled up at him, looked over her shoulder at James standing there, alone, and she wanted him so much, loved him so desperately she could scarcely believe she could feel it at the same time as the hatred.

The next day he phoned her. 'I just wanted to say I was sorry.'

'For what, James? For not marrying me? For marrying Maggie? For being such a bastard. Could you expand a little, please?'

'All of those things,' he said. 'But really for upsetting you yesterday.'

'Yes, well. Don't do it again.' But she could hear her voice lighten, ease, hating it for doing so. 'Goodbye, James.'

Three months later, they met again. At a charity ball. Fate in the form of Janet Beaumont had put them at the same table. Susie was pregnant.

'I'm pregnant,' she said to James.

'Congratulations. Alistair must be very pleased.'

'Yes he is. I hear you have a daughter.'

'Yes indeed. Sweet little thing. Would you like to dance?'

'No. No thank you.'

But later Alistair was dancing with someone else and she was alone at the table; he came over. 'Come along, one dance won't hurt you.'

But it did.

She stood in his arms, felt him, smelt him, wanted him.

'You don't feel very pregnant,' he said.

'Well I'm not very pregnant. Only five months.'

'You don't look more than five days.'

'Yes, well, I've been working at it.'

'You would,' he said.

Maggie thought she was lovely, James said; wanted to ask her to dinner.

'You mustn't let her.'

'How can I stop her?'

'We won't come.'

'Darling, I see we've been invited to the Forrests' for New Year's Eve. Might be fun. I like James.'

'Really?'

'Yes, don't you?'

'No, not much.'

'Well, I'd like to go. The Beaumonts will be there, and he was saying he had a big land-law case coming up, looking for advice. It's a field that interests me.'

'Alistair, do we have to? I feel so enormous and I'd rather stay at home.'

'I'd rather you didn't.'

When it came to his career Alistair was ruthless. Like James, she thought to herself.

She arrived at the party feeling odd. She was eight months pregnant, she was tired, she was edgy. She found it hard to sparkle.

Halfway through the evening she started having contractions. Sure they were nothing, she found a room and lay down on the floor, doing her relaxing exercises. The pain got worse.

The room happened to be James's study; he came in and found her there.

'What on earth are you doing?'

'Having a baby,' said Susie through gritted teeth.

He was concerned, professional, soothing. He felt her tummy, listened to the baby's heartbeat, timed a couple of contractions and phoned the local hospital. He drove her over himself, relaxed, cheerful, cheering. She was shivery, said she wanted to push; he told her to pant and to hang on. Alistair sat in the back of the car, panicking.

At the hospital James found a wheelchair, pushed her through reception towards the labour ward himself. 'She's in transition,' he said calmly to the nurse. 'Get a delivery room ready. The baby's premature.' Alistair had disappeared.

Through her pain, her fear, her confusion, he was there: level, steady, reassuring.

'You'll be fine,' he kept saying, 'and the baby will be fine. Just hang on. Hang on to me. Hold my hand.'

They reached the delivery room; three nurses were ready, eager to serve the great god, the consultant.

James helped them lift her onto the bed. He bent over her, smiled into her eyes. 'Yell if you want to,' he said, 'no one will mind.'

'No,' said Susie, clenching her fists. 'I don't approve of making a fuss. Just don't go away, that's all.'

'I won't,' he said, smiling down at her again, 'I won't,' and in spite of everything she saw the humour in the situation, smiled back.

And so it was that when Susie Headleigh Drayton gave birth to her first baby, James Forrest was there with her.

After that it was hopeless really. He saw her through the two desperate days after the birth when the tiny four-pound Lucy struggled to survive. He wheeled her down himself to the prem unit when the baby was out of danger, so that she might sit with her. He dried her eyes when she wept with third-day blues, and he laughed at her discomfiture when the milk arrived and leaked all over her nightie.

'Don't laugh,' she said crossly. 'It's not very pretty.'

'It's quite nice, Susie, to see you out of control just for once, even if only of your boobs.'

She scowled at him, then smiled.

'I love you,' he said gently and bent and kissed her forehead.

Alistair had gone back to London.

Two months later they were lunching regularly, a month after that they were in bed. It was wonderful. Susie thought she had never been so happy.

'A lovely baby, a sweet husband and you,' she said one afternoon after some particularly good sex. 'What more could I ask?'

James turned away from her.

'What's the matter?'

'That wasn't the most tactful thing you could have said. At such a time.'

'Jamie,' said Susie, propping herself up on her elbow, fixing her dark eyes on him, 'Jamie, I really don't think you have any right to complain about my being tactless. You've got a pretty good deal, it seems to me. Don't knock it.'

'I can't help it,' he said, 'You're so fucking – pragmatic.'

'And I can't help that,' she said, bending over, kissing his shoulder, 'it's what I'm all about, pragmatisim. Be grateful. I might just be pragmatic, without the fucking.'

And then she got pregnant. With James's baby. While Alistair had been away in the north of England.

'I don't see how it could have happened,' he said fretfully. 'You're on the pill –'

'Yes, I know, James, but I had a tummy upset that week. Quite a bad one. It must have cancelled out the pill or whatever –'

'You should have mentioned it.'

'Oh don't be ridiculous.'

'I'm not being ridiculous. What are we going to do?'

'I don't know, Jamie. You tell me.'

She drove herself to the nursing home; she had insisted on it.

'I want to be by myself, completely by myself. I'll be fine by tomorrow.'

'What have you told Alistair?'

'That I'm staying with Mummy.'

'And what have you told Mummy?'

'That I'm going to a health farm for forty-eight hours, and I don't want Alistair to know. He genuinely doesn't approve of them. Luckily.'

'And does Mummy believe you?'

'Mummy's like me. She's a pragmatist. Anyway, she's fielding phone calls. Don't worry, Jamie, it'll all be fine.'

The nursing home was a large mock-tudor house just outside Luton. The staff were polite, efficient, detached.

'Here's your room, Mrs – Henderson. Perhaps you'll get undressed for me, and then Doctor will come and examine you.'

Susie undressed, got into bed. A nurse shaved her pudenda, gave her an enema. It was horrible. She felt very odd, light-headed, slightly sick.

Doctor was an iron-grey man with a sickly manner.

'Mrs Henderson. Good morning. What a cold one. I'm Brian Miller. Now if I can just –'

He smiled rather condescendingly at her when he had finished. 'Yes. About eleven weeks. Just in time. Have you had anything by mouth this morning?'

Susie shook her head.

'Good. All over by lunchtime then. Your doctor is quite right, much too soon for you to be having another baby, you're still not fully recovered from the last one. Now you won't know anything about it, of course, you'll need a very light anaesthetic and you'll be in theatre for about twenty minutes. A simple D and C. You know what that is?'

'No,' said Susie. She did, but for some reason she wanted to hear it.

'Dilatation and curettage.' He looked a little impatient.

'I understand dilatation, but what's curettage?'

'Well – the strict definition is a scraping. To remove tissue. And – er – any growths.'

'Oh,' said Susie. She pulled the sheet up higher over her body. 'Yes I see.'

'Right then.' He picked up his notes. 'Any more questions?'

'No. No, I don't think so.'

'Good. Well, I'll pop in and see you afterwards. When it's all over. Nurse will be in to give you your pre-med in a little while.'

Susie lay there, trying not to think. The phone by her bed rang.

'Darling? It's me.'

'Oh – Jamie. Hallo.'

'Are you all right?'

'Yes. Yes, I think so.'

'He's a very, very good chap, Miller. You really don't have to worry.'

'I don't?'

'No.'

'Good.'

'I love you, Susie. I'll ring you later.'

'All right, Jamie.'

She lay there and thought about her baby. Hers and James's baby. Conceived in a moment of such fierce, flying, tearing rapture there was a physical remembrance of it; her body stirred at it even now. And it was still there, the rapture. It had become something real, something living, had not just passed away into nothingness. She had it within her, she surrounded it; it was hers.

She thought of it, what it was to her in truth: not a cluster of cells, not even the strange primeval being she knew it to be, but an embodiment of happiness, of pleasure, of love.

The nurse came in. 'Right, Mrs Henderson, ready for your pre-med?'

'Oh – yes.' She put on the hospital gown, open at the back, the paper hat, surrendered her rings.

'Just pop onto your side for me then.'

Susie rolled obediently onto her side, felt the needle jab into her buttocks. The nurse dabbed at it with a swab, smiled at her distantly.

'We'll be back for you soon then. Have a little sleep, I would.'

No you wouldn't, you silly bitch, thought Susie, you wouldn't at all, you'd lie here, like I am, thinking of what you were doing, what you were allowing them to do. To dilate you, to open you up, and then to – what was the word he had used? – oh yes, scrape, scrape away this baby, this little living thing, that she knew, she knew although she had tried not to think about it, who already had a head, eyes, hands, feet. Christ, she must stop this, stop thinking of the sweet smiling blunt foetus-face that she had seen so many pictures of, stop thinking of what she was doing to it, killing it, dragging it from the snug, safe darkness of her womb into the light and then – what? What did they do, what did they do to these babies, these little tiny half-people, how did they get rid – No, Susie, don't, you mustn't, it's only a few cells, only a dot, don't think about it, don't, don't, don't, you have to go through with this, you have to.

The door opened. A porter came in with a trolley, the nurse helped her onto it. She felt dizzy, confused, far away from them. They began to wheel her down the corridor. She felt panicky suddenly, sick, frightened of what was going to happen.

She closed her eyes; the corridor spun. Oh God, this was horrible, horrible. 'I feel sick,' she said.

'Don't worry,' said the nurse. 'It'll pass in a moment.'

She was pushed into the anteroom of the theatre; Dr Miller was there.

'Ah, Mrs Henderson. All right?'

'No,' croaked Susie. Her lips were very dry, she was having trouble framing her words.

'You will be soon.' He smiled at her, patted her hand.

Yes, she thought, I will be. But *it* won't. My baby won't. It won't be a baby any more. It won't be anything.

'Right,' he said, 'right, Nurse. Let's get this good lady into the theatre, shall we?' He had his needle poised; he was smiling at her, his awful steely sickly smile. 'Now, when I've given you this injection, Mrs Henderson, I want you to count for me.' Susie nodded feebly. She would count, and the baby would be gone. One, two, three, bye-bye, baby. Oh God, it was horrible. Horrible. Why did she have to do this? Why had she ever agreed?

'Right.' He rubbed a swab over her hand. 'Ready? Now remember, count for me, one, two –'

'No!' she screamed, managed to find the strength to sit up, thrust his hand and the needle away. 'No, no, no. Don't do it. I don't want you to do it. Stop. I forbid it. Stop.'

'Now, Mrs Henderson. Don't be silly –' The nurse looked alarmed, tried to push her down again.

'Come along, Mrs Henderson. This isn't very sensible, is it? You wanted this, it's much for the best. Now let me –'

'No. I said no.' She was lying down now, hanging onto the sides of the trolley to try and stop the dizziness, but she was totally awake. 'Don't. Don't you dare. I shall sue if you do. I don't want you to. I forbid it. It's my body, my baby. You are not to. Take me back to my room, at once. At once.'

'Dr Miller, I think perhaps –' The nurse was looking uncomfortable. Miller looked at her, and Susie thought she had never seen such distaste, such cold fury on any face.

'Very well. Take her back. Get her out of here quickly. Mrs Henderson, I hope you realize you are still liable for the full fee. I would be grateful for your acknowledgment of that in writing, along with your cheque.'

'You'll have your fucking cheque,' said Susie politely. 'And your fucking acknowledgment. Get me a bowl, would you?' she added to the nurse. 'Quickly. I'm going to be sick.'

The nurse wasn't quick enough. With something very close to pleasure, Susie threw up all over Dr Miller's white theatre shoes.

'Susie! Susie, we're here.' Harriet patted her hand gently. Susie opened her eyes, smiled at her.

'Sorry. Didn't mean to go to sleep on you.'

'That's OK. You look better.'

'I feel better.' She did. Much better. And James was walking towards them. Susie's heart lifted, as it always had, always would, at the sight of him.

'Hallo, Jamie.'

'Hallo, you two. No, no news. I've been over to see the Bergins. Josh is very upset.'

'And Julia?'

'Well she's upset too, but she seems to be what she calls handling it. She says she's quite sure Cressida will be back, as soon as she has had a little – space, I think the word was.'

'Oh God,' said Harriet. She smiled at her father. 'She is something else, as they say. What about the bank manager, Daddy?'

'He still hasn't called.'

'How's Mummy?'

'Asleep finally. Janine as well.'

'I'll go and make us some tea,' said Harriet.

They looked fondly after her. 'She's a glorious girl,' said Susie.

'I know. I know she is.'

'I wish –' She looked at him and laughed. 'No I don't.'

'What?'

'I was going to say I wish Rufus wanted to marry her.'

'That would never do. One of my nightmares, actually.'

'Really? Do you know, it never occurred to me.'

'Yes, well,' he said, and his voice was heavy, almost bitter, 'bad things never do occur to you.'

And then fear and what she realized was anger hit her and her eyes filled with tears; the golden day, Jamie's face, blurred and she looked away.

He took her arm, gentle suddenly. 'What is it? Darling Susie, what is it? I'm sorry if all this has upset you.'

'No, Jamie, it's not this. Really. Can we – can we talk?'

'Yes of course. Let's go down to the bridge.'

They walked down slowly. Susie was silent for a while. Then she began to tell him. She didn't look at him, didn't touch him. When she had finished he sat down heavily on the seat, started stripping a large daisy of its petals, one by one.

'Is that my prognosis?'

'Don't be silly.'

There was a long silence; then he said, 'Have you told Alistair?'

'I haven't told anyone.'

'But you'll have to. Tomorrow.'

'Yes, I suppose so,' she said. 'I needed to tell you first.'

'Of course.'

He picked up one of her hands, turned it over, raised it to his lips. 'I'm so sorry,' he said, 'so terribly sorry.'

'I love you,' she said.

'I love you too.'

'Jamie –'

'Yes?'

'What is the prognosis?'

'Oh – I don't know. Not my field really.'

'Don't lie to me.'

'Sorry. Well, it's not great. But it does depend on what they find. It could be dealt with fairly swiftly or –'

'You mean a mastectomy?'

A long silence. Then, 'From what you've told me, possibly. And chemotherapy. But it might not come to that –'

'And it might be worse?'

'Susie, this is impossible. I haven't seen your X-rays, haven't talked to your consultant. Don't make me say things that may be wrong, irresponsible, please.'

'Sorry.'

She sat there, and looked down the years, the long, happy years, at closeness, sweetness, love, and wondered how she could have found them wanting. There had been shadows, to be sure, gentle difficulties, slight pain; they had quarrelled occasionally, longed for one another often, been forced to share one child across two sets of lives. But there had been so much good, so much joy; they had lain so often, shaken after love, smiling at one another, taking happiness for granted, pleasure as a right, and been careless of it all. And now they were to lose it, lose certainty, closeness, and she was to go alone and fearful into a new dark destiny.

'I shall need you now,' she said suddenly, before she had meant to, but the fear took her, chilled her. 'All the time, for as long as we can have. You won't leave me, will you, not any more, Jamie, you'll be there with me? I mean really with me, living with me? It's the only way I can bear it.'

She waited for him to answer and realized she had never known true fear before; she had experienced its lesser compatriots, panic, apprehension, even dread, but not this, this ugly, driving invasion of her body as well as her mind, and the fear itself frightened her.

She felt tears rising again, felt at the same time nausea, faintness; her mouth was dry, her throat closed with terror. She knew she could not have moved, could not have cried out even, no matter what might happen to her; and then he smiled at her, gently, tenderly, and as always her self-control, her courage came back to her, and she looked at him, at her love, and gripped his hand and clung to it, as she had when Lucy had been born, and said as she had then, 'Don't go away, will you? Whatever they say or do.' And he said, 'No, Susie, I won't go away. I'll stay with you now, for as long as you need me.'

And the fear receded quite quickly then, just as pain can sometimes do, leaving only a sweet weariness behind it, and she sat with her head on his shoulder, staring at the water, and trying not to wonder how short a time together they might actually have.

Chapter 13

Harriet 4:30pm

The cups of tea looked horrible when she poured them out. Dark, with a floating scum on them. Harriet stared at them, amazed as always by her inability to accomplish the simplest domestic task. It was a family joke that she couldn't even make a nice jug of water. Things burnt while she watched them, remained raw however long she consigned them to the oven; any bed she made was lumpy, anything she ironed looked creased. Her only near-culinary skill was mixing martinis, which she did superbly; Merlin Reid had been her tutor and Theodore Buchan was one of her most appreciative customers. He said not even at the Ritz in Paris, or the Polo Lounge at the Beverly Hills, had he experienced such martinis. 'Not tasted, Harriet, experienced. There is a great difference. It is a rare talent in a woman.'

Harriet told him cheerfully he was a sexist pig but she liked the appreciation nonetheless.

Having made the stuff, she couldn't even find Susie or her father: how irritating. They'd probably gone for a walk: they were good friends those two. Cressida had often hinted they were more than that, but then Cressida was like that, finding intrigue, scandal where there was none. It was wishful thinking, an attempt to make them all more glamorous and interesting. Like her absurd idea that their mother was in love with Theo. 'You can laugh,' she'd said to Harriet, the first time she'd propounded it, when she was about fifteen, 'but I know I'm right. And it's so embarrassing for poor Theo. I mean Mummy's lovely, but she's hardly – sexy, is she?'

'Honestly, Cressida,' Harriet had said, 'you read too many romantic novels.' And Cressida had shrugged and told her to watch her mother next time Theo came to the house. 'She blushes a lot and sort of looks at him under her eyelashes. It's so sad.'

Harriet watched in spite of herself and could see what Cressida meant. 'But he's such a terrible old flirt himself, Mummy's only responding, and she hasn't had much practice. Anyway she's only got eyes for Daddy, you know that.'

As she grew up, Harriet had become increasingly aware of an oddness in her parents' marriage. It was not so much that her father was so extremely good-looking still, and so easy and amusing, while her mother was (despite a sweetly pretty face) so overweight and clumsy and frumpily dressed. That happened in a lot of middle-aged marriages; in the end they levelled out again. It was more that her father, against all logic, tried so much harder than her mother: he paid her compliments, teased her, kissed her, always invited her opinions, asked for her company if he was going for a walk, a drive, a drink. And her mother was cool, almost indifferent, made no effort with her appearance, no attempt to respond to him.

'I really would rather not come,' she would say to many of his invitations, or 'I really don't have an opinion' to his promptings. She was pleasant, but treated him rather as if he was a brother she was not particularly fond of, and he continued to work away at her, meeting detachment with affection, dullness with sparkle, apathy with interest. He never criticized her, either openly or behind her back, never indicated for a moment that he might deserve better. His patience with her seemed infinite, his acceptance of her without limit. It was as if, Harriet thought, he had drawn up some kind of contract and these were the terms and he had accepted them without question.

She had always adored her father; the constant acceptance by everyone when they were small that Cressida was Daddy's girl hurt her every hour of every day. Sometimes, as she watched Cressida snuggled deep into his lap, her great blue eyes sleepily contented, she hated her so much she could easily have killed her, dragged her onto the floor and pulled off her hair ribbon and wound it round and round her neck until she choked, until those eyes bulged, those cherubic features turned blue. And then he would notice, and set Cressida gently down, tell her to go to Mummy, and hold out his arms to her, and say 'Come on, Harriet, grown-up girl's time now.' But although she would flash a triumphant look at Cressida as she scrambled up, and snuggle into his arms herself, she knew it wasn't really quite a victory, that he did it out of duty, out of a sense of rightness, that he had had to notice, to remember her, whereas Cressida seemed always there first, by right.

When she was older she felt in some way she had become the son he hadn't had; she walked with him, played tennis with him, sailed with him, discussed things with him, and that was wonderful, but it was still Cressida who charmed him and sparkled for him, flattered him, flirted with him. It was Cressida who went to official dinners with him or played hostess at home when Maggie had one of her many migraines, Cressida who jumped up and made him soup, a drink, a sandwich when he arrived at the Court House late on Friday nights, Cressida who ran up and down endlessly with trays on the rare occasions when he was ill. 'I honestly don't mind, Mummy,' she would say, 'you look tired, and I'm not. And he's such a bad-tempered old bugger when he's ill, and it just rolls off my back, and I know it upsets you.'

It was Harriet's observation that her father's bad temper had no effect on her mother either but it led to a quieter life not to argue with Cressida.

The roles intensified as they grew up and left home. 'Harriet has a career,' Cressida would say, smiling sweetly, self-deprecatingly, 'and I've got a job.' This was true, but it was certainly of her own making; she had, Harriet knew, a brain as sharp and as effective as her own. She had done modestly well in her A-levels (3 Cs) and could perfectly well have gone to university. But she had chosen to do a secretarial course and after a rather large number of run-of-the-mill jobs, had become secretary/receptionist to a large paediatric practice in Harley Street, where her charming manners, genuine fondness for children and sympathetic efficiency had made her (as more than one of them had remarked) as crucial to its success as any of the doctors themselves. The same qualities and the knowledge she had absorbed in her time there would of course equip her even more perfectly to be the wife of an upwardly mobile young medic.

She was jealous of Harriet's success, of course, but cheerfully, supportively so; and she was openly and intensely proud of her. 'She always had the brains,' she would say, 'and the drive and the energy. She's the new woman. Bit of an anachronism I am.' And she would smile at whoever was listening, and they would hasten to assure her that she was nothing of the sort, and if her audience included any of the older generation (particularly if it was male) they would frequently say something that implied it was she who had actually got it right and Harriet wrong.

Harriet could never quite remember when she decided she wanted to get into the fashion business, but she was certainly still quite small. She would wait for her mother's *Vogue* and *Harper's* to arrive each month (for a comparatively unfashionable woman, Maggie was an avid consumer of the glossy press) as eagerly as if they were a present for herself, and by the time she was eleven or twelve was making dresses for herself with astonishing skill. What was more, she made up her own patterns; she kept a store of old basic Simplicities (a dress, a skirt, a shirt) and worked on them, adding and subtracting with huge ingenuity. She raided her mother's wardrobe, the village drapery shop, jumble sales for fabric and old clothes; her greatest triumph was a party dress she made for Annabel Headleigh Drayton, aged three (when Harriet had been only fifteen herself), a gloriously simple Kate Greenaway creation, puff-sleeved and high-waisted, out of an old 1940s print dress she had found at a village sale. It had been a surprise Christmas present for Annabel, who loved it so much she wore it night and day for months. With a final touch of inspiration Harriet had used the leftover fabric to cover a pair of Annabel's dancing shoes.

Janine had been her great ally in those early days, not only having her to stay in Paris, walking her tirelessly round the shops (Harriet especially loved the stock shops on the long, dull-looking rue d'Alesia, where so many of the chic-est, most magical names, Dorothée Bis, Cacherel, Lapidus, sold their last-season's stock for a fraction of its original cost) and arranging for her to see the occasional couture show, but almost more importantly, taking an intense interest in what she was doing, happy to talk far into the night over the relative merits of Karl Lagerfeld and Vivienne Westwood, pure cotton as opposed to cotton polyester mix and the status of American couture vis-à-vis French and English. It was

Janine, not Maggie or James, who had encouraged Harriet to take art at A-level, Janine who had argued with them both to let her go to St Martin's to do a foundation course, Janine who had persuaded them (with still more difficulty) that she should be allowed to go and work as a stitcher at Jean Muir, rather than carry on with a more conventional education.

From there, working long, hard, badly paid hours, learning in a week what she knew college could not teach her in a month, possibly a year, studying not only technique but the necessity for a pursuit of perfection that was unarguably religious in its fervour, she found herself by a series of extraordinary accidents answering the phone to one of the great fashion editors of her day: Caroline Baker, ex-*Nova*, then working on *Cosmopolitan*. A dress Caroline had asked to borrow for a session had not turned up; Harriet was told to take it personally in a taxi to the studio. There, relieved of the dress and her responsibilities, she stood in the back of the studio unobserved watching entranced as Caroline selected, added to, subtracted from, built on a series of garments, with shirts, jackets, sweaters, shoes, scarves, jewellery, hats, hairstyles, creating looks that were at the same time unique to her and her magazine and yet remained faithful to the spirit of the designers; and she saw too how the sparkiness of a good model, the care of a talented make-up artist, the energy of a creative photographer could intensify, bring further alive an already dazzling picture. She forgot everything, what she was meant to be doing (finishing a hem), where she was meant to be (back in the workroom); she could scarcely have told you her name. At the end of the afternoon (which was actually eight thirty in the evening), as Caroline and her two assistants were packing up the clothes and the photographer had embarked on an apparently endless conversation with a model agency in New York, she emerged timidly from her shadow and asked Caroline if she could talk to her.

Caroline smiled her rather vague, sweet smile and said of course she could; she listened to Harriet's halting explanation of her ambitions to be a designer, her slowly growing frustration with what was the painstaking discipline of couture, and her enchantment with what she had seen that day. Caroline laughed and said it wasn't always like that, but why didn't she go and talk to a girl she knew, a stylist, who was looking for a dogsbody. 'It will be just that, I warn you, trailing round

London finding things like scarves and bracelets and berets, nothing glamorous, and I think she wants experience anyway, but it's worth a try, you could go and talk to her. Oh, and learn to type, then you could work for someone like me.'

The stylist took Harriet on (being more in need of cheap labour than experience). Caroline had been right: it was backbreaking, thankless work and most of the time everything Harriet contributed was discarded; but she made contacts at every manufacturer, every retail outlet in London, and on a great many magazines and several advertising agencies as well. She took Caroline's advice and taught herself to type, and on her twenty-first birthday her present from fate was a job as personal assistant to a firm called Jon Jonathan. Jon Jonathan was the pseudonym for two brothers, who designed the kind of evening dresses that fill the tables at charity balls and the social pages of the glossy magazines.

They were successful, clever and fun; Harriet had a wonderful eighteen months with them, gaining first-hand experience in running a business, made a lot more contacts, and was allowed to put a couple of dresses into a new line they were doing for the booming teenage ball market. Her dresses sold out in days, and the following season she did several more, all of which were best sellers. A year later, she got a job as a designer for a new young high street chain of upmarket leisurewear called Freetime. Working on those clothes, aiming for a line as clean-cut, as classically perfect in its own way as Jean Muir's, and yet as breezily commercial as Jon Jonathan's, Harriet felt she had established a concept that she could make her own. She turned out coordinates of shirts, sweaters, leggings, chinos, with matching hats, caps, scarves, socks. She put stinging colour with cool neutrals, outrageous detail with classic style. She finally knew where her talents fused; she knew now what she wanted to do. The Freetime studios were in Wandsworth; while she was working for them, a tiny shop became empty in the increasingly fashionable high street. With the courage, vision and refusal to look down that had characterized her working life so far, Harriet sold her car, her flat, bought the lease and opened under the name of Harry's (Mungo Buchan's childhood name for her) on her twenty-fourth birthday. For a year she lived and worked there, some weeks scarcely even leaving the four walls. She was exhausted, poor, frightened and permanently exhilarated, flying on adrenalin: cashing in shamelessly on the contacts she had made over the years. Previous customers bought from her, journalists wrote about her (she was a great story), the Jons once bailed her out when she was in a real crisis and put money into her business, in return for a ten per cent share. 'Don't ask for more,' she said coolly, the first time. 'I'd rather go under altogether than lose control of Harry's.' She refused to take money from Theo, from Merlin, from her father, even when she wanted to expand, to get another shop. Theo was particularly pressing, said he had always wanted a foot in the fashion market, that she would be doing him a favour. 'I'm sorry, Theo,' she said collectedly, sipping at the champagne over which he put to her his proposition (£1 million investment in return for a forty-nine per cent stake). 'I'm going to make it on my own.'

'Harriet, Harriet,' he said, shaking his head at her, 'it's impossible without investment. I've forgotten more about starting a company than you've even learnt yet. You'll starve from underfunding, and then you'll come back, crawling to me.' He winked at her through a cloud of cigar smoke; Harriet didn't even smile back.

'Never, Theo,' she said, 'never ever. Thank you for the offer, but it isn't even tempting.'

She was lying; it was. She was desperate for her second shop, a perfect site in the Fulham Road (where she knew her customers lived in droves), and she didn't have anything like the money. Interest rates were soaring (this was 1988), Theo's offer was as insanely generous as it was tempting. But she wouldn't take it. She went to the bank and took out a loan, and she opened the second Harry's just before she was twenty-five; she followed it with shops in Bath, Birmingham, Edinburgh and Exeter. A year after that she had her own design studio in Covent Garden, with two assistants; her turnover was £10 million. And then she looked at Paris, and saw how well shops like Laura Ashley and The Gap were doing there, and with Janine's help found a tiny shop in Passy, with a flat over it. She loved Paris, she had always loved it. She began to spend half her time there.

And still her luck held, and the economy boomed, and her clothes echoed the joyous, extravagant optimism of the era and its devotion to the fitness creed, and sold and sold, not only to the young, but to the newly young thirty- and even forty-somethings. There seemed to be no stopping her.

And then she fell in love.

It was so ridiculous when she had known him so long.

'It's so ridiculous when I've known you so long,' she said, staring at him, her heart churning, her head in turmoil, feeling her body wildly weak with longing, and shock as well that it had happened at all, looking at her hand in his across the table, as if she had never seen it, seen either of them before, feeling the hot, twisting, leaping shafts of desire between them, savouring the delicious, sweetly strange knowledge that soon, astonishingly soon, she would be in bed with him, learning of him, discovering him, feeling him, and he raised her hand and held it against his cheek, while looking at her with something that was close to amusement mixed nonetheless with love, holding her eyes with his.

'So long, all your life in fact,' he said, smiling, beginning to kiss her palm, and fronds of hot sweet excitement began to forge their way through her, and she smiled back, and said, 'What would they say to us, whatever would they say?' And he said (reaching out with the other hand, stroking her cheek, slowly, lingeringly, and then pushing her hair back, and his hand in her hair, on her head, was somehow the most sensuous thing she had ever known), 'They'd say it was dreadful, terrible, completely unsuitable,' and she said, (turning her head, leaning it on his hand, closing her eyes briefly with the effort of sitting still), 'And it is, it is terrible, it's awful, what would my father say? I can't even begin to think about it.'

'Your father,' he said simply, 'is much more of a pragmatist than you might think.' And she stared at him, arrested briefly in her delicious progress into love, and said, 'What do you mean? I don't understand,' and he said, 'I mean exactly that and don't let it trouble you.' She would have pressed him further, demanded an explanation, only he dropped her hand suddenly, and placed his hand on her thigh under the table, and she felt his fingers, his strong, thrusting fingers moving on it, stroking it, and then working upwards, slowly, inexorably, towards the tender liquid place that was yearning for him, unable to wait for him, and she forgot everything, only stood up abruptly, and said, her eyes fixed on his, 'Shit, we have to go, we have to go now, quickly,' and he threw a thousand francs onto the table (in payment for what was at the most a four-hundred franc bill) and took her elbow and guided her out of the restaurant and into the car he had waiting outside. 'My hotel,' he said briefly to the driver, then lay back and took her in his arms, and began to kiss her; hot, hungry, probing kisses. When they reached the hotel they went in quickly, through the foyer and up in the lift, and he took her hand and half dragged her out of it and into his suite.

He pushed her in impatiently, almost roughly, and slammed the door behind him, stood there leaning against it, breathing heavily, staring at her, his eyes moving all over her, her face, her breasts, her legs as if he had never seen her before, and she was panting too, staring at him, filled with excitement and fear at the same time, many fears, of what she was doing, of whether he really wanted her, of how she would be for him.

'This is bad of us,' he said, 'really bad,' (still smiling, knowing he didn't mean it, knowing she knew it too). 'Maybe even now we shouldn't, I shouldn't, not to you, you of all people.' And, 'Yes we should, we should and me of all people, it will be all right, I know it will,' and she was dragging off her shirt, fighting out of her trousers, her eyes still fixed on him.

'Yes, but he's my best friend,' he said, tearing off his tie, his shirt, struggling with his zip.

'I know, I know, and what does it matter?' she said, tearing off her tights, her pants.

'He'd be so shocked, so angry,' he said, moving forward, bending, starting to lick at her nipples, her erect, hard nipples. 'You said he was a pragmatist just now, you know you did,' she said, and her hands were in his hair, pushing at his head, pushing his mouth onto hers and he said, 'God, your breasts are so beautiful,' and then raising his head, smiling at her like a delighted child, 'I knew it, I always thought they would be.' And he pushed her down onto the bed, kissing her, his hands everywhere, on her stomach, her buttocks, her thighs, and she was writhing, moaning for him, her hands on him, too, stroking, feeling, exploring, the big firm buttocks, the surprisingly flat stomach, the soft, heavy balls, the wet, quivering penis, and then he said, 'Christ, Harriet, Christ, I can't, I can't stand it,' and it was there, his penis, in her, swiftly, impatiently, thick, heavy, reaching far far into her, urging her into sensations, hot piercing liquid sensations, and she lay back, her arms flung wide, her eyes closed, not touching him, not doing anything, just opening, opening to him and her pleasure, and there was a great white-hot brightness ahead of her, above her, and she was reaching, grasping, climbing to it, and she had never imagined, never known such strength, such power, and she thought she would tear, break with it, and then suddenly there it was, a great wild roar of joy and she realized there was indeed a great noise and it was her own voice, crying out with triumph, and for what seemed like a long long time her body gradually fell away from its climax in sweet, slow tumblings of pleasure and into peace. And then she opened her eyes, and saw him looking at her, and there was such tenderness, such love in his eyes, and she could not, would not, feel anything but triumph and joy. And 'Was that good for you?' he asked, and she smiled and said, 'Theo, you know how good it was.'

It had started with dinner, a perfectly ordinary dinner. He had phoned her at the shop in Passy, said he was alone in Paris staying at the Crillon while some work was done on his house, could she spare him the evening, and she had said delighted (for she had always loved him, adored him even, had grown up thinking how wonderful it must be to be the sort of woman he would want, fall in love with, had thought also that she was exactly the sort of woman he would not, had said of course she could, but he must come down to her, she had something to finish first. His car, an absurdly extended Mercedes, arrived forty minutes later, and the shop was locked; she went to the door and smiled up at him through the glass, thinking not for the first time, not even for the hundred and first, that he really was the most extraordinarily good-looking man even at the age he must be (well into his fifties), and quite absurdly sexy too, with his wild black hair, his burning, brilliant brown eyes, his permanently tanned skin. He was very tall and big, heavy even, but not fat; and he was of course, as always, beautifully dressed, not as so many middle-aged men dressed, trying to look young, but carelessly careful, in a fine lawn shirt, a silk tie, a dark jacket, perfectly cut grey trousers, and as he bent to kiss her she could smell very faintly the unmistakable scent of the Hermès Equipage he always wore.

'You look tired,' he said, half severely, 'and you've lost weight, I shall take you out and spoil you,' and she said, smiling, that that would be lovely, and he sat patiently for a while as she finished a drawing, wrote a letter, faxed them both to the studio in London, and then less patiently as she made a couple of phone calls.

'Come on, come on,' he said, 'don't you ever stop?' 'No' she said, firmly, 'not till I've finished, do you?'

'Never finish,' he said, 'actually. Can I use your phone?' And then it was her turn to wait while he called first London, then New York and Sydney, until finally, impatient herself, and irritated at his wanton and expensive use of her phone, she said, 'Theo, for Christ's sake, stop it,' and he laughed and said, 'Sorry, I'll pay for the calls,' and wrote her a cheque there and then for 300 francs.

'That's much too much,' she said, 'don't be absurd,' and he told her to shut up, it was hush money, and took her elbow and eased her out of the shop.

They ate in one of her favourite restaurants, just round the corner from her shop, classically perfect French food, the tables set with baskets of bread and jugs of wine and water, the first course brought swiftly (she had mushrooms à la Grecque, he a goat's cheese salad) and then a long wait for a shared carré d'agneau, as they talked, finished one jug of wine, and he ordered another ('Can't we have something better?' 'No, Theo, we can't and anyway, it wouldn't be'). He was slightly depressed, lonely (the fourth divorce was hitting him, he said, and he was feeling his age) and had just been trumped in a deal to buy an Australian property company. Harriet listened, politely at first, then more patiently, tenderly almost, recognizing for the first time at least with her heart what her head and her father had frequently told her: that this great ebullient, badly behaved, overindulged spoilt child of a man was in fact strangely vulnerable, oddly sad.

And then, 'How about you?' he asked, as finally the carré arrived, and he began to carve it, to put slices of it, pinkly perfect, onto her plate. 'How is it going, the great fashion empire that I'm not allowed even a smidgeon of?' And she said oh, fine, really, but it really was one long crisis after another, the latest being that the new line of cotton knits she was doing for the spring, absolutely dependent on some yarn arriving undyed from Hong Kong, had in fact gone horribly wrong because the yarn had been dyed and half the colours were totally out and she had sent them back and was battling for redress, and meanwhile time was hurtling by and she had already passed one deadline and if Benetton got what she knew was something very similar into their shops long before she did, she would lose considerable sales, and she was also in dispute with the landlord in Bristol where she was hoping to open in the spring. 'But you know,' she said, 'one fights on. It's half the – well, I was going to say fun, which of course it isn't, but it sharpens everything, I find, makes me go on caring a hundred and one per cent.'

'Absolutely right,' he said, munching through a huge mouthful of spinach. 'Of course it does. Christ, Harriet, I'm proud of you. You're a – what is it Mungo says? A star. A real star. Brave and tough and clever. I wish you were my daughter.' Harriet blushed, surprised at the praise, and dropped her fork.

'Goodness, Theo,' she said, 'praise indeed. Shit, that was my last bite of lamb.'

'Here,' he said, holding out his own fork to her mouth, a slice of succulent lamb on it, 'have mine,' and she opened her mouth to take it and, as she did so, met his eyes, and they were very strange those eyes, tender, amused and at the same time thoughtful, and distinctly sensuous, moving over her face as if for the first time, drinking her in, and it was one of the most sexually disturbing incidents she had ever known. Then she shook herself and thought that this was Theo, for Christ's sake, Theo who had been around for always, her father's best friend, an old man, and then she met his eyes again, probing hers, and she knew of course that he wasn't an old man at all, he was a vital, forceful, very sexy, oddly ageless one, and it was as if she had only just met him. She looked down and pushed what was left of the food on her plate with her knife and when she looked up again he was still staring at her, half amused, half startled, just as she was.

'Harriet?' he said gently, and it was both question and statement, and she said 'Yes, what?' quite aggressively, but he was not deceived, merely smiled rather self-confidently, called the waiter over and said, 'Do you have any champagne?'

'Theo!' said Harriet reprovingly. 'Really! At the end of the meal!'

'Why not?' he said. 'Champagne is wonderful at the end of the meal. And besides, we have something to celebrate, don't we?'

'What?' she said, deliberately misunderstanding.

'Recognizing each other,' he said simply, 'after all these years. Now then, what shall we talk about?'

'Mungo?' said Harriet hopefully, thinking that this would restore him to his rightful position as father figure, generations older.

'If you like. What shall we say about him?'

'Well –' She was more flustered still, anxious, her pleasure gone. 'Well, I just thought –'

'I know what you thought, my darling. You thought you would remind me that Mungo is your age, and I am his father. Right?'

'No of course not,' said Harriet irritably, trying to crush the joy at being called his darling. 'Don't be silly.'

'All right. We'll talk about Mungo. Do you like Mungo?'

'Yes of course I do. I think he's lovely.'

'But you've never been in love with him?'

'No, never. I've never been in love with any of them,' she said, relaxing again, the champagne lifting, easing her.

'Any of who?'

'The three of them. Mungo, Rufus, Oliver. They all seem like – well, like brothers. Baby brothers.'

'Ah. We used to dream of you falling in love with Mungo, your father and I. I can see it's a nonsense now. That you don't like young men very much at all.'

'No,' she said, 'no I don't. I like people who've done things, know things, fought, suffered a bit.'

'Ah. Like Bill Bryant.'

'Yes,' she said, with a heavy sigh, 'yes, that's right. Daddy told you, I suppose? The whole sad story?'

'He did. And I was sorry. And sad. But you're better without him, Harriet.'

'Oh don't!' she said, angry suddenly, 'don't you start, Theo.'

'Start what?'

'Telling me he's a bad lot, that I should never have got involved, that he's famously charming, famously wicked, plays around, likes young girls –'

'Oh no,' he said, 'nothing like that. Of course he is, of course he does. But I'm like that myself, I play around, I like young girls, I certainly wouldn't criticize that. No, it's that he's a playboy, he drifts about, he's not a worker, a fighter like you, Harriet, not what you want, not what you need.'

'Yes he was,' she said, stubbornly, 'you don't understand, nobody could.' She scowled at him, angry that he dared to pronounce on her, remembering Bill Bryant, rich, hedonistic, with whom she'd had an affair the year before, with his easy lazy charm, his dazzling lifestyle, his prodigious appetite for pleasure, in and out of bed. She would have died for Bill, given up everything for him, had he asked her, but he hadn't; it had ended in horrific grief because he had not loved her, had only used her, and then moved on. But suddenly now, in a moment of pure revelation, she realized that Theo was right, that had Bill asked her to marry him (unthinkable, unimaginable) it would have been a disaster, a dreadful awful mistake, he would never have accepted her as she was, would have wanted to change her, possess her totally.

'It wouldn't have worked, would it?' she said, staring at Theo, and he said no, of course it wouldn't, and there was a long silence and then she said, 'God, I should have talked to you before,' and he said, 'Oh, you wouldn't have listened, you'd have said I was a silly old fart.' 'Quite probably,' she said, and laughed, and he patted her hand and refilled her glass.

'You seem to understand me rather well,' she said, half amused, half serious. 'I hadn't realized.'

'I think I understand you very well.'

'But not as well as Cressida?'

'Oh, there's not a lot to understand about Cressida,' he said, 'just a sweet, straightforward, nicely brought-up girl.'

'Your favourite.'

'Of course not my favourite.'

'You always acted like she was.'

'Well,' he said, 'you were always going off with Merlin. And it was awful for me. I had to settle for what was left.'

'You're a devious old bastard,' she said lightly, 'but you're lovely.'

'I wish you really thought so,' he said.

'I do.'

'No you don't.'

'Theo, I do,' said Harriet, smiling at him rather determinedly, trying desperately to keep the mood light, easy. 'And what does it matter anyway?'

'It matters,' he said, very low, very serious suddenly, 'because I care about you. I think you're glorious.'

'Theo, don't,' said Harriet, feeling within the depths of her something lurch, rise unbidden, against her will.

'Why not? Why the hell not?'

'Well, because – oh you know why not.'

'Oh, for God's sake,' he said suddenly, 'this is absurd. Let's go.'

'All right,' said Harriet quietly. 'All right, Theo. It might be best.' She signalled to the waiter for the bill.

'What the hell are you doing?'

'Asking for the bill.'

'What for?'

'I want to pay it. I'd like to. Please.'

'Oh, for Christ's sake, Harriet.' He stood up; his hand as he drained his glass was shaking.

'Why are you so angry?' she said, startled.

'I'm angry,' he said, 'because I'm hurt. Because you so plainly think I'm a fool. Because you're so ready to dismiss me. I don't like it. I don't like it at all.'

'Theo,' said Harriet reaching out, trying to take his hand, pulling him down again, 'the last thing I think you is a fool. I was just trying to – to handle things. Badly, obviously. I was – well, I was very shaken myself just now.'

'When?'

'A little while ago. While we were still eating. I realized –'

'What?'

'I realized what – what might happen. If I let it. Let myself.'

'And you won't?'

'Theo, how can I? How can I possibly? When you're –'

'When I'm an old man?' His eyes were angry again, hurt, harsh.

'No. Not an old man. But you are practically another father to me. When you've seen me learn to walk, talk, lose my teeth –'

'Get your bosoms,' he said suddenly.

'What!' said Harriet, laughing, blushing at the same time.

'I shall never forget you getting your bosoms.'

'Theo! You really are a dirty old man.'

'I'm sorry. But I'd been away for six months, and I'd left a little girl behind, miserable, awkward – God, you were awkward, Harriet.'

'You'd have been awkward with –'

'I know, with Cressida for a sister.'

'You knew!'

'Of course I knew. Anyone would have known. Don't be absurd. Anyway, I came down for the day and went into the garden to find your parents, and there you were standing by the swimming pool, with just knickers on and two gorgeous little rosy buds, slightly uneven, they were, one bigger than the other, see how well I remember, and you didn't see me, and I stood there and got the most enormous erection, I couldn't move, and you dived into the pool and I turned away and stood there, taking deep breaths and thinking Christ Almighty, she's grown up, and then your mother appeared, and I somehow managed to talk myself down. It was one of the most profoundly moving moments of my life.'

'Literally,' said Harriet. She felt very odd, excited, touched, almost tearful.

'Literally. And ever since –'

'Don't tell me. Ever since you've been hoping to catch me by the pool again just in my knickers.'

'Or anywhere. Without them as well. If possible. Shit,' he said suddenly.

'What's the matter?'

'Same old thing,' he said, grinning slightly shamefacedly. 'Just remembering it all. Remembering you. I do have trouble with it.'

'Oh, Theo,' said Harriet helplessly, feeling herself softening, moistening, dangerously sweet. 'If only.'

'If only what?'

'If only I'd only just met you.'

'Would that be different?' he asked and his voice was odd, wary.

'Of course it would. Quite different.'

'And what would you want to do? If you'd only just met me?'

'I would want,' she said in a great surge of courage mixed with a rush of desire, 'I would want to go to bed with you.'

'Oh my God,' he said, 'dear God. Dear sweet Jesus. Look at me, Harriet, look at me.'

And she looked at him. And then she was lost.

It was so ridiculous when she had known him so long . . .

It was doomed of course; there was no way it could work. James would have been outraged, Maggie appalled, all the young horrified. 'Mungo would lynch me if he knew,' Theo said as they lay one night entwined in one another's arms, kissing lazily in the sweet aftermath of love.

'They'd all lynch us.'

'Does it matter?'

'Probably not. No. No, not at all.'

The sex was wonderful: wild, clever, original, beautiful. But it wasn't just sex, it was his very self, she told him, in all his complex, difficult, absorbed, absorbing passions. He took her to the opera in San Francisco, in Sydney, to the ballet in New York, and once in London, greatly daring, he made love to her in his box at the Opera House during a performance of *Salome*. 'Listen,' he said, as the curtain came down to great roars of applause, 'they must all have been watching us.' He took her to the races with him in Sydney and Longchamps, shouting, punching the air with excitement when the horses he had backed won, growling, scowling when they did not, and he also read aloud to her in bed, poetry usually, but sometimes from Hemingway, Tom Wolfe, Dylan Thomas, his hands moving idly over her, filling her body with longing even as his deep musical voice filled her head. Seldom was a poem, a chapter, a passage completed, the book would be dropped, flung aside, or simply lost in the bed. 'I wonder how many copies of *For Whom the Bell Tolls* have been fucked on,' Theo said one night, fishing the crushed copy from beneath him, laughing, 'and how pleased dear old Papa would have been had he only known.' They could seldom meet in London, and so she met him in a myriad different places all over the world, making long, exhausting plane journeys to Australia, to Mexico, to Barbados just to spend perhaps forty-eight hours with him. She realized again and again how vulnerable he was, even in his immense selfishness, how badly he needed people, needed affection, tenderness, how great his capacity for giving it. He cared for her as she had never been cared for, not dutifully, not mechanically, but thoughtfully, imaginatively, delightedly. 'I want to spoil you,' he said simply one night, as they shared a rare dinner in London. 'You deserve it, and you need it.'

She found that as arousing as his intense, burning sensuality, the fact that he should mind about her so much. She told him everything, trusted him with her very soul: with all her most intimate, private fears, joys, griefs, from her earliest childhood. She told him of her jealousy of Cressida, her unrequited adoration for her father, her desperate need for success. She even told him about Biggles, fearing even as she did so that he would belittle the grief and pain of that loss. He didn't. 'I had a puppy once,' he said smiling at her, wiping the tears that still flowed at the dreadful memory, 'my father sent him away, while I was at school. I just came home one day and he was gone, I never knew where. I thought I would like to kill myself.'

She could not have enough of him; she was distracted from everything, from her work, her friends, her very self. Always vain, concerned about her appearance, her style, she failed for months to go shopping, even to get her hair done. Everyone noticed, teased her about what was obviously a secret lover; she smiled, carefully vague, terrified they would guess. She had, Theo told her, accomplished the impossible and made him neglect his work too.

'I love you,' he said one night, as they sat watching the sun sink into the Mexican ocean. 'I love you as I haven't loved anyone since Deirdre. You fill my heart, Harriet, and I simply can't believe it.'

'You fill mine too,' she said, putting her hand into his. 'Absolutely and utterly.'

But things went wrong. They began to fight, angry with themselves and one another; starved of one another so much of the time, when they managed to be together they were frantic, desperate, overpossessive.

He found her youth troubling, hurtful, tormenting, she found his past, his experience worse. 'How can you wonder that I'm jealous, that I wonder where you've been, when you've had all these women, all these wives?' she would cry, when he'd been missing, hadn't phoned, hadn't been where he'd said he would be, and 'Sweet Jesus, Harriet,' he would say, 'I love you, how can you even imply I'm playing around?' And 'For Christ's sake,' he would shout at her, 'do you know how hard it is to believe you're not in bed with some boy, some beautiful young boy,' and she would cry, 'But Theo, I love you, only you, and I don't sleep around.' They agreed, after a while, that they must tell everyone, make it official, but they put it off, over and over again, afraid of ridicule, of outrage, and then fought because the fear was greater than the love.

'All right,' he said one night, as they sat seething and apart, after a dinner with Mungo and Cressida and James and Maggie, after agreeing to tell them, after totally failing, after a harrowingly complex ruse to meet later, at his house in The Boltons, 'all right, we're cowardly and feeble and pathetic and all the things you say. I'm sorry for my share in that. I'm sorry. You're not so brave either, are you? Are you, Harriet? The fault is in both of us.'

'I know, I know it is,' she said, brushing away the hot angry tears. 'I'm sorry too. I don't know why it's so hard. I can't understand it. Can't understand myself.'

'I understand it,' he said, suddenly gentle, coming over to her, wiping away the tears with his finger. 'It's because it does seem so wrong, so incestuous somehow.'

'Yes,' she said, 'yes, that's exactly right. Of course it does.'

'We've let ourselves think that. But it isn't. It isn't at all. Harriet, look at me. I love you. I love you very much.'

'I love you too,' she said, 'I really really do.'

'Perhaps we should get married,' he said suddenly, and staring at him, her eyes wide with astonishment and something close to horror, she said, 'Now that really would be awful, terrible.'

'I've never had quite such a turndown,' he said, trying to make light of it and then seeing she was deathly, deadly serious, 'Why?' he asked. 'Why so awful, why terrible? What's so wrong with it?'

'Theo, I'm not going to be Mrs Buchan the Fifth,' said Harriet with something close to distaste.

'Why not, for Christ's sake?'

'Because it's – well, it's not what I'm about. I'm not going to be Mrs anybody, and especially not Mrs Buchan the Fifth.'

'That's a filthy thing to say.'

'Well it's true.'

'I thought you loved me.'

'I do love you. But I don't want to be your wife.'

'Why the hell not?'

'Because it's – well, it's a label. Something close to absurd.'

'How very charming you are,' he said and walked out of the room, the house, and she didn't hear from him for days.

She could see why he was so hurt, so angry, but she had felt it very strongly, had had to explain. Being Theo's wife seemed to her a great deal less meaningful, less dignified than being his mistress. It seemed to her a public acceptance of submission, of selling out. When finally he took her phone call, agreed to listen, she said, 'Theo, I love you, I love you so much. I'd love to live with you. Really I would. But – shit, Theo, you've degraded marriage, it doesn't mean anything. Not in your life. I want to be your equal, not your wife,'

'Well, thanks for nothing,' he said and rang off.

Slowly, painfully, they came together again, but the rows increased. Wounded by her reaction he became obsessed with the idea of marriage; he asked her again and again, again and again she refused. She offered to live with him, but he was wounded now, savagely hurt. 'If marriage is such an awful prospect then I must be too,' he said, and try as she would, she couldn't convince or persuade him otherwise. And in the end their relationship – still new, after all, fragile, vulnerable – could not sustain the pain, and in a wretchedness of rage and misery they parted, more afraid of ridicule and outrage than of separation and grief.

'It is absurd, dreadful,' said Harriet, tears streaming down her face, her body drained, dry with hurt as they finally agreed to part, and 'That's what you said when I first told you I loved you,' said Theo, his own face ravaged with pain, and 'I know, I know,' she said, 'but it can't, it won't work, will it?' and 'No,' he said, 'no, I don't think it will.'

It was a long time before Harriet began to heal, and the agony when she heard Theo was going to marry Sasha was so frightful she seriously doubted if she could stand it; she was unable to sleep without pills for six months, and to contemplate so much as speaking to him for twelve. Indeed their first meeting after his wedding upset her so much she was physically sick. She still found herself unable to meet his eyes, or to be next to him. 'I actually now know,' she said to Tilly, who was the only person she had ever confided in about the whole wretched affair, 'how people can commit murder. I would gladly kill first him and then her, given the opportunity.'

Tilly remarked with her usual clear-sightedness that from what Harriet had told her, the break-up had been as much at her instigation as Theo's. 'I know, I know,' wailed Harriet, 'but at least I haven't married some bimbo less than a year later.'

'Maybe he's more desperate than you are,' said Tilly. 'And what's the male for bimbo?'

'Himbo?' said Harriet, and first shrieked with hysterical laughter and then burst into tears. But just the same Tilly's words had been oddly comforting.

She decided to go and find her father and Susie, with the tea; they'd seemed to want it so much and they couldn't be far away. She put two of the cups on a tray and went out of the back door, across the yard and into the garden, but they were not on the lawn or in the rose garden, or by the tennis court; maybe then by the bridge. Cressida was not the only person who liked to be by the bridge. She pushed open the little gate that led into the field; her thoughts (occupied with her problems, with her business, with Theo, with Cressida) distracting her so thoroughly that she had almost forgotten where she was going when she reached the bridge. And she saw then, sitting on the seat, in a position that spoke somehow most clearly of a long intimacy, Susie and her father, Susie's head on his shoulder, his arm around her, his hand in hers.

It was unmistakable, that pose; it was not one of friendship (despite its lack of passion), nor was he comforting her over the events of the day. These were two people as close, as familiar as if they had been married a long time, the image made the more forceful because her parents never sat like that, nor had she ever seen Susie and Alistair do more than exchange the briefest touch. And as she stood there, staring at them, they sensed her presence and turned round, simultaneously, and saw her, and on Susie's face at least there was some amusement mixed with her dismay, and she seemed to hear Theo's voice (and she could remember the precise words and his tone too) in the restaurant that first night. 'Your father,' he'd said, 'is much more of a pragmatist than you might think,' and she heard Susie's voice too, much more recently – 'I'm very good at keeping secrets' – and in a blinding, white-hot revelation she understood, saw down the years the pleasure, the happiness, the closeness between them, and understood too in the same moment the strange relationship between her parents, her father's patience, kindness, courtesy, her mother's coolness, distancing, lack of response, saw it for what it was, part of a complex, well-negotiated deal, and while she wondered exactly, precisely how she felt about it, her father spoke.

'Harriet,' he said, 'Harriet, I think we should – talk.'

'No,' she said, 'I don't think we should, I really haven't got time. I – brought you some tea. It's a bit strong, and a bit cold now. I'm sorry.' And she set the tray down on the grass and turned and walked very swiftly towards the house, wondering why it should have disturbed her so much, when she was grown-up, quite grown-up, sophisticated, experienced, that her father had a mistress (even if she was supposed to be a great family friend) and realized it was because, quite simply, all the security, the absolute knowledge of her childhood that her parents loved one another, had been faithful to one another, was lost to her, wiped out in a single moment, and that Theo, whom she'd loved so much, been so close to, had clearly known all along and had not told her.

She found it hard to see as she walked back into the kitchen; it seemed somehow dim. Maybe it was getting dark, she thought irrelevantly, looking at her watch, but that was blurred too, and she realized she was crying. Furious, she brushed the tears away, picked up the cup of tea she had made and sat down at the table, sipping at it, wondering what she should do. And then she saw that there was a letter on the table, propped against the toast rack, a white envelope with what was – couldn't be, couldn't possibly be, but yes it was, Cressida's rather neat writing on it. 'The Forrests' it said, 'Urgent.'

Harriet reached out and picked it up, cautiously, as if it might be hot, might burn her, and sat staring at it, turning it over without opening it. Then she got up and walked over to the door, called gently into the hall, 'Cress? Are you there?'

There was no answer, as she had expected, of course, nothing, so she went back to the table, sat down and with immense difficulty opened the envelope and took out the sheet of paper inside.

'Mummy, Daddy and Harriet' (it said), 'I'm very sorry about today. Please believe me. I seemed to have no choice. I'm fine, and not in any danger. I'll phone you when I can. Much love, Cressida.'

Chapter 14

James 5pm

'Daddy, don't talk to me like that.' Harriet was flushed, breathing heavily. She was clearly very upset, near to frightened. 'I told you, the fucking letter wasn't there before.'

He knew why she was using language like that; it was not about the letter, it was about him and Susie, about betrayal. Just the same he hated it.

'Harriet, darling, there's no need for that.'

'Sorry,' she said, and her tone made it clear she wasn't, not in the least. 'It was horrible, you know. Like seeing – hearing – a ghost.'

'Yes, of course.' James sighed; he felt terribly tired, drained of sympathy, patience, understanding. Even for Susie. He had had too much, too much of all of them. He just wanted to go away, leave them, do something nice and straightforward that he could control, like play tennis, or take out his boat or even deliver a baby. To a sensible mother who had been to all her antenatal check-ups and wanted an epidural, with a midwife in attendance who thought he was wonderful. The thought was so ridiculous he smiled in spite of himself.

'I'm glad you think it's funny,' said Harriet. She sounded extraordinarily angry.

'Darling, I don't think it's funny. I – well, I was thinking about something else.'

'I wish I could. Incidentally Susie thinks we should tell the police about the passport business. And I think she's right.'

'Why?'

'Well, because if she has got a duplicate passport, she can get abroad. It's obvious.'

'Yes. Yes of course you're right,' said James. He sounded very vague. 'I'll call them very soon. Let's try and get this letter business sorted first.'

'Well,' Susie said, her tone forcedly bright, 'obviously someone put it there. None of us actually believes in ghosts. Someone must have come in. It hasn't been through the post. Is it dated, Harriet?'

Harriet shook her head. 'No. But it says today.'

'It still could have been written yesterday.'

'Now that is really unbelievable,' said James. 'She couldn't have planned this, couldn't have been so deliberately – cruel.'

'Why not?' said Harriet, and her voice was even harsher. 'Why do you say that? She took her dress, she seems to have got a second passport organized –'

'I suppose so,' said James. 'I suppose so. I'm just still trying to resist the idea, that's all. And of course there was what Oliver said this morning when I – well, when I told him what had happened.'

'What did he say?' asked Harriet sharply. 'And why didn't you tell us before?'

'Because I honestly didn't – still don't – think it was important. But he said, "She hasn't actually gone, has she?" Or something like that?'

'James, how can you not think that was important?' Susie's voice was shocked. 'How could you have kept that to yourself? If Oliver knew –'

'Susie, Oliver didn't know anything. Do you think I'd have kept quiet about it if he had? But he did say that she'd had a bad panic attack about three or four days ago, and said she felt like running away. She'd been very tearful apparently. But that was all. I'm sure there aren't many brides who haven't threatened to run away, a few days before the wedding.'

He hoped he sounded convincing, as convinced as he wanted to be; he was still thoughtful about Oliver's response, but the subsequent conversation had been too distressing to allow for cross-questioning. And then there'd been the dress business and the passport–

'It sounds to me,' said Susie slowly, looking up from the letter, 'as if she was under some appalling pressure. Something she couldn't escape from.'

'Well, she has escaped,' said Harriet. 'Very nicely. As usual.'

'Darling, why are you sounding so hostile? You've never talked about Cressida like this before.'

'Yes, well, it always seemed best to keep quiet before,' said Harriet. 'It never did me any good to say anything. I just got sent away to school or out of the room.'

She sounded suddenly like the small hurt child he had left at St Madeleine's all those years ago; looked like her too, with a white face and hard, desperate eyes.

'Harriet, what are you saying?'

'Oh, it doesn't matter,' said Harriet wearily. 'This isn't getting us anywhere.' She sighed, rubbed her eyes. 'I want a drink.'

'It's a little early for that, isn't it?' said James. He looked at his watch: five past five. Christ Almighty. Cressida had been missing for almost twelve hours.

'I don't care if it's early,' said Harriet. 'I want one. Just because you never drink, you never think other people might want to.' She walked over to the fridge. 'Susie, how about you? Glass of wine?'

'Yes, I think it might be nice,' said Susie.

Harriet poured two glasses of wine, handed her one. They stood there, sipping slightly awkwardly. 'This is very nice wine,' said Susie.

'Isn't it?' said Harriet. 'Lovely and fruity.'

James looked at them, thought how absurd it all was and laughed suddenly.

'You seem to be finding this whole thing very funny,' said Harriet irritably.

'It's so ridiculous, that's all. Here we are, a missing bride, a banquet for three hundred slowly going off, flowers wilting, the police alerted, a letter appearing as if from the ether, and you're suddenly discussing the merits of Californian chardonnay.'

'Yes, well, we didn't seem to be getting far discussing anything else,' said Harriet.

'Look,' said Susie suddenly, 'look, Harriet, perhaps we should – well, what you saw just now. Your father and me. It doesn't – didn't mean –'

'Susie, please. I'm not stupid,' said Harriet briskly. 'I could see what it meant. Thank you. I really don't think we should talk about it. What we have to decide is what to do about this note. Do we tell the police? Or try and find out if anyone came in? What? We can't just stand here drinking.'

'It was your idea to drink,' said James mildly.

'Oh, for Christ's sake!' said Harriet. 'Can we just –'

The door opened and Maggie came in. She looked very pale and her fair hair was slightly damp around her face, but she smiled almost cheerfully at them.

'I just woke up. I feel – much calmer. I'm sorry I – well, is there any news?'

Harriet and Susie were silent; they both looked at James.

'What is it?' asked Maggie. 'What's happened?'

'Nothing – really,' said James. He felt almost inclined to hide the letter, not tell Maggie, he so dreaded the descent back into hysteria.

'Yes, it has,' said Harriet. She stared at him stony-eyed. 'Of course it has. Mummy, there's a letter. Look, from Cressida.'

Maggie sat down heavily and took the letter. She read it slowly several times, and then said, 'Where was it?'

'On the kitchen table. It just appeared.'

'It can't have just appeared. Don't be ridiculous. She must be here, Cressida must have brought it. Have you looked for her, called her –'

'Maggie, of course we have,' said James, realizing suddenly that they'd done nothing of the sort, not really. 'She isn't here. Nobody's here.'

'They must be. Janine's here, for a start. Where is she? Maybe she saw Cressida –'

'She's lying down,' said Harriet. 'She's exhausted.'

'She's exhausted!' said Maggie. She sounded angry. 'I really can't imagine why Janine should be exhausted. She hasn't done anything. Anything at all.'

'Maggie, of course she has. She's lived through this whole thing with us, she's been a tower of strength, she only arrived from Paris yesterday and besides she's quite an old lady now –'

'Yes, all right, all right,' said Maggie. 'Well, we must get her up, talk to her. She might have heard, seen someone –'

'Maggie, I really don't think –'

'Jamie, I don't care what you really don't think. I really do think. Harriet, could you go and get Janine, please? And who else is in the house?'

'No one. Everyone's gone. No cars, nothing.'

'Leaving the sinking ship,' said Maggie. 'Susie, give me a glass of that wine would you? Is Alistair here?'

'No,' said Susie, quickly. 'No, he's gone back to London.'

'Ah,' said Maggie. 'Ah yes, of course.'

James looked at her sharply, but her face was blank, stony.

Harriet came in, looked at them both, went to sit near her mother. It was an oddly symbolic gesture. 'Janine's just washing her face,' she said, 'then she'll be down. But she really hasn't heard anything.'

'We should have let her be,' said James. He felt irritated, upset on Janine's behalf.

'Yes, that's what you always like to do, isn't it?' said Maggie. 'Leave things be. Carefully covered, so they aren't any trouble. To you at least.'

James felt the familiar pang of sheer, icy panic, and at the same time the equally familiar flash of hope, of relief. Christ Almighty, was she going to say something now, confront him, confront them both? All his life, all their lives, he'd been waiting for it, waiting for the confrontation, and it never came; she sat there, like a great fat cat, toying with him, with the knowledge she must surely have, and made him wait. Often he almost wanted her to face him with it, yearned for the end of the sham, the games they all had to play, wished he could start it off himself, say something, force her to say something back. But he never did and he never would. He liked to think it was his alter ego, his better self, doing that, sparing Maggie, allowing her some kind of dignity, of status at least; but he knew that actually it was nothing of the sort. James had a great talent for self-deception, but it did not extend quite this far. He played the game Maggie's way to buy her silence, her acceptance of what he had done to her; he simply could not face the ugliness of a scandal, of divorce. It was not perfect, of course, the situation; he would have been much happier married neatly, respectably to Susie, but the opportunity for that had been lost to him thirty years earlier, and in the event it had all turned out very satisfactorily. He saw Susie almost as much as he wanted to, he had plenty of freedom, he had a fair amount of money (but it was only money, only salary, not wealth, and it would diminish quite painfully, supporting two households). But now, with Susie, with the promise he had made her – Christ, how was he going to get out of that one? A great deal of very skilful talking and manoeuvring would be necessary. He had no intention of actually setting up house with her, it was an absurd, romantic notion, but she hadn't thought it through, hadn't seen that it would cause great grief and stress to herself as well as her family, would quite possibly exacerbate her condition. When she was feeling less shocked, when they had a clearer idea of what her prospects were, then he could put that to her, make her see it wasn't such a good idea. God in heaven, it was a hideous thought. He was genuinely and deeply shocked himself; he loved Susie very much, had loved her all his life. The thought of her dying, lost to him, no longer there for him was ghastly. He looked at her now, so lovely still, her face strangely serene. She had great courage, Susie, always had. Well, she was going to need it, every last final shred of it. He must not completely fail her, must do all that he possibly could.

He stared at Maggie, wondering what she might say next, feeling her hostile bitterness almost tangibly in the room; but she suddenly smiled at him with the extreme sweetness she always seemed able to summon out of somewhere and said, 'Sorry, James. I didn't mean to be cross. Ah Janine, come in, dear. Would you like a glass of wine?'

For ten, fifteen minutes they talked, argued, read and reread the letter, propounded theories as to how it had got there (paper boys, post office messengers, passing strangers), debated calling the police, the hospital, the Bergins, examined the silent afternoon behind them now for sounds of footsteps, car engines, even bicycles. 'Well, I do think we have to tell the police,' said James finally. 'We can't not, really. They're looking for Cressida, and this is a clue. Of a sort. I'll go and ring them now, tell them – Good Lord, Merlin, where have you sprung from?'

Merlin walked into the kitchen with his quick, light tread, smiling sweetly at them all. He had discarded his morning coat and was wearing a khaki safari shirt and a long white cricket cardigan over his shorts.

'Been for a walk. Felt a bit restless. Got a drink for me, Harriet? Something long, if you don't mind. A beer perhaps. That lovely creature Tilly gave me some beer in the car, and I've been dreaming of another ever since. Find the note, did you? I dropped it off on my way. I thought you'd see it if I left it on the table.'

'Merlin, did you put that note there?' said Harriet. She looked almost angry, James thought, ready to explode.

'Yes, well I couldn't find any of you. Knew you'd be back.'

'Merlin, it's from Cressida.'

'Yes, I realized that,' said Merlin impatiently. 'Know her writing perfectly well. Better than yours, Harriet, look like unravelled knitting your letters do –'

'And you just left it on the table. Merlin, how could you?'

'Harriet, calm down,' said James. 'Merlin, where did you get it from? Who gave it to you?'

'Nobody gave it to me,' said Merlin. 'I found it.'

'Yes, but where? Where was it?'

'In the lavatory,' said Merlin. He spoke as if it was the most natural place in the world to find a letter. 'Fallen on the floor, behind the cistern. Only noticed it because I dropped my compass. Can't think why I brought it today, but still. Force of habit I suppose. Anyway, just as well, wasn't it? Otherwise –'

'Yes, yes, Merlin, which lavatory?'

'The one down here,' said Merlin. 'Does it matter? Suppose the silly girl left it there on her way out. Forgot it. This is jolly good beer, Jamie. Pay a lot for it, did you?'

'Quite a bit, yes,' said James.

'Let me come with you next time. See if I can beat them down a bit. Now then –'

'Merlin,' said Maggie, her voice slightly shaky, 'I really think we have more important things to discuss than the price of beer.'

'Sorry,' said Merlin cheerfully. 'Any other news is there?'

'No, I'm afraid not,' said James. 'We were debating whether we should give that note to the police. We thought it had just arrived you see. But –'

'It must have been there all day,' said Harriet. 'She must have left it there when she went. Early. It does seem odd though –'

'Yes, but I told you, she was unwell,' said Janine. 'I heard her vomiting. The *pauvre petite*.'

'Well, there you are,' said Merlin. 'Takes it out of you, that sort of thing. Tends to happen in a rush, doesn't it? Suppose she parked the letter on the cistern while she –'

'Yes, I suppose so,' said Harriet hastily. They were all patently trying not to think too hard about the sequence of events that led to Cressida leaving her letter behind. Poor child, thought James, vomiting repeatedly, exhausted, frightened; no doubt she heard someone moving upstairs, thought she wouldn't get away and just fled. He sighed. 'Poor child,' he said aloud. 'Poor little thing.'

'I still do think,' said Susie, 'that all this points to her being under some kind of intolerable strain. That there was something she was running away from. Some kind of trouble. Incidentally, has anyone phoned her flat lately?'

'We do it every hour, on the hour,' said Maggie. 'There's just no answer. I think maybe someone ought to go up there, perhaps Rufus or maybe Mungo – it seems crazy not just to check she's not there. None of us have been there for ages, anyway, you never know what clues we might find there. I know we haven't got a key, but – oh, if only she'd had a flatmate, it would have been such a help. I always said she should and now –'

'Yes, well, she could hardly have been expected to get a flatmate simply to be helpful to us in the event of her possible disappearance off the earth,' said James. He could hear the exasperation in his own voice, but he couldn't help it.

'Jamie, don't be difficult,' said Susie. 'Maggie's right, we should check the flat out. I'll ask Rufus if you like.'

'Thank you. Anyway, I don't know about strain, Susie, she seemed so happy, so calm last night. There was no sign –'

'She was a bloody good actress,' said Merlin. 'Never saw anyone turn on the tap like Cressida could.'

'Merlin!' said Maggie. 'Please!'

'Well, why not? Jolly useful attribute. I'll have another of these beers, if you don't mind, Harriet. Got her out of trouble plenty of times, I expect. And it got her things. Remember that business with the shrunken head, Harriet?'

'Merlin, not now,' said James heavily.

'Yes,' said Harriet quietly. Everyone looked at her. 'Yes, of course I do.'

'What was that?' asked Susie. She sounded genuinely interested.

'Merlin –'

'Oh, what's it matter now, James? I brought back a shrunken head for Harriet once. Knew she'd like it. Swapped it for a little transistor radio in some village in the bush. She was thrilled. Said she was going to start a collection. Only I hadn't got anything for Cressida. Well, I never saw the sort of things she liked, national dolls and all that nonsense. She didn't seem to mind too much, until her mother came in. Then she was off, weeping and wailing. Put Garbo to shame. Said I was always forgetting her, that I never brought her anything, and she wanted the head. Don't you remember, Maggie?'

'No, not really,' said Maggie. She sounded very tense. 'Merlin, do we have to –'

'Surprised. You made a bit of a scene. Told me to give her the head. Said I always brought Harriet things, and that hurt Cressida. Anyway, a week later she gave it to the dog. We saw her, didn't we, Harriet? And when she realized we'd seen her she was off again, never seen anything like it, great tears, it was giving her nightmares, she hadn't known what to do. You had to admire her. I wouldn't have minded, only it was a damn fine head.'

'I don't think this is getting us anywhere at all,' said Maggie coldly.

'No, of course it isn't. I was just saying she was a fine actress, that's all.'

'I think,' said Maggie glaring at him, 'I think Susie's right. It's the only explanation really. That she was feeling so under pressure that the only way out was – escape. Poor darling,' she added. Her voice was low and slightly shaky; she looked very pale.

'Well – none of this has got us any further. Do we tell the police about the note or not?' said James. His head was aching horribly; he felt sick.

'I think we should,' said Maggie. 'I really do. And – well, maybe try the hospitals again. Especially if she was ill. She might be in terrible trouble by now.'

'I think we should talk to Oliver first,' said Harriet. 'I really don't believe he didn't even suspect there was something wrong. Can't we get him over? Or go there?'

'He was off for a walk with Tilly earlier,' said James. He tried to sound relaxed, natural, but he hated even saying the name; it made him feel uneasy.

'Well, I expect they're back now. Let's phone the hotel.'

'Tell you what,' said Merlin suddenly. 'I don't trust that mother of his. I think she might know something about it all.'

They all stared at him.

'Julia! Merlin, why?' Harriet sounded astounded, almost shocked.

'Don't like her. Damn silly fool of a woman. Always talking rubbish in that absurd language of hers.'

'Merlin, American is the same language as ours,' said Susie laughing.

'Rubbish. Ever listened to them properly? Babbling on about prioritization and fitness programmes and being in touch with themselves and all that poppycock. Do you know, she once asked me if I felt diminished as a person by never marrying. Diminished! Bloody nerve! I told her I'd be a lot more diminished if I had married, and lost my freedom and spent all my money on some bloody silly girl.'

'Merlin,' said Harriet, looking more cheerful suddenly, 'I love you. And I'd love to diminish you. But I can't see any of that is grounds for her knowing where Cressida is.'

'I didn't say that. You don't listen, Harriet. Never did. I said she might know something about it all. Someone should question her.'

James looked at Janine, remembering what she had said earlier, about not liking, not trusting Julia. It was interesting that, but they could scarcely start cross-questioning her on that basis.

'I agree with Harriet, that we should tell Oliver about the letter,' he said, 'and perhaps we should ask all the Bergins over here. It seems almost discourteous not to. Maggie, can you cope with that?'

'I suppose so,' said Maggie. Her voice was heavy, dull, but she smiled at him again, her good-wife smile. 'Yes, of course I can.'

He decided to change again; his clothes felt frowsty, over-worn. While he was upstairs the phone rang: 'James? Tony Bacon. Sorry, heavy day.'

Yes, thought James, very heavy, on the golf course. 'That's OK.'

'What can I do for you?' His voice was carefully cheerful, expressionless; he knew then.

'Tell me something, Tony, if you will.'

'Will if I can.'

'Look, I'm sure you've heard. Cressida's disappeared. Early this morning.'

'Yes, James, I had. I'm sorry. No news of her then?'

'No, not yet. The police are being very helpful. But –'

'Hell of a worry for you.'

'Yes, it is rather. Look, I know this is classified information, but the circumstances are exceptional and it would help a lot if we knew. Has there been any undue activity in her bank account recently?'

'Wish there had, old boy. Yes, of course I'll tell you. It's been a bit – moribund lately. Ever since she cleared her overdraft.'

'Her overdraft?' said James. 'I didn't know she had one.'

'Well I rather assumed you didn't. It was quite big, you know, last year, bigger than I should have let her have actually, but you know how it is, you weren't going to run away, and she's always been a bit of a favourite of mine, ever since she used to come in with her pocket money every week and pay in five bob.'

'Er – how big is big?' asked James. 'A few hundred?'

'Well – rather more than that. In the end I had to take a charge on her flat. I'd actually asked her to come and have a chat. It wasn't just the overdraft, her credit card borrowing was very high, and she sold her shares as well –'

'When was this?' asked James. 'Exactly? Christ, I wish I'd known.'

'Oh – last summer. Right up to Christmas actually. Then she cleared it completely, and closed the account altogether for a while. That was when she had her windfall, came into that money –'

'What money?' said James sharply. 'I don't know anything about money –'

'You didn't? How extraordinary. Her great-aunt, leaving her all that money . . .'

'She – hasn't got a great-aunt,' said James. 'Look, Tony, I'm sorry, but I really didn't –'

'Ah,' said Tony Bacon. He was clearly embarrassed. 'Ah, I see. Well, someone must have died, or she must have broken the bank at Monte Carlo or something. A hundred thousand pounds was wired to us, on a CHAPS payment, from some solicitor. Only at the time she didn't have an account here, so we returned it to the solicitor.'

'Look,' said James, 'can we just go over that again, Tony? Someone paid Cressida a hundred thousand pounds into your bank and you returned it?'

'Yes, that's right. Because she'd just closed her bank account with us. A few weeks later she opened it again, with a small deposit, and she's hardly used it since.'

'And you have no idea where this money came from?'

'Well, I told you, she said it was a legacy. She specifically – although quite casually – asked me not to mention it since it was a bit of a sore point in the family. Her getting it, I mean.'

'It might have been,' said James, 'if we'd known about it. How extraordinary. How absolutely extraordinary. When was this, Tony? Around Christmas, you said?'

'No, a bit later than that. February, early February.'

'I see. And – and since then, nothing untoward at all?'

'No, not at all. I was slightly anxious when she came back to us, to be honest, because I thought the borrowing might start again. But it hasn't. Look, I do hope you get some news soon, and I hope I haven't made things worse.'

'Yes,' said James absently. 'Yes, thank you. I mean, no, no, of course you haven't.'

He put the phone down and sat down heavily on the bed, staring at the telephone. How in God's name, he wondered, had Cressida got hold of £100,000 and what if anything did it have to do with her disappearance? He felt suddenly and sharply as if the Cressida he had known and loved and lived with for twenty-seven years had entirely ceased to exist, had been replaced by a total stranger.

The Bergins' car pulled into the drive thirty minutes later. Oliver was driving it, with Tilly beside him. 'I thought I'd come and see Harry,' she said by way of explanation as she walked in. 'I hope that's OK.' James looked at her and felt absurdly nervous. Pull yourself together, Forrest. What can she do to you now?

'Hi, Tilly,' said Harriet, giving her a hug. 'I'm not sure if you've met my father . . .'

'Yeah, we've met,' said Tilly, smiling rather coolly at James. 'A couple of times actually.'

'Dad's still walking with Theo,' said Oliver into the slightly tense silence, 'and mother is resting. They may be over later. But thanks for inviting them.'

He looked terrible, pale and wild-eyed; he refused the drink Harriet offered, asked for tea. She filled one of the maxi-sized teacups that she kept for herself and gave it to him. 'I thought it was only the British who wanted tea in a crisis,' she said.

'I'm a Brit by marriage,' said Oliver. 'Or at least I thought I was.'

'You will be,' said Harriet cheerfully.

James led them all into the drawing room; he felt he had spent too many traumatic hours in the kitchen that day. He told Oliver about Cressida's letter, about where Merlin had found it. Oliver's reaction was dull, almost uninterested. He was clearly exhausted, unable to cope with anything more. 'It doesn't get us anywhere, does it?' was all he could say.

'Well – at least it means she wasn't abducted or has met with some horrible accident,' said Harriet. 'We found it kind of faintly comforting. The thing is, Oliver, do you think we should tell the police?'

'Oh – I don't know,' he said. 'Whatever you think.' He put his head in his hands, pushing them through his hair; Harriet went over to him, put her arms round his shoulders.

'Oliver darling, you mustn't despair. I know she'll turn up. She'll be all right. She'll just walk in here and laugh and say "you're never going to believe this" and it will all make sense.'

Oliver shook his head; he looked up at her and there was a darkness, a bleakness in his eyes that reached out to them all.

'I don't think so,' he said.

Harriet looked rather uncertainly at Tilly; she was sitting in the depths of the huge sofa, her endless legs wrapped round one another, her huge almond eyes calmly, almost lazily absorbing the scene. She was an amazing creature, James thought; quite unlike anyone he had ever known. Well, that was absurd: how many – what were they called? – Super-models? – had he known anyway? But she had a tranquillity about her, an easiness that was highly engaging. He tried to remember her mother; she had certainly not been tranquil. But then the circumstances under which they had met had hardly been tranquil, nor the ensuing ones either. Well, she had certainly made a good job of Tilly. In the most difficult of conditions. On her own, no money. James crushed determinedly the thought of what some financial damages for the loss of Rosemary Mills's other baby might have done to make things easier for her, and smiled at Tilly rather awkwardly. She looked levelly back at him, her arched eyebrows just slightly higher. What the hell did she have in mind for him, and how was he going to handle her? Christ Almighty, what a day.

As if in response to his thoughts, Tilly suddenly stood up and walked over to him. 'I'm very interested in gardens, in growing things, Mr Forrest,' she said. 'Would you like to show me yours?'

They all looked up, startled: Maggie especially. Susie's eyes were wary, watchful. She half stood up herself. Jamie shook his head at her imperceptibly, smiled his careful consultant's smile at Tilly, trying to equate this glorious creature with the tiny scrawny baby he had laid so exhaustedly and thankfully on her mother's breast. And who now, it seemed, might quite possibly become his daughter-in-law – albeit unofficially. How the hell was he going to deal with it all?

'I would be delighted,' he said, 'there's nothing I like more than showing off my roses. Let's go.'

He stood back for her as she walked through the door; in her stack-soled boots she was at least two inches taller than he was.

'We'll be back in a minute,' he said into the room. He could see Harriet watching them both, clearly baffled.

She walked slowly, gracefully, leading the way across the lawn; she seemed to glide. He followed her, feeling like some small eager pony in the wake of some great beautiful thoroughbred. When they were out of hearing distance of the house, she turned and waited for him, pointed at the field.

'Can we go there?'

'Yes,' he said, 'and into the woods. It's a nice walk.'

'Oh good,' she said, and her tone was heavy, ironic. 'I like a nice walk.'

She was silent for a few more minutes; then as they reached the trees she turned to him again and said, 'Well, Mr Forrest. What a long time it's been.'

'Yes, I suppose it has. You're – what? Nineteen?'

'Twenty,' she said, 'as you very well know.'

'Ah. Twenty is it?'

'Twenty years. Tough ones for my mother. Very tough.'

'Yes, I'm afraid they must have been.'

'It's been OK for you,' she said, 'by the look of things.'

'In some ways yes.'

'In most ways, I would say, Mr Forrest. I mean we're talking material

here. I'm not interested in any other kind of problems you might have
had. Except that I hope you've had a few.'

'Miss Mills –'

'Oh, puh-leeze, Mr Forrest! Tilly. We're going to get to know one
another pretty well, I think, you can't keep on calling me Miss Mills. I
mean, Rufus wants to marry me. And he's family, isn't he?'

'Not quite. Not strictly speaking,' said James carefully, 'but I know
what you mean.'

'The hell you know what I mean. And strictly doesn't seem to have a
lot to do with it. Are you really telling me no one else in this gilded cage
you all live in has noticed what Rufus looks like? Very interesting I found
that. Shocking even – for a moment.'

'I – don't quite understand.' Jesus, this was worse than he'd expected.

'I think you do.'

'Miss Mills – Tilly, I assure you –'

'OK,' said Tilly, suddenly cheerful, polite even, 'let's leave that for
now. I just wanted to ask you how you could possibly, possibly have done
what you did to my mother. It may sound like I'm raking over old
ground, but it's what I've been walking on all my life and it really does
intrigue me.' She smiled at him, a great warm engulfing smile.

James stared at her, his mouth dry. 'Perhaps,' he said after a moment,
'perhaps you could clarify that question just a little. If you mean the
birth, the death of your sister –'

'Yeah, I mean that. But that's not the main thing. I suppose if I was to
be really really charitable, I could tell myself it was possible that my
sister's death was unavoidable. I mean I don't really think so, but I could
keep on telling it, and maybe in the end I'd get to believe it. I talked to
Oliver about it, I thought as he was a doctor he'd know –'

'You talked to Oliver about your delivery – your birth,' said James and
he felt so angry, so hot with rage he had to stop and take several deep
breaths.

'No, it's OK, calm down, not mine,' said Tilly. She stopped and waited
for him, smiling her odd, aloof smile. 'Just the birth of twins. I said how
complicated was it, could it be, and he said these days not so difficult,
but it was still tricky, still a process he hadn't liked when he'd had to do
it, that often the second twin was a breech, that then there was always
the danger of brain damage –'

James thanked God for any difficulties Oliver had clearly had in the delivery room during his training, and started to walk again.

'Then you can accept that there was a problem . . .'

'Yeah, I can. And I can imagine my mother might have been difficult. She can be very stubborn and she's heavily into all that natural business. With that silly cow Tamsin. And I know it kept coming up that she hadn't been for her prenatals –'

James was beginning to feel more easy; maybe she had just wanted to clear the air, maybe he could persuade her that he had acted properly, in good faith . . .

'Well then –'

'No, Mr Forrest, not well. Because you'd been drinking, hadn't you?'

'I beg your pardon!'

'I said you'd been drinking. You were drunk.'

'How dare you!' said James. 'How dare you stand there, in all your crass ignorance, and accuse me of being drunk when I was working. Of course I –'

'*I'm* not accusing you,' said Tilly easily. '*I'm* not saying it. It was the little student nurse who did that. She went to Tamsin, told her. When Tamsin was trying to get evidence together.'

'I don't recall her saying that at the inquiry,' said James smoothly. He was in control of himself again now. 'And I have to tell you that –'

'I'll do the telling, Mr Forrest. And no, she didn't say it at the inquiry. She just said you were very tired. I wonder how that happened. Not because it was her word against yours and the other medical people. No, no, of course not. She must have been wrong in the first place. Or thought she was wrong.'

'Miss Mills, you're making some very serious accusations here. I have to tell you –'

'I'm not making any accusations,' said Tilly, and her voice was icy, filled with contempt. 'Well, not yet. I can't quite decide who I'm going to talk to first about all of this: Rufus maybe. Maybe not. I can't decide. Does that lovely Susie know about it incidentally?'

'Yes, of course she does. Everyone knows. It was a widely reported case. And everyone knows also –'

'Yeah, that you were cleared absolutely. Well, bully for you. And then back to the treadmill, eh? The five-star consulting rooms and the expensive suits and the big bucks and the big career.'

'It wasn't quite that simple,' said James, fighting to keep indignation out of his voice. 'It was a considerable setback. And a very, very traumatic experience, I might add. You may find it hard to believe but I was deeply upset by the whole thing. Very deeply. It was the first and only time I ever lost a baby . . .'

'Oh, *you* lost it, did you?' said Tilly and her voice was heavy with scorn and a stony, harsh hatred. 'Do you know, I didn't realize that. I always thought it was my mother who lost it. I didn't realize it was you who went through all that pain and hell, who saw my sister born dead, dragged out of her like a rat. I didn't realize it was you who cried every night for years and years, and had nightmares and felt terrible awful guilt for not doing the right things when you were pregnant. I didn't know that it was you who needed some kind of recompense for it, for all that pain and misery, so that your life wasn't so hard. I didn't realize it was you who were made to feel irresponsible and foolish by the hospital and you who had to take the crap in that awful letter they sent. How stupid of me. How exceedingly stupid.'

'Well, I –'

'You bastard,' said Tilly. She had stopped walking now and had turned to face him, barring his way. 'You pathetic lying bastard. I wasn't sure until today what I was going to do. I thought I'd like to see what you said about it all. Now I've seen, and heard, and I feel sick.'

'How dare you!' said James. 'How dare you talk to me like this!'

'Oh, quite easily,' said Tilly more cheerfully. 'I'm quite brave altogether. You'd be surprised. I expect it's in my blood. Lots of my forebears were spear-carrying warriors. Anyway, now I know exactly what I'm going to do. I'm going to tell every single person in this family of yours what you did, what really happened.'

'You can't,' said James, an icy sickness in his veins.

'Why not?'

'It would be slanderous.'

'Oh, for God's sake,' said Tilly, 'what are you going to do, sue me? That would be very interesting. No Mr Forrest, you can't do that. And I'm going to make very sure they all know the truth. That poor cow of a wife of yours, I bet she thinks the sun shines out of your anus, doesn't she? I bet she'll be shocked rigid.'

'Miss Mills, I warn you –'

'And Susie? Your lovely friend? And your children? Christ, Harry idolizes you, thinks you're the next best thing to Jesus.'

'Not any more, I fear,' said James.

'Oh really? She seems pretty obsessed with you. And Rufus. What does Rufus think?'

'What I do is of little concern to Rufus,' said James, fighting for dignity.

'Oh really? What I see makes me doubt that. And that lovely old duffer, Merlin, he's your godfather, isn't he? Bet he thinks you're no end of a fine fellow.'

'Look – what do you want?' said James. He knew it was dangerous, knew he was placing himself at her mercy, appearing to be ready to do a deal, but he was desperate.

'I want justice, Mr Forrest. I want my mother convinced that it was all your fault, all of it, I want you to go and see her and tell her the truth, tell her it would have made no difference if she'd gone to her prenatal classes or not, that you were drunk and bungling and incompetent, and if you hadn't been my sister would have been alive today. And I want your family to know what a shit you are, how you lied and cheated and intimidated that poor little nurse –'

'How dare you!' James was shouting now, his rage suddenly converted into physical energy. 'How dare you say such things?'

'I dare,' she said, 'I dare quite easily. I told you – I'm quite a brave person really. And I'll tell you something else, Mr Forrest. If you don't do what I say, then you're going to be reading all about it in the tabloids. Very soon.'

'Oh, for God's sake,' he said, 'why on earth do you think they'd be interested in it? After all this time.'

'Because it's me,' she said, her eyes wide, innocent as a child's. 'I have a way of making headlines, you know. I'm what's known as good copy. And so is this. I think the fact I should have been twins is a terrific story. I can see them now, all the headlines, the picture editors getting their computers to work out what she might have looked like. I think people would really love to read why there's only one of me. And about the struggle my mother's had to raise me all on her own. Don't you?'

James had never known such rage; he felt self-control leave him suddenly. He stepped forward, raised his hand to hit her. She stood there calmly, her eyes heavily contemptuous, her lips curved in a half-smile.

He pulled himself together, dropped his arm, stood looking at her.

'You're disgusting,' she said simply. 'Quite disgusting.'

And she turned and stalked off into the woods.

When he got back to the house – shaking, exhausted, fearful – Julia Bergin was standing on the back lawn. She was wearing a white polo shirt and madras bermudas; her face was porcelain-smooth, her brown hair looked freshly set.

'James! So sweet of you to ask us over. I was sent to try and find you.'

She sounded, looked even, as if she had come for drinks, or a barbecue; her studied casualness seemed an affront to their distress, an insult to Cressida.

'Oh really?' he said, and it was difficult to speak, his tongue seemed disconnected to his brain. He felt dreadful, scarcely conscious. He had to pull himself together, work out what he was going to do. 'Any reason in particular?'

'Maggie has made some sandwiches. She thought we should all eat something.'

Bloody Maggie and her obsession with food; didn't she ever concern herself with anything else? Then he realized that he hadn't eaten all day, and was in fact something close to hungry.

He managed to smile at Julia. 'She's probably right. Is everyone still here?'

'Yes, of course. Your wonderful godfather is making everyone drinks. Such a sweetheart. Such an original. Many people would find his frankness rather rude, but I like it. I appreciate honesty, as I'm sure you do, James. It was one of the first lessons I learnt when I went into analysis, to confront the truth and then convey it.'

'Oh really?' said James. 'Good.'

She linked her arm in his, led him towards the house. 'You must try not to worry too much,' she said. 'I just know Cressida is fine. That she'll be safely back.'

'I hope you're right. And I wish I shared your optimism.'

'Well, I have feminine intuition on my side,' said Julia, 'and it tells me that there is nothing seriously wrong. I got very close to Cressida, you know. She and I were like sisters. She was a very strong, sensible girl. She wouldn't do anything stupid. I know it. Trust me.'

Nobody seemed to have moved when they went back into the drawing room. James was faintly surprised; it seemed hours, days since he had left for his walk with Tilly.

'James, are you all right? You look terrible,' said Susie.

'Yes, I'm fine.'

'Where's Tilly?' asked Harriet, surprised.

'She went for a walk,' said James briefly. 'She felt she needed the exercise.'

'She's amazing,' said Harriet fondly. 'She runs at least five miles a day you know.'

'How very energetic of her,' said James coldly.

Harriet looked at him, puzzled; he returned her stare, his face ironed blank.

'I say,' said Merlin, who had sat himself down next to Janine, in between Harriet and Josh, 'these are good, Maggie. Part of lunch I suppose. Well, it'll keep you going for months, that food, won't it? Needn't go to waste. Put it all in the freezer. Wonderful things, aren't they, freezers?' he said to Susie. 'I've got two. Only shop twice a year now.'

'Good heavens,' cried Julia, clearly relieved by the distraction. 'How amazing. What about fresh fruit and vegetables?'

·'Never touch the stuff,' said Merlin. 'Can't stand any of it. Except for red peppers. Eat several peppers a day. Buy them fresh of course. Did you know,' he said to the room in general, 'there's more vitamin C in half a red pepper than three oranges? You'd know all about that, of course,' he added to Janine. 'Can't teach your lot anything about food. When all this nonsense is over you must let me cook you a meal one night. I do a very good ratatouille, though I say it myself.'

There was an awkward silence as everyone ignored Merlin's slightly unfortunate phraseology, then Julia spoke.

'Well, I am truly amazed you're so healthy. You could be in danger of severe tissue damage. No, not prawns, Maggie dear, I have a shellfish allergy. Just a little cucumber perhaps –'

'Tissue damage pah!' said Merlin. 'I'm eighty-four years old, woman, and a damn sight healthier than most of your compatriots. Look at them, obese, pasty-faced, mass of allergies like you, obsessed with their bowels –'

'Talking of health,' said Harriet, rather desperately, 'Oliver, we didn't tell you. We think Cressida was ill on the – God, it was this morning, wasn't it? It seems weeks ago. Well anyway, she was ill. Janine heard her – heard her being sick once or twice, and – well, sorry everyone, not a very nice topic. Did you have any idea she was ill, Ollie, or maybe it was just nerves –'

Oliver stood up suddenly. He walked over to the window and stared out for a few moments. Then he turned round and faced them.

'She wasn't ill,' he said finally, his voice shaking. 'She was perfectly well. She was pregnant, that's all. I think I'll have another drink, James, if you don't mind.'

James, looking at Oliver over the whisky bottle, wondering how many more revelations he could take about his beloved daughter, saw a very odd expression in his eyes. It wasn't embarrassment, or even bravado; it was something extraordinarily close to anger. And then thirty years of absorbing announcements of pregnancies, the near-subconscious computing of dates, symptoms, probabilities, told him something that he found almost unendurable, something he crushed hastily, ruthlessly, without even beginning to acknowledge it further. And then he looked at Harriet, who was staring at Oliver, her face very pale, and he knew she had reached the very same realization as swiftly and as certainly as he had.

Chapter 15

Mungo 6:30pm

More than anything in the world, he wanted to see Alice. The events of the past twenty-four hours had been so surreal, so nightmarish that he desperately needed some of the cool common sense she brought so efficiently into his life. Maybe he could get away that evening, get to London, have dinner with her even. There was no way Cressida was going to turn up now; his role as best man had been written out of the script. And now that Tilly was here, she was looking after Oliver far more competently than he could, she and Rufus. God, it was a strange partnership, that one: nice, but totally unpredictable. Mungo thought of Tilly's two previous lovers, a wildly eccentric French film director who had recently embarked on a second career as a Formula Two racing driver, and a black bisexual interior designer who had shot to fame with a simple if slightly esoteric corner in executive jet decor. And here she was, madly in love with a beautifully behaved English lawyer, an ex-public schoolboy who was polite to his parents, held doors open for women and stood up when his elders came into the room. Oh well. Love did strange things to people: as he knew. He could have had the pick of every nubile twenty-something on several continents, and what did he do? Fall head over heels – and that was such a good expression that exactly described how he felt half the time, shaken to pieces and totally disorientated – with a woman of nearly forty with three children. Well, if nothing else, it certainly made you believe in the thing, in love. Rufus, who was a great believer in love, was always talking about it, had indeed first experienced it at the age of seventeen, had talked endlessly and tediously about it right through one summer when Mungo stayed with him and his family in France and Rufus had been forced to leave the beloved behind in London. Mungo had listened to his ramblings, impressed mainly by the fact that Rufus had insisted (shocked) that he and the beloved had not even been to bed together, that she didn't want to yet; and right up to the time that Mungo had met Alice he had thought it was a myth, a label stuck on sex, sex with possibly a bit of shared interest and background thrown in. Now he knew differently. Love, it seemed, was losing control.

He picked up the phone, dialled Alice's number. Jemima answered the phone.

'Hi, Mimi. It's Mungo.'

'Oh hi, Mungo. How was the wedding?'

'Er – interesting. Is your mother there?'

'I'll get her for you.'

Alice's low, slightly husky voice came down the line; if you could see that voice, Mungo thought, it would have a cleavage.

'Hallo, Mungo. I'm surprised you're free so soon. How did your speech go?'

'Well – it's been a funny old day. I need to see you.'

'Tonight? But Mungo, I thought –'

'Alice, it hasn't happened.'

'What hasn't?'

'The wedding. The bride ran away.'

'What!'

'Yes. Nightmare stuff. Christ, it's been awful. Anyway, I think I can get to London. There really isn't much point me being here any more. Are you free this evening?'

'Well – I could be. But –'

'Good. I'll disentangle myself and phone you when I'm on my way. It might be quite late. Does it matter?'

She hesitated slightly. Then, 'No. No of course not. But ring me first, won't you?'

'Yes of course. Bye, Alice. I love you.'

He felt instantly better: in touch with reality. He phoned the Bergins' hotel and was told they had all gone out. Great: that let him off the hook a bit. It would seem less uncaring to disappear if they'd all disappeared as well. And he could phone from Alice's, could always come back if he was needed.

Mungo showered, changed into a clean white shirt and his beloved 501s, the ones with the rip at the knee and the tear at the crotch, and put everything else into the big leather Gladstone Sasha had given him for his last birthday. Nice girl, Sasha: he hoped she'd last. For some reason, he wasn't sure what, he feared she wouldn't.

He decided he'd better at least tell his father he was leaving; as far as he knew both he and Sasha were in the bar. He went downstairs; they weren't there.

'Mr Buchan is in the pool, sir,' said the barman, 'and Mrs Buchan has gone for a walk in the grounds.'

Mungo sighed, decided it would cause less trouble to leave a message with Sasha than his father and went to look for her.

It took a little while to find her; she was well out of sight of the hotel, sitting on a low wall beyond the tennis courts. She was talking on her mobile phone, no doubt gossiping with a girlfriend or fixing up to see some frocks, and she looked somehow different from how she usually did; Mungo, trying to analyse it, could only define it as an alertness, an air of purpose. She didn't see him coming for a while, she was engrossed in her conversation, but he didn't get near enough to hear what she was saying before she saw him, smiled, said *Ciao* – God, it was bimbo talk that – and switched the phone off.

'Hi, Mungo. How are you doing?'

'Oh – fine. You know. It's been a funny old day.'

'Certainly has. Where do you think she went?'

'Oh – God knows. The general idea seems to be she was under some kind of terrible strain and she just scarpered, couldn't take any more, but I think there's more to it than that.'

'Really? Like what?' The blue eyes were sharp, watchful suddenly, beneath the long sweeping lashes; the sugary smile just slightly set.

'I'm not sure,' said Mungo quickly. He certainly wasn't about to tell Sasha about Oliver's panic the night before, about the overdose. She was sweet, but he didn't absolutely trust her. 'What do you think?'

'I think she was certainly under a lot of strain. I talked to her yesterday. More than just normal wedding nerves, I would have said. I spoke to her briefly yesterday, in the garden here. I was quite struck by it.'

'What did she say?' asked Mungo, intrigued.

'It wasn't what she said. It was how she was. Tense, and – I don't know – odd. She had a long rambling conversation with me about make-up, and then just casually at the end she asked me if Theo was around, she wanted to ask him for something.'

'For something or just something?' said Mungo. 'There's quite a difference.'

'For. Definitely for. Anyway, he wasn't here, he'd gone into Oxford, but I said I could call him, give him a message. She said no, she'd speak to him later. But she never did. I asked him. He even rang her, but she said it was nothing, nothing at all.'

'And you've no idea what it was?'

'No idea at all. But I didn't get the impression it was nothing. At the time. I wondered if she needed money. Anyway, whatever it was all about, it's certainly a fairly drastic thing to do, run away on your wedding day. I would say she was pushed into it, that she didn't have any real choice.'

'What – you mean some kind of – well, blackmail?' Mungo was increasingly intrigued, excited even.

'Maybe not blackmail. But there has to be another element in it all somewhere, I think, some other person or factor forcing her hand. She really didn't seem to me the sort of person to just crack.'

'Oh I don't know,' said Mungo. 'She was very gentle, you know, very – well, soft, and sweet. Not a bit like Harry.'

'No, she didn't seem a bit like Harriet.'

'Now that sounded interesting,' said Mungo, grinning at her, sitting down beside her on the wall.

'What do you mean?'

'I mean it sounded as if you'd rather she had been like Harriet.'

'No. I mean I don't know either of them well,' said Sasha. 'But I like Harriet – what I've seen of her. I think she's clever and gutsy. She's got balls.'

'And you like your women with balls, do you?'

'Yes I do,' said Sasha, smiling at him.

'I'm surprised.'

'Why?'

'Oh – I don't know. You seem more of a Cressida to me. Than a Harriet.'

'Oh really? You mean you don't think I've got balls?' She was relaxed now, smiling more broadly; she was obviously enjoying herself. She seemed a rather different person suddenly. Mungo stared at her.

'Well, I –'

'I do hope, Mungo,' said Sasha gently, 'that you don't think I'm just a pretty little bimbo, with nothing in my head but getting my hands on your father's money.'

'What? No, of course not.'

'I think you do,' she said with a sigh, 'but it doesn't terribly matter.'

'Yes it does,' said Mungo, finding somewhat to his surprise that it did. 'If it matters to you, then it matters to me.'

'Oh Mungo, why?'

'Because you've been so nice to me,' said Mungo, suddenly picking up one of her hands. She had beautiful hands, very slender and delicate, the nails just a tiny bit too long (they were always a giveaway, nails, he was amazed girls never realized), longer than Susie or Alice would have worn them. She looked at him, startled, and then smiled again.

'Well, it wasn't very difficult,' she said, 'being nice to you. You were nice to me. Most people weren't.'

'Who wasn't?'

'Oh – most of your father's friends. Most of his business colleagues. All his employees. His dear son, Michael.'

'Michael sucks,' said Mungo briefly. 'You don't want to take any notice of him.'

'I try not to. Anyway, I've got used to it. But it isn't very nice. People are polite of course, but that really is all. It's a very – thin politeness, most of it.'

'I'm sure –'

'Mungo, it's inevitable. Everyone thought I was a gold-digger looking for a sugar daddy. And I suppose they were right. In a way. Although when I met him, I did genuinely fall in love with him. I found him irresistible. I suppose most women do. But of course money is very nice. Nobody could pretend it wasn't. And later, when it all began –'

'When what began?'

'Oh, you know, the patronizing, both by him and everyone else, and knowing he wasn't in love with me –'

'Sasha, I'm sure he is.' Mungo was beginning to feel uncomfortable now, felt she was telling him too much.

'Mungo, he isn't. He's only been in love twice. Once with your mother and once with – well, it doesn't matter who.'

'Tell me.'

'No. I won't. It's not my secret.'

Mungo felt a fierce curiosity. 'Did he tell you?'

'No. No of course not. I found out.'

'God. Sasha, please tell me. I won't tell anyone.'

'No, Mungo, I'm not going to. Now listen, this is getting out of hand. You look as if you're going somewhere.'

'I – well, I do want to go somewhere. Yes. To London. Do you think it would be all right?'

'And what's in London, Mungo?' She was grinning at him again, that easy, casual grin, so different from her careful neat smile. 'Love?'

'Yes. Actually. But don't tell Dad. Please.'

'I won't. As long as she's nice.'

'She's wonderful,' said Mungo simply. 'I'm going to marry her.'

'My goodness. Don't you think –' Suddenly, sharply the phone rang; she looked at him quickly, said excuse me, turned just slightly away. 'Hallo. Yes, yes of course. Good. That's excellent. Fine. Yes, later tonight. Lovely, thanks for calling. Have to go now. Oh, Mungo, there's your father, coming now. You can tell him yourself.'

'Tell me what?' Theo's voice was good-natured, indulgent. 'Sasha darling, what on earth are you doing out here? I thought we had a tryst in the bar.'

'We did, but I got tired of waiting for you.' Sasha's voice was clear, surprisingly firm. 'And it is a lovely evening.'

Theo was silent; his face was hard to read. Then he said, clearly with an effort, 'Yes of course. Shall we have drinks out here? Mungo, will you join us?'

'Well –'

'Mungo wants to go to London,' said Sasha. 'Is there any reason why he shouldn't?'

'London? Well – I don't know. It seems a little – odd. We are in the middle of a very complex situation here, Mungo. Your friends need you; I need you. I really think it would be better if you stayed.'

'But Dad –'

'Mungo, I said I thought you should stay. All right?'

'But I don't see the point, what on earth can I do?' said Mungo. 'They've all gone out and –'

'Mungo, please. I said I'd rather you stayed.'

'Well I'm not going to stay,' said Mungo, his skin pricking with the familiar violent irritation that his father should still seek to control his actions. 'I've done my bit today. And last night. You have no idea –' He stopped suddenly. He really didn't want to start discussing the events of the night before with his father and Sasha, didn't want to hear them start conjecturing, analysing it all.

'That's an extraordinarily selfish way of looking at it,' said Theo. 'I don't think I like that very much, Mungo.'

'Well I'm extremely sorry I can't aspire to your own high standards,' said Mungo. He knew he was sounding more and more like a spoilt sulky child, but he couldn't help it. 'But I have something important to do.'

'Yes,' said Theo heavily. 'I can imagine.'

'Theo,' said Sasha suddenly. 'Theo, I really do think –'

'Sasha, this is nothing to do with you.'

Sasha got up in silence and walked over to the high fence that bordered the garden, stood looking out beyond it; Theo looked after her, seemed about to follow, then turned his attention back to Mungo.

'Right then. Are you going to have a drink with us?'

'No,' said Mungo. 'I'm not. I'm going to London.'

There was a silence, then Theo said, clearly struggling to keep his temper, 'Then perhaps I could ask why? What is so important? I do hope it's not just another poker game.'

'No, of course not. I – want to see someone.'

'Oh really? Who?'

'Do I have to tell you that as well?' said Mungo wearily.

'You don't have to, but I'd like to know.'

Theo's voice was suddenly quieter, more reasonable again. Mungo looked at him; he was half smiling, seemed genuinely interested. Go on, Mungo, go for it. You have to do it some time. Tell him, break the news.

'All right, I'll tell you. She's called Alice.'

'Pretty name. What does she do?'

'Works for a charity.'

'Oh, very debby.'

'She's – not a deb.'

'Ah. A power-suited executive then?'

'Not exactly. She – well, she's supporting her family.'

'Her family! What, you mean her parents?'

'No, her children.'

'Her children! Mungo, what are you trying to tell me? That you've got involved with some single parent? Very fashionable, very – what's the phrase – politically correct.' He was smiling now, his slightly dangerous, glittering smile.

Mungo swallowed. 'Yes,' he said, 'yes I have. Alice is divorced.'

'I see.' Theo looked genuinely nonplussed for a moment, not sure how to react. Sasha had come back to join them, was listening intently. She smiled at Mungo; it gave him courage, that smile, hope.

'How old is she, your Alice?' said Theo. 'How long has she been divorced?'

'Quite a long time. She's – she's thirty-nine.'

'Thirty-nine,' said Theo very quietly. He seemed to be thinking, processing the information. The phone still in Sasha's hand rang again; she switched it on, listened for a moment, said, 'I'll call you back.'

'Who was that?' asked Theo.

'It was Jackie.'

Jackie was their housekeeper in London; Sasha's unkinder critics had been heard to remark that she was a blonde version of Jackie.

'Oh really? Well, I'll speak to her later.'

'Theo, she called me.'

'Yes, so you said. Look, Mungo, I hope you know what you're doing with this relationship. Not getting in too deep.'

'Dad,' said Mungo, a sweep of rage, of outrage flooding through him, as he thought of how his father conducted his own private life, of the trail of misery, humiliation and chaos he left in his wake, 'Dad, I know exactly what I'm doing with the relationship. And I am getting in very deep as you put it. I'm going to marry Alice. Actually.'

'Oh really? I rather think you're not.'

'That's up to me, Dad. And I rather think I am.'

'That is a little open to debate, I would suggest,' said Theo. 'That it is up to you. Actually.' His sentences were growing shorter, as they did when he was really angry. Mungo looked at him, defiant, hoping his fear didn't show.

'Of course it's up to me. I'm twenty-seven years old. I can do what I like.'

'Is that so? Are you really? Twenty-seven, eh? Good Lord. That's hard to believe, Mungo, it really is. I mean the majority of twenty-seven year-olds are standing on their own feet, supporting themselves. I –'

'Don't start that,' said Mungo, 'don't throw that garbage at me about supporting myself. My agency is –'

'Oh Mungo, Mungo. You really are a child, aren't you? Do you realize what that office alone costs? And who's actually paying for it? Who put up the money for the lease, to pay your staff –'

'Theo, don't,' said Sasha. She sounded very upset.

'Stay out of this, Sasha. You don't know what you're talking about.'

Sasha looked at him, then at Mungo and turned and walked away towards the hotel. Mungo stood staring at his father, trying not to lose his temper, trying to be calm, rational.

'Look,' he said, his voice shaky with the effort of keeping it level. 'Look, Dad, let's start this again, shall we? I – know you're very generous. I know I'm very fortunate. But I really am making my own way now. I'd like that at least acknowledged.'

'OK,' said Theo. His voice suddenly sounded more even. 'I'll acknowledge that. You're making your own way. Tell me, how old are Alice's children?'

'Jemima's fifteen and –'

'Fifteen! For God's sake, Mungo, she's almost as old as you are. You can't be serious about this. You really can't.'

'I'm totally serious. I love Alice.'

'And I suppose she loves you?'

'Yes, she does. She's agreed to marry me.'

'Marry you! For Christ's sake, Mungo, what are you talking about? Marriage! How long have you known this woman?'

'Since the New Year.'

'Well that's a very long time. A very long time indeed. God Almighty, you're more of a child than I even thought. What are you playing at?'

'I'm not playing as a matter of fact,' said Mungo, making an immense effort not to shout. 'I'm being very serious. Trying to be responsible.'

'Look,' said Theo, sitting down gently on the wall, clearly struggling to control himself. 'Look, Mungo, what's the rush, for heaven's sake? Why do you have to marry this – person? I'm sure she's extremely nice, but six months really isn't a very long time. Can't you just – enjoy one another for a while? Why do you have to marry her? It's crazy.'

'You always do,' said Mungo. 'You always have to marry them. However crazy.'

He felt sick as he said it, knowing where it would lead. Many things made Theo angry, but being confronted by the truth about himself was the worst provocation. He had once hit Mungo when he was a little boy because he'd told his father he ate too much and that was why he was so fat. On the whole people went along with the comfortable untruths Theo managed to believe about himself.

But for some reason Theo seemed in no danger of hitting him, not even of shouting at him. He just looked at him with an infinite sadness and said, 'Yes and sometimes it's the wrong decision.'

Mungo was silent; he still felt slightly sick. Thank God Sasha had gone back to the hotel.

'And I don't mean Sasha,' said Theo, 'in case you thought I did. Now then, please, Mungo, please wait. For a while. Apart from anything else, and I'm sure you won't have thought this one through, you'll want children one day. And if your Alice is –'

'Of course I've thought it through,' said Mungo, angry again, 'and it's fine. Alice can still have children. She's checked it out. I wish you had some respect for me, for what I want, for what I'm doing. Alice is – well, she's very special. And I'm going to marry her. As soon as possible.'

There was a long, leaden silence. Then: 'Mungo,' said Theo quietly. 'Mungo, you simply can't do this. You can't.'

'Dad, I can. You can't stop me.'

'Well,' said Theo, 'maybe not. But I intend to go on trying. I cannot and will not go along with this madness.'

'It is not madness.'

'It's madness. On both your parts. And I wonder how influenced this woman –'

'Her name is Alice.'

'All right. I wonder how influenced Alice is by your situation.'

'What situation?'

'Oh Mungo, don't be so naive. You are an extremely wealthy young man. A very good catch for someone –'

'Dad,' said Mungo, 'just don't. Don't insult Alice. I'm in love with her and she's in love with me.'

'Oh really?' said Theo. He had a very odd expression on his face.

'Yes, really. I can't expect you to understand that, of course, because you're too bloody selfish and self-centred ever to have experienced it. You have to buy your wives.'

'Mungo,' said Theo, very quietly, 'Mungo, I would advise you to be careful what you say to me.'

'I won't be careful because you don't seem to understand. I don't have to buy Alice, she's going to marry me because she loves me, and just to prove it to you, I'm not going to take another penny from you as long as I live. I'm going to make my own way. With Alice's help. And I'll tell you something else, I'm glad. I've spent my whole life taking from you, being told by the whole bloody world how spoilt, how advantaged I was. Well in future that'll stop, because I'm going to be standing on my own feet, making my own way, and I can tell you that's a huge relief. You'd better remember this conversation, Dad, because it's the last one we're ever going to have. I'm going now, to London, and I won't be back.'

'Fine,' said Theo calmly. 'Absolutely fine. Bye, Mungo. Tell Sasha if you see her that I'd like her back out here, would you?'

'Deliver your own messages,' said Mungo.

He was back in reception carrying his bag when he remembered that he had no car. Well, that was all right. He could call a minicab. It was a pity, it meant a delay, but there was no real problem. On the other hand he didn't want to be hanging around the hotel waiting, quite possibly having to see his father again. Maybe he should get over to Oxford, take the train. He'd get Brian to take him to the station. Mungo was about to have Brian paged when he realized he was already doing exactly what his father had thought he would: calling on the apparently infinite resources that had been available to him all his life. Right, no Brian.

He'd have to get a cab then. He picked up his bag and was about to walk out when he remembered the hotel bill. There was no way he was going to afford his father the satisfaction of picking up that one. He went over to reception, asked them to make out his share of the bill.

'Certainly, Mr Buchan.' The girl was wearing a tailored red suit and a striped shirt, the crisp neatness at odds with her wildly crinkly hair and heavily made-up face. She addressed herself to her computer with great self-importance; there was the usual delay, the endless whirring and spewing of paper out of the machine. As Mungo stood there, trying to look calm, still shaking with emotion, with rage and something worse now, with grief, hurt, a call came in to the switchboard.

'Royal Hotel, Woodstock, how may I help you?' said the girl, passing up the bill to Mungo with a smile. (Three hundred and eighty pounds. Shit, couldn't be right, not for twenty-four hours.) 'I think he's in the grounds somewhere. I'll see if I can have him paged. What name shall I say?'

She looked up at Mungo again, said, 'Your father is still outside, isn't he, Mr Buchan?'

'Yes, I think so,' said Mungo shortly, 'by the tennis courts.'

'Miss Forrest, if you could just hold on a moment, I'll –'

'Hey, I'll take that,' said Mungo, his heart lifting at the thought of Harriet's slightly tough clear-sightedness. 'Tell her I'll take it. I need to talk to her anyway.'

'Well – Miss Forrest, Mr Buchan junior is here. Can he help you at all? Oh I see. Right. Well, then, if you'll hold, as I said I'll have him paged.' She looked up at Mungo, her face carefully, politely blank. 'I'm sorry, Mr Buchan, she said it was specifically your father she wished to speak to.'

'Oh,' said Mungo. 'Oh all right.' He felt disproportionately put out. 'Er – this bill. I don't quite see why it's so high –'

'Ah, well, let me just go through it for you,' said the girl, sweetly deadpan. 'There's the room, of course, that's a hundred and eighty. Your luncheon yesterday, for yourself and your friend, seventy pounds, that was mostly the wines of course, then the bar last night before dinner, thirty pounds, and the two bottles of champagne through room service, they came to sixty, and then –'

'Yes, yes, of course,' said Mungo, passing her his gold Amex card.

'Sorry. That's fine. Right. Well I'm off now. To Oxford,' he added, not sure why he should feel it necessary to tell her that.

'Can I call you a taxi, Mr Buchan? I can have it here in about three minutes.'

'Oh – yes. Yes, that would be very kind.'

He sat down again, picked up a copy of *The Field* and started thumbing through it. The girl was engrossed with her switchboard; taking calls, putting them through, taking messages; then he heard her saying, 'I'm sorry, Miss Forrest, we can't find him at the moment. Can I have him call you? I see. Well, all right, fine. You could try in half an hour maybe.'

What on earth was Harriet doing, refusing to speak to him, refusing to let Theo call her back? It was so unlike her. Well, they were all upset, nobody was behaving quite normally; if only Cressida would – Mungo suddenly went very cold. He stood up and walked over to the desk. 'Excuse me,' he said, 'but that call, from Miss Forrest, for my father, did she give another name? A first name? Or did she just say Miss Forrest?'

'Oh no,' said the girl, and he realized how silly he had been, that the hotel staff would surely have picked up on the drama, would have known Cressida had disappeared, would certainly have reacted to her name. 'No, just Miss Forrest.'

'And you have no idea where the call came from?'

'No, I'm afraid not. You never can now, not with direct dialling.'

'No, no, of course not. And it was a good line?'

'Yes, very good.'

'Oh. Oh, I see. Well – well, never mind. Could I just – make a call please?'

'Yes, certainly. If you go into that booth over there, I'll give you a line.'

He stood there, dialling the Court House, stood waiting, his heart thudding. It was just a chance, a very very slight chance, but he had to check up on it. It was too important not to.

'Wedbourne 356. James Forrest speaking.'

'Oh – James. This is Mungo. Could I – could I speak to Harriet please?'

'Yes of course. I'll get her.'

There was a long silence: then Harriet came on the line. 'Mungo, hi.'

'You're – you're speaking to me now then?' he said, trying to sound light-hearted, afraid of creating a drama before it was necessary.

'What? What are you talking about, Mungo?'

'You didn't just ring? Ask to speak to Dad?'

'No. No of course I didn't.'

'Well in that case Cressida did.'

'I don't understand.'

'A call just came through. From a Miss Forrest. I thought it must be you.'

'Shit. And she wouldn't speak to you?'

'No. And they couldn't find Dad. So she rang off. She's ringing back, though.'

'Oh God, Mungo, what do we do now?' Harriet's voice was very quiet. 'Oh how awful to have missed her. So near and yet so far. Can you find your father, talk to him? He must know something, he must.'

'Well – it might be difficult,' said Mungo. 'We just had a major fight.'

'Why? Has he gone back to London or something?'

'No. No he's here. I think. But we just had a mega fight.'

'What about?'

'Oh – I'll tell you when I see you.'

'Well, I think this has to be more important. There's some fairly staggering news this end too. I'll tell you when I see you.'

'Well –'

'Mungo, really. Look, I'll come over. But I don't want to raise any hopes here. I'll make some excuse. OK?'

'Yes. Yes, OK. I was just – going to London actually.'

'Oh Mungo, you can't. Not now. Can't it wait?'

'Yes,' he said, 'yes, of course it can.'

Alice was very sweet about it. He told her he couldn't get away after all, that there was some family conference going on about Cressida.

'Oh, and I told my father about us.'

'What about us?'

'That I intend to marry you.'

There was a long silence, then she said, 'And?'

'And he didn't take it too well, I'm afraid.'

'Well – I'm not surprised. Mungo, you shouldn't have rushed it. You should have introduced him to the idea slowly.'

'I couldn't. I wanted to tell him. I want to tell everyone. Well, I've done it now. I want us to get married very very soon.'

'Well – yes.'

'You want that too, don't you?'

'Yes. Yes, of course I do. Well, quite soon. When you say he didn't take it too well, what did you mean?'

'Oh – huge dramatics. But he's like that. He's like a child. He says I am, but he's worse. Anyway, I've told him that as far as I'm concerned we're finished. I don't ever want to see him or have anything to do with him again. Or take anything from him. He thinks I won't be able to manage, but I will. I'm sick of living in his pocket anyway, being beholden to him. This is my big chance, Alice, to prove myself. With your help. And I feel really good about it. As if I'm starting all over again.'

'Well,' said Alice, her voice soothing, 'I don't believe either of you meant it. I'm sure you'll be friends again soon.'

'Alice, I meant it and he meant it. And, like I said, I'm glad. I don't want any of his charity.'

'Hardly charity, Mungo. He is your father.'

'He sees it as charity, I can tell you. He sees it as one big handout. Which I'm just not going to take any more.'

'Well,' said Alice gently, 'well, we'll see.'

'Alice, there's nothing to see about. You seem rather concerned about all this. If –'

'Of course I'm concerned. But only for you. It seems so – sad.'

'Not sad at all. My father's a monster. And I find the thought of it all, of managing on my own, very exciting. Challenging. So what if he pays the rent on my office and lets me use his executive jet? Who needs it? I certainly don't. We can get married next weekend, if you like. In fact I think we should. Now look, I'll see you tomorrow. I really don't see myself getting up tonight, I'm afraid. But I can ring you, can't I? Any time?'

'Of course you can. Well, maybe not much after ten. I'm very tired. Tough day at the office.'

'Poor baby. Well, you'll be able to give all that up soon.'

'Yes,' said Alice. 'Yes, of course. Goodbye, Mungo.'

'Bye, darling.'

He didn't know quite what to do until Harriet arrived; he certainly didn't want to risk bumping into his father. He went into the bar, and saw Sasha sitting there alone. She was drinking champagne and flicking through *Tatler*; she had changed into a brilliant blue silk suit with a very short skirt, her tanned legs bare. She really was gorgeous, thought Mungo; if it wasn't for Alice he would quite seriously fancy her.

'Hi, Sasha.'

'Hallo, Mungo. Are you – OK?'

'Oh yes,' he said, smiling at her. 'Very much so. I'm sorry about the scene.'

'I felt so sorry for you, Mungo. But –'

'Let's not talk about it. What are your plans?'

'Long-term? Or right now?'

'Right now,' said Mungo, slightly surprised that Sasha should have anything as impressive as long-term plans.

'Oh, I think we're going to have dinner quite early. And then the idea is we go over to the Forrests. Theo feels he ought to be with them.'

'Harriet's actually on her way over here,' said Mungo. He felt Sasha stiffen slightly, and looked at her interestedly. 'You really don't like Harriet very much, do you?'

'Yes, of course I do,' said Sasha briefly. 'She's fun.'

'But you prefer Cress?'

Sasha looked at him thoughtfully, clearly debating something. Then she said, 'Actually, Mungo, between you and me, I can't stand Cressida.'

'You can't stand Cressida? Why on earth not?'

'I think she's devious and manipulative. And she did something totally out of order to me.'

Mungo was so astonished he didn't notice that Sasha was sounding quite different from her usual self.

'What?'

'I can't tell you. Now. But it was malicious and very destructive. I couldn't believe it at the time. I can hardly believe it now.'

'Sasha, you can't do this,' said Mungo. 'Give me tantalizing little morsels so that I'm drooling and then declare the banquet's over for the day.'

'I'm sorry, Mungo. I really can't say any more. Maybe one day. I probably shouldn't have said that much actually. It just came out.'

'I think,' said Mungo, deciding she was after all to be trusted, thinking it might prompt further revelations, 'that she just phoned.'

'Phoned? Cressida phoned here?'

'Yes. Asked for Dad. Wouldn't speak to me. But they couldn't find him. And I didn't realize until she'd rung off that it was her. Thought it was Harriet. Do you know where he is?'

'He's gone for a walk. A long walk, he said.'

'Uh-huh. No doubt reflecting upon the incompetence and ingratitude of his younger son.'

'Mungo, he loves you so much. You mustn't let it get to you. And you know he doesn't mean it.'

'Sasha, I really don't care if he means it. I mean it.'

'I'm sorry?'

'I'm absolutely determined to manage on my own. I don't want to have anything more to do with him. Or his lousy money. I don't need it.'

'Mungo –'

'And don't try telling me I do, there's a good girl.'

'Mungo,' said Sasha mildly, 'I do hate being talked to like that.'

'Like what?'

'Down to. Please don't do it.'

'Sorry,' said Mungo. Sasha was suddenly proving very unpredictable.

Theo and Harriet arrived almost simultaneously. They nodded and smiled briefly at one another; things were clearly not entirely happy between them. His father had probably been trying to tell Harriet how to run her business, thought Mungo; as if she needed that kind of advice.

Theo nodded equally curtly at Mungo. 'Thought you'd gone.'

'I was just leaving,' said Mungo, 'but there's been a development.'

'What kind of development?'

'Cressida phoned you.'

'What do you mean she phoned me? Why wasn't I told?'

'They paged you. They couldn't find you.'

'Christ,' said Theo. 'Christ Almighty. They can't have tried very hard. Why didn't you come and look for me, or Sasha?'

'We didn't realize it was her, for God's sake,' said Mungo, 'until she'd rung off. But she's phoning again. Quite soon hopefully.'

'And there's something else,' said Harriet, 'something totally unexpected, something you have to know. Apparently she's –'

'Oh Theo,' said Sasha and her expression was sweetly, carefully contrite. 'Sorry to interrupt, Harriet. I'm so sorry, Theo, I almost forgot with all the excitement. Could you call Mark? He said it was very urgent. Very urgent indeed. I tried to find you but –' her voice trailed away.

Mungo looked at her. The coolly composed woman who had been sitting in the bar half an hour earlier reading *Tatler* and drinking champagne had not seemed too much like someone anxious to give her husband a very urgent message. The fifth Mrs Buchan had stepped sharply out of character; he wondered suddenly if it could possibly have anything to do with Cressida's disappearance.

'For Christ's sake when?' said Theo. 'When did he call? You don't have a great deal to remember, Sasha, I wish you'd – look, I'm going upstairs to call him. If Cressida phones, they can just interrupt the call, put her through. All right?'

'All right,' said Harriet. She had an odd expression on her face. Theo disappeared; they all sat picking compulsively at peanuts, not looking at one another. Not for the first time that day Mungo felt as if he was caught up in some rather strange film.

'Apparently,' Harriet said abruptly, in between munches, and Mungo never forgot that moment as long as he lived, the almost casual way she dropped her bombshell, 'apparently Cressida was pregnant.' She smiled brightly at them both, brushed some salt off her navy shorts. They stared at her.

'Well,' said Sasha finally, 'well, she won't be the first pregnant bride. Where I come from, it's considered rather posh to get married when you're not pregnant.'

Harriet smiled at her uncertainly. 'Yes of course,' she said politely. 'I mean, no of course she won't. It's just – well –'

'Not terribly like Cressida,' said Mungo.

He was, against all logic, rather shocked. He knew it was absurd, but he couldn't help it. Of course Sasha was right, of course it wasn't unusual, and not even Cressida, sweet, slightly shy, absolutely conventional Cressida would be going to the altar a virgin; but – pregnant? He thought of the drama of the night before, with Oliver, and tried to put it together with this new piece of information. It just didn't fit. None of it fitted.

'Harriet, how do you know anyway?' asked Sasha. 'Who told you and when?'

'Oliver told us,' said Harriet casually, 'about an hour ago.'

'I see,' said Sasha, her fine eyebrows arched, her voice slightly thoughtful. 'Poor Oliver. Poor, poor Oliver. It gets worse and worse, doesn't it?'

'Yes,' said Harriet. 'Yes it does. Poor Oliver,' she added dutifully, but she sounded almost impatient suddenly.

'And how did everyone take this announcement?' asked Mungo. He was trying to imagine Julia's reaction, Maggie's. 'Were they all very shocked?'

'Well, there wasn't time really,' said Harriet. 'I mean, he'd only just announced this when you phoned. I came haring over. Bit of a bomb-shell, though.'

'Yes,' said Mungo, 'it is a bit.'

They sat looking at one another, embarrassed without knowing why.

Then Harriet got up; it was a very decisive gesture, as if she'd just made a difficult decision and had to act on it. 'Excuse me,' she said, and walked out into reception; Mungo followed her. She went over to the desk, spoke to the girl.

'If my sister phones for Mr Buchan, could you let me speak to her first?' she said. 'It's important.'

The girl looked doubtful. 'Well, she was very emphatic last time, Miss Forrest, that she spoke to –'

'Look,' said Harriet, 'I wasn't here then. She's my sister. I need to speak to her. You can put her through to Mr Buchan after that.'

'Harry,' said Mungo. 'Harry, I don't think that's a good idea. This is such a delicate situation. Why don't you just let Cressida speak to Dad? That's what she wants.'

'Look,' said Harriet, and her face was tense, her voice shaky. 'Look, Mungo, I'm sorry, but this is nothing to do with you. Cressida will speak to me. Of course she will. She's my sister, for God's sake. She just doesn't know I'm here, that's all. If she did, she'd ask for me.' Her face was very white, her eyes huge and dark.

Mungo hesitated, then he said, 'Harriet, I'm sorry, I'm really sorry to say this, but if she'd wanted to speak to you she'd have rung you at home. At the Court House. Don't you think?'

'No I don't,' said Harriet, and her voice was icy cold. 'Of course she wouldn't. She might have got Daddy, Mummy, anybody. Now please stay out of this, Mungo, I really don't think it has anything to do with you.'

Mungo shrugged and went back into the bar. Harriet's stubbornness, her blind pursuit of what she knew was best, was legendary. There was absolutely no point pursuing this one any further.

Sasha looked up at him, raised her eyebrows. 'Problem?'

'Not yet,' said Mungo. 'Would you like another drink, Sasha?'

'No, thank you,' said Sasha. 'I have to keep a clear head for the next couple of hours.'

Mungo, intrigued, was about to ask her what for, apart from what she might choose to wear for dinner, when Harriet came back in. She gave them a faint smile and sat down, fiddling with the gold link bracelet she always wore. She didn't say anything. Mungo looked at her, and he knew what had happened. He put his hand on her arm, patted it gently, offered her her glass. She shook her head rather feebly.

And then Theo came back into the bar. Looking surprisingly cheerful. Maybe, thought Mungo, his heart lifting, maybe Cressida had phoned back, spoken to him, told him where she was; maybe she had, after all, only been in some minor accident, been taken ill, had some personal crisis to deal with that was now over.

But: 'Nothing from Cressida then?' said Theo. 'Bloody Mark, gone out for a meal. Won't be available for another hour. We'd better all have another drink and wait for her. Why don't we all go up to our room, darling, it's nicer up there?'

Mungo was not looking at Harriet, but he felt her start forward and then withdraw again in a swift involuntary response to – what? Then he looked at Sasha and she was staring at Harriet too, a most odd expression in her big blue eyes, thoughtful, watchful and somehow compassionate. What was this? What was going on here? And then Harriet stood up, faced Theo full square, visibly braced for battle, and said, 'Theo, I'm sorry, I've made a bit of a hash of things.'

'Oh really?' he said lightly, but his voice had an edge to it. 'How unlike you, Harriet. What is it this time?'

'Cressida did ring,' said Harriet, her voice very calm, 'and I – I took the call.'

'I'm sorry?' said Theo. 'You took it? But it was for me. I gave strict instructions for it to be put through.'

'Yes I know that, Theo, but I knew – well, I thought – that Cressida would want to speak to me. You were engaged anyway,' she added, her eyes just slightly defiant, 'and she wouldn't have held on. Obviously.'

'I don't quite see that,' said Theo. 'But anyway, do go on. You took my telephone call and then what happened?'

'Well, she – she said –'

'Harriet, a few simple words should suffice here,' said Theo. He smiled at her, an icy, cold-faced smile. His voice was deathly heavy. 'Do try to put them together for us.'

'She rang off,' said Harriet. 'I said it was me and she just rang off.'

'And then?'

'Well, and then nothing.'

'Nothing at all?'

'No.'

'Nothing about where she is, how she is, what she might like us to do?'

'No.'

'You bloody fool,' said Theo quietly. 'You bloody, arrogant little fool.'

'I thought,' said Harriet, and her eyes were blank now as she faced him, 'I thought it would be better. I thought she'd want to talk to me.'

'Oh really? You thought that, did you? You thought. So you take my telephone call, override my instructions, intrude into my affairs, because you thought. Well, you didn't think, Harriet, did you? You didn't think at all. Actually.'

Christ, thought Mungo, it was foul beyond belief the way his father treated people, adult people, as if they were just mindless incompetents, but mindless incompetents who were his property, who owed him respect, obedience, allegiance. There was some slight excuse, he supposed, when those adults were in fact his own children, his employees, even to a faint, albeit arguable degree, his wives, but someone like Harriet, over whom he had no authority, no hold, that was seriously outrageous. He waited, as she stood there taking it, taking the distaste, the contempt, the – what was it? – the sheer dislike, wondering why she took it, why she didn't walk away, answer back, stop what was a most public humiliation. But she didn't.

'I'm sorry,' she said.

'Yes, well, I expect you are. Unfortunately your sorrow is not going to be a great deal of help to us. Jesus, Harriet, she could be anywhere, anywhere at all, she could be in danger, in trouble, she could be hurt, she could be ill, and she reaches out to ask for help, in her own way, and you ride in with your fucking, mindless arrogance and pull all the plugs on her. I don't understand you, I don't understand you at all.'

'I know that,' said Harriet quietly, and Mungo thought what an odd thing it was for her to say, and in such a way, then he realized, confusedly, that despite his father's rage and Harriet's defiance there was a strange intimacy between them, an undercurrent of emotion that he could not, did not want to, analyse.

'Well,' said Theo, 'well, that's that, I would imagine. She won't ring again. She'll be afraid to ring again. You'd better get back to your family, Harriet, tell them what's happened, tell them we had a chance of helping her, of knowing where she was, and that you've wrecked it. They may not be entirely pleased with you, but I think that's what you should do. I'm going back upstairs, I have other calls to make. Sasha, you'd better come up with me. Now just in case you should be passing the switchboard when any calls, any calls at all, come through for me, Harriet, would you be good enough not to take them? It might conceivably be better that way. Mungo, you can do what you like. I really don't care.'

'That's extremely good of you,' said Mungo icily.

Sasha stood up. She looked heavily, dreadfully sad. She put her hand out briefly to touch Harriet's arm, then followed Theo out of the bar. Mungo went rather helplessly towards Harriet, put his arms round her shoulder and gave her a hug.

'I'm so sorry,' he said, 'he's such a bastard. He had no right to talk to you like that.'

'Oh but he did, Mungo,' said Harriet, with a great tear-filled sigh. 'He had every right. You have no idea how much right he has. To talk to me any way he pleases.'

Chapter 16

Theo 7pm

'That was a terrible way to behave,' said Sasha.

She had closed the door behind her; she stood leaning against it, staring at him. 'Really terrible. Poor Harriet.'

'I'm sorry you should think that,' said Theo. 'I personally think it was Harriet who behaved terribly as you put it. High-handed, thoughtless.'

'Yes, Theo, I heard you. We all did. The entire hotel did, I would imagine. Mindless fucking arrogance I think was your precise phrase. Not pretty.'

Theo looked at her. He was feeling disorientated already, and Sasha was hardly helping.

'I'd rather you didn't criticize me,' he said. 'What Harriet did was absolutely out of order. And, as it turns out, disastrous. You have to see that.' He went over to the drinks tray, poured himself a large whisky and started to light a cigar.

'I think disastrous is a rather strong word,' said Sasha. 'Unfortunate, maybe, but not a lot more than that.'

Theo felt a surge of irritation; he drew on his cigar, looked at her through the smoke.

'Sasha, I don't think you quite appreciate the full extent of what's happened today. I –'

'Theo, I perfectly appreciate it. Cressida has run away. She didn't want to marry Oliver, so she removed herself from the possibility. She's obviously been planning it for some time.'

'Why do you say that?'

'Well, it's so obvious. There's the pilot's licence, the letter –'

'Sasha, I don't think you know what you're talking about. Of course she wasn't planning it. Something pushed her into it at the last minute –'

'Or someone –'

'What do you mean, someone?'

'I think there was someone else,' said Sasha. 'I think she was in love with someone else. Did you know she was pregnant?'

Her words hit him like a slug in the stomach; he put down his glass, stared at her.

'Pregnant? Of course she wasn't pregnant.'

'Yes she was,' said Sasha coolly. 'Harriet told us. Just before you had your little tantrum.'

'Sasha, please don't speak to me like that.'

'Theo, I shall speak to you how I like.'

Theo looked at her. It was like being in a room with a stranger. A stranger he wasn't at all sure that he liked very much. He hung onto what was relevant with a great effort.

'OK, so she was pregnant. A lot of brides are –'

'And just suppose the baby isn't – Oliver's.'

'Oh don't be absurd. Why the hell shouldn't it be Oliver's?'

'Why the hell should it? Since she's run away from him.'

'Sasha, do you know anything about all this? You seem remarkably well informed.'

'I don't know any more than you do, Theo. But I have feminine intuition on my side.'

'Ah,' he said, 'that old thing.'

'Yes, that old thing. I happen to put quite a lot of faith in it. And I also have common sense. If you thought about it all a bit, Theo, I think you'd probably concede it was quite likely that the baby is someone else's.'

'And whose do you suppose it is then?'

'Theo, I don't know. I only just heard about it a few minutes ago. Oliver had apparently only just mentioned it when Harriet came over here.'

'Pity she didn't stay there,' said Theo heavily. He had to admit that Sasha's theory made sense and he felt very shocked and very upset. Cressida, sleeping with someone else – rather seriously sleeping with them – when she was engaged to be married to Oliver. Cressida, whom he'd known all her life, since she was a tiny, unbelievably beautiful baby, lying in a frilled crib in the nursery at the Court House. And suddenly he was there, smiling down at her, his arm round Maggie's shoulders, and she had asked him to be godfather and he had said . . .

'I'm not a very suitable person to be anyone's godfather, Maggie,' he said. 'Immoral, amoral, you name it –'

'I'd still like it,' said Maggie. 'Very much. Besides, you'll do all the other things so well, make a fuss of her, give her lovely presents, throw parties for her . . .'

He laughed suddenly. 'You're quite pragmatic, aren't you really, Maggie?'

'Yes,' she said, 'very, actually.' And burst into tears.

'Hey,' he said, 'what's this, postnatal depression?'

'No,' she said, 'just the good old-fashioned kind.' And then she looked at him and said, 'You know, Theo, don't you? About why he married me?'

'Yes,' he said, 'yes of course I do. Because he loves you. That's why.'

'No,' she said, 'no, Theo, that's not why. He married me to please my father. To get his consultancy. All that.'

'Maggie, that is nonsense,' said Theo, feeling panic clutch at his heart and his vitals at the same instant. 'Absolute nonsense. Jamie loves you. Very much. He wanted to marry you. He's very happy. Look at the pair of you. You're such a success. Two lovely little girls, a thriving career, this lovely house –'

'Yes, and no love,' said Maggie. 'No love at all. Well, I love him, but he doesn't love me. Don't, Theo, please don't. I'd rather you were honest, actually. It would make me feel better, less insulted. I feel at the moment there's a kind of conspiracy between you –'

'Oh, Maggie,' said Theo, taking her in his arms, giving her a rib-crushing hug. 'Maggie, there is no conspiracy. I swear. And I certainly love you. Very much.'

'Well,' she said, 'at least that's something. It's quite hard, Theo. To know you were simply chosen for your dowry. That's what it was, you know. My dowry. The job at St Edmund's. Oh, I'm sure he's fond of me. I know he is. But he doesn't love me. Not how I love him. He didn't choose me for the – the right reasons.' Her voice shook; she tried to smile at him. 'And that's hard, Theo. It's very hard.'

'Well,' he said carefully (mindful that he must not sound dishonest, and therefore insulting), 'well, maybe there is some truth in it. But I do know his world revolves around you, Maggie. He does love you. Maybe – at the time – it wasn't an earth-moving kind of a thing. But I've known him a long time. And I can see when he's happy, the old bugger. And he's happy and he's fulfilled and for Christ's sake, Maggie, isn't that what marriage is really about?'

'Yes,' she said, with a heavy sigh. 'But you both need to be happy and fulfilled, wouldn't you say? And I'm really not.'

There was a silence. Then she said, 'But anyway, I'm not about to give up on him. On it. On the marriage. I've got what I wanted, in a way. And Cressida is a symbol of that.'

'Why?' he said, interested. 'Why do you say that?'

'Oh – I told him I knew. Just about nine and a half months ago now, actually. I told him I knew why he'd married me. And that even so I was going to make it work. And he cried and said he would make it up to me somehow. And that very night, Cressida was conceived. So you see how special she is, don't you?'

'Yes,' he said, 'yes, Maggie, I do.'

And a quarter of a century later, it seemed, she was indeed a symbol. A symbol of faithlessness, of manipulativeness, of sexual infidelity: of all the things her father displayed every day of his life. Theo felt sick at heart. He stared at Sasha, and his feelings obviously showed in his face for she came towards him, and kissed him quite gently on the lips.

'Poor Theo,' she said, 'you look upset. I'm so sorry.'

'Well,' he said, 'well, there's no point in conjecturing about any of it.'

'Not really.'

'And she gave you no clue yesterday when she talked to you? That she was frightened, anxious – pregnant?'

'None at all. She was jumpy, I told you that. Unsettled. But that was all.'

'Well,' said Theo with a sigh. 'No doubt we shall find out in due course. About all of it. Although –'

'I know,' said Sasha. 'We might be nearer, if Harriet hadn't done what she did. I can see why you were so angry.'

'It's just if she needs us. Needs help. And of course it would be good to know where she is.'

'You really don't think she'll ring again?'

'Not now. Not tonight. She'll be afraid of – well, of having to speak to anyone. Anyone she doesn't want to. Of having the call traced. All sorts of things.'

He finished his whisky, poured himself another, sat down and started playing with the remote control of the television. Sasha walked forward and gently removed it from him.

'I want to talk to you. What did Mark want?'

'Oh – business. Nothing for you to worry about.'

'Theo, I am growing a little tired of this,' she said.

Theo smiled up at her, put out his hand and took hers. He raised it to his lips. 'Of what, my love?'

'Of being treated like some little tart who's only fit for one thing.'

'But my darling, you're so very fit for it,' said Theo. He suddenly wanted her, wanted to be in bed with her, wanted to be taken away, however briefly, from this dreadful day. 'So beautifully, wonderfully fit. Come and sit down here. I want you to distract me.'

She looked at him and he thought for a moment she was going to refuse, then she sat down beside him and smiled at him very sweetly.

'The silly thing is,' she said thoughtfully, 'I'm really rather fond of you.'

Theo stroked her hair. 'I don't see why that's silly,' he said.

'You will,' said Sasha, 'I'm afraid.'

'Sasha, what are you talking about?' said Theo. He felt very tired and slightly drunk, and he was finding Sasha's behaviour disturbing. 'Look, let's go to bed. You look gorgeous and I need a fuck.'

'But I don't,' said Sasha.

Theo felt as if he had been hit. In the whole nine months of their marriage, Sasha had never refused him, had never even hinted that she was not one hundred and one per cent ready for him.

'What is this?' he said, trying to smile. 'What's wrong? Do I have bad breath or something? Should I have a shower?'

'No,' said Sasha coolly, 'but I should.'

She stood up, walked into the bathroom and shut the door. Theo poured himself another whisky, and sat trying to pretend that this was absolutely par for the course, that women were unpredictable, sexually quixotic, not to mention slaves to their hormones, that it had been a tough day, he should take this like a man. And the more he told himself all this, the more he knew there was something wrong. Most women were unpredictable and sexually quixotic (Harriet particularly so, her mood swings and libido fiercely, erotically interesting, and why was he thinking about Harriet and sex in one breath at this moment when, if she had walked through the door, he would have hit her?), but Sasha was not. Sasha was a constant flame, a lovely liquid, constant flame, it was the greatest source of his fondness for her, it had healed and soothed him after the pain of Harriet. And now, in his hour of great need, she was failing him. Well, she couldn't. It was unendurable.

Theo stubbed out his cigar, took a last swig of whisky and walked into the bathroom.

Sasha was in the shower; he could see the outline of her slender body against the glass door. God, she was gorgeous. The mind, the soul might not be quite there, but the body was. Theo stood staring through the glass, thinking about Sasha, about the feel of her, the look of her, the gently golden all-over tan, the firm, high breasts (there had to be a bit of silicone there, she denied it absolutely but he still suspected it), her slightly bony hips, her flat stomach, and her surprisingly thick golden-brown bush. And within the bush, behind it – Theo felt his heart beginning to beat uncomfortably hard; desire ripped through him. He tore off his belt, his trousers, his shirt, opened the shower door; and Sasha stood there, looking at him, her eyes moving thoughtfully over him, lingering contemplatively, almost amusedly on his erect cock. But she did not reach out for it, as she usually did, did not press her small, greedy body against him, onto him, but turned her back towards him, and stood there, her face raised into the thudding water.

Theo suddenly lost not just his temper but his senses. He stepped forward into the shower, pulled her round and started to kiss her, ramming his penis against her. She pulled back, startled; he went on. He knew he was being stupid, brutal even, but he couldn't help it. He had to have her, had to lose himself in her hot sweetness, had to try to forget the dreadful day.

'Theo!' said Sasha, her voice very calm, very loud against the background of the thudding water. 'Theo, stop it. Please. I don't – I don't want to. Stop it.'

But he couldn't stop; he was in the grip of a wild, angry hunger, a hunger that was totally out of control, and he was out of control with it, grasping, pushing, thrusting at her; and still she resisted, stayed closed to him. And then he was in her; and it was wrong, different, she was tight, hard, hostile, not the Sasha he knew, not fluid, not welcoming, her mouth lifeless under his, her hands hanging motionless at her sides. And still he went on, he had to, pushing into her, rising, falling, and then quite quickly it was over, he felt the rush, the flooding, the release, and felt something else too, almost at once, something rare and ugly and unfamiliar; shame he supposed it was. And he withdrew from her and stepped back out of the shower and shut the door without meeting her eyes.

He pulled on a robe, and went and lay down on the bed; he felt sick and wretched and very tired. After a long time she came in too, a towel wrapped round her sarong style, and started to rummage through the cupboard for something to wear without looking at him.

'I'm sorry,' he said suddenly, startled to hear the words. 'So sorry, Sasha. Please forgive me. I won't do it again.'

She looked at him rather distantly. 'Good,' she said. 'I'm pleased to hear it.'

'I was – upset,' he said.

'Oh dear.'

Shit, who was this? This coolly controlled woman, with no apparent desire to please, to say the right thing, to comfort him, to screw him, for God's sake.

She looked at him across the room. 'Would you like a drink?' she said, in the same distant tone. 'Because I would.'

'Yes,' said Theo, 'Yes I would. Scotch. No ice. Thank you,' he added as an afterthought.

She gave him a look of half amusement; half dislike as she handed him the glass. She sat down on a chair in the corner of the room with a glass of white wine and sipped it slowly and carefully, as if it was important what it tasted like.

'I'm sorry,' he said again. He had lit another cigar.

'That's all right,' said Sasha, 'I'll get over it. So what are you upset about?'

'Mark had news for me,' said Theo, 'quite bad news as a matter of fact. On a small scale.'

'What sort of bad news?'

'Sasha, I don't want to talk about it.'

'Theo, I do. All right?'

The same detached look, the distant coolness. For some reason it worried him. What the hell was going on? Well, it might actually help to tell her, to talk about it. Set it in perspective, clarify what he might do next.

'Oh – yes, all right. There was a company I very much wanted to get hold of.'

'Called?'

'CalVin.'

'Ah. The wine company.'

'Yes. How do you know that?'

'I know lots of things, Theo. You'd be surprised.'

'I'm beginning to be. Anyway, it was – is – in California.'

'Yes, I know. In the Napa Valley.'

'That's right,' said Theo. 'In the most beautiful spot. I'd rather fancied building a house there as a matter of fact.'

'Oh really? For whom?'

'For you and me of course.' Now what was going on? He looked at her, but her eyes were clear, wide, unreadable.

'I see. Well, so what's happened?'

'What's happened is that some other bastard has got hold of it. Well, of a lot of it. Bought a huge block of shares just today. God knows why, and it doesn't really matter, but – but –'

'It hurts,' said Sasha with that same distant look, 'doesn't it, Theo? Seeing your plans scuppered, all awry? Seeing someone playing with you, with what you want to do? It hurts.'

'Yes,' said Theo, 'it hurts. It hurts like hell. And it makes me very angry.'

'With whom?'

'With a great many people. With Mark, for letting this thing slip through his fingers. With whoever bought the fucking thing. With myself, I suppose.'

'I see,' said Sasha. 'Well, I'm sorry.'

She got up again and pulled the big leather case she had brought with her out of the clothes cupboard. She opened it, and then began taking things out of drawers and off hangers and piling them on the bed beside the case. Theo looked at her irritably.

'What the hell are you doing? I don't want to leave. We have to stay here with James.'

'You do,' said Sasha. 'I don't.' She was dressing now, pulling on some leggings and a T-shirt; she sprayed herself with perfume, brushed her hair, started checking through her handbag.

'I beg your pardon?' Theo put the cigar down in the ashtray by the bed, and stared at her.

'I don't want to stay here. I can't do anything. Sorry as I feel for everyone. So I'm going back to London.'

'You are doing nothing of the sort,' said Theo. 'I need you here with me.'

'Well, you'll have to make do without,' said Sasha sweetly.

'Sasha, you are not to go back to London. Absolutely not.'

'Theo, I'm going.'

A black, rising rage took hold of Theo. He stood up, moved across to her, took her arm in a violent grip. It was very thin, that arm, he noticed, little bigger than one of his own wrists, but it was extremely strong.

'You're staying, Sasha.'

'Theo, I'm going. For good. And let go of me. Now.'

Theo felt the ground shifting beneath him; the walls seemed to be moving before his eyes. Sasha's face, on the other hand, was quite still, gazing up at him, the eyes calm and contemptuous in the eye of the storm.

'Theo, I think I should tell you something. The – er – bastard who bought all those shares in CalVin. It was me.'

'You! Oh don't be so ridiculous.'

'I'm not,' she said. 'I bought them. They're mine.'

'But you haven't got any money.'

'Yes I have.'

'Well it's my money, if you have. And if you've used my money to do that, then the company is mine.'

'No, Theo, I think not.'

He stared at her; she was smiling gently, almost pityingly at him. He got up, refilled his glass, sat down again, without taking his eyes from her. She hadn't moved.

'I think I'd better explain.'

'I think you had.'

'You've been very generous to me, Theo. Very. Given me lots of lovely things. Lots. Except –'

'Except what, Sasha?'

'Except any kind of respect. Any real emotion. Just – what? – indulgence. And it wasn't very nice, Theo, actually. I didn't like it. I'm not a stupid woman, I don't enjoy being put down at dinner tables, belittled at parties, treated like some kind of pet poodle. I don't like being told I won't understand things I'm well able to understand and to stay out of things I would really enjoy being involved in. It's hurtful and humiliating. I did actually love you at first, Theo. You might find that hard to believe but it's true. I would have married you if you hadn't had any money at all actually. I thought you were lovely. Clever and charming and witty. And very very sexy of course. But it's worn out, that love. You've wrecked it, Theo, by the way you've treated me. It's not just me either, it's Mungo and Mark and – well, almost everyone. I just can't respect you. I really don't even like you any more.'

Theo wanted to speak but he couldn't. If his entire life had depended on his getting out a dozen sensible consecutive words, he would have died then and there. He just sat, taking slug after slug of whisky, staring at her.

'Anyway,' she went on more briskly, starting to put things neatly into her case. 'Anyway, I thought I'd show you that I wasn't as stupid as you thought. And do something for myself into the bargain. So I sold lots of the things you'd given me. Jewellery mostly, I had copies made, but a few clothes too, the really wonderful things, the Saint-Laurent evening dresses and the Chanel suits. Of course I didn't get very much for them, but it was enough. And I invested the money, did quite well.'

'How did you know what to – buy?' asked Theo. His voice was hoarse, rasping.

'Theo, don't be silly! I live with a master. I only had to listen and then instruct my broker. It was easy. Anyway, this was the big one, buying CalVin. Or most of CalVin. I bought that share in Tealing Mills yesterday, and sold it this morning. That's why I went out early, to find a phone. And then with that money, I bought CalVin. I'm sorry, Theo, but I really wanted it. I think I'll keep it. Of course I haven't been out there yet, to look at it, at the vineyard, but I will now. Maybe tomorrow if I can get a flight.'

Theo managed to speak again. 'I'll sue you,' he said simply, 'I'll sue you until you can't afford a drink of water.'

'Theo, what for? I haven't done anything wrong. Well, I suppose it was morally wrong, to sell the jewellery, but not legally. I don't think. It was all gifts, surely, you didn't plan on wearing any of it, or giving it to the next Mrs Buchan? And anyway, think how stupid you'd look, Theo, if you did sue me. Outwitted by your bimbo of a wife. I think you should keep very very quiet, actually. In any case' – she walked over to him, kissed him gently on the forehead – 'I don't terribly mind if you do. I'm a survivor, and it will have been worth it. I'm off now. To London. Goodbye, Theo. It's been a lot of fun. Say goodbye to Mungo for me. He's a lovely boy. He's been really kind to me. Oh, and Theo, I think you should get together with Harriet again. She's obviously still in love with you, and you've never begun to get over her. Have you?'

'Did she tell you about it?' said Theo, hanging onto sanity with immense effort. 'Because if she did –'

'No, Theo, of course she didn't. Harriet would never do anything so tacky.'

'So who . . .?'

'Oh,' said Sasha, and there was an expression of immense distaste on her face, 'it was Cressida, Theo. Sweet, lovely, too-good-to-be-true Cressida. She told me, very soon after we were married, actually. It wasn't very nice of her, was it? And my goodness she enjoyed it. Anyway, I must go now. I have a taxi ordered, and a train to catch. Bye, Theo. Thank you for everything.'

Chapter 17

Tilly 7pm

Tilly was in the nursery bathroom, lying in the bath, her Walkman turned right up, her eyes closed, concentrating on keeping her mind blank, not thinking even about Rosenthal (she was in no state to make that sort of decision), when Mungo came in. She wouldn't have known he was there at all had he not turned off the taps and in doing so knocked one of her feet. She opened her eyes with a snap and saw him looking down at her, his black curls even wilder than usual, smiling slightly apologetically. She switched off the Walkman and smiled back.

'Hi, Mungo.'

'Hi, Til. Sorry to – er – disturb you. I came in for a pee. And you were about to flood the entire place.'

'That's OK,' said Tilly equably. 'You go ahead and have your pee. Fine by me. I should have locked the door.'

'There would certainly have been a flood in that case, and anyway you couldn't have,' said Mungo. 'One of Nanny Horrocks's rules. No locks on her bathroom doors. You'd have liked Nanny Horrocks. She was ace. Tough as old boots, terribly strict, but such fun. She could play football better than the master at my prep school, and she was brilliant at poker too. I taught her, but she was better than me in no time.'

'Really? Well, I haven't known many nannies to compare her with,' said Tilly. 'How are things, and what are you doing here anyway? Apart from having a pee?'

'I brought Harry back. From our hotel. She had a mega bust-up with Dad. She's very upset.'

'Ah,' said Tilly. 'Poor baby. What about?'

'Well, she did do something a bit unfortunate. Cress phoned for Dad and Harriet insisted on taking the call and Cress rang off. So it looks like we lost her.'

'Silly bitch,' said Tilly amiably.

'Who, Harry?'

'No, of course not. Cressida. The more I hear of her, the more I discover, the less I like her. I mean, what a way to behave. God, I must sound like Nanny whatsername. But for heaven's sake, Mungo, if she didn't want to marry Oliver why couldn't she just have said so weeks ago?'

'Oh, I think there's probably a bit more to it than that,' said Mungo. He sat down on the side of the bath. 'From everything I've heard. Mind if I stay? It's not a lot of fun down there.'

'Of course not,' said Tilly.

'I've never seen you naked in the flesh before,' he said, looking at her contemplatively. 'Only shared you with millions of others in replicate.' He smiled down at her, his dark eyes flicking over what was visible of her, her boobs and her knees.

Tilly grinned back. 'I hope I don't disappoint you.'

'Not at all. You look absolutely gorgeous. If I wasn't seriously in love with someone else, I'd be in there with you.'

'Then there'd really be a flood,' said Tilly. 'And don't forget I'm seriously in love too. But it would distract them all a bit from their problems.'

'Yeah. What are you actually doing here, Til? And where's Rufus?'

'Rufus is downstairs. Doing what he does best. Being charming, and soothing. And I was desperate for a bath and that old darling Merlin showed me in here, said it was the biggest bath in the place. He's a peach.'

'Yes he is. Harry says he's working himself up for a romance with Janine. Pretty cool, eh?'

'Ah, Janine. Cressida's godmother? She's very stylish.'

'Yes she is. My dad told me she and James had a thing once, when James was very young.'

'You're kidding me!'

'Not at all. He was a virgin of eighteen and she was a worldly Parisian of thirty-five, or something.'

'Ugh,' said Tilly and shuddered.

'You don't like James, I gather?'

'I do not.'

'He's OK,' said Mungo.

'He's not OK. I may tell you why one day.'

'You know him?'

'You could say that. We have a deal on, and I'm waiting to see if he delivers.'

'Tilly, this is unfair. Exciting me like this.'

'No it's not. It's very fair actually. Let's change the subject. What's happening?'

'Well, Harriet's come back to confess, and to see what if anything needs doing, and I'm taking her car on to London.'

'I might come with you,' said Tilly, plunging her small neat head under the water, emerging and shampooing it furiously. 'Would you mind? Why are you going to London anyway?'

'I can't take much more of this. I've had a huge row with my father, and I want to see my girlfriend.'

'Your girlfriend? Is she nice?'

'She's glorious,' said Mungo simply. 'I told you, she's the only reason I'm not in that bath with you.'

'You can tell me more in the car. Pass me that towel, would you?'

'What about Rufus? Won't he want to come?'

'Maybe, maybe not,' said Tilly briefly, 'but he's not coming.'

'Why not?'

'Can't tell you. Well, partly because he knows he has to stay here and be a soothing presence. Alongside his beloved mother.'

'Don't you like Susie?' said Mungo surprised.

'Yes, of course I do. Why?'

'You sounded a bit – disapproving suddenly.'

'You're imagining things' said Tilly briefly, but Mungo, who could be surprisingly perceptive, had touched a nerve. She was in fact still to establish exactly how she felt about Susie in the light of her discovery about Rufus's undoubted parentage; more amused than shocked certainly, concerned over Rufus rather than any major moral issue, but just the same her instant liking for Susie had cooled, dimmed.

She looked at Mungo and smiled reassuringly. 'Now could you maybe go and find him and ask him to come up and see me here?'

※　※　※

There was a gentle knock on the door. 'Come in,' said Tilly. Only Rufus would have knocked like that.

He came in smiling, pushed the door shut behind him. 'Hallo,' he said.

'Hallo,' said Tilly, and thought how for the first time in her life the expression 'My heart turned over' meant something, meant exactly in fact what she was experiencing now.

'Nice bath? Merlin told me he'd shown you up here.'

'Very. I feel a lot better.' She put out her hand, stroked his face. He caught the hand, kissed her palm. Sensation soared through Tilly, echoing down her body. 'Shit,' she said. 'Shit, Rufus.'

'What did I do?'

'Made me want to fuck you,' she said simply.

'Now?'

'No,' she said, thinking with sorrow of the conversation they had to have, as soon as possible, 'no, not now, it wouldn't be very proper, would it?'

'Ottoline Mills, when were you concerned about being proper?' asked Rufus, smiling. He put his hand out again, undid the towel, pulled it off, touched her breasts. 'Lovely,' he said, 'so lovely, I love those breasts so much.'

Tilly was silent. His hand moved down, over her body, smoothing her stomach, his fingers strong, rhythmic. He bypassed her bush briefly, started stroking her thighs, moved forward, started to kiss her. He kissed very skilfully, Rufus did, Tilly thought, hanging confusedly to her determination through the whirlwind of beating, throbbing sensation travelling through her; slowly, carefully, and yet with immense pleasure. 'You kiss with your cock, did you know that?' she had said the very first time he had ever kissed her and he had laughed and said how novel. He was kissing her with his cock now, it was all she could think of, his strong, pleasure-bringing, powerful cock. She felt herself begin to tremble, her invariable signal of sexual arousal, and despite her resolve, pressed very gently, tremulously even, pressed her hips against his, pulled his head harder onto hers, pushed a hand down the front of his trousers, seeking, finding, caressing his penis.

'God,' said Rufus, 'God, Tilly, come on, let's find somewhere,' and he took her hand and she pulled the towel around her again, and he led her along the corridor and up the back stairs to the big attic room, locked it behind them.

'Oh my darling, darling Tilly,' he said, 'I love you so much, so very, very much.'

Tilly said nothing, but she smiled at him and lay down instantly on the dusty floor, opening her arms; he was pulling off his clothes, dragging off shirt, jeans, shoes, pants, his eyes locked with hers, and then he lay down beside her, and very gently began to kiss her breasts again.

Tilly threw back her head, her eyes closed, feeling his tongue circling her nipples, pushing herself against him, feeling his penis growing, growing against her; she loved this moment almost best, when he was still outside her, when every atom of her energy was absorbed in reaching for him, wanting him, urging towards him, when she could think, see herself opening to him, awaiting him, and then, then he was in her, sinking in, into her fathomless wet softness, his penis reaching into her charged, innermost places, and then she turned, rose, knelt above him, riding him, wildly, almost angrily, rising and falling with her own pleasure, feeling the circles begin, the whirling, powerful circles drawing her in, faster, faster, into a vortex of sensation, and she was plunging now, pulling at him, dragging him after her, forcing his own pleasure into her, and she heard herself cry out sharply, felt herself rising finally into the bright darkness, and then the tumbling of release, endless sweet falling, and she fell on him, kissing him, stroking him, loving him and wondering how she could possibly ever have thought of leaving him.

And then she opened her eyes and looked at him, looked at James Forrest's face, and knew that that was what she had to do.

'Now listen,' she said to Harriet who was sitting tearstained in the kitchen, drinking a cup of tea with Merlin, 'you are not to let them upset you. You did what you thought you had to do, and you've taken a lot of shit today – sorry, Merlin – and if Cressida doesn't want to talk to you, frankly, that's her loss. OK?'

'Well spoken,' said Merlin. 'Couldn't have put it better myself. Don't you worry, Tilly, I'll see they don't give her a hard time. Silly little thing. Needs her bottom smacked if you ask me.'

Tilly and Harriet both smiled at him, Harriet rather weakly.

'Pity you're going,' said Merlin to Tilly, 'I would have liked to get to know you better. Another time, perhaps.'

'That'd be good,' said Tilly. 'I'd like it too.'

'And you will go to Cressida's flat, won't you?' said Harriet. 'Just to make sure. Not that you'll be able to get in. But the caretaker might – well, you could explain.'

'Sure,' said Tilly, 'I'll explain. Don't worry. And I'll call you when I get home. Sure you won't come with me?'

'I'd love to,' said Harriet wistfully, 'but it would be running away. And whatever else, I've never done that.'

'Pity you didn't run away from the awful school,' said Merlin. 'Dreadful place. Cruelty to children sending you there.'

'Janine tried to save me too,' said Harriet, blowing her nose. 'What would I have done without the pair of you? She spent hours arguing with Daddy. I heard her once. And she wrote me more letters when I was there than anybody.'

'Did she by Jove?' said Merlin, his old head lifting and almost visibly sniffing the air with pleasure. 'What a girl, eh? Can't think why I never got together with her before. Anyway, I'm taking her out to dinner tonight, what do you think about that, both of you? Your mother didn't seem too pleased, but by my reckoning Janine's earned it.'

'Oh, Merlin, no, don't go out,' wailed Harriet. 'I need you here.'

'Come with us,' said Merlin.

'Darling Merlin, I wouldn't dream of playing gooseberry. But you will be back, won't you?'

'Of course. Not too late either. Got to get going in the morning.'

'Tilly,' said Harriet suddenly, 'do you know anyone at Cotton Fields? The American leisurewear chain?'

'Sure,' said Tilly, 'I did some pictures for them a few weeks ago in Mexico. Nice things. A bit like yours, only not such quality. They're doing a really great catalogue.'

'So who was there from the company?'

'Guy called Ken Lazard, the head of marketing, and the chief designer, poisonous little tart called tony joel without capital letters. If he said "tony written in lower case" once he said it a hundred times. I was ready to kick him in the balls, sorry, Merlin, by the end of day one.'

'But Lazard was nice?'

'Yeah, he was a honey. Why?'

'Well, I wondered if you could do a tiny bit of research for me. Some time. Thing is, they were going to come in with me, you know –'

'Harry! What the hell are you going in with anyone for?'

'Oh – it's called salvation, I think,' said Harriet. She looked into her mug.

'You in trouble?' asked Merlin sharply.

'You could say that, Merlin, yes. Just a tad. Only please don't say anything to anyone yet, will you? Specially not Janine, I don't want her worried.'

'No, no of course not. How bad are things, though?'

'About as bad as they can be. I have to – well, I have to go into liquidation in the next forty-eight hours, I would say.'

'Shit, Harry, why didn't you say so before? That's really terrible, and it's so unfair.'

'Yes, well, life's not fair, is it?' said Harriet, determinedly calm. 'And I have to say I've been extremely stupid. I probably deserve it. But –'

'Nonsense,' said Merlin, 'of course you don't. Look, anything I can do, Harriet, talk to a few people, beat them down, you know I will.'

'Merlin, I do know,' said Harriet, patting his hand, 'and thank you. Anyway the Cotton people seemed really keen until a couple of days ago. Practically signing. Then they just seemed to pull the plug, wouldn't talk to me, wouldn't return my calls. I just wanted to find out why.'

'Harry,' said Tilly slowly, 'how much money do you need?'

'Oh – about a million,' said Harriet cheerfully. 'See me through. Got it on you?'

'Not exactly,' said Tilly. 'But –'

'Tilly, what on earth are you hatching?' said Harriet. 'I know you earn a bob or two, but –'

'Oh, I might be able to help,' said Tilly. 'Tell you how another time. Anyway, I'll call Ken now. No time like the present, and it's a good time, mid-afternoon there. Otherwise we'll miss them. Got the number?'

'Tilly, you will be discreet, won't you?' said Harriet, thumbing through her filofax. 'I don't want to upset them if there's even the remotest chance.'

'Yeah, yeah,' said Tilly impatiently. 'Can I use this phone, do you think?'

'No, use my mobile. It's up in my room.'

Ken Lazard was in a meeting, his secretary said, and she didn't know when he might be out, could she say who was calling and maybe have him call her back when he had the time?

'Sure, tell him Tilly Mills,' said Tilly cheerfully, 'and I'd like to speak to him pretty soon – I have a message from Patsy Torminster.' Patsy Torminster had been her co-model on the shoot: as tall as she was, ash-blonde and drop-dead gorgeous.

'I really don't see him able to call you before tomorrow soonest,' said the girl, a heavy frost descending on her voice, 'he is really very busy indeed.'

'OK, OK,' said Tilly. 'Just deliver the message, would you?'

Ken Lazard was on the line inside thirty seconds; Tilly grinned into the phone.

'Hi, Ken. That must be a very important meeting.'

'It is,' said Ken. 'How are you, Tilly?'

'I'm good, thank you. How are you?'

'Fine, fine. God, that was a good week. Didn't we have fun? What's this message from Patsy?'

'Well, there isn't exactly one,' said Tilly, a rather vivid memory rising in front of her eyes of Ken Lazard andPatsy Torminster writhing around in the Mexican surf, 'but she'll be in New York next week. And I'll remind her to look you up.'

'Bitch,' said Ken Lazard amiably. 'So what do you want, Tilly?'

'I want you to do a little research for me,' said Tilly. 'And then get back to me quickly. And I really will get you the name of Patsy's hotel in return. Now this is for a friend of mine . . .'

'Ken Lazard will ring me before the end of the day,' she said to Harriet, walking back into the kitchen. 'Their day. So in around three or four hours. OK? And don't worry, he will. He's very well motivated.'

'Tilly,' said Harriet, 'I love you.'

* * *

'Tilly,' said Rufus, 'I love you. And I don't know why you have to go.'

'Because I have to work tomorrow,' said Tilly, 'and because this is family business. I did what I could for Oliver, which wasn't much. He wasn't talking.'

'He really wasn't? I thought he would to you,' said Rufus.

'No, he's scared,' said Tilly. 'Scared to start, you know? I mean he didn't even tell me Cressida was pregnant. He's a very screwed-up guy, that one.'

'Do you think so?'

'Yeah. Mind you, if I had Julia for a mother I'd be screwed-up.'

'Nothing would screw you up,' said Rufus fondly.

'You'd be surprised,' said Tilly.

Mungo talked about Alice all the way to London. Tilly was intrigued by the affair. Given Mungo's past and reputation, Alice must be one hell of a woman. Although of course it didn't exactly take Sigmund Freud to see why Mungo would be in love with someone almost old enough to be his mother. Just the same –

'What about children, Mungo?' she asked, as they began to hit the hideous outer reaches of London on the M40. 'Don't you want them?'

'Yes, of course I do,' said Mungo slightly irritably, 'but we can have them. Alice is only thirty-nine, for God's sake. She's not a menopausal old crone. Anyway, she's had it checked out.'

'Oh really? Good. Well, I can't wait to meet her.'

'You'd love her,' said Mungo, 'you really would. I've never felt so – oh, I don't know, safe before. I'd take you there with me now, but I'm surprising her, she doesn't think I'm coming and – well –'

'Of course not,' said Tilly, 'I wouldn't dream of it. Anyway, I have to get back. I'm expecting lots of calls. Including one from Mick McGrath. Fucking *Sept Jours* may want to shoot another two wedding dresses, in which case I'll have to go back tomorrow afternoon.'

'What, to Paris? Bloody hell. Pretty hectic your life, isn't it?' said Mungo.

'Tell me about it,' said Tilly. 'Now look, Mungo, I'd like you to come with me to Cressida's flat. It won't take long and it's on the way to your Alice. OK?'

'Sure. Why isn't Rufus coming up with you, as a matter of interest?'

'Because he felt he should stay down. Do his bit. You know how Rufus is about doing his bit.'

'Sure,' said Mungo. 'Are you guys going to get it properly together then?'

'Shouldn't think so,' said Tilly. She felt him look at her, fixed her eyes firmly on the architectural splendours of the Hoover factory they were passing.

'Why not? You seem pretty good together to me.'

'Yeah, well, we may be,' said Tilly, 'but that doesn't mean our lives exactly gel. Think about it. Anyway, why should we want to change things? They're OK how they are.'

'Sure.' There was a silence, then Mungo said, 'So how did you like his Mum? Now there is one nice lady.'

'Yeah,' said Tilly briefly.

Mungo looked at her again. 'But? What is it with you and her?'

'Look, Mungo,' said Tilly, 'can we drop all this? I'm tired. Let's just concentrate on getting to Cressida's flat, and then home, OK?'

'OK,' said Mungo.

Cressida's flat was in Chelsea, in a small modern block just off World's End.

'I think it's the first floor,' said Mungo, looking up at it slightly nervously. 'I've never actually been there, but it's number 2B.'

'And what do we do if we do get in? Look for clues? God, this is like that board game, what's it called, with Miss Scarlett and the Rev somebody.'

'Cluedo,' said Mungo, pulling up outside the block. 'I always rather liked it. I don't know what to do, Tilly. Let's worry about that when it happens. Shall we go up to the flat first? You never know, she might be there, and we'd look pretty silly asking the caretaker to let us in if she was.'

'Sure.'

But the door to the street was locked, with an entryphone for each flat; they tried 2B without success.

'The caretaker then,' said Mungo, ringing that bell. No answer; he rang it again without success.

'Shit. Must have gone out.'

'Excuse me,' said a girl's voice. 'Can I just –'

'Sure,' said Mungo, stepping aside to let her unlock the door; it was easy to catch it after her and let themselves in.

'Come on,' said Tilly, 'let's go up.'

The building was clean, clinical; there was a small lift. They stood in it not looking at one another; Tilly felt increasingly nervous without knowing quite why.

The landing was more of a lobby, with the doors to Flats A and B opposite one another; there was loud orchestral music coming from B, and a light showing through the small frosted-glass window in the door.

'Christ,' said Mungo, 'Christ, she's here.'

Tilly felt her heart begin to thud, her palms suddenly moist. 'You ring,' she said. 'I can't.'

Mungo looked at her. 'OK,' he said. But he didn't do anything either. 'What are we going to say to her, Tilly? What are we going to do?'

'I don't know,' said Tilly. They stared at each other, frozen into stillness.

'What are we afraid of?' said Mungo. 'What is it?'

'I don't know,' said Tilly again. 'But we can't just stay here. Come on, Mungo, be a man.'

He still didn't move. Tilly sighed, raised her hand and rang the bell. It was a very ugly loud buzz; nothing happened. She did it again for longer. Still no answer.

'She must have gone out and left the radio on,' she said, relief making her weak. 'We'd better come back.'

'No, we might miss her.'

A man emerged from the lift, stood at the door of 2A, fiddling with his keys. 'Keep trying,' he said, 'she never hears anything. She's definitely there. I saw her go in with the dog.'

'The dog?' said Mungo. 'But she – she hasn't got a dog.'

'I wish,' said the man and disappeared.

Tilly started hammering on the door with her fists, in between ringing the bell. 'This is hopeless,' said Mungo, 'why don't we go and phone again?'

'No.' She rang the bell again, left her finger on it. 'Cressida!' she shouted as loudly as she could. 'Cressida, open the door.'

A dog started barking furiously. The music stopped; they heard footsteps coming towards the door, an inside key in the lock; a handle turned. Tilly swallowed, tried to ease her dry mouth. Then: 'All right, all right,' said a voice, 'just hang on a minute. Who is it?'

A rather hard voice it was, with a South London twang to it: a voice that certainly wasn't Cressida's. A face looked through the crack of the door, past the chain, a pale slightly peevish face that wasn't Cressida's either. A dog's nose thrust its way out at knee level. Tilly stood there, staring into the crack; then she said, 'I'm sorry. We're friends of Cressida Forrest's. Is she there?'

'Cressida Forrest?' said the voice. 'No, of course she's not here. She hasn't been here for over six months.'

She was a very good-natured woman actually in spite of her peevish face; she asked them in, gave them a cup of tea, told them everything she knew, which wasn't much. Her name was Sally Hawkins, she was recently divorced, and Cressida had sold the flat to her soon after Christmas, had advertised it privately in *Loot*. She had taken the phone number with her, and had given the woman the Court House as her forwarding address.

'She was a very nice girl,' said Sally Hawkins, 'a very nice girl indeed. She got on very well with Benjy,' she added, looking fondly at the dog, an extremely shaggy black mongrel. 'She said she'd always wanted a dog as a child and hadn't been allowed one.'

'Oh really?' said Mungo. 'Er – was there ever anyone here with her, when you came to see the flat and so on?'

'No. She lived alone here, as you probably know. She seemed a very lonely person.'

'Did you – that is, was the flat expensive?' asked Tilly. 'For what it was, I mean?'

'No, not really. About average, maybe a bit below. But it's hard to tell these days, with the state of the market, isn't it?'

'Yes, I guess it is. Do you think any of the neighbours might have known her?'

'Well, I don't know. This isn't a very friendly place. The guy next door moved in after me, and all he ever does is complain about Benjy and my music. And I've never got to know anyone else at all.'

'We could ask the caretaker, I suppose,' said Tilly. 'But thanks anyway. Er – here's my number. If by any chance you think of anything, remember any clues she might have given you as to where she's gone, could you ring me?'

'Yes, of course,' said Sally Hawkins.

They tried the caretaker again; he was still out. Tilly looked at Mungo. He was very pale, clearly shaken.

'I need a drink,' she said.

'Me too. Let's find a pub. And then we should call Harry.'

Tilly opened her front door with a hand so weak it could hardly turn the key, and walked very slowly into her flat. She loved it, a white shell of a place, too big for her really, with very little furniture because she'd never had time to buy any, just a few couches and low glass tables, and a big iron bed, a present from Rufus ('mostly selfish' he'd said to her tenderly, 'now I want you to burn that horrible futon.') She stood there smiling round at it, feeling immediately better, and then noticed it smelt very fusty. Well, it wasn't really surprising. She hadn't been in it for three days, a hot three days; the windows were all tightly closed, the pile of dirty laundry she had meant to put into the machine before she'd left was still sitting on the bedroom floor, and the half-finished bottle of milk she'd left out on the draining board had separated into a watery rancid mess. She'd have to get a proper housekeeper or something rather than just dear Betty who came in once a week for what she called a whip-round. Tilly poured the offending milk down the sink, ran the cold tap fiercely to get rid of the smell, dumped the laundry into the washing machine and plugged in the kettle. At least she'd got some Long Life; if there was one thing she really hated it was black coffee.

She kicked off her boots, poured herself a glass of wine to go with the instant coffee and cigarette that frequently served her for a meal, and stood staring out of her small kitchen window. What a shit of a day. She couldn't ever remember one like it. It really had had the lot, that day: work, airports, hangover, sex, love, shock (several doses), new encounters, old friends, rage, confrontation – and great sadness. She wasn't sure what the deepest impression was, but it sure as hell wasn't making her feel good now. She decided that it was probably the sadness:

sadness for Harriet, for her family, for Mungo, for Cressida even – but most of all for Rufus and for herself.

There could be no happy ending to their particular little story, she thought to herself, pouring the water into the mug, adding five sweeteners (God, to think that used to be three spoons of sugar), carrying it over to the white leather sofa by the window, scooping up the telephone as she went. She loved Rufus, she loved him almost beyond endurance, and he loved her as much in return; and she had to end it, end the whole thing quickly before it grew and strengthened so that there could be no hope of revival, no tender, delicate little shoots and roots left. It was the only way, she had seen that as she walked through the lovely Oxfordshire countryside with Oliver that afternoon – God, it felt like months ago – trying to concentrate on what he was saying. There was no good thinking she could live with it, avoid James, ignore Rufus's origins, turn her back on his family, because it wasn't going to work. Apart from anything else it wasn't in Rufus's nature to do that; he was in essence a family person, he adored his mother, and the man he thought was his father, he loved his home, he belonged to his background. And there was no way either she could keep her new knowledge about him, about his parentage, to herself; her intrinsic honesty would never allow it. Even if James Forrest did what she had asked – and she was very doubtful that he would, and that matters would end there – she would have to tell Rufus what she knew. And that would spread pain, misery into so many lives, and while she felt no concern for James, for Susie, she cared very very much for Harriet, and for Rufus himself. He would be upset when she told him she couldn't marry him, didn't want to see him any more, but it would be normal healthy pain, he would get over it, find some other girl to love and to marry, some suitable, well-bred blonde, who would choose pretty chintzy furniture for his pretty, smartly based house, bear him pretty blond children, and wear pretty, dull clothes at her charming important dinner parties.

It would all be much much better and she would be over it in no time, indeed be back where she wanted to be, free, untied, in charge once more. She was tough, she had a most vulgarly iron constitution, she would find some new lover, from her own world, who understood her life and whose life she understood, and in a year, probably less, she would be thinking of Rufus fondly but slightly detachedly and she would hardly be able to remember how his eyes looked when they rested upon her, how he smiled with pure childish pleasure just at her very presence, how her heart lurched and her head spun when she saw him again after some parting, however brief, how she felt somehow warmed and cared for when she was near to him, how his voice seemed to reach out and caress her, how the gentlest, most casual touch left her shaken and moved, how when she was apart from him she felt not quite whole, not quite herself: all these things, she thought, told herself, forced herself to know, would pass, would become a memory, a part of her own history. But first, first there was the pain. And she shrank from it.

She knew when she must do it, had arranged it even, there was no sense in postponing it. Every day she left it, every hour she put it off, made it worse, deeper, crueller. Rufus was coming to see her in the morning (it wasn't true that she had to work) after driving his mother back to town; she would tell him then. Not the whole truth, there would be no sense in that; she would tell him instead that they had no future with one another and their affair was best ended at once. And then she would take up the Rosenthal offer, and go to New York, quickly – and that was another thing; if she did that she could put some money into Harriet's company, that would make it seem a little more worthwhile, would ease her homesickness – it was all going to be vile; he would argue, protest, and so she would have to hurt him further, be vicious to be kind, tell him she was already half involved with someone else, some photographer, designer, spare him hope. Tilly poured herself another glass of wine, lit another cigarette, put REM onto her stero. And then the phone rang. It was Ken Lazard.

'Harry? It's Tilly. Any news? Oh, I see. Well, I have some. No, nothing about Cressida. Did you tell the police about the flat? And what did they say? That is so strange. I mean it's all so complicated. Harriet, don't sound so despairing. The more we learn, the more it's obvious that Cressida planned this whole thing. Has been planning it for months. Yes, I know it's terrible, but at least you can assume she's safe. I mean she hasn't been kidnapped or run over. Try to be positive. What? Yeah, I know you do. Now listen, Harry. Have I got news for you. As they say.

Ken Lazard called me just now. Apparently – Harry, are you sitting down? Well, I really think you should – apparently your Mr Cotton, he's called Hayden by the way, Mr Cotton had dinner with – shit, Harry, I can hardly bear to tell you this – dinner with Theo Buchan three nights ago.'

There was a very long silence. Tilly could feel the shock coming down the phone; it was a physical force.

Then: 'But he can't have done. Theo was in London.'

'So was Hayden. For twenty-four hours.'

'But how does he know Theo?'

'Oh Harry, you know how all these guys link up. Theo has a textile division, for God's sake. And Theo told him not to get into bed with you. Figuratively of course.'

'What!'

'Yes, I know. I know. Harry, try to keep calm. Don't go and shoot him yet. I want to help.'

'But Tilly – oh, I can't believe it. I just can't think Theo would have been that – that unscrupulous. That evil.'

'You'd better believe it. Anyway, it fits. Think about it. The timing, everything. You said they were about to sign what? – forty-eight hours ago, that you'd agreed terms, everything.'

'But what grounds did Theo give him?'

'I don't know. Obviously it was complex and Ken couldn't find out any more. I expect he said you were incompetent – or anything really.'

'God,' said Harriet. 'Tilly, do you think he stopped the other two deals as well?'

'Don't know. Sounds possible. He's obviously been monitoring you and your plans quite closely.'

'But how –'

'Harry, it really isn't very difficult. Honestly. You know what a tiny world it is.'

'Oh my God. Tilly, thank you so much. So much. I don't know quite what I'm going to do, but – well, I'll think of something. But I tell you what. I feel an awful lot better suddenly.'

'Good. Get him by the goolies, Harry, squeeze them till he screams.'

'I couldn't bear to touch them,' said Harriet simply.

* * *

The substitute food wasn't working; Tilly decided she needed the real
thing. She dialled the local pizza delivery company, but it was engaged;
suddenly going out, walking a few streets seemed like a good idea.

The air was very warm still, but not close; the sky was almost dark. The
streets were packed, a mass of people walking, shopping, sitting outside
pubs, at pavement tables, smiling, friendly people. It was true what everyone
said, Tilly thought, the weather played a huge part in the English reserve.

She walked down to the Kings Road, into the Europa supermarket,
bought a basketload of vegetables and some eggs. A huge Spanish
omelette was exactly what she fancied. She wandered back slowly,
enjoying the evening, feeling better. It was ten o'clock: an endless day.

As she ran up the stairs to her flat, she heard the phone ringing, then
stop as the answering machine took the call. She couldn't hear what the
person was saying, but it was a female voice. Probably Harriet, calling to
talk about Theo again.

She pressed the playback button: there were three lights flashing.
The first message was from James Forrest.

'Miss Mills? This is James Forrest. I've thought over what you had to
say, and I agree it would be nice if I talked to your mother. Perhaps
you'd like to let me have her number some time so that I can call her.
Thank you.'

'Well, well, well,' said Tilly aloud. 'You must be a very frightened
man.' Even to her it seemed remarkable that he should move into action
on such a day. She debated ringing her mother, then decided it would
possibly upset her to get such a call, to be forced into recollection; she
needed to be with her, to explain, to talk it over. She would go over at
the weekend to Peckham and sit with her and tell her about it, tell her
that James Forrest wanted to see her and reassure her after all this time
that she had not been at fault.

The second call was from Felicity Livesey. 'Tilly, it's Felicity. Mick
said you were back in London. Sorry to hound you, but I'd like to give
some kind of indication at least to Meg Rosenthal on how you feel about
her offer. Could you give me a ring at home? Thanks.'

Then the third message.

'Tilly? This is Cressida Forrest. When you get back, could you please
just call my family and tell them I'm fine, and they are not to worry
about me. Thanks.'

Chapter 18

Harriet 9pm

Mr Buchan was out, they told her, in their blank, courteous way, had taken his car and gone out. No, he hadn't checked out of the hotel, but they really couldn't say when he would be back. They were so sorry. No, Mrs Buchan wasn't there either. Yes, of course they would give him a message. And yes, they would make sure he got it, no matter what time he came in.

Harriet put down the phone and wondered how on earth she was going to stand the raging mass that was centred somewhere in the area of her stomach for however long it took before she was able to confront Theo. She felt quite literally possessed; she knew now how people could kill.

She stared at the closed door of the drawing room; from behind it she could hear – what? Dear God, the television. How on earth could they watch television, all of them, when Cressida had gone missing? Then she considered the alternatives they had all been pursuing for the past two hours, and decided it was actually quite sensible. If one more person put forward a theory, she knew she would scream. She felt like screaming anyway; indeed it began to seem rather difficult to imagine that she would be able to endure many more minutes of this day without doing so.

It was almost dusk now, the sky deep brilliant turquoise, the sun sinking in a glory of orange behind the hills. The stillness was almost tangible; she felt if she went outside she would be able to put out her hand and touch it, feel it. It would be cool, she thought, slightly silken in texture; soothing, gentle. She decided to go down to the bridge and watch the sun finally settle into the night, see the stars come up. It was lovely down there in the darkness; when she and Cressida had been little they had crept out sometimes, greatly daring, and sat there, listening to the night sounds, the owls, the horses occasionally nickering, the water rats plopping into the stream. It was one of the few experiences that united them; they would snuggle together on the stone seat, holding hands, sharing a sense of courage, of adventure. They had only been caught twice (and of course she'd been blamed, being the eldest, and indubitably the instigator of the expeditions), but had gone out many times, every summer.

She went to the back door, and was about to cross the yard when she remembered Theo; she didn't want to miss his call. And they might be worried if they didn't know where she was. She went back, put her head round the drawing-room door. They all looked up slightly guiltily from what they were watching (some costume drama, she noticed confusedly, a re-run of something like *Middlemarch*). She smiled at them, as cheerfully as she could.

'I'm just going for a breath of air,' she said, 'down to the bridge. If there are any calls, any news, will you call me?'

They nodded; a heaviness had settled on them all. Since the message from Cressida there was a sense of anticlimax, a loss of adrenalin. Only Julia smiled brightly. 'I'll come and get you personally, dear,' she said. She looked marvellous, Harriet thought, as if the day had been a great success, her son safely dispatched with his bride across the Atlantic, instead of publicly humiliated, deserted almost literally at the altar.

Oliver looked at her, then at Harriet, rather uncertainly. 'Would you mind if I came with you?' he asked. 'I won't if you'd rather not –'

Harriet did mind, she minded very much, but she could scarcely say so. She forced a smile. 'No, Oliver, of course not. Really. I'm just going to get a sweater. I'll see you in the kitchen.'

She went out into the utility room; there was nothing there except Barbours and anoraks, all much too warm, and an old, rather holey cardigan of her father's that they all wore from time to time. It seemed to belong to quite a different time: when everything had been simple, straightforward, happy. A time that belonged to another age: when Cressida was engaged to Oliver and her parents had a good marriage and she had a company that might yet survive. Years and years ago that was, that other age, yet actually only yesterday.

Harriet shivered, physically chilled by what had happened to them all that day, what might happen yet; she pulled the cardigan on, noticing she ached, ached all over, and stood there patiently, waiting for Oliver.

He came out still looking slightly doubtful. 'You sure this is all right? Because you don't have to be kind – '

'Ollie,' said Harriet, slipping her arm through his, 'I think you've earned a bit of kindness. Actually. Come on, let's get the hell out of here.'

They sat on the bridge, staring up at the brightening stars. 'Does this remind you of the desert?' he said suddenly. 'You know, when Merlin took us. God, we were so happy then. Life was so straightforward. I should have married you, Harriet, not Cressida. Well, not that I married Cressida.'

'No,' said Harriet, 'and if this is a proposal I have to tell you I'm going to turn you down. I expect you wish right now Cressida had turned you down as well.'

There was a long silence, then he said. 'There was no question of her turning me down, Harriet. She proposed to me. And there was no question of my turning her down either.'

Harriet stared at him, trying to make out if he was joking, but his face in the near darkness was very serious.

'I don't understand,' she said. 'Why? What happened?'

'Oh God,' said Oliver, 'I shouldn't have started this. Sorry, Harriet. Forget it.'

'Ollie, don't be ridiculous. How can I forget it? You have to go on now. Why couldn't you refuse her? If you didn't want to marry her?'

'Oh Harriet,' he said, 'the oldest reason in the world. She was pregnant.'

The bridge seemed to shake under Harriet. She put out her hand, but the parapet seemed reassuringly steady.

'Oliver, I'm sorry, but you've lost me. I'm a simple soul. Could you start at the beginning please? I thought we were talking a year ago, not now – '

'Sorry, Harriet. I'm fairly lost myself. Go back a year. Nearly a year. Cressida and I had been having an affair for a while. I was very fond of her, she seemed very fond of me, she was pretty, fun – '

'Yes, all right, you don't have to go into justifications,' said Harriet impatiently.

'Sorry. Start again. Cressida and I had been having an affair. She came over for a few weeks in August, do you remember, stayed with us at Bar Harbor, sailed a lot, had a lovely time. It wasn't at all serious. We agreed it wasn't. I honestly don't think I was taking advantage of her in any way. She was twenty-six years old, for God's sake. And – she certainly wasn't a – a – '

'Virgin?' said Harriet gently. She smiled at Oliver; it was so like him, like his serious, conscientious approach to life, that he shouldn't be seen as a seducer, even of someone who had most efficiently and ruthlessly humiliated him that day.

'Yes. I mean, she wasn't. Well, anyway, in October she wrote to me, and said she had some holiday and could she maybe come over for a few days. I said of course. I was actually seeing someone else by then but not – well, you know what I mean?'

'Yes, Oliver,' said Harriet, putting her hand on his arm, 'I know what you mean.'

'So I met her at Kennedy, and I did think she seemed a bit – well, tense. But no more. That night we went out to dinner, all of us, Mother and Dad as well, and it was really good fun. When we got back we all had a nightcap and then they went on up to bed. Cressida suddenly said she had some news. She said she was pregnant, that it was definitely mine, and she thought we should hurry things along and announce our engagement. Harriet, I swear to God it had never ever been mentioned, never considered an option, even in the vaguest terms. I knew I didn't really love her, and I knew I didn't really want to marry her. I – well, I kind of said that. And she was terribly upset. She started crying and carrying on, then she rushed out of the room. She came back and said she'd been sick, that she was being sick all the time, that she felt terrible. I felt so awful, Harriet, so ashamed. I sat and talked to her for a long time, and said I would do everything I could to help her, but I really didn't think we should get married, and she said didn't I care for her at all, and I said of course I did. And she said what options did I see for her, did I think she should have an abortion? I said, quite carefully, that it was certainly something we should look at, and she started crying again, and saying how could I even think of getting rid of our baby. Then she was sick again, and then she came back and started all over. Christ, Harriet, it was terrible. Whenever I read about the police interrogating witnesses and making them confess to things they haven't done, I know how they do it.'

'Oh Oliver,' said Harriet, 'oh Ollie, I'm so sorry.'

'Yes, well. Maybe our parents were right when they told us not to sleep around,' he said with an attempt at a laugh. 'It certainly doesn't make for an easy life. You can imagine the rest. I lay awake all night, thinking what a heel I was, what a lovely girl she was, how fond of her I was, what a wonderful time we'd had in the summer, what a good wife she'd make me, how happy everyone in the family would be, and about the alternative, and in the morning I went to see her in her room and said that of course I'd marry her, it was a very good idea, I'd just been a bit taken aback the night before, that was all. And she went flying down to my parents and told them, and of course they were pleased – well, Dad was pleased, Mother seemed a little reserved about it – and then she put in a call to your parents and – well, you know the rest. It's a very heavy steamroller that, Harriet, and it's very hard to get out from under it.'

'But Ollie, I don't know the rest. What happened to that – baby?'

'Oh,' he said, and his voice was heavy, infinitely sad. 'No, of course you don't. Sorry. She lost it. A couple of weeks later. She hadn't even broken the news to our parents, we were trying to decide what to do, how to handle it, whether we should get married quickly and quietly or – well, anyway, she lost it.'

'What, when she was back in London?'

'Yes.'

'Well,' said Harriet and her own voice was bitter now, 'how very convenient for her.'

'No,' he said, 'no, I know what you're thinking and you're wrong. She really was pregnant, she really was feeling terrible, she – well, she had all the symptoms. I'm a doctor, Harriet, not so easy to deceive, and she had a letter from the hospital. You don't remember her being – well, ill? Away from home? Anything like that?'

'No,' said Harriet, stifling her doubts, her suspicion that it would have been quite easy, with her connections, for this new, devious Cressida, the one they had never known, to fake a hospital letter. 'No, I don't, but then, to be fair, I'm away a lot. Last autumn I was in Paris practically all the time. But Mummy never said anything – oh for God's sake, what am I talking about? This is a girl who has just disappeared on her wedding day piloting her own plane when none of us thought she could even ride a bicycle, who sold her flat months ago and let us think she was still living in it. ('That explains the mysterious legacy at least,' James had said when she told him.) I guess a little miscarriage would hardly seem very difficult to conceal. But then, why didn't you – '

'Call it off? I couldn't, Harriet. I thought I would, of course, it was a huge relief to me, actually, but she was so miserable, so depressed. She came over the week after, and she did look awful, so thin and pale, and she was crying a lot and she said the only thing that was keeping her going now was the thought of our being married. She – well, she really did seem to love me. And need me. It's not the best time to dump someone, you must see that. And then – well, you know, I'm actually quite an easy-going guy. I had a lot to worry about, my research work, my first big job. I went along with it, and just kept telling myself how lucky I was.'

'Oh, Oliver,' said Harriet. The story was making her flesh creep slightly; she felt sick. 'What a nightmare.'

'Well it was a bit. But not bad enough, you know? For me to do anything. I think I just kept hoping for a miracle. And my parents seemed so pleased, and yours were delighted, it's a tough one that, Harriet. Don't ever get into anything like it.'

'I don't think it's very likely,' said Harriet with a sigh. 'But then, here you were, getting married, and she was pregnant for real. And presumably by then it didn't matter – '

'No,' he said heavily. 'It didn't matter. Or doesn't now.'

'And when did she tell you?'

'When I arrived here,' he said briefly. 'Last week.'

Harriet looked at him, and saw on his face the same anger, the same sick distaste that had been there when he had made his announcement earlier, and the strange sense of wrongness, of disorder resurfaced, and she said, 'Oliver, forgive me, but – '

And 'Yes,' he said, 'I know what you're going to say. It doesn't make sense. I just kept trying not to think about it. The dates don't work, don't fit in with the times we were together recently. She swears they do, but they don't. She should either be quite a bit further along, or – what? – three weeks at the most. Hardly pregnant. I mean I have to believe her, well, I had to, there didn't seem to be an alternative, but – I knew it wasn't right. It just wasn't. I'm sorry, Harriet, I know she's your sister and you love her and you've always been terribly close, but –'

'I'm not sure that I do actually,' said Harriet. 'Love her. In fact,' she added in a rush of courage, 'most of the time I don't even like her very much. And we certainly aren't close. We just pretend, act out this stupid charade.'

'Well,' said Oliver, 'she's good at acting. Very good.'

'Yes. As Merlin said earlier. Dear Merlin. Oliver, you should have said something, you shouldn't have gone along with it all, you really shouldn't. It would have been so terrible.'

'Oh, I know,' he said, his face pallid in the moonlight, 'and of course even now I can't imagine why I didn't, why I let things go on. But it's not an easy thing to do, Harriet, disrupt things, stop arrangements on this scale, publicly humiliate someone –'

'She has,' said Harriet. 'My God, she has.'

'Yes, well. I'm going to be grateful. I know I am. I took an overdose last night,' he added conversationally.

Harriet stared at him. She felt very sick.

'You did what?'

'I swallowed a bottle of aspirin. With some whisky. Oh, it was only a yell for help. I knew that. And Rufus and Mungo took care of me. They were fantastic.'

'Oh, Oliver,' said Harriet and she suddenly burst into tears. 'Oh, Oliver, I feel so ashamed for her. So sad for you.'

'Well don't be,' he said almost cheerfully, putting his arm round her, 'because it's actually going to be all right. I mean I don't have to marry her now, and when this awful day is over, I can get on a plane and fly back to New York and get on with my life, and we can tell some cosmetic lie about the whole thing. I'm very lucky I don't live here, it would be a lot more difficult. Honestly, Harriet, I *am* beginning to feel much better. Certainly better than the way I'd feel if we were on the plane en route to a honeymoon.'

'I suppose so. Oh God.' She sniffed loudly. 'What a day. What a bitch of a day. Sorry. Have you got a handkerchief?'

'Sure. Are you all right?'

'Not really,' said Harriet and burst into tears again.

'Harry, darling, don't cry. There's something else, isn't there? What is it, tell me?'

'Oh, Oliver, I can't. Not all of it. It's too horrible, and too humiliating and – well, I just don't think I can face talking about it now. I'm sorry. Maybe tomorrow. Or something.'

'OK,' he said equably. 'But please do tell me if you want to. And if there's anything I can do –'

'How are you on murder?' said Harriet briefly.

When they got back to the house, James was in the kitchen making some tea.

'Your mother's gone to bed,' he said heavily. 'I'm making her this.'

'You'd better give her something to help her sleep,' said Harriet.

'I have. Your parents are moving off,' he added to Oliver, 'do you want to go with them? You're very welcome to stay here, of course.'

'No, it's kind of you, James, but I think I should go,' said Oliver. 'Harriet is that all right with you –'

'What? Oh, yes,' said Harriet. 'Yes, of course. Ring me in the morning.' She looked at her father coldly. 'What are you going to do?'

'Oh, I don't know,' he said, 'wait up for a while. In case there's still some news. Merlin and Janine still aren't back, I think I should check them in,' he added with the echo of a smile. 'And I have to run Susie back to the Beaumonts', of course.'

'Of course –'

'Harriet, I think perhaps we should talk –'

'Daddy, there's nothing to talk about. I'm not stupid, I can see what's been happening. And I don't want to hear any more about it. OK? I think I'll go up and say goodnight to Mummy.'

'All right,' he said.

Maggie was lying in bed, awake but very still. She put out her hand and smiled weakly as Harriet looked round the door. She looked rather as if she had had a serious operation, Harriet thought, and went to kiss her. Maggie took her hand gently.

'You've been wonderful today,' she said, 'so good. Thank you.'

'Mummy, it was no more than anyone else did. Honestly.'

'Yes it was. You've kept me sane.' She sighed. 'Where do you think she is, Harriet, why do you think she did it? What could have happened to her, was it our fault, do you think?'

'So you do think now that she – chose to go?' said Harriet carefully.

'Yes, I do. The second message, from your friend Tilly, that really did confirm it. But I think I knew really, as soon as I heard about the plane. It's all so strange, such a nightmare. She must have been so desperate, so unhappy. And pregnant too. Oh God, who will be looking after her now?'

'Mummy, try to be calm,' said Harriet. 'The new Cressida, the one we didn't know about, she's able to look after herself I think. She'll manage.'

'Yes, but – pregnant,' said Maggie again. 'And what can she be doing for money?'

'Well, I should think she had plenty of that,' said Harriet. 'She got a hundred thousand for her flat, don't forget. That should pay for a bit of looking after.'

'Darling, don't sound so hard.'

'Sorry,' said Harriet. 'I feel a bit hard.'

'Yes, well, you always were a lot tougher than she was,' said Maggie, 'she was so easily upset always, so sensitive. She felt so bad, you know, about your puppy.'

'What puppy?' asked Harriet.

'There you are, I told her you'd forgotten all about it. Biggles. The sweet little puppy who was run over. She always felt it was her fault, you know, because she'd left the gate open. Nanny told me that night, she saw her, and of course we did speak to her about it, and she was so upset, just couldn't stop crying, begged me not to tell you. We told her we wouldn't, that it was just an accident, it could have been any of us, and of course it was much better that you didn't know, but –'

'Oh God,' said Harriet, 'oh my God. I always knew, I knew it wasn't me.'

'Now, darling, don't start getting upset about it. It wasn't anybody, I just said it was an accident.' She was getting drowsy now, her eyes closing. 'Goodnight, Harriet, thank you again. Let's hope tomorrow is a better day.'

'Poor little Biggles,' said Harriet. 'Oh God, poor sweet little Biggles.' And of all the things she had learnt about Cressida that day, this was the most shocking: that anybody, anybody at all, least of all a small child, could deliberately, cold-bloodedly, arrange things so that a round, golden, velvety-pawed and totally trusting puppy should be sent to a certain and most horrible death.

She went into Cressida's room and looked around it; she felt like smashing it up, hurling all its charming accessories, its lace-covered pillows and Victorian pin-cushions and antique scent bottles out of a broken window. And then she went into her own room and got out the photo of Biggles that she still kept, in its old leather frame in the top drawer of her desk, and he looked at her adoringly, with his squashed puppy face, his floppity ears pricked up, his fat paws hooked over the arm of the big chair he was sitting in, and even after all that time it hurt, it hurt so much, more than ever in fact, knowing now that it hadn't been an accident, need never have happened. 'Oh, Biggles,' she said to the photograph, seeing it through blurred eyes, 'oh, Biggles, I'm so sorry.'

It suddenly seemed very hot; she opened the window wider to air the room and then realized she was still wearing the thick cardigan. She pulled it off and started to straighten it out; it was still covered in bits of grass clippings from when her father had been cutting the grass ready for the marquee. He always cut it himself; he took an immense pride in his lawn, Cressida always said he regarded it as another child, so concerned was he over its welfare. She began to brush the grass off and as she did so saw a piece of paper in the top inside pocket. Probably nothing, she thought, pulling it out, a shopping list or a vet's bill, probably been there for years, but you never knew –

And 'Cressida,' she said aloud, staring at the note, reading and rereading it, as if the words might vanish if she looked at them long enough, 'oh, Cressida. What was the matter with you, for God's sake, what were you up to?'

For it was not a shopping list or a vet's bill, it was a letter from a gynaecologist at somewhere called the Brompton Clinic, dated the previous October.

Dear Miss Forrest (it said),

This is just to confirm what I told you on the phone this morning, that although your pregnancy test showed a negative result, I see no reason to suppose there is any cause for anxiety. Many women have some difficulty in conceiving, and you are extremely healthy and have time on your side. I suggest that if after six months you are still not pregnant, you come and see me again, perhaps with your fiancé, and we can discuss whether some investigations might be appropriate then. But I really think that for the time being you should just try to relax and enjoy your forthcoming trip to New York.

Yours sincerely

Jennifer Bradman, F R C O G

Chapter 19

Susie 10pm

'Jamie, I think I'd like to ring Alistair now,' said Susie.

She knew she was behaving totally out of character, that Susie Headleigh Drayton, always so serene, so in control, would never have even considered late-night panic phone calls, soul-baring sessions, ultimatums; but she didn't feel serene or in control and she didn't really feel like Susie Headleigh Drayton either, she felt like some alien creature, someone floundering in a nightmare, someone afraid.

'Ah,' said James. 'Ah, yes of course. If that's what you really want.'

'Well, yes, it is what I really want. You know that.'

She had found him in his study, sitting staring out of the window, his hand on the telephone; he had just made, he said, yet another phone call to the police. 'No news. Not from anywhere. Apparently in the morning, they can step up the search. And the Missing Persons have been very good. Tried to be soothing, reassuring. So many people do this apparently, Susie, just vanish into thin air, hundreds every year. Nobody knows why.'

'And do they return, these hundreds of people?'

'Some of them, yes.'

'Well then,' she said, 'you have some hope.'

That was when she had made her announcement, that she wanted to talk to Alistair, to tell him that she and James wanted to be together, for however long she had left.

He looked at her now, carefully, consideringly, and said, 'Susie, are you really sure about this?' and for a long, dreadful moment she thought he was going to fail her, was going to say he didn't think after all it was such a good idea, and she knew what people meant when they said their hearts stopped. But then: 'I mean, my darling,' he said, his eyes moving over her tenderly, lovingly, his hand drifting out to take hers, 'if you really want to do it now. When it's late. When you're exhausted, when I'm exhausted, when Alistair may be asleep. It's after ten. I would have thought tomorrow maybe would be better.'

'But Jamie,' she said, relief flooding her, warm and soothing, her heart starting again, steady, strong, 'Jamie, maybe it would, but I have to go in for the biopsy in the morning, and he wants Alistair to come with me, and I don't think I could face that, go through that sham. And besides, I'm so frightened, so afraid. I'll need you with me then. And afterwards, when I've had the biopsy, I want you to be there, I want you to be there when I wake up and have to hear the news and –' She heard her voice quiver, shatter; she bit her lip, looked at him, willing the tears not to come.

'Susie,' said James, 'Susie darling, of course I'll come with you. Incidentally I've looked Hobson up, and he is absolutely the best man. So you're lucky there. But after that –'

'Yes,' she said, 'yes, after that? After that what? Jamie, you promised, you promised this afternoon, that from this day forward –' she paused, realized she had unwittingly quoted from the marriage service, half smiled – 'you would be with me, would look after me.'

'Yes, and I will. Darling, don't look like that. I will. But it is bound to take a little time, the disentanglement. Nobody, nobody at all can just walk out of a marriage, a household, at a moment's notice. Or into another. What would I say to Alistair? Shove out, old chap, it's my turn now. There has to be a little space, a little room for manoeuvre, surely you can see that?'

'Yes,' she said with a sigh, 'yes, I suppose I can. But time is exactly what I haven't got. So even if we can't be physically together yet, all the time, I want everyone to know that's what's going to happen. So we do have to tell Alistair, yes.'

'Right,' said James, and there was an uncertainty in his voice that frightened her again, 'right, yes. I suppose we do. But does it really have to be tonight? Consider the ructions, darling, the implications. And I can't possibly tell Maggie, she's asleep, I've given her something very strong. And even tomorrow, do you really think she can take this news, on top of Cressida's disappearance, is it really fair?'

'Jamie, it may not be fair, but I think I do have absolutely first claim here,' said Susie. Her fear was growing. 'In a year, six months, I could be dead. I really can't wait for you, for happiness, until Maggie can handle it. I'm sorry.'

James looked at her again, and he was clearly thinking: thinking fast. She watched him in a kind of frozen fascination, fighting back the tears. What was this, what was he doing to her?

'Susie, darling, don't you think also you're being slightly premature about the whole thing? It may prove after all this to be a false alarm: just a lump, just a cyst. You don't know. Hobson doesn't know, nobody knows. Why not wait at least until tomorrow?'

'Jamie,' said Susie very quietly, 'I know. I know there's something wrong. I don't feel well, I'm terribly tired, I've lost weight. I can't allow myself to –'

The phone shrilled out sharply in the silence. James picked it up, she sat there looking at him, watched his face change from fear to a careful blank.

'Yes, Annabel, she's here. I'm about to bring her back. What? Well, in about half an hour I suppose. Oh, all right, I'll put her on. It's your daughter,' he said, handing Susie the phone. 'She says it's urgent.'

'Oh God,' said Susie, 'God, I hope it's not Tom, or Alistair. Annabel, yes, darling, what is it?'

Annabel's voice, husky, sexy, expensively educated, came down the phone. 'Mummy, some of us want to go to a club in Oxford. Is that OK?'

'What?' said Susie. She felt confused, disorientated, wrenched from fears for herself into fears for her children and husband, and thence into trivia, literally unable to believe what she was hearing. 'Annabel, what did you say?'

'I said some of us want to go to a club in Oxford,' said Annabel irritably. 'Well we have to do something to cheer ourselves up, it's been a pretty bloody awful day.'

'Annabel,' said Susie, trying to keep her voice level. 'I rather think it's been a better day for you than for most of the people concerned. Anyway, I thought you said this was urgent.'

'Yes, all right, all right,' said Annabel. 'Sorry. The thing is I haven't got any money, and my cash card's gone missing. Can you let me have some cash? Daddy said he'd give me some and then he just went off without doing it. He's so hopeless. If you hurry back now, we can go in about fifteen minutes, I don't want to hold everyone up.'

Susie carefully counted to ten. She had always found it helped enormously in the past, had enabled her to deal with her children in a calm and reasonable way, even when they were enraging her. For some reason it wasn't working.

'Annabel,' she said, and she could hear her voice rising, 'Annabel, I'm having a little trouble following this. You want to go to a club in Oxford and you haven't got any money. Is that right?'

'Yes,' said Annabel, 'I really can't see what's so complicated. If you could just –'

'What's complicated,' said Susie, settling her voice lower down the vocal range again, 'what's hard for me to believe is that you could see that as an emergency. How could you ring me up here, late, when everyone could well have been asleep, when everyone has been through the kind of day that's normally confined to nightmares, when several people are feeling literally heartbroken, and tell me it's really urgent that you have some money to go to a club. You shock me, Annabel, you really do. I'm ashamed of being your mother. Now you can go to a club if you want to, I really don't care, but you'll have to get your financing from someone else. And if I find you've asked Janet or Brian Beaumont for it, I do assure you it will be a very long time before you get another penny from either your father or me. Goodnight, Annabel. I suppose I'll have to see you in the morning.'

She put down the phone, looked at James and grinned rather shakily. 'I don't usually do that sort of thing. I rather enjoyed it. You got the drift, I suppose?'

'Yes, I did. They're all the same, these children. We spoil them. I remember Cressida ringing Maggie from a party at two in the morning once when she was only a bit younger than Annabel, to tell her she'd broken the zip on her dress and could we take another one over. It was a round trip of about thirty miles.'

'And did you?'

'Well I had a lot of trouble preventing Maggie from doing it,' he said. 'She always was ridiculously indulgent with Cressida.'

'You both were,' said Susie, 'I was always telling you.'

'Yes, but it didn't seem to do her any harm.' There was a long silence. 'Well, that was a particularly bright remark,' he said, with a heavy sigh. 'Obviously it did. A lot of harm. Oh Christ. Do you think she's seriously psychologically disturbed, Susie, or just a drama queen?'

'Oh, Jamie, I don't know,' said Susie, 'that is such an impossible judgment to make. Unfair to ask me.'

'I'm sorry. Bit of both, I suppose. God, where do you think she is, what can she be doing? I'm so frightened even now of hearing she's been found – beaten up somewhere, in an accident, dead even. It's such a dreadful, ghastly nightmare.'

'Jamie, she may be hurt, or worse, I suppose,' said Susie, speaking carefully, 'but I do think it's unlikely. I think actually it's far more possible that she's just run away, to escape. Taken herself off. She's sent two messages to you after all.'

'I know, I know, but they could be fakes, bluffs, she could have been forced into sending them. You just don't know, do you? The police were reassuring, but they would be. That's their job. And if she had run off, Christ, what kind of a state must she have been in? Pregnant, frightened – What did we do to her? I've made a terrible hash of parenthood, Susie. Of everything.'

'You've done pretty well with Harriet,' said Susie. 'The sort of daughter everyone dreams of. Successful, clever, nice – Jamie –'

'Yes, darling?'

'I know this is all terrible for you. But I have something terrible to deal with too. And I really can't wait. Please let me ring Alistair.'

She watched James disentangle himself from his thoughts with a great effort, turn to her. There was something in his eyes, apart from love, apart from sympathy, that troubled her. Trying to analyse, she realized that he looked trapped, cornered, almost desperate.

'Jamie, what is it? You don't have any – doubts about this, do you? You're not going to fail me. Because I don't think I could bear it if you do, don't think I could handle it.'

'No', he said smiling at her, holding out his hand, 'no, of course not. No doubts at all. Come over here. God, Susie, I love you. I love you so much.'

She went over to where he sat at his big desk, took his hand, bent down to kiss him. His mouth as always was very warm, very dry and firm.

'You taste of peppermint,' she said.

'Peppermint tea. My mainstay.'

'God,' she said, 'I don't know how Alistair would get by without his booze. Aren't you ever tempted?'

'Yes of course,' he said simply. 'Every day, almost.'

'Then why don't you ever –'

'Oh,' he said, lightly, 'it just doesn't agree with me. That's all. It just isn't worth it.'

'Tilly's lovely, isn't she?' she said. She felt him tense slightly.

'Why did you say that. Then?'

'No reason,' she said, surprised. 'I was just thinking about her. How strange it is that all our lives have intertwined. I often think about her mother, poor woman, how dreadful that must have been.'

'Yes,' he said, 'so do I. Of course.'

'Dreadful for you, too, though. But I've always hoped she does realize that it really wasn't your fault that the other little baby died. In any way. When – when Tilly asked you to show her the garden, she didn't –'

'No,' he said quickly. 'No, she didn't say anything. Of course she knows about it, knows I delivered her. But she certainly doesn't seem to hold it against me.'

'Well, she shouldn't,' said Susie, 'you were completely exonerated, at the inquiry. Just the same –'

'Susie, can we stop this please? You know it upsets me, talking about it.'

'Sorry,' she said, startled. 'Look, why don't I make us some tea – peppermint if you like – and we can sit in the drawing room and talk sensibly. I'm feeling calmer now. I'm sorry if I seemed hysterical earlier. Not like me.'

'No,' he said, 'not like you at all. It's one of the things I most love about you, Susie, your serenity. It's beautiful. It restores me. It's been restoring me today.'

'Good,' she said, and bent to kiss him, feeling in spite of everything suddenly happy, light-hearted, thinking how much she loved him, how wonderful it was that they were finally going to be together, all the time, openly, peacefully, no more concealment, no more pretence.

She went out to the kitchen, made some tea, carried it into the drawing room. 'Merlin and Janine are late.'

'He's probably arguing over the bill,' said James.

'Yes, probably.' She took a sip of her tea, waited, looking at him, willing him to take up the subject of herself and their future, wondering why she felt so nervous. Well, it was not entirely surprising: under the circumstances. She was not in any way herself.

There was a long silence: he said nothing. He didn't even look at her. Susie felt her skin begin to crawl; finally she took a deep breath, said, 'Jamie, Jamie please. Can we talk about this? Can I ring Alistair?'

'Susie, I don't know. I'm not sure.'

And now panic did hit her, hot, liquid panic, filling her head and her chest, making her limbs feel light and odd.

'Jamie, what do you mean, you're not sure? Not sure about what?'

'About the way you want to handle this.'

Well, that was better; not totally all right, but better.

'You mean we should wait till tomorrow? Well, maybe if it was really early, but –'

'Well, possibly, yes.'

'Jamie, what are you saying?' She heard an edge enter her voice, hated it, couldn't control it. 'Jamie, look at me.'

He looked at her, briefly, before she could read his eyes, then looked away again.

There was a long, frozen silence; she felt suddenly still and calm, the panic gone.

'You're not going to do it, are you?' she said finally. 'You're not going to leave her, not going to be with me.'

'Susie, there's no need to sound quite so dramatic. I'm not saying that at all. I'm just not convinced that it's actually the best thing for us to do.'

'Oh, really?' she said. 'And would you like to tell me why that is, why you're lacking in this conviction?'

'Darling, I – oh, for God's sake, come over here, let me hold you.'

'I think I need a little more than holding,' she said, and she could hear her voice exactly as it had been when she spoke to Annabel, oddly controlled and cold. 'I'd rather you didn't try to confuse the issue that way, James. I think we have a little straight talking to do here. You promised me earlier that you would be with me, leave Maggie, and now –'

'I didn't actually,' he said. 'I said I would be with you as long as you needed me. And I will. That isn't quite the same thing as disrupting two marriages, two households at a time when –'

'At a time what? Jamie, what are you saying? I don't understand. The only time I have is now and it's possibly very short, and I need you, and as far as I'm concerned you promised me – Jamie, for Christ's sake, explain, because I –' She stopped, biting her lip, looked at him, willing his absolute reassurance, knowing with the same icy certainty that it wasn't going to come.

'Look,' he said, and his voice was steady, level, patient, 'look, Susie, I know how frightened you must be, and I really do want to help you all I can. But you could be in for quite a tough time and I'm not entirely convinced that ripping two families apart is quite the best background for it.'

'James, I –'

'Susie, let me finish. You wanted me to explain. If you do what you say you want to do, then you're going to cause so much unhappiness, so much pain. You're such a family person, Susie, do you really want to add to your children's grief? Because that is what you'll do. They won't just be afraid of losing you, grieving for you, they'll be grieving at the break-up of their family, they'll be angry at what you've done to their father. Who incidentally they do adore. Is that really fair? Is that really going to make you feel better, stronger, more able to cope? Because I don't think so. And all right, you don't love Alistair, but do you really want to hurt him like this? Is it really the legacy you want to leave him? I can't believe it is, Susie, I can't believe it of you.'

There was a long silence; through the roar of confusion in her head, Susie dimly heard a car pull into the drive: a tiny piece of her brain thought it must be Merlin and Janine, home from their date – God, don't let them come in here – but the rest of her was still focused entirely on James and her pain.

'All right,' she said firmly, 'all right, you can't believe it. And I know it's true, what you're saying. But the thing is, James, they're strong, they'll survive. Whatever I do to them. And I can help them, I can try to explain. But I have to think of myself, because I'm not strong, I've discovered, not at all, and the only way I'm going to get through this is with you. All my life I've had to share you, James, had to live out this long charade, and OK, it's worked very nicely on the whole. I haven't exactly liked a lot of it, it's been quite hard watching you, thinking of you with Maggie, however much I've smiled and known that was a charade too, I haven't liked never spending a night with you, or almost never, haven't liked a lot of the sneaking off and the lying, certainly haven't liked pretending even to myself quite a lot of the time that Rufus was nothing to do with you, haven't liked not being able to share him, enjoy him with you. But I've put up with it, because I've loved you so much it seemed worth it. Better than the alternative. Now everything's changed. I'm frightened and I feel very alone and, like I said, I need you, I need you badly.'

'But Susie, have you really thought what this means? Especially to Rufus. That you're going to tell him that he's my child, my son, that you've lied to him, to Alistair all these years? Do you think he deserves that, do you think any of them do? Please, darling, please consider terribly carefully.'

'Jamie,' said Susie, and in spite of herself she felt swayed by his argument, his logic, 'Jamie, all right, I will think, I will consider. I promise. But you have to promise me something too. If I do decide I want you, that I want to be with you, will you do that, will you be there for me?'

James looked at her, and she saw it again, that expression in his eyes, the trapped, almost frightened expression, and as she waited for his answer, she knew, even as she shrank from it, what it would be: more prevarication, more equivocation, after all the loyalty, all the years, he was going to fail her when she needed him. And then she heard a sound behind her, and there in the doorway was Rufus, standing frozen still, and she could see perfectly clearly from his face that he had heard every single word.

'I'm sorry,' he said, gently polite as always, 'I'm sorry if I startled you. I came over to fetch you, I thought it would save James the trip.'

'That was – very kind,' said Susie, 'very thoughtful. Thank you. I –'

'Yes, I can see you're – busy. Stupid of me not to have phoned first. To check.'

'Rufus, I think perhaps –' said James.

'James, it's all right. I'll just go again. Leave you in peace. No doubt you'll bring Mum back in your own good time. Is – is Harry around?'

'Well, she is somewhere,' said James. 'But I'm not quite sure where – in her room I expect – shall I –'

'No, no, she's probably asleep,' said Rufus hastily. 'Don't disturb her. Not on my account.'

There was a silence; then Susie said, 'Would you like a drink or something, darling? Or a – a sandwich?'

It was farcical, she knew, she could hear herself sounding like something in a very bad drawing-room comedy, but she had to say something, had to try to distract herself from the awful pain on Rufus's face.

'No,' he said, 'no really, I'm fine. Thanks. Er – I'll be off, I think. Probably go back to London.'

'Rufus,' said James, 'Rufus, I really don't want you to –'

'Don't want me to what?' said Rufus and for the first time there was some emotion in his voice, he sounded alive, angry, 'tell anyone? Say anything? Well I –'

'Good Lord!' It was Merlin; he and Janine had come in, smiling, through the back door, they hadn't heard his car. 'Looks like a party in here. Pour us both a drink, Jamie, there's a good chap. No news I suppose? We've had the most marvellous evening, haven't we, Janine, absurd price they charged us for the meal, had a few words to say about that, got a few quid knocked off as a matter of fact, but otherwise, it's been –'

'Merlin, Janine,' said Susie, knowing that if she didn't do something, anything, quickly, she would scream very loudly, 'would you excuse us, Rufus and me, he's come to collect me very sweetly and he's been waiting for ages already, I really do want to get back, I'm terribly tired.' She went over and kissed them both briefly, then, not looking at James, 'Rufus, darling, let's go, we can't keep Janet up all night waiting for us.'

And amidst a blur of goodnights, of well-wishing, of admonishments to Rufus to drive carefully, of James's face, startled, almost ashamed, she walked quickly out of the room, and at last they were in the car, she could never remember afterwards getting there, and Rufus who always drove so carefully, so considerately put his foot down and screeched out of the drive, gravel flying, and up the lane. It was only when they reached the more major road that led into Woodstock that he stopped, lurched to a halt, and put his head on his arms on the steering wheel.

'Rufus,' said Susie, 'Rufus darling, I –'

'Don't,' he said, 'don't please. Say anything. I couldn't bear it. I can't bear any of it. Just let me take you back to the Beaumonts and then I'm going to London.'

'Take me with you,' said Susie, and she was surprised by how much it mattered, how much she wanted it, 'please. I want to go home. I won't say a single word all the way, but I want to go home.'

Her only fear was that Alistair wouldn't be there, but as she got out of the car, thanked Rufus, made him promise to ring her in the morning, tried to kiss him (but he turned his face away), she saw the light on in the first-floor study, saw Alistair walk over to the window and look out. She ran up the steps, fumbling with her key; by the time she had it in the lock, had managed to turn it, he was there, opening it for her, looking at her surprised, puzzled.

'Darling!' he said. 'What on earth are you doing here? And why didn't you ring me, tell me you were coming?'

'I couldn't,' said Susie, 'well, not easily.' She walked past him, into the kitchen. 'I'd love a drink, Alistair. Just some white wine or something.'

'Of course. I presume there's no news?'

'No, nothing. Well, there was apparently, on Tilly Mills's answering machine. From Cressida, saying she was fine.'

God, it seemed so long ago, all that, another lifetime, another life.

'Girl's cracked,' said Alistair cheerfully, handing her a glass. 'Needs her bottom smacked.'

'That's what Merlin said,' said Susie, and giggled; the giggle got slightly out of hand, she couldn't stop. She looked at Alistair and saw he was looking at her rather oddly.

'It's not that funny,' he said.

'No,' she said, 'no, I know,' and realized she was crying instead. She struggled back into control, sat down abruptly at the table.

'Alistair, I have to talk to you.'

'Oh dear,' he said, 'sounds heavy. Is it?'

'A bit. Yes.'

'Is it one of the children? I wondered why Rufus –'

'No,' she said, 'well, not really. It's – well, it's us.'

There was a silence. Then he said, carefully, 'Do we really have to, Susie? I mean, really have to?'

Susie stared at him. It was an extraordinary moment; for she saw in it, reading his eyes, his watchful eyes, what she had always suspected: that he had known much of it all along. Exactly how much, precisely what details, she had no idea, but certainly he had never been properly in ignorance, totally deceived. And against all odds she smiled at him, just a little, amazed, awed even, not only that their marriage could sustain such a thing, but that they could so perfectly and tacitly agree that it should.

'Well –' she said, 'well, but you see –'

'Susie,' he said, 'Susie, let's not. I'm so very very fond of you, I've been extremely happy with you. I'd rather leave it like that if we possibly can.'

'But Alistair –'

'Susie, let me finish please. You've been very clever, I think, made a very happy family. Much happier than most. We all love you. Don't spoil it, unless you really have to. There isn't any point.'

Susie drained her glass, poured herself another. 'There is a bit of point,' she said quietly. 'Things have changed today, I'm afraid. I'm sorry.' 'It's Rufus,' she had been about to say, but decided she must go further back, explain how she had come to be behaving so out of character, so differently from herself. 'I'm ill,' she said, and her voice was steady, its old self. 'That's the thing. I possibly – probably, actually – have cancer. Breast cancer. I heard this morning. I'm so sorry, Alistair.'

She meant it; she *was* sorry. It was going to be a dreadful nuisance for everybody; she would be no use to Alistair, to any of them. All the things he relied on her for, running the house, taking care of the children, entertaining, arranging holidays, she would be able to do none of it. It was a terrible prospect; she didn't see how they would be able to bear it.

She looked at him; he was staring at her as if he had never seen her before, his face ashen, his mouth taut. He put out his hand as if to touch her, then dropped it again, sat down heavily in a chair beside her at the table.

'How – how bad is it?' he said.

'I don't know yet. Mr Hobson spoke to me this morning. I have to go in tomorrow for a biopsy, first thing. He wants to see you too. Of course. He wanted us both to go in today, but of course we couldn't. Well, it didn't seem the best day. Really. So – it's tomorrow.'

'But it might be – nothing?'

'I don't think it's nothing,' said Susie, speaking carefully, 'and he doesn't think so either. I know he doesn't. Well, he said so. He's drawn off some fluid and looked at that, I don't quite understand, and done a mammogram, and he's worried. I can tell. But we won't know for sure until tomorrow.'

'Does it – are you in pain?'

'No. No, not really. But I don't feel terribly well. I'm very tired all the time, which isn't me, and I've lost some weight. I'm sorry, I'm not trying to worry you, but it seems best to be honest. In this instance,' she added and smiled at him, wryly ironic.

'Oh God,' said Alistair, and this time he did touch her, just very gently, took her hand and stared down at it. 'Oh God, Susie, I wish you'd told me. I wish to God you'd told me.'

'But why, what good would it have done? I only found the damn thing a week ago and then it might have been nothing, and then you'd have been worried quite needlessly, and –'

'Yes, yes, I know, but you must have been so – well, so – frightened,' he said. It was not the kind of word Alistair used; he looked, she thought, quite frightened himself. And thought, even in her pain and misery, that he was actually being more thoughtful, more imaginatively caring than James had been. Well, James had had rather more on his mind. To be fair.

'I was frightened,' she said, realizing with something of a shock that that particular emotion was, briefly at any rate, in the past, 'but I'm not any more. I feel quite resigned. I'm sure it won't last though. I'm sure I'll get scared again.'

'And what did he say, your Mr Hobson, how – well, bad did he think it was, what could it entail?'

'Alistair, he didn't know, he won't know anything until he's done the biopsy. I'm sorry.'

'Oh Christ,' he said, 'oh dear Christ, Susie, I don't like this.'

He put his arms round her, cradled her head. Susie sat quite still, numb to any emotions of her own, absorbing his fear, his raw, naked terror, without being able in any way to respond to it, and realized properly and for the first time in their lives together that Alistair did actually love her.

Chapter 20

Harriet 11pm

Harriet was doing a cash-flow forecast for the year 2001 (with a discharged bankruptcy and with new backing, staff and premises; she was nothing, she kept telling herself, if not positive) when she heard the phone ringing. She had stayed up in her room ever since she had found the note from the gynaecologist; she couldn't face sharing it with anyone, not even Oliver, couldn't face any more emotion, recrimination, theorizing. In the morning, perhaps, she would tell them; not now. She simply wanted to get away from the whole damn thing, to concentrate on her own problems, her own future. She had been aware, but only half consciously, of the occasional car coming and going, of voices downstairs, but she ignored it all. If they wanted her, they could find her, but she had had enough of them; they had worn her out, along with the day. Only the phone call, waiting for its ring, occupied her attention, consumed her energies. The cash flow had been a good idea; it focused her mind absolutely. Reading, watching television, listening to the radio were all futile, she would just have sat there fretting, raging silently over Theo. Well, at least it was distracting her from the duller, more wretched pain of her discovery about her father; that would have to wait, until she could set aside the time to examine it, to grieve, to decide what to do. One thing at a time; one hurt at a time.

She had been half afraid Theo wouldn't ring, would continue to avoid her; she was strangely relieved to find she did not have to add cowardice at least to his list of faults.

She ran down the stairs, seized the phone in the hall. 'Harriet Forrest,' she said, hating her voice for its slight tremor, despising herself for the harsh thudding of her heart. Bloody Theo, bloody Theo, how he could–

Only it wasn't Theo; it was Tilly.

'Harry, hi. You weren't asleep, were you?'

'Asleep? I'm still waiting for that bastard to phone. I thought it was him then –'

'Sorry. Listen, something extraordinary has happened. I've found – no I haven't, let me start again. Harry, do you know anyone called Eloise Renaud?'

'No. No I don't think so. I'm sure I don't. Unless she's a supplier or something, but I can't think of anyone called that. Why?'

'Well, whoever she is, she's Cressida's double. Or – something.'

'What? Tilly, what are you on about?'

'Sorry, Harry, but this is very hard to make any sense of. In fact it's seriously strange. I –'

'Tilly, please,' said Harriet in agony, 'start at the beginning or something. What's happened, who –?'

'OK, OK, Mick McGrath just phoned.'

'From Paris?'

'Yeah, from Paris.'

'What's that got to do with Cressida?'

'I'm trying to tell you. Just listen.'

'I'm listening.' Harriet sat down abruptly on the hall floor, cradling the phone on her lap.

'Mick went into the *Figaro* offices this evening. He had some pictures to deliver. He was waiting to see the picture editor and there was a load of stuff on his desk, you know, that hacks had brought in.'

'Yes, yes, I know. Get on with it, Tilly, for God's sake.'

'I'm trying. Well, anyway, there was one picture of a couple running down the steps of Sacré-Coeur. It was really sweet, he said, she was in a wedding dress, and laughing, and the pigeons were everywhere, and everyone round them was staring at them and smiling. Very Robert Doisneau.'

'Who?'

'Robert Doisneau. You know, the guy who did that famous picture of the boy and girl kissing in the middle of Paris, it's everywhere at the moment –'

'Tilly, what's that got to do with it?'

'Well, nothing, except the poor schmuck who took it thought that was why it might get published. Anyway, Mick suddenly realized that the girl was Cressida.'

'Cressida! In her wedding dress in Paris. But –' The room whirled. Tilly's voice down the phone seemed to be ebbing and flowing. Hang on, Harriet, she thought, this time you really do have to be dreaming, you'll wake up in a minute. She waited, staring ahead, holding her breath, she wasn't sure why, waiting for an awakening; but only heard, still in the same strange whirling space, Tilly's voice in her head again.

'Harry, are you all right, are you there?'

'Yes,' she said, her breath coming out in a rush, 'yes I'm here. I think. Tilly, was he sure? Really sure? He wasn't on anything?'

'He was quite sure. Well, he was sure until he looked at the caption on the back. Which said the girl was Eloise Renaud. After her wedding at Sacré-Coeur today. It didn't give the guy's name.'

'But Tilly, it couldn't have been. It just couldn't. I mean – well, Mick doesn't know Cressida very well. It must be a mistake.'

'Of course he knows her. Well enough to recognize her anyway. We all had dinner a few weeks ago, for Christ's sake. Only problem is, of course, she isn't called Eloise Renaud.'

'No,' said Harriet. 'No she isn't. Oh God. God, Tilly, I really think we're all going mad. She's driven us mad.' She felt horribly near to tears; she took a deep breath, tried to steady herself.

'Look, can you get somewhere where there's a fax?' said Tilly. 'Because Mick took one of the prints, he can fax it to you.'

'Well, I don't know. I could go up to London, I suppose. Bit of a long way . . .'

'What about a hotel? They all have them now. Couldn't you bribe someone to let you use –'

'That's a brilliant idea, Til,' said Harriet slowly. 'I'll do that.'

The Royal Hotel at Woodstock certainly contained a fax. It also contained Theo Buchan.

She was halfway out of the kitchen when she realized she had lent her car to Mungo. Shit. It was going to mean taking her father's, and she would have to tell him at least. Then he'd want to know why, and – 'Oh God,' said Harriet aloud. 'Oh God.'

'Got a problem?'

It was Merlin, his blue eyes particularly brilliant, sparkling at her. He had a glass of whisky in his hand. 'Wanted a drop of water to put in this. Can I help?'

'Well –' said Harriet, 'well, you could. But I don't know if you would. It's a huge favour.'

'Try me. Feeling pretty good as a matter of fact.'

'You look good,' said Harriet, smiling at him, distracted from her anguish briefly by the sheer happiness radiating from him. 'What's happened?'

'Tell you what's happened,' said Merlin, 'gone the same way as the birds and the bees and the educated fleas, that's what.'

'Sorry, Merlin, I don't quite follow you.'

'Don't you ever listen to any decent music, Harriet? Little number by Cole Porter. "Let's Do It", it's called. Fine song. Anyway, that's it. Waited a bit of a time but here I am, helpless as a kitten up a tree, to quote another one.'

'Merlin, are you trying to tell me you've – well, you've fallen in love?'

'That's it. Head over heels. Well, you can guess who with, of course. Janine. She's a wonderful girl. What an evening we've had. Could have stayed out with her forever, but didn't want to start any talk, ruin her reputation, that kind of thing.'

'No, of course not,' said Harriet, keeping her expression sober with great difficulty.

'Can't believe my luck,' he said, taking a large slug of whisky. 'She's damn fine-looking, isn't she, and extremely sharp. And a wonderful listener. But I let her talk too. Told me about her husbands, all three of them, and her life. Very interesting. One thing she's never done enough, she says, is travel. Can't wait to show her the bush. And the rain forests. Anyway, I've proposed and she's accepted. What do you think, eh?'

'Merlin, I think it's wonderful,' said Harriet, reaching up to kiss him on the cheek. 'Er – how official is it? I mean am I to keep it a secret?'

'Good Lord, no. Don't want to waste any time. Don't believe in long engagements, never did. No, I'll put it in the *Telegraph* tomorrow and we'll apply for a special licence. Apparently she's got a frock she can wear, so that'll cut out a lot of messing about.'

'Good gracious,' said Harriet. 'You really are serious, aren't you?'

'Of course I am. Look, I've always said once I found the right woman I wouldn't let her get away again. She made up her mind pretty quickly too. I asked her just before they brought the pudding and by the time we'd had coffee, she'd said yes.'

'Well, I think it's lovely,' said Harriet. 'Can I say anything to her?'

'Maybe not tonight,' said Merlin. 'She seems a bit tired. All this nonsense today has taken it out of her a bit. Gone up to bed now. But in the morning, of course you can. In fact she said she'd like to tell you before anyone else.'

'Oh, Merlin,' said Harriet. Tears had filled her eyes. 'Oh, Merlin, I think it's so lovely. I'm so pleased for you.'

'Yes, well, I'm a fool not to have realized before,' he said, blushing slightly. 'Wasted a bit of time, I suppose. But never mind, we're not in our dotage yet, plenty of years ahead of us. Pity we can't have children, but there it is, not much chance of that I'm afraid. We could adopt I suppose,' he added suddenly. 'What would you think of that? Or do you think they'd say we were too old? The authorities, I mean?'

'Merlin,' said Harriet, kissing him again, 'I'd back you against the authorities any day. But I should wait a little while if I were you. Best to have a bit of time just the two of you on your own, don't you think?'

'I suppose so,' he said. 'Now what was this favour you wanted to ask me?'

Harriet felt absurdly happy as she drove the Lagonda down the winding lane. The pure charm of a romance between Merlin and Janine had lifted her spirits as nothing else could have done. She had longed to go and talk to Janine herself, but the door to her room had been firmly closed and no light showed under the door; she would see her in the morning. She wondered suddenly if Janine would let her design a dress, but if Merlin was in that much of a hurry, maybe it wasn't such a good idea. What a wedding it would be. She wondered who would give Janine away, and who Merlin would have as his best man. He surely couldn't have that many able-bodied surviving friends; people of his age generally spent their time attending funerals rather than weddings. Maybe, she thought, smiling fondly, he would bring over some exotic figure from his travels, some tribal chieftain. It would be exactly like him. Janine would like that, too.

Behind her in the darkness someone was flashing her, clearly someone who had no knowledge of the dangerous narrow winding lanes. 'Just you wait,' she said aloud, 'and learn some manners,' and to distract herself from the irritation started to sing 'Let's Do It', that being the first song that came into her head. Rather to her surprise she realized she knew almost all the words: 'Argentines without means do it, Down in Boston even beans do it' . . . something about English soles do it, and what came next, oh, yes, 'Goldfish in the privacy of bowls do it.' Well, it wasn't surprising, she'd been raised on those songs, Merlin had boxes full of old 78s in his dusty flat and one of her treats when she stayed with him had been playing them on his wind-up gramophone. By the time she reached the forecourt of the Royal Hotel she had moved through 'Putting on my Top Hat' and 'Isn't It a Lovely Day' to 'Just the Way You Look Tonight'; so who needed a car stereo? She had just parked the Lagonda and was patting its wooden dashboard lovingly when she saw that it was Theo Buchan's Bentley that had been following her and flashing at her; the expression on his face when he saw her, rather than Merlin, climb out made up for quite a lot of the wretchedness of her day.

Harriet walked over to the car and smiled sweetly down at him.

'Theo,' she said, 'fancy seeing you here.'

'Yes,' he said, and even allowing for the ghastly yellow lighting of the Royal Hotel car park he looked terrible, ashen-pale with great hollows under his nearly black eyes.

'It's terribly bad manners, you know, to flash endlessly at someone like that.'

'Oh, for God's sake,' he said, getting rather slowly out of the car; he looked at that moment, she thought, like an old man. 'I thought you were Merlin. What on earth are you doing, driving his car?'

'Oh, I stole it,' she said, 'while he was asleep. I'm going to run away with it actually, sell it to a dealer in the Old Kent Road. Merlin lent it to me, that's what I'm doing with it. I lent my car to your son.'

'How kind,' said Theo, 'but I wish you hadn't.'

'Why not?'

'Oh – doesn't matter. Merlin must love you very much,' he added, 'he's never let me even drive it.'

'Yes, well, some of us are more deserving than others,' said Harriet, 'and I might add more trustworthy.'

'Right,' said Theo. 'Well, you must excuse me, Harriet, I'm very tired. It's been a long day. I'm going to bed.'

'No you're not,' said Harriet, 'we have things to discuss, Theo. Actually.'

'Oh, really? In the nature of?'

'In the nature of business, of course. There's certainly nothing else I would wish to discuss with you.'

'Harriet, I don't know what you're talking about.'

'Yes you do,' said Harriet briefly. 'Cotton Fields.'

'I beg your pardon?'

'I think you heard. I'll say it again, though, just in case. Cotton Fields. Fashion chain. Leisurewear. Hugely successful. Any bells ringing yet?'

'I don't think so.'

'Liar,' said Harriet shortly. 'Well, anyway, I have something else to do first, and then I'll be up to your room. Or maybe we should talk in the bar, if you think Sasha might prefer that. But it could get noisy.'

'Sasha isn't here,' said Theo tersely.

'Really?'

'No. She's gone up to London.'

'I see. Without you. How enterprising.'

Theo didn't answer. He walked to the front door of the Royal, held it open for her. 'I'll see you later then. I look forward to it.'

'I wouldn't,' said Harriet.

She went over to the reception desk. The crinkly-haired girl had been replaced by a young man of immense superiority. He was dressed in a rather sharp light grey suit; he had a smooth pale face and smooth pale hair, and an extremely flashy signet ring. Harriet didn't like him.

'I wonder,' she said, struggling to overcome what she knew was prejudice, largely engendered by the suit, 'if I could ask you a huge favour.'

A chilly, half-smile crossed his face and he was clearly shaping up some bland piece of unhelpfulness when the phone rang. 'Excuse me one moment,' he said, and picked up the receiver. The call was evidently from his girlfriend; he turned away from Harriet and spoke at some length. Harriet waited, trying to hang onto her temper. Finally he turned back to her. 'Now,' he said, 'you were saying?'

'I wasn't,' said Harriet, 'actually. But what I was going to say was, could I possibly use your fax? There's something I urgently need to receive from France, and this was the nearest fax I could think of. I live at Wedbourne,' she added, anxious to impress upon him that she was not some passing tourist, 'in the Court House.'

He looked at her oddly. 'I don't know this area,' he said, 'I come from Birmingham.' He made it plain that anyone who didn't come from Birmingham was a person of very little importance.

'Yes, well, we all –' 'have our problems' she was going to say, but bit the words back. 'That is, well, could I use the fax? Obviously I'll pay for it, but I need to phone someone in Paris and give him this number.'

'But you're not a resident of the hotel?'

'No,' said Harriet patiently, 'no, I told you, I live in Wedbourne.'

'Well in that case,' he said, 'I don't think I can possibly help you. I'm not empowered to give you access to our fax.'

'But it's there,' she said, leaning over the counter, 'I can see it. You don't have to give me access, just the number.'

'Which you would then pass on to your friend,' he said. He made it sound as if Harriet was about to do a heavy trade in drugs in the reception area.

'Yes.'

'I'm sorry, that's against management rules. The fax is for residents only,' he added carefully.

'But I'm not going to be using it all night,' said Harriet. 'I just want to receive one thing.'

'Yes, but while you're using it, a resident can't. You must see that.'

'Look,' said Harriet. 'It's eleven thirty at night. I don't see a lot of residents milling about and certainly not waving bits of paper they want to fax. It will take roughly thirty seconds to do this. Please, it's very important.'

'I'm sorry, but I really am not empowered to break management rules,' he said. 'They are very clear and – Ah, good evening, Mr Buchan, sir, can I get you anything?'

Harriet hadn't seen Theo reappear behind her; shit, he must have heard the whole humiliating episode.

'I cannot imagine that I'd want anything at all that you could get me,' said Theo in the heavy voice that made his staff the world over extremely nervous, and indeed start planning alternative employment immediately. 'Harriet, I have a fax upstairs, you can use that.'

'I'd rather use this one,' said Harriet firmly.

'Well, you're not going to be allowed to. Clearly. Some piss-pathetic management rule, I seemed to understand. So it's mine or nothing.'

Harriet looked at him. Behind the heaviness, the seriousness, there was a sparkle in the dark eyes; he had her, and he knew it. She felt furiously angry: with the young man, with herself for not handling him better, with management for having the stupid rule, but most of all with Theo for finding her at such a disadvantage and using it. 'Couldn't you – couldn't you ask him if you could use it? For me?' she said.

'Now why should I want to do that? They charge the earth, these people, for doing absolutely nothing. It would add a tenner, I daresay, to my bill, with VAT and God knows what.'

'I'll give you a tenner,' said Harriet desperately.

'Well, that would be interesting. But our young friend here would still know he was breaking his management rules. I imagine he would find that very difficult. Unethical even. No, you'd better use mine. Oh come along, Harriet, for Christ's sake. Get me a bottle of brandy sent up, would you?' he added to the young man. 'And let me have your name. I would hate to inadvertently employ you in one of my companies at some future date.'

'Poor little sod,' he said as they walked into his suite. 'Shitting bricks down there I should think.'

'How unlike you to show such concern,' said Harriet, 'and I don't know why you should either. He was horrible.'

'I agree. But it really wasn't entirely his own fault, I suppose. He had certain genetic and educational disadvantages to overcome.'

'Theo, don't be altruistic. It doesn't agree with you.'

'Oh, I don't know. I think I'm being fairly altruistic, letting you use my fax machine. Now then, what is it you want so urgently? From Paris.'

'A picture,' said Harriet, giving in, 'a picture of Cressida. Well, we think it might be Cressida. I have to phone the photographer and he'll fax it over.'

'Cressida? Doing what?'

'Getting married.'

'Dear God. What's his number? I'll do it.'

Somehow, until she saw the picture, she hadn't believed it. She'd thought Mick McGrath must have been mistaken, that it was a photograph of someone who looked very like Cressida; but there was no doubt, no doubt at all, even on the slightly smudgy fax. It was her, wearing the dress that had been hanging in the attic room for weeks, not the veil to be sure, but it was Cressida's hair, her bloody perfect blonde hair, thought Harriet, falling loosely on her shoulders, Cressida's face, smiling joyously up at the man whose hand she was holding, Cressida's pretty profile with its just turned-up nose, its neatly carved little chin, Cressida's tall, slender body, frozen forever in its joyous flight down the endless steps that led down from the great south door of Sacré-Coeur. She held not a traditional bouquet but a small bunch of what looked like sweet peas; her bridegroom (if such he was) was classically French-looking, with a darkly handsome, scrunched-up face and black curly hair, and he wore not a morning coat but a dark suit, over a white collarless shirt, open at the neck. There seemed to be no wedding guests with them, but small groups of tourists were staring at them, smiling benevolently; and around their heads, and on the steps below them, were the omnipresent, unconcerned pigeons of Paris.

'Dear God,' said Theo. 'Dear, dear God.'

'Theo,' said Harriet, 'Theo, at least try and think of something else to say.'

'I can't. I really can't. It is her, isn't it? There's no doubt at all.'

Harriet looked at him. He seemed very shaken. 'No, no doubt. It's totally nightmarish, isn't it? I feel absolutely shattered by the whole thing. Apparently the name she gave the photographer was Eloise Renaud. Maybe if we went through all the directories or something.'

'Hardly an unusual name. It would take forever.'

'Well, maybe we should go over there, see the priest at Sacré-Coeur – how did they manage to arrange that, it's a huge cathedral for God's sake – get the name of the man. Who doesn't seem quite dressed for the part, I must say.'

'Yes, we could. Obviously we should. We have to. But not tonight. I'll take my plane over early in the morning.' There was a silence while he looked at her. 'I don't think we tell your parents, do you?'

'God, no,' said Harriet with a shudder. 'All right, Theo, yes, that would be best. We'll wait till the morning. I'll just ring Mick McGrath, say thank you.'

'OK. Drink?'

'Coffee'd be good.'

She phoned Mick. 'Thank you. It's a nice picture. Are they going to use it?'

'No. No they're not. Look, if there's anything I can do –'

'There might be. I'll be over in the morning. I'll ring you then.'

'Yeah, OK. I tell you, Harriet, this is one weird business.'

'Oh, Mick,' said Harriet, 'tell me about it.'

She put the phone down, stared at Theo. Somehow, briefly, he had ceased to be her enemy, had become divorced from any past they might have had, was simply her travelling companion in this strange new journey.

'You OK?'

'Yes. Yes I think so.'

He poured them both a coffee from the big jug that had arrived with his bottle of Martel Cordon Bleu. 'What the hell was she up to?' he said. 'What the hell?'

'Theo, I don't know. I can't make any sense of it. Any sense at all. OK, she wasn't quite the Miss Goody Two-Shoes everyone thought but – this is so – well, awful. And cruel. Wickedly cruel. She looks so happy. That's almost the worst thing. Knowing what she's done to us all –'

'Well,' he said, with a heavy sigh, 'love, if that is what she felt for this man, love does strange things. To us all.' His eyes, looking at her, were remote, brooding; she met them for as long as she could, then turned away.

'You think that's what it was then? She was in love with someone else, with this person, and finally –'

'I don't know. I really don't. I can't begin to imagine. I've done some fairly – well, unpleasant things in my life, but this is beyond even my imagining. Your parents, what they have endured today, it's unthinkable –'

'I know. I know.'

'And to think I helped her do this.'

'Theo, of course you didn't.'

'Yes I did. I paid for those flying lessons, I gave her money –'

'You gave her money? When?'

'Oh – quite often. Well, she was my goddaughter, I was very fond of her. She was hopeless with money, you know, always getting into debt, running up bills in shops and on her credit cards, in spite of her allowance and her salary and so on. Always begged me not to tell your father and of course I didn't. But it did worry me. I used to lecture her from time to time. Just as well Oliver had plenty of money –'

'He didn't have a lot,' said Harriet. 'I mean they're well-off, but they're not rich.'

'Oliver's going to be. Very rich.'

Harriet stared at him. 'I didn't know that.'

'Oh, you must have done,' he said, looking at her in genuine astonishment. 'Cressida certainly did. And your parents did I'm sure. But I suppose it wasn't common knowledge. Josh liked it played down. And you know how modest Oliver is, the opposite of flashy. Anyway, he was due to inherit an enormous sum from his grandfather. Julia's father. Serious money. All tied up in trusts of course, but –'

'I knew about the trust fund, but I didn't realize it was so big. I wonder why they didn't tell me. Maybe they thought – oh well –' She smiled rather shakily; it hurt her, hurt and humiliated her, that her parents should have thought she must be protected from the knowledge that Cressida was going to be seriously rich, that she would be jealous or upset. How much more pain was she going to have to take today? She pulled back abruptly to the present, to more immediate, more relevant questions. 'Why wasn't Julia getting it, Theo, this money? I don't understand . . .'

'Old chap didn't like Josh. Doesn't like him, rather. Never wanted Julia to marry him. Thought he was a loser.'

'I see,' said Harriet slowly. 'Well, he was wrong there, wasn't he?'

'Not really. Josh is one of my dearest friends, Harriet, but I wouldn't give him a job as my office boy. He's no real business sense. He's only held that job in the bank by the old virtues.'

'What old virtues?'

'Oh, you know, family connections, contacts, charm. They've lived off Julia's income to a large extent.'

'Which explains why Josh doesn't like talking about the money. Makes him look bad.'

'Yes, that's right.'

'Good Lord,' said Harriet. 'Oh Theo. Oh shit. This has been such a truly shocking day.'

'Yes it has.' He looked at her carefully. 'You OK?'

'Yes. Yes, I'm OK. Just. Maybe Sacré-Coeur will yield an answer tomorrow. Only I don't know if the priest or whoever will be able to help.'

'Oh, he'll help,' said Theo. There was a darkness in his voice. 'I'm quite good at persuading people to – help.'

And the expression on his face, the tone of his voice, replaced him for her, made him again the person he truly was, set him in his proper context, as tyrant, tormentor, arch-manipulator, and 'Yes,' she said, 'yes, Theo, you are, aren't you? Let's change the subject briefly, shall we? Let's talk Cotton Fields.'

'Harriet, haven't we got enough to worry about for now? I really don't know what you're talking about. Where it's leading –'

'I rather think you do, Theo. And from where I'm sitting it leads ultimately to my going absolutely and finally bust. In total humiliation. Unless of course I come crawling to you for money. Which I suspect might just be what you have in mind. Well, I can tell you, Theo, I would rather die from a thousand cuts.'

'I don't think you would,' he said, 'but still.'

'I would. Now then. Did you or did you not tell Hayden Cotton not to back me?'

There was a long silence. Then Theo said, 'Not exactly . . .'

'I see. Perhaps you could enlighten me on exactly what you did say then. It must have been fairly specific. He disappeared from the negotiating table faster than a snowflake in hell. Rather suddenly.'

'Harriet, I –'

'Yes Theo?'

'OK. I'll tell you. I told him to take a very hard look at the figures.'

'Theo, he'd *taken* a very hard look at the figures. And he seemed to be able to handle them.'

'Yes, well, I had a look at them too. He showed them to me.'

'What? Why?'

'We're old allies. He knows I know you. He wanted my advice.'

'I see. And?'

'And I thought they'd been massaged. A bit. And I said so.'

'They'd *what*! Massaged!' Harriet stood up. 'Theo, how dare you! How dare you even imply such a thing? There are slander laws in this country, as you very well know. I intend to use them.'

'Difficult,' he said, 'when you're bankrupt.'

'You bastard,' she said, 'you rotten, filthy bastard. What's it to you, Theo Buchan, why do you want me bankrupt? What will it do for you? Flatter your grotesque ego? Take you one step nearer your ambition to rule the world? You disgust me, Theo, you really do. I'm ashamed to have ever had anything to do with you.'

'Harriet,' he said, and there was real, raw pain at the back of his dark eyes, 'Harriet, don't say that. Please.'

'I'm afraid I have to say it, because it's true. I am ashamed. It makes me feel sick.'

'Oh God,' he said, and put his head in his hands suddenly.

'And don't,' she said, 'don't call in the throbbing strings, Theo, because they're sounding fairly badly out of tune. I find it hard to imagine that you could say anything, anything at all, that would change the way I'm feeling about you right now. Which is above all nauseated.'

He looked up at her, and his face was literally grey; he reached out for his glass and his hand was shaking so violently he had to put it down again. 'Harriet, I –'

'Theo, don't. Just don't. I've seen them all, all the routines, heard all the scripts. I'm leaving. Now.' (So why aren't you going, Harriet, why are you still standing there looking at him? Just walk out, walk away. Maybe kick him in the balls for good measure.)

'No,' he said, getting up. 'No, Harriet, don't go. I want to talk to you –'

'Well, I don't want to talk to you. Ever again. Except just possibly in court. Goodbye, Theo.' (Well, go on, Harriet, go, leave, you don't want to talk to him, you want to get out of this room, full of his bloody arrogant, manipulative presence. What's stopping you? God, Harriet, don't, don't walk forward, don't whatever you do let him touch you, take your hand away from his –)

'Oh God,' he said, and the words were a great echo of misery, 'oh God, Harriet, please, please stay, don't leave me, I'll do anything, anything at all, but don't go.'

'Theo,' she said, and she put out her other hand now, the one he wasn't holding, and to her own intense astonishment gently, tenderly touched his hair, 'Theo, we can't –' and the words came slowly, falteringly, she had to struggle with every one, and there was something else going on now, a warmth, that bloody, dangerous, flooding warmth that he could always create in her, the prelude to something fiercer, stronger. Her body throbbed once, twice, sweetly, powerfully, and she was afraid, afraid of its betrayal, of its longing for him. 'Theo,' she said, 'Theo, we can't let it begin again. We really really can't.'

And she pulled her hand away then, hard, roughly, and looked away from him, and the effort was so intense she felt it physically, and then she turned her back on him and walked swiftly, desperately fast, to the door, wrenched it open, ran down the stairs, through the front door, across the courtyard to Merlin's car and struggled to start it, frantically fearful that he would follow her, catch her, knowing that if he did, she would be lost, helplessly, hopelessly lost, and that if he touched her once more, however lightly, she would take all her clothes off there and then, and just lie down on the hard stones and fuck him and fuck him until they were both senseless.

Chapter 21

Mungo 11:30pm

Financial reality was not something Mungo was overfamiliar with. Like most people who have grown up cushioned by apparently limitless wealth, he had really very little idea what anything cost: he had once been asked how much his weekly outgoings were and he had replied with charming naiveté that he thought about £5. His flat in Sloane Street had been bought for him out of his trust fund; its outgoings were paid for from the same source. Such food as he ate at home he had delivered from Harrods and Fortnums, on the Buchan account, his clothes were all made by the various tailors who served his father, or from establishments where a Buchan charge account had been run for decades, Harrods, Fortnums, Simpsons and Paul Smith in London, Brooks Brothers and Paul Stuart in New York, Trimingham Brothers in Bermuda. His shoes were all made by Lobb. His cars were provided and serviced by his father's garage, he bought air tickets on his father's accounts with various airlines, hired cars on his father's account with Hertz. Many of the world's great hotels welcomed him, and simply presented him with a bill to sign as he left; the same applied to a large number of restaurants. Theo had accounts with cab companies, florists, theatre ticket agencies; Berry Brothers of St James's had supplied the Buchan family with wine and spirits for three generations. For several days at a time, the only cash Mungo ever had to produce was for an evening paper or a packet of Polos. Indeed one of the more educational aspects of his affair with Alice had been discovering the cost of eating at places like McDonald's and Pizza Hut. Mungo was not stupid or even thoughtless; he knew perfectly well what an inordinate amount of money he must work his way through in the course of a year, or even a month, but there was a faceless quality to the money, it didn't mean anything, no thought went into its coming and going, it was simply part of the process by which he procured things. He thought, he chose, he signed; no decisions were necessary, no choices made, he wanted therefore he had.

And now suddenly, he could see quite a lot was going to change and there might, for a while at any rate, be a great deal he wanted and would not be able to have.

Of course, any such deprivation was not strictly necessary: when it came to Mungo, Theo's memory was famously short, his attitude notoriously liberal. Had Mungo not gone into battle so vigorously, taken Theo on so valiantly, had he told Alice that it might be politic for them to wait a while before actually getting married, had he seen his property company safely through a full financial year or maybe two, then he could have continued with his way of life more or less unthreatened. But battle, and the more vigorous the better, was Mungo's style; and having forced the confrontation, made all those brave statements, there could be no going back. Even if he'd wanted it: which he most emphatically didn't. It was going to be tough, making out on his own, but it would be very very good. There would be no more insinuations about his inadequacy, no more references to his dependency; for the first time in his twenty-seven years he would feel like an adult. And he was hardly going to be destitute: he still had a sizeable income from the capital in his trust fund, he had his flat, his car, enough clothes to see him through the next twenty years, and he had a viable – well, potentially viable – business. He would be all right.

He had spent the past hour in his office in Carlos Place, looking at business in hand, studying the cash flow, doing projections. And confronting a truth that had confronted a great many people running companies over the past thirty-six months: that his incomings simply didn't begin to match his outgoings. The costs of the offices, staff and advertising were, month on month, roughly double what they were earning. It hadn't mattered before: Theo had simply made up the shortfall. Now it mattered a lot. Mungo stared out of his window at the subtle opulence of the Connaught Hotel and realized that he would have to get rid of the office and most of the staff. He and the two Sloaney girls he had hired as negotiators (extremely effective as well as pretty) would have to run the business from his flat. It wouldn't be ideal, but it would be all right. The marketing and advertising manager, the surveyor and the interior designer would have to go; they simply weren't earning their keep. They were useful in promoting the company, but he could cope without them. He'd have to put a lot more hours in, of course, but that would be OK; he'd enjoy it. Looking through his books, his files, that night, he realized how much he loved his company, already, how much the business fascinated him, how much he wanted to develop it. And he knew he could. He might even study for a degree in estate management in his spare time: Roddy Fairfield, his rather flashy young assistant (he'd have to go too) had one, and there was no doubt he was not only very knowledgeable, he had all the jargon. People liked jargon. And it would be good to study, good to learn something again. He went off into a brief reverie, imagining himself working every night in Alice's little house while she read and did her tapestry. Well, he would get off to the little house now; it was late, but she wouldn't mind. She hardly ever went to bed before midnight, usually well after. He'd said he wouldn't be coming, so she wouldn't be expecting him of course, but that would make his arrival all the nicer, more fun.

Mungo went down the stairs and locked the heavy front door behind him; the street was deserted and very quiet. The crime wave that was theatening to engulf London, if the media were to be believed, certainly hadn't broken on Carlos Place. Now he had to get a cab; well, there were plenty outside the Connaught. He might just have a drink there, before he went to Alice. He felt he needed one suddenly; it had been a bit of a bitch of a day.

It was almost midnight when he left the Connaught, two glasses of champagne later. Maybe he should ring Alice, warn her he was coming. Then he thought that if she was asleep, the phone would wake her; he would go to the house and if all the lights were out, he would restrain himself.

'Nine, Chatto Street please,' he said to the driver and sat back.

'Lovely evening,' said the cabbie.

'Lovely,' said Mungo.

'Long day,' said the cabbie. 'Been driving tourists round since lunchtime. Can't stand them. Except the Americans of course. They're all right. Speak English as well. Mind you, why they go on coming here I can't think, the filth in the streets, and the traffic, beats me, when they've got the whole of the United States to look at. Course they haven't got the royal family, that's what brings them in, and that's a mystery too, the way they've all gone downhill, well, not the Queen herself, but the rest of them, specially the young ones, no sense of duty any more, no real class, terrible, and I'll tell you something else, I don't think she should be charging for seeing over the palace, doesn't seem right somehow, makes the whole thing too commercial, we shall be having a republic soon, I'm sure of it, and then we'll be sorry, specially when she's gone, it'll be Mrs Thatcher all over again, Lady I should say –'

Mercifully Mungo was saved from hearing how the downfall of the monarchy might be paralleled in some way with Lady Thatcher's demise; they had reached Chatto Street and he was about to pay the driver off and get out when he saw that the small house was indeed in total darkness. Shit. That was seriously irritating. Oh, well, he told himself, if he was going to be a proper businessman in future, he was going to have to get used to keeping more demanding hours. He was about to tell the cabbie to turn around and go back to Sloane Street when he realized he had only just enough money to pay the fare as it was.

'Thanks, that's fine,' he said. 'Look, I'm terribly sorry, I don't have any spare change at all, I can only give you a 5p tip, bit of an insult I'm afraid, but –'

'You keep your bloody 5p, mate,' said the cabbie, reversing viciously, preparatory to turning round, 'you must need it more than I do.'

'I'm terribly sorry,' said Mungo again. 'I thought –'

'I wouldn't try,' said the cabbie, 'thinking I mean, you might find it too much of a strain.'

And he was gone with a squeal of tyres and a blare on his horn as he reached the junction with the Kings Road.

Mungo looked after him, and sighed, and then thought he might as well just walk home. There was no point waking Alice up, she was bound to be tired, and they had all the time in the world after today. It wasn't far to Sloane Street, only about ten minutes; he would get a good night's sleep and then – His plans for the next day were gently disturbed by the quiet clunk of a door being shut. Someone leaving a dinner party, no doubt, although there was no shouted bonhomie, no 'thank yous', no 'lovely evenings'. Just the clunk.

Vaguely intrigued he turned round, and saw a figure walking away from Alice's house. A male figure. One of Jemima's friends, Mungo told himself firmly, ignoring the tiny movement, a minute curl of fear stirring somewhere in the region of his stomach; she was home for the holidays after all. Considerate of them to be so quiet: unlike Jemima that. Much of Jemima's behaviour made Annabel Headleigh Drayton appear a dead ringer for Mother Theresa by comparison. He didn't slow down, then, in order to get a better look at the person; of course he didn't. He was tired and it was very hot and he just didn't want to get any hotter, that was all. A nice gentle unwinding walk was what he wanted; the fact that the man was catching him up, about to overtake him, was neither here nor there. There really was a dinner party going on in the house he was passing now; the dining room was at street level, the light flooding out onto the dark pavement. It lit up the man's face as he passed Mungo, and he didn't look too much like one of Jemima's friends: he was at least thirty years old, extremely good-looking, his jacket was slung across his shoulders, his tie hung loosely round his neck and he was whistling 'Candle in the Wind' very quietly under his breath. 'Candle in the Wind' was one of Alice's favourite songs.

Mungo took a deep breath and walked straight back to number 9.

The house was not in total darkness any more; Alice's bedroom (front, first floor) had a light in it. Well, maybe whoever'd just left had woken her and now she was reading. She was a very light sleeper. He rang the bell gently, hardly to be heard. He wished Alice would let him have a key; he felt so foolish, having to be let in like a casual visitor. But she was very protective, possessive even, about her domain, her personal space; she told him it was on account of living alone for so long. Well, now they were definitely going to be married, she would surely agree to let him have one. Until they got a place of their own. He'd been thinking of a house, on the Kensington–Chelsea borders, maybe near The Boltons, nothing too grand, but big enough for all of them. Shit, even that would be more complicated now, he'd have to get the trustees' permission and – What on earth was she doing, why was she so long? Maybe she hadn't heard him. He rang again, a little more firmly. Ah, there were footsteps now. The door opened; Jemima's face appeared in the crack above the chain. She looked confused, embarrassed.

'Oh – Mungo. Hi. What are you doing here?'

'Visiting your mother, I hope.'

'But I thought –'

'Yes, I know, but I had to come up to town, so I just dropped by on the off-chance. Aren't you going to ask me in?'

'Oh – sorry, I wasn't thinking – but the thing is, Mungo, well, that is Mummy isn't here.'

'Isn't here? But her bedroom light's on.'

'Yes I know. I was in there myself, just – oh, you know, looking at her dresses. Seeing if there was anything I could borrow for a – a dance I'm going to.' She pushed her heavy hair back; smiled at him awkwardly.

'Well, where's your mother?'

'She's gone out to dinner. With – with a friend.'

'Oh, I see.' Well, that was all right. Alice had every right to go out to dinner. With anyone really, and certainly with a girlfriend. Even if she hadn't mentioned it. It was probably a last-minute invitation.

'When do you think she'll be back? I really do want to see her.'

'Oh – I don't know. Not for ages probably. She's with her very best friend. They just talk and talk for hours.'

'Who, Anouska?' said Mungo. He didn't quite know why he said that: he wasn't really checking up, of course not, he just wanted to make sure, to be able to go home to bed with an absolutely easy mind.

'Yes,' said Jemima. 'Yes, that's right, Anouska.'

'I see,' said Mungo. Anouska was away with her husband for a long weekend in France; Alice had told him herself.

* * *

He stood there for a long minute, trying to convince himself that it still didn't mean anything, that Jemima was simply trying to come up with an answer, to please him, to get rid of him. He failed. 'Well, I think if you don't mind, Jemima,' he said, 'I'll come in and wait for your mother. I've got something terribly important to talk to her about. You just get off to bed and I'll sit and read or something.'

'But –'

'Jemima,' said Mungo. 'I really do want to come in. Friend of yours just leaving, was it?'

Jemima looked at him; her face in the street light was startled, guilty. 'No. Yes. Well, an old friend of the family. Of Mummy's, really.'

'I see. And you were entertaining him with all the lights out, were you?'

'Mungo, I – oh shit, I –'

She looked very scared. Mungo smiled at her suddenly, conspiratorially. 'Listen, Jemima, I'm not so much of a grown-up I'm going to tell on you. But I would like to come in.'

'Oh, all right,' said Jemima, and smiled, slightly uncertainly, back. She undid the chain and unlocked the door; Mungo wondered vaguely how Alice might have been supposed to get in, but then dismissed the thought. He had more important things on his mind.

'Thank you.' He looked at her; under her long dark lashes her eyes were knowing, defiant. She led him into the kitchen. 'Coffee? Drink?'

'I'd love a coffee. Thank you.'

She made two cups, slightly to his surprise, put them on the table, sat down on a chair opposite him. She was wearing a silk robe; her cleavage was very visible, her hair, thick, blonde, tousled, tumbled over her shoulders. One long brown leg was crossed over the other, revealed almost to the crotch. God, she was gorgeous. Talk about jail bait. Mungo concentrated very hard on his mug of coffee. 'You don't have to worry,' he said again, 'I really am not going to tell on you.'

'Thank you. Of course we weren't –'

'Of course you weren't.'

'But he's much older than me and Mummy doesn't really approve.'

'I see. Is it – quite serious?'

'Well, a bit. But only a bit. I've got another year at school yet and –'

'Three surely. Three years. With A-levels.'

'Oh, I'm not going to do A-levels,' said Jemima, with as much scorn in her voice as if he had suggested she might take up cleaning or pig farming. 'I'm going to do modelling.'

'Oh really? Well, you'll make a lot of money. If you do well.'

'Yes, I know. And it's obviously great fun. You know Ottoline, don't you? What's she like?'

'She's gorgeous,' said Mungo simply, 'and fun, and really nice. But she works like a dog.'

'Oh, really? How?'

'Hours and hours on end in boiling studios. And freezing clifftops and things. And twenty-hour days in fashion showrooms, for weeks at a time. It's tough.'

'I don't call that tough,' said Jemima carelessly, 'and she gets bloody well paid for it, doesn't she?'

'Yes she does. Tell me, Jemima, what would you call tough?'

'Oh God, studying. I loathe it. And looking after kids. That's what I'm doing these holidays until we go away. It's gross. I hate it.'

'Well, I presume it's earning you a bit of money.'

'A bit. Mummy won't put my allowance up, and I just don't get enough –'

'I think it's more that she can't, Mimi, isn't it, she really doesn't have a lot of money.'

'I'm sure she could if she wanted to. She seems to have plenty of money to spend on herself. She's always buying clothes and things.'

'She seems to me to buy you quite a lot,' said Mungo, 'you and the others. So where is she then?'

He shot the question out quickly, catching her off her guard. Her voice was nervous, a bit too loud. 'I told you. She's gone out to dinner with Anouska.'

'Jemima, Anouska is in France. I happen to know. So who is your mother with?'

'Mungo, I don't know. I wasn't really listening. She's with friends, anyway.'

'Uh-huh. Look, do you want to go up and finish changing the sheets on your mother's bed? I'd hate to be responsible for your getting caught out –'

Jemima stared at him, her eyes filled with fear. 'How did you –'

'Oh Jemima, I've been fifteen too, you know. Not so long ago. You didn't invent naughty behaviour. Go on, go and get on with it.'

'OK,' she said, looking at him uncertainly, 'OK. Thanks. I won't be long.'

He sat drinking his coffee, feeling increasingly disorientated. He looked at his watch: one o'clock. Late. Well, quite late. Late for an impromptu dinner with a girlfriend. Or was it? Maybe not. Late for something Jemima was covering up anyway. Very late. He sighed, got a half-drunk bottle of wine out of the fridge and poured himself a glass. It was extremely good: expensive. Very expensive, he thought, looking at the label. Maybe one of the ones he'd bought. No, it wasn't, it was a French burgundy, he never bought French wine these days. Californian was a lot more interesting. She must have bought it herself. Maybe for a dinner party. Or maybe Jemima's friend had brought it. Yes, that was it. He drank the glass very quickly, finished the bottle, put it down under the sink. Alice was very strict about empties, taking them all to the bottle bank on Saturday mornings. There was another identical one there, plus a champagne bottle, and a bottle of red as well, a Penfold, 1989. Jemima and her friend must have had quite an evening. And he must be pretty well-heeled. Well, he'd looked well-heeled. And pleased with himself as well. Disgusting, fucking schoolgirls. Mungo felt angry suddenly, angry with all of them; he ran up the stairs and stood in the doorway of Alice's bedroom. Jemima had her back to him; she had nearly finished her task, was pulling the duvet cover finally into place. She hadn't heard him. 'Who's she with?' said Mungo. It was a dirty trick, but he couldn't help it. She jumped, spun round.

'Mungo, don't, please don't. I can't tell you. It's – it's not fair.'

He sighed. 'I suppose not. All right. Well, I'm going to wait. As long as it takes.'

'Mungo, there's not much point,' said Jemima, and for the first time that evening her large blue eyes – beautiful eyes, he noticed, irrelevantly, flecked with darker blue still – were soft, concerned.

'Why not?'

'Because – because she won't be back. Not until the morning. Oh Mungo, don't look like that. I'm so sorry.'

'That's all right, Jemima. Thank you for telling me. I think I'll still wait, though, if you don't mind. You go to bed, I'll be quite all right on the sofa.'

He was sitting there, staring into the darkness when she came in ten minutes later, bringing him a brandy and a cup of coffee. 'There you are. A nightcap.' She bent down and kissed him very gently on the cheek.

'I'm sorry, Mungo. She doesn't deserve you, she really doesn't. And you certainly don't deserve her.'

Chapter 22

Tilly 12:30am

Considering she stood to make several hundred thousand dollars out of it herself, Felicity had been very noble about Tilly's decision. 'I really am not at all sure you should do it,' she said, when Tilly told her. 'You know how homesick you get, you know how you hate being tied down. There's more to life than money, Tilly.'

'You're kidding me,' said Tilly grinning into the phone. 'Yeah, I know. And the reason I want to do this – correction, the reason I *am* doing this – is exactly that. I have to get away, Felicity, away from London, out of this whole thing. And besides, I have plans for the money.'

'Tilly, don't get too excited about the money. It will go fast enough. Hideous tax bills, horrible expenses –'

'Yeah, outrageous commission to my agent, don't forget that. Don't fuss, Felicity, I know what I'm doing.'

'And you're sure?'

'I'm sure.'

'Can I call Meg? I mean you still won't be totally committed, not till you've signed, but she's going to start getting very wound up –'

'Sure,' said Tilly. 'Tell her. It's fine. Really.'

Felicity rang back five minutes later. 'She's so excited. She asked me to tell you she never felt more happy about anything in her life.'

'She must have had a pretty crap life,' said Tilly. Then she poured herself a very large glass of wine, and sat down to watch the last vestiges of day leave the sky.

She was woken by the entryphone ringing. She stumbled over to the door, stupid with sleep, picked it up. 'Yeah?'

'Tilly. It's Rufus.'

'I thought you were still in Wedbourne.'

'You thought wrong. Please, Tilly, let me in. I have to talk to you.'

'Rufus, I –' God, she didn't need this. Not now. Not tonight. She needed her strength, her sleep.

'Tilly, please.'

'Oh – all right.'

She pressed the entryphone, went into the bathroom. God, she looked terrible; great hollow eyes, saggy skin, and she had a spot, for Christ's sake, coming on her chin. Thank God they didn't have to reshoot any of the wedding dresses. Tilly dragged a comb through her cropped hair and cleaned her teeth. When she came out Rufus was standing in the sitting room. He had a bunch of rather tacky-looking flowers in his hand, wrapped in the lace-printed plastic garages use as substitute for wrapping paper. He was deathly pale. He tried to smile at her.

'Hallo, Tilly. These are for you.'

'Rufus, you really shouldn't have got Pulbrook and Gould out of bed at this time of night,' said Tilly, trying to sound light-hearted. She took the flowers, kissed him briefly. 'Drink?'

'Yes please. Well, if I can stay.'

Tilly took a deep breath. There was no point in postponing the agony longer than necessary. The swifter and cleaner the surgery the better.

'I – don't know. I have a six o'clock call.'

'Oh.' He looked confused. 'That never stopped you before.'

'I know, but I'm fucking tired.'

'Oh. Oh I see.' His eyes were so dark, his face so collapsed with hurt she could hardly stand it. She went into the kitchen quickly, poured two glasses of wine, handed him one. 'Here you are. I guess you could sleep on the couch.'

'Tilly! Tilly, whatever is it? What did I do?'

'Nothing. I told you, I'm just wrecked.'

'Too wrecked to talk to me?'

'No, of course not. But I have to talk to you too.'

'Oh. Well, all right. Of course. You go first.'

Oh God, he was such a nice man. Here he was, exhausted, clearly upset, desperate to talk to her, and she was treating him like some kind of pervert, and he was politely prepared to listen to her. How was she going to do this; and did she really really have to?

'No. No, you have first claim. Go ahead. I'm all yours.' She smiled at him, settled in the sofa opposite him.

'Are you, Tilly? Are you really? Because that's, at rock bottom, what I want to talk to you about. Well, there is something else, connected to it, but – before I start on that I just have to know, Tilly. Whether you'll marry me. I need you so much. More than ever now. You see –'

Right. This was it. She couldn't let this one go. Whatever else was going on. She took a deep breath, lit a cigarette, offered him one. He shook his head; he hated her smoking, she was always promising, without really meaning it, to give it up. 'Well, Rufus,' she said, not trying to be careful, tactful (for what was the point, what good would it possibly do?), 'Rufus, I've had an offer.'

'Ah.' She sensed him bracing himself, watched his eyes darken with alarm.

'What kind of offer?' he said clearly struggling to sound relaxed. 'From another man?'

God, Rufus, don't do this to me, don't try to be so nice, so brave.

'No. Well, from a whole load of men.'

'I'm sorry, Tilly, I don't follow.'

'From a cosmetics company. Called Rosenthal. I'm sure you won't have heard of them.'

'I – don't think I have. No.'

'Well, they're big. Very big. And they want to sign me up.'

'And is that what you want?'

'Yes. Yes it is.'

'Well, I should let them. If I were you. You want to get a good lawyer to look at the contract though.' He managed to smile at her; she didn't smile back.

'Yeah, I probably will. It's very big.' Might as well make herself sound as bad as possible. It would help him through it.

'How big?'

'Around two million dollars.'

Rufus whistled. 'That's a lot of dollars.'

Tilly shrugged. 'Yeah, well.'

'Tilly, what's the matter? You just don't seem yourself.'

'I'm myself,' said Tilly, beginning to believe it, 'probably more myself than I've been for a while.'

'So what does this have to do with us?' asked Rufus quietly.

'Well, I have to move to New York basically. For at least a year.'

'And?'

'And what?'

'Are you going to?'

'Yes, of course I am. Rufus, I really can't turn down two million bucks.'

'You could have talked to me about it. We could have discussed it, I would have thought.'

He looked so desperate, so bewildered, Tilly relented just a little. 'Rufus, I'm sorry. But I had to decide today. And there was rather a lot going on, it didn't seem quite the sort of thing to bother you with.'

'Tilly, anything to do with you is the sort of thing to bother me with. You know that.'

'Yes, I suppose it is. Yes of course. But – well, I do think it's for the best. In the long run.'

'Why?' He came over to her, took her hand, kissed it tenderly. Tilly looked at him, into his brown eyes, so full of love for her, and her heart quite literally seemed to be dying, choking to death. 'I'm sorry,' she said again, 'I'm so sorry. It just seemed – well, like I said, the best thing. To me.'

'Well,' he said, 'it doesn't to me. And I think you should have talked to me.'

'But Rufus, why?'

'Because I love you, Tilly. Because I want to marry you. To be with you. You know that.'

'Yes, Rufus, of course I do and –'

'Don't you love me? Is that what this is all about, is that what you're trying to tell me suddenly?'

'Yes,' she said, unable to lie about such an important, such a lovely thing, 'yes, Rufus, of course I love you. You know I do. But – well, love isn't everything. Is it?'

'For me it is. Everything.'

'Well, you're not very sensible, in that case,' said Tilly, getting up, fetching the wine bottle.

'No I'm not. I never thought being sensible was very important.'

'Well, I'm afraid I do. Rufus, we can't get married. I've told you so many times. It's hopeless. It would be like – I don't know. Pushing water uphill. Every day. Our lives wouldn't work together, Rufus. You'd want me to be what I'm not and I'd want you to be what you're not. It isn't practical, Rufus, I know it isn't. And in the end you'd know it too. We'd make each other so unhappy. So it's best to end it now. Before everything stops being good. And I've had this offer, and I've said I'm going. It's the right thing for both of us, Rufus, don't you see?'

'No,' he said, 'no I don't. I can't believe I'm hearing this, Tilly, I really can't. It's unbelievable.'

'I don't know why,' she said, irritated in spite of herself, in spite of her love for him. 'I've said all along that any idea of our being together, properly together, was hopeless. I think fate's come along and given us a bit of a shove.'

'And that's it, is it?' he said. 'Goodbye, baby, and amen. Just like that. You've decided it's not going to work, and so you're going. Have I got this right, Tilly?'

'Well,' she said, and she was having to drag the words out now, one by one, each more painful than the last, 'well yes, Rufus, actually, you have. I'm sorry, I'm really sorry.'

'Yes,' he said, standing up, staring down at her, 'yes I can see that. Terribly sorry. Nothing two million dollars can't fix though. Well, good. Tilly, I think there's something more to all this. I don't know what. And I don't know that I want to hear it, but I suppose I have to ask. Good lawyer that I am, I want to examine all the facts. Has something happened today, in this bloody awful day we've all been through, that's made you feel differently about me? Apart from the prospect of being a millionaire? Like have you met someone? Or –'

And 'No,' she said, 'no of course not. Although – well, in a way, I suppose I have. I mean I've met your mother, seen how she is, what she has obviously done for your – your father. I can't do that, Rufus, and I can't be part of your world. Not ever. It's impossible.'

'And you're not prepared to try? Because,' he added, his voice infinitely heavy with sadness, 'I've tried very hard to be part of yours. And not done entirely badly, I don't think.'

'That's different,' said Tilly.

'Why? Why is it different?'

'Well, it's easier, more fluid. The people I know and work with don't wear a uniform, and talk with the same accent, and go to the same schools, and serve up the same food on the same tablecloths and talk the same fucking shorthand.'

'Yes they do,' said Rufus, 'of course they do. And I've found it quite hard, some of it. I don't even like a lot of it. I don't like people saying fuck all the time for a start. And thinking it was terribly terribly important to be wearing the right jacket and having the right haircut, and to know who did those wonderful pictures in British *Vogue* this month. But it's been worth it, to feel part of you, to feel I'm helping you. You obviously don't have the same concerns. So maybe you're right, Tilly, maybe it's better we do part. Especially if you can make a major decision like going away for twelve months without any reference to me whatsoever.'

To her horror, she realized he was going, and in spite of the heat, the flat seemed suddenly cold, deathly, horribly still and cold; and although she knew it was the right, the only thing to do, she was more afraid than she had ever been in her life. She sat there staring at him, and panic rose in her, a huge, choking panic, at the thought of life without him, without his company, his comfort, his love for her. It seemed incredible to her suddenly that she had got through nineteen of her twenty years without him, and impossible that she would get through more than another hour of the rest of her life on her own. And yet, and yet the alternative was impossible, unthinkable; and so she didn't do what she longed to, didn't explain, didn't try to tell him what she was thinking, what she knew, just sat there, willing herself to be silent, to be still.

'Well,' he said, after a very long time, 'well, I might as well leave. Goodbye then, Tilly.' He walked over to the door, turned and looked at her; she saw there were tears in his brown eyes, that one was actually rolling down his face. She clenched her fists until her long nails dug into her palms, folded her lips together, terrified that some word, some noise even, would betray her.

He opened the door, waited another moment, then walked out and shut it quietly behind him, and she heard his feet going down the stairs and knew what it must feel like to be bleeding to death, to feel life ebbing away; and still she sat motionless, enduring it. And then as she heard the outside door shut (for the night was very still now), heard his car start, heard it drive slowly away, away, she remembered that she had never heard, had never asked even, what it was he actually wanted to talk to her about.

The Next Day

Chapter 23

Theo 5:30am

Flying, Theo Buchan had been often heard to say, was the greatest physical pleasure, next to sex. Flying yourself of course, he would add, not sitting in some godawful lorry in the sky, drinking inferior champagne; many, many parallels could be drawn, he would go on to say, the intense concentration, the surging, soaring exhilaration, the sense of absolute release – and afterwards the sweet, sweet peace. It was famously said of Theo that if he was serious about a woman, he took her flying; that was how she knew.

He was flying to Paris that morning: the physical presence beside him was that of James Forrest, but it was Harriet Forrest who filled his head and his heart and his senses, Harriet who was haunting the strange beautiful other-world he had up here, Harriet's lovely, slightly gaunt face he saw, as he had last seen it, with its extra-ordinary, fearful blend of hatred and desire, Harriet's voice he heard, harsh with anger, with scorn, and yet heavy with yearning, Harriet's body, its joyous, intent hunger denied him totally, and yet greedy for him still.

James had called him soon after she left, as he'd sat shaking with despair, with helplessness, said he had to talk to him, and 'Not now, James,' he'd said, 'Please not now, I'm done for.' But James had begged him, said he had to have companionship or he would go mad, and Theo had finally, wearily, agreed.

James, coming in drawn, grey-faced, had told him at once about Susie, about Rufus: 'What do I do, Theo, what the hell do I do?' and

Theo, shocked himself, had counselled caution, restraint: 'Leave him to think about it, James, to come to terms with it. Don't rush in with justifications, explanations, for Christ's sake. And certainly not fatherly sentiments.'

'Christ Almighty, Theo, what do you think I am?' said James, genuinely shocked, and Theo said, not entirely seriously, an insensitive egotist with a talent for trouble.

'Do you think he'll talk to people, want his family, my family to know?' said James, draining a second jug of coffee, reaching for the phone to order a third.

'Probably not,' said Theo coolly, knowing why he asked, thinking that he should, indeed did, despise James for the question, the reasons behind it, forty years of friendship holding him loyal. 'He's not a child, and he's a very conventional young man. And sensitive. I daresay he'll tell Tilly Mills though.'

'Christ,' said James, 'dear Christ,' and added suddenly, with a look of desperation at Theo that was truly childlike, 'Theo, you'll see me through this, won't you? You won't let me down?'

And Theo said of course he would stand by him, would see him through; and the conversation had then switched to Cressida, to what she had done, was doing, where she might be, and he had listened for a while to James agonizing, theorizing, before pleading exhaustion and then suggesting he came with him next morning on his quest for Cressida, his pilgrimage to Sacré-Coeur. 'I had thought that Harriet might come, but – well, I think perhaps it would be better if it was you.'

James had not known about the photograph; he was shocked, shaken, not only by what it revealed, but because Harriet hadn't told him. 'We are not friends just at the moment, she and I,' he said, and Theo, struggling to keep emotion from his voice, said it was much the same for him.

'Oh really? Why's that, do you think?' James asked, and 'Oh, I tried to interfere in her business,' Theo said casually, thanking God that James had clearly never had the slightest shadow of suspicion that there had been anything remotely more than paternal in his love for Harriet, no inkling of the glorious, dreadful love affair that would surely and finally have shaken their friendship to death. And still might, he thought, still might. 'And of course she's angry with me about the flying lessons, I suppose. As well she should be.'

'Yes, well I'm not,' said James with a sigh. 'At first, perhaps, but after all I've learnt about Cressida today, Theo, how capable she is of such infinite deceit, I could blame no one for any of it. I'd like to come to Paris with you, like to try and find her.'

Theo had driven to the Court House to collect him at 4.30 in the morning, as another perfect day was breaking through the mists, and together they drove to the small airfield near Kidlington where Theo had had his plane taken during the night, and climbed into the plane and took off feeling, against all possible odds, strangely and cheerfully excited as if they were on some schoolboy adventure. 'Where it all started, Paris, wasn't it?' said Theo, setting the plane at a steady 90 knots and visibly relaxing for the first time. 'Our lives together, that first holiday, when we went to stay in my father's apartment and you met Janine. Do you remember eating that bad oyster?'

'Yes, and you deserted me, left me with my head down the pan.'

'Well you got the best of it in the end. Initiation in Janine's hands. Literally. You've always been a lucky bugger.'

'I think my luck's run out finally,' said James. 'Finally and forever.'

'Get any sleep?'

'Not much.'

'Poor sod,' said Theo. 'Pour me some coffee, would you, out of that flask? I feel half dead. There should be some croissants in that picnic bag. And some pains au chocolat, I hope. Myra usually organizes those as well.'

'She's some secretary,' said James. 'Yes, here they are. Want one? One of each?'

'What do you think?'

'You eat too much,' said James, looking at him. 'How much do you weigh?'

'None of your bloody business.'

'Yes it is. I don't want to lose you yet.'

'I had a fitness test only the other day,' said Theo cheerfully, 'heart, lungs, cholesterol, the lot. The guy said I was absolutely fine. It's all muscle, you know, not fat. Hit me, go on.'

'No thanks,' said James, 'I don't want the plane to crash. There's some orange juice here. Want some? Oh, and two half-bottles of bubbly. For Buck's fizz I suppose. Christ, Theo, you're spoilt. Do I detect Sasha's hand in this?'

'No you don't,' said Theo briefly.

'Where is she?'

'I haven't a clue. I don't care.' He was extremely surprised to find it was true. Well, he supposed he knew why. The confrontation with love, raw, real, unarguable last night, had left Sasha already a shadow. 'She's left me,' he added, forestalling an interrogation. 'Yesterday. Taken a whole lot of goods, including a company I wanted, and scarpered. And before you say anything, I want you to know I deserved it. I treated her very badly. And not how you think either.'

'How then?' asked James.

'I put her down. Belittled her. Underrated her. Bad thing to do that, James. Don't ever do it yourself.'

'I won't get much chance, will I?' said James. His voice was heavy, full of pain.

Theo turned to look at him. 'I was wondering about you and – and Susie. If –'

'Yes?'

'If – oh, I don't know, that this might be a time for honesty. So you could be together for a bit. Concentrates the mind, that sort of thing. Makes life seem more precious.'

'Good God, no,' said James, 'Susie would never want to do anything like that. Rock her beloved family. No, I just have to go on biting the bullet and taking it. Playing understudy to bloody Alistair. Hopefully she'll come through.'

'Shit,' said Theo. 'Life's a bitch, isn't it? A real bitch. I'm sorry, James. So sorry.'

'Yes, well.' James was quiet for a moment, then he said, clearly with immense difficulty, 'So – any more thoughts on Rufus?'

'Not really. Just – leave things be. For a while. I suspect he'll want to do the same. Poor little bugger. Bit of a shock.'

'Yes,' said James shortly.

'I always liked Rufus,' said Theo thoughtfully. He grinned at James. 'Chip off the old block.'

'It's not funny, Theo, for Christ's sake.'

'No, no, of course not. Sorry.'

There was a silence.

'When will you hear about – about Susie?'

'Later this morning.'

'Ah.'

Another silence. Then: 'What do you think Cressida might be up to?'

It was obviously an easier subject, horrible as it was. Theo's heart went out to James; as he'd said his luck had finally run out. 'God knows,' he said, 'but whatever it is, I really don't think we've begun to scratch the surface of it. She must be very seriously mixed up.'

'Yes,' said James, 'and Theo, what really scares me is what the hell happens if we find her? We can hardly just take her home as if nothing had happened and rearrange the wedding, can we?'

'Not really,' said Theo. 'Not now.'

They landed at a small airfield outside Paris just before six, seven French time. The admirable Myra Hartman had organized a car, a large Mercedes. 'You drive,' said Theo, 'we've hit the rush hour, it's going to be hell, and I'm bushed.'

He went to sleep almost at once, to dream not of Harriet, nor even of Sasha, but of Cressida. She was sitting on the bridge in her wedding dress, laughing at them all. He woke up angry, to realize they had arrived at the Butte, the street below Sacré-Coeur. He felt very hot and sick. James was easing the Mercedes into a spot far too small for it.

'You'll never get it in there.'

'Yes I will.'

'Arrogant bugger. Christ, I feel terrible.'

'Should we have coffee somewhere? I'm sure the priest won't be there yet.'

'No, let's go up. Someone will be there. It opens at six forty-five. Is the funicular working?'

'Doesn't seem to be. Come on, Theo, I thought you were fit.'

'I am,' he said, and ran up the first fifty steps to prove it, then sat down, fighting for breath, waiting for James who was proceeding more slowly and steadily. Theo looked round and up at the exquisite pictures behind him, the stark white domes of Sacré-Coeur carved out of the blue, blue sky. It was like a vision, like something in a children's Bible. You could see why the Church got such a hold on people: it was enough to make you believe in God. He said as much to James, who looked up at it and grinned. 'Harriet loathes it. Says it's kitsch. That's the smart view generally, I'm told.'

'Yes, well, we can't all be smart. Bloody snobbery if you ask me,' said Theo irritably and continued his climb. For some reason it eased the pain Harriet had caused, was causing him, to criticize her, however mildly.

Illogically, and without admitting it, Theo felt nervous as he walked slowly into the cathedral through the great south door: absurd, he told himself, as if Cressida might still be there, waiting for them. After the brilliance of the morning, the dimness engulfed him; he could see nothing, nothing at all, only smell the familiar cathedral blend of incense and slight mustiness and the faint smokiness of the banks of candles, already lit, and the equally familiar sounds of oddly distant organ music and muffled voices and shuffling footsteps. He looked up, into the soaring dome, and then ahead at the great mosaic above the high altar, the golden Christ figure, arms outstretched; and then glanced behind him and saw James also gazing up, an expression on his face of reluctant awe mingled with a dreadful sadness.

A young priest was walking swiftly up the main aisle, his face wearing the careful, courteous smile that seemed as crucial an appurtenance of his calling as faith, his eyes fixed several yards ahead; Theo stepped out and said, '*Bonjour, mon père. Parlez-vous anglais?*'

'A little, yes.'

'Yesterday, a young girl was married here. In the afternoon. You were here, perhaps?'

The priest shook his head. 'We had no weddings here yesterday. Not at all. I am sorry.'

'Are you sure?'

'Quite sure, *monsieur*. No wedding.' He smiled rather blankly.

Theo fumbled in his pocket, produced the photograph of Cressida. 'Here, you see. This was taken yesterday. We know, because it was a friend.'

'No, *monsieur*. It cannot have been a wedding. There were none. I am sorry. Now if you will excuse me . . .'

He hurried away, up towards the altar; James and Theo looked at one another. 'Now what?' said Theo.

'He could have been wrong.'

'He didn't sound as if he was wrong. Let's ask someone else.'

One of the cathedral officials was standing at the back near the racks of postcards. '*Monsieur*,' said Theo, '*monsieur, parlez-vous anglais?*'

'*Non*,' said the man briefly.

Parisian charm, thought Theo, smiling at him. '*Monsieur, hier, l'après-midi, une jeune fille était mariée dans cette cathédrale . . .*'

'*Non*,' said the man, '*Il n'y a eu absolument aucun mariage.*'

Theo produced the photograph again, showed it to the man; he looked at it, shook his head, shrugged, and walked briskly away.

'Little sweetie,' said Theo. 'How I hate the French.'

They approached an old nun, who was lighting a candle, carefully, with a shaky hand; she smiled at them sweetly. '*Bonjour, ma soeur*,' said Theo. '*Est-ce que . . .*'

But she put her fingers over her lips, shook her head, sank onto her knees. Theo looked at her, wondering how it must feel to possess such faith, reflecting how greatly simplified life must be.

'Excuse me, *monsieur*.' Standing behind them was a plump, smiling old priest; he smelt of garlic and his complexion owed more than a little to a lifetime of good French wine. 'I heard what you were saying. I think perhaps I can help.'

'Oh really?' Theo held out his hand. 'How very kind. My name is Theo Buchan, and this is my friend James Forrest.'

'*Messieurs*,' said the old man courteously, with a slight bow. His robe, strained over his large somach, was threadbare, his shoes beneath it cracked and worn, but he carried with him an air of great contentment.

'We have reason to believe a young girl was married here yesterday. We have a picture of her leaving the cathedral in her wedding dress, see.'

'Yes, yes, I see. And I saw her, too. Yesterday. She was here, with her husband. A lovely girl. And a charming young man.'

'You saw them – married?' said James. His voice shook slightly.

'*Non, non*, that was not possible, I am afraid. It is not easy to be married here. They knew that, of course. But they asked me if I would give them God's blessing.'

'Oh God,' said James. His face was grey; he sat down suddenly.

'Are you all right, *monsieur*?'

'Yes, yes, I'm fine. Thank you. Do please go on.'

'Very well. I saw no harm in that. After all, who am I to keep God's love from a young couple? I asked them to come to one of the side chapels, this one here, and they knelt together and we said a prayer and I blessed them. That is all.' He smiled his sweet, slightly conspiratorial smile. 'There may be some here who might have felt I should have asked permission but I do not think I shall do too many extra years of purgatory for it.' He smiled again. 'They seemed very happy. She wore a wedding ring, I noticed that. Perhaps they had already been to the Bureau de l'Etat. There is not a problem, I hope.'

'No, not really,' said Theo. 'So you don't have any record of her – their name?'

'No, *monsieur*, I do not. They were gone very quickly after that. I am sorry.'

'Thank you, Father, very much. You've been most kind. And thank you for what you did for them. We are very grateful.' Theo took out his wallet, started riffling through notes. 'I would like to – for the church, of course –'

'*Merci, monsieur*. In the box, over there. Goodbye, *messieurs*. God bless you.'

'Goodbye, Father.'

Theo went over to the collection box, put a 500-franc note in it, stood looking at the bank of candles for a moment. Then he went forward and lit one. 'Cressida,' he said quietly, 'this is all I can do for you now. I hope, in spite of everything, you will be happy.'

He went back for James who was sitting absolutely still, staring ahead of him. His mouth was set.

'Come on,' Theo said gently, 'there's nothing more we can do for now. No point staying, trying to find her. She's all right, James, she's safe.

That's the main thing, really. She's happy and safe. Let's go.'

James nodded, stood up and walked very slowly to the door of the cathedral. When they got outside, Theo saw that his face was wet with tears. 'I'd like to go home, Theo, please,' he said.

And all the way home, the long drive out on the nightmare of the Périphérique, and the flight back through the blue morning, Theo thought not of Cressida at all, nor of his wild and wilful son, not even of his friend and his dreadful bleak misery, but of Harriet, and how in God's name he was going to get her back.

Chapter 24

Mungo 7am

He had slept. It seemed impossible, but he had. He woke, stiff-necked, his head aching unbearably, to hear the throbbing of a taxi outside in the street. The rest of the house was silent; Jemima and the two younger ones were clearly still asleep.

Mungo sat up, holding his aching head, pushed back his hair. He must look ghastly, he thought: unshaven, red-eyed, slightly grubby. Well, it didn't matter; he was hardly planning on seduction.

He crossed to the window, looked outside; Alice was paying off the taxi. She was wearing a light floaty dress, under a man's dinner jacket; he recognized the dress, they'd bought it together in Harvey Nichols, she'd needed something desperately, she said, for a duty party – 'Can't take you, it's business.' He had insisted on paying for it. She came to show it to him, outside the changing room, barefooted, the chiffon clinging to her slender body, her ice-blonde hair tousled with pulling things over her head. 'You look great,' he'd said, 'get that one' and 'It's terribly expensive,' she'd said, and 'You're worth it,' said Mungo, and he'd signed the slip (quite a lot for a rather insubstantial dress, even he'd thought that, £1,400, but of course she was worth it) and she'd come out and hugged him, and said 'Let's go home, I want to say thank you. Quickly.'

And they had rushed out of the shop, hailed a taxi, told the cabbie to go to Chatto Street, kissed all the way there, and when they got to the house, she'd dropped everything in the hall, and after calling the children's names briefly, to check they weren't at home, stood there, tearing off her clothes, and lay down on the stairs, quite naked, holding out her arms to him, and he came towards her laughing, pulling off his own clothes, and knelt astride her at the bottom of the stairs and started to kiss her again, slowly, very slowly and deliberately, and she raised herself up to him, her wet, greedy self, pulling herself onto him, pulling him into her, and he felt her closing round him, tightly, tuggingly, and she began to push, push, faster, faster up at him, and the familiar noisy cries began, and far far within the depths of himself Mungo felt the rising, the inexorable, rushing rise of his orgasm, and she said as she so often did, 'Wait, Mungo, wait, be still,' and as he paused somehow, forced its delay, savouring the sweet suspended pleasure, the time-stood-stillness, he had opened his eyes and looked at her, and she had looked back, and for just a moment then he had seen something watchful, wary, and then it was gone, and her head was thrown back again so that he couldn't see her face, and she was thrusting, pulling, enfolding him absolutely, and then he felt her coming, in her great powerful greedy waves, and he lay, his head on her breast, releasing his own pleasure, loving her and making himself forget what he had seen.

But he remembered it now.

'Hallo, Alice,' he said. He had opened the door, was standing smiling like a dutiful husband welcoming home his wife. 'How nice to see you.'

Alice's face was absolutely expressionless; it was a gift of hers that he had often envied, to be able to make it thus to order (except when she was in mid-orgasm). 'How do you do that?' he would say. 'Show me how to do it.' And she would laugh and say, 'You don't want to do that, Mungo, I love your face, it's so easy to read.'

'Hallo,' she said pleasantly, as if he were some neighbour, some casual friend, 'what are you doing here?'

'I came to see you last night. You'd gone out. With Anouska, I think.'

'No, not Anouska. She's away.' There she goes, he thought, bloody clever, just one jump ahead of him. 'I thought you were staying down in the country.'

'I was. But I couldn't stand it any longer. And I wanted to go to the office, and after that I came to see you.'

'And how did you get in?'

'Jemima let me in.'

'She's not supposed to,' said Alice. 'She's not supposed to let anyone in. I shall have to speak to her.'

'Don't. It wasn't her fault,' said Mungo. 'I – made her.'

'Well, that was unfair of you. But it was also naughty of her.'

'I don't think any reproaches are in order,' said Mungo, 'and I think she's very young to be left alone in the house all night. Actually.'

'Yes, well, I don't think I need advice on childcare from you,' said Alice. 'When you've spent a few years as a single parent, you'll be qualified to comment, but until then . . . Excuse me, please, I really want to make myself a cup of coffee.'

'I'll make you some coffee,' said Mungo. 'You go and sit down.'

He was surprised to find he didn't feel anything like he might have expected; he seemed to be in control, to know what to do, how to act. He was almost enjoying it. Alice went into the kitchen ahead of him and sat down. She looked very composed and orderly; her face was freshly made-up, her hair neatly done. She didn't even look tired; she had obviously had a good night's sleep.

'Nice time?' said Mungo casually, handing her the coffee.

'Yes, very nice, thank you. Mungo, this is instant. You know I don't like instant coffee.'

'It's what I've made,' he said, 'and it's what you'll have to drink, I'm afraid. I'm not messing about with that stupid grinder thing at this time in the morning. Anyway it might wake the children.'

She looked at him and though her eyes were blank there was a watchfulness behind them.

'Did you – talk to Jemima last night?'

'Oh, a bit. But not about you. We were both very loyal.'

'Ah.'

'Which is more than I can say for you,' he said. Anger suddenly hit him, took him unawares. 'Where the fuck were you, and who with?'

'Don't use that horrible language in my house,' said Alice.

'I'll use what I like. Where were you?'

'I was out. With some old friends.'

'Oh, really?'

'Yes, really. If you like I'll give you their number and you can ring and check. Giles and Fanny Brentwood. This is Giles's dinner jacket I'm wearing.'

'I see,' said Mungo. He was beginning to feel a little uncertain. 'Do you often stay out all night with people? Leaving your daughter on her own?'

'Yes, sometimes. She has to put the chain on the door, double-lock it, and if I want to come back I have to ring her. Last night it was so late, it seemed unfair to wake her. But you did, it seems, so I needn't have been so scrupulous.'

'Why didn't you tell her you were with these old friends? Why did she have to tell me some lie about Anouska?'

'I didn't tell her anything. Just that I was going out. She was engrossed on the phone with some boy, and had her stereo on at full blast, it was just too much hassle. No doubt she thought you'd be upset unless I was with some woman. Oh, Mungo, for God's sake, you can't think – look, ring Giles. Or Fanny. They won't mind. Here's the number. Go on. I'll dial it for you –'

'No,' he said hastily. 'No, Alice, don't. I really don't want to –'

'You look worn out,' she said suddenly, 'much tireder than I am. Let's go into the drawing room. I do want to talk to you. Actually. But I'm going to make some decent coffee first.'

'All right,' he said, 'all right.'

He sat on the sofa where he had spent the night staring ahead of him; he had stopped enjoying himself, the numbness was wearing off. He wasn't sure how much of this he could take. Alice came in, sat down beside him, kissed him gently on the cheek.

'You've got it all wrong you know,' she said quite cheerfully.

'Have I? Have I really?'

'Yes. You really have. And a few other things too. Are you sitting comfortably?'

'Yes thank you,' said Mungo.

Alice looked at him. 'Then I'll begin.' There was a silence. Then: 'Mungo, I did do something you wouldn't have liked last night,' she said, 'I phoned your father.'

The sofa rocked gently under Mungo; he tightened his grip on the mug of coffee she had handed him. 'What did you say?' he said finally.

'You heard. You heard right. I phoned your father. He was extremely nice to me.'

'Yes, I expect he was,' said Mungo bitterly. 'He can be very charming when it suits him. The fact remains he's a –'

'Mungo, I can see what he is. He's manipulative, and he's immensely arrogant and possessive and he doesn't like being crossed. But he loves you, Mungo, my God he loves you.'

'Yes,' said Mungo tersely, 'when I do what he wants. I don't know how you could have done that, Alice, I really don't.'

'Well,' she said simply, 'I had to do something. There you were, falling out with him, setting yourself on the path to financial ruin, probably wrecking that extremely promising little business of yours, all because of me.'

'Alice, it isn't like that. You're not just some game or toy I'm playing with.'

'I should certainly hope not,' she said lightly.

'I love you. I want to marry you. Well, I thought I did.'

'And what's changed that? Me being out when you came to call? Really, Mungo, this certainly can't be love. Love is about trust. I thought.'

'I know but –'

Christ, she was clever. She was tying him up in knots, just as his father did.

'Mungo, I give you my word, I'll swear on the Bible if you like, if I can find it, that I was simply out to dinner with my friends last night. I was not in any other man's bed, I don't have an interest in any other man. I love you. There. Does that make you feel better?'

He looked at her, and against all the odds he found himself believing her. 'Jemima seemed to think –' he started, and then stopped.

'Seemed to think what? That I was plying a brisk trade in Piccadilly? That I was in some hotel in King's Cross with three other men?'

'No, of course not, but she –'

'Mungo, Mungo, Jemima is a very naughty, manipulative little girl. She would get on wonderfully well with your father. She has just discovered her own sexuality, and she's jealous of mine. She also has a bit of a crush on you. And what was she up to last night anyway? Entertaining a gentleman far too old for her?'

'No,' said Mungo quickly, and then wondered if he was being irresponsible, immature, taking the side of youth against the grown-ups. 'Well, that is –'

'I thought so. You're right, I shouldn't leave her alone. She's trouble, Mungo, much as I love her.'

'Don't say anything to her, will you? Not about last night specifically.

She was very sweet to me, and I'd hate her to think I'd – well –'

'Sneaked on her,' said Alice tartly. 'No, I won't. Unless I find evidence on my own account. The laundry bills have gone up a lot lately, I've noticed. Lot of sheet changing going on . . . Anyway, let's not talk about Jemima. You and me is a much more agreeable subject. And I want to tell you what we talked about, your father and I.'

'What then?' said Mungo sulkily. He hated to think of the pair of them discussing him, agreeing no doubt that he was a silly, reckless child. 'I suppose you had a little laugh about it all, and then you said that of course you wouldn't marry me if he didn't want you to, that it was a crazy idea.'

'No, we didn't laugh and I didn't say I wouldn't marry you. Although we did agree it was a crazy idea. And then he said –'

'Yes?'

'He said he liked crazy ideas. That a lot of his were fairly crazy. Especially when it came to what he called entanglements. I liked that word.'

'You obviously got on very well,' said Mungo. He felt wretchedly, horribly foolish.

'Yes, I think we did. We agreed that we would meet. And –'

'Oh, well, that's great,' said Mungo, standing up. 'The two of you meeting, talking about me, the silly little boy, discussing what it would be best to do, how you could distract me.' He felt violently hurt, abused almost; he had to get out, quickly. He slammed his coffee mug down, and the contents slopped over the coffee table onto Alice's beige carpet. He looked at it, at the dark spattered stain, and he thought that was what had happened to his love for her; it had been treated roughly, spilt, become something dirty, messy, spoiling everything.

'I'm so glad you've been able to discuss our future with my father,' he said. 'What a pity it's all become irrelevant. Because I really don't want to see you again, Alice. Perhaps he'd be a better friend for you. I don't know how you could do it to me, when I loved you so much. And trusted you. Goodbye, Alice.'

He walked over to the door, then turned to look back at her. She was staring up at him, startled, shocked almost, her face concerned, no longer carefully blank. 'Mungo,' she said, 'Mungo, please. You don't understand. Please don't go.'

'I want to go,' he said, 'and I do understand, I'm afraid.'

He walked out of the front door, slammed it behind him, and then leant against it briefly, thinking of all the happiness he had had in the little house, the lovely Sundays, the golden evenings, the rapturous love-making, and for just an instant he was amazed that he could leave it, walk away. Then he thought of Alice, Alice and his father, talking, laughing indulgently about him, and he ran, ran away from her, away from both of them, as fast as he could down the street and into the Kings Road, and hailed a taxi, and told the driver to take him to the one place where he wanted to be at that moment, the one place where he was a person in his own right, the one place he felt was his own: his office in Carlos Place.

Chapter 25

Tilly 8am

'Yeah, I'll go,' said Tilly, 'if you want me to. The sooner the better.'

'You don't sound very enthusiastic.'

'Felicity, right this minute I'd find it hard to be enthusiastic if Brad Pitt and Keanu Reeves asked me to spend a year on a desert island with them both. Sorry. I'm just gutted. I'd actually love to go to New York. Anything to get out of this place.'

'I can get you on a flight at noon. You'll have to be at Heathrow at ten. I'll send a car.'

'OK. Fine.'

'And the Rosenthal people will meet you at Kennedy. They said they'd book you into the Pierre. For three nights, I think.'

'Fine.'

'Right then. Take a couple of slightly smart outfits. You can't meet le tout New York in those torn cut-offs.'

'Felicity, as if I would . . .'

'Tilly, you know you would. Anyway, I'll confirm your flight. Call me when you get there. I hope you feel better soon. Lots of love.'

'Thanks. Bye, Felicity.'

She hauled herself out of bed: just under two hours till she had to go. Bit of careful packing. Slightly smart. What did that mean, for God's sake? The Karan probably, the black silk jersey suit, and the glorious new stuff from Claude Montana, the white linen crepe Nehru jacket and trousers. That would do for le tout New York, surely. If it didn't, they could go play with themselves. She needed some shoes, but she could get them when she got there. Fuck, it was going to be hot . . . she suddenly heard Rufus's voice saying 'I don't like people saying fuck all the time,' and a spasm of such intense pain took hold of her heart that her eyes filled with tears. Now, Tilly, don't start. It's over now, he belongs in the past. A lovely, loving, joyful past, but the past. The future's what you have to think about now. The immediate future first, just getting things into your bag, yourself into the car, onto the plane – 'Shit,' she said aloud, 'shit, I have to see my mum.' That was essential; and she had to phone James too, with the phone number. She had victory in her hands; she mustn't let it go. She could call at her mother's house on her way to the airport; she would tell Felicity to send the car there. That would be good. And she could phone James Forrest right now.

She dialled the number; Harriet answered the phone. She sounded calmer than she had last night; she had called Tilly when she got back from seeing Theo. It had taken Tilly half an hour to talk her down. 'I hate him,' she kept saying, 'I hate him so much, Tilly, I can hardly bear to think about him.' And Tilly had made soothing, calming, sympathetic noises into the phone, listening, listening to the half-truth, to the anger, to the passion in Harriet's voice, and wondered how long it would be before Harriet admitted even to herself how much she still loved Theo.

'Hi, Harry, it's Tilly. How are you today?'

'OK, I think.'

'No news?'

'No. My father's gone off with Theo to Paris. They left at dawn in Theo's plane. Seem to think they'll find Cressida still sitting at Sacré-Coeur, waiting for them.'

Her voice was immensely, heavily scornful; her hostility seemed to extend to her father, as well as Theo. Tilly did not, could not pursue that one; she lacked the strength.

'Well,' she said, for want of something more intelligent to say, 'maybe they will.'

'Yeah yeah. But there is one delicious piece of news. It's not all gloom and doom here. We have an engagement to celebrate.'

'An engagement! Don't tell me Mungo –'

'No. Why should it be Mungo? Much more exciting. Merlin and

Janine. Getting married by special licence, wandering round the garden holding hands like a couple of kids.'

'Now that is seriously nice,' said Tilly. 'That I like. Give him a huge hug from me.'

'I will. Mind you, I think it was a toss-up whether he proposed to you or Janine. He's very taken with you.'

'Tell him it's mutual. Next time around. No seriously, I think it's wild. Harry, I'm off to New York.'

'Now?'

'Yes, now. I'm signing with Rosenthal and they want to inspect the goods. Or something like that.'

'Tilly, are you sure it's a good idea? You know how homesick you get, and what will Rufus say?'

'Rufus is history,' said Tilly and burst into tears.

'Tilly, don't. You can't do that. Why, Tilly, why? He loves you and you love him and –'

'Yeah, and we get married and start hating each other. It isn't any good, Harriet, really it isn't.'

'Oh, Tilly, are you sure? Really sure? Couldn't you try –'

'Try what? Becoming someone else? Taking a course in legal wifehood?' Thank God she's always made a lot of the differences between her and Rufus, had said repeatedly that their lives could never work together. And anyway, it was true: they never could. 'There's nothing to try. Honestly.'

'Did you tell him?'

'Yes, I told him. Last night.'

'And?'

'And nothing really. We parted. Said goodbye. That was it.' She groped for a Kleenex, blew her nose. 'Now listen, I don't want to talk about that. I *can't* talk about that. But there's something else that I do want to talk about. If you need some money, I mean real money for your company, I can let you have it.'

'Tilly, don't be absurd.'

'I'm not being absurd. I mean it. What do you need, a million? It's yours. You can pay me back some time. OK?'

'Tilly, darling –'

'Think about it. I have to go. Oh, that's reminded me, that's why I called really. I'm leaving in a couple of hours, but I'm going to my mum's house first. Could you' – she thought fast – 'could you give her number to your dad?'

'My father? What on earth for?'

'Well, it's kind of complicated. But she has a little – female trouble, and I'm worried about her. He said he'd give me the name and number of the best person in town for her.'

'Tilly, this is the most extraordinary thing I ever heard. When on earth did you get to talk female trouble with my father?'

'When we were out in the garden yesterday, you know?'

'Oh – yes. Yes, all right.' She was clearly baffled. 'And you're going there now, you say?'

'Yes, to say hallo and goodbye. How's *your* mother?'

'Still asleep. My father gave her a mega shot of something last night.'

'And when are you seeing Mr Buchan again?'

'Never, I hope. Unless it's in hell.'

'Cool. Bye, Harry. And I meant it about the money.'

'Bye, Tilly. Thank you, but I really couldn't. And take care.'

Tilly had a shower, dressed (not in the torn cut-offs but leggings and an oversized T-shirt), called a cab, grabbed her big leather Gladstone, and her Gucci leather rucksack that was never really unpacked, just occasionally cleared out, which carried all her needs, money, credit cards, make-up, cigarettes, chewing gum, passport, keys, appointment book, set her answering machine, looked round her flat and went out, locking the door after her. She was halfway down the stairs when she heard the phone ringing; she simply couldn't go back now, she was running quite late enough already.

'Tilly, you look terrible,' said Rosemary Mills. 'I'm going to make you some camomile tea. It will calm you down.'

'Mum, I hate camomile tea. And rosehip tea and peppermint tea. They all make me want to throw up. What I need is a seriously strong cup of coffee. Do you have any real or is it all that decaff rubbish?'

'It's all decaff,' said Rosemary, 'and it will have to do.'

Tilly sat drinking the coffee, studying her mother. She really was looking good. She looked about ten years younger; she was happy, busy, her aromatherapy practice growing fast. She had had a haircut (Nicky Clarke had done it as a favour to Tilly: 'Pity you don't know what a fortune you're carrying about on your head, Mum') and although she still favoured her rather droopy ethnic clothes, they were at least new and pretty, not bought at jumbles and Oxfam shops.

'So where are you off to now?'

'New York. Midday.'

'New York! Paris yesterday, Mexico the week before. Tilly, I wish you'd settle down a bit. It's so bad for your body clock, all this.'

'Mum, my body clock's fine.'

'It doesn't look fine,' said Rosemary Mills. 'What about the boyfriend?'

'The boyfriend's finished,' said Tilly, 'and don't start, or I shall cry. It wasn't going to work, Mum, and that's all there is to it. Now listen, I have something much more important to talk to you about.'

'What's that?'

'James Forrest will be coming to see you.'

'James Forrest? What on earth for?'

'He wants to explain a few things to you,' said Tilly briefly. 'Like –'

The phone rang suddenly. 'Excuse me, dear,' said Rosemary. 'Peckham 4111. Rosemary Mills speaking. Yes, that's right. Yes, she's here. It's for you,' she said, holding the phone out to Tilly, 'a woman.'

'I expect it's Felicity,' said Tilly, 'or Harry.'

It wasn't. It was Susie Headleigh Drayton and she sounded as if she had been crying.

'Tilly? Sorry to bother you at your mother's. Your agent told me you were there. I thought you might know where Rufus is?'

'No,' said Tilly, 'no, I don't. I'm sorry. Isn't he – still in the country?'

'No,' said Susie, 'no he isn't. He brought me up to London last night. I've got to – well, have a little op this morning. Nothing serious, I'm sure. But I'm worried about Rufus. I can't find him anywhere. Not at his flat, not at Harriet's place, not in the office – well, I suppose he wouldn't have been there yet, but –'

'Oh, I'm sure he's fine,' said Tilly, trying to sound as if she meant it. 'He was fine last night.'

'So you did see him last night? When was that? I'm sorry to ask you, Tilly, but what with my going into hospital and – well, he was a bit upset about something, I'm afraid. I just wanted to speak to him, make sure he was all right before I went in.'

'If he was upset,' said Tilly, 'it was probably my fault. I – well, we – I told him I thought we shouldn't see each other any more.'

'Oh Tilly! Oh no.' Susie's voice rose on a panicky note. 'Not last night.'

'Yes, but –'

'That's not why he was upset, Tilly. Well, obviously he would have been very much more upset then. But there was something – something that happened yesterday. Earlier. Before we left Wedbourne.'

'He didn't mention it,' said Tilly slowly. No, because she hadn't let him, poor sod, hadn't listened, had just sat there dealing out body blows. Shit. *Fuck* . . . 'I don't like people saying fuck all the time.' Sorry, Rufus, sorry, sorry. For everything.

'I see. Oh dear. Well, if he does get in touch will you ask him to come and see me? I'll be in the Princess Diana Hospital. He – well, he doesn't know. I hadn't told him. I hadn't told anyone.'

'I'm so sorry,' said Tilly, and meant it. 'Is it – I mean is it serious?'

'Oh, I shouldn't think so.' Susie's voice had recovered itself, was its level, slightly husky self. 'I hope not anyway. Just a little lump. You know how careful they like to be.'

'Yes,' said Tilly, 'yes of course. Well, good luck. I really will be thinking of you. I'd come and see you, but I'm going to New York.'

'Today?'

'Yes, in a little while actually. I've been signed up by Rosenthal. Their new face. You know?' Now why the hell was she telling her that? Why should Susie care? With a son gone missing and what was clearly a cancer scare? Silly self-centred bitch, Ottoline, that's what you are.

'Oh, how exciting, Tilly. Congratulations.' How did she manage it, thought Tilly, how could she even sound as if she cared about something so idiotic?

'Yeah, well. It's all crazy really. I don't actually want to do it at all.' Now why had she said that, to Susie Headleigh Drayton of all people? Of course she wanted to do it. 'Er – I don't suppose you want to tell me what Rufus was upset about? Just in case I can help?'

'No. No, I don't think so. I don't want to sound rude, but it was – well, quite private. Family business.'

'Of course,' said Tilly. 'I'm sorry, I didn't mean to –'

'No, I know you didn't. Goodbye, Tilly. Please come and see me when you get back. I'd like to get to know you. And I hope you didn't make your decision too hastily. Rufus loves you very much, you know.'

'Yeah,' said Tilly. Then, and she really hadn't meant to say it, she added, 'And I love him too. Very much. But it couldn't possibly work. Anyway – yes, of course I'll come and see you. Good luck. Goodbye, Mrs Headleigh Drayton.'

'Please call me Susie. Goodbye, Tilly.'

'Now then,' said Rosemary Mills, 'what's all this James Forrest business. I don't want to see him, Tilly. I really don't. It just – reminds me, brings it back. Why is he coming anyway, after all these years?'

'I met him,' said Tilly briefly. 'He's Harriet Forrest's dad. Harriet of Harry's you know? My friend. The one whose sister was getting married yesterday. Only she didn't. Well, maybe she did. Oh God.' She lit a cigarette; she suddenly felt very frightened about Rufus. Where was he, what had happened to him?

'Tilly, dear, you really aren't making any sense,' said her mother. 'Why is James Forrest coming to see me?'

'He's coming to tell you some things,' said Tilly shortly. 'About – well, you know what about. Beatrice and everything. He wants to make sure you understand that it wasn't your fault, and –'

'But Tilly, it was. To an extent. Oh, I hate going over this awful old ground. He was right – I should have gone to the antenatal clinic. And all right, maybe he was incompetent, maybe he had been drinking. I don't know. He was very kind to me at the time, which was important. He did his best. I just don't want to drag it all up again, Tilly. Beatrice died, but you lived and we've been very happy together, and you've done wonderfully well. Why can't you leave it alone, just drop this dreadful obsession? It's me that should have the obsession anyway, not you. Now please tell him that I really would rather not speak to him. I appreciate his kindness and generosity, but –'

'Oh, yes,' said Tilly bitterly, 'very kind, very generous. After – what? – nearly twenty years. Bastard.'

'Tilly, don't. Don't spoil everything. You have so much, and so do I now – just let it rest.'

'Mum, you don't –' said Tilly. There was a knock at the door; it was the car to take her to the airport. She gave her mother a hug. 'You're the best,' she said suddenly, 'the very best. Bye, Mum. I'll – I'll think about James Forrest some more –'

'It would be better,' said Rosemary Mills, 'if you stopped thinking about him altogether. And I think you've made a mistake about that boyfriend too.'

'Mum, it wouldn't have worked,' said Tilly patiently. 'I'm too fond of my independence, you know I am. And he's a white upper-class lawyer and I'm a black working-class girl. Where's the future in that?'

'In some beautiful, clever, middle-class children,' said Rosemary, giving her a hug back. 'We're in the nineties, Tilly. You're sounding very out of date. And he loves you, and I think you love him. And independence is a very lonely commodity. You shouldn't let love go. It doesn't often come back. Goodbye, Tilly. Take care of yourself. Eat something now and again, there's a good girl. And try to –'

'Yes, all right, Mum. I'll try. I'll leave them all here, look.'

Tilly tipped sixty Marlborough out of her bag onto her mother's kitchen table. 'Throw them away. I won't buy any more.'

'Promise?'

'No,' said Tilly, thinking gratefully of the two full packs in her rucksack. 'I don't make promises unless I know I can keep them. But I will try.'

'And think some more about Rufus.'

'I wish I could stop,' said Tilly.

Chapter 26

Susie 9am

Susie thought how odd it was, how relevant, that her heart and her breast, situated so conviently near one another, should both be aching so much. She wasn't quite sure which was worse, only that the confusion was somehow helpful. She was surprised that the breast should be so sore; she had always heard that cancer, in its early stages, was painless.

She said as much, hopefully, to Mr Hobson, as she sat up in her room at the Princess Diana Hospital; they were waiting for Alistair who had disappeared briefly to make a phone call.

'I'm afraid it doesn't really mean very much either way,' he said, 'it's wrong to read anything into it. If there is inflammation of any kind, the result can be discomfort. Simple as that. How are you feeling?'

'Oh, wonderful,' said Susie, 'absolutely wonderful,' and burst into tears. Mr Hobson, who had never seen the serene Mrs Headleigh Drayton in any kind of disarray, but who was used to his patients becoming emotionally labile, sat down on the bed and took her hand. 'Hope Matron doesn't catch me doing this,' he said. 'Absolutely not allowed. Now you have a good cry. It always helps. I'm not going to come up with any bloody silly nonsense about not worrying and all that, because of course you're worried. You'd be a fool not to be. I'm worried, we're all worried. But the sooner we get this over and know what we're actually up against the better.' He handed her his handkerchief. 'Blow hard.'

'Yes I know,' said Susie, blowing obediently, 'thank you. It's just that I've tried so hard to be brave, but I have other problems, other worries.'

'Oh, really? Want to tell me about them?'

'Um – no, I don't think I can. Well, I've lost Rufus. My son,' she added. 'I'm a bit worried.'

'And how old is Rufus?'

'Well – he's twenty-seven,' said Susie, feeling suddenly foolish.

'And where is he? In the Himalayas or wherever it is they all go these days?'

'No, no, he's in London somewhere,' said Susie, 'but I don't know where. And he's very upset about something.'

'I think,' said Mr Hobson, 'that if he's twenty-seven he can handle a bit of upsetness. Worried about you, is he?'

'No, no, he doesn't even know. There was some – some family thing yesterday –'

'What, this wedding? Dreadful things weddings, always get people churned up.'

'No, not the wedding. He – well, he found something out. And –'

'Mrs Headleigh Drayton – or may I call you Susie –?'

'Yes, of course. I'd like that.'

'I think you can let your little twenty-seven-year-old boy take care of himself, and concentrate all your energies on yourself. If he's reached that age and not been badly upset yet, he's very lucky. You could even say it's time he learnt a bit about real life. All right?'

Susie was about to argue with him, to protest, to say that Rufus really couldn't take care of himself, not in this instance, when she found that not only did she not have the strength, she felt Mr Hobson might just possibly be right. She thought of herself at twenty-seven, dealing with most complex emotional matters, quite competently; was Rufus, her son, the most like her of all her children, really so different? She blew her nose again, smiled at Mr Hobson weakly. 'Maybe.'

'That's better. Now you don't want to be crying when your husband comes in, do you? He's quite worried enough. You're very lucky to have a husband who loves you so much, after such a long marriage, you know. Quite rare. Lucky and clever I'd say you were, Susie. In equal proportions. Ah, Mr Headleigh Drayton. Good morning. Do sit down. I'd offer you coffee, but your poor wife is thirsty enough without having to watch us drinking it. Now, I just want to take you through her case as I see it thus far, so that at least we all know what we're talking about, and don't have any misconceptions . . .'

Susie looked at Alistair and wanted James so much she could hardly bear it. She closed her eyes briefly, then smiled at him and took the hand he held out to her. Lucky and clever, was she? With a son shocked into disappearance, a lover who had deserted her in her hour of great need, and a husband who knew she had been unfaithful to him for most of their marriage. Dear God. Very lucky, and very clever.

Alistair had gone now, with a tender kiss and a promise to be there when she woke up. She felt fiercely, terribly alone. And dreadfully afraid. Afraid of what they would find, what they would do, that in spite of Mr Hobson's reassurances she would wake up without her breast. And what would there be? A great wound? A cobbling together of her flesh? A mutilation, pain, ugliness. Panic rose in her, she began to sweat.

The nurse came in with the pre-med tray; suddenly, vividly she remembered the other time, all those years ago, when she had been pregnant with Rufus, when there was nearly no Rufus. Thank God, thank God there had been. Her lovely, gentle, handsome, clever son. Who had disappeared. Who no longer trusted her. No longer loved her . . .

A moan escaped Susie, a low quiet moan; the nurse was alarmed. 'I'm sorry, Mrs Headleigh Drayton. Did I hurt you?'

'No. No, it's all right. Could I – could I have the phone? I'll be quick, before this takes effect.'

'Yes of course. Here, let me dial the number.'

'No, no, it's all right.' Hang on, Susie, hang on, don't let go; just once more, that was all she asked, just to hear his voice once more, to take with her into this awful, ugly darkness . . .

'Wedbourne 240.' It was Harriet's voice.

'Harriet, it's Susie.'

'Ah. Hallo.' Hostility, polite but unmistakable.

'Harriet, could I speak to your father? I'm sorry to ask you but . . .'

'He's not here I'm afraid. He's gone to Paris. With Theo.'

'To Paris! Why?' God, she was feeling strange already: hazy, confused, dry-mouthed. Her tongue seemed thick, out of control.

'Yes. To look for Cressida.'

'Oh, yes. Yes, of course. Cressida. Poor Cressida.' Her eyes were getting heavy, she felt very dizzy, even though she was lying down.

'Is mother there?' That wasn't quite right; the words weren't properly ordered.

'My mother? Yes. Susie, are you all right? Where are you?' The hostility was gone, she sounded alarmed.

'I'm hospital Harriet. In operation. Princess Diana. Good – breast.'

Somehow then the receiver was gone, taken gently from her, and she was drifting, drifting down a long, dark corridor, and the fear was gone and the pain too, just a lovely lightness, and oh God, this was what happened when people died, she had read it so often, people saw a bright light at the end of a dark tunnel, and how lovely it was, she was safe now, quite safe, safe from all of them, just her and the soothing quietness, and there was Mr Hobson smiling at her, so kindly, saying, 'Good, good, can you hear me?' And she tried to say 'yes' but she couldn't, she couldn't speak, she couldn't move, obviously she was really dying, and she suddenly thought how awful, how awful to die in this horrible green paper hat, she couldn't, what would everyone think, and suppose some of the children saw her, and she was wrenching it off, tugging it, and it hurt, it really hurt trying to do it, her hand hurt, and someone was holding it now, holding it gently, telling her to relax, and she did, falling sweetly into darkness, falling, falling, and now even the bright light was gone . . .

Chapter 27

Harriet 9am

'So we thought a very quiet wedding.'

'Don't talk about weddings,' said Harriet with a shudder.

'Sorry, *mon ange*. A very quiet ceremony. In Paris. Which I hope very much you will attend. And then Merlin wishes to take me to see a rain forest. Or perhaps China. What do you think?'

'I think it all sounds wonderful. So wonderful. I'm really very very happy for you, Janine.'

'*Bon*. I am happy for myself.' Jannie smiled at her, her dark eyes brilliant. 'And a little surprised. It was, what do you say, an arrow from the blue –'

'Bolt, Janine. You're getting confused with Cupid.'

'And why not? Very well, a bolt from the blue. You do not think we will seem a little ridiculous?'

'Janine, really! Neither of you could ever seem that.'

'I am not so sure,' said Janine quietly. She looked troubled. 'Both of us quite old people. Very different. And to get married, to set up home together like twenty-year-olds, it seems so – I don't know, so foolish somehow.'

'Janine, not foolish at all. Lovely. Sweet and lovely. And anyway, why should you care what it seems? You're going to be terribly happy, I know you are, and that's what matters.'

'Yes,' said Janine, suddenly relaxing, smiling at her. 'Yes, I think we will be. I am sure we will be. And one should take happiness, should one not? With both arms. While one can.'

'One should,' said Harriet, with a sigh, 'with both arms. And hold onto it.'

She thought of her own difficult happiness the year before, wondering if she should have clung to it more tightly; too late now, it was gone, long, long gone.

'What a sigh, Harriet darling. You are not happy, I think?'

'Oh, I'm all right, Janine. Worried obviously. But all right. Thank you. And certainly very happy for you. Really. Where are you going to live?'

'In Paris,' said Janine firmly. 'I could not be happy living anywhere else. And Merlin doesn't mind where he lives. Besides, if he has his way we won't be there so very much. We have several continents to look at.'

Harriet was silent for a moment, smiling at the vision of Merlin and Janine looking at continents together. 'It sounds lovely,' she said, 'as if you were going to be on a magic carpet.'

'I am sure we would be,' said Janine, 'if Merlin could get one at half price.'

'Where is he now?'

'He has gone out on a mysterious errand. I have an inkling as to what it is, but we must wait and see.' She put out her hand, stroked Harriet's check. 'You look so tired, *chérie*. It was a terrible day yesterday, was it not?'

'It was,' said Harriet with a sigh, 'truly terrible. And I –' She took a deep breath. She had to confess to Janine some time, had to get it over, had to tell her what had happened to her money. 'Janine, there's something else as well. You see I –'

'Just look at this!' It was Merlin, stalking into the kitchen flushed, his white hair standing up round his head like a halo. 'Hope you like it, my dear. Chap said he'd take it back if you didn't.'

With a proud beam he handed Janine a small, rather worn leather ring box. She looked at him, then opened it very carefully. Inside was a ring: a lover's knot worked in gold, with a flower of garnets and diamonds at its centre.

'Merlin, it's beautiful,' said Janine. She put it on her long slender wedding finger; amazingly it fitted. She reached up and kissed his cheek. 'Thank you. Does this make it official?'

'I should hope so. Glad you like it. Victorian. Beat the chap down a lot, ridiculous price he was asking, told him I'd –'

'Merlin,' said Harriet gently, 'you really can't tell your fiancée her engagement ring was a bargain. It just isn't done.'

'Oh really? Suppose I've got a lot to learn. Sorry, my dear. Well, it still cost a lot of money. Does that make you feel any better?'

'I did not feel bad in the first place,' said Janine. 'Isn't this a beautiful ring, Harriet? Am I not a lucky woman?'

'Yes,' said Harriet, 'you are. But you deserve it. Both of you. And I hope you'll be terribly happy.'

'Oh, no doubt about that,' said Merlin. 'Got it right, I can see it. Thank goodness I was still free, waited for the real thing . . . Nearly married a dreadful girl I met in India, just after the war . . .'

'Good gracious,' said Harriet, 'that was a narrow escape.'

'Yes, well, she wasn't really dreadful of course, but she certainly couldn't hold a candle to Janine. Isn't she lovely?' he said to Harriet, a sweet soft smile on his handsome old face. 'Isn't she fine?'

'Merlin, you speak of me as if I were a horse,' said Janine briskly.

'No, Janine, that's not fair,' said Harriet. 'That's exactly what you are, fine. A fine person. It's a good description.'

'Well, all this is making me blush,' said Janine. 'Harriet, my darling, should I go and see your mother, do you think?'

'No, she's still asleep, thank goodness,' said Harriet, 'and I honestly think when she does wake up she'll feel better. Be able to come to terms with it a bit more. Poor Mummy. She dreamed of yesterday for so long . . .'

'Lot of bloody nonsense,' said Merlin suddenly. 'Silly spoilt little girl. Needs her bottom smacked. Where's your father, Harriet?'

'Oh – he's – he's gone to see Theo,' said Harriet quickly.

'Good chap, Theo,' said Merlin. 'Always liked him. Needs the right woman, that's all. That little thing he's got with him now, very pretty, but no good for him.'

'Merlin, he isn't very nice to her,' said Harriet.

'That's what I mean. He needs someone who'll stand up to him. Give as good as she gets.'

'That's what all those wives try to do. He just sends them packing.'

'Well that's because he knows they don't really give two figs for him,' said Merlin. 'Most of 'em married him for his money. Damn shame. Must hurt, that.'

'Yes, I suppose so,' said Harriet slowly. 'I'd never thought of it like that.'

'Merlin, you have been engaged for less than twelve hours and you are already an expert on marriage,' said Janine, laughing. She stood up and gave him another kiss. 'Now, Harriet, *ma chère*, what do you think I should do? Should I stay here with your mother for a day or two longer, or would it be better if I left? I am willing to do whatever is best.'

'That's sweet of you, Janine, but I think she'll probably be best left in peace. She's so hurt, so humiliated, as well as frightened and worried – she has to come to terms with it by herself.'

'Yes, and of course Cressida may yet come back. I have heard of these things, where people go away, disappear, it is a little like a suicide. They reach the end of their rope –'

'Tether, Janine.'

'All right, tether. They cannot cope. A cry for help, that is what this might be.'

'It might, I suppose,' said Harriet, trying to sound convinced, thinking of the picture of the radiant Cressida running down the steps of Sacré-Coeur in her wedding dress. 'It might indeed. Well, we must wait and see.'

'And you? What will you do?'

'Oh, I have to get back to London,' said Harriet. Her voice sounded taut, strained, even to her.

'Today?'

'Yes, I'm afraid so. My business is – well, anyway, I do have to go. I have an appointment with a man about an overdraft at two –'

'Now look, Harriet,' said Merlin, 'the offer stands. Anything I can do . . .'

'Is there a real problem?' asked Janine. Her eyes were brilliant, thoughtful.

'Yes, Janine, there is.' Harriet faced her, looked at her very levelly. 'There's something I have to tell you. I was going to do it just now, when Merlin came in. I may have to ask you to bear with me for a while before I can give you your money back. I'm so sorry. I've fought so hard to be able to save it, tried everything, but you see –'

'My darling child, I don't want my money back. It was an investment I made, and if it was a bad one, that is my problem. Well, it is yours as well of course, but anyway, I certainly do not want to hear the details now. Another time. We will go through it all and you can tell me what has happened, and what should be done. But just now, clearly you must go and see this bank manager.'

'Think young Tilly could help?' said Merlin. 'Said she would, didn't she? Lovely girl, don't you think, my dear? Just right for young Rufus. Maybe we could make it a double wedding. There's an idea now.'

'Merlin, it's a terrible idea,' said Harriet, laughing, 'and I'm afraid there won't be any wedding there, double or otherwise. Tilly is hell-bent on finishing the whole thing. Oh God, I completely forgot. Janine, did you know Susie was in hospital?'

'Susie? No, of course not. What's wrong? It must have been very sudden. She looked well yesterday. Thin, of course, but –'

'She phoned my – well, she phoned a little while ago. From the hospital. She sounded very strange. I told Rufus, he phoned about Annabel and Tom, he didn't know either.'

'Let us hope it is not serious,' said Janine. 'Such a nice woman.'

'Yes,' said Harriet shortly. Janine looked at her sharply; Harriet looked back, her eyes a careful blank. 'Well, I must go and sort out a few things. Excuse me. And congratulations to you both again. That ring is heaven, Merlin.'

She was on her way upstairs when the phone rang; it was James. 'Harriet, darling, we're almost back.'

'Back! But you've only just gone.'

'I know. Let's just say there didn't seem any future in staying.'

'No Cressida?'

'Well – no. Not really. Certainly she won't be back. Not for a while. I'll explain when we get there. There's a lot of talking to do.'

'I'm sorry,' said Harriet, 'but I may have gone. I simply have to get to town. Meeting with the bank. Obviously I'll come back tonight if I possibly can. I'll have to take Mummy's car.'

'All right,' said James with a sigh. 'Is Mummy awake?'

'Not yet. Well, she wasn't twenty minutes ago.' Don't ask me what my problem is, will you, thought Harriet, don't worry about me. There's Cressida and Mummy and Susie to think about, quite enough for one day. No wonder I'm so obsessed with success, with proving myself.

'Good. What was that, Theo? Ah, Harriet, Theo wants to know if he could have a word with you.'

'He couldn't,' said Harriet and put the phone down.

She went up to her room, repacked her briefcase, then sat down on the bed and picked up the letter from the gynaecologist she had found in the cardigan pocket.

Jennifer Bradman, FRCOG, said she could see her around midday: 'I'm sorry it can't be before. Full morning. I don't know how much I can help, but I'll certainly try.'

'Thank you,' said Harriet.

She looked in at her mother on her way down. Maggie was lying awake but calm; she gazed rather hopelessly at Harriet from her mound of pillows.

'I'll get you some tea, Mummy. Then I really have to go up to London. I'm sorry. Urgent business. I'll be back tonight if I possibly can.'

'You always have urgent business,' said Maggie fretfully. 'Don't delay yourself on my account, Harriet, I'll get my own tea.'

Harriet walked out in silence, closing the door with acute care behind her. Otherwise she would have slammed it.

Chapter 28

James 10am

'You drive,' Theo had said, when they finally reached Kidlington, fell exhaustedly into the Bentley. 'I want to hit the phone.'

'You sound like a character in a TV drama,' said James, grinning at him.

'I am like a character in a TV drama,' said Theo rather grimly. 'Ridiculous. Absurd. Hard to believe in.' He was punching out numbers. James, aware of how tired he was, how upset, desperately trying to concentrate on the road, heard a long trail of conversations: with Myra Hartman, about faxes, letters, appointments, flowers (flowers?); with Mark Protheroe, about prices, selling, buying, markets; with Jackie the housekeeper, about arrivals, departures, guests, the weekend; and then a brief heated exchange clearly with Mungo, and another, brief as well, but coolly level, with his elder son Michael. 'I've got to do something about that boy,' he said, finally hanging up the phone.

'Which one? Mungo?'

'Oh, I can't do anything with Mungo. He's absolutely impossible. Pig-headed, arrogant, totally absurd –'

'Like a character in a TV drama,' said James mildly.

'What? Oh, for God's sake, James. Mungo is nothing, nothing in the least like me. I'm talking about Michael. He's thirty-two now, you know. Got to give him something to run.'

'Well, is that a problem?'

'Yes it is. He's efficient, shrewd, conscientious, got an excellent business head.'

'So what's the problem?'

'He's got no passion. No style. None at all. Never does anything on impulse. He's all brain.'

'Isn't that a good thing in business?' asked James, genuinely intrigued.

'No of course not,' said Theo. He sounded astonished, as if James had suggested that a good businessman should possess a talent for ballet or pottery. 'Passion is what makes it all work, James. You can get other people to crunch numbers and deal with contracts and contacts, but it's what you do with your heart and your instinct that wins you the day. It's like falling in love, James, it's like sex, it's an excitement, a thud of the heart. Michael's heart doesn't thud. Ever.'

'What about Mungo's?'

'Thuds too bloody much,' said Theo and picked up the phone again.

'Can you drop me at the Bergins' hotel?' said James. 'I left my jacket there yesterday and I can see how they're coping at the same time. I hope quite honestly they go home very soon – there's no point their hanging around. Or do you think there is? Do you think she might even now come back?' he added, hearing the note of hopeful pain in his own voice as he said it, feeling foolish.

Theo looked at him. 'Honestly,' he said, 'I don't. It's a bitch of a thing to admit, but I don't.'

James was silent.

'James! Good morning. How are you?' Julia was as china-doll perfect as ever, smiling, holding out her hand as she came across the hotel lounge.

'Oh – all right,' said James wearily. He was too tired, too wretched to keep up any pretences, to try to sound positive.

'You look exhausted,' said Julia Bergin severely. 'Has there been any development?'

'Yes,' said James, and told her what it was.

He didn't look at her as he talked; he couldn't. When he finally lifted his head, met her eyes, there was a moment of appalling truth. Before shock, distress, disbelief carefully took over, for just one second Julia Bergin looked complacently, smugly self-satisfied.

Then: 'Poor Oliver,' she said quietly. 'My poor poor Oliver. And you James, and Maggie, what you must be going through. I only wish –'

'Maggie doesn't know yet,' said James briefly. What was it with Julia, was Merlin right, did she know something? No, she couldn't, she couldn't. It must have been one of those inappropriate shock reactions, like giggling when you heard that someone had died.

'Maggie doesn't know?' repeated Julia.

'No. I gave her some very heavy sedation last night. I've rung home and apparently she's only just woken. I'm going home to tell her now.'

'Oh, James. How terrible. That lovely little girl – what she must have gone through.'

'That's very charitable of you,' said James. 'To take that view.'

'Well, one has to try to understand. To imagine what might have led her to do such a thing. What unhappiness, what confusion.'

'Yes, yes,' said James, 'and what selfishness, what cruelty.' He didn't want Cressida defended; had she walked into the lounge then he would have hit her.

'Well, there had to be more to it than that.'

'I don't think so. Is Oliver about?'

'He's gone for a walk. With his father.'

'I see. I really wanted to tell him myself.'

'James, I think it would be better if I told him. He's been through such a terrible time. He's very hurt. I think I would know how to break it to him –'

'Yes, all right,' said James. He found he was grateful for an escape route; telling Oliver how nearly he had married a liar and a cheat who happened to be his daughter was not a pleasant prospect.

'So if you want to get off home to Maggie, then do please feel free. She needs you more than Oliver does, James. Poor woman. As a mother, I feel for her so much. If you think I could help in any way –'

She sat down abruptly, buried her face in her hands. James stood looking down at her helplessly. 'Julia, please – I'm so sorry –'

'Oh James, don't feel – it's all right – I –' She looked up again; her eyes were brilliant with unshed tears, her mouth taut with an attempt at control. 'Suddenly I – so silly – shock, I suppose. Please excuse me.'

She was gone, leaving James staring after her with nothing left to do now but go home and tell Maggie the horrible thing her beloved daughter had done.

Chapter 29

Mungo 10:30am

'Mungo! Call for you on Two.'

It was Belinda, one of the Sloaney negotiators; she was moderately pretty, extremely charming and very sexy, with good legs, long blonde hair (which Mungo swore actually grew attached to the black velvet hairband which held it off her high forehead), a hugely infectious laugh and a fine line in dirty jokes. Her pedigree was impeccable: her father worked for Lloyd's, her boyfriend at Christie's and her mother had been deb of the year. The clients all adored her; Mungo adored her too. If he hadn't been so much in love with Alice, he thought he might well have gone into battle for her with the Christie's boyfriend.

'Thanks. It's not my father, is it?'

'No, Mungo, it's not your father. It's a female. Didn't give a name.'

Wouldn't be Alice; she always rang on his mobile. 'If you think I'm giving those girls the pleasure of knowing how often I want to talk to you, you don't know me very well,' she'd said to him when he pointed out that if she used the office line she could leave messages. He picked the phone up. He felt very tired suddenly; his arms were leaden and his head ached.

'Mungo Buchan.'

It was Jemima. 'Mungo, sorry to ring you in the office. Is this all right?'

'Depends what you're going to say,' said Mungo.

'I'm going to say thank you,' said Jemima.

'What on earth for?'

'For not ratting on me to Mummy. It was really nice of you.'

'That's OK,' said Mungo wearily. 'But if you want a bit of advice from an old man, Jemima, you'll find somewhere else to conduct your love life in future. Somewhere a bit more discreet.'

'Yes, I know. I will. Promise. Um – there's something else, Mungo. I – I might have given you the wrong impression last night. About Mummy. I was – angry with her, we'd had a fight.'

'What kind of wrong impression?'

'Well, that she – you know. She – well, she isn't – she doesn't –'

'Jemima, what are you trying to say?'

'Well, that she's really really fond of you. And she – well, she wouldn't do anything to hurt you. I know she wouldn't.'

'I'm afraid, Jemima, she already has,' said Mungo and put the phone down. 'Get me some coffee, Carol, would you?' he shouted through the door. Carol was his long-suffering secretary: more conventionally pretty, but rather less well connected than Belinda and plainly and helplessly in love with him. She came in early, worked through most of her lunch hours, left late and had more than once worked until long after Mungo had left and she had missed her last train home if there was an urgent brochure or prospectus to prepare, and then paid for a taxi back to Ealing with her own money rather than cause Mungo any more trouble. She found the things he had lost, remembered the things he had forgotten and enjoyed nothing more than performing such politically incorrect secretarial duties as sewing on his buttons and taking his clothes to the cleaners. She came in now looking slightly nervous, the coffee in a large mug and a plate of Jaffa cakes in her other hand. Mungo's devotion to Jaffa cakes was well known, and Carol made frequent pilgrimages to Selfridge's Food Hall to keep the supply topped up. It was usually worth the effort, he would smile and thank her, but this morning he simply took the mug and waved the plate away without a word.

'Er – how was the wedding, Mungo? You look tired.'

'Lousy and I am tired. Get me the file on the Bruton Lane building, Carol, and get the bank on the phone.'

'Yes, Mungo, of course.'

Mungo looked at her as she half ran out of the office; she'd have to go, he couldn't stand the sense of guilt she engendered any longer. Well, that would be easily effected; she could be part of the cost-cutting exercise. He'd talk to her at lunchtime.

* * *

'You,' said Alice, 'are a brat.'

She was standing in the doorway of the office, Belinda hovering uncertainly behind her.

Mungo looked up at her. 'Please leave,' he said coldly.

'Mungo, I have no intention of leaving.'

'Well in that case I will.'

'No you won't,' said Alice, and closed the door behind her. She leant against it, looking at him thoughtfully, then she said, 'Mungo, we have to talk.'

'There's nothing to talk about as far as I can see,' said Mungo icily. 'Now if you will excuse me, I have work to do.' He started tapping at his keyboard, calling up details of properties; then he picked up the phone and punched out a number rather too viciously. 'Mrs Packard? Mungo Buchan. Mrs Packard, I think we might have a very interesting property for you. In –'

'Mrs Packard will have to wait, I'm afraid,' said Alice coolly. She had come over to his desk and cut him off. 'Mungo, do you have to be so rude? I thought you were supposed to love me.'

'You thought wrong, I'm afraid. Well, I suppose I did, but you've fucked it up rather neatly.'

'Mungo, the only fucking up that's being done is by you. Of just about everything. Your life, your work, your relationships, not just with me but with your father. And –'

'Please don't talk to me about my father,' said Mungo. 'What you did, phoning him like that, was absolutely unforgivable. And you're doing a pretty good job of fucking up my work yourself. Please go away. I have clients to attend to.'

'No, Mungo, I won't go. And I'd like you to tell that poor little soul out there who seems to have the misguided idea that you're some kind of a cross between Tom Cruise and the Messiah to hold all your calls for a while.'

'I'll do nothing of the sort.'

'In that case,' said Alice, starting to unbutton her dress, 'I shall scream and say you were assaulting me.'

Mungo looked at her. There was an expression in her blue eyes that he had come to know very well: one of absolute steely determination. He picked up the phone. 'Carol,' he said, 'hold all the calls for now, please. And ask Roddy Fairfield to talk to Mrs Packard urgently. If she hasn't already gone to another agent,' he added, glaring at Alice.

'Yes, Mungo. Er – would you like some more coffee in there?'

'No I wouldn't,' said Mungo.

As he put the phone down again, he heard muffled giggles; he looked up at Alice. 'How dare you,' he said, 'how dare you come in here and disrupt my business and make a fool of me in front of my staff?'

'Oh don't be so pompous,' said Alice. 'I dare, as you put it, because it's very important you hear what I have to say. I want your undivided attention. It won't take long.'

'All right. Get on with it. And then get out.'

'Mungo, do look at me please, stop sulking. It's impossible to talk to the top of someone's head.'

Mungo looked at her and scowled. She laughed. 'You really look very like your father when you do that.'

'How do you know what he looks like, Alice? If you've been to see him –'

'Oh, Mungo, don't be ridiculous. Of course I haven't been to see him. But he is quite famous, you know. I've seen him on things like the *Money Programme*, and he was on *Panorama* the other night.'

'Was he?' said Mungo, genuinely surprised. 'I didn't know.'

'Yes, a programme about the Third World. He was giving his views on the food surplus here and in the States. It was very interesting. You should have watched it.'

'No thanks,' said Mungo. 'I know most of his interesting views off by heart. They bore me.'

'What a little charmer you are,' said Alice lightly. 'Let's talk about you, shall we, Mungo? That will presumably interest you more.'

'Alice,' said Mungo, losing his temper suddenly, 'Alice, last night I told my father how much I loved you and that I wanted to marry you. He was foul to me. He talked to me as if I was six years old, it was patronizing to me, insulting to you, and –'

'Yes, he knows that, and he was very sorry,' said Alice.

Mungo could not have been more astonished if she had told him his father was taking up ice skating or social work.

'He was what?'

'He was sorry.'

'My father doesn't know the meaning of the word.'

'Mungo, I think he does. He sounded very sorry indeed to me. He said he wasn't very good at apologizing, but he was going to have a go at doing it to you. He's a honey. I really liked him.'

'Oh,' said Mungo, 'oh, shit.'

'What?'

'He phoned – earlier. Tried to speak to me. I told him to – well, I told him to fuck off.'

'Well,' said Alice, 'that was very charming. And it probably won't encourage him to pursue the art of contrition.'

'Sorry?'

'I don't suppose he'll try apologizing to you again.'

'Did you – did you have to point it out to him?' said Mungo.

'Point what out?'

'Well, that he's been patronizing and insulting?'

'No, of course not.'

'If you knew him,' said Mungo, 'you'd know there was no "of course" about it.'

'You may be right. I happen to think you're wrong. Anyway, I'm hoping to get to know him.'

'Oh, really? Over cosy little dinners while you discuss my appalling behaviour and what you're both going to do about it?'

'Oh, don't be so childish,' she said wearily.

'I'm not being childish. Maybe you should set your sights on him, rather than me. He's a lot nearer your age, and he's not exactly picky. I'm sure you could get rid of the current Mrs Buchan in no time, if you set your mind to it –'

Alice walked over to the desk and hit him; first she slapped him extremely hard across the face, and then she drew her arm back and punched him with surprising force on the nose. The room went briefly black and then a few lights danced in front of his eyes; the famous stars, he thought confusedly. He felt something warm trickling down his upper lip: blood he supposed. He sat slumped back in his chair, staring at her. He felt very odd.

'Right then,' she said. She stood over him, her hands on the arms of his chair, her eyes blazing in her white face. He could feel the heat of her, could smell her, not just her perfume but something else, a hot musky smell, the smell of rage. 'Right then, Mungo, I've got a few things to tell you and then I'll go. First of all, I don't go round setting my sights on anyone. I actually thoroughly enjoy being single. It's fun and it's easy. I didn't want to fall in love with you, Mungo, I fought it very hard. For a long time. As for marrying you, it still seems the most ridiculous, the most impractical, the most appalling idea.'

'Well, then,' he said, and his voice was somehow quieter than he had expected it to be, 'if it seems so appalling why did you say you would?'

There was a very long silence; he stared up at her. Her eyes, holding his, were still hostile, still furious.

'Because I couldn't help it,' she said finally. 'I simply couldn't help it. Because I do love you. I think you're spoilt and self-centred and childish and dreadful and yet you make me terribly happy. And I love you. I weakened. I just couldn't hold out any longer.'

'Oh,' said Mungo, his voice quieter still. The blood was pouring down his nose now, and onto his shirt; he reached for his handkerchief, mopped at it rather helplessly. 'I've fucked this up rather, haven't I?'

'Just a bit,' said Alice. 'But since I told your father last night I wasn't going to marry you, it doesn't really matter what you did. Or said.'

'Ah,' said Mungo, 'ah, I thought so. He did talk you out of it. Somehow or another.'

'No, Mungo, he didn't. I talked me out of it. He hardly said a word. I heard myself saying, and thinking how sensible of me it was, that I wouldn't marry you. That it was a stupid idea.'

'Appalling,' said Mungo mechanically.

'Appalling. Yes. That I must have been out of such mind as I have, agreeing to it in the first place. And I also said that if he thought it would be better for you, I would go away altogether.'

'Well, I'm very glad you consulted him so fully about our lives, rather than me,' said Mungo. 'And what did he say to that?'

'He said it was no business of his,' she said. 'Absolutely none at all.'

'He did?' said Mungo, staring up at her. 'My father said that?'

'Yes he did. He said he had absolutely no intention of telling me what I should or shouldn't do.'

'He didn't even express a view?'

'No he didn't.'

'I don't believe I'm hearing this,' said Mungo. 'My father spends his entire life telling people what to do. Expressing very strong views indeed. He was just being clever, stringing you along –'

'Mungo, I told you, he was really sorry about – about what he said to you. About us. I don't know why you can't believe it.'

'I can't believe it,' said Mungo, 'because I know him so well. I've lived with him for twenty-seven years. I tell you, Alice, every leopard on the face of this planet is more likely to change its spots to sky-blue pink than my father is to stop interfering in everyone's lives. Especially mine.'

'There are some white leopards, you know,' she said quietly.

'I'm sorry?'

'I mean some leopards have actually changed their spots. Well, lost them anyway. In response to certain situations.'

'Yes, maybe, but not overnight.'

'You're very hard on him, aren't you?'

'Yes, I am. I've learnt to be.'

'He's very proud of you, you know.'

'Yeah, yeah,' said Mungo, 'when I'm being a good boy, doing what I'm told.'

'No, not really. He told me last night how proud of you he was. Of the way you've built this business up. He said he hadn't actually thought you'd got what it takes, but he was wrong. That you've done it without any input from him at all. It was one of the things he was most sorry about, implying that you couldn't. And he also said he was very proud of the way you'd stood up to him. He said' – she smiled at what was obviously a funny memory – 'he said he knew it took some doing.'

'Good God,' said Mungo, 'this really was some conversation.'

'Yes it was. Anyway –'

'And he actually said that? That I've got what it takes?'

'Mungo, how many more times do I have to tell you? That's what he said.'

Mungo looked at her. He felt very powerful suddenly, very joyful, as if he could do anything, anything at all. And he felt something else, too, a sense of immense, heady freedom.

'Shit,' he said, 'shit.'

'Is that all you have to say?'

'No,' said Mungo, 'no it isn't.' He looked at Alice and thought how it had taken her and her clear-sightedness and courage to do this for him, to cut into the complex, cross-purposed lines that lay between him and his father and to deliver each of them safely, if a little shamefaced, back to one another.

'I love you,' he said to her, 'I really really love you.'

'And I really love you too. Like I said.'

'But you won't marry me?'

'No, Mungo, I won't marry you. I can't. I told you, it's an –'

'Yes, yes, all right, it's an appalling idea. You're going to have to work quite hard to convince me of that.'

'No,' she said, 'no, not really. I won't have to. Because what I'm going to do is go away, leave London.'

'What do you mean, you're going away? Going away where? I don't understand, you weren't going away yesterday.'

'Mungo, I know. But I did a lot of thinking yesterday. And – well, I am. I'm going to Italy.'

'Italy? What the fuck for?'

'Not fucking,' she said smiling, touching his face gently. 'Oh, Mungo, your poor, poor nose.'

'Never mind my nose,' he said, rummaging in his pocket for another handkerchief. 'What's with this Italy business?'

'Business actually,' she said. 'Exactly that. Here, let me clean you up.' She bent over him, started tenderly wiping his face; she was very near him, he could smell the warmth of her, smell her skin, her hair. He put out his hand, gently touched one of her breasts, clearly defined beneath the white silk jersey.

'Alice,' he said, 'oh, Alice –'

And 'Mungo,' she said, 'Mungo, don't. Please don't.'

'Why not?' he said and he could hear the pain deep down in his voice. 'Don't you like it? Don't you want me any more, is that it, are you tired of me, Alice, are you in love with someone else?'

'Mungo darling, I do want you, and I do love you, and I'm not tired of you. It's none of those things. That's what makes it all so difficult. That's why I'm going away.'

'Oh, Alice, please. Don't be ridiculous. You can't go away. What would you do?'

'Work. My friends of last night, the ones you didn't believe in, Giles and Fanny, they've bought a big house in Tuscany and they want to turn it into a small, very luxurious hotel. They want me to run it for them. For a while at least.'

'You can't do that,' he said, 'you don't know anything about hotels, you don't speak Italian, it's nonsense.'

'I know quite a lot about hotels actually, Mungo, and I *can* speak Italian. I think I'll be very good at it.'

'What about the children? You can't leave them.'

'I'm not going to leave them. The little ones will come with me, go to the International School in Florence, and Jemima will come out in the holidays, practise her burgeoning sexual talents in a different language. It'll do them good, to discover there's a world beyond SW3.'

Mungo felt panic, clammy, cold, clutching at him. 'Alice, you can't. You can't do this to me.'

'I'm doing it *for* you,' she said, with a peculiarly sweet smile. She reached out, touched his cheek very gently. 'Because I love you so much. And for me, actually. It'll be wonderful.'

'Alice, please don't go. Please. I need you.'

'Mungo, I have to go. It really is the only thing to do.'

'Well then, I'll come too. I want some European business, I could be your agent, find more places to let and –'

'Mungo, no. That is really not the idea. Much as I'd love it.'

'Well, if you'd love it,' he said, feeling in spite of himself that he was losing ground, 'why don't you let me?'

'Mungo, listen to me.' She took his face between her hands, looked into his eyes. 'I can't let you because it wouldn't work. We have lives to live, you and I, and they don't go together too well. It's been lovely having you all this time, and the children have adored it and so have I, but it hasn't been about real life. You couldn't fit permanently into my life, Mungo, and, much more importantly, I couldn't fit into yours. I should never have let you think so, never have let myself think so. And I'm more sorry than I can tell you. And I do love you very, very much.'

'But I need you. I need you so much.'

'Not really. You can manage beautifully without me. You're a very special person, Mungo. Just don't forget it, that's all. Don't – er – fuck the very special person up, OK?'

'Oh God,' he said, staring at her, a clutch of misery starting at his heart, realizing she meant it. 'Oh God, Alice. I don't know if I can do this. Say goodbye to you. Live without you. And it seems so unnecessary somehow.'

'Nonsense,' she said, 'of course you can. And it isn't unnecessary, actually, Mungo. Not at all.'

'And this is it? I'm not to see you any more?'

'Not any more,' she said.

'You seem very cheerful about it.'

'Mungo, I'm not cheerful at all. I'm going to be very unhappy for quite a long time. But I'll survive. And so will you.'

'Well – can't we still be friends? At least?'

'Mungo,' she said, bending down, kissing him very gently on the lips, his sore, bloody, cracked lips; her own mouth was cool, soft. 'Mungo, I would love to be your friend. In time. But not just yet. It wouldn't work and I –' Her voice cracked, she stood up quickly, decisively, her eyes brilliant with tears. 'I couldn't bear it,' she said quietly. 'Goodbye, Mungo. I'll see you – I'll see you maybe next year? Come and find me, then, in Italy. If you still want to.'

'Of course I'll want to,' he said slowly, staring at her. He felt as if he was seeing her for the first time, not the last, discovering her all over again, her lovely face, with its high cheekbones, its curvy mouth, her blue eyes, brilliant, tender, fixed on him, her ice-blonde hair (more dishevelled than usual) and – oh God, her perfect slender body, the body he knew so well, how it felt, smelt, how it welcomed him, loved him, wanted him; and he knew she meant what she said, that there would be no dissuading her, that he had to say goodbye to her, for a long while.

'You'd better go,' he said, 'I think you'd better go quickly. Goodbye, Alice. I love you. I love you so much.'

'I love you too,' she said, 'and I'm sorry about your face.'

'Oh,' he said, 'don't worry about that. I expect I deserved it.'

'Yes, you did,' she said, and smiled again, gaily, bravely. 'Darling Mungo. Take care. Goodbye.'

And she was gone, closing the door quietly behind her, and Mungo sat at his desk, just looking, staring at the space where she had been, thinking of the space in his life she had filled, empty of her, empty of everything about her, and he couldn't see how he was going to bear it, even while he knew he had to, and he buried his head in his arms and wept like a child.

'Mungo.' It was Belinda; she was standing in front of him, looking very tender, very concerned. 'Mungo, I've brought you some coffee. Is there anything else I can do for you, get you?'

'Yes,' said Mungo, taking a gulp of coffee, blowing his nose hard on his bloodstained handkerchief, 'Yes, Belinda, there is. Could you please get hold of my father? And tell him I'd like to buy him dinner tonight.'

Chapter 30

James 10:30am

James was half a mile down the lane in the cab the hotel called for him when he realized he still hadn't picked up the jacket he had left there yesterday. Bloody hell. The last thing he wanted to do was go back to that place. On the other hand, he did have to get it, and retrieving it would postpone the conversation with Maggie a little while longer. On balance probably better to turn around.

'I'm terribly sorry,' he said to the cab driver. 'I've left something behind. Could we go back please?'

'I'm sorry, Mr Forrest, the Bergins are all out. Mrs Bergin has gone for a walk with Dr Bergin and Mr Bergin has gone into Oxford. I'm sorry, sir. Is there anything we can do to help?'

'Well, yes, there is actually,' said James. 'I left my jacket in Mr Bergin's room yesterday. I do rather want it. Could one of your staff fetch it for me?'

'Certainly, sir.' He called a young man in a striped waistcoat who was standing in the hall trying to look importantly busy. 'Michael! Would you go and get Mr Forrest's jacket from Mr and Mrs Bergin's room, please? He left it there yesterday.'

'Certainly, Mr Rogers. Er – how will I know which jacket it is, Mr Forrest? Is it distinctive in any way at all, sir?'

'Oh Lord, I don't know,' said James. 'No – yes – look, I'll come up with you. All right?'

'Well, sir, I don't know –' The young man in reception looked dubious. 'We're really not supposed –'

'Oh, for God's sake,' said James, feeling nearer to a loss of control than he had for twenty-four hours. 'Mr Bergin is a very old friend of mine, his son was about to marry my daughter, my daughter's gone missing, now will you, for Christ's sake, let me go and retrieve my own jacket from his room?'

'Yes, sir. I'm sorry, sir. Michael, go along please, don't keep Mr Forrest waiting.'

James followed the unfortunate Michael into the lift and out again, along the first-floor corridor into the Bergins' room; Michael stood awkwardly silent while James walked over to the cupboard. His jacket was there, hanging neatly next to Josh's morning coat, still in its plastic cover. The sight of that, forlornly unworn, brought back more poignantly than anything what had happened, the loss of Cressida, the heartache and the grief of the day. Tears rushed to his eyes; he sank down on the bed and buried his head in his hands. To his horror and humiliation he began to cry, loud racking sobs. Michael coughed gently, discreetly.

'Oh for God's sake,' James shouted, his voice rich with tears and pain, 'for God's sake get the hell out of here. I'm not going to rob the bloody room. Get out.'

Michael withdrew and closed the door very quietly; James continued to sob. After a while he felt better, lay back exhausted, staring at the ceiling. Why had she done it, why, why? Was she really so bad, so totally devoid of morals? Was it his fault, Maggie's fault, for spoiling her, loving her too much? Was it his bad genes, his own lack of morality, passed on to her? Christ Almighty, was this his judgment, his punishment? Or was Susie's illness that, a punishment for them both? He suddenly felt filled with terror for Susie, for the danger she was in, with shame too, at what he had done to her, for failing her. Christ, he was a mess, an appalling, amoral mess. He looked at his watch: she would be out of theatre by now; maybe he could phone.

He went over to the bedside table, picked up the phone, dialled the number of the Princess Diana Hospital. 'Is Mr Hobson out of theatre, please?' he asked. 'This is James Forrest, obstetrics consultant at St Edmund's. I'm a colleague of his.'

'Just a moment, please, Mr Forrest,' said the girl. There were a few clicks, then she said, 'I'm sorry, Mr Forrest, Mr Hobson is still in theatre. Can I ask him to call you?'

'No, it's all right,' said James, 'I won't be here. I'll call back in about an hour. Will he be there?'

More clicks. 'I'm sorry, Mr Forrest, Mr Hobson won't be here in an hour, his secretary says he'll be in his consulting rooms. Can I give you the number?'

'Yes, please,' said James. He had no pen or paper on him; he rummaged in the small drawer of the bedside table, found a pad, took it out, pulling half the contents of the drawer with it. 'OK, fire away, yes, 934–2268. Thank you very much.'

He tore the piece of paper off the pad, replaced the rather florid gold-plated biro that was clearly Julia's and started picking up the papers from the floor. Lists in Julia's spidery American writing; a note from Maggie, giving the name and address of the hotel; a – James suddenly sat down on the bed staring, staring at the letter in a hand that had begun to shake, fallen from inside a leather-bound notebook of Julia's.

The writing paper was headed with an address in Palm Beach, Florida, and the letter was written in a slightly shaky but absolutely legible hand. It was dated a week earlier.

My darling girl (it said)

So very lovely to see you the other day. I wish you could come more often, but of course I know you have your duties to your husband. He is extremely fortunate to have you, to ease his path so loyally and effectively. I hope he recognizes his good fortune.

I was very distressed to hear that this girl is proving to be so unsuitable for Oliver. It seems tragic that such a brilliant and charming young man should have his future endangered by falling into the hands of someone so amoral and, if it is not too strong a word, dangerous. How foolish love makes one; even you, my darling.

Of course I am more than happy to extend what I am pleased to see you now perceive as the favour I did you, in keeping the Coleridge fortune safe from incompetent hands. I have spoken to my lawyers and changed my will. Under the new terms, Oliver is no longer a beneficiary, of either capital or income, and will not be one for so long as he remains married to this creature; should the marriage end, as I know you pray it will, then we can review the situation. I enclose a photocopy of the relevant passage; the fully revised document is now lodged, as always, with the trustees.

I have done as you advised and not written to Oliver myself. I trust you, in your wonderfully charming and tactful way, to break the news to him. He may be a little hurt and even angry, as you were so many years ago, my dearest, but I am sure he will come in the fullness of time to see the wisdom of what we have done. We have a duty to protect and care for our children for as long as God grants us; I thank Him daily that I have been able to do that for you.

My fondest love,
Dada

'Dear Christ,' said James aloud, putting the piece of paper down, 'dear Christ in heaven.'

He went over to the mini-bar and, for the first time in twenty years, poured himself a drink.

Chapter 31

Susie 10:30am

Maybe she hadn't died yet. The darkness was somehow softening. And the light was back, a faint pinprick now, but getting bigger. She was drifting towards it rather fast, so obviously she hadn't got long. Her arm and her breast hurt; hurt quite a lot. Well, that would be over soon, at least. You didn't feel pain if you were dead. Oh God, she was thirsty, her mouth was so dry. She wondered if you had drinks in heaven, and what they were. Would there be champagne? She wouldn't think much of a heaven without it. And would James be there? If she was going to be happy, she'd need him. But he couldn't be, because he hadn't died. And he didn't love her anyway. She knew that now. He didn't love her and he probably never had. The whole of her grown-up life had been lived on a lie. It hurt so much to think that. And all that time Alistair had loved her, and she hadn't realized it. And that hurt, too. She'd wasted him, and wasted herself on James. 'Oh God,' she said fretfully, through dry, thick lips, finding her throat was sore. 'Oh God, I'm so sorry.'

'Darling,' a voice said, very gently, 'darling Susie. Hallo.'

She hadn't expected God to use that sort of endearment; she'd thought He'd be rather gruff. Kind but gruff. The light got bigger suddenly, brighter; she braced herself to open her eyes, look at Him, look at God. And found herself looking at Alistair.

He was smiling very tenderly at her; he put out his hand and stroked her hair. Then he picked up her hand and kissed it. 'Hallo,' he said.

'Alistair,' said Susie, 'Alistair, aren't I dead?'

'Not in the least,' he said, 'I'm happy to say. Very much alive.'

'Hi, Mum,' said another voice. It was Rufus.

Susie turned her head to the other side of the bed; he was sitting there, smiling down at her with equal tenderness. He took her other hand.

'Ouch,' said Susie, 'that hurts. So does my arm.'

'Sorry. How are you feeling?'

'All right I think. Bit woozy. I –' She remembered suddenly the fear, the awful fear that it would be gone, and tried unsuccessfully to move her good arm, her right arm, over to try to feel if it was still there, her precious, treacherous breast. It was too much of an effort; she relaxed again, biting her lip. Alistair kissed her again.

'It's all right, darling. It's still there.' He knew, had realized what she was trying to do. She was so touched by that, and by a great flood of relief, of joy, her eyes filled with tears; she closed them briefly. They stung; they hurt. Everything hurt. Maybe if she kept them closed for just a second, it would be better . . .

When she opened them again, Mr Hobson was standing at the foot of her bed; he was wearing his green gown, and he was looking rather pleased with himself. A nurse was taking her pulse. 'Good,' she said. Definitely not dead then, thought Susie, smiling at Mr Hobson.

'Your husband's popped off to make a quick phone call,' he said. 'He was getting just a tiny bit restive, watching you sleep.'

'Watching me sleep! I just woke up.'

'Half an hour ago. Then you promptly went off again.'

'No I didn't,' said Susie, indignantly.

'Yes you did, Mum.' Rufus's face was very solemn, very loving. 'Honestly.'

'Rufus, what are you doing here? How did you know? I told your father –' She bit her lip, realizing she would never be able to say that again to Rufus without guilt, without shame. But he didn't seem to react any differently from usual. 'I told Alistair not to tell any of you.'

'Dad didn't.' Did she imagine it, or was there just a slight emphasis on the word Dad? She hoped so. 'Harriet told me.'

'Harriet! How did she know?'

'You rang her up. Don't you remember?'

'No. I'm sure I didn't. I –' And then she did remember, struggling to speak to Harriet through the fog of her pre-med, wanting, needing to speak to James. For the last time. And failing.

'Mum, why didn't you tell me? How do you think I'd have felt if – well, if I hadn't – oh, you know what I mean.'

'I know what you mean,' said Susie, smiling rather uncertainly at him.

He bent to kiss her. 'Love you loads,' he said. He had always said that, ever since he was a tiny little boy, whenever they said hallo or goodbye.

'Love you too,' said Susie, hoping Rufus was telling the truth.

Mr Hobson cleared his throat. 'I hate to intrude on this touching family scene, but there's something I have to tell you.'

Susie braced herself; even that very tiny movement hurt. 'What?' she said, and a sickening, dreadful fear took hold of her. She gripped Rufus's hand, and realized to her immense surprise that it wasn't enough. She wanted Alistair, wanted him to be there, to hear her sentence. Maybe, she thought confusedly, through her terror, maybe this whole thing was a judgment on her, a punishment for all her wickedness.

'Mr Hobson, could you wait until my husband gets back, please? I want –' she corrected herself – 'I need him to be here.'

'Yes, of course you do. The only thing is you're not my only patient. I should be down in theatre again now.'

'I'll go and find him,' said Rufus.

'Oh Rufus, darling, thank you. Could I have a drink of water, Mr Hobson? I'm so terribly thirsty.'

'What do you think, Nurse?'

'Should be all right,' said the nurse. 'Just a sip.'

Susie sipped. Her throat really hurt. 'What's the time?' she asked, trying to see what the nurse's upside-down watch said.

'Almost eleven.'

'Oh my God,' said Susie. She suddenly remembered everything. Tilly. The flight. Rufus. 'Oh God, where's my son?'

'Gone to find his father,' said Mr Hobson. 'What is it, what's the matter?'

'I have to tell him something urgently. Very, very urgently. Nurse, could you – please –'

She lay back on her pillows, exhausted. The nurse on a nod from Mr Hobson hurried out of the room.

'Mum, what is it? What's wrong? Dad's just coming, he –'

'It's not me, Rufus, not Dad. Listen, you have to get to Heathrow fast.'

'Why?' said Rufus.

'You have to catch Tilly.'

'Tilly won't want to catch me. Or see me,' said Rufus flatly. For the first time Susie looked at him, looked at him properly. He was very white; he looked as if he hadn't slept.

'Rufus, she will. I know she will.'

'No she won't. Last night I wanted to talk to her so badly about – well, it doesn't matter what about –'

'Me,' said Susie quietly.

'Well – yes.'

'Rufus, I'm so –'

'Mum, I really don't want to talk about it. Sorry.'

'All right, darling. Maybe another time. Well, anyway, I spoke to Tilly this morning. When I couldn't find you. She was at her mother's house. She sounded very down. And she's going to New York this morning. In – in an hour. Rufus, you've got to stop her. You've got to explain things to her.'

'Mum, I told you, she doesn't want to hear. She doesn't want to see me any more.'

'Oh, I think she does,' said Susie. 'She may not quite know it but she does. And she loves you very much. And cares about you.'

'No she doesn't. She just wants to sign this bloody stupid contract.'

'Rufus, she does care about you. She told me so, and she doesn't actually want to sign the contract. But she will if you don't stop her. Rufus, darling, please, go and catch her. You should be able to, if you break a few speed limits.'

'I want to hear what Mr Hobson has to say.'

'Well then, will you go after that? Rufus, I'm beginning to feel very upset. That's bad for people after surgery, you know.'

'All right, Mum, all right, I'll go. After that.'

Mr Hobson came in with Alistair. Alistair looked very drawn. He sat down in the chair beside the bed and took Susie's hand.

She clung to it.

'Well now,' he said, 'the news is – what can I say?'

'Please say it,' said Susie.

'The news is – fairly good. It's not excellent, but it's good. The biopsy showed that the lump was benign; but some of the surrounding tissues have undergone changes which could lead to malignancy later on. In other words, it's something we need to keep an eye on, and long term we might need to consider a subcutaneous mastectomy –' Susie caught her breath in swiftly, felt Alistair's hold on her hand tighten – Mr Hobson smiled, patted the bedclothes. 'It's not as bad as it sounds, it means in its simplest terms a mastectomy beneath the skin. Which means inevitably that reconstruction is a great deal easier, and you'd be surprised how good you'd look again. And that would remove any possible danger. But there's no hurry, you have plenty of time to think about it. I'm sorry you had to be so worried, but –'

'Oh dear God,' said Alistair. He stared at Susie, then got up and walked over to the window, gazed out. He doesn't know what to do, thought Susie confusedly, he isn't pleased, he's turned against me. And who could blame him? She herself felt nothing, nothing at all.

'Thank God,' said Rufus. 'That is just so wonderful.' He was looking down at her, and his expression wasn't hostile or angry, just very very happy.

'Oh, Mum, I'm so pleased, so relieved. Thank God. Listen, I'll go now, try and catch Tilly. Heathrow, yes?'

'Yes. Midday flight to New York,' said Susie dully, staring at Alistair's back.

'Bye, Mum. Love you.'

'I love you too,' said Susie quietly.

'Well,' said Mr Hobson, 'I must go. I'll pop in and see you later, Susie. Goodbye. Well done. You were very brave. Let us know if you want anything for the pain. Bound to be sore. Goodbye, Mr Headleigh Drayton.'

'Goodbye,' said Alistair. He sounded very strained. 'Thank you so much.'

He still hadn't moved. Mr Hobson went out, closed the door noiselessly behind him.

'Alistair,' said Susie, 'Alistair, please do go if you want to. You must be –'

'Oh, Susie,' he said, 'oh, Susie, I –'

And then he turned, and there were tears, tears pouring down his face, and he came over to her and sank onto his knees by the bed and took both her hands and kissed them.

'I love you so much,' he said, 'so very much. I didn't realize it, but I do. I thought we had – well, we both had – a – a marriage of convenience. Neat, functional, highly suitable. But I know now it wasn't that at all. Not for me at any rate. I couldn't have lived without you, Susie. I really couldn't.'

'But Alistair –'

'Don't,' he said, 'please don't. Don't start on it all. As long as I've got you, Susie, I don't care. I've been able to live with it all these years, and I'm sure I still can. As long as you're alive, as long as I have you. That's what matters. That's all that matters.'

'No, Alistair,' said Susie, reaching out her good arm, stroking his hair gently, wiping away his tears with her finger. 'No, it isn't all that matters. You matter very much and I don't deserve you. And I'm going to –'

'Don't,' he said again, 'please don't.'

'Alistair,' said Susie, with an effort so immense it startled her (but she had to begin, begin now putting things right, making it up to him), 'you're what matters to me now. You and making you happy. We won't ever talk about this again, I promise, but I just have to say one thing. I – did want some – something else. As you know. But now – well, I realize what I wanted wasn't what I'd thought it was. And that what I'd got was actually better. So that's it really. I'm sorry to have been so stupid. Sorry to have made you unhappy if I did.'

'You didn't,' he said quite cheerfully. 'In fact, I'm an uncomplicated sort of chap. I'd got so absolutely used to it. Had my own little arrangements of course. As I'm sure you knew. And you were always so extremely nice to me. Give me a kiss.' He leant over, kissed her on the mouth, very, very tenderly.

'And – Rufus?' said Susie.

'Rufus?' said Alistair, deliberately vague. 'My darling Susie, Rufus is old enough and ugly enough as they say to take care of himself.'

'He's not ugly,' said Susie defensively.

'You're his mother, you would say that. Anyway, he's got your looks and my brains, as GBS so neatly encapsulated it. And both of our happy dispositions. No doubt whatsoever about his genealogy.' He met her eyes with a look that said let us leave it at that. Forever.

'Well,' said Susie, taking her cue from him, 'I just hope he catches that plane and marries that gorgeous Tilly.'

'So do I. Then I shall die a contented man.'

'Don't talk about dying,' said Susie with a shudder. She felt terribly tired suddenly, tired and still emotionally in turmoil. She meant what she said: she would remove James from her life as resolutely, as thoroughly as Mr Hobson had removed her tumour. But he would not be as neatly removed from her thinking, from her heart; it would be hard, there would be struggles and pain and much confusion. She hoped she was equal to the task.

There was a knock at the door. The nurse stood there with an enormous bunch of roses. 'For you,' she said. 'Aren't they lovely?'

Susie looked at Alistair; he had got to his feet and was picking up his coat. The knuckles on his hands were white. He didn't look at her.

She looked at the card. 'For my darling,' it said, 'with all my love.'

'I'm sorry,' she said to the nurse, 'there's been a mistake. These aren't for me. Please send them back to the florist, and make sure the person who sent them knows that. Thank you.'

'But Mrs Headleigh Drayton –'

'Nurse,' said Susie, and was surprised at the firmness in her own voice, 'please take them away. I really really don't want them.'

Chapter 32

James 11am

'Really, James. Do you make a habit of rifling through other people's possessions?' said Julia. She was standing in the doorway; she looked from the letter in his hand to his face, and smiled, her carefully placed, dazzling smile. 'Perhaps I see now where Cressida got some of her unfortunate genes from –'

'Please don't insult my daughter,' said James.

'James, I have every right to insult your daughter. And I am hugely relieved that in the end I was able to save my son from a marriage that even he had become deeply unhappy about.'

'What the hell do you mean?' said James. He sat down again on the bed, drained his glass. It had helped; he walked over to the bar and poured another one.

'I've never seen you drink,' said Julia.

'You've never seen me in need of a drink before,' said James. 'Now, would you like to explain what this' – he shook the letter at her – 'was all about?'

'I would have thought it was self-explanatory,' said Julia. 'My father, God bless him, was deeply worried at the prospect of Cressida getting her hands on his money. He had left it all to Oliver, as you know, although held in trust until after my death.'

'I did, but I didn't think it was so very much,' said James.

'It was an enormous amount. We – he always tried to play it down, in fact it was quite a well-kept secret, but we're talking real money. We had even kept from Oliver how much was involved until after his twenty-fifth birthday. I think it's very bad for young people to get the idea that they don't need to work, or to make their own way in the world. But

Cressida did know. I'm not sure how she found out, but she certainly knew. I think perhaps your extremely overpowering friend Mr Buchan might have told her. These millionaires all know one another, know what they're worth.'

'Why are you so convinced that she knew?' asked James.

'Because she asked Oliver about it. If he was really going to inherit that much money. He told me, he seemed slightly bemused by it, and by the fact that she knew.'

'Oh, really? And when was this rather strange conversation?'

'A year ago. When she was staying with us at Bar Harbor.'

'I see,' said James. He felt slightly sick. 'Well anyway, I don't quite follow –'

'Oh, James, really. Cressida was marrying Oliver entirely for his money.'

'Julia, I won't –'

'James, please be quiet. She didn't love him. She certainly had a bit of a crush on him, maybe last summer when she was staying with us, but no more than that. But she decided to marry him and she manipulated him into it. I could tell, the morning they announced that they were engaged, that he was uncertain, not quite happy, but he's so loyal, Oliver, such a gentleman, he would never admit it. I tried to get him to talk about it, but he wouldn't.'

'I think,' said James, speaking with difficulty, 'he is probably old enough to make up his own mind.'

'Oh, really? How very naive of you, James. But then your marriage to Maggie has been so perfectly happy, hasn't it, you probably don't understand the complexities of lesser mortals.'

Shit, thought James, does she know about that as well? He took another slug of whisky. He was beginning to feel very strange.

'Anyway, gradually I discovered it wasn't just maternal anxiety. I was right. Your daughter was – is – a tramp, James. A slut.'

'Julia, please be careful what you say.'

'I shall say what I please. She had several – what shall I say – lovers. One of them in New York, while she was staying with us.'

'This is absurd. How do you know?'

'Because I followed her. There was just something about her. I was suspicious, once I had established that she knew about the money.

And every other day she went off on long shopping and sightseeing expeditions, saying very charmingly, I have to say, that she liked to be alone. And of course she was extremely hostile to me. When we were alone. To the point of rudeness.'

'I can't imagine why,' said James dryly.

Julia ignored him. 'I tried to talk to Josh about it, but he wouldn't take any notice. Of course, he'll trust anyone with a pretty face and nice manners. So I followed her one day. She went down to Gramercy Park, spent the day in some man's apartment. I saw him open the door to her, saw her kiss him, go inside.'

'Julia, this is horrible. I'm not going to listen.'

'Nobody would listen to me. I tried to tell Oliver, after she'd gone home, but he just got angry. There was another incident as well, some nonsense about an attack. Josh thought I knew nothing about it, but the hall porter mentioned it, and I put two and two together, phoned the limo hire company. It wasn't very difficult. Finally I made Oliver confront Cressida next time he saw her. She denied it, of course, wept, stormed, said I hated her, that she'd kill herself if he didn't believe her, or walked out on her. He was still unhappy, but he was completely in her thrall, you know. Even though he didn't actually love her, she had some strange influence over him, he wanted to make her happy. She was a very emotionally powerful girl, James. And very neurotic of course. Before I despaired of her, I begged her to see my analyst –'

'Oh, for God's sake,' said James, 'you and your analysts.'

'She agreed actually,' said Julia quietly. 'She went a few times, then said it was too much for her.'

'So you really expect me to believe that Oliver went ahead with this marriage, knowing that Cressida was sleeping around –'

'James, he didn't actually know it. Well, not until the end. He wouldn't know it. He blinded himself to it. And don't forget they weren't seeing a lot of one another. There was a lot of pride involved by then, pride and kindness, and an innate decency. Oliver is a very trusting, straightforward person. There was nothing I could do with him. He got angry with me, told me it was I who was obsessed. He just kept saying "Mother, I'm going to marry her, I love her, she needs me." The more I tried to tell him, the less he believed me. Although I think at the end, when he knew about this pregnancy, he must have done. But by then it was too late. It was only days before the wedding.'

'And what makes you so sure, Julia, that it wasn't Oliver's baby?'

'James, it couldn't have been. You should know that. The dates don't make any kind of sense.'

James was silent, knowing she was right; remembering his own unacknowledged certainty of the night before.

'So – I realized there was nothing I could do. Except appeal to Cressida.'

'Which you did?'

'Yes, of course I did. And she did what she does with Oliver, cried, told me I hated her, that I was crazy, jealous because I was taking Oliver away from her. And then she said, and I'll never forget it, "Julia, you can't stop it now. You just can't. He'll never back out now. Never." So then I knew I had to try and do something myself. I just wanted to hurt her, to make this marriage less what she had hoped, stop her getting her hands on what she wanted. Stop her going down the aisle feeling quite so triumphant. I did think that way the marriage would be a lot less likely to last. If I couldn't stop her marrying Oliver, I could make sure she divorced him pretty damn quick. Which I was sure she would.'

'So you told your father he had to change his will?'

'Yes. I just don't know why I didn't think of it before. I went to see him, down in Palm Beach, and I told him everything, and he agreed to do it. He's a very – amenable old man.'

'I can see that,' said James, thinking of the almost psychotic adoration that the letter had exuded.

'And I thought I would just let Cressida know.'

'On the night before the wedding? That was unspeakable. Cruel.'

'Oh really, James. You can say that still, in the light of what she did to you? How blind you all are about her. She's rotten, James, thoroughly rotten. And you're all taken in by her, by that sweet little face, those charming little ways. All of you. Except maybe that old Merlin fellow. He seemed to see through her. Anyway, when I went up to say goodnight to her – maybe you'll remember – I showed her the letter. She just read it in silence, there was no reaction whatsoever, she just threw it onto the bed. And then she said "Goodnight, Julia" and went over to the dressing table and started cleaning her face. And I picked up the letter and went out, and that was the last time, thank God, I ever saw her. But obviously she decided after all that it wasn't worth it . . .'

'No,' said James, slowly, 'even then surely she wouldn't have decided not to go through with the wedding. Surely. It's just – oh, I can't believe it, Julia. I can't believe any of it.'

Julia shrugged. 'Well, the facts speak for themselves, I think. I can only tell you that I think this is the happiest outcome. Under the circumstances. For us all. Even you. And of course you will remain quiet about it. About what I did.'

'Of course I won't,' said James. 'Why should I? I shall make quite sure that everyone knows –'

'Yes, James? Yes? Knows what?'

And then he realized that of course he would have to remain silent; that he was trapped into silence by the possible truth of the story, and indeed by what was unarguably the truth of much that had happened anyway; that Cressida had in fact run away, on her wedding day, to marry someone else, for whatever reasons, had betrayed and savaged them all, and the more of the story that could remain in obscurity the better.

'I'm going,' he said heavily. 'Home to Maggie. To tell her – I don't know what. Does – does Josh know about all this?'

'No, of course not. He's such a fool, James. He'd just start babbling it out. And he wouldn't understand. Nor would Oliver. Oliver is so much happier this morning. Really, James, you should be grateful to me. She is no loss to any of us. I know it's painful to recognize, but if she never comes back, that will be a very, very great blessing.'

'Julia,' said James, 'Julia, I don't know how you can even think that, let alone say it. You must surely know that to a parent a child is always welcomed, always loved, whatever it has done. We forgive our children anything, anything at all. If we are human. Which I begin to doubt you are. Goodbye, Julia. I hope we never have to meet again.'

Chapter 33

Harriet 11:30am

'How about if I slept with you?' said Harriet pleasantly.

'I beg your pardon?'

'I said how about if I slept with you. You know, went to bed with you, had sex, that kind of thing. Would that make any difference? Change your decision?'

'Miss Forrest, I do assure you – that is, I –'

'Well, would it?' She smiled sweetly at him.

He was visibly flushed, beads of sweat on his pale forehead. He shifted uneasily in his seat. 'Miss Forrest –'

'I'm told I'm not entirely without talent in that area. It wouldn't be that bad – oh, Mr Carter, don't look so frightened. I find it insulting. Of course I'm not serious. Well, I don't think I am. I suppose if you'd agreed to a further two million I might have been. But I can see you wouldn't. Sorry, Mr Carter. Bad joke. Bad.'

Geoffrey Carter visibly relaxed. He wiped his forehead with his initialled handkerchief, eased his slightly over-floral tie. He had not enjoyed the past half-hour; the past half-minute had been very bad for him indeed. The training he had been given in business banking had just about equipped him for telling highly attractive and patently emotional young women that their business futures were over for the foreseeable future; what it had not equipped him for was to deal with sexual propositioning.

Harriet smiled at him. The past half-minute had quite cheered her up. 'I understand. You're only doing your job. And throwing good money after bad is clearly not what the bank would see as doing it. Oh well. What next?'

'Well, I'm afraid I have no alternative but to appoint a receiver.'

'And what precisely will he do? This receiver?'

Geoffrey Carter cleared his throat. 'Well, he'll arrive at your company some time later today.'

'Today!' said Harriet, thinking of her staff, her beloved, loyal, self-sacrificing staff, who had taken salary cuts, worked uncomplainingly harder as she laid the less vital amongst them off, refused, in two cases, tempting offers, who had no idea that this final awful thing was to happen. 'Why today? Why so soon? It's brutal. Horrible.'

'I'm afraid this is a rather brutal world, Miss Forrest. But, well, you see, the thing is that in some cases people have been known to dispatch their employees with equipment and other assests, such as company cars. Now I'm sure you wouldn't think –'

'What a good idea,' said Harriet cheerfully. 'I'd never have thought of that. Thank you, Mr Carter. Don't look like that, it's all right, I'm only joking.'

'Yes. Yes, of course. And he will also want the keys to the building. He will lock it up, to safeguard it. We will also, of course, be calling in any personal guarantees, which includes your flat, and inform your debtors and creditors.'

'I have a lot of both,' said Harriet. 'And if the debtors had behaved a bit better I wouldn't be here now. Well, I might be, but – anyway, Mr Carter, thank you for at least listening to me. How long have I got?'

'No longer at all, I'm afraid, Miss Forrest. You are legally obliged to cease trading as from now. I'm sorry.'

'Mr Carter, you don't want to go to the toilet or anything, do you?'

'I beg your pardon?' said Geoffrey Carter. The sweat broke out again, this time under the armpits of his monogrammed cotton polyester City Style shirt.

'There's a last call I really would like to make. You don't have to pay for it, I have a charge card.'

'Well, I –'

'Please Mr Carter, you've drunk all that tea. Just a few moments –'

Geoffrey Carter began to feel he really did need the lavatory; a churning was taking place somewhere in his stomach. He took a deep breath. Harriet smiled at him encouragingly. 'Mr Carter?'

He stood up. She could have sworn he almost smiled. 'Miss Forrest,

I will just go and – ask my secretary to get the receiver on the phone. I won't be more than a moment.'

'Thank you, Mr Carter. You're a star. I'll take you to lunch at the Caprice if – well, I'll take you anyway.'

Geoffrey Carter hurried out of the office; Harriet rang the studio. 'Kitty? It's me. Nothing from Cotton Fields?'

'No. I'm sorry, Harry. Nothing at all. Theo Buchan rang though. He's ringing back. What shall I –'

'Just tell him to go away and leave me alone,' said Harriet. She felt totally dispirited; her emotions resembled a foot that had gone to sleep, as Nanny Horrocks used to call it. In time, no doubt, the pain would start, shooting, agonizing pain, but just now she felt nothing, only a great swollen numbness.

Geoffrey Carter came back into the room, complete with secretary, presumably, she thought, more as chaperone than anything else. He looked at her warily, clearly nervous of what she might say or do next. 'Right, Miss Forrest. I presume you have no further – observations to make?'

'No,' said Harriet, 'none at all.'

'I think that's all then. I'll call the receiver now.'

'Yes,' said Harriet, 'er – thank you.' She sat staring at him, as he lifted the phone, wondered if she was actually going to throw up all over the desk. She picked up the file on his desk: her file, labelled 'Harriet Forrest – Harry's Fashion Retail Business', and the life of Harry's began to roll before her eyes, in painfully slow motion: the tiny shop in Wandsworth, the twenty-four-hour shifts she worked all on her own, her head aching, fighting sleep; the exhilaration of her very first sale, the rapture of reading her first editorial: 'Harriet Forrest's designs show a clean-cut originality, an extraordinarily daring sense of colour. Do go and visit her small treasure trove of a shop, Harry's, in newly fashionable Wandsworth High Street for coordinated casual classics . . .'

And then there had been the next shop, and the next, full of eager customers, and the shock of excitement at realizing she really did have something to offer that people wanted; and hiring staff, doing cash flows, more sleepless nights, raising money, putting it to work, feeling the ideas burgeon, grow, more shops, bigger shops, her own small factory, the design studio, her first modest show – oh, that show, with

Tilly gliding down the studio, laughing, on the catwalk that the four of them, she and Tilly and Rufus and Mungo, had built right through the night, people clapping, actually standing up and clapping.

And then moving into Paris, Paris! home of fashion, the heady wonder of girls in Paris wanting, buying her clothes. By then there had been Theo too, taking hold of her life, turning it upside-down, loving her, driving her to all kinds of new intensities, making her happy as she had never been before, and disturbed and disorientated too, and then – shit – and then overreaching herself, getting into trouble. Real trouble. And it wasn't the fault of the clothes, her lovely, witty, charming, beautifully cut, perfectly coordinating clothes, nor of Theo for distracting her, taking her mind from its total concentration; it was her fault, her fault for being vain and self-important and egotistical. She had let them all down, everyone who worked for her, who had lent her money, encouraged her, praised her, supported her; failed them through her own foolishness. She deserved this, she thought, this moment of absolute misery and humiliation, deserved it well.

She looked at Geoffrey Carter and his secretary, and they were blurred, and so was the paper as she looked down at it, and a great tear fell on her file and smudged the label. 'Sorry,' she said, groping for a tissue, blotting at the paper, and had just wiped her face with the same tissue when Geoffrey Carter's other phone rang. She stopped, froze; it might, it just might be Cotton Fields. Miracles did still happen. Even to the undeserving.

'Geoffrey Carter. Yes. Yes, she's here. I'll just see if –' He looked at Harriet rather uncertainly. 'It's a Mr Buchan. Mr Theodore Buchan. He wants to speak to you.'

'Tell him I'd rather die,' said Harriet firmly, putting the file down.

'Miss Forrest can't speak to you at the moment, she's – oh, I see. Ah, yes of course. Yes. Miss Forrest, Mr Buchan says he would like to put the necessary money into your company. Er – will you speak to him now?'

'Tell him I'd still rather die,' said Harriet and turned and walked out of the office, feeling that just for one moment the whole dreadful thing had been worthwhile.

Chapter 34

Tilly 12 noon

'I hope you're good at sweet-talking,' said the cab driver to Tilly. They were sitting in a traffic jam on the A4. Heathrow was two miles away; it might as well have been two hundred.

'I am,' said Tilly, 'but how long do you reckon now?'

'Well – I could try the back doubles, go round the back of the airport. If we're lucky, fifteen minutes. But there's no telling really, you never know in this game. And that'll be only fifteen before you fly.'

'That'll be OK,' said Tilly. 'I've phoned them, and I have an instant check-in gold card, you know? They know I'm going to be late. I've no luggage, it'll be fine. Yeah, try the back doubles. And just keep going, OK? Never say die, that's my motto.'

'Wish it was never say fly,' said the cabbie and spent the next five minutes patently enjoying his own joke. Tilly smiled politely and lit a cigarette; he turned round, looking pained. 'Don't do that if you don't mind, love,' he said, 'I'm a non-smoker, there's a sign up in the cab, and it makes me feel sick. Can't concentrate, you see. And with the passive smoking and all that, I don't want to –'

'OK, OK. Sorry,' said Tilly and stubbed it out again.

She didn't really feel calm, she felt sick and her head ached. What the hell was she putting herself through this for? Why was she tearing herself away from London, which she loved so much, and Rufus, whom she loved so much, to go and sign a contract to do a lot of boring things: beauty sessions were always the least fun, and there were going to be endless in-store events and God knew what else, personal appearances everywhere, videos: hell on earth. She must be mad.

'No, I'm not actually,' said Tilly aloud. 'I'm not.'

'What's that, love?'

'Nothing,' said Tilly and spent the next ten minutes rehearsing the reasons for her lack of madness: James Forrest's treatment of her mother, her intense, almost fanatical desire to be her own mistress, unarguably in charge of her own life, her recognition of Rufus's undoubted parentage, and finally, and probably most importantly, her total unsuitability to be Mrs Rufus Headleigh Drayton. She had to go: she had no choice. And she could help Harriet, give her some money, and she'd get over Rufus much more quickly and – and – God, she didn't want to go. She just didn't want to go. 'Fuck,' she said aloud. 'Sorry, Rufus. Sorry.'

The back double way was clear; but then the tunnel was jammed. 'You sure you've got this right?' said the driver. 'Sounds funny to me. Usually Terminal Four for the States.'

'Yes, yes, it's Air America,' said Tilly irritably. 'It's OK, we'll make it. Maybe I should get out and run.'

'Don't. You'll be had up.'

It was seven minutes to twelve when she finally shot into the departures terminal, tore over to the information desk. The girl was charmingly helpful. 'That's OK, Miss Mills, we've been expecting you. Just go right over to departures and through. Gate thirty-nine. Have a good trip.'

The man at departures was slightly less helpful and a lot less charming. 'Final call ten minutes ago,' he said.

'I'm sorry,' said Tilly, handing him her boarding card. 'I'm really sorry.'

'You should be, they're practically holding the plane for you.'

'I run fast. I'll make it. Here's my boarding card and here's my – shit, where is it, where's the bloody thing? Hold on, I have it, I have it, it never leaves this bag, it's here, it has to be . . .'

She turned the leather rucksack upside-down, shook the contents out onto the man's desk; her wallet opened, coins spattered every-where, mingling with the chewing gum, the make-up, the cigarettes, Polaroids from recent sessions, the odd battered Tampax – it would have been funny if it hadn't been so awful. But no passport. For her passport, she realized, staring at the mess on the desk, must still be in Merlin Reid's Lagonda (placed, she remembered now, on the dashboard shelf as she rummaged for his second beer) and it was two minutes to twelve and she heard her name now on the tannoy: 'Would Ottoline Mills, passenger to New York on American Airlines Flight 279, proceed immediately to gate thirty-nine.' But the man was shaking his head, saying she couldn't proceed anywhere, not without a passport, couldn't go through, no, couldn't even try, it was more than his job was worth. And so it was that as Rufus Headleigh Drayton came haring into the terminal, knocking over an elderly Asian cleaning lady and picking her up with most uncharacteristic brusqueness, as he looked up and saw the words 'Flight Closed on Air American Flight 279 to New York' on the indicator, and as he uttered a loud roar of despair that made everyone in the vicinity stare at him, and draw their baggage and their children closer to them, Tilly Mills appeared before him as if in a vision, clutching what looked like the contents of an entire rubbish bin in her arms, and said, 'Fu – I mean good gracious, Rufus, what on earth are you doing here?'

They went and rescued his Porsche from a double yellow line (no warden, the fates were famously kind to Rufus) and drove extremely fast and in complete silence out onto the hideous wastelands of the A4, rather more slowly up to the concrete mountains of what the traffic officials call the elevated section of the M4, and eventually reached the long car park that is the Cromwell Road extension, where finally Rufus spoke.

'I still can't believe you did that,' he said.

'Did what?'

'Oh, for God's sake, Tilly, do I have to spell it out to you?'

'Yes you do. Traffic's moving, Rufus.'

She got out a cigarette and lit it; Rufus sighed and wound down his window. 'You know I hate you smoking in the car,' he said, 'I hate you smoking altogether, but particularly in the car.'

'First the cab driver, then you,' said Tilly. 'I think I might get out and walk.'

'If you like,' said Rufus, glaring at her. 'Shall I stop?'

'You'd better,' said Tilly, 'if you're not going to hit the car in front of you.'

'Fuck,' said Rufus and hit the brakes just in time.

'I've never seen you in a temper before,' said Tilly thoughtfully.

'I've never been angry with you before.'

'But why, Rufus, why? Why are you so angry?'

'Oh, for God's sake, Tilly. I can't believe you're that stupid. There are several things actually. First you just take this decision, all on your own, without consulting me, to sign this ridiculous contract and go and live in New York. Then you're so bloody full of your own problems you don't even notice I have some that I want to talk to you about. Plus you persist in this ridiculous obsession that a marriage between us couldn't ever work, when you really ought to see that I'm the best judge of that. It's outrageous, Tilly, the way you shut me out, just go on your own sweet way, do what you think is best. I'm absolutely fucking fed up with it.'

'Rufus,' said Tilly, 'that's the second time you've used that word in five minutes. I thought you hated it. You'll be smoking next.'

'I might be driven to it,' said Rufus.

Tilly was silent. She reached out to put the radio on; Rufus pushed her hand away. 'And don't do that either. I cannot face that bloody mindless rubbish you listen to.'

'Dear, dear,' said Tilly. She was beginning to find it all rather funny.

'And don't patronize me.'

'Rufus, I'm not patronizing you.'

'Yes you are. That's what all this is about. You deciding you know best for us without even consulting me. It's horrible. It's unkind and it's insulting. I hate it.'

'All right,' said Tilly, 'I get the idea. Rufus –'

'Just shut up,' he said, 'just don't say anything.'

'Where are we going?'

'To my flat.'

'Oh.'

She sat in silence for a minute, then with a sickening thud remembered Susie, Susie sick and frightened and going to hospital. 'Shit, Rufus, I'm so sorry. I'd forgotten about your mum. Is she going to be all right?'

'Yes, thank God,' he said, sounding more normal suddenly, more himself. 'Well, we think so. The surgeon is – what shall we say? – cautiously optimistic. Anyway –'

'And she didn't say anything about it before?'

'No.'

'Brave lady.'

'Yes,' said Rufus briefly.

His jaw was very tightly clenched, his eyes fixed determinedly on the traffic ahead. Tilly put her hand tentatively on his knee.

'Don't,' he said, 'don't do that. I can't stand it.'

'Rufus, I'm not at all sure I want to go to your flat. With you in this mood.'

'You'll do what I decide,' he said. 'For once. I spend my life doing what you say, having to abide by your decisions. And I've decided we're going to my flat.'

'Oh, all right,' said Tilly meekly.

Rufus's flat was in Brook Green, ten minutes' drive from Chiswick Mall. Tilly had often teased him about being tied to his mother's apron strings. It was a very nice flat, charmingly furnished by Susie, kept spick and span by Susie's cleaning lady; for the hundredth, the thousandth time, looking round at the furniture (Victorian), the pictures (watercolours), the photographs (family groups, silver-framed), the gleaming wooden floors, the flourishing plants, Tilly wondered how Rufus could possibly imagine she could be moved into this world that he inhabited so easily and unquestioningly, its tribal customs so clearly defined, its tribal members so carefully initiated; and she decided also for the hundredth, the thousandth time, that she absolutely couldn't.

'Rufus, I really must phone Felicity. She'll be so cross with me.'

'Yes, of course.' He was still tense with rage. Tilly looked at him and then went to the phone. This was proving an extremely uncomfortable morning.

Felicity was cross: so cross Tilly was quite startled. 'The Rosenthal people have a reception committee laid on for you, and an incredible programme. It's appalling, Tilly, what am I going to tell them?'

'Felicity, I don't know. Tell them I got sick or something. I'm so sorry.'

'It's so unprofessional. So unlike you, Tilly. I just can't think what's got into you.'

'Felicity, I said I'm sorry. Anyone can make a mistake.'

'People being paid two million dollars don't make mistakes, Tilly. They just don't. Look, I'll see if I can organize a flight for tomorrow. Can you get your passport back by then?'

'Yeah, I – I think so.'

'OK, I'll call you later. Where are you?'

'Um – in Rufus's flat. You have the number. I'm really really sorry, Felicity.'

Felicity had put the phone down.

'I'll make some coffee,' said Rufus, 'but first I'd like to call the hospital again.'

'Of course.'

He made the call, looked at her slightly more cheerfully. 'She's fine. I said I'd go in later. She sent her love.'

'Ah,' said Tilly. Then, 'She's great,' she said carefully, 'I really really like her. I can see why you love her so much.'

'Yes, well. I –'

'What?'

'Oh, it doesn't matter.'

'Is your dad there with her?'

'Yes,' said Rufus briefly. Then he said, 'Actually, he's not my dad.'

Tilly was silent; she didn't say anything, anything at all, just looked at him, her face carefully blank.

'Excuse me,' he said, 'I'll just get that coffee.'

He was a while; he came back looking suspiciously moist-eyed, sat down on the leather chesterfield by the window.

Tilly went over, sat down, took his hand. 'Do you want to tell me about it?'

'Yes,' he said, and for the first time that morning he looked at her without hostility, without anger. 'Yes please, Tilly, I do.'

He told her: how he had heard his mother and James Forrest talking late the evening before, how he felt, shattered, betrayed, totally bewildered.

'I just can't believe it, Tilly, you know? I can't. She's always been so lovely, so perfect –'

'Nobody's perfect,' said Tilly evenly.

'She was. For me. And now – I just feel so disorientated. As if everything I thought, everything I knew, was wrong. I think if you told me the earth was flat I'd believe you today. And my father – I mean Alistair – oh God, I don't know, Tilly: how must he feel? Such a fool, so betrayed, how has he stood it all these years? I hate it all so much, it's so different from everything I thought – oh God, I'm not making any sense, am I? I'm sorry. But, oh Tilly, I needed you so much, to tell me what to think, what to do. And you weren't there for me, and I couldn't stand it.'

He stared at her, his eyes full of such bewilderment Tilly's own filled with tears. She reached out, touched his face very gently, leant forward, kissed him lightly on the lips; and all the time her mind was racing, flailing around, trying frantically to work out what to say, what would best help him.

'Listen,' she said carefully, finally, 'listen. This is what I think. Which is not telling you what to think. I think your mother is just great. OK, so she's been unfaithful to your dad. That's not the biggest thing in a marriage. Not really. Your dad isn't a fool, he must have known. Don't tell me he didn't, Rufus, that really is like thinking the earth's flat. He must have known and he must have decided she was worth it. Which I think she most certainly is. It hasn't made her less good to you, has it? It hasn't suddenly meant all these years she hasn't loved you and cared for you and changed your shitty nappies – although I suppose Nanny did that for you –'

'Sometimes,' said Rufus with a faint smile.

'OK, and she wiped your snotty nose and drove you to your poncey school every day, and read you bedtime stories and made sure you knew the facts of life, and laughed at your jokes and listened to your troubles, and furnished this bloody place for you and made it so perfect it scares the fuck out of me. Didn't she, Rufus? It didn't stop her being brave enough not to tell you all about her cancer, and not making a fuss yesterday when she must have been shitting herself, sorry, Rufus, and it didn't stop her being out of her head because she didn't know where you were this morning. She's still the same person, nothing's changed –'

'Yes,' he said, 'yes, it has changed, of course it has.'

'Only if you let it. Listen. This time yesterday you were the nicest, cleverest, best-adjusted most – fuck it, sorry, Rufus, but I have to say it – most decent person I ever met. Has that changed? Has it? Not at all. You're still that person, and it was your mother made you that person. Don't be too hard on her, Rufus. You don't know what made her do what she did. But she's never let you down. You or any of the rest of that spoilt tribe of yours. Which includes your father. Yes, your father, he's your father, he raised you, as they say where I come from, not that self-important, jumped-up –'

She stopped. Rufus was looking at her oddly.

'You don't like him, do you? James?'

'No,' said Tilly flatly, 'I don't. But I like him a lot better now I know he's your dad. How's that?'

'That sounds – interesting. Oh God, Tilly, I wish I could think it was all as simple as you make it, but –' He got up, walked round the room in silence. He seemed filled with a feverish distress. Tilly watched, wishing as she had never wished for anything that she could help him, do, say something positive, something healing. He sat down again, took her hand, sighed, looking down at it. 'Maybe I will in time. Right now – oh God, I don't know, I just can't. See it that way. I can't have it how I want it, how I thought it was, and that's that. It's so bloody hard to come to terms with. I wish I had your pragmatism. Maybe you can teach it to me.'

'I would if I knew what it meant,' said Tilly.

Rufus laughed suddenly; he looked better, the colour had come back into his face. 'Oh Tilly, Tilly, why couldn't you have done this for me last night?'

'Because I'm a self-centred bitch,' said Tilly cheerfully. 'Rufus, could we possibly go to bed?'

She fell asleep briefly afterwards, worn out with love, with care, with soaring, singing, wonderful sex. She woke to see him sitting on the bed looking at her.

'I love you,' he said.

'I love you too.'

'Tilly, what happened yesterday? What happened, for God's sake, that you suddenly felt it – us – was so impossible? You've got to tell me, we've got to talk about it. It wasn't – it wasn't the contract, was it?' He gazed at her, his dark eyes full of pain; it was clearly what he most dreaded.

'No,' said Tilly, 'no, it wasn't the contract. Honestly.'

'Well, what was it then?'

Tilly looked at him. She thought of James Forrest, of how she had hated him for as long as she had been able to understand what he had done: of what he had put her mother through, of her grief and pain, her guilt and her ruined health, and what James Forrest could have done to make their lives easier, with a little compassion and generosity and honesty. She thought of her mother, toiling in the sweatshop, sewing sequins onto dresses for twelve hours a day, and she thought of the small plaque with 'Beatrice Mills' on it, all the result of bungling, of incompetence, of dishonesty and cowardice. And she thought of Rufus being the son of this man, and she hardly knew how to bear it.

'Well, Rufus, you see, it's very complicated,' she said. 'There's something –' And then she thought of how much he must have endured himself, making the discovery about his mother, his father and the man he had always thought to be his father, the man he adored and idolized, and how he would feel if she added to the knowledge of his beloved mother's adultery by telling him that the man who was truly his father had done this awful thing to her and her family. And she knew she could never tell him, that it would be the depths of cruelty, brutal, awful cruelty, to tell him, she must not, could not do it; she sat there, staring at him, at the bewilderment, the pain in his eyes, and love held her silent, love helped her to lie.

'I suppose,' she said carefully and truthfully, 'I suppose I panicked. You know. I'm so frightened of getting married, Rufus, of having to totally belong to anyone, it isn't just that it's you, although a lot of it is that it's you –'

'Thanks,' he said, amusement and hurt mixing on his face.

'Please, Rufus, listen, try to understand.'

'I am listening, I am trying to understand.'

'OK. I just get so scared when I think of that degree of handing over. You know?'

'No,' he said, 'I don't know.'

'Look,' she said, taking his hand, 'look. It's all right now. I love you,

you love me, we have a great time, we have wonderful sex, it's all perfect. What could anyone want more than that?'

'I want to know you're there for me. Always. I want you to know I'm there for you. That's what marriage is, in my book. A commitment. A total commitment. It's saying look, everyone, we're an entity. Not just two people having a good time.'

'That's what I'm scared of.'

'But why? What can go wrong?'

'Life,' she said, 'and if it does go wrong, I want to decide how to put it right.'

'And why can't we do that together?'

'Because I want to deal with life my way. It's so important to me, Rufus, to be able to do what I think best, and not have to ask, fit in, say "would it be all right if". I need to be in control. Of everything. To be able to run my life on my terms. I suppose it's seeing my mum all those years, not in control, forced to do awful demeaning things –'

'Tilly,' said Rufus gently, 'you're not seeing this thing straight. What took your mother out of control of your life was the sort of person she was. Not her situation. If you'd been in her position, you'd have got it all sorted in no time. You wouldn't have been doing demeaning things, as you put it. Whether you'd been on your own or not, had me, had a baby to care for or not. You'd have been running the dressmaking business or whatever it was, no time at all. And I'd have been standing on the sidelines cheering.'

'No, no, you don't understand,' said Tilly. 'You're being dense, Rufus.'

'Maybe I am. Try again.'

'Listen, you might not have wanted me to run the dressmaking business. Or you might have wanted it run differently from how I was going to do it. That's what I'm scared of. Having to fit in, compromise. Surely you understand that.'

'I do understand,' said Rufus, 'and it's you being dense. Stubborn. Stupid. And besides, Tilly, where does all that leave love? If you love someone, surely you have to fit in and compromise anyway. Because you care about that person, what they think, what they need. Is it really worth being able to run the whole world your way if you're doing it on your own, with no one to turn to when things get tough, no one to talk to at the end of the day, no one to care about, to care for? I just don't see the connection.'

'Well, you wouldn't,' said Tilly crossly, 'you're in control of your life, always will be.'

'Oh, really?' he said. 'You say that to me now, when I'm falling apart, when I have all this wretched situation to cope with? Do you really think I can sort all this mess out on my own? Of course I can't. Maybe I can with your help. But not on my own.'

'That's what I mean,' she said in an agony, 'I don't want to be dependent. Even emotionally. Even on you.'

'But you have to be dependent when you love someone. You can't take them out of the equation, by refusing to commit yourself to them. Not if they're there at all. You can cut them completely out of your life, but that's the only way. And where's the sense in that, the happiness, keeping them at arm's length, not letting them near you? It just doesn't work. The only way you can be independent is never to care for anyone. Where's the joy in that, Tilly? It seems pretty sterile and miserable to me.'

'You don't understand,' she said again, growing angry now. 'You just don't.'

'All right, I don't. Let's leave that one for now. Let's look at the other nonsense, shall we? About this obsession that you're not good enough for me.'

'Not *not* good enough,' she said indignantly, 'just terribly different.'

'Wonderfully wonderfully different. That's good, it's healthy. I don't want to marry a clone. Which is what you seem to think. I want to marry *you*, Tilly. I love you and you love me. That's what matters.'

'No, Rufus, it isn't. What matters is what you are, how you are. And however I'm going to fit into all this. You need a proper wife, Rufus, someone who'll say all the right things, in the right accent to the right people. Not a jumped-up black girl from Brixton.'

'You are amazingly bigoted,' he said, smiling at her, 'and you're sounding so terribly out of date.' (Someone else had said that to her, what seemed like years ago: who was it, who was it?) 'You're not a jumped-up black girl from Brixton, you're one of the most beautiful women in the world. No contest, as you would say. And I have somehow managed to make you fall in love with me. You could have any man you wanted, and for some inexplicable reason you've settled on me. It's me that should be feeling panicky and scared. Not you. Now get real, Tilly, as you would also say, I think, and stop talking this bloody prejudiced rubbish.'

Tilly stared at him. 'But Rufus, you don't' – she said, and then she remembered who'd said these things earlier that day, her mother: 'We're in the nineties, Tilly, you're sounding very out of date.' And she remembered something else her mother had said, that she should try to drop her obsession about James Forrest and what he had done. She sat there, thinking, very carefully and clearly, thinking about what Rufus had said, knowing it was quite possibly true, all of it, that love, real love as she knew she felt for Rufus, was worth giving up her independence for (albeit not without a fight, lots of fights, probably), that love could maybe even teach her somehow to be a good, supportive wife to him, even persuade her to give a dinner party once in a while, say the right important things to the right important people; but thinking too about the greatest reason for her inability to commit herself to him, the one she hadn't even known about twenty-four hours earlier, about James Forrest, who had dominated her life for so long; and she didn't want to let that go, let him go, let him get away with it, this monster of a man. It hurt, the very thought of it, it was like giving something away that had been important to her ever since she could remember. But then, she thought, was her mother right, saying that it was no longer important, that it was in the past, that no good could come of her pursuing him? Would it really help her, help any of them, publicly to humiliate James Forrest, castigate him in the press? Wouldn't it just hurt Rufus further, and her mother, and indeed herself? But – well – maybe – if – 'Shit,' she said aloud. 'Oh shit.'

'Tilly,' said Rufus, very gently, 'Tilly, please, please, Tilly, will you marry me? I love you so very much. And I need you so much too, more than ever now. You can't not marry me. And you can go on smoking and saying fuck and listening to that dreadful music and you can stay independent, go where you like, do what you like, make all the important decisions in our lives if you really want to, and you needn't have any babies, but please, please marry me.'

Tilly looked at him, in silence; and still she couldn't quite do it, couldn't quite give it all away. And after another moment or two a terrible sadness came into his eyes and he stood up, visibly withdrawing from her.

'You'd better go,' he said, 'I really think you'd better go.'

The phone rang, sharply; Rufus answered it.

'Hallo. Yes, she's here, Felicity. Hold on. It's for you,' he said to Tilly. His voice was very heavy.

'Hi,' said Tilly. 'What? Oh I see. Well –' She looked at Rufus, and he was picking up her clothes from the floor where she had thrown them as she had feverishly dragged them off an hour earlier; he was folding them up very carefully and neatly, and then he suddenly sighed and sat down, hugging them to him, staring at them as if he was holding her for the last time, and 'Felicity,' she said, 'Felicity, I don't know quite how you're going to take this, but I've changed my mind. I'm not going to New York. Please tell them how sorry I am, will you? And – what? Oh, I see. Well, let's just put it this way, Felicity, I'm going to get married. Rufus, for fu – for heaven's sake, Rufus, that's a Joseph T-shirt you're blowing your nose on . . .'

Chapter 35

Harriet Midday

'I'm so sorry,' said Jennifer Bradman. 'How dreadful for you.'

'Thank you,' said Harriet. The morning had taken on a surreal air; she was having difficulty in properly realizing that the rather dazzling and glamorous Mrs Bradman, who did not conform too closely to the traditional image of a gynaecologist, was referring to Cressida's disappearance rather than the death of her company. 'It was – is – terrible actually.'

'Your parents must be so upset.'

'Yes, they are. We all are. And I'm here because – well, I'm just looking for clues really. To where she might have gone. And why. I know you're not supposed to talk to me but –'

'Oh, don't worry about that,' said Jennifer Bradman. 'This is an exceptional case. Besides, I won't be giving away any secrets, or indeed helping you very much, when I say first that your sister was a very mixed-up girl, and second I'm afraid I don't have the faintest idea where she is.'

'But she was – pregnant this time?'

'Oh, definitely. About fourteen weeks. And wretchedly sick, poor girl.' She looked at Harriet sharply. 'Why do you say this time?'

'Because I found a letter from you, saying that she wasn't pregnant last year. That's how I found you. Not that any of us knew anything about it.'

'I see. That was a very strange thing,' said Jennifer Bradman. 'It was a genuine phantom, if that is not a contradiction in terms. They do happen, you know. She had every symptom, her periods had stopped, her breasts were swollen, she was being terribly sick –'

'She's always had a dodgy tummy,' said Harriet. 'Ever since she was quite a little girl. Anything remotely difficult and Cressida started throwing up.'

'Yes, well, it goes with the syndrome.'

'What syndrome?'

'Of a hysterical personality. Which is what I would say she suffered from. Did she have other health problems?'

'Oh God, yes,' said Harriet. 'She was allergic to dairy products, she could only wear cotton next to her skin, you name it, she had it.'

'Ah yes. And the dysmenorrhoea – painful periods –'

'Yes,' said Harriet, thinking of the countless dinners, tennis games, picnics, cycle rides that had had to be cancelled while Cressida lay white-faced, unarguably in pain, a hot-water bottle on her tummy, Maggie sitting by her, stroking her head. 'So – um, what happened with the phantom pregnancy?'

'Well, she was desperately upset. When it proved not to be a pregnancy. She came to me, telling me she and her fiancé were about to be married anyway –'

'This was last September or thereabouts?'

'Er – October,' said Jennifer Bradman, consulting her notes. 'She was just off to New York to see him anyway. She was excited, happy, in spite of feeling so wretched. But when I examined her, I found that in spite of the other symptoms her uterus was not at all enlarged. I did a test – negative. She broke down. Became actually quite hysterical. I couldn't understand it at all. She told me there was a history of infertility in her – in your family, that your mother had had to have all kinds of treatment before becoming pregnant, and she was terrified that the same thing was going to happen to her.'

'Total garbage,' said Harriet. She felt very angry suddenly, without being sure why. 'I'm absolutely sure my mother never had to have any kind of fertility treatment, and Cressida wasn't even engaged to Oliver then. She really is – oh, I don't know –'

'I can see this is all very hard for you,' said Mrs Bradman gently. 'As I told you, she has, I believe, a very complex personality. She displayed a lot of what I think the psychiatrists would call histrionic behaviour. Even this flying is a classic indication. Of a desire for escape, for getting away from everything.' She smiled at Harriet suddenly. 'It sounds very corny, I know, but it's true.'

'So what does that mean exactly? With relation to what happened yesterday?'

'It means, I would guess, that she simply couldn't cope with life. All of it. Not just with regard to yesterday, but to everything. Running away like that – I think again the technical term is a hysterical fugue.'

'You seem to know a lot about it,' said Harriet.

'Yes, well, I'm married to a psychiatrist. It tends to rub off. Oh dear, I'm rather aware I'm not being very constructive. I do wish I could help more. I wish I could have helped your sister more. I did suggest she had some sort of help, counselling perhaps, but she refused.'

'Really?' said Harriet.

'Yes. I even suggested she came to see me with her mother, or you – she spoke about you quite a lot.'

'Really?' said Harriet again, genuinely surprised, almost startled.

'Oh yes. She's terribly fond of you. She admires you a great deal. And I would say she's very – what shall I say? – overawed by you. By your success. She feels she has a lot to live up to.'

'I can't think why,' said Harriet, 'she was always the favourite, always the perfect daughter. Never in trouble.'

'That's not the impression I got. She seemed to feel herself a failure.'

'Well, that's absurd,' said Harriet, 'of course she wasn't. And she was making this wonderful marriage, everyone was over the moon about it, and her –'

'Miss Forrest,' said Jennifer Bradman, 'whether or not we are failures depends on our own self-perception, our self-image. And I would say your sister's self-image was not very good.'

'I see,' said Harriet slowly. Cressida seemed to be falling into fragments, in front of her eyes, re-forming differently, awkwardly.

'You see,' said Jennifer Bradman, 'this kind of thing, this running away, is very often a cry for help. An alternative to suicide if you like.'

'But –' Harriet paused. She didn't really want to get into a complex discussion with the slightly daunting Jennifer Bradman, to confess to any more perfidy on Cressida's behalf, start telling her about the photograph, the other wedding.

'I'm simply trying to help you find explanations – understandable explanations,' said Mrs Bradman. 'The human personality, Miss Forrest, even at its most healthy, is a very complex thing. And Cressida's was not entirely heathy.'

'No,' said Harriet, 'no, I can see that. But – she didn't give you any indication that there was a problem with – with this pregnancy?'

'No, not at all. She seemed very happy about it. In spite of feeling so unwell. Mind you, the approaching wedding must have been something of a strain for her. Under the circumstances. Why do you ask?'

'Oh, nothing,' said Harriet. She suddenly felt sickened by the whole thing, wanted to get away from Jennifer Bradman and her reasonable, pragmatic approach. 'I just wondered. But you did say she was happy about it –'

'Oh, very happy. And her fiancé was delighted too, I understand. Hoping for a boy!'

'Oh really?' said Harriet. 'I didn't know that. I don't think he did either.'

She reached Covent Garden just before one; her studio, converted from one of the old warehouses, was on the first floor, just off the central piazza. She stood outside it looking up, thinking how much she loved it, how much it meant to her, how it was truly home to her (and she was going to mind losing it a great deal more than she would her flat), and that this was the last time she would ever come back to it as hers, that in future it would be literally barred to her, the locks changed, strangers inside, and – 'Shit,' she said aloud, recognizing the car parked on the double yellow line outside her door, recognizing the large figure at the wheel, and turned away, ready to run, but he was out of it, had grabbed her arm.

'Harriet,' he said.

'Theo, go away.'

'Harriet, I just have to talk to you.'

'Theo, there's nothing to talk about.'

'There's a great deal to talk about.'

'No, Theo, there isn't. And let go of my arm, or I shall scream and have you up for assault.'

'The way London is these days,' he said, 'no one would take the slightest notice of your screaming. I'm certainly prepared to take my chance on it. I don't think I look too much like a rapist.'

Harriet looked at him: he was immaculately dressed, as always, his huge frame oddly elegant in a grey pinstripe suit, cream shirt, silk tie –

even in her rage and misery Harriet found herself noticing the print of the tie, half floral, half abstract, thinking how good it was.

'That's a very naive remark,' she said coolly. 'Rapists come in all shapes and sizes, you know.'

'Yes,' he said, suddenly subdued, 'yes, I do know.'

There was an expression on his face Harriet had not often seen there; it was wretchedness. It was unlike him. Grief, fury, despondency, but not that absolutely dispirited near-defeated look. 'Please,' he said, sensing a softening, a concern, 'please Harriet, come and have lunch with me.'

'I couldn't eat lunch, Theo, I feel as if I shall never eat again. I probably will never eat again, I won't be able to afford it.'

'Oh, don't be ridiculous,' he said, 'you'll rise again from this little heap of ashes you've made for yourself, and –'

'Theo, I didn't make it,' said Harriet.

'Yes you did. You have to recognize that, it's important. You overreached yourself, Harriet, overspent. You're a brilliant designer, but you're a bad businesswoman. I've seen the figures, don't forget. I'm ready to help, but I'm not prepared to heap sympathy upon you, because you don't actually deserve it. I stand by what I said to Hayden Cotton, you did massage those figures . . . a little . . .'

Harriet looked at him, then up at the window of her studio, thought of what she had endured that morning at the bank, what she was to endure that afternoon, and a violent rage swept over her. She wanted to hurt him, really hurt him; she knew then what the expression 'beside herself with rage' meant, for she stood beside herself and watched as she drew back her fist and hit him, hard, twice, in the crotch. She saw him wince, draw back; then 'I wouldn't do that again,' he said quietly.

'I will do it again,' she said, and did.

He reached out, took hold of her, put his arms round her and pushed her into the car, then, with a speed extraordinary in so large a man, ran round to the other side, started the engine and drove off down Floral Street at some speed. He had been right, she thought, about people's reaction: most of them had hurried carefully past, a few had stopped to watch interestedly, a couple had laughed, but nobody had been even remotely near to coming to her aid.

'That was a foul, filthy thing to do,' he said. He was obviously in pain; he was white, his jaw set.

'So was what you did to me. Stop this car, Theo, I want to get out.'

'I will not stop it.'

'You have to. There's a red light ahead,' she said, looking at the traffic lights at the bottom of Bedford Street where it met the Strand.

'Fuck the red light,' he said and paused briefly to check, then drove through it, turning left up towards Fleet Street and the City. There was a screech of brakes; a van driver swerved violently to avoid him. 'Bloody wanker,' shouted the driver, his face distorted with rage, 'bloody great poofter, look where you're bloody going.' Theo ignored him, put his foot down, drove through the next lights (orange) and extremely fast round the Aldwych.

'Theo, for Christ's sake, you'll get arrested,' said Harriet.

'Oh, shut up,' he said. 'Just shut up. Leave me alone.'

They had swerved back into the Strand, and were crossing Waterloo Bridge when a policeman came up behind them on a motorbike, blue light flashing, and waved them over to the side. Theo wound down his window resignedly.

'Yes?'

'Did you realize you just drove through a red light, sir?' said the policeman. He looked about sixteen years old.

'Yes, of course I did,' said Theo. 'I'm extremely sorry, I was in appalling pain and I really wasn't concentrating.'

'I'm sorry to hear that, sir. Would you mind telling me the nature of this pain, sir?'

'Yes, certainly,' said Theo. 'This young lady here had just punched me in the balls.'

Harriet looked at him in total disbelief.

'Is this true, madam?'

'No! Well – yes. Yes, I suppose so. In a way.'

'Harriet,' said Theo, 'you can't punch someone in the balls in a way. Either you do or you don't.'

'Was there a problem, madam? Was the gentleman making a nuisance of himself?'

'Er – no,' said Harriet hastily. Much as she hated Theo, she didn't actually want him had up for sexual assault.

'Not threatening you in any way?'

'No. Not really.'

'Do you know the gentleman well then, madam?'

'Yes,' said Harriet, wearily, 'very well. Too well.'

'So it was just a straightforward argument, was it, madam? Which caused you to strike the gentleman?'

'Not straightforward,' said Harriet, with dignity, 'but an argument, yes.'

'It's very dangerous to engage in physical violence with the driver of a moving vehicle, madam. I'm sure you must realize that.'

'Look,' said Harriet, seeing she was rapidly becoming the culprit rather than the victim in this exchange, 'he wasn't driving at the time.'

'He wasn't?'

'No.'

'What were you doing, sir?'

'Standing by my car. Talking to her.'

'I see, sir. So you were able to get into your car and drive it away. You were not incapacitated?'

'No, not entirely.'

'And you got into the car beside him, madam?'

'I was pushed into the car,' said Harriet, 'and driven off. Abducted, I would imagine the word would be.'

'I see,' said the policeman. He was clearly out of his depth; he looked rather less than sixteen. 'Do you have your driving licence on you, sir?'

'Yes,' said Theo gloomily. He produced his wallet, took out his licence.

The policeman got out his notebook and started filling in what seemed to be a very elaborate form. Harriet sat staring straight in front of her; the sense of total unreality the day had taken on had intensified dramatically. Surely, surely, she thought, I shall wake up in a minute, find it's all perfectly all right, that it's yesterday morning, that Cressida's in the next room, that Mummy's bringing us both a cup of tea . . .

'If I could just have your name and address as well, madam. You may be needed as a witness.'

Harriet gave him her name and address. It certainly wasn't yesterday, and she wasn't dreaming. It was today and she was very much awake . . .

* * *

'Right,' said Theo, as they pulled round onto the Embankment, 'now let's have lunch.'

'There's nowhere decent to have lunch round here,' said Harriet sulkily, 'and I don't want to have lunch with you anyway.'

'There's the Tate,' said Theo, 'restaurant there. Very good wine list. How would that be?'

'Theo, it wouldn't be at all. I'm not coming.'

'We'll have a bottle of the Bollinger,' said Theo, handing back the menu to the waiter, 'and just some smoked salmon and scrambled eggs. Thank you.'

'How do you know I just want smoked salmon and scrambled eggs?' asked Harriet irritably.

'Because I know you so terribly well. Intimately would not be an inaccurate description. Look at me.'

She looked at him. His almost black eyes were probing, intense. She felt a distraction from herself and her misery, a faint turning to him; memories stirred, physical memories. She looked resolutely away, pushed back her hair.

'I felt that,' he said, quietly, gently.

'Felt what?'

'You know.'

'Theo, I don't know. I don't know anything any more.'

'You look tired,' he said.

'I feel tired. Terribly tired. It's been a fairly shitty twenty-four hours.'

'It has indeed.' The champagne arrived; he tasted it, nodded to have it poured. 'Drink it, Harriet. It will do you good.'

She drank obediently; the champagne hit her bloodstream, lifted her awareness.

'That was terribly painful,' he said, suddenly more light-hearted, 'what you did to me back there. It's like being hit all over, you know, very hard, very deep down. Did you realize that?'

'No, but I'm glad,' she said briefly. 'That's exactly how I felt when I heard about you. Telling your friend about me massaging the figures.'

'Well,' he said, 'we'd better leave that one for now.'

'Fortunately for you,' said Harriet, 'you can. You don't know a lot about humiliation.'

'Now there you are mistaken,' said Theo, refilling her glass. 'I was well and truly humiliated about – oh, twelve hours ago. Do you want to hear about it?'

'No.'

'I think you should. Sit quietly and listen.'

'Well,' said Harriet, 'good for Sasha.' She was shovelling smoked salmon into her mouth with some relish.

'Yes, I suppose so. I suppose, too, you think I deserved it.'

'I certainly do.'

'Well,' he said with a sigh, 'I expect you're right.'

'Are you upset? That she's gone?'

'No,' he said and sounded faintly surprised, 'no, I'm not upset, I find. Not in the least.'

'Why not?'

'Because,' he said very quietly, 'because I still love you.'

'Oh, Theo, stop it. Stop it, stop it.'

'Why?'

'Because it's pointless. And stupid. And insulting.'

'Why insulting?'

'Because if you still loved me, you shouldn't have married her.'

'I know that. But –'

'Yes?'

'I had to do something,' he said more quietly still, 'to ease the pain.'

'Oh, for God's sake, I can't believe you said that. That you married someone you didn't love just to get over someone else. You're so self-centred, Theo, so appallingly, childishly, self-centred.'

'I know, I know.'

She wasn't looking at him. 'The universe revolves round you, doesn't it, Theo?'

'I'm working on making it that way.'

She looked up sharply; his eyes were amused. 'It isn't funny.'

'I didn't mean to imply it was.'

Harriet gave up.

'Sasha knew,' he said.

'Knew what?'

'About us.'

Harriet felt very odd; she stared at him, trying to take in what he had just said. 'Who told her?'

'Cressida.'

'Oh God,' she said and burst into tears.

'She was so awful,' she said, 'so awful. I can't believe how awful she was.'

They had left the restaurant and were sitting in the gallery with the Degas; Harriet was gazing determinedly at the sculpture of the little ballerina and moving determinedly away from Theo every time he tried to get closer to her.

'I've learnt so many terrible things about her. It's as if she was someone else altogether, another woman, someone none of us really knew. Living a secret life, an appalling secret life, all lies and cruelty. It's horrible. Poor Oliver, poor poor Oliver. She was pregnant, you know, but not by him – by this man in Paris, I suppose. Who knows? The one she's married to. Or isn't married to. Who knows that either? And last year she told Oliver she was pregnant and she wasn't. I don't understand it, Theo, I really don't. How could she have done all that, Theo, lied to us all, to me, to you, to Oliver, and especially to my parents, who loved her so much? The gynaecologist said she was a hysterical personality, she said even the flying was – what was it? – oh yes, symptomatic of her condition, and I was beginning to think the same, to be sorry for her, but now you've told me that, I think she was just vile.'

'Maybe a bit of both,' said Theo mildly. 'What gynaecologist?'

'Oh, the one she was seeing. I found a letter in the pocket of a cardigan. I went to see her this morning. She was very nice. Tried to make me see Cressida as sick rather than bad, but I –'

'She must be,' said Theo.

'She's not,' said Harriet fretfully, 'and don't you start feeling sorry for her. I couldn't bear it. She's done that all her life and –'

'Harriet, if she is sick, if she is psychiatrically disturbed, it does put a very different complexion on all this. Explains it to an extent.'

'Not to me,' said Harriet. The latest disclosure about Cressida had re-formed her yet again in her mind.

'How would you feel if she came back?'

'I don't know, but I hope she never does. I honestly think I'd kill her if she did. I learnt something else about her the other night, something my mother told me. You know my puppy, Biggles, remember?'

'Yes,' he said gently, 'of course I do, of course I remember.'

'It was her fault all along. She opened the gate deliberately, so he could get out, could be run over. She –'

'Harriet, I can't believe that –'

'You have to believe it,' she cried, and was startled at the anguish in her voice. 'You have to, because I always knew in my heart that that's what happened. She told my mother that it was an accident, that she just forgot, but of course it wasn't. She hated me and she wanted to hurt me. It was –'

'Harriet, Harriet, don't –'

'Don't what?' she said. 'Don't mind? Don't blame her? Don't reproach her? Theo, you don't understand, you just don't understand the wickedness of her. I suppose it's not surprising really. She could twist you round her little finger more easily than anyone. Bat those long eyelashes at you –'

'Oh, shut up,' he said wearily, 'don't be so bitter, Harriet. It won't help.'

'Oh, really,' she said, angry again, 'how can I not be bitter? I feel so betrayed, so – oh, this is ridiculous, I don't know what I'm doing even sitting here talking to you. You of all people.'

'Harriet,' he said, and his voice was heavy with emotion, with pain. 'Harriet, I of all people probably know you best, understand you best, love you best. It is me of all people you should be talking to.'

'No, Theo, it isn't.'

She got up, walked over to the little ballerina, stood looking at her, at her awkward grace, her almost simian beauty, the stalklike neck, the hands clasped behind her back; he followed her over.

'Harriet, please –'

'No,' she cried, loudly, passionately hostile. The gallery guard looked at her, raised his eyebrows warningly; she felt herself flush. 'I have to get back,' she said, 'please take me. The man from the receiver's office will be there, impounding all my stuff. If you remember.'

'Harriet,' he said, 'let me help you at least. Let me give you the money. Sorry. Lend you the money. At very stiff terms if you like. You should be able to buy the company back from the receiver, you know. Let me do it for you. Please.'

'Theo,' she said, 'you really don't understand me at all, do you? Don't know what I want. Of course I won't take your money, of course I won't let you help me.'

'Why not?'

'Because,' she said, 'because then you'd have won. Beaten me. Forced me to do what you want. And I meant what I said to the bank manager. I really would rather die. Now please, Theo, leave me alone. I don't want you. Or anything you might possibly do for me. Is that really so beyond your comprehension?'

'Harriet,' he said, very quietly now, putting his hand out to touch her, then dropping it again in an oddly helpless gesture. 'Harriet, please don't do this. Please. I love you. I love you more even than I ever knew.'

There was a very long silence, while she stood there, staring at him, thinking, remembering love, Theo loving her; physically shaken by the force of her longing for it, yearning for it, for him.

'Please,' he said again, absolutely still, 'please, Harriet. I want you so.'

It was that word that changed it, changed everything; that one word, *want*. That was the whole thing about Theo, the key to him: he wanted, and he had to have. Houses, land, works of art; cars, planes, horses; companies, people, power; women, sex, love. And she would not, could not, join his catalogue of possessions, of things he wanted, and thus of things that then belonged to him.

'Theo,' said Harriet, 'you don't know anything about love, I'm afraid. Anything at all.'

She turned then and left him, ran out of the room and out of the front door, down the steps of the Tate, hailed a taxi, got into it, managed not to look back, despite a dreadful yearning just for the sight of him, until they were driving quite quickly away from the gallery, away from him, away from comfort, from help, from love. When she did, he was walking down the steps, his hands in his pockets, his head bent, utterly dispirited, looking drained, bereft of power and strength.

'Bastard,' said Harriet aloud. 'Fucking bastard.'

Then she burst into tears.

Chapter 36

James 1pm

The house was terribly quiet, its stillness a tangible, heavy thing. Everyone had gone, even Janine and Merlin. James sat in his study, trying to recover just a little from the previous hour before going to find Maggie, to talk to her, to tell her what? That her beloved daughter was a manipulative promiscuous monster, greedy, ruthless, using her, using all of them, careless of their feelings, their love, their concern for her, heedless of their humiliation, their pain. He tried to remember her as she had been, only thirty-six hours earlier, her sweetness, her thoughtfulness to him, the way she fussed over him, so patently enjoyed his company, asked to go for walks with him, loved to hear about his work, how she would sit on the arm of his chair, chatting to him, as Maggie and Harriet never would. Remembered how proud of her he had always been, how he loved to show her off to friends and colleagues, how deep-down sad he had been at the thought of losing her to Oliver, to her new life, three thousand miles away. Remembered her charm, her lovely smiling prettiness, her grace; and yes, of course he loved Harriet too, was desperately proud of her, admired what she had done, could do, but Harriet was different – Harriet was tough, clever, ambitious, self-sufficient; she didn't need an adoring, protective father.

There was a collage of pictures of Cressida on his desk that Maggie had made for him once: a snapshot of her life, composed of many snapshots: Cressida lying in Maggie's arms in the hospital, Cressida toddling across the garden, her fair curls haloed round her face, Cressida in her school uniform, in tennis clothes, in party dresses – the frillier the better she liked them, unlike Harriet who had always chosen plainer, starker clothes – Cressida blowing out candles on her birthday cake, sitting by the Christmas tree, building sandcastles, in her first grown-up party dress, on Theo's yacht, and his favourite picture of all, the two of them together, him and her, walking arm in arm along a wintry beach somewhere, laughing, their hair blowing in the wind.

And as he looked, as he tried to equate her with the person he now knew about, he realized she was gone, gone forever and the pain in his heart was as great, greater even, than if she had truly died, if she was lying in front of him white and still. He had lost her, lost her completely; she was no longer his child, and he buried his head in his hands on the desk and started to weep.

The phone rang, sharply; he sat looking at it, lacking the strength even to reach out and pick it up. It stopped again, after a few rings. Maggie must have answered it. It was probably yet another well-meaning friend, another well-wishing enquiry. It was so kind of people to phone, so kind, and so appallingly, stupidly insensitive. Well, it looked as if Maggie would be able to cope with some of it at least today; her sleep must have done her good. Poor Maggie: poor hopeless hapless Maggie. He should be grateful she was so hopeless and so hapless, he supposed; otherwise she would be demanding her own life, revenge, recompense. As it was, she accepted it all, accepted her role, did what he needed her to do, in return for a home, security, status, and a life she managed, although God knew how, to enjoy. He supposed it was much the same for Alistair, in a totally different way: if he did know anything, suspect it even (and James felt he must, although Susie swore he didn't), he presumably preferred the status quo, the unarguable value of a beautiful charming wife who ran his home and his life, was the perfect consort and mother. Why exchange those benefits for scandal, disruption, hideous expense? He was not in love with Susie, never had been: theirs was a shining, exemplary version of the marriage of convenience. God, he hoped Susie would come back to recognizing the value of the same thing; he had been badly shaken by her demands. His mind (distracted briefly by the events of the morning) returned to the nightmare of Rufus, the new but already familiar panic rising and falling in his chest. He stared out of the window, thinking about it, about Rufus, and into his head came the memory of a survey done on inherited characteristics in Birmingham or some such place, that over half the children were fathered by men other than their mothers' husbands: they'd had to abandon the survey for that very reason. He clung to the memory, finding it oddly comforting, easing his panic. Maybe he was overreacting, maybe Rufus and his generation were overfamiliar with such things, had grown up in such knowledge that he would take it all in his stride, maybe Maggie, Alistair, Harriet, the other children would just laugh – 'Christ,' he said aloud, shocked at his own crassness, 'Christ Almighty, James, what are you thinking about –'

Suddenly, desperately, he wanted Susie, wanted to hear her voice, know how she was, tell her he loved her. He dialled the Princess Diana Hospital on his own line; he couldn't have Maggie picking it up in error, listening to him.

'Could I speak to Mrs Headleigh Drayton? In room fifteen. This is James Forrest again.'

'I'll see. One moment please, Mr Forrest.'

He waited, seeing as he waited Susie's lovely face, her soft dark eyes, heard, before she spoke, her pretty, husky voice. Christ, he was missing her already.

'Mr Forrest?' It wasn't Susie's voice. It was the receptionist again.

'Yes?'

'Mrs Headleigh Drayton says she can't speak to you, I'm afraid. She's very tired.'

'I see,' said James. He felt a slug of shock. Susie had always wanted to speak to him, however exhausted: hours after the birth of all her children, immediately after the funeral of her mother, leaving the deathbed of her father, she had been on the phone, wanting him, wanting the comfort of him. 'Are you sure?'

'I'm quite sure, Mr Forrest.'

'Did she send any message?'

'No, Mr Forrest.'

'Is Mr Hobson there?'

'Yes he is. I'll put you through.'

'Martin? James Forrest.'

'Ah, James. Good to hear from you. How's things? Surviving dear Mrs Bumley's reforms, are you?'

'Don't start me on that,' said James. 'I might get violent. Er – Martin. You operated on an old friend of mine this morning. Well, an old family friend. Susie Headleigh Drayton. I – can't get hold of Alistair and she's tired of course. I just wondered if she was OK.'

'Yes, she's absolutely fine. Well, almost, I'm happy to say. She'll give you the details, no doubt. Pretty woman, liked her. I thought the husband was with her as a matter of fact. They were holding hands like a couple of teenagers a bit earlier. Gives you hope, that sort of thing. Shall I ask him to ring you if I see him?'

'No, no, it's all right,' said James hastily. 'I'm just going out. Thanks anyway.'

'That's OK, old chap. You going to that conference in Bournemouth next month? The one on pre-malignancy? I'm presenting a paper. Try and make it. Should be quite a good bash.'

'I'm not sure,' said James. 'Thanks anyway, Martin. Goodbye.' He put the phone down: it rang again almost immediately.

'Mr Forrest? This is Crowthorne's Florists here. Mr Forrest, there seems to be some confusion about the flowers you ordered for Mrs Headleigh Drayton. At the Princess Diana Hospital. The hospital have just asked us to query the order with you. Apparently Mrs Headleigh Drayton sent the flowers back. Insisted they were not for her. We wondered if we had the right Mrs Headleigh Drayton, or even the right hospital?'

James felt very sick suddenly. 'Oh, no,' he said, 'must have been my mistake. Tell – tell the hospital to keep them anyway, put them in reception or something. Goodbye.'

The feeling of panic was increasing. Cressida, Rufus, Susie. Christ, what was happening to him, to his well-ordered life? His head was beating extremely hard; it almost hurt. The pain reached downwards, towards his churning stomach. He felt very physically shaky, and horribly near tears again. He thought how wonderful the drink he'd had earlier had been, and longed sharply, desperately for another.

'God,' he said aloud, throwing back his head, closing his eyes. 'God help me.'

Dimly in the distance he heard the phone ringing again. He could not, would not answer it. He couldn't take any more. He sat, his hands clasped tightly together, trying to stop his teeth from chattering. His legs were shaking violently. The ringing stopped: Maggie had obviously answered it. Thank God. He lit a cigarette, drew on it heavily. He didn't often smoke, maybe once a week, after dinner. It helped.

He had stubbed out the second before Maggie came into the room. She was smiling; she looked radiant. James stared at her.

'What is it?' he asked. 'What's happened?'

Maggie sat down, and just looked at him, her eyes bright, studded with tears. Happy tears. 'That was Cressida,' she said simply.

'Cressida! What do you mean it was Cressida?'

'It was Cressida. She phoned. She's in Paris. We had a long talk.'

'Oh, for Christ's sake,' he said, 'what did she say? What is going on, I don't –'

'Nothing's going on,' said Maggie, 'except that she is ill and frightened and terribly terribly upset. She needed to talk. I think I helped her a little. She is desperately sorry about it all.'

'Well, I'm so glad to hear that,' said James. Rage was flooding him, hot, dangerous. 'Absolutely delighted. She walks out on a wedding and a husband and a family and terrifies us and humiliates us but she's terribly terribly sorry about it. Well, that makes it perfectly all right then, doesn't it? Let's all relax and hang out the welcome home banner.'

'James, don't. You don't understand.'

'Oh, really?' he said. 'Is that right? Well, I don't think you can make me understand, Maggie. Not just now. I don't think you can even make me want to understand. As far as I'm concerned, Cressida is –'

'James, listen! Please. She's desperate.'

'All right,' he said, 'all right, I'm listening. But not exactly sympathetically. If she's desperate that's fine by me.'

'James, she's pregnant. Well, we knew that –'

'Yes, we did.'

'It – it isn't Oliver's. She – she's in love with someone else.'

'Oh, right. So far I'm not bowled over with sympathy by this story.'

'James, please. She never wanted to marry Oliver. She felt under tremendous pressure, poor darling. He was so passionately in love with her, and she thought she was with him. By the time she realized she'd made a mistake it was too late. Everything was planned, everyone was so happy, she didn't have the heart to pull out.'

'Well, bully for her.'

'James, try to understand. You know how sensitive she is, how she can't bear to hurt anyone. Well, early this year, she met this man in Paris. Fell passionately in love with him. She tried to break off with Oliver, but he was beside himself. She just didn't have the heart to do it to him.'

'Why didn't she talk to us?'

'She said she did try, again and again, but it always seemed impossible. The arrangements were going ahead so fast, we were all so excited, you'd spent so much money, and she just got deeper and deeper in the mire. I feel so dreadful, James, that she had no one to turn to, no one understood how desperate she was. What kind of a mother am I, to fail her like that? To make her think a wedding was more important than her happiness?'

'A foolish, gullible one, I should think,' said James, but a stab of hope, a faint stirring of relief was rising in him. Maybe, just maybe Cressida wasn't so bad, maybe Julia had been lying, it was possible, maybe the letter had had nothing to do with it.

'Anyway, early in May, she broke off with this man in Paris. His name was Gérard. Gérard –' She looked down at a piece of paper in her hand; there was a name written on it, over and over again. 'Gérard Renaud. He's a writer of some kind. A journalist.'

'Really?'

'Yes. Anyway, she told him she had to do the right thing, go ahead, marry Oliver. She still didn't realize she was pregnant then, you see. She thought she would be able to cope, that it was an infatuation she was going through, a sort of last fling, that she would settle down and be happy with Oliver. Gérard was heartbroken, but he understood. He went away, on some assignment his paper sent him on, to South Africa. He was gone for weeks. She couldn't trace him.'

'Not through the paper? How extraordinary.'

'No. Oh, James, I don't know. Stop putting me in the witness box. And when she discovered she was pregnant she just didn't know what to do. She panicked, she arranged a termination but she couldn't go through with it. Oh, James, why couldn't she have come to us, why couldn't we have been there for her?'

'We were there for her,' said James grimly.

'Not enough. So then she – she told Oliver the baby was his.'

'Poor old Oliver.'

'Yes. Yes, that was bad of her. Of course I agree. But she was frightened, feeling so wretchedly unwell –'

'Maggie, not even you should be falling for this garbage. And she didn't look unwell –'

'James, she was. She was so terribly pale, and tired-looking. And she has got very thin. You know the dress had to be taken in. We all thought it was exhaustion and nerves and of course all brides lose weight. I swear to you it isn't garbage as you call it. You didn't speak to her, you didn't hear her voice. She was beside herself with remorse, with guilt – and there's something else –'

'Yes?'

'Very late on the night before the wedding, this man – this Gérard – phoned her. I do remember a call. I was half asleep. He was back in Paris. He said he had to speak to her, he had something to tell her. Something dreadful, that she had to know.'

'His story wasn't going to be published? Oh all right, I'm sorry, what was it?'

'He's ill, James. I mean really ill. He has leukaemia. He'll probably be dead in three months, certainly six. He told Cressida he wanted to see her just once more. He said he could wait until after the wedding but – well, that was the last straw, she said. She had to be with him, for the time they had left, had to let him know about their child, had to care for him.'

'But Maggie –'

'She said she felt she had absolutely no choice. She had to go. She said it was as if she became someone else, watching herself. She said she felt fate had stepped in and saved her from something she knew anyway was wrong, terribly wrong.'

'So why couldn't she have come to us, talked to us, told us what she was going to do? Spared us at least some of the misery, the anguish –'

'I asked her that. She said she knew that if she even just began talking to us she'd find herself weakening, giving in. And she'd written the letter, don't forget. I know it got lost, but she thought we'd find it much earlier and we wouldn't be so worried. That wasn't her fault.'

'No,' said James. 'No, I suppose it wasn't.'

His mind was whirling. Who should he believe? He wanted to believe Maggie, Cressida; the story was so wild, so absurd it almost made sense.

Almost. On the other hand, it was very carefully constructed, perfectly designed to melt her mother's heart. But then – what of Julia's version? She surely wouldn't have made that up. It was too checkable. The opposite of carefully constructed. But then, maybe – maybe Julia herself was mad. Knocked off-balance by a psychotically overprotective adoring father, herself overpossessive and protective of her own son. Josh had said himself she could hardly be described as well adjusted, was permanently in analysis. She might well have shown Cressida the letter and Cressida would simply have shrugged it off.

'Did she –' his voice cracked, he cleared his throat, started again – 'did she say anything about Julia?'

'Julia? No, why should she? What did Julia have to do with it?'

'Oh,' he said, his voice as casual as he could manage, 'oh, nothing really. I just wondered. Julia said something about her seeming upset when she went up to say goodnight to her.'

'Julia is about as perceptive as a rhinoceros,' said Maggie. 'I really don't think she –'

'No, all right. So what's happened? Where is she?'

'She's at Gérard's flat. In Paris. She's alone, he's gone back into hospital for more tests. She's desperately worried, she just wanted to talk to me.'

'I'd like to talk to her,' said James grimly. 'Give me the number, would you?'

'No, James, I won't.'

'I'm sorry?' He stared at her blankly. 'Of course you must give it to me.'

'No, I'm not going to. Not yet at any rate, until she's settled down, come to terms with it all, feels a little better. I'm not having you upsetting her, making her feel worse, more guilty. She's in a bad enough state already. Poor child.'

'Maggie, she is not a child. At best she's a mixed-up woman. I actually think she is rather worse than that –'

'I knew you'd say that, think that,' said Maggie. 'That's precisely why I have no intention of giving you the number.'

'Oh, for God's sake. You're crazy about that child. You always were. Could never see any harm in anything she did. Did you know she actually married this man yesterday?'

'What?'

She faltered then, her mother's faith plainly momentarily shattered.

'She married him. Does that tally with her story about rushing off to a desperately sick boyfriend?'

'James, that's ridiculous. She can't have done.'

'She did.'

'How do you know?'

'There was a photograph of her somebody saw, running down the steps of Sacré-Coeur, presumably with him, wearing her wedding dress. Oh, she didn't marry him there, of course –'

'Oh, that,' said Maggie. She was patently relieved. 'Oh, it was just something they decided to do. She took her dress with her, and they went to Sacré-Coeur to ask a priest for a blessing. She told me that. She wanted to do something to mark the day –'

'Oh, for Christ's sake,' said James, 'this pantomime has gone on long enough – let's leave it there. I'm terribly tired, Maggie, I can't take much more of this.' Just the same, the story was beginning to sound better, more feasible. The cracks in it were being filled. It didn't excuse what Cressida had done but it made her less evil, less immoral.

'But she's not actually married,' said Maggie. 'She couldn't be. There wasn't time for them to arrange it. Anyway,' – she stared at him – 'how do you know all this?'

'A photographer friend of Tilly Mills saw the picture at some newspaper where he was delivering his own pictures. Faxed it to Harriet last night.'

'To Harriet?'

'Yes.'

'Have you seen it?'

'Yes. And I went to Paris this morning –'

'You went to Paris?' Her face was grey with shock.

'Yes, with Theo. We went in his plane. We went to Sacré-Coeur and found the priest who'd blessed them, as a matter of fact. I have to say he does confirm something of this story. He –'

'And you didn't tell me, neither of you did, that you went to Paris looking for Cressida, didn't even show me the picture –?'

'Maggie, you were asleep. Drugged. I was going to, of course I was. I didn't know myself until about two this morning. What good would it have done to have woken you, upset you all over again? And we left here at four-thirty. I was back on English soil before you'd woken up, and then –'

'It all sounds very par for the course, I have to say,' said Maggie. She had an expression on her face James had not seen before: a hard, cool look, absolutely sure of herself, utterly in command. 'Keep Maggie in the dark. Lie and keep on lying. Keep her out of it, and she'll come to heel. Well finally, James, I won't. I'm leaving you.'

'Oh, don't be absurd,' said James. He hardly took the words in, they were just another set of Maggie's histrionics.

'Yes I am. I'd decided anyway, before all this. That as soon as the wedding was over I was going.'

'Oh, Maggie, really. Of course you can't go. What would I do without you, how could I –'

'James, you'll do fine without me. You'll have exactly what you wanted. Freedom to do what you want, sort yourself out. Live with Susie if she'll have you.'

'Susie?' said James. He had rehearsed this conversation in his head so often he was word-perfect. 'Susie? What has Susie got to do with it?'

'James, please. Don't insult me. Don't start play-acting.'

'But Maggie –'

'James, I know. Of course I know. And the way I feel right now, you're very welcome to each other. Do what you fucking well like. I simply don't care.'

It was the word fucking that made James realize she meant it. Maggie hated bad language, never swore; the harshest word he had ever heard on her lips had been bloody and that was only about once every five years and then under the most dire provocation. He stared at her, trying to take in what she was saying, absolutely silent. He could not have spoken if his life depended on it.

'I hate you,' she said simply. 'I really do hate you. It's a strong word, but that's what I feel. For all these years you've made a fool of me. With your mistress, God how I hate her too, bloody Susie with her perfect figure and her lovely face, taking you away from me, poor fat stupid Maggie. Of course I knew, I knew quite quickly, and presumably you either thought I didn't or I'd accept it for all the dubious benefits of having you as my husband. Well I did accept it, in a way, because I never made a fuss or threw wobbles. How could I? I'd have looked even more stupid. Everyone would have said poor old Maggie, how can she expect to keep a husband like James, behaving like that? And I had the girls to think of, and they both adored you. I couldn't have broken things up before.'

James looked at her. She had changed. Overnight she had changed. She was still Maggie, still fat, still awkward, and she was pale and tired-looking, but she had clearly washed her hair, and she had put on a nice dress, and even some make-up. She was a pretty woman, still; her plumpness had safeguarded her face, she had fewer lines, her skin was fresher and younger-looking than most of her contemporaries', and her eyes, large, black-lashed eyes, so like Cressida's, were still a clear cornflower blue. He felt an odd rush of panic at the thought of her leaving; he didn't love her but he needed her, she was important to him, to his life.

'Don't talk like this,' he said finally. 'I hate it.'

'Well, that's very unfortunate for you, James, but I'm afraid you'll just have to hate it. I need to explain, to tell you what I'm doing and why.'

'You mustn't go,' he said. 'You mustn't leave. It's a terrible idea. Go and see Cressida if you must, but come back.'

'Why, James? I really don't see why.'

'Well,' he said, 'because we're married. We've been married a long time. And we –'

'No we haven't,' said Maggie, 'not what I call married. I've run the house and looked after the children and organized our social life and seen to your laundry and so on, but we haven't been married. We haven't slept together for years – no, James, we haven't. Well, hardly ever, and when we do I hate it, because I know you think it's time and you ought to and you're thinking about Susie –'

'Maggie, please – this isn't fair.'

'It's perfectly fair. I don't even blame you for it, I'm just explaining why it's not a marriage. We don't talk, we don't ever go out on our own, not even to the cinema, we don't do anything together, except have meals, and then I know you're watching me, thinking I eat too much.'

'Maggie, I don't –'

'Yes you do. And thinking about Susie and her bloody perfect figure, and the way she takes care of herself and watches what she eats and –'

'When did you find out about her? How?' he said, curious in spite of himself.

'Oh – very early on. I suppose before Rufus was born.'

James held his breath. Did she know about that, had she suspected?

'I used to wonder about Tom, you know,' she said conversationally, 'fantasize that maybe he was yours. But he does look so exactly like Alistair, doesn't he?'

'Yes,' said James, relief flooding hard into his lungs, 'yes, of course he does. What an extraordinary idea.'

'Not really. These things do happen. And I did so long for a boy, for more children, it seemed just the kind of thing that would have happened. But I suppose if Susie had been going to have your child she would have had an abortion. Not gone ahead with it. She's hardly the maternal type, is she?'

James didn't answer. He couldn't defend Susie; it would be too dangerous.

'I tried to ignore it, to tell myself I was being neurotic, that you were just flirting with her because she was so lovely and everything I wasn't, but I could see. I watched you together, and I listened to your excuses for being away, and I went through your wallet for clues, and checked up on you both occasionally, phoned your flat or your secretary, and then her home, and you were always missing together. Or the answering machine at the flat was on when I knew you were there. I used to sit and listen to your voice saying you were out, while I knew you must be in bed with her, making love to her, and I hated you so much for a while I wanted to kill you. I actually thought about it sometimes. Well, not really of course, but I did occasionally wonder about poisoning your food. Or hers.'

'Why did you never say anything? I can't understand it.'

'Because,' she said simply, 'I knew it wouldn't do me any good. I knew you wouldn't give her up, whatever I said, and I knew I didn't want a divorce. Not when the girls were young. So I just waited. Hurt and cried and ate a lot and waited. Until now. And it's been worth it. It's been worth it just to have this conversation, James. I've really enjoyed it.'

'Oh God,' he said, 'oh, Maggie, I'm so sorry.'

'What for?' she said in genuine puzzlement. 'Whatever for?'

'For hurting you so much.'

'James, really! You wouldn't have stopped it though, would you? Even if you'd known how much it hurt.'

'I don't know,' he said. 'I might have tried.'

'James, you wouldn't. You're too absolutely selfish. And too much in love with her, I suppose. Well, it doesn't hurt me any more. I don't give a toss. I really really don't. She's very welcome to you. And you'll be able to have her now. To marry her. If you want her.'

James said nothing, just stared out of the window.

'Anyway,' said Maggie brightly, 'I'm lucky. Just when I thought I was really going to be on the scrap heap, I have a role to play again. Cressida needs me, and that's wonderful.'

'What? You're going to go and live with her, in Paris, with this man? Do you really think that's a good idea?'

'No, I won't live with them, of course I won't. What a very low opinion you must have of me, James. I'm not that stupid. I shall get a little flat near London, Putney, Wimbledon, somewhere like that, I've still got friends there, and I'll rebuild my life. I've been planning it for quite a long time. Cressida wants me to go and visit, meet Gérard, so when the baby arrives I shall maybe go and stay with her, and when – well, when she's alone, she can decide where she wants to be. And where she wants me to be.'

'So you really believe this story?' said James. He had shut his mind to Maggie's announcement for a while; his consciousness had closed down, he simply couldn't cope with any more.

'Yes, I believe it. Of course I do. Why shouldn't I? I'm a truthful person, James. Unlike you. I recognize and respect it in others. Or is there something else you know that I don't?'

'No,' said James hastily, 'no, there isn't.'

'Well,' she said, 'I'm going now. I'm just sorting out a few clothes.'

'You're going today?' said James. 'Where, how?'

'I'm going to stay with an old nursing friend, in Guildford. That will be convenient for my house-hunting. Sarah Jennings, you know?' He nodded silently. 'You never liked her. She never liked you either,' she added. 'She's delighted at my decision. Anyway, she's on her own, her husband died last year, and she says I can stay as long as I like. And then, as I say, I shall be available for Cressida as and when she wants me. Don't look like that, James. She's very upset and frightened. Waiting for the results of these tests on – on Gérard. I feel I've failed her enough. Quite enough. Now then, I'll need some money from you, of course, and I think I've earned it, but I don't want either this house or the flat. I'll come and say goodbye before I go.'

And she walked out of the room and out of his life, as he had so often dreamed of her doing, longed for her to do, leaving him utterly chilled, utterly alone.

Chapter 37

Theo 2:30pm

Like Queen Victoria, Theodore Buchan was not interested in the possibilities of defeat; he was reminded of her words to Lord Balfour on the subject that afternoon as he sat in a traffic jam outside Buckingham Palace looking broodingly up at it. He was a great fan of the old Queen; he admired her stubbornness, her shrewdness, her political flair, and above all her preference for conservative principles. He often said he and she would have got on famously; there were those, Harriet amongst them, who observed that the Queen was scarcely likely to have received a man with five wives, let alone got on with him famously, but Theo was quite undeterred by this, explained that he would have won her heart Disraeli-style by making her Empress of his Scottish island and wearing a kilt in the manner of her beloved ghillie, John Brown.

'Theo,' Harriet had said, 'not a kilt. Not you.'

This conversation had led on to a subsequent one of some lewdness, on the subject of what he might have worn under the kilt, and that had led in turn to some fairly intense physical pleasure, as they contemplated together the area under discussion. All this flooded back into his bleak mind, making him first smile and then wince as he remembered Harriet's most recent assault on his person. It also made him still less interested in the possibility of defeat. He wanted her, he needed her, he loved her; and he was going to have her. It was perfectly simple: merely a matter of patience and logistics. Being strong on logistics he could not see that a great deal of patience should be called for.

He reached for his car phone, to call his office; the movement hurt his tender balls.

'Bitch,' he said aloud, 'bitch.'

'Who, me, Mr Buchan?' said Myra. 'What did I do?'

'Nothing, Myra, nothing. Sorry. I'm on my way in.'

'Where are you?'

'In the Mall. Any messages?'

'A few. Mungo called about six times, he wanted to have dinner with you. Hayden Cotton called, can you ring back soonest, he said.' Myra didn't like Americans, her clipped upper-class English voice disdainful when she relayed messages, absolutely verbatim, and she spoke to them politely but slightly condescendingly; Theo teased her about it and referred to them in her presence as colonials.

'Mark Protheroe's rung several times, please ring him, most specifically about CalVin. A Mr Hennessy called, he's acting for Mrs Buchan, he says, can you call him urgently. James Forrest rang, he wants to see you, maybe this evening. Everything else can wait.'

'Fine. Tell Mungo I'm not sure about dinner, but I'd love to see him and I'll ring him the minute I'm free. I'll get the rest when I arrive.'

He rang off, found himself in another traffic jam in St James's and rang James.

'James? Theo. You OK? I can't do dinner, sorry, but –'

'Maggie's left me,' said James flatly.

'She's what?'

'Left me.'

'Why?'

'She says she hates me.'

'Well, I suppose that could be called a reason,' said Theo carefully. He eased a cigar out of his top pocket, clipped the end with some difficulty and pushed it into the lighter on the car dashboard.

'It isn't funny.'

'Of course it isn't. I'm sorry. Really sorry. Unless it's what you want, of course . . .'

'I don't know what I want,' said James, and Theo realized he was crying.

'Jamie, what is it? Not Susie?'

There was a silence; he heard James blowing his nose. 'Sorry,' he said, 'sorry, Theo. No, no, Susie's fine. False alarm.'

'Rufus?'

'No, not Rufus either.'

'Where – where is Maggie going?'

'Well, she's talking of buying a flat in London. And then spending a lot of time in Paris, looking after Cressida.'

'Cressida?' Theo almost drove into a taxi, jammed on his brakes. 'Sorry,' he shouted at the cabbie, 'sorry, mate.'

'Keep your bleeding eyes open,' said the cabbie equably.

'Theo, what is going on?' asked James.

'I'm in the car. Almost had an accident. You did say Cressida, James? Really? Have you found her?'

'No. Well, yes, I suppose. She rang Maggie. Told her some extraordinary story and – well, I won't go into it now.'

'You might as well,' said Theo, 'I'm not going anywhere.'

And he sat there in the midst of the thick Friday afternoon traffic, surrounded by hooting, swearing drivers, a light rain falling now onto the windscreen, listening as James told him Cressida's story and then, falteringly, clearly upset, Julia's story. Theo put them together in his mind with Harriet's story and not for the first time in the past thirty-six hours wondered if he was dreaming.

'Oh, and Theo, did you really ever tell Cressida the full extent of Julia's father's wealth? I really had no idea it was such serious money.'

'Yes I did,' said Theo with a sigh. 'I didn't mean to, but she was very good at wheedling information out of one. I told her I'd just seen the old bugger, at a convention in Palm Beach. He's virtually a recluse these days, but still obsessed with the heart of his business which is computer technology.'

'Well, I'm afraid that rather confirms Julia's story,' said James wearily. 'She said she thought it was you who'd told Cressida.'

'Mea culpa,' said Theo, 'I'm sorry, James.'

There was a silence. Then James said, 'Well, I don't suppose it would have made that much difference. She'd have found out somehow. If Julia's right.'

'I don't think you should assume that.'

'Maybe not. I'm trying not to.' There was another silence, then he said, 'And Maggie's gone. She wants a divorce.'

* * *

'Oh Jamie,' Theo said finally, as he eased the Bentley into the car park beneath his office, 'I'm sorry. We seem to have made a bit of a hash of things, you and I. If only we could go back to that weekend in Paris and start again –'

And as he said that he knew who he could talk to, who would advise him about Harriet.

Janine had returned to the Basil Street Hotel; she said she was delighted to hear from him, but that she was busy just at the moment and would he like to have tea with her.

'And I am not sure if you have heard the news, *chéri*. I am engaged to be married.'

'Janine, you're not, you're supposed to be keeping yourself for me. Who is the swine?'

'The swine is Merlin. Are you not happy for me?'

'Merlin! The old bugger. Janine, that's the most wonderful thing I've heard for – well, for years. Of course I'm happy for you, very happy, delirious in fact. And him. How amazingly cheering. Whenever did that happen?'

'Rather swiftly. Yesterday. Last night. Merlin took me out to dinner and in between bargaining with the waiters he asked me to marry him. You do not think we are a little old for it?'

'Janine, you are two of the youngest people I know. Give the old boy a hug from me. Will he be there at teatime?'

'No, Theo, he will not. He is going off to some unfortunate travel agency to book our honeymoon trip. We are going to China.'

'China! God, I'm jealous. Terribly jealous. But you did promise to marry me next, you know.'

'Well, I am sorry, Theo, but you are married already, are you not?'

'Not for very much longer, Janine,' said Theo soberly.

'Oh really? And what have you done to the lovely Sasha?'

'She's done it to me. Taught me a lesson.'

'Then she is a clever girl,' said Janine. 'You are not quick to learn lessons, Theo. But I am sorry if you are upset.'

'I'm not,' said Theo, 'but I do need advice.'

'Then you shall have it. For what it is worth.'

He put the phone down and sat smiling at it. Nothing, with the exception of hearing Harriet tell him she loved him, could have made him feel more cheerful.

Hayden Cotton had wanted to confirm that he was not putting any money into Harry's.

'It's not the figures. Sure, she's worked them over a bit, but nothing serious. That's not really the problem, it's just that the business is no use to me. Not big enough, and she duplicates what we do. And we're already strong in the UK. It's a lot of hassle for no real return. Pity, she's a bright girl, and a brilliant designer. She just isn't a businesswoman. I'd like to hire her, but I don't think she'd come.'

'Hire her as what?' asked Theo.

'As a designer. I'm thinking of launching a new range. More upmarket. Think of Ralph Lauren. Well, Diffusion Ralph Lauren.'

'What's Diffusion?'

'Oh, it's a kind of a budget line for the top designers. Jean Muir does Studio, Lagerfeld does KL, that sort of thing. And then think evening too. Not frocks, exactly, more tailored. Female dinner jackets.'

'Tough one to crack I'd have thought,' said Theo.

'I know. But it's there. The potential. And I think she could be my girl.'

'Mm,' said Theo thoughtfully. 'Based where?'

'Oh, over here, it would have to be here. I could put together a terrific package for her. But she's such an independent creature, I really don't think she'd come.'

'I don't think she would either,' said Theo, 'but it's exactly right for her. And she's right for you and the idea. And it could altogether – Actually, Hayden –'

'Yeah?'

'I tell you what would make her come.'

Michael Hennessy, representing Mrs Sasha Buchan, was humourless, pompous and extremely efficient. Mrs Buchan wanted a divorce, a quick, no-fault divorce, she had no desire to be vindictive, but she said that if Mr Buchan was going to contest it she would tell the press how she had acquired CalVin. Mr Buchan said he had no intention whatsoever of contesting it, and that he was very happy to go along with Mrs Buchan's request. Mr Hennessy said Mrs Buchan was prepared to be reasonable on the matter of settlement, in fact her demands were extremely modest, she would like a small London house, and a realistic income – 'The word realistic is of course open to interpretation and discussion,' said Mr Hennessy. 'Indeed,' said Theo – 'and she would also like you to give bank guarantees as and when required for the business she intends to set up, as an independent financial adviser, and she wants a flat sum, in the region of a hundred thousand pounds, with which to set up the business.'

'The hell she does,' said Theo. 'She can find her own banker.'

'She said you might say that, Mr Buchan, and in that eventuality, asked me to remind you again about the matter of the CalVin company.'

'This is blackmail,' said Theo.

'That is a very serious allegation, Mr Buchan.'

'It's a statement of fact. But –' He paused, thinking, then grinned into the phone. 'OK. Tell her – tell her she can have all that in exchange for a ten per cent share in her company. And a directorship. Strictly non-executive, of course.'

'I will certainly tell her that, Mr Buchan. But I don't know if Mrs Buchan will agree to it.'

'I think she'll agree,' said Theo, 'she's a good business-woman, and a good sport. And tell her I'll throw a copy of the original version of her engagement ring into the melting pot for good measure. On condition she doesn't sell this one.'

This obviously defeated Mr Hennessy; Theo bade him good afternoon and put the phone down, smiling. He loved getting the better of lawyers, however briefly.

He rang Mungo; he was out, Belinda said, showing someone round a new property.

'He'll be sorry to have missed you, Mr Buchan, he's been trying to get you all day. Shall I call him on his mobile?'

'Good God, no,' said Theo, 'what he's doing is much more important.

Just ask him to call me when he gets back. Tell him I'd love to have dinner with him.'

'Certainly, Mr Buchan.'

'I knew there was someone,' said Janine, 'I knew there had to be. She looked so different for a while. She was warmer, softer, she glowed. Sex is very good for the looks, all Frenchwomen know that.'

'Oh, really?' said Theo. 'I don't think it's ever done a lot for mine.'

'You are not a woman, *chéri.*'

'That's true.'

'Besides, I think you are wrong. Anyone can see you are a man of great passion. It shows.'

'*Tiens!*' said Theo.

'But of course I did not think it was you. You did well. Nobody knew? Nobody at all?'

'My staff.'

'What, the terrifying Mme Hartman, she knew?'

'She did. And several others. Brian, of course. He spent a lot of time collecting Harriet, driving her to airports, that sort of thing. Various housekeepers. But nobody else – I don't think. I like running secrets. It appeals to me.'

'And Cressida?'

'Ah,' said Theo, 'yes.'

He had told Janine, because he'd wanted to, because he thought she had earned it, because he trusted her, all the Cressida stories. 'Which one do you favour, Janine?'

'I agree certainly with the doctor, that she was disturbed. A very difficult personality. She always was. A charming, difficult, disruptive child.'

'I would have thought Harriet was the disruptive one,' said Theo.

'No, no, not at all. You were all so wrong about that. Harriet suffered greatly from Cressida. She seemed difficult herself, yes, and her parents could never see anything really wrong with Cressida's behaviour, it was always, every time, a surprise, they would say oh, but she has always been so good, how strange that her teacher should say she is being naughty in the classroom and not working at school, or how can it be, when she is normally so thoughtful and sensible, that she failed to come home until almost half past three? They never put two and three together –'

'Two and two, Janine.'

'Oh, well, whatever. And the squabbling with Harriet, they always thought it was her fault, because Harriet was the one caught shouting, or hitting her, and Cressida would be sitting there crying. I could see Cressida very often started these things, but they would not accept it. She was very good at appearing to be the victim, indeed thinking herself the victim. But she was so loving, so sweet to them, could wrap Maggie especially right round her thumb.'

'Finger.'

'Finger then. One of the reasons I have fallen in love with Merlin, Theo, is that he never corrects my English.'

'Sorry, Janine.'

'And now she is doing it again. She could lie and lie, with those great eyes of hers wide. I often caught her out, I have sharp eyes of my own, but again her parents nearly always believed her. And if they didn't, then she could turn on the shower and win them round.'

'Oh, really?' said Theo with a heavy sigh, silently translating shower into tap and thinking that Cressida's light, cosmetic tears were actually more reminiscent of a shower, and at the end of them she looked as pretty as when she started. Harriet on the other hand cried noisily, heavily and messily and ended up with red eyes, smudged mascara and a runny nose.

'I'm afraid,' he said, 'she took me in very thoroughly too. I loved her, loved her company, enjoyed taking her away with me.'

'She had – has great charm,' said Janine. 'I enjoyed her company too. In spite of everything. And remembering things you had said to her, which is always enchanting, and making small pretty gestures. She never forgot my birthday, always wrote sweet thankyou notes – she was easy to love. And Harriet – more difficult. She kept you at a distance.'

'Well, I found Harriet very easy to love,' said Theo mournfully. 'Dreadfully, dangerously easy to love. Merlin always adored her,' he added, 'never really liked Cressida.'

'Merlin is a man of great perception,' said Janine with a slight complacency.

'You sound as if you'd been married to him for years and years already,' said Theo laughing.

'I only wish we had. But I tell you, Theo, I cannot quite accept this story of the belle Julia's. I do not believe Cressida is so bad as that.'

'Well, whether it was true or not, Julia believed it. Believed Cressida could be bought off. Or at any rate a variation on that theme. James saw the letter. Oh, Janine, I don't know. Poor old Jamie's in a terrible state.'

'I know it,' said Janine, 'and he has other problems as well, I think. I expect he too will be here before very long.' She smiled at Theo wryly. 'He always comes to me when things go wrong for him; when they are right, I do not hear from him. Cressida has much of that quality too, I think. But Theo, you are not here to discuss Cressida or James. What can we do to help *you*? And Harriet?'

'You don't think it's a disgraceful idea then?' said Theo cautiously.

'Absolutely disgraceful,' said Janine, smiling again. 'Unsuitable, impractical, almost incestuous. What her father will have to say I really hate to think. But I cannot think of two people better suited to loving one another. Except for me and Merlin of course. Two delightful surprises in one day. Now let us put ourselves together and think how you can overcome this little temporary problem you have run into.'

'Not so little or so temporary,' said Theo with a sigh. 'She's told me on three separate occasions in the last twenty-four hours that she hates me and never wants to see me again.'

'You cannot be surprised, I think. You have done some terrible things to her. Marrying someone else within months of the break-up, the pauvre Sasha –'

'Not so pauvre.'

'*Comment?*'

'Oh, I'll tell you another time. Let's just say the pauvre Sasha can take care of herself.'

'I'm pleased to hear it,' said Janine. 'Harriet must be able to do the same, I think. It was not nice or kind to tell your friend not to put his money into her company . . .'

'Janine, it would not be nice or kind to encourage Harriet into thinking she was a good businesswoman when in the last resort she is not. Or of allowing my friend to waste what was actually a great deal of money –'

'Well, perhaps. But it could have been done with more finesse. You lack tact, my Theo.'

'I'm afraid, Janine, you're absolutely right.'

'And how do you know that Harriet does not mean it when she says she hates you?'

'I just do,' said Theo simply. 'I know it. I feel it and I know it.'

'Then we have to help her to find out for herself. But it will not be easy. You cannot tell Harriet anything. She does not listen.'

'No. Well, she certainly doesn't listen to me.' The small phone in his pocket rang shrilly. 'Excuse me, Janine. Can I take that? It's probably Mungo.'

It wasn't Mungo, it was Mr Hennessy. 'Mrs Buchan asked me to tell you that she accepts all your terms, Mr Buchan.'

'That's very good of her,' said Theo.

'She is particularly happy with your offer of the ring. She says she will send the one she is currently wearing over to my office this afternoon in order that you may get it copied.'

'How helpful of her,' said Theo. He grinned suddenly into the phone; the irony of having a genuine diamond ring made to match a fake greatly charmed him. He suddenly remembered rather sharply why he had married Sasha in the first place: she was sexy, she was pretty, she was charming, but she was also a lot of fun. For the first time since she had walked out, he felt a pang of loss.

'Indeed. There is an additional matter, Mr Buchan. Mrs Buchan has found a house and is anxious to proceed with the purchase as soon as possible. A cheque from you is therefore required. Perhaps if you could see your way to coming to my office –'

'Mr Hennessy, I'm an extremely busy man. I really can't drop everything at a moment's notice to come and sign cheques at your office. Besides, I need to see the details of this house, I need to be sure it's a good investment and –'

'May I remind you, Mr Buchan, the house will be for Mrs Buchan, not yourself. She did ask me to remind you again that she thought the story about the CalVin deal would be very interesting –'

'I don't give a shit about the CalVin deal,' said Theo, and then after a moment's thought realized he did. 'All right, Mr Hennessy, but I'm not prepared to come to your office. You can come to mine. In an hour. You have the address, I imagine. Dover Street. Yes, that's right. Good afternoon.'

'What was that about?' asked Janine.

'Oh – Sasha playing games. Clever games, I have to say. Clever girl. And I'm a fool not to have realized it.' He sighed. 'I'd better go, Janine. Ring me if you have any good ideas. I'll be at my office and then –'

There was a knock at the door; Janine went over and opened it. Merlin stood on the threshold beaming, holding a very large bunch of red roses.

'Merlin!' said Theo, giving him one of his bear hugs. 'Let me congratulate you. It's wonderful news. Couldn't be more delighted.'

'Thank you,' said Merlin. 'Pretty delighted myself. Can't think why I couldn't have sorted it out before. Love is blind, I suppose. These are for you, my dear. Got them just down the street on my way back from the travel agent. Terrible price, and the chap wasn't budging, but I thought you deserved them.'

'They're beautiful,' said Theo. 'Perhaps I'd better get some for Sasha. Might sweeten her up a bit. Off to meet her –' His phone rang again. 'Sorry, Merlin. Hallo? Yes, Myra, I'm on my way. Yes, yes, of course, immediately. Merlin, I'd like to buy you both dinner, maybe tomorrow? But I have to rush now. I'll call you. I wouldn't mind coming on your honeymoon with you either. Don't look so alarmed, Merlin, I didn't mean it . . .'

Chapter 38

Harriet 4pm

'You all right, miss?'

Harriet looked up from where she was sitting, hunched up in the doorway of what had been her studio until three o'clock that afternoon, and found herself staring into the eyes of a policeman. Or was it a small boy dressed in policeman's uniform? No, it was a real one. God, it was true, the joke about policemen getting younger; first the one who had stopped her and Theo on the bridge, now this one. She must be getting old. She certainly felt it now. She smiled at him slightly uncertainly, struggled to her feet.

'Yes. Yes, I'm fine. Thank you.'

'Can I call you a taxi or something?'

'No, thank you. I'll be fine. Really.' Well at least the £550 she'd spent on her Nicole Fahri suit hadn't been wasted, if even a policeman could tell she wasn't actually a vagrant, could afford a taxi. Only she couldn't of course; she couldn't afford anything. She was bankrupt, she would shortly be homeless, and she was all alone in the world. She might as well settle back into her doorway and make that her home. It might be quite clever actually; it would cause the receiver a bit of trouble when he came back again to try to sell her offices. Then a cleaning lorry rumbled past, spraying a mixture of rain and dust across the pavement, and she thought perhaps there might be a better option. She realized suddenly she was very thirsty; she walked slowly down to the Strand and into McDonald's and ordered an orange juice and thence headed for Charing Cross station and the uncertain haven of the underground and finally her flat. Her car was parked outside it, returned by Mungo, with a note and a red rose tucked under the windscreen wiper. He was

getting as dangerous as his father, she thought, smiling at the gesture as
she read the note: 'Keys in the letterbox. Thank you for lending it. I'd
love to see you soon.'

It was a very nice flat, but it was blank, anonymous, in a small
purpose-built block near Kensington High Street. She had furnished it
at high speed from John Lewis and Habitat; it was rather dully tasteful
in all shades of beige, its only really interesting feature a dark blue gas-
powered Aga which Theo had had installed for her in the kitchen at
considerable cost, replacing the immensely more practical Neff wall
cooker that had come with the flat. She had gone to be with him for a
few days on the island near Mustique, and when she had come back it
had been there, waiting for her, the ravages of installing it immaculately
put to rights, with a card standing on the top that said, 'I could get
jealous of this. Theo.'

She had once told him that what she most associated with love and
comfort was her mother's Aga, standing in the kitchen at the Court
House and never going out, summer or winter. She had grown up by
that Aga, she said, warming her hands over it when she got in from
school, leaning against its comfort when she had a tummyache, drying
her wet clothes on its rail, opening the oven to see what was in it for
dinner, watching happily as Christmas puddings bubbled on its hob,
Christmas and birthday cakes went in and out of it, had sat in Purdey's
basket for long hours beside it, reading (and before that, for a brief,
joyous time, had cradled the tiny Biggles in her lap by it, actually slept
there with him on his first night, after creeping down in the stillness of
the sleeping house, hearing him, frightened, bewildered, whimpering
for his mother); had brought half-dead animals to lie in soft boxes by its
warmth, birds, two of the farm cat's abandoned kittens, and once even a
small fox cub she had found lying by its dead mother near the bridge.
She made her first disastrous forays into cooking in it (but they'd been
more successful than any of her other efforts since in more sophisticated
stoves). She and Cressida had always hung their stockings on it, rather
than the conventional fireplaces in the house (ignoring the fact that
Santa would have had more than a little trouble negotiating its
chimney), and whenever there was a family conference (sadly an
increasingly rare event) it was in the kitchen, near the Aga, that it took
place.

Nothing, she'd told Theo on the phone that night, half laughing, half crying, could have made her realize how much he loved her, nothing could have made her love him more. 'Next time you're here, I shall cook you a meal on it,' she said, and 'Good God, I hope not,' he said in alarm (having sampled her cooking once or twice). 'It's just to remind you of me. We could have some sex with it,' he'd added more cheerfully, 'I'd much rather that,' and sure enough, they had. She'd dragged the mattress from her bed and laid it in front of the cooker, heaped with cushions and pillows, had greeted him at the door wearing nothing but a striped cook's apron, had led him to it and then removed the apron and lain down, watching him undress, hurling his clothes onto the floor, feeling her body warming, softening, opening to him before he even touched her, seeing the pleasure ahead, his mouth on hers, his hands everywhere on her, unfolding joy, the sweet heavy settlement of him within her, the clenching, the gathering round him, the pushing, the pulling of desire, the leaping and falling of delight, and then the last slow, sure climb into orgasm, hearing the great roar of her own voice as she reached, accomplished, conquered, and then the oddly quieter cry in his own. And then much much later, as she lay beside him, her body throbbing into quietness, she looked at him and smiled and he smiled back and said, 'That's quite a cooker you have there, Miss Forrest.' And she thought, reaching out and touching the warm sides of the Aga, that she had never been so happy.

She'd intended to have it ripped out when the affair was over, as a final, painful gesture, but it proved so complicated and so expensive that she'd abandoned the attempt. It seemed to her absolutely symptomatic of Theo that he had managed to bestow upon her something that she couldn't get rid of without enormous difficulty and expense; other girls wrapped up their engagement rings, their necklaces, their bracelets and sent them back, and she had to sit, day after day, staring at a love token that weighed half a ton.

Well, it would go now, she thought, along with the flat, and it might even be a selling point, would actually have a cash value. What should have been a cheering prospect made her sit down and burst into tears. She cried for a long time; racking sobs, cathartic, almost pleasurable, and so loud they almost drowned the ring of her phone. 'Shit,' she said and decided to leave it, to let the answering machine take it; but her rush of tears once halted refused to start again and she grabbed a tea towel to wipe her eyes on and ran into the tiny bedroom she had converted into a study. A female American voice was telling her to ring Mr Hayden Cotton most urgently, and issuing an endless list of numbers which Harriet wrote down in the wrong order twice so that she made two extremely expensive calls first to a truck company in Ohio and then a health club in Miami before finally reaching the haven of Mr Cotton's office just off Delancey Street, Manhattan. Hayden Cotton insisted on remaining in Delancey Street, where he had launched his empire in a small sweatshop and where it now occupied an entire block.

'Why quadruple overheads?' he would growl whenever (as they frequently did) one of his executives suggested moving up-town, or even further down towards the Seaport area. 'Or are you offering to take a salary cut?'

They never were, and so he never moved, and never would, it was famously said, until he had to leave feet first; and it was true, he saved hundreds of thousands of dollars a year, and since all his employees, even the most humble stitcher, operated under a profit-sharing scheme, they did not argue too much about it.

Harriet, who had visited the Cotton Fields offices, would not always have agreed with him, would have protested that a good address, a glamorous image, were essential. Having been forced to see that a good address and a glamorous image had done her very little good at all, possibly very much the reverse, she would now have consented to run her company from Cardboard City had she been given the opportunity. Waiting now to be put through to Hayden Cotton, she wondered if she was to be given the opportunity, and if maybe it wasn't too late: Theo had said companies could be bought back from receivership. Perhaps . . .

'Harriet Forrest?'

'Yes, speaking.'

'Hayden Cotton. You get a backer yet?'

'No, Mr Cotton, I haven't, I'm afraid. And my company's gone into receivership today.'

'Uh-huh. That's a shame. And I'm sorry we didn't get a chance to do business together.'

'So am I, Mr Cotton.'

'However, I have another proposition for you.'

'Yes?' Could the sound of a heart thudding be heard down the phone? Did a voice strangled with excitement, with emotion, give you away?

'How would you like to come and work for me?'

'For you? In what way?'

'I'm thinking of launching a new range. Tell you more about it if and when you want to talk. I need a designer for it. A chief designer. I'd like that person to be you.'

'Oh,' said Harriet, 'Oh I see. Well, Mr Cotton, I don't know. I mean I'd love it and I'm terribly flattered to have been asked, but I've got used to working for myself, you see, and –'

'I do see and I greatly admire what you've done. But I think, with the greatest respect, Miss Forrest, your talents are ninety-nine per cent in the design field. Running a business just distracts you from that.'

'Oh,' said Harriet. 'Well, I haven't done that badly, Mr Cotton. I mean –'

'I think you've done extremely well. All you needed was a really good business manager. But even so, designing is what you were made for. And what you should do for me. I could make you a very good offer. Harriet. Very good indeed.'

'Well – I don't know. It's not something I – I ever thought of –' Harriet started again, trying to sound more efficient, less daffy. 'Where would I work? In London?'

'No. That wouldn't be any good. You'd have to come over here. I'd want you working closely with me.'

'Oh, I see.' Her mind was racing, raking over his offer, thinking of all the implications. They were scary, they weren't what she wanted at all: but then was she really in a position to argue? A new city, a new lifestyle, a new life; it could be exactly, exactly what she needed

'The pay'd be good,' said Hayden Cotton, 'I thought quarter of a million for starters.'

Quarter of a million dollars a year! That was at least, at least £150,000. And the low tax structure in the States, the lower cost of living, would make it worth far, far more than the same sum in England. She'd be – 'With profit-sharing, of course,' said Hayden Cotton, cutting into her thoughts. 'And there'd be a lot of potential built in. Maybe a partnership one day. And narurally a car and an interest-free loan to buy an apartment or whatever. And you'd be able to get home to London often, obviously. Think about it, Harriet. At least come and talk to me.'

Harriet thought. She thought of the pleasure of designing clothes, her own collection, with none of the attendant headaches of cost, cash flow, financial forecasting, VAT returns; she thought of the heady lifestyle that would surely ensue; she thought of having more money, real money, to spend on herself, not plough endlessly back into the company, of freedom to enjoy herself, of not having to work through weekends and nights, not having to find staff, get rid of staff, find more staff. She thought of living in New York, a city she loved, of jetting backwards and forwards across the Atlantic, and she thought of getting away from England, from the pain of her discovery about her father, the nightmare of Cressida – and from Theo. Theo hated New York, visited it as rarely as he could. The opportunities for bumping into him, for being pursued by him, would undoubtedly be fewer. It was very, very attractive. And then she thought of the joy, the pure, unalloyed pleasure of having her own business, of seeing it grow, of doing what she wanted, what she thought best; and yes, she had made mistakes, but she had learnt from them, she wouldn't make the same ones again, and she would do it again, somehow, she would get hold of some more money. Owning a company was like having a garden, planting things in it, ideas, talent, skills, risk, courage, and seeing them grow in entirely your own way, and however hard, however exhausting, however at times unrewarding, the pleasure was heady, and the rewards, however meagre, were absolutely your own, absolutely personal. Working for Hayden Cotton, as his chief gardener, might be a lot easier, but the end result, however grand and splendid, would still be his.

'I really don't think I could,' she said finally. 'I have to do things my way, Mr Cotton. I've made lots of mistakes, and I'm sure I'll make lots more, but they'll be different ones. Thank you for asking me, but I have to stick it out here.'

'Oh well,' he said with a sigh, 'pity. I thought you just might. Mind you, Theo said you wouldn't, said you'd never come.'

'Theo! Theo Buchan?'

'That's the one.'

'You discussed this with Theo?'

'I mentioned it. We talk a lot, you know. We go back a long way, to when I dealt direct and bought textiles from him.'

'Yes I know,' said Harriet bitterly.

'He thought it was a great idea for you, but he told me I was wasting my time. I guess he knows you better than I thought he did.'

'Oh, he does?' said Harriet. 'I think not. You can tell Theo Buchan I –' She stopped, confused. It was hardly Hayden Cotton's fault that Theo still saw it as his prerogative to go around trying to run her life for her. It was outrageous, but –

'I'm sorry,' she said carefully. 'I didn't mean to sound rude, Mr Cotton. I really didn't.'

'That's OK, I understand. Listen, Harriet, don't rush this. Take a day or two thinking about it. It may seem better when you've slept on it. Come and talk to me, spend a few days here.'

'Well – yes, all right,' said Harriet slowly. 'Maybe I should. That'd be good.'

It still didn't feel right, but she wasn't going to give Theo the satisfaction of knowing what was best for her, what suited her. And she could do it for a year or two maybe, get some money together and then start again. Bloody, bloody overbearing, officious man; he would not, could not go on behaving as if he owned her, as if she still loved him.

'Good. Very good. You call me tomorrow and we'll fix a trip. Goodbye, Miss Forrest. You'll like New York. You'd suit it.'

'Yes,' said Harriet thoughtfully, 'yes, I think maybe I would. And I'll ring you in the morning. Goodbye, Mr Cotton.'

'Oh, and by the way,' he said suddenly, as she was about to put the phone down. 'In case you thought otherwise, I took no notice of Theo's views when I was making my decision as to whether or not I bought your company. I make my own decisions, too, you know.'

'Oh,' said Harriet, 'oh, I see.'

She ran herself a bath and lay in it, thinking; she woke up an hour later, freezing cold, to hear the phone ringing again. She dragged on her bathrobe and sat hugging the radiator, looking at her interestingly wrinkled feet and hands, feeling rather sick. It was her father.

'Darling. Can I come and see you?'

'I'd rather you didn't, if you don't mind,' said Harriet. 'Not tonight. I'm terribly tired.'

'Oh,' said James. It was a small, hurt little sound. Harriet didn't care. She felt a cold, hard hostility towards him; she didn't want to see him, didn't want either alternative, of confrontation or pretence. She supposed she might get used to the idea of his having an affair with Susie, but she would never get over it. It was too hurtful, too literally shocking.

'Surely Mummy needs you?'

'No,' he said very quietly, 'no, Harriet, she doesn't.'

'Daddy, what is it?' she said.

'Your mother's gone.'

'Gone? Gone where?'

'She's left me.'

'Oh', said Harriet. 'Oh I see.' She knew she sounded dull, absurdly uninterested, but she couldn't help it. She wasn't quite sure what she should feel, what she did feel, but whatever it was, she wasn't feeling it. Her prime emotion, she discovered, exploring her mood briefly, was admiration for her mother. Certainly not sympathy for her father.

'You don't sound very surprised.'

'I'm sorry,' she said with an effort. 'Very sorry. Er – where exactly has she gone?'

God, she hoped her mother wasn't coming to her. Sympathize with her she might, but that would truly be more than she could stand. She had had enough: enough of all of them.

'To stay with a friend,' said James. 'And quite soon, I fancy, to visit Cressida.'

'Cressida? Cressida! You mean you've found her?'

'She rang up.'

'Where from? Paris?'

'Yes.'

'Well, is she all right?'

'Yes and no,' he said.

'Can't you tell me about it?'

'Not on the phone. It's too complex, too difficult. I just need to talk to you, Harriet, so badly.'

He sounded terrible; in spite of everything, Harriet felt a pang of alarm. 'Look,' she said, 'I'm frozen, I went to sleep in the bath. Give me five minutes to get dressed, and I'll ring you back.'

'Can't I come and see you, Harriet? Please?'

'Maybe,' she said, 'but don't leave yet. I really have to sort out what I'm doing.'

She put the phone down feeling utterly chilled; not just physically, her heart seemed to have ice round it too, heavy grey ice, and there was ice in her veins and ice in her head. Everywhere she looked there was betrayal, loneliness, no one seemed to be there for her. She was very happy for Rufus and Tilly (who had phoned to tell her they were getting married, Tilly full of remorse that she would not after all be able to lend her any money; Harriet told her not to be crazy and she'd never have taken it anyway), very glad for Janine and Merlin (who had also phoned and asked her out to dinner, which she had rather half-heartedly refused), very sorry for Mungo (who, Rufus told her, had had his heart broken by his mysterious lady-love, but was burying himself in his work: 'Mungo!' said Harriet. 'Working!'), very sympathetic with a shattered Oliver who had rung from the airport to say goodbye, a swift careful phone call, thanking her for her help, not talking about Cressida, about what might have happened. She even now felt the stirrings of pity for her father; faint, echo-y but there. You couldn't adore someone for twenty-nine years and then feel nothing for them, just abandon them.

She went to her room, pulled out some leggings and a big sweater and some thick socks, dried her hair – God, it looked awful, wispier than ever, maybe she should have it cut off again – then went back into the kitchen and made herself a cup of tea. As she got warmer, began to come back to life, the numbness left her and she began to ache. She ached with weariness and loneliness and misery, she ached in every bone, every muscle, in her head, in her stomach and in the very heart of herself. She was very tired, she would have liked to go to sleep, but every time she closed her eyes she lived again the awful scene when the receiver, having arranged for the phones, the electricity to be cut off, having picked up all her books, all her files, all her chequebooks and bank statements, asked everyone to leave the building with him, and they filed out, her and her four girls (none of whom would go without her: 'We're all in this,' they said to her, 'we're all in this with you'), taking

with them only their personal possessions, and some work folders –
'they're personal,' Harriet said defiantly, 'pictures of our own, to hang on
our own walls in our own homes.' She could see he didn't believe her,
but he allowed them to take the folders all the same; he was not an
unreasonable man, just a very dry and precise one. But as he stood
there, screwing a padlock onto the door, snapping it shut, looking up at
the building with a strangely satisfied expression, as if it had somehow
become his, all the work, all the love she had put into it negated by that
one action, she could gladly have killed him.

The girls had asked her to go for a drink, but she refused; she said she
had things to do; and that was when she had settled in the doorway and
the policeman had found her.

She sat in the kitchen, drinking the tea, putting off without knowing
quite why the moment when she had to phone her father again, staring
out at the misty rain, wondering what was to become of her. Was she to
end up one of those powerful, rich New York women who returned at
night alone to empty, stylish apartments after long days of ruling
companies and running lives? Or was she to stay here in England,
following her instinct, picking up a myriad of untidy tangled ends,
battling to get back to where she had been before? Here she was,
twenty-nine years old, bankrupt – well, maybe that was an achievement
in itself, at so tender an age – absolutely alone, or so it felt, her mother
concerned only with her sister, her father become someone she
preferred not to see, her friends scattering – 'Now don't start, Harriet,'
she said aloud, feeling the treacherous tears rising, the choking
sensation in her chest, 'don't start.'

The phone rang sharply; God, it must be her father again, she'd
promised him five minutes and it was almost twenty-five. It was.

'Harriet –'

'Sorry, Daddy,' she said. 'Listen, you stay there. I'll come down. It'll
only take me an hour or so. And I'd like to come home.'

'You would?' He sounded touchingly, frighteningly grateful.

'Yes, I really would,' she said, and found to her surprise it was true.
She wanted to go home: to go home to the Court House. This flat wasn't
home, even with the Aga; the only other home she had was her studio

and that was barred to her, its locks changed, the heart ripped out of it. She would go home and see her father, spend a few days with him, perhaps discover why he had done what he had; and there, where she had grown up, where she had become what she was, with all the good and all the bad, she could decide what she wanted and what she should do. She felt more cheerful straight away; journeys always lifted her spirits, distracted her. She would play some really nice music, and stop on the way at a service station – Harriet was always surprised by how much people disliked service stations, they seemed to her lovely warm womblike places, faintly reminiscent of fairgrounds with all the cheerful tat and rubbish for sale, and she liked the food too, cheerful rubbishy food – and she would arrive at the Court House and her father would be waiting for her and she would at least be somewhere she belonged, where someone cared about her.

That reminded her of Janine; she ought to ring her, tell her she definitely wouldn't be going to dinner with her.

Merlin answered the phone: Janine had gone out, he said, gone shopping: 'Oh, I see. Well, look, Merlin, I'm going home. Now. To Wedbourne, so I definitely won't be joining you for dinner. My father sounds pretty low. Thank you anyway, and I'll see you soon.'

'Quite all right, Harriet. I'll tell Janine. Your father does sound bad. He phoned here, wanted Theo –'

'Theo!' said Harriet. 'What was Theo doing there?'

'Oh, he came to see Janine. Not sure why. Anyway he's gone now, rushing off to see Sasha, apparently.'

'Sasha! Theo's gone to see Sasha? Merlin, are you sure?'

'Quite sure. He said something about buying her some roses, I'd got some for Janine you see, and –'

'Yes, I see, Merlin,' said Harriet very quietly. 'Well, send my love to Janine. Goodbye.'

'Bye, my dear. Are you all right? You sound a bit down. Not surprising really, I suppose.'

'No,' said Harriet, 'not really.'

She put the phone down, picked up her car keys and her bag, and, keeping her mind carefully blank, walked out of the door.

* * *

Harriet had had her appendix out when she'd been eleven; due to the bungling of an inefficient anaesthetist (whom her father had had removed from his hospital within the week), she came round from the anaesthetic a little too soon, before she was even out of the theatre. She had never forgotten it, the way she was hurtled from darkness into white-hot pain; she had screamed, and then was dispatched swiftly back into the darkness and awoke again hours later, safely and aware only of mild discomfort, but traumatized nonetheless. Her experience that evening was much the same: one moment she was driving automatically and dully down the Cromwell Road extension and the next she was in such emotional pain that she almost crashed the car.

Theo back with Sasha. Taking roses to Sasha, rushing to meet Sasha, only – what? – two hours after he had told her he loved her still, that he had always loved her, that he felt nothing for Sasha, never had, had only married her to ease the pain of losing her, losing Harriet. 'Christ!' she yelled aloud, throwing her head back, trying to concentrate, to keep at least most of her mind on the road, the traffic. 'Christ, Theo, how could you, how could you?'

Chapter 39

Theo 6:30pm

Theo sat at his desk looking at the relics of his marriage to Sasha: a large fake diamond engagement ring, her keys to the house in The Boltons, the Daimler and the Range Rover (he had never allowed her to drive the Bentley) and a rough draft of the articles of association of her new company. Mr Hennessy had proved to be younger and better-looking than he had expected, and possessed of a redoubtable legal mind, but he was more than a little out of his depth with his new client. Theo felt almost sorry for him.

Right. He would phone Mungo, fix a place for dinner, go back to the office and do some work, and then maybe try, just try phoning Harriet again.

Mungo sounded subdued but no more; he said it had been a bitch of a day but he was looking forward to seeing his father. 'Me too,' said Theo. 'Ritz, eight o'clock?'

'Fine,' said Mungo.

Theo spent two hours trying to distract himself from the thought of Harriet, and then rang her flat. No answer. The studio. No answer. He tried Rufus, Tilly, the Headleigh Drayton house: Annabel told him sulkily that everyone was at the hospital visiting her mother and she had been left to answer the phone. 'And before you ask, she's fine.'

'Good,' said Theo, 'send her my love. Harriet's not there?'

'No, I don't think so. I'm sure she's not, it's family only tonight.'

'All right, Annabel. If by chance she phones, get her to call me.'

'I will if I'm here,' said Annabel. 'I'm hoping to go out.'

'Love you too,' said Theo and rang off. He had forgotten briefly about

Susie; he ordered some flowers for her, and then rang Janine again. She was out, but Merlin answered the phone.

'She rang – oh, about half an hour ago. Said she was going home to Wedbourne. I told her you'd been here, said you were off to see Sasha –'

'You what? Merlin, I wasn't.'

'But you said you were, my boy. I heard you. You said you were going to take her some roses.'

'No, Merlin, I said I was going to see Sasha's lawyer. You must have misunderstood. Sasha and I are getting divorced. It was a joke about the roses.'

'What, already? That's a pity. Quite liked Sasha. I'd have liked to have her around for a bit longer. Oh dear, well, I've given some duff information then.'

'You have a bit.'

'Even told her you were taking flowers along,' said Merlin cheerfully. 'She will be confused. Better get onto her.'

'Oh Merlin,' said Theo in agony, 'Merlin, this is terrible. And I can't get onto her. If she's on the way to Wedbourne.'

On the M40, in the pouring rain, in that bloody Peugeot of hers, that went so much too fast, that she never had serviced; upset, angry, thinking he was rushing off to see Sasha with flowers. Christ Almighty, what a mess.

'Better get after her then,' said Merlin. 'You can catch her up easily. Bit of sport. I'd come with you if I didn't have so much to do here. Very complicated, getting married. Can't think how you've managed it five times.'

Theo ran out of his office, tore down the stairs, into the car park, into the Bentley, roared out into Dover Street. It was raining; the traffic was appalling.

An hour later he was still not even on the motorway.

He rang James. 'Is Harriet there?'

'No, not yet. I'm getting worried about her actually. The weather's frightful and she's been over two hours already.'

'Can't you ring her on her mobile?'

'She doesn't seem to have it with her.'

'Oh Christ,' said Theo.

After the Beaconsfield turn-off, the traffic eased. Theo put his foot down, tried to tell himself she was all right. It wasn't dark, she was a good driver, she wasn't hysterical, she'd be fine. Probably just stopped for a coffee or something. Or run out of petrol, she was always doing that. Silly girl. Stupid girl. Why couldn't she have listened to him at lunchtime, then she'd be all right, safe, with him – His car phone rang. 'Yes?'

It was Janine. 'Theo, I am so sorry. I just heard what Merlin did. The stupid, stupid old man –'

Even in his anguish Theo was amused to hear Merlin, who was only a little more than ten years Janine's senior, described by her as an old man.

'It's all right, Janine. I remember how it happened. I was talking and my phone rang mid-sentence. He meant well.'

'He should not have meddled. We have just had our first quarrel. I have told him –'

'Janine darling, not now.' He really couldn't face the details of a lover's tiff. 'Have you spoken to James?'

'Yes, and she is still not there. He is very worried.'

'Me too,' said Theo and rang off.

It was round the next corner, between the huge white chalk cliffs near the Thames turn-off, that he hit the tailback to the crash. It was maybe half a mile ahead: he could see it, several cars and a lorry packed together, police lights flashing, two ambulances. The traffic was at a complete standstill. Theo sat there for roughly thirty seconds, thinking he was going to throw up, then got out of the Bentley, just left it in the fast lane, and ran, ran down the hard shoulder, his lungs straining, his heart bursting, until he reached the heap of cars. One of the ambulances was just pulling away; a policeman waved him back.

'Not now, sir, if you don't mind. Keep the area clear. Terrible mess.'

'I can see that,' said Theo. He walked forward slowly, peering terrified into the wreckage. Two of the cars were unrecognizable. The third was a Peugeot. Crumpled, mangled, standing almost on its tail, but still indisputably a Peugeot. A Peugeot 205. Black. Christ Almighty. A K-reg black Peugeot 205.

'Not now, sir,' said the policeman again.

Theo ignored him, went on.

'For God's sake, sir.'

'I think,' said Theo, speaking with immense difficulty, 'in fact, no, I know – that's my girlfriend's car.'

A police car took him to the hospital; he stood in the doorway of casualty while the young sergeant went up to the desk, made inquiries. He looked over his shoulder at Theo, then turned his back on him and followed a nurse into the netherland beyond the waiting room. Theo knew then; he knew that she had died. She had died, and she had died thinking he was a cheap, tacky boor who lied and fucked around and did not, as she had said so often, know the meaning of love. She was lost to him now, lost forever, and he would never get the chance to be with her again, talk to her again, hold her, care for her, love her. She was gone, in all her passionate, lovely courage, gone in a tangle of metal, crushed, brutally murdered by a mistake, by a misunderstanding. Theo felt suddenly violently sick; he rushed outside and threw up, over and over again, then walked very slowly back into casualty, into reception, sat down and put his face in his hands.

A young nurse, the one who had led the policeman off, came over to him, put her hand gently on his shoulder. 'Mr Buchan is it?'

'Yes,' said Theo, 'yes, that's right.'

Every word was an enormous struggle to get out; it was as if some huge pressure was constricting his throat.

'Would you like a cup of tea?'

They always did that, offered relatives tea. It was supposed to help, God knows why. He shook his head at her dumbly.

'Well, if you wait just a little while, someone will see you. Are you sure you're all right?'

He nodded again. The doctor, he supposed: to tell him. All the usual clichés, that they had done all they could, that she hadn't suffered, hadn't known anything about it; maybe he would even have to identify her, someone had to, he knew that. He found the thought of looking at Harriet, a suddenly dead Harriet, quite horrific. It was not death itself, Deirdre had died, she had died in his arms, he had held her for hours, and for hours after she died had sat looking at her, wondering where she had actually gone, why he could not have gone with her; but they'd said all the right things, he and she, all the things that needed to be said, had reassured, tried to comfort one another, and he'd had Mungo at least, had that much of Deirdre left to him. He'd said nothing to Harriet that was right, and he had nothing left of her, only her face, raw with misery when she told him to get out of her life and leave her alone. And now she had got out of his.

'Mr Buchan?' It was a young doctor; he looked, Theo thought, like an extra in *Casualty*, with his white coat and his stethoscope and his carefully arranged face.

'Yes?'

'Mr Buchan, if you come with me you can see Miss Forrest now.'

So he *was* going to have to identify her. How bad would she look, how badly mutilated would she be? Was he going to be able to stand it? He stood up, and felt suddenly very dizzy.

'Are you all right, Mr Buchan? Did anyone give you tea?'

'No. Yes. Well –'

'This is a terrible ordeal, I know,' said the doctor. 'Nothing can really prepare you for it. I'm so sorry. Now, I think you should be ready for a bit of a shock, but –'

Theo wasn't listening. He was standing outside the cubicle and nothing he had ever done in his life had required this kind of courage. He raised his hand to pull back the curtain, and it fell again; he simply couldn't do it. 'I'm sorry,' he mumbled to the doctor. 'I don't seem to be able to –'

'That's all right,' said the doctor. 'Let me.'

Theo looked away, hearing the curtain pulled back, knowing he must turn, look at her, what was left of her, still unable to do it.

'Just a moment,' he mumbled to the doctor. 'Just a moment. Sorry.'

Go on, Theo, do it, do it, man, for Christ's sake, look at her, get it over, do it, do it–

'Theo.' It was Harriet's voice, weak, slightly slurred, but still her voice, unmistakably hers, unmistakably real. 'Theo, what on earth are you doing here?'

Epilogue

He drove her home next morning to Wedbourne, his car retrieved from the fast lane of the M40 and brought to the hospital by a reproachful policeman who told him he was lucky, it could well have caused another accident.

James followed in his car; he had arrived at the hospital in response to Theo's phone call, and they had sat together through the night while Harriet slept, checked on hourly for concussion and a suspected fractured skull. They all said it was a miracle she had come out alive; two people had died, three had sustained major injuries, and she had suffered only a fractured ankle (although broken in two places, possibly requiring surgery), a broken arm, two cracked ribs, a great many cuts and bruises on her face and what they were assured was a comparatively mild concussion.

The police came in the morning to question her, but there was no question of any of the blame being hers; several witnesses had seen the lorry (going in any case far too fast) swerve from the middle lane straight across the road, and go into a skid and then a spin, hitting the first car head-on, and then Harriet's. She had crashed onto the hard shoulder and into the barrier, and the car behind her had hit her tail sideways. She had been saved by her seat belt and the fact that she had been skidding so fast her brakes had been useless.

'If they'd worked, the car, and therefore you, might have been hit much nearer the centre,' said James, stroking her head tenderly.

'Oh God,' said Harriet, 'and you know what I thought? The last thing I thought? That I really should have had the car serviced, then I could have stopped.'

'Wouldn't have made any difference,' said Theo.

'What I don't understand,' said James, 'is why you were here at all, Theo. I thought you were having dinner with Mungo.'

'Oh God,' said Theo, 'he's probably still sitting at the Ritz.'

They set her up in the drawing room, made a bed for her there, since she couldn't handle the stairs. She slept a lot for the first few days, her head gave her a lot of pain, but then she became more cheerful and a great deal more demanding, wanted to be out in the garden (summer had returned), wanted a phone, wanted endless jugs of fresh iced lemonade, wanted very specific kinds of food, mainly rather spicy things, curries and chillies. They raided Maggie's freezer, then moved on to takeaways and the food department at Marks and Spencers.

James provided her with crutches, but her broken arm prevented her from using them, so he got her a wheelchair, which she rather liked but still needed help with; she couldn't propel it efficiently herself (again because of her arm) and sat crossly dependent while they wheeled her about the house and garden, and even on occasions down the lane.

Theo refused to leave her; he nursed her and cared for her with surprising sweetness, performing the most intimate tasks with a detached competence, anticipating her needs with extraordinary perception. It was only after a week of this that Harriet properly realized that the sickroom was familiar territory to him, that he had nursed Deirdre, Mungo's mother, almost single-handed during her illness. She found the thought infinitely moving, found, too, that her emotions towards him shifted, softened, found herself in those first shocked, pain-filled days dangerously near to admitting love. Then as she recovered, began to gain strength, physical and emotional, as thought took over from reaction, she struggled to put herself back into a more objective mode. Theo observing all this, recognizing the conflicts, was at once amused and touched by it.

She woke one night, hot, aching, thirsty, reached out for the glass of water by her bed, and knocked it over. 'Shit,' she said aloud, but quite quietly, her sense of helplessness adding to the blanket of misery, wondering if she felt bad enough, desperate enough to ring the little bell Theo had supplied her with to summon them. But before she'd had time to decide he was there, sleepily alert, struggling into his dressing gown, and 'What is it, Harriet?' he said. 'Is the pain bad, do you want me to get you something?' And she stared at him, so awed by his response to her need, his sensitivity to her pain that she was unable to speak, unable to do anything but smile and reach out for his hand.

'I seem to be making progress,' was all he said, smiling back at her, and was gone, to return with more iced water, her painkillers, and a quiet swift neatening of the bed; and then he sat beside her, waiting for her misery to ease.

'You're wonderful,' was the last thing she said, drifting back to sleep. 'Dear Theo. Thank you.'

In the morning her mood had changed; she was irritable, tired, and anxious too that he should not think she and her resolve were weakening. Always one jump ahead of her, he teased her, said it was all right. He wasn't going to cash in on any goodwill he might have engendered, he was going to London for the day, so she could relax.

'I'm perfectly relaxed,' said Harriet petulantly, aware of a distinct lack of such a quality in almost every area of herself.

'You don't look it,' he said mildly and bent to kiss her cheek. Harriet turned away.

Mostly he stayed at the Court House, conducted his business from there, moving Myra Harman and Mark Protheroe into the Royal Hotel for several days a week, using both the phone lines, one for his fax, as well as his own mobile and car phone.

'You must be singly responsible for most of Telecom's profits,' said James plaintively after three days of this. 'I really can't go on, Theo, having to go out to the village post office to make a call.'

'Sorry, James. It's not for long.'

He had told James on the long night at the hospital about Harriet, told him he loved her, that he wanted to marry her. James had taken the news with interesting calm.

'I can't imagine what she sees in you, and it had better be the last marriage you ever make, or I swear to God I'll kill you, but if that's what she wants –'

'She does, but she doesn't know it yet,' said Theo.

At Harriet's request, her accident was played down to Maggie. 'I know she'll want to come home and look after me, but that will be difficult for everyone and probably most of all me. I shall have to be fussed over which I hate and listen to her telling me how wonderful Cressida is being and I just shan't be able to stand it.' So Theo phoned and simply told Maggie that Harriet had had a bit of a bump in her car and hurt her arm and was taking a few days off to recuperate. Maggie was happy, he reported, with her friend and was house-hunting. Cressida, it seemed, was also happy, feeling better, coping with her situation. Maggie was probably going over for a few days in September. 'She says,' he added, his dark eyes gleaming with malice, 'that Cressida has written to Oliver, trying to explain. Your mother says she is sure Oliver will understand and see that it's for the best.'

'I'm sure it is,' said Harriet, hitting her pillow viciously, 'but not for the reasons Mummy thinks. I wonder what this person is like. A sucker I should think.'

A week after the wedding day a letter arrived from Cressida for James, begging his forgiveness, hoping he would understand. 'We plan to be married in the Bureau de l'Etat (that's the registry office) as soon as he is out of hospital. I wish you could meet Gérard, but I expect you would prefer not to. He is very ill, I'm afraid, he's having treatment, transfusions, they're seeking a bone-marrow donor for him. But he's not expected to live for very long. The best we can hope is that he will survive to see his child born.'

James was clearly distressed by the letter; he went for a long walk and came back his face drawn and grey.

'Do you want to talk about it?' said Harriet.

'No,' he said, 'no, not now.'

He spent the rest of the day in his study, only emerging for supper which he ate in almost complete silence.

'It sounds a terrible thing to say but this is a perfect scenario for Cressida,' said Harriet to Theo later. 'It's got everything, romance, tragedy, mystery. She must be very happy.'

'You sound very cynical,' said Theo.

'Cressida makes me feel cynical,' said Harriet. 'I can't help it.'

Slowly, painfully, she was coming to terms with her father's long relationship with Susie.

He broached the subject one evening when Theo was in London, and oddly, after an initial resistance, she found it helped her, eased her hostility to him, to air it, to hear his halting apologies.

'I can't excuse it, can't explain it,' he said simply. 'I was in love with her. I behaved very badly for a long long time. Now I'm getting my just desserts.'

'You are.'

'Yes, I've lost them both. I'm going to be very lonely. It's a fitting punishment for me.'

Harriet was silent.

Tilly and Rufus came down to visit. Tilly was wearing a large engagement ring, a futuristic sculptured gold design, set with tiny spangled diamonds. She said she had given up swearing, and planned on giving up smoking for Rufus, but it was too much to ask her to do both things at once.

'And what are you giving up, Rufus?' asked Theo.

'I couldn't think of anything,' he said. 'I seem to be perfect already. But I've promised Tilly we won't send our sons to public school.'

'Sons? Tilly, this is a huge change of heart,' said Harriet laughing.

'Yeah, I know, I know. I think maybe, one day, with a Caesarian under a double general anaesthetic I might be able to manage something. I really am quite interested to see what we might produce between the two of us.'

'Me too,' said Rufus. He pushed back his fair hair, smiled his lovely, gentle smile at her, his dark eyes soft with love.

'Rufus, you look more and more like your mother every day,' said Harriet.

Susie was recovered, but had agreed to have the surgery Mr Hobson recommended. Another lump had appeared – still benign but none the less worrying.

'I can have a reconstruction done,' she said to Alistair, 'I hate the thought of it so much, but I think I should. And I shouldn't be so vain, it's terribly wrong of me. Anyway, no one but you will see it, and if you can cope with it then so can I.'

'Is that a promise, my darling?' said Alistair lightly. Susie looked at him; he was smiling carefully, but his eyes were unreadable.

'Yes, Alistair, it's a promise.'

Mungo came to visit too, bearing a jeroboam of champagne, a bunch of three dozen roses and a sheaf of details of studios and offices where Harriet might start up her next business. 'Special rates to you, madam, and we'd waive our usual insistence on a year's rent in advance.'

He looked vaguely different, Harriet thought; more sober, more grown-up. The wild black hair was shorter, neater-looking, he was wearing a suit (linen to be sure, but still a suit) and a tie, and he produced the studio details from a formal-looking briefcase, rather than the canvas bag he had always used before. But he looked happy, more self-confident than she could remember, and the hug he gave his father was unmistakably affectionate.

'Mungo, you're sweet,' said Harriet laughing, flicking through the papers, lingering longingly over a studio in Bloomsbury, 'but I'm an undischarged bankrupt. I can't possibly start taking on expensive new premises. If I do start again, it will have to be from the kitchen table here, I should think. I've even got to sell my flat.'

'That's ridiculous, there must be dozens of people who'd make you a loan. Dad for a start, why don't –'

'Mungo, no,' said Harriet hastily. 'Your dad is the last person I'd take money from.'

'Why?'

'Well, because – just because.'

'You're mad,' said Mungo. 'He'd like to do it and he's very fond of you, you know.'

'Yes,' said Harriet, 'yes, I know he is.'

* * *

Janine and Merlin also came to visit several times. They'd set their wedding date for the end of August. They were having a small civil ceremony in Paris, followed by a luncheon at the Meurice and a large party in London, before leaving for their journey through China. Merlin was remorseful, still convinced he had been instrumental in causing Harriet's accident. 'Darling Merlin, you weren't. Don't flatter yourself. And don't flatter Theo either. As if I'd care if he was going back to Sasha or not anyway.'

'Not what he's hoping to hear, I understand,' said Merlin, and received a sharp kick on the ankle from Janine. 'Sorry, my dear. Can't do a thing right these days,' he said to Harriet plaintively; but he winked at her and then at Janine, and took her small white hand and kissed it tenderly.

'Have you been saying things to Merlin?' said Harriet crossly to Theo that evening, as she lay in the garden on a chaise longue, drinking her way through yet another jugful of lemonade.

'I say a lot of things to Merlin.'

'You know perfectly well what I mean. About me. Us.'

'No, but Janine might have. Why don't you have some champagne in that?'

'You know I'm not allowed alcohol. Theo, you are appalling. How dare you discuss our lives with other people?'

'Well, I'm not allowed to discuss them with you.'

'There's nothing to discuss,' said Harriet.

They talked for hours, night after night, the three of them, about Cressida: whose story to believe, which explanation might be the right one, tracking backwards and forwards over the same ground, the same details, the story each of them wanted to believe, the story that to each of them seemed the most likely.

'A combination of them all, perhaps?' said Theo. 'There is no doubt she is in love with this man, that he is ill –'

'He doesn't look ill,' said Harriet sharply, 'in that photograph.'

'Harriet, you're being very hard,' said James. 'You can't tell from a photograph, and besides leukaemia patients often look comparatively normal until very near – well, for a long time. He's in hospital –'

'How do you know that?' said Harriet. 'We have Cressida's word for it. Oliver had her word that she was pregnant last year and she wasn't, we had her word she loved Oliver, was going to marry him. For God's sake, you're all obsessed with her, duped by her –' Angry tears had filled her eyes; she struggled to stand up on her crutches, to leave the room, almost fell over.

'Harriet,' said Theo gently, easing her back into her chair, 'Harriet, don't be so hostile. It doesn't help.'

'I can't help it,' she said, 'I am hostile. I can't forgive her, I can't even think about forgiving her. How you can, Daddy, I really don't know. At best, at very best, even if we believe her wonderful, romantic story, she still hurt you so much that day. And Mummy too, who adored her so. She could have talked to you, discussed it, told you what she felt she had to do. I just don't understand you.'

'Well,' said James, 'the human psyche is very complex. And she was in crisis. Try to put yourself in her position, Harriet, desperate, pregnant, trapped. What would you have done?'

'That's an impossible question for her to answer,' said Theo quietly. 'Harriet would not, could not, have been in that kind of situation. She's too honest even to imagine it.'

Harriet stared at him, surprised as always by the depth of his knowledge of her family, the daily conflict of her feelings towards him intensifying sharply.

'Theo, don't speak for me,' she said finally. 'My brain hasn't been affected by the accident, you know.'

'No,' he said, 'I can see that. James, can I take some more of that excellent Armagnac?'

'Yes, of course,' said James. He seemed distracted, scarcely aware of where he was. 'It's so odd talking about her like this, I feel somehow I don't know her at all any more, that she can in no way be my child, the one I loved and cared for and endeavoured to bring up well and did so badly with. It's as you said to your mother, Harriet, she has become another woman altogether, one we simply don't know any more. And conjecture as we may, we can't properly understand her or why she did what she did. But I – I have to share that woman's view – what was her name, Harriet, the gynaecologist –'

'Bradman,' said Harriet. 'Jennifer Bradman.'

'Yes. I have to share her view, looking at Cressida from this viewpoint, that she was – well, disturbed. With hindsight, she did display a classic personality disorder. The near compulsion to lie, the complex deceptions – those flying lessons she talked you into are classic, Theo, there was no real reason for secrecy there, after all, her constant health problems, her ineptness with money.'

'You say that,' said Harriet, 'but I've been pretty inept with it myself. No one suggests I have a personality disorder. Or perhaps you do,' she said, glaring at Theo.

'Harriet, of course we don't,' said James. 'Don't be silly. You've just made some bad business decisions. That's completely different.'

'Oh, well, good,' said Harriet, her voice loaded with sarcasm. 'That's all right then, I can relax. Well, I think that selling the flat, for instance, keeping that a secret, just proves she was planning on doing something drastic.'

'Not at all,' said Theo. 'She would have had to sell her flat anyway, what use would it have been to her if she was living in New York? She could have explained it away so easily.'

'You're all obsessed with her,' said Harriet. She felt the tears rising again. 'Here we are still making excuses for her, saying poor Cressida, there must have been something wrong with her, when she was just a – a brat, a spoilt, self-centred girl, who you all adored.'

'She was indeed,' said James, his face heavy with pain, 'and it hurts me to say it, but that is another reason for not being too hard on her now. Being overindulged, the spoilt baby as she undoubtedly was, the youngest, having excuses made for her all the time, does predispose to that sort of condition. I've talked to people about it.'

'Well,' said Theo, 'as I said, I personally take the view the answer is not simple. That we have to accept an amalgam of all three explanations.'

'Not, surely not, Julia's?' said James, desolation in his voice.

'I'd say not, I'd like to think not,' said Theo, 'but it's an extraordinary lie on Julia's part, and if she did show Cressida the letter and Cressida had no interest in the money, then surely she would have told Oliver, would have laughed – or even cried about it.'

'Maybe,' said Harriet slowly, 'that was the last straw. Maybe she was desperate anyway, and Julia's hostility tipped her over into going. '

Theo was staring into his glass, his dark eyes very sombre, his face infinitely sad. 'I think,' he said, 'I think the truth is that none of us will ever really know. Only Cressida knows. And she will never tell.'

'Listen,' said Theo one evening, sitting down by Harriet, taking her hand, 'there's a lot to discuss. I don't understand you, Harriet. I love you. I know you love me –'

'Theo, I don't. Well, of course I do, but not like that. It's over. It was a lovely time, a lovely experience, but – well, it just wouldn't work. It couldn't. I know.'

'How do you know?'

'Because – because I just do. Our lives won't, can't go together. You'd start taking me over, owning me, and I won't be owned.'

'I don't want to own you.'

'Theo, you can't help owning things. It's in your very soul.'

'Harriet, I swear I won't even try to take you over. I won't ask you to marry me, I won't suggest I give you any money for your wretched company, I won't even suggest I give you money for anything. You can live in some hovel in Brixton or somewhere like that and I'll come and visit you sometimes and we can eat baked beans and drink bitter paid for out of your social security money. How's that? As long as I can love you, that's all I ask.'

'Oh, don't be ridiculous,' said Harriet. 'And anyway, you know perfectly well I'm probably going to New York.'

'Good God,' he said. 'I'd forgotten about that. I thought you'd given the whole idea up.'

'Well I haven't. You were wrong. Wrong about the whole thing.'

'What do you mean?'

'Telling Hayden Cotton I'd never go.'

'Oh,' he said, 'oh, yes. I'd forgotten that too. It seemed like a good idea at the time – and it worked, didn't it?'

'What do you mean it worked? What worked?'

'I told him to tell you I'd said you'd never go, because I knew that was the one thing that would change your mind. And I was right.'

'You what!' said Harriet. 'Theo, you are absolutely outrageous. Playing with my life as if it was some kind of a – a computer game.'

Rage swept over her, pure, sweet rage, hot, liquid. All he had done for her since her accident, all the care he had lavished on her, the thoughtfulness, the love, was blotted out, and she could have, given the strength, killed him. Her voice rose, shook with fury. 'How dare you, Theo, how could you? I'm not one of your businesses, one of your projects that you can just push around however and whenever you like. Dear God, you've made a mistake telling me that. If anything, anything could have convinced me I was right, that we could never –'

He looked at her, and saw she was actually near to tears, her face white and tense.

'Harriet I –'

'Theo, for God's sake just leave me alone. Leave me alone.' She was shouting now, her fists clenched. 'All right? Get out of my life. I keep saying it, and you won't take any notice. Get out, go back to London, go to New York, just go anywhere, but please please stop this, I can't stand it.'

'All right,' he said quietly. 'I'll stop it. I'll go. I'll go now. You win, Harriet. It's over.'

Looking after him as he left the room, seeing his great shoulders drooped in misery, hearing his voice, his deep, resonant voice, harsh with pain, she had to put her hand over her mouth to stop herself calling out, calling that she knew she was wrong, that she knew she loved him.

He was gone within the hour, everything packed into the Bentley. He didn't even say goodbye to her, just left. The house seemed bleak, bereft of him.

Harriet went to bed early; she was tired, but slept badly, and when she did sleep she had dreadful, complex dark dreams, with Theo at the heart of them. She woke late, feeling exhausted, shattered; her father helped her downstairs. She sat drinking cup after cup of coffee, staring morosely out of the window, trying not to think too much about what she had done, trying to convince herself that she'd been right, that she was actually feeling much better. It was a lovely day, rather like Cressida's wedding day, mistily golden, but summer was almost over now, the roses were drooping, dropping, and the lawn looked parched. Only a few weeks, but a whole life ago; and here she was still hurting, still angry, still lonely. Why did she have to do this, behave as she did, so sure she knew what was best for her when she didn't know at all? She suddenly wanted Theo so much, so badly, just wanted him there, near her, that she moaned aloud.

James looked up startled from the paper. 'Ankle hurting?'

'No.'

'Head hurting?'

'No. Just my heart.'

'Ah,' he said, 'that old thing.'

He paused, then said, 'You love him, don't you?'

'Yes,' she said, 'yes, I'm afraid I do. So much. So very much. But –'

'But what?'

'Oh – nothing. It could never ever work out. And it's too late, I'm afraid.'

'It's never too late.'

'It is this time. And I know it's for the best really. We could never, ever have had a life together. We'd have killed each other.'

'Well,' he said, 'it might have been fun for a while. Until you did.'

'No. No, I don't think so. The thing is, Daddy, he's got me wrong. He's never done anything really, not a single thing, that showed he properly understood me. And what I'm about. He thinks he does, but he just doesn't.'

'It isn't easy,' said James, 'understanding someone properly.'

There was a silence, then she said, 'I think I'd really like to go down and sit by the bridge. I love it there, it always makes me feel better, and I haven't been since – well, since Cressida's wedding day. Could you help me down there?'

'Yes, of course I will. Get your crutches and we'll hobble down together.'

It was very quiet at the bridge; the water was low after the summer drought, and there was a mass of weed muffling the small waterfall. But it was cool there, and comforting. She sat on the stone seat and threw bits of twig into the water, and smiled at a particularly foolish moorhen trying to walk on the weed. 'You really should know better than that,' she said.

'I could say the same to you,' said Theo.

She turned; he was standing there, on the other side of the bridge, looking at her very seriously. He looked slightly odd, slightly misshapen; he seemed to have something buttoned into his jacket.

'Theo,' she said, with an immense effort, 'Theo, I wish you'd stop prolonging the agony. How many more times do I have to say it? It really would be much better if you'd just go away.'

'It's all right,' he said, 'I've only come to say goodbye. I think we owe each other that.'

'Oh,' said Harriet uncertainly. 'Yes, yes of course we do.'

'Can I come and shake hands,' he said. 'Would that be all right?'

'Yes, yes of course,' she said, smiling brightly. 'Please do.'

He walked slowly over the bridge, stood in front of her.

She looked up at him, studying him for the last time, still carefully smiling. He looked back at her very solemnly.

Finally he said, 'I've got something for you here. A good-bye present. I can't really shake hands until I give it to you.' There was a silence as he started to undo the buttons of the jacket.

'You're always saying,' he said, 'that I don't understand you, don't know what you really want. This might make you change your mind. God, I wish you'd help me with the bloody thing.'

Harriet sat wordless, staring at the bundle, the bump wriggling inside his jacket, realizing slowly that it was moving, was wriggling slightly, that emerging from the darkness of the jacket came first a small wet black nose then a golden rumpled face, then two fat blunt paws.

'Here you are,' said Theo. 'Something I do know you really want. He comes with all my love. He's called Biggles.'

BURK PICS